Maybe Not

Also by Colleen Hoover

Slammed
Point of Retreat
This Girl
Hopeless
Losing Hope
Finding Cinderella
Maybe Someday
Ugly Love
Confess

Maybe Not

A Novella

Colleen Hoover

ATRIA PAPERBACK

NEW YORK LONDON TORONTO SYDNEY NEW DELHI

ATRIA PAPERBACK

An Imprint of Simon & Schuster, Inc.
1230 Avenue of the Americas
New York, NY 10020

First Atria Paperback edition December 2015

ATRIA PAPERBACK and colophon are trademarks of
Simon & Schuster, Inc.

The Simon & Schuster Speakers Bureau can bring authors to your live event. For more information or to book an event, contact the Simon & Schuster Speakers Bureau at 1-866-248-3049 or visit our website at www.simonspeakers.com.

Manufactured in China

10 9 8 7 6 5 4 3 2 1

ISBN 978-1-5011-2571-3
ISBN 978-1-4767-9984-1 (ebook)

To Kendall Smith, one of my very best friends. You've been by my side since we were kids, and I couldn't do any of this without you.

Maybe Not

Chapter One

I'm convinced that hell has an intercom system and the buzz of my alarm clock is played at full volume on repeat against the screams of all the lost souls.

Which is why I'll never murder anyone, because there's no way I can live with this sound for eternity. I can't even live with it for five seconds.

I reach over and stop the alarm, dreading another day at work. I hate that I have to keep this shitty barista job just to pay for school. At least Ridge lets my sporadic rent checks slide in exchange for my managing his band. It works for now, but *God, I hate mornings.*

I stretch my arms, bring my hands to my eyes, and begin rubbing the sleep out of them. When my fingers meet my eyes, for a split second I think maybe my worst fears have come true and I'm actually burning in hell, because *SHIT! Motherfucker! I'm going to kill him!*

"Ridge!" I scream.

Oh, God. It burns.

I stand up and attempt to open my eyes, but they're stinging too badly for them to be of any use. It's the oldest prank in the book, and I can't believe I fell for it. *Again.*

I can't find my shorts—*God, it hurts so bad*—so I stumble my way to the bathroom in order to wash the pepper juice from my eyes and hands. I find the doorknob and swing the door open, rushing straight to the sink. I'm pretty sure I hear a girl screaming, but that very well could be *me* screaming.

I cup my hands beneath the stream of water and bring them up to my eyes, rinsing them over and over until the burn starts to subside. Once my eyes begin to feel relief, my shoulder starts to ache from the repeated blows being delivered to it.

"Get out, you pervert!"

I'm awake enough now to know that I actually did hear a girl screaming, and now that girl is hitting me. In *my* bathroom.

I grab a hand towel and press it to my eyes while I shield her punches with my elbow.

"I was peeing, you sick bastard! Get out!"

Shit, she hits hard. I still can't really see her, but I can recognize fists when they're flying at me. I grab both of her wrists to keep her from assaulting me even more.

"Stop hitting me!" I yell.

The bathroom door that leads to the living room swings open and my left eye is working enough that I can tell Brennan is standing there. "What the hell is going on?" He walks toward us and removes my hands from her wrists and then stands between us. I bring the towel back to my eyes and squeeze them shut.

"He barged in on me while I was peeing!" the girl yells. "And he's naked!"

I open one eye and glance down. I am, in fact, completely naked.

"Jesus, Warren. Put on some clothes," Brennan says.

"How was I supposed to know I'd be attacked in my own bathroom?" I say, pointing at her. "Why the hell is she using my bathroom, anyway? Your guests can use *your* bathroom."

Brennan immediately holds up two defensive palms. "She didn't spend the night with me."

"Gross," the girl mutters.

I don't know why Ridge thought it would be a good idea to rent a four-bedroom apartment. Even though one of the bedrooms is empty, that's still two people too many. Especially when guests spend the night and don't know about the designated bathrooms.

"Look," I say, pushing both of them toward the door that leads to the living room. "This is my bathroom and I'd like to use it. I don't care where she slept or who she slept with; she can use your bathroom. This one's mine."

Brennan holds up a finger and turns to face me. "Actually," he says, "this is a *shared* bathroom. With *that* bedroom." He points to the door that leads to the other bedroom. "And that bedroom now belongs to . . ." He points to the girl. "Bridgette. Your new roommate."

I pause.

Why did he just call her my roommate?

"What do you mean, *roommate*? No one asked me if I wanted a new roommate."

Brennan shrugs. "You rarely pay rent, Warren. You don't really have a say in who lives here."

He knows I don't pay rent because I help manage their band, but Ridge does take on the brunt of the financial expenses. He makes a good point, unfortunately.

This isn't good. I can't share a bathroom with a girl.

Especially a girl with that good of an arm. And especially a girl with all that bronzed skin.

I look away from her. I hate that she's hot. I hate that she's a brunette, because I really like her long, light brown hair and the way it's pulled back, all messy and shit.

Dammit!

"Well, this has been a really fun bonding moment," Bridgette says, walking toward me. She shoves my shoulders, pushing me back toward my bedroom. "Now wait your turn, *Roomie.*"

The bathroom door closes in my face and I'm standing in my room again. Still naked. And maybe a little emasculated.

"You can leave, too," I hear her say to Brennan, right before the door to the living room slams shut. Seconds later, the water begins running in the shower.

She's in the shower.

My shower.

She's probably taking off her shirt right now, tossing it on the floor, pulling her panties down over her hips.

I'm fucked.

My apartment is my sanctuary. My man cave. The only place I can go where my life isn't ruled by women. My boss is a woman, all my professors are women, my sister and my mother are both women. Once Bridgette steps into my shower and makes it her own with all her girly shampoos and razors and shit, I'm screwed. That's *my* shower.

I walk to Ridge's bedroom and flip the light switch a couple of times to give him warning that I'm coming in, since he's deaf and can't hear me knocking or stomping toward his room like a kid about to tattle on his little brother.

I flip the switch two more times and then swing his door open. He's lifting up onto his elbows, groggy-eyed. He sees the anger on my face and he begins to laugh, incorrectly assuming I'm here about the pepper-juice prank.

I hate that I fell for it. I'm such a deep sleeper though, and he gets me every damn time.

"That prank was stupid," I sign to him. "But I'm not here because of that. We need to talk."

He sits up in bed and reaches over to tilt his alarm clock so that he can check the time. He looks back at me, agitated. "It's six-thirty in the morning," he signs. "What the hell do you want to talk about at six-thirty in the morning?"

I point in the direction of the new roommate's bedroom. *Bridgette.*

I hate her name.

"You let a *girl* move in?" I make the sign for roommate and continue. "Why in the world would you let a *girl* move in with us?"

Ridge makes the sign for Brennan's name. "That's all him. I don't think he would have accepted no for an answer."

I laugh. "Since when are girls important to Brennan?"

"I heard that," Brennan says from behind me. "*And* saw you sign it."

I face him. "Good. So answer the question."

He glares at me and then looks at Ridge. "Go back to sleep. I'll handle the five-year-old." He motions for me to follow him into the living room, turning out Ridge's bedroom light as he exits.

I like Brennan, but the fact that we've known each other for so long makes me feel like he's my little brother sometimes. My *annoying-as-fuck* little brother. My little brother who thinks moving his women into our apartment is a good idea.

"It's just for a few months," Brennan says, continuing toward the kitchen. "She's in a rough spot and needs a place to stay."

I follow Brennan into the kitchen. "Since when did you start providing rescue homes? You don't even let girls spend the night when you're done with them, much less move in with you. Are you in love with her or something? Because if that's the case, this is the stupidest decision you've ever made. You'll get tired of her in a week, and then what?"

Brennan faces me and calmly holds up a finger. "I told you earlier, it's not like that. We aren't together and we never will be together. But she's important to me and she's in a tough spot and we're going to help her, okay?" He takes a bottle of water out of the fridge and opens the cap. "It won't be that bad. She's in school and works full-time, so she'll hardly ever be here. You won't even notice."

I groan, frustrated, and run my hands down my face. "This is great," I mumble. "The last thing I need right now is some chick taking over my entire bathroom."

Brennan rolls his eyes and begins walking back toward his bedroom. "It's a *bathroom*, Warren. You're acting like a little shit."

"She *hit* me!" I say in defense.

Brennan turns and cocks an eyebrow. "See what I mean?" He walks into his bedroom and closes the door behind him.

The water turns off in the shower, and I hear the curtain slide open. As soon as the door to her bedroom shuts, I walk toward the bathroom. *My* bathroom. I try to open the door from the living room, but it's locked from the inside. I walk through my bedroom and check that door, but it's locked, too. I walk out of my room, straight into her bedroom. My eyes catch a glimpse of her before she screams and pulls a towel in front of her.

"What the hell are you *doing*?"

She picks up a shoe and tosses it at me. It hits me in the shoulder, but I don't even flinch. I ignore her and walk into the bathroom and slam the door shut. I lean against it, lock it behind me, and then close my eyes.

Dammit, she's hot.

Why does she have to be hot?

And I know it was just a glimpse but . . . she shaves. *Everywhere.*

It's bad enough I have to share a bathroom with a girl, but now I have to share it with a *hot* girl? A hot girl who has a severe mean streak? A hot girl with a sick tan and hair so long and thick, it covers up her breasts when it's wet, and *shit, shit, shit.*

I hate Brennan. I hate Ridge. I also love them for doing this to me.

Maybe having her for a roommate could be a good thing.

"Hey, asshole!" she yells through the door. "I used all the hot water. Have fun."

Maybe not.

I walk to Brennan's room and swing open the door. He's packing a suitcase and doesn't even look at me when I stalk over to him.

"What now?" he asks, annoyed.

"I need to ask you something and I need you to be completely honest with me."

He sighs and turns to face me. "What is it?"

"Have you slept with her?"

He looks at me like I'm an idiot. "I already told you no."

I hate that he's acting so mature and calm about this situation, because my reaction is making me feel really immature. Brennan has always been the immature one. Since the moment I met Ridge . . . *God, how long ago was that? Ten years? I'm twenty-four, Brennan's twenty-one . . . yeah. Ten years.* I've been best friends with them for a decade, and this is the first time I've actually felt inferior to Brennan.

I don't like it. *I'm* the responsible one. Well, not as responsible as Ridge, obviously, but no one is. I do manage Brennan's band, and I do a hell of a good job of it, so why can't I seem to control my reactions right now?

Because. I know myself, and if I can't get rid of the new roommate right away, then I'll more than likely become infatuated with her. And if I'll be infatuated with her, I need to make sure Brennan *isn't.*

"You have to be honest with me, because I think you might be in love with her and I need you to tell me you're not, because I think I might want to kiss her. And touch her. A lot. Like, everywhere."

Brennan's hands fly to his forehead and he looks at me like I've lost my mind. He takes several steps back.

"Are you listening to yourself, Warren? I mean, *fuck,* man! You yell at me three minutes ago because you hate her and don't want her here, and now you're saying you want her? Are you bipolar?"

He makes a good point.

Jesus, what's wrong with me?

I pace the room, trying to figure out a solution. She can't stay here. But I want her to stay. I can't share a bathroom with her, but I don't really want anyone else to share a bathroom with her, either. I'm a little bit selfish, apparently.

I pause my frantic pacing and look at Brennan. "Why is she so *mean?*"

Brennan walks over to me and calmly places two hands on my shoulders. "Warren Russell, you need to calm the hell down. You're starting to freak me out."

I shake my head. "I know. I'm sorry, I just. I don't want to be attracted to a girl that you're involved with, so I need to know now if that's the case because we go too far back to let something like this mess us up. But you also know you can't just drop a girl that looks like her in my lap, and expect me not to go there in my head. And I just saw her naked and now I'm useless. Ruined. She's so damn perfect beneath all those clothes and . . ." I look up at him. "I just want to make sure I'm not stepping on any toes when I fantasize about her tonight."

Brennan stares at me, mulling over my admission. He pats me twice on the shoulder and returns to his suitcase. "She's mean, Warren. Probably the meanest girl I've ever met in my life. So if she murders you in your sleep, don't say I didn't warn you." He closes his suitcase and begins to zip it. "She needed a place to stay and we have an extra room. Her life makes mine and Ridge's look like a cakewalk, so go easy on her."

I take a seat on the edge of his bed. I'm trying to be sympathetic to the situation, but the business manager in me is skeptical. "She just called you out of the blue and asked if she could move in with you? Don't you think that's a little suspicious, Brennan? You don't think it has to do with the band finally making a name for itself?"

Brennan glares at me. "She's not an opportunist, Warren. Trust me on that. And hit on her if you want, I couldn't care less."

He walks toward the door and grabs his keys off the dresser. "I'll be back next week after the last show. Do you have our hotel rooms squared up?"

I nod. "I emailed you all the confirmation numbers."

"Thanks," he says as he walks out of the room.

I fall back onto the bed and hate the fact that Brennan isn't into her. That means she's fair game.

I was kind of hoping she wasn't.

But then I smile, because she is.

Chapter Two

"What are you doing?" Ridge signs.

I walk back to Bridgette's bedroom with another glass of water. Once I carefully place it on the floor with all the others, I come back to the living room. "She's lived here two weeks," I tell Ridge. "If she wants to be a roommate, she has to live with the pranks. It's the rule."

Ridge shakes his head disapprovingly.

"What?" I say defensively.

He sighs heavily. "She hardly seems like the type to embrace pranks. This will backfire on you. She hasn't even spoken to us since she moved in."

I disagree with a shake of my head. "She hasn't spoken to *you* because you're deaf and she doesn't know sign language. She hasn't spoken to me because I'm pretty sure I intimidate her."

"You *annoy* her," Ridge signs. "I don't think that girl is capable of being intimidated."

I shake my head. "I don't annoy her. I think she might be attracted to me and that's why she's avoiding me. Because she knows it's not a good idea for roommates to hook up."

Ridge points to her bedroom. "Then why are you making an effort to prank her? Do you *want* her to speak to you? Because if you think roommates shouldn't hook up, then you probably shouldn't be . . ."

I interrupt him. "I didn't say *I* think roommates shouldn't hook up. I said I think that's why she's avoiding me."

"So you want to hook up with her?"

I roll my eyes. "You don't get it. No, I don't want to hook up with her. Yes, I like staring at her ass. And I'm only pranking her because if she's going to live here, she needs to get used to it. When in Rome . . ."

Ridge throws his hands up in defeat and heads toward his room, just as the front door begins to open. I rush to my bedroom and shut the door before she sees me.

I sit on the bed and wait.

And I wait.

And I wait some more.

I lie down on the bed. I wait some more.

She never makes a sound. I don't hear her getting angry that I just filled over fifty cups of water and placed them strategically around her entire bedroom. I don't hear her stomping into the kitchen to pour them out. I don't hear her beating on my door to throw the cups of water at my face in retaliation.

I'm so confused.

I stand up and walk out of my bedroom, but she's not in the kitchen or living room. Her work shoes are by the front door where she keeps them, so I know she came home. I know she went into her room.

What a disappointment. Her lack of response makes me feel like my prank was a failure, when I know it wasn't. It was epic. There's no way she could have made it one foot into her room without having to move all those cups of water.

I stalk back to my bedroom and lie down on the bed.

I want to be pissed at her. I want to hate her for sucking at prank retaliation.

But I don't. I can't stop smiling because I love that her response caught me off guard. She's unexpected, and I like that.

•   •   •

"Warren."

Her voice sounds so sweet. I must be dreaming.

"Warren, wake up."

So, so sweet. Angelic, even.

I give myself a few seconds to adjust to her voice, to the fact that she's waking me up, to the randomness of her being at my bedroom door, calling out my name. I slowly open my eyes and roll onto my back. I lift up onto my elbows and look at her. She's standing in the doorway between the bedroom and our bathroom. She's wearing an oversized Sounds of Cedar T-shirt, and it doesn't even look like she's wearing anything underneath it.

"What's up?" I ask her.

She wants me. She totally wants me.

She folds her arms tightly over her chest. She tilts her head to the side, and I watch as her eyes narrow into tiny, angry slits. "Don't ever step foot inside my bedroom again. *Ass*hole." She straightens up and backs into the bathroom, slamming the door.

I glance at the clock, and it's two in the morning. That was an extremely delayed reaction to my prank. Was she just waiting for me to fall asleep so she could wake me up and yell at me? Is that her idea of revenge?

She's such an amateur.

I smile to myself and roll over, shifting on the bed. I gasp when a rush of water pours down on top of me.

What the fuck?

I look up, just as an empty cup falls from the edge of the headboard and hits me square between the eyes.

I close my eyes, ashamed that I didn't see that coming. I'm so disappointed in myself. And now I'll have to sleep on towels, because my mattress is soaking wet.

I throw the covers off and swing my legs over the bed, only for my feet to be met with even more cups of water. I knock several of them over in my attempt to stand and it creates a sort of domino effect. I bend over and try to stop them from falling over, but I just make it worse. She's placed them so close together, all over my bedroom floor, and I can't find a safe spot to step.

I try to reach for the nightstand while at the same time lifting my right leg so that it doesn't hit any more cups, but I lose my balance in the process and . . . *yes.* I fall down. Onto the remaining pile of cups that are full of water. Water that is now all over my carpet.

Touché, Bridgette.

·   ·   ·

I'm carrying the cups of water from my bedroom to the kitchen, back and forth, back and forth. Ridge is sitting at the table, staring at me. I know he wants to ask why the cups are now in my room, but he better not. I'm sure he can see by the look on my face that I don't need his *"I told you so."*

The door to Bridgette's bedroom opens and she walks

out with her backpack slung over her shoulder. I pause and stare at her for a few seconds. Her hair is pulled back into a ponytail. She has on a pair of jeans and a blue tank top. She's usually wearing her Hooters uniform, which, don't get me wrong, is fantastic. But this? Seeing her dressed down with her flip-flops on and no makeup is just . . . *Stop looking at her.*

"Good morning, Warren," she says, shooting daggers in my direction. She glances at the cups in my hands. "Sleep well?"

I smile at her with vengeance. "Screw you, Bridgette."

She crinkles up her nose and gives her head a quick shake. "No thanks," she says, heading toward the front door. "Oh, by the way. We're out of toilet paper. Also, I couldn't find my razor, so I hope you don't mind that I used yours." She opens the front door and turns to face me. "And . . ." She scrunches up her nose again. "I accidentally knocked your toothbrush into the toilet. Sorry. I rinsed it off for you, though."

She closes the door right when one of the cups of water flies out of my hand and meets the back of the door.

She's such a bitch.

Ridge calmly walks past me, straight to his bedroom. He doesn't even look at me, because he knows me better than anyone, and therefore, he knows not to speak to me right now.

I wish Brennan knew me that well, because he's laughing, making his way into the kitchen. Every time he glances up at me, he laughs even harder. "I know she's mean, but Christ, Warren. She *hates* you." He's still laughing as he opens the dishwasher to unload it. "I mean, really hates you."

I finish the trek across the living room and set the empty cups next to the sink. "I can't do this anymore," I say to him. "I can't live with a girl."

Brennan glances at me, amused. He doesn't think I'm serious.

"Tonight. I want her out tonight. She can move in with a friend, or with that sister of hers she's always on the phone with. I want her gone, Brennan."

He can see that I'm not kidding. He straightens up and presses his hands onto the counter behind him, eyeing me. He shakes his head. "She's not leaving."

He reaches down and closes the dishwasher and presses the button to start it. He begins to walk away so I follow after him. "You can't have final say in who lives here. I've tried for two weeks to get along with her, and she's fucking impossible."

Brennan glances at all the cups lining the countertop. "You think pranking her is making an effort to get along with her?" He looks back at me. "You have a hell of a lot to learn about women, Warren." He turns away from me and walks back toward his room. "She's not leaving. She's our roommate now, so *deal* with it."

He slams his door, and it pisses me off even more because I'm really tired of everyone slamming doors lately. I stomp across the living room and swing his door open. "Either she goes or I go!"

As soon as I say it, I regret it. Actually, I don't. I'm not going anywhere, but maybe the threat will change his mind. He shrugs.

"See ya," he says casually.

I turn around and punch the door. "Seriously, Brennan? You would let me leave over her?"

He stands and walks toward me, not stopping until we're eye to eye. "Yes, Warren. I would. So go think it over and let me know when you're moving out." His hand grips the door and he tries to close it in my face, but I slap my palm against it and push it back open.

"You're fucking her," I say.

"Stop it, already! I'm not fucking her."

My jaw is clenched tightly and I'm nodding my head slowly. That's the only explanation for why he's endlessly defending her. "I don't know why you won't just admit it, Brennan. It's fine. You're in love with Bridgette and you don't want her to move out. If you would just admit it, I'd stop."

Brennan's jaw tenses and he expels a quick, frustrated breath. He runs his hands through his hair, and that's when I see it. I see it written all over his face.

Brennan is in love with Bridgette.

I don't know how I feel about that, which makes no sense, since I'm trying to kick her out.

"Warren," he says calmly. He backs into the room and motions for me to step inside. I don't know why he thinks he needs privacy when the only other person in this apartment is Ridge. He closes the door behind me once I'm inside his bedroom. He puts his hands on his hips and stares at the floor for several seconds. When his eyes finally meet mine again, they're full of defeat.

I knew it.

"I'm not in love with Bridgette," he says calmly. "She's my sister."

Chapter Three

I'm pacing the room, holding my forehead, pausing every few feet to look at Brennan and shake my head, only to continue pacing again.

I liked it better when I thought he was fucking her.

"How?" I ask. "How is that even possible?" I pause again and face him. "And why didn't you guys tell me before now?" I feel slightly excluded, like Ridge and Brennan were trying to keep some big family secret from me. That isn't right, because *I'm* their family. They lived with me after they left home. My parents took them in and gave them a roof over their heads and food on the table.

"Ridge doesn't know," Brennan says. "And I don't want him to know until we find out for sure. We'll have a paternity test done soon, but our schedules just haven't worked out yet and it's kind of expensive."

Great. I can't keep secrets from Ridge. We've been best friends since we were ten. I've never kept a secret from him, especially one this big.

"Warren, swear to me you won't tell him. The last thing he needs right now is more stress, and if he finds out I've been in touch with our father, he'll take it personally."

My hands fly up in the air. "Your father, Brennan? Why in the hell would you ever want to contact that bastard again?"

He shakes his head. "I didn't. After Bridgette found out that her biological mother had an affair with our father, she found me and asked me to help her find him." He folds his arms over his chest and looks down at the floor. "I warned her, but she had to see it for herself. I won't be seeing my father again, but if Ridge knows I even took her to see him, he would think I was going behind his back to reach out to our parents, and I wasn't."

"What did your father say when you showed up after all these years?"

Ridge and Brennan moved in with me and my parents when they were only seventeen and fourteen, so it's been about seven years since either of them has had contact with their father.

Brennan shakes his head. "He hasn't changed. He barely said two sentences to us before he sent us on our way. I think it disappointed her so much, she'd be fine not having a paternity test completed if it weren't for Ridge and me possibly being her brothers. I think she just wants someone she can call family, which is why I'm helping her out with all this. I feel bad for her."

I can't believe this. I never would have guessed it. "She doesn't even look like either of you." Brennan and Ridge look almost identical, and they both look just like their father. If their father is the common link between them and Bridgette, you would think she'd have some form of similarity to them. Other than her brown hair, there's nothing about her that looks like Ridge or Brennan. Her green eyes aren't even close to their dark brown eyes, so if she is their sister, she must have taken a hundred percent after her mother. I could just be justifying the fact that I don't want them to look alike. That would be a little strange for me.

Brennan shrugs. "We still don't know for sure, Warren. If it turns out she's not his daughter, then Ridge will never even have to know about this."

I nod, knowing full well that Brennan is right. Ridge has enough on his plate having to deal with Maggie's issues, and until they know for sure, this isn't something he should have to stress over.

"What happens to Bridgette?" I ask him. "If it turns out she's not your sister."

Brennan shrugs. "Then I guess she's just our new roommate."

I sit down on the bed and try to soak everything in. This changes everything. If she's Ridge and Brennan's sister, she won't just be my roommate. She and her attitude and her tiny little Hooters shorts will be part of our lives forever.

I don't really know how I feel about that.

"Are you sure she's not just trying to swindle you?"

Brennan rolls his eyes. "That girl is just trying to survive, Warren. She's had a really fucked-up life, and even if it turns out we're not related, she just needs someone to give her a chance. So please. You don't even have to be nice to her. Just be understanding enough to allow her to live here."

I nod and fall back onto the bed. *Sister?*

"So," I say to Brennan. "I guess that means you definitely aren't into her. Which means I *can* be."

Brennan's pillow meets my face. "You're disgusting."

Chapter Four

Brennan was right. I'm disgusting. I've never felt more disappointed in myself than I have these past two weeks. Since the moment I found out she might be Ridge and Brennan's sister, I haven't been able to stop staring at her. I keep trying to pinpoint mannerisms they have in common, or physical features, but the only thing I've noticed is how hot she looks in that Hooters outfit.

Which, in turn, makes me disgusted with myself, because thoughts of her in her uniform lead to some really strange dreams. Last night I dreamt I walked into the apartment and she was standing in the kitchen in those tiny orange shorts with her midriff showing. But when my eyes made it to her face, it wasn't her face I was looking at. It was Brennan's. He was smiling at me with a shit-eating grin, and right when I started gagging, Ridge walked out of his room wearing the same Hooters outfit.

I woke up after that and had to immediately go to the bathroom and brush my teeth. I don't know why I thought brushing my teeth would help me, but whatever. This sibling thing is fucking with my head in more ways than it should. On the one hand, I think it would be cool if Ridge and Brennan had a sister. On the other hand, I don't want that sister to be Bridgette. Mainly because I'm skeptical of the reasons she's showing up out of the blue right when Brennan begins to make a name for himself. Does she have ulterior motives? Does she think he's made of money?

Because as the band's manager, I can assure her, he's not. The money the band brings in goes right back into promotion and travel expenses. It's at the point where they're putting in so much time and effort, if it doesn't start paying off during this next scheduled tour, it may be the last one they go on. Which is why I'm a little bitter when it comes to Bridgette, because I need Brennan's focus to be on Sounds of Cedar and Ridge's focus to be on writing the songs. I don't want them caught up in family drama.

But dammit. Those shorts.

I'm standing in my bedroom doorway, watching her. She's in the kitchen, talking on the phone while she makes herself something to eat. The phone is sitting on the counter and she's on speaker with whoever is on the other line.

Bridgette hasn't noticed I'm standing here, so until she does, I'm staying right here. Because seeing her have a normal, human conversation is something I've never witnessed before, and I can't stop watching. Which is strange, because how many times a day do I see people having typical interactions with other humans? It says a lot about Bridgette's personality that seeing her do something like this could actually be fascinating. She'd make an interesting anthropological study, considering she doesn't seem to conform to how society expects a young woman to act.

"I can't take living in this dorm," the voice on speaker says. "My roommate's a fruit loop dingus."

Bridgette tilts her head toward the direction of the

phone, but still doesn't turn around to see me. "You can make it until you graduate."

"And then we can get our own place?"

My ears perk up, hearing her mention the possibility of moving out. "We can't afford our own place," Bridgette says.

"We could if you would go back into doing porn films."

"It was one porn," Bridgette says defensively. "We needed the money. Besides, I was in it for all of three minutes, so will you please stop bringing it up."

Holy shit. *Please say the name, please say the name.* I have to know the name of this porn.

"Okay, okay," the girl says, laughing. "I'll stop bringing it up if you can promise I'll be out of the dorms in three months."

Bridgette shakes her head. "You know I don't make promises. And are you forgetting about the time we tried living together for three months? Because I'm still shocked either of us came out alive. We get along better with distance, and you're better off in the dorms, believe me."

"Ugh. I know you're right," the girl says. "I just need to get off my ass and get a job. How's that Hooters gig working out for you?"

Bridgette scoffs. "It's the worst job I've ever had." She turns around to pick up her phone and her eyes meet mine. I don't even try to hide the fact that I was listening to her conversation. She glares at me as she picks up the phone and holds it to her mouth. "I'll call you later, Brandi." She ends her call and slaps her phone against the counter. "What's your problem?"

I shrug. "Nothing," I say, straightening up and walking toward the kitchen.

Don't look at her shorts, don't look at her shorts.

"I just didn't realize you were capable of normal human interaction."

Bridgette rolls her eyes and picks up the plate of food she just finished preparing. She begins walking toward her bedroom. "I can be pleasant to people who deserve it."

When she reaches her door, she turns around and faces me. "I need you to drop me off at work in an hour. My car's in the shop." She disappears into her bedroom.

I grimace, because for some reason the thought of taking her to work excites me, and my excitement disappoints me. I feel like I'm two different people right now. I'm a guy who finds his new roommate insanely attractive, but I'm also a guy who can't stand to be around his bitchy new roommate.

I'm also a guy who's about to do some heavy research into the porn industry, because I have to find that movie. *Have* to. It's all I'm gonna be able to think about until I see it with my own eyes.

· · ·

"What's Bridgette's last name?" I ask Brennan. I've texted him five times in the last half hour, trying to figure it out, but he hasn't texted me back, so now I'm on the phone with him. I'm sure a little Google search of her name could help me find the title.

"Cox. Why?"

I laugh. "Bridgette Cox? Seriously?"

There's a pause on his end of the line. "What's so funny? And why do you need her last name?"

"No reason," I say. "Thanks."

I hang up the phone without giving him an explanation. The last thing Brennan needs to know is that his possible sister was in a porn film.

But *Cox*? That's way too easy.

I spend the next fifteen minutes googling her name, looking for anything porn-related. I come up empty-handed. She must have used a fake name.

I slam my laptop shut when my bedroom door swings open. "Let's go," she says.

I stand up and slip on my shoes. "Ever heard of knocking?" I ask as I follow her through the living room.

"Really, Warren? Coming from the guy who's walked in on me in the bathroom no less than three times in the past two weeks?"

"Ever heard of locking doors?" I say in response.

She doesn't reply as she makes her way outside. I grab my keys off the bar and follow her. I am curious as to why she never locks the doors when she's in the shower. My first thought leads me to believe that maybe she likes it when I walk in on her. Why else would she leave them unlocked?

Come to think of it, she also wears that damn uniform way longer than she needs to. She puts it on a good two hours before going to work and she leaves it on just as long when she gets home. Most people spend as little time as possible in their work clothes, but Bridgette seems to like flaunting her ass in my face.

I pause at the bottom of the stairs and watch as her ass makes its way toward my car.

Holy shit. I think Bridgette is into me.

She turns around after she tries to open the locked door. She looks at me expectantly and I'm still frozen at the bottom of the stairs, staring at her, my mouth agape.

Bridgette likes me.

"Unlock the car, Warren. Jesus."

I lift the key fob and point it at the car to unlock the doors. Bridgette slides into her seat and flips the visor down, fingering at her hair. A smile slowly spreads across my face as I make my way to the driver's side.

Bridgette wants me.

This is gonna be fun.

After I back the car out, I keep half of my focus on the road and half of it on her legs. She has one propped up on the dash and she keeps running her hand up and down her thigh. I can't tell if she's doing it in a seductive way or because she likes the sound of her fingernails scraping over her panty hose.

I have to adjust in my seat and swallow the lump in my throat, because we've never actually been this close before for this long. The tension is thick, and I can't tell if it's all mine or if it's a shared tension. I clear my throat and do what I can to not make this the most awkward ten miles I've ever had to drive.

"So," I say, attempting to think of something to break the ice. "Do you like your job?"

Bridgette laughs under her breath. "Yes, Warren. I *love* it. I love when disgusting old men grab my ass night after night, and I especially love it when drunk guys think my boobs are an accessory and not an extension of my body."

I shake my head. I don't know why I thought it would be a good idea to speak to her. I exhale and don't bother asking her any more questions. She's impossible to talk to.

Silence engulfs the car for another two miles. I hear her sigh heavily and I turn and glance at her, but she's staring out the window. "The tips are good," she says quietly.

I smile and look back at the road. I smile, because I know that's as close to an apology as Bridgette is capable of giving. "That's good," I say to her, my way of telling her I accept her apology.

We're quiet until we reach her work. I stop out front and she gets out of the car and then leans down and looks at me. "I need you to pick me up at eleven tonight."

She slams the door shut without saying please or thank you or goodbye. And even though she's the most inconsiderate person I've ever met in real life, I can't stop smiling.

I think we may have just bonded.

•   •   •

After I make it home, the first thing I do is set timers on every single porn on pay-per-view. I spend the next few hours fast-forwarding through most of them, pausing it any time it lands on a girl that even remotely resembles her. I take into account that she may have been wearing a wig, so I can't rule women out simply based on their hair color.

Ridge takes a seat next to me on the couch and I consider putting the TV on caption for him, but I don't. Let's be honest, pornos aren't known for their riveting story lines.

Ridge elbows me to get my attention. "What's with this new fascination?" he asks, referring to the fact that I've done nothing today other than watch porn after porn.

I don't want to be honest, so I just shrug. "I like porn."

He nods his head slowly and then stands up. "I'm not gonna lie," he signs. "It's really awkward. I'll be out on my balcony if you need me."

I pause the TV. "You worked out any new songs yet?"

Ridge looks frustrated when I ask him this. He shakes his head. "Not yet." He walks away and I feel bad for asking. I don't know what's changed over the last few months, but he's not the same. He seems more stressed out than usual, and it makes me wonder if he and Maggie have been fighting. He says they're fine, but he's never had a problem writing music for the band before, and everyone knows the number one source for musical inspiration comes from relationships.

Ridge and Brennan are both musically inclined and I've always been a little bit jealous in that regard. Granted, I'm jealous of Ridge in a lot of ways. He just seems to have been born with a certain level of maturity, and I've always envied that about him. He's not impulsive like I am and he also seems to take people's feelings into consideration more than I do. I know Brennan has always looked up to him and I definitely do, too, so seeing him struggling with whatever is going on in that head of his is tough. He knew what he was getting into when he began dating Maggie, so I'm not sure if he's growing unhappy in his relationship with her or if maybe he's concerned she's unhappy with him. Whatever it is, I'm not sure what I can do to help him.

I don't think I *can* help him.

I give my focus back to the TV and fast-forward through at least three more films before I realize it's already eleven and I'm late picking up Bridgette.

Shit. Time flies when you're watching porn.

I spend the next several minutes in fast-forward, making it the ten miles to Hooters in record time. When I pull up, she's standing outside with her arms folded across her chest, shooting daggers at my car. She swings the door open and climbs in. "You're late."

I wait until she slams the door before pressing on the gas. "You're welcome for the ride, Bridgette."

I can feel the anger radiating from her. I don't know if it's simply because I'm late picking her up or because she had a shitty night at work, but I'm not about to ask. When we pull into the complex, she jumps out of my car before I even have it in park. She stalks up the stairs and slams the front door shut.

When I reach the apartment, she's already in her bedroom. I try to be understanding, but this is just . . . *it's fucking rude.* I give her a ride to and from work and all she does is bitch at me? You don't have to be taught manners to know how inappropriate that kind of behavior is. Hell, I'm one of the most inconsiderate people I know, and I would never treat someone like she's treating me.

I walk to my bedroom and head straight for the bathroom. She's already in there, standing at the sink, washing her face. "Again with the failure to knock?" she says with a dramatic roll of her eyes.

I ignore her and walk to the toilet. I lift the lid and unzip my pants. I try to keep my smile in check when I hear her scoff at the fact that I just started taking a piss with her in the bathroom.

"Are you serious?"

I continue to ignore her comments and flush the toilet when I'm finished. I leave the lid up on purpose and step over to the sink, right next to her. *Two can play at this asshole game, Bridgette.*

I grab my toothbrush and squirt toothpaste on it and then start brushing my teeth. She elbows me when I get in the way of the sink, attempting to push me aside. I elbow her right back and continue brushing. I look up at our reflection in the mirror and like what I see. I'm several inches taller than her. My hair is darker than hers, and my eyes are brown compared to her greens. We complement each other, though. Standing next to each other like this, I can see how we could make a good-looking couple. We'd probably even make some good-looking children.

Shit.

Why am I allowing thoughts like this to fester in my brain?

She finishes wiping the makeup from her face before grabbing her own toothbrush. Now we're both fighting for sink space, brushing with more force than our teeth have probably ever been brushed. We take turns angrily spitting into the sink, throwing elbows at each other between every turn.

When I'm finished, I rinse off my toothbrush and put it back in the holder. She does the same. I cup my hands under the stream of water and bend forward to take a sip when she shoves me aside, causing me to splash water all over the counter. I wait until she has water in her own hands, then I shove her arms, watching the water splash everywhere.

She grips the counter and takes a deep, calming breath. It doesn't help, though, because she splashes her hand through the faucet stream, sending a handful of water straight at my face.

I close my eyes and try to put myself in her shoes. Maybe she's had a rough day. Maybe she hates her job. Maybe she hates her life.

Whatever her reason for acting the way she does doesn't excuse the fact that she still didn't say thank you for the ride. She's treating me like I ruined her life, and all I've done is try to accommodate her.

I open my eyes and don't even look at her. I reach over, turn the sink faucet off, and then grab the hand towel and begin drying my face. She's watching me closely, waiting for me to retaliate. I take a slow step toward her, towering over her. She presses her back against the sink and keeps her eyes focused on mine as I lean forward.

Our chests are almost touching now. I can feel the heat radiating from her as her lips slowly part. She's not pushing me away this time. In fact, it looks like she's daring me to keep going. To come closer.

I place my hands on either side of her, locking her in. She still doesn't resist and I know if I tried to kiss her right now, she wouldn't resist that, either. Under any other circumstance, I *would* be kissing her right now. My tongue would be as far into that mouth as I could get it, because *fuck it's a nice mouth*. I don't know how so much venom can spew from lips as soft as hers.

"Bridgette," I say, very calmly.

I can see the roll of her throat as she swallows, still looking up at me. "Warren," she says, her voice a mix between resolved and desperate.

I smile at her, just inches from her face. The fact that she's allowing me this close only proves that my theory earlier this afternoon is correct. She wants me. She wants me to touch her, to kiss her, to carry her to my bed. I wonder if she's as mean in the bedroom as she is out of the bedroom.

I lean in another inch and she gasps quietly, trading glances between my eyes and my lips. I pull my bottom lip into my mouth, slowly sliding my teeth across it. She watches my mouth with fascination. My heart is in my throat and my palms are sweating, because I'm not sure I can do this. I'm not so sure I can resist her.

I lean in even closer, reaching around her with my right hand until I find the mouthwash on the counter. Just when our lips would meet if I were to kiss her, I pull back and step away, removing the lid from the mouthwash. I keep my eyes focused on hers and take a sip before putting the lid back on it and setting it down on the counter.

I can see the desire in her eyes become swallowed up by fury. She's pissed at me, pissed at herself. Possibly even embarrassed. When she sees I was teasing her, the corners of her eyes crinkle with her intense glare. I step up to the sink and spit the mouthwash out, wiping my mouth with the hand towel again. I turn toward my bedroom. "Goodnight, Bridgette."

I close the door and lean against it and squeeze my eyes shut. Her bedroom door slams shut and I blow out a steady breath. I've never been more turned on than I am right now. I've also never been more proud of myself than I am right now. Walking away from that mouth and those hungry eyes was the hardest thing I've had to do, but also the most important. I have to keep the upper hand, because that girl has way too much power over me, and she doesn't even know it.

I turn out my bedroom light and walk to my bed, trying to get the image of what almost just happened out of my head. After several minutes, I give up trying to fight it. I decide to use the thoughts of her to my advantage as I slip my hand into my boxers, thinking about those orange shorts. That mouth. The small gasp of breath she took when I leaned in toward her.

I close my eyes and think about what could have happened if I wasn't so stubborn. If I would have just kissed her. I also think about the fact that she's just a few feet away, hopefully just as sexually frustrated as I am right now.

Why does she have to be so damn mean? Mean girls are my weakness, and I think I just now figured that out.

Chapter Five

It's been three days since our moment in the bathroom. I've noticed she keeps the doors locked now, which is fine. I'm sure she's pissed off that she allowed herself to have a moment of weakness. She doesn't seem like the type to give in as easily as she almost did.

Either way, I can't decide if I made the right move. Half of me rejoices in the fact that I was able to walk away, but the other half of me can't believe how stupid I was for passing up an opportunity like that. I could have had her, and now I more than likely won't ever. But it's for the best, because the last thing I need is to hook up with a roommate who could potentially be the sister of my best friend. But she makes it hard, pun intended, when she walks into the living room looking like she does right now. She's not in her work clothes, but what she does have on doesn't make it any better. She's wearing a thin tank top over a barely there pair of pajama shorts, and she's walked between me and the TV more times than I can count.

Shit.

Now she's heading toward me with books in her hands.

Shit.

She's sitting on the couch. Next to me. In that thin tank top. Without a bra.

I can handle this. I force my eyes on the TV, still in

search of whatever porn she was in. I could just ask her, but that's not a good idea. If she knows I know she was in a porn film, she'd probably do everything she could to make sure I never find out.

She leans forward and picks up the remote, and then points it at the TV to mute it. I don't know who she thinks she is, but if she doesn't want to hear the TV, she can go to her room. I grab the remote and turn the sound back on. She sighs and opens one of her textbooks and begins reading.

I pretend I'm paying attention to the TV, but I can't stop stealing glances at her, because *holy shit, I can't believe I walked away from her.* I'm an idiot.

She grabs the remote and mutes the TV again, possibly because one of the girls was screaming at the top of her lungs. I wonder if Bridgette is loud during sex? Probably not. She's more than likely stubborn, refusing to give up any of her sounds.

I unmute the TV again and she reaches her breaking point. "I'm trying to study, Warren. For fuck's sake, you still get the same effect when it's on mute."

I eye her curiously. "How would you know? Are you a porn expert?"

She glances at me, a flash of suspicion in her eyes. "Can you please, for one night, forgo your addiction so I can study in peace and quiet?"

Bridgette said "please."

"Go study in your bedroom," I say.

Her mouth presses into a tight, thin line. She pushes her book off her lap and stands. She walks toward the TV and reaches behind it, pulling the plug. After returning to the couch, she pulls her book back onto her lap and resumes studying.

I don't know how I ever got beyond her horrible attitude enough to even be attracted to her. She's vile. I don't care how good she looks, she'll never find anyone who can put up with her personality.

"You can be a real bitch sometimes, you know that?"

She releases an exasperated breath. "Yeah, well. You're addicted to porn."

I laugh under my breath. "At least I wasn't *in* a porn."

Her eyes swing in my direction. "I knew you were eaves-dropping."

I shrug. "I couldn't help it. You were having a conversation like you were an actual human being. It was fascinating."

Her focus falls back onto the pages of the textbook. "You're an asshole."

"You're an opportunist."

She slams her book shut and turns to face me on the couch. "An opportunist? Are you kidding me?"

I pull my knee up and turn and face her. "You don't think it seems a little fishy that you show up out of the blue and claim to be the long-lost sister to the most popular local band in Austin?"

She looks capable of murder. "Warren, I suggest you stop making accusations against people you know absolutely nothing about."

I grin, because I know that got to her. I might come out victorious again.

"I've learned enough about you to know you don't deserve to be trusted." I pick up her book and put it back in her lap and point to her bedroom. "Now take your homework and go back to your borrowed room."

"*My* borrowed room? You don't even pay rent, Warren."

"Neither do you, Bridgette."

"All you do is watch porn and stare at my ass. You're a lazy pervert."

"All you do is *flaunt* your ass and fantasize about me kissing you."

"You're disgusting," she says. "As a matter of fact, *watch* the porn. I'm sure you need all the pointers you can get."

Okay, that's low. She can insult my laziness, my finances, my new porn addiction, but she cannot insult my bedroom skills. Especially when she doesn't have firsthand experience. "I don't need pointers to please a woman, Bridgette. I was born with natural talent."

She's eyeing me like she's about to punch me, but I can't stop staring at her mouth, hoping she insults me again. Somewhere between being called an asshole and this moment, I've become more turned on than I've ever been in my life. I'm hoping she's about to storm off to her bedroom because I've already met my quota for restraint when it comes to her.

She licks her bottom lip, and I have to grip the couch cushion to keep myself from attacking that mouth. Her eyes are focused intensely on mine, and we're both breathing so heavily from our verbal attacks, I can taste her breath on my lips.

"I hate you," she says through clenched teeth.

"I hated you first," I hiss back.

Her focus falls on my mouth and as soon as I see the tiniest flash of desire in her eyes, I lunge forward. I grab her face and press my lips to hers as I shove her back against the couch. She's pushing me away with her knees while pulling me to her with her hands. My tongue forces through the barrier of her lips and she devours me in response. I kiss her hard, and she kisses me even harder. I'm pulling at a fistful of her hair while she scratches down my neck with her fingernails. *Fuck,* it hurts. *She* hurts.

I want more.

I'm hovering over her and then pressing myself against her, pulling her knee up so she can wrap it around my waist. Her hands are in my hair, and I don't want her to move out. I want her to stay. I want her to be my roommate forever. She's the best fucking roommate I've ever had and, my God, she's so *nice.* How did I ever think she was mean? She's so, so sweet, and her lips are sweet and *Bridgette, I love your name.*

"Bridgette," I whisper, wanting to say her name out loud. I don't know how I hated her name before this moment, because it's the most beautiful name I've ever said out loud.

I pull away from her mouth and begin working my way down her sweet, sweet neck. As soon as I make it to her shoulder, she begins to push me away with her hands.

Just like that, I snap back to reality and separate from her willingly.

I move to the other end of the couch, needing the space to wrap my head around *what the hell just happened?*

She quickly sits up on the couch. She wipes her mouth and I run my hands through my hair, doing whatever I can to process this.

She's an evil vixen. I close my eyes and squeeze my forehead, trying to figure out how I just lost complete control of myself simply because I was kissing her. I think of all the lies that were just passing through my head as my dick tried to convince me she was actually a decent person.

I'm weak. I'm so weak, and she just gained the upper hand again.

"Don't do that again," she says, angry and breathless.

Her voice makes me wince. "You started it," I say defensively.

Did she? I can't remember. It might have been mutual.

"You kiss like you're trying to resuscitate a dead cat," she says, disgusted.

"You kiss like you *are* a dead cat."

She pulls her knees up to her chest and wraps her arms around them. She looks extremely uncomfortable in the silence, so it doesn't surprise me when she spits out another insult. "You probably fuck like a limp noodle."

"I fuck like I'm Thor."

I'm not looking at her, but I know that comment had to make her smile. If she's even capable of smiling. The silence grows heavier and neither of us moves, making it even more apparent that what just happened was a mistake.

"Why do you taste like onions?" she asks.

I shrug. "I just ate pizza."

She glances into the kitchen. "Is there any left?"

I nod. "It's in the fridge."

She immediately stands up to walk to the kitchen, and I hate that I'm staring at her shirt. I can see her nipples poking through the thin fabric, and I want to point at her and say, *"I did that! That's all me!"*

Instead, I close my eyes and try to think about whatever

will stop my wanting to follow her into that kitchen and bend her over the counter. Luckily, Ridge's bedroom door opens, so I give my full attention to him as he walks into the living room. He pauses when he sees me sitting on the couch. He glances at the TV that isn't even on. "Why do you look so guilty?"

I shake my head shamefully. "I think I just made out with Bridgette," I sign.

Ridge looks at Bridgette, who is standing in the kitchen with her back to us. He shakes his head in disappointment. Or confusion.

"Why?" he asks, perplexed. "Did she do it willingly?"

I grab one of the couch pillows and throw it at him. "Yes, she did it willingly, asshole. She wants me."

"Do you want her?" He seems genuinely shocked, like he didn't see this coming at all.

I shake my head. "No, I don't want her," I sign. "But I feel like I need her. So bad. She's so . . ." I pause my hands for a few seconds before continuing. "She's the best worst thing that's ever happened to me."

Ridge backs up until his hand is on the front door. "I'm going to Maggie's for the night," he signs. "We'll pray for you."

I flip him off as he makes his way out. When I turn back to face Bridgette, she's walking toward her bedroom. She passes the TV and doesn't even have the audacity to plug it back in.

I plug in the TV, because there isn't a doubt in my mind now. I *have* to find that porno, because after experiencing that kiss, I'm addicted. Addicted to all things Bridgette.

• • •

I barely slept last night. Being in the same apartment with her, knowing Ridge and Brennan were both gone, was too much. It took all I had not to make an excuse to knock on her bedroom door. But I'm learning how her mind works, and I know she'd turn me down in a heartbeat just to stay in control.

And now, Ridge and Brennan are both still gone and she's at work and I've exhausted all the porn on pay-per-view. I can't keep track of how much porn I've watched in the past two weeks. It's ridiculous. How many could there possibly be? And I've narrowed it down to the ones that have been recorded in the last few years, because she had to be over eighteen when she filmed it. She's twenty-two now, so that's four years of porn films to sift through.

Oh, my God. I'm obsessed.

I'm like a stalker.

I *am* a stalker.

The front door swings open and Bridgette walks in. She slams it shut so hard, I flinch. She walks to the kitchen and begins opening cabinets and banging them shut. She finally rests her palms on the bar and looks straight at me. "Where the hell do you keep the alcohol?"

Bad day, I guess.

I stand up and walk over to the sink. I open the cabinet beneath it and take out the bottle of Pine-Sol. I don't even bother grabbing her a glass. She looks like the type who can take a good swig.

"Are you trying to kill me?" she asks, staring at the bottle in my hands.

I push it into her hand. "Ridge thinks he's clever by hiding it in old cleaner bottles. He doesn't like it when I drink all his alcohol."

She brings the bottle to her nose and winces. "Is whiskey the only thing you have?"

I nod. She shrugs and brings the bottle to her lips, tilts her head back, and takes a long swig.

She hands the bottle back to me as she wipes her mouth with the back of her hand. I take a sip from the bottle myself and then hand it back to her. We do this several times until her anger seems to have subsided, as much as anger can subside in Bridgette's world. I put the top back on the bottle and return it to the cabinet.

"Bad day?" I ask.

She leans against the counter and pulls at the elastic of her orange shorts. "The worst."

"Want to talk about it?"

She looks up at me through her lashes and then rolls her eyes. "No," she says flatly.

I don't push it. I don't even know that I really want to know about her day. Anything and everything seems to set her off, so she's probably pissed over something stupid, like a red light on her way home. It has to be exhausting to respond to all aspects of life with so much anger.

"Why are you always so mad?"

She laughs under her breath. "That's easy," she says. "Assholes, stupid customers, a shitty job, worthless parents, crappy friends, bad weather, annoying roommates who don't know how to kiss."

I laugh at the last comment, which I'm sure was supposed to be a dig, but it felt more like an underhanded flirt.

"How are you so happy all the time?" she asks. "You think everything is funny."

"That's easy," I say. "Great parents, being lucky enough to have a job, loyal friends, sunny days, and roommates who starred in porn films."

She glances away quickly in an attempt to hide a smile that almost appeared on her face. God, I wish she would let that smile out, because I'm dying to see what it looks like. As long as she's lived here, I'm not sure that I've ever seen her smile.

"Is that why you watch so much porn? Because you're hoping to find out which one I was in?"

I don't nod, but I don't shake my head, either. I lean my hip into the counter and fold my arms over my chest. "Just tell me the name of it."

"No," she says quickly. "Besides, I was just an extra. I didn't even really do anything."

An extra. That helps narrow down my search a little.

"*Didn't really* do anything doesn't mean *didn't*."

She rolls her eyes at me, but she's still standing here, so I keep going. "Were you naked?"

"It was a porn, Warren. I wasn't wearing a sweater."

That means yes.

"Did you have sex on camera?"

She shakes her head. "No."

"But you made out with a guy?"

She shakes her head again. "Wasn't a guy."

Holy fuck.

I turn around and grip the bar with one hand while

making the form of a cross over my body with the other. When I turn back around, she's still standing in the same spot, but she actually looks relaxed. She should drink whiskey every day.

"So you're telling me you made out with another girl? And it's documented somewhere? On film?"

The corner of her mouth curls up into a ghostly smile.

"You smiled."

She stops smiling immediately. "I did not."

I take a step toward her and nod my head. "Yes, you did. I made you smile."

She begins to shake her head in disagreement, so I slip my hand behind her neck. Her eyes widen, and I'm almost positive she's about to push me away, but I can't help it. *That smile.*

"You *did* smile, Bridgette," I whisper. "And you need to own it, because it was fucking beautiful."

She gasps in shock right before my lips crash against hers. I don't think she was expecting this kiss to happen, but she certainly isn't objecting. Her mouth is warm and responsive and when I part her lips with my tongue, she actually lets me.

I don't know if it's the whiskey or her, but my heart is thrashing around in my chest like a caged beast. I slide my hands down her back until they meet her ass and I squeeze as I pick her up and set her back down on the bar.

Our lips separate, and we stare at each other silently, each of us hesitant to believe that the other isn't about to walk away again. When I realize that neither of us seems to want to stop this, I bring my hands up to her cheeks and lean in again, taking her lips between mine.

This is different from our kiss the other night. Our first kiss was quick and frantic, because we knew that's where it would end.

This one is slow and deep, and feels like it's just the beginning of what we're about to experience tonight. This time when I leave her mouth to taste her neck, she doesn't push me away. She pulls me closer, wanting me to kiss her harder.

"Warren," she whispers, tilting her neck to the side, allowing me free rein of her skin. "If I have sex with you, you have to promise you won't get clingy afterward."

I laugh, but I don't move away from her neck. "If you have sex with me, Bridgette, *you're* the one in danger of becoming clingy. You'll want so much more of me, I won't be able to tell the difference between you and Saran Wrap."

She laughs, and I pull away from her. I look down at her mouth and then into her eyes. *"My God."*

She shakes her head, confused. "What?"

"Your laugh." I kiss her on the lips. "Fucking phenomenal," I whisper into her mouth. I lift her off the counter and keep her wrapped around me as I make my way across the living room. As soon as we're in my bedroom, I close the door and push her against it. I keep her pressed against the door with my body while I remove my shirt. I find the hem of her shirt and begin to pull it over her head. "I can't tell you how many times I've fantasized about this, Bridgette."

She helps me pull her shirt over her head. "I haven't fantasized about it at all," she says.

I smile. "Bullshit."

I lift her again and carry her to the bed. As soon as I lay her on it and begin to crawl on top of her, she pushes my shoulders and shoves me onto my back. Her hands meet the button on my jeans and she undoes them. I attempt to take control again by pushing her onto her back, but she's not having it. She straddles me and places her hands on my biceps, pushing my arms against the bed. "I make the calls," she says.

I don't argue. If she wants to be in charge, I'll absolutely let her.

She sits up straight and brings her hands around to her back to undo her bra. I lift up and begin to reach around to assist her, but her hands are back on my arms in a flash. She pushes me to the mattress again. "What did I just say, Warren?"

Holy shit. She's not kidding.

I nod and focus my attention back to her bra as she lifts up and unfastens it. She slides the straps slowly down her arms and I can't keep my eyes off her. I want to touch her, to help her, to be the one to remove her bra, but she's not allowing me to do anything.

My breath catches in my chest when she flings the bra away.

My God, she's perfect. Her breasts are the perfect size, appearing as if they would fit right in the palms of my hands. But I wouldn't know, because I'm not allowed to touch them.

Am I?

I hesitantly lift my hands to feel the softness of her skin, but she immediately shoves my arms away from her, back to the bed.

God, it's torture. Her breasts are *right here*, inches from me, and I can't even touch them.

"Where are your condoms?"

I point to the nightstand on the opposite side of the bed. She slides off me and I watch her closely as she walks to my nightstand. She opens the drawer and sifts around until she finds one. She puts it between her teeth as she walks back toward the foot of the bed. She doesn't climb back on top of me. Instead, she hooks her thumbs into the waistband of her shorts and begins to shimmy out of them.

I'm harder than I've ever been, and I can feel my pulse throbbing throughout my whole body. She needs to hurry the hell up and climb back on top of me.

She leaves her panties on as she bends over and begins to pull my jeans the rest of the way off. She hooks her hands in my underwear and pulls them down as well, the condom wrapper still dangling between her teeth. Her hair is the perfect length, trailing lightly over my skin like feathers every time she leans over me.

Once all my clothes are off, her eyes focus on the hardest part of me. A smile tugs at her lips and her eyes meet mine. She pulls the condom out of her mouth.

"Impressive," she says. "This definitely explains your inflated ego."

I take the insult with the compliment, because I already know Bridgette isn't the type to dish them out.

She straddles me again, still wearing her panties. She leans forward and presses her palms into my forearms. Her mouth meets mine, and her breasts press against my chest, causing me to groan. She feels incredible. So good. I'm worried now, because we haven't even had sex yet and I can already tell I'm ruined.

I can feel her wetness through her panties as she torturously slides up and down, up and down, as slow as she possibly can. Her tongue is in my mouth, and I keep trying to grab the back of her head, or grip her by the waist, but every time I move, she stops me.

I imagined she would be bossy in the bedroom, but nothing like this. She won't even let me touch her, and it's fucking killing me.

"Open your mouth," she whispers into my ear. I do, and she places the condom wrapper between my teeth. I bite down on it and she uses her own teeth to grip the other end of it as she pulls away from me, tearing the wrapper open between both our mouths.

Okay, that was hot.

So hot.

We should quit our jobs and do this full-time.

She pulls out the condom and sits straight up. She looks down and licks her lips as she slides the condom over me and I moan, because her hands are *fuck. They're too much. I want them everywhere.*

I understand how guys can say stupid shit in the throes of passion, because I want to say so much to her right now. I want to tell her I love her and that we're soul mates and that she should marry me, because her hands make me think stupid, stupid, untrue thoughts like this.

She lifts up higher on her knees and pulls her panties to the side, leaving them on as she begins to lower herself on top of me.

It's official. She's the best roommate I've ever had in my life.

She winces slightly when she begins to take me inside

her, and I feel kind of bad that it hurts her. But not bad enough to stop myself from lifting my hips and sliding into her the rest of the way.

As soon as we're flush together, we moan in unison.

I've never felt anything like it.

It's as if her body contours perfectly to mine, fitting every line and curve and dip. Neither of us moves an inch while we fill the room with heavy gasps, giving ourselves a moment to adjust to the sheer perfection we just created.

"Fuck," I whisper.

"Okay," she replies.

She begins to move, and I don't know what to do with myself. My hands want to hold her by the waist as she slides up and down, but I also know I'm not allowed to touch her. My eyes take her in as she continues her movements, her perfect, methodical, sweet movements.

After several minutes of watching her on top of me with her eyes closed and her lips parted, I give up. I can't not touch her. My hands grip her waist and she tries to pull them away but I just grip harder, lifting her when she rises and pulling her down when she falls. She gives up trying to fight me after seeing how much better my strength can make it feel.

I want to hear her moan and I want to hear her fall apart on top of me, but she's holding it all back, just like I knew she would.

I slide my hands up her back and pull her forward until our mouths meet. I keep one hand on the back of her head and one on her waist as she continues her rhythm on top of me.

I curve my hand around her hip and slowly slide it over her stomach, until I'm touching her. I slide a finger between us, separating her, feeling her warmth and wetness surround me. She moans into my mouth and I begin to rub her, but she immediately stops moving. She grabs my wrist and pulls it away from her, slapping my arm against the mattress again.

Her eyes open and focus firmly on mine as she slowly begins to move again. "Keep your hands on the mattress, Warren," she warns.

Dammit, she's making this difficult. I need to feel her again, and when I'm done touching her, I want to taste her. I want that wetness and warmth all over my tongue.

But first, I'll let her have her way. I close my eyes and stop trying to take control. I focus on her tightness, swallowing me up. I focus on the fact that each time her body meets mine, I'm as deep inside her as I can possibly go.

She leans forward and her breasts dance back and forth across my chest as she moves on top of me.

Heaven is *definitely* for real.

My legs begin to tense and my hands are searching for something to grip as I feel myself building. She can sense I'm near release, so she tightens around me and her thrusts become faster and harder. I keep my eyes closed as my body begins to shake beneath her.

I want to cuss and groan, and let her know how good this feels as I release inside of her, but I don't make a single noise. If I'm not allowed to touch her while I come, then she's not allowed to hear how much I fucking love every second of it.

She continues to move over me as I quietly succumb to the tremors. When it's over, she comes to a stop on top of me. I open my eyes and look up at her and catch her smiling down at me. As soon as she realizes I'm looking at her, the smile is gone.

I want her to collapse against my chest. I want to roll her onto her back and take her in my mouth until she's screaming my name out in ecstasy, rather than anger.

Instead, she slowly slides off of me. She stands and turns toward the bathroom. "Goodnight, Warren."

The door closes behind her and I'm lying here in complete confusion. I would be running after her right about now, but I'm still too weak to move.

I give myself time to regroup, and then I remove the condom and toss it into the bathroom trash can on my way to her bedroom. I swing open the door just as she's crawling into her bed. As soon as her head meets her pillow, I'm on top of her, kissing her. As expected, she pushes me away.

"What did I say about being clingy?" she says, pulling her face from mine.

"I'm not being clingy," I say, kissing my way down her neck. "We're not finished."

She pulls away even farther and pushes my face back. "I'm pretty sure we finished, Warren. About three minutes ago."

"*I* finished," I say, looking her in the eyes. "But *you* didn't finish." I can feel her resistance as she attempts to roll over.

"Warren, stop," she says, pushing me away.

I don't pull away from her. Instead, I wrap my arm around her and slowly move my hand across her stomach.

That's when she slaps me.

I immediately pull back and look down at her in shock.

She pushes me away and scoots up on her bed until her

back meets the headboard. "I said stop," she says, defending her slap.

I work my jaw back and forth, not sure what to do. In all my years of experience with girls and even in all the recent porn I've been watching, this isn't how sex usually goes. People are selfish by nature and the fact that she doesn't even want me to get her off is confusing the hell out of me.

"Am I . . ." I pause and look at her. "Am I misreading something here? Because I thought . . ."

"We fucked, Warren. It's over, now go to sleep."

I shake my head. "No, Bridgette. *You* fucked. *You* did all the work and you didn't even get to enjoy it. I don't understand why you won't let me touch you."

She groans, frustrated. "Warren, it's fine. It was fun." She looks away from me. "I just don't like the other part, so go to bed."

She doesn't like the other part? The part where she has an amazing, mind-blowing orgasm?

"Okay," I say. "I'll go to bed."

"Thank you," she mutters.

"But first," I say, holding up my finger. "I need to know something."

She rolls her eyes. "What?"

I lean toward her and look at her with fascination. "Is this how sex *always* is with you? You have to be in complete control, to the point where you don't even allow someone to get you off?"

She kicks at me with her foot, trying to get me to leave her bed. "I'm not discussing my sex life with you, Warren. Go back to your room."

She scoots down on her bed until her head meets her pillow. She rolls over until her back is to me and she pulls the covers up over her head.

Holy shit. This is . . . I don't even know what to think. I've never met anyone like her. She has some serious control issues.

"Bridgette," I whisper, needing her to roll over and talk to me again. She ignores me, but I can't leave because this conversation needs to happen. "Are you telling me you've never had an orgasm during sex?"

The covers fly off her head and she rolls onto her back. "It's never been an issue with anyone until you," she says angrily.

I laugh and shake my head and for some reason, feel extremely happy about this. Because she's apparently been with some really selfish assholes in the past, and I'm about to show her what she's been missing.

She pulls the covers back over her head and faces the opposite direction again. Rather than stand and walk back to my room like I know she wants me to do, I lift the covers and slide in behind her. I wrap my arm over her, pressing my palm against her stomach, pulling her against my chest.

She practically growls at me. "Believe it or not, I'm perfectly happy with my sex life, and I don't need you to *Oh, my God.*" She stops mid-rant as soon as I cup her between the legs.

I rest my cheek against hers. "I need you to shut up, Bridgette."

She doesn't move, so I roll her onto her stomach and slide on top of her. I pin her arms beneath my hands, just like she did me earlier. "Please don't resist me," I whisper into her ear. "I want to be in control, and I want you to do what I say." I run my tongue across her ear and watch as the chills break out on her neck. "Understood?"

Her breaths are shallow, and she squeezes her eyes shut with her nod.

"Thank you," I tell her. I kiss my way down her neck and shoulder, and then work my kisses slowly across her back. Her entire body is tense and knowing that she's never experienced an orgasm at the hands of another guy already has me hard again.

I reach down to her thighs and spread her legs with my hand. She buries her face into her pillow and it makes me smile. She's never been this vulnerable with someone else, and she doesn't want to give me the pleasure of seeing how much she enjoys it.

I keep my eyes focused on her anyway as I slowly push two fingers inside of her, waiting for her to moan into her pillow.

She doesn't make a sound, so I pull them out and re-enter her with three fingers this time.

I press my forehead into her pillow, right next to her face, and I wait for the sounds to escape.

Nothing. I laugh quietly, because I really have my work cut out for me.

I pull my hand away from her and flip her onto her back. Her eyes are still closed tightly so I grab her jaw and press my lips to hers. I kiss her hard and deep, until she begins to kiss me back with just as much anger. She pulls at my hair and spreads her legs for me, wanting me to bury myself inside of her.

I do. I push her panties aside and shove into her so hard and fast, she lets out a moan and *my God, I need more of that. So much more.* But I don't have on a condom, and this time isn't about me, so I pull out of her. I take one of her breasts in my hands and bring it to my mouth.

I slowly kiss my way down her stomach, and the lower I get, the tenser her body grows. I can feel her hesitation, and part of me wants to devour her immediately, but part of me needs to know that I'm not going too far, too fast. I can tell by the stiffness in her posture that she's nervous now. I position both my hands on her waist and look up at her. She's chewing nervously on her bottom lip and her eyes are terrified.

"Have you never let anyone do this to you?" I whisper.

She releases her bottom lip with the shake of her head.

I pull her hips down several inches on the bed. "You're too stubborn for your own good." I lift her and begin to lower my mouth to her, but she pulls back and sits up.

I grip her hips and pull her back down. "Lie back and close your eyes, Bridgette."

She continues to look at me with fear in her eyes, refusing to lie back down, so I lift up onto the palms of my hands. "Will you please stop being so stubborn and just relax? *Fuck*, woman. I want to give you the best ten minutes you've ever had in your life, but you're making it really difficult."

She bites her lip hesitantly, but she does as I say and slowly lowers herself to the bed, relaxing into her pillow.

I smile triumphantly and press my lips to her stomach again. I start just below her belly button and trail slow kisses all the way down until I meet her panties. I hook my fingers into the waistband and pull them down, over her hips, over her thighs, and I continue to slowly remove them until I'm at her ankles. Once I toss them on the floor, I lift her leg and press a soft kiss against her ankle, then her calf, then the inside of her knee, repeating the kisses all the way up her thigh, until I'm inches from sliding my tongue against her. As soon as I position my mouth over her, I can feel her warmth beckoning me.

"Warren, please . . ." she begins to protest. As soon as the word *please* leaves her mouth, my tongue slides against her, separating her. She lifts her hips several inches off the bed and cries out, so I grip her waist and pull her back down to the bed.

She's sweet and salty, and as soon as my mouth is against her, I'm convinced she could satiate every ounce of hunger I'll feel for the rest of my life.

She cries out again, still trying to pull away from me. "What . . . God . . . Warren . . ."

I continue to lick her, devour her, run my tongue over every bare part of her so that I leave no inch of her untasted. Her hands find their way back to my hair just as my fingers find their way back inside of her. I'm filling her, consuming her with my tongue, and she's taking every ounce of me she can get. She's no longer trying to scoot away from me. Now she's pressing my face into her, begging me to go faster.

Her hands leave my hair and meet her headboard as she grips it tightly and locks her legs around my shoulders. I keep my fingers buried inside of her as she cries out my name with each tremor that racks her body. I continue to please her until her shudders subside and her moans fade into silence.

I kiss the inside of her thigh as I pull my fingers out of her. I kiss all the way up her stomach until I'm pressed against her again, wanting to slide inside of her and stay the night.

I want to kiss her, but I don't know if she'd want that. Some girls prefer not to be kissed afterward, but my mouth is aching with a need to feel her lips against mine.

Apparently she wants the same thing, because she doesn't even hesitate when she pulls my face to hers and kisses me with a moan. There's so much pressure in every inch of my body, because I want to take her again. The only thing that can relieve that pressure is to push into her, which is exactly what I do.

She lifts her hips and meets my thrusts and I know I should stop. I have to stop.

I don't know why I can't stop.

I've never been inside a girl without a condom before, but she makes me stupid. She renders my conscience useless, and all I can think about is how incredible she feels.

And also how much I need to stop.

Stop, Warren. Stop.

I somehow pull out of her and press my face against her chest, gasping for air.

It hurts. God, it hurts. I live in the next room, where there's a drawer full of condoms, but I'm not sure I'd make it that far if I tried to stand.

She pulls my face back to hers and presses her lips to mine. She slides her hands down to my lower back and she pulls me against her, pressing her warmth against me as she urges me to move with her.

She feels incredible. It's not the same as being inside her, but the way she's moving against me feels pretty damn close. I close my eyes and bury my face against her neck as I work to increase the pace between us.

I grab a fistful of her hair and tilt her face to mine as I look down on her, watching as we both grow nearer to yet another release. She winces and I feel the first of her shudders pass through her. "Warren," she whispers. "Kiss me."

I do.

I cover her mouth with mine and drown out her moans with my own as I feel the warmth of my release spread between us. I'm holding her as tight as I can, kissing her as hard as I can.

All my weight is against her now that I'm physically incapable of holding myself up for another second. Her hands slide from my neck and fall to the bed. I'm too weak to speak, or I would be telling her how amazing she is. How good she feels. How perfect her body is and how she just single-handedly got the upper hand for all of eternity.

I can't speak, though. My eyes fall shut from pure exhaustion.

Pure, blissful exhaustion.

•   •   •

"Warren."

I try to open my eyes, but I can't. Or I just don't want to. I don't think I've ever experienced as deep of a sleep as the one I'm being torn from right now.

Her hand is on my shoulder and she's shaking me. I lift my head and turn to face her, curious if she's ready for another round. I smile at her through sleepy eyes.

"Go to your room," she says, kicking me with her feet. "You're snoring."

My eyes fall shut again but they fly open when her cold feet meet my stomach. She uses the strength of her legs to try and push me out of her bed. *"Go,"* she groans. "I can't sleep."

I somehow push myself into a standing position. I look down at her and she rolls onto her stomach, flips her pillow over, and sprawls out across her mattress.

I shuffle my way across her bedroom, through our bathroom and to my own bed. I fall onto it and close my eyes, taking all of three seconds to fall right back to sleep.

Chapter Six

I'm convinced that I've never slept as well as I did last night. And even though she kicked me out of her bed, I still feel victorious. Like royalty.

After I'm showered and dressed, I join Ridge in the kitchen. He's cleaning up what looks like breakfast, which is odd, because neither of us ever cooks breakfast. But then I understand when Maggie emerges from his room.

"Morning, Maggie," I say to her with a smile.

She eyes me cautiously. "What's with you?"

Right at that moment, Bridgette's bedroom door opens. We all watch her walk into the living room. She pauses when she looks up and sees us all staring at her.

"Morning, Bridgette," I say with a triumphant smile. "Sleep well?"

She sees the look on my face and immediately rolls her eyes. "Screw you, Warren." She walks into the kitchen and begins rummaging through the refrigerator, searching for something to eat. I watch her the entire time, until Ridge taps me on the shoulder.

"You had sex with her?" he signs.

I immediately shake my head in defense. "No," I sign back. "Maybe. I don't know. It was an accident."

Maggie and Ridge both laugh. He grabs Maggie's hand and pulls her toward his bedroom. "Come on," he signs. "I don't want to be in here when Bridgette realizes her mistake."

I watch them retreat back to Ridge's room, and then I turn and face Bridgette. She's glaring at me.

"Did you just tell him we had sex?"

I find myself once again shaking my head. "He already knew. I told him the other day."

Bridgette tilts her head to the side. "We had sex last *night*. How did you tell him before it happened?"

I grin. "I had a good feeling."

She lets her head drop back in defeat, until she's staring up at the ceiling. "I knew it was a bad idea."

"It was a *great* idea," I interject.

She looks at me with as much seriousness as she can muster. "It was a onetime thing, Warren."

I hold up two fingers. "It was twice, actually."

She makes a face that lets me know just how much I'm irritating her. "I'm serious, Warren. We're not doing it again."

"Thank God," I say, slowly stepping toward her. "Because it was awful, wasn't it? I could tell you weren't enjoying it." I continue across the kitchen until I'm less than a foot from touching her. "You especially weren't enjoying the part when you were on your back, and my tongue was . . ."

She slaps her hand over my mouth to shut me up. She's looking at me, narrow-eyed. "I'm serious, Warren. This changes nothing. We aren't a couple. In fact, I'll probably bring other guys home and you need to be prepared for that."

She removes her hand from my mouth and I disagree. "You will not."

She looks at me with a competitive gleam in her eyes. "I will. This is why I warned you not to get clingy."

Ha. She thinks this is clingy? If she smiles and laughs like she did last night, she'll find out just how clingy I can be.

"If you don't want me to want you anymore, it's not that hard," I tell her. "Just don't smile at me." I lean forward until my lips are at her ear. "If you don't smile at me, I won't have the urge to do all those bad things to you. Because your smile is incredible, Bridgette."

I pull away slowly and look down at her. She's attempting to control the rise and fall of her chest, but she's not fooling me. I grin, and the faintest of smiles appears on her lips. I reach my hand up and touch the corner of her mouth with my finger. "You're such a tease."

She pulls away from me and calmly pushes against my chest. She grabs her drink and returns to her bedroom without another word.

I press my head against the cabinet door and sigh heavily. What have I done? What in God's name have I done to myself?

•   •   •

Bridgette and I both had the day off today, and I was positive that after our interaction this morning, and especially after last night, that she'd be all over me by nightfall. However, she completely ignored me. She stayed in her room most of the day, and she wouldn't even acknowledge me. Now it's after eleven at night. I have to be at work tomorrow morning, and I know she has an early class, so my hope for a round three is swiftly dwindling.

She even locked the door when she took a shower earlier.

I sit on the edge of my bed and contemplate the night before, going over every single move in my head, wondering where I went wrong. The only thing I can conclude is that I did nothing wrong. I did everything right, and this scared her, because she's not used to guys taking control over her. I made her feel weak.

She doesn't like to feel weak. She obviously has serious power issues and I messed with her head. This should probably make me feel guilty, but actually I'm proud. I love that I got to her. I love that I'm slowly figuring her out. And the best part is, I have a feeling that she'll be coming back for a repeat. Maybe not tonight, but she'll be back, because she's human. Every human has a weakness and I think I just discovered what hers is.

Me.

I crawl under the covers and close my eyes, but I can already tell I won't be able to sleep. It's as if last night awakened this hunger inside of me and if I don't feed it every night before I go to bed, I'll never fall asleep. I count sheep, I count stars, I repeat Bible verses in my head that I learned when I was five. None of it works, because I'm still here an hour later and I'm still wide awake.

I wonder if *she's* awake.

I wonder if she would open her door if I knocked.

I toss the covers off and begin to walk to my door, but immediately U-turn to the nightstand for a condom. All I have on are boxers, so I slip it beneath the elastic band and open my bedroom door.

Boobs.

Her boobs.

They're right here.

Her hand is in the air, poised to knock on my door. She looks just as shocked that I opened it as I am that she's standing here. She's wearing a black lace bra and the tiniest pair of panties I've ever seen in my life. She lowers her arm and we stare at each other for a solid five seconds before I'm pulling her inside, slamming my door and pushing her up against it. Her tongue is in my mouth faster than I can slip my hand beneath her bra.

"Is this what you sleep in?" I say against her mouth, pulling the straps of her bra down.

"Yes," she says breathlessly. She tilts her head and pushes my face against her neck. "But sometimes I sleep naked."

I groan and press myself against her, ready to sink myself inside her. "I like it." I spin her around until her chest is pressed against the door and her back is to me. I wrap my arm around her and grab one of her breasts while I slide my other hand down to her ass. She's in a thong. A teeny, tiny, black, lacy, beautiful thong. I rub my hand over her and then slip my fingers beneath the thin veil of fabric, pulling it down to her knees. I watch as the thong falls to her ankles and she kicks it aside.

I position myself directly behind her and run my hands down her back and to her waist. "Put your palms against the door."

She doesn't move them right away. I can feel her hesitation. I'm sure she doesn't want to hand over control again, but she needs to realize she lost control the second she showed up at my bedroom door.

I watch as she slowly presses her palms against my bedroom door. I lean forward and brush her hair away from her neck, dropping it over her shoulder. "Thank you," I whisper against her neck. I pull her hips until she's flush against me, and then I remove my boxers and open the condom.

"Bend over a little more," I tell her.

She does. She's such a fast learner.

I wrap my fingers in her hair and twist my hand around until I have a fistful of it, and then I tug just enough to get her to lift her face. She whimpers when I do this, and that little whimper is all it takes for me to push into her, as far as I can go until she's completely full.

"Make that sound again," I whisper.

She doesn't, so I tug at her hair. The noise escapes her throat and it's so beautiful and full of desire. I pull out and push back into her, and the same sound passes her lips. *I can't take it.* I don't know if I can do this standing up, because that sound is making me dizzy.

I cover one of her hands with mine and squeeze, giving myself the wall support I need to continue moving in and out of her. Every time she whimpers, I push into her a little bit harder. She begins to whimper, over and over, occasionally replacing that sound with my name, and *I already know I'm gonna sleep like a rock tonight.*

Right when I feel myself growing close to release, I pull out of her and reposition her so that her back is against the door. I lift her legs and wrap them around my waist, sliding back inside her with ease. I keep one arm wrapped around her waist to hold her up and my other hand pressed against the door for support. My tongue is fighting hers, and I'm swallowing every sound she's willing to give me.

Her hands are gripping my neck, so I reach behind me and pull one of her hands away. I press her palm against her chest and slide it slowly down her stomach. My forehead meets hers, and I look her hard in the eyes. "Touch yourself."

Her eyes grow wide, and she begins to shake her head. I place my hand on top of hers and I look down at where are bodies join together. I move her hand a few more inches until her fingers are right where I want them. "Please," I breathe out, desperately.

I need my hand for support, so I pull it away and press it against the door beside her head. I'm still holding her around the waist with my other arm and slowly pushing in and out of her. Our foreheads are still pressed together, but now my eyes are planted on her hand as she timidly begins to move her fingers in a slow, circular motion.

"Holy shit," I exhale. I watch her for a minute longer, until she starts to relax against her hand, and then I move my eyes back to her face. I pull away and stare down at her, watching as her head falls back against the door. Her eyes are closed and her lips are slightly parted and all I can feel in my heart is *kiss her, kiss her.*

My lips come down gently against hers and she moans softly into my mouth. I tease her lips with the tip of my tongue, sliding it across her top lip and then her bottom. Her moans are becoming more frequent, and the more I press her against the door, the better I can feel her hand moving between us.

I can't believe this is real life. I can't believe she lives five feet away from me and she's willing to give me this part of her. I'm the luckiest man in the world.

She starts to whimper again, but this time my mouth is resting against hers and I take in every single one of the sounds she makes. She tilts her face more and more to mine, wanting me to kiss her hard, but I'm enjoying this too much. I love the way she looks right now, eyes closed, mouth open, heart exposed. I don't want to kiss her. I want to keep my eyes open and watch every second of this.

I stop moving inside her and wait for her to finish, because if I keep moving, I won't last another second. She begins to open her eyes, wondering why I stopped, so I lean in to her ear. "You're almost there," I whisper. "I just want to watch you."

She relaxes again and I continue to watch her, soaking up every whimper and every moan and every movement she makes like I'm a sponge and she's my water.

As soon as her legs begin to tighten around my waist, I grip her hips with both hands and resume moving inside her. Her whimpers turn into moans, and her moans turn into my name and it takes us all of ten seconds before we're both shaking and gasping for breath and kissing and groping and then finally, sighing.

Her body weakens in my arms and she lays her head against my chest. I bring my hand up to her neck and kiss her softly on top of the head.

After a solid minute of working to catch our breath and regain the ability to move, I slowly begin to pull out of her. She lowers her feet to the floor and looks up at me. She's not smiling, but I can see the calmness behind her eyes. This was exactly what she needed. Exactly what *I* needed.

"Thank you," she says, matter-of-factly.

I grin. "You're welcome."

She ducks her head as soon as she begins to smile, and slips under my arm. She enters the bathroom and closes the door behind her. I lean against the wall and slide down to the floor, completely unable to will my legs to make it back to the bed. If I didn't have to wait on her to finish in the bathroom, I'd fall asleep right here on the floor.

Chapter Seven

Three solid weeks.

Twenty-one nights.

Over thirty times we've had sex.

Absolutely zero interaction during the day.

I don't really understand her. I don't know her well enough to know what sets her off or, in turn, what makes her so quiet. I don't know why she refuses to treat what's going on between us like it's anything remotely significant, but I'm not complaining. I mean, come on. We have sex every night and I don't have to dote on her during the day. I would have the perfect setup if I didn't want just a little bit more from her. But until I can get to another level with Bridgette, I know nothing better come in between us. Especially a new roommate, which is what I'm afraid might happen. Brennan has officially gone on tour and moved out, which means his room is now up for grabs. I can't take the idea of Bridgette's sister moving in, which is something I've heard them discussing on the phone. I don't know what or whom Ridge has in mind, but I for sure don't think I can take the possibility of another guy moving in. As much as I want to pretend I'm as casual with this arrangement as Bridgette is, if another guy even looks at her ass in those shorts, I won't be able to refrain from beating his ass. And I'm not even the type of guy who fights other guys, but Bridgette makes me want to fight everyone. Even the nerdy guys. I'll hit all the humans if it means keeping up the arrangement I've got going with her.

Which is why I can't stop staring at the couch right now. There's a person on it. I think it's a girl, because I see blond hair peeking out from under the pillow pulled over her face, but it could be a long-haired guy. A guy I don't want to be our next roommate. I continue to watch the couch, waiting for the person to wake up. I'm loud enough in the kitchen to wake up the whole apartment, but whoever is on this couch is sleeping like a rock.

I finish pouring my bowl of cereal and bring it into the living room. Since whoever this is has decided to take up residence where I eat breakfast, I take a seat on the floor, right in front of the couch. I begin eating, crunching as loud as I can.

I wonder if she or he is a friend of Bridgette's.

No, Bridgette didn't bring anyone home last night. I know this because I picked her up after I got off work and we came straight home and went straight to my bed. Come to think of it, we didn't even turn on the living room lights, so I'm pretty sure whoever this is was probably on the couch last night, we just didn't notice.

Oh, man. I wonder if we were loud? We never have to worry about how loud we are when Ridge is home.

A groan comes from beneath the pillow and the body rolls over, facing me so I can see it is, in fact, a girl. I continue to sit on the floor, eating my cereal. I watch her attempt to open her eyes.

"Who are you and why are you asleep on my couch?" I finally ask her.

Her whole body jerks at the sound of my voice. She lifts the pillow and backs away, making eye contact with me. I have to stifle a laugh, because someone has written *Someone wrote on your forehead* on her face with a Sharpie.

It was more than likely Ridge, so I do what I can to avoid looking at it and stare at her eyes instead.

"Are you the new roommate?" I say with a mouthful of cereal.

She shakes her head. "No," she says. "I'm a friend of Ridge's."

Hmmm. Didn't see that one coming.

"Ridge only has one friend. Me."

She rolls her eyes and sits up on the couch. She's cute. *Very impressive, Ridge.*

"Jealous?" she asks, stretching into a yawn.

"What's his last name?"

"Whose last name?"

"Your very good friend, Ridge."

She sighs and her head falls against the back of the couch. "I don't know Ridge's last name," she says. "I don't even know his middle name. The only thing I know about him is he's got a mean right hook. And I'm only asleep on your couch because my boyfriend of two years decided it would be fun to screw my roommate and I really didn't want to stick around to watch."

I like this girl. She could give Bridgette a run for her money. And I don't mean with *me*, I just mean because Bridgette is mean and probably doesn't meet a lot of girls who would stand up to her. This could be fun. "It's Lawson," I say. "And he doesn't have a middle name."

I hear Bridgette's bedroom door open and I immediately turn around to face her. She's still wearing my boxer shorts from last night, but she's put her own T-shirt over them. *God, she looks good.* "Good morning, Bridgette. Sleep well?"

She looks at me briefly and rolls her eyes. "Screw you, Warren."

Which, in Bridgette speak means, *Yes, Warren. I slept like a baby, thanks to you.*

"That's Bridgette," I whisper, turning back to the girl on the couch. "She pretends to hate me during the day, but at night she *loves* me."

The girl laughs and makes a face like she doesn't believe me.

"Shit!" Bridgette yells. I turn around in time to watch her catch herself by grabbing the bar. "Jesus Christ!" She kicks one of the suitcases that are still on the floor next to the bar. "Tell your little friend if she's staying here she needs to take her shit to her room!"

My little friend? I turn to face the girl on the couch again, wide-eyed. I think Bridgette already has an issue with this girl. All the more reason to make sure she becomes the new roommate, because I like an angry Bridgette. I'm also willing to bet a jealous Bridgette will be a lot more clingy, which could work in my favor. I turn and glare at Bridgette from where I'm seated. "What am I, your bitch? Tell her yourself."

Bridgette glances at the girl on the couch, then points to the suitcase she almost tripped over. "GET . . . YOUR . . . SHIT . . . OUT . . . OF . . . THE . . . KITCHEN!" she says before marching back to her bedroom.

I slowly turn my head to face the girl again. "Why does she think you're deaf?"

She shrugs. "I have no idea. She came to that conclusion last night and I failed to correct her."

I laugh. What a perfect prank, and I didn't even have to think of it. "Oh, this is classic," I say to her. "Do you have any pets?"

She shakes her head.

"Are you opposed to porn?"

"Not opposed to the principle of porn, but slightly opposed to being *featured* in one." I nod, because that's probably a good thing. At least I won't have double the reason to watch every porn I can get my hands on.

"Do you have annoying friends?"

"My best friend is a backstabbing whore and I'm no longer speaking to her."

"What are your showering habits?"

She laughs. "Once a day, with a skipped day every now and then. No more than fifteen minutes."

"Do you cook?"

"Only when I'm hungry."

"Do you clean up after yourself?"

"Probably better than you," she says, glancing at my shirt, which I've used for a napkin several times during this conversation.

"Do you listen to disco?"

"I'd rather eat barbed wire."

She's perfect for us.

"All right, then," I tell her. "I guess you can stay."

She sits up straighter and pulls her legs onto the couch. "I didn't realize I was being interviewed."

I look at her suitcase and then back at her. Most people don't travel with all their belongings, and if she's in search of somewhere to live, I want it to be here so I can ensure the new roommate doesn't have a dick. "It's obvious you need a place to stay, and we've got an empty room. If you don't take it, Bridgette wants to move her sister in next month and that's the *last* thing Ridge and I need."

"I can't stay here," she says, shaking her head.

"Why not? From the sound of it, you're about to spend the day searching for an apartment anyway. What's wrong with this one? You won't even have to walk very far to get here."

The door to Ridge's bedroom opens and I can see the girl's eyes widen slightly, as if she's nervous. That's probably not a good sign for Ridge, but he's so hung up on Maggie, adding this chick as a roommate shouldn't be an issue for any of us. I wink at her and stand up to walk my bowl back to the kitchen. I speak and sign at the same time. "Have you met our new roommate?"

Ridge glances at her and then looks back at me. "Yeah," he signs. "She needs a place to stay, so I'll probably just let her use Brennan's room. Or if you want, she can take your room and you can take Brennan's, so we both aren't having to share a bathroom with girls."

I shake my head. "No way are you putting me further away from Bridgette. Our bathroom sex is my favorite."

Ridge shakes his head. "You're pathetic." He walks back to his room and I look at our new roommate.

"What did he say?" she asks, nervously.

"Exactly what I thought he'd say," I tell her. I walk to my room and grab my keys off the dresser. I glance into the bathroom and see Bridgette at the sink. I swing the door open and give her a quick kiss on the cheek. She tries to pull away from me, but I also see the smile tugging at her lips.

My eyes fall to the black Sharpie sitting next to the sink. I pick it up and eye Bridgette suspiciously. She shrugs her shoulders and I laugh.

I didn't think she had it in her, but after the water cup prank and now this, I fear I might have met my match. At least the new roommate is being hazed early.

I close the bathroom door and head back out into the living room. "He says you two already worked out a deal." I point to Brennan's old room. "Heading to work now. That's your room if you want to put your stuff in it. You might have to throw all Brennan's shit in the corner, though." I open the door and step outside, but turn around before I close it. "Oh. What's your name?"

"Sydney."

"Well, Sydney. Welcome to the weirdest place you'll ever live."

I close the door behind me, feeling slightly guilty that I may have swayed this roommate thing a little in my favor. But seriously. Not only does this ensure our new roommate won't be putting the moves on Bridgette, it also makes for an interesting dynamic. Two girls in a prank war may be the best thing that ever happened to Ridge and me.

Chapter Eight

"So, what's with the new roommate?" I sign to Ridge when I walk in the door.

"She lives in the complex. Her boyfriend cheated on her and she needed a place to stay."

I walk over to the table he's seated at and pull the chair out. "She still here?"

He looks up from the laptop and nods. "Yeah, she'll probably be here for a few weeks, at least. That okay?"

Something is off with him. When you've known someone most of your life, you can almost feel their unease. This Sydney girl makes him nervous, and I don't know why.

"Is Maggie okay with it?"

His attention quickly moves back to his laptop. He nods his head and stops signing. I push my chair out and glance at the door to see if Bridgette's shoes are where she always keeps them. They aren't. I tap Ridge on the shoulder. "Where's Bridgette?" I sign.

He shifts in his seat. "Out."

"Out where?"

He shrugs. "Warren, do you really want to know? Because you aren't going to like it."

I sit in the chair again. "Hell yes, I want to know. Where is she?"

He leans back in his chair and sighs. "A guy picked her up about three hours ago. It looked like they were going out."

"Out," I sign. "Out like on a date?"

He nods.

I suddenly want to punch Ridge, but I know he has nothing to do with it. I stand up and push the chair back under the table.

She's on a date. Bridgette is on a fucking date.

This is such bullshit. Why didn't I set boundaries? Why didn't I tell her she couldn't see other guys?

What if she brings him back here? She will. She's so mean, she probably will.

I grab my keys and sign to Ridge that I'll be back in a little while.

I'll fix this.

Somehow.

•   •   •

I'm seated on the couch two hours later when the door opens. As expected, she doesn't walk in alone. A guy is following behind her, way too close. His hand is on her lower back as she slips her shoes off at the door and looks straight at me. "Oh. Hey, Warren."

She points to me. "Guy, this is Warren. Warren, this is Guy."

I look at him. At all six-metrosexual-douchebag-feet of him. "Your name is *Guy*?"

He doesn't respond. He just looks at Bridgette like he's a little uncomfortable that he just walked into her apartment and a guy is sitting on her couch. I bet he'd be really uncomfortable to know what I was doing on this same couch with Bridgette just twenty-four hours ago.

"Warren," Bridgette says in a sickeningly fake, sweet voice. "Do you mind giving us some privacy?" She glances toward my bedroom, silently asking if I'll go wait it out in there while she flirts in my living room with *Guy*. I narrow my eyes at her. She's doing this on purpose. She's testing me, and I'm about to ace this test.

"Sure will, Bridgette," I say with a smile. I stand up and walk over to Guy, reaching out for his hand. "Good to meet you," I say to him. He smiles and his apprehension eases when he sees I've loosened up. "You kiddos have fun. I'll leave the bathroom door unlocked in case either of you needs to use it." I point toward the bathroom, planting the seed.

Please, let him have to use the restroom. Please.

Bridgette can see that my last comment was out of character. She squints her eyes at me as I retreat to my room. I close the door and stay right next to it. I'm not about to miss a second of this. If she's going to try and test me or torture me by bringing another guy home, she has to expect I'll eavesdrop on their entire conversation.

I stand with my ear pressed to the door for at least fifteen minutes. In those fifteen minutes, I hear him go on and on about everything he's good at.

Baseball.

Football.

Tennis.

Trivia. (He actually forced her to quiz him.)

Work. (He's a salesman. He's the best, apparently. Highest sales for the last four quarters.)

He's a world traveler, *of course.*

He speaks French, *of course.*

Bridgette yawns four times during their conversation. I feel like this act she's putting on is exhausting her more than it is me.

"Mind if I use your restroom?" Guy says.

Finally.

A few seconds later, I hear the door close to the restroom and I immediately open my bedroom door and walk to the kitchen. Bridgette is seated on the couch with her feet propped up on the coffee table. "You look bored to death," I tell her.

"He's riveting," she says with a fake smile. "I'm having so much fun, I'll probably ask him to stay the night."

I smile, knowing that won't happen. "He'll never agree to that, Bridgette," I tell her. "In fact"—I look down at my wrist and tap it—"I'm pretty sure he'll be leaving as soon as he exits the restroom."

She sits up straight on the couch and then comes to a quick stand. She stalks over to me, pointing her finger, pushing it against my chest. "What did you do, Warren?"

The bathroom door opens and Guy walks out. Bridgette faces him with her obnoxious, fake smile. "Want to hang out in my room?" she says, walking toward him.

He glances at me and I shake my head, quickly. For all he knows, I'm just warning him, man-to-man, that he better run while he still can.

I can tell he's terrified after seeing what all I've planted in the restroom. He glances at the door and back at Bridgette. "Actually, I was just about to leave," he says. "I'll call you."

The next few seconds are the most awkward seconds I've ever seen play out between two people. He reaches in for a handshake, she goes in for a hug, he backs away, afraid she's about to try to kiss him, and his eyes grow wide with fear. He rushes around her and heads straight for the door. "Nice to meet you, Warren. I'll call you later, Bridgette."

And he's gone.

She slowly turns to face me. Her eyes are as sharp as diamonds. I'm scared they're sharp enough to slit my throat. I wipe the smile from my face and walk toward my bedroom. "Good night, Bridgette."

Nice try, Bridgette.

Nice try.

.   .   .

"Son of a bitch!"

My bathroom door swings open and she marches straight toward my bed. I was studying, but I quickly throw my books aside when I see her coming at me. She jumps onto the bed, standing, and walks across it. She holds her hands up in the air and that's when I notice she's holding something. I notice it too late, though, because the cream squirts out of the tube and onto the top of my head.

"*Hemorrhoid* cream?" she yells, tossing it aside. She grabs another tube of cream that was tucked under her arm.

"*Wart* remover?" She squeezes it onto my pillow. I'm trying to cover my head with the blanket, but she's getting the stuff everywhere. I pull her legs out from under her and she falls on the bed, then she starts kicking me, and throwing the tubes at me.

"Cold sore relief?" She squirts that one right in my face. "I can't believe you put all these in our bathroom! I swear to God, you're a little boy, Warren. A jealous little boy!"

I pull the rest of the tubes from her hands and I wrestle her onto her back, locking her arms to the mattress.

"You're such an *ass*hole," she yells.

I struggle to hold her still. "If I'm an asshole, then you're a coldhearted, calculating, ruthless *bitch!*"

She grunts, trying to free herself from my grip. I refuse to budge, but I also do my best to remove the anger from my voice and speak to her calmly.

"What was that about, Bridgette? Huh? Why the hell did you bring him here?"

She stops struggling long enough to smile in my face. Knowing that my jealousy makes her smile pisses me off even more. I hold both of her wrists with one hand and reach beside her head, grabbing a tube of the cream. I flip the lid open and squirt it in her hair. She starts thrashing beneath me and *God, I'm so mad at her.*

Why would she do that?

I grab her jaw and hold her face so she'll look at me. She realizes she's not overpowering me physically, so she relents. Her chest is heaving and she's gasping for breath. I can see anger in her eyes. I have no idea what gives her the right to be mad, when she's the one fucking with my head.

I lower my forehead to hers and close my eyes. "Why?" I say, breathless. The room grows quiet. "Why did you bring him here?"

She sighs and turns her head. I pull back and look down on her, convinced I see more pain in her features than anger. Her voice is quiet when she speaks. "Why'd you let another girl move in today?"

I know that was hard for her, because her question proves that she cares. That question proves that I wasn't the only one fearing a new roommate would come between us. She's scared I'll move on. She's scared that Sydney is going to come between us, so she tried to hurt me first.

"You think things might change between us just because another girl moved in?" I ask her. She looks over my shoulder so she doesn't have to look me in the eyes. I tilt her jaw and make her look at me. "Is that why you brought him here?"

Her eyes narrow and she tightens her lips, refusing to admit she was hurt.

"Just say it," I beg. I need her to say it out loud. All I need is for her to admit she brought him here because she was hurt and scared. I need her to admit that there's an actual heart inside her chest. And that sometimes it beats for me.

Since she won't admit it, I'll admit it *for* her. "You've never let anyone close enough to where their absence could hurt you. But it would hurt you if I left you, so you wanted to hurt me first." I press my lips closer to her ear. "You did," I whisper. "Seeing you walk through that door with him hurt like hell. But I'm not going anywhere, Bridgette, and I'm not interested in anyone else. So that little game you tried to play backfired, because from now on, the only man you're allowed to bring home is the one who already lives here." I slowly pull back and look her in the eyes. "Understood?"

In true Bridgette form, she refuses to answer. But I also

know that her refusal to answer is her way of saying I'm right and that she agrees.

She's breathing so much heavier than she was a few minutes ago. I'm almost certain I am, too, because it doesn't feel like my lungs are working anymore. I can't inhale, no matter how hard I try, because the need to kiss her has taken over my passageways. *I need her air.*

I force my mouth against hers and I kiss her with a possessiveness I didn't even know was in me. I kiss her so desperately, I forget that I'm still mad at her. My tongue dives into her mouth and she takes it, giving me her own desperate kiss in return, grabbing at my face, pulling me closer. I can feel her in this kiss like I've never felt her before. It's probably the best kiss I've ever experienced with her, because it's the first kiss with actual emotions behind it.

Even though it's the best kiss, it's also one of the shortest. She shoves me away from her. She's out of my bed, out of my bedroom, and out of my line of sight as the bathroom door slams behind her. I roll onto my back and stare up at the ceiling.

She's so confusing. She's so frustrating. She's so damn unpredictable.

She's nothing I've ever wanted in a girl. And absolutely everything I need.

I hear the water in the shower start running, so I immediately roll off the bed and walk into the bathroom. My heart tightens a little when the doorknob turns and I realize she didn't lock it behind her. I know this sign means she wants me to follow her. What she wants me to do once I'm inside this bathroom is a mystery, though. Does she want me to take her against the shower wall? Does she want me to apologize to her? Does she want me to talk to her?

I don't know with her. I never know. So, I do what I always do and wait for her to show me what she needs. I walk into the bathroom and grab a towel to wipe all the damn cream out of my hair. I get as much out as I can and then close the lid to the toilet and take a seat on it, listening quietly as she continues her shower. I know she knows I'm in here, but she doesn't speak. I'd even take her insults right now if it meant she would say something to alleviate the silence.

I lean forward and clasp my hands between my knees. "Does this scare you, Bridgette?"

I know she hears me, but she doesn't answer. *That means yes.*

I let my head fall into my hands and I vow to remain calm. This is how she relates. She doesn't know any different. Somehow, over the course of her twenty-two years, she's never learned how to love, or even communicate, really. That's not her fault.

"Have you ever been in love before?"

It's a slightly generic question. I don't ask if she could fall in love with me *specifically*, so maybe the question won't piss her off.

I hear a relenting sigh come from behind the shower curtain. "I think it takes *being* loved in order to know *how* to love," she says quietly. "So I guess that's a no."

I wince at her answer. What a sad, sad answer. One I wasn't expecting.

"You can't really believe that, Bridgette."

Silence follows. She doesn't reply.

"Your mother loved you," I say to her.

"My mother gave me to my grandmother when I was six months old."

"I'm sure your grandmother loved you."

A quiet, pained laugh comes from the shower. "I'm sure she did, but not enough to stay alive for more than a year. After she died I lived with my aunt, who made it very obvious that she didn't love me. My *uncle* did, though. Just in all the wrong ways."

I squeeze my eyes shut and allow her words to sink in. Brennan wasn't kidding when he said she's had a rough life. And she's so casual about it, like she's just accepted that this is the kind of life she was given and there's nothing she can do about it. A mixture of anger and sadness consumes me.

"Bridgette . . ."

"Don't bother, Warren. I've dealt with my life the only way I know how. It works for me, and I don't need you or anyone else to try and figure me out, or fix me. I am who I am and I've accepted that."

I clamp my mouth shut and don't offer her words of advice. I wouldn't know what to say anyway. I feel awful for wanting to prod her with more questions after that revelation, but I'm not sure when I'll get this side of her again. Bridgette doesn't open up easily, and now I can see why. She doesn't seem to have had anyone to open up to, so this might be a first for her.

"What about your sister?"

Bridgette releases a sigh. "She's not even my real sister. We're stepsisters, and we didn't even grow up in the same house."

I should stop with the questions. I know I should, but I can't. To know that she's probably never spoken or heard the words "I love you" from anyone in her life is affecting me way more than I imagined it could.

"I'm sure you've had boyfriends who have loved you in the past."

She laughs a really sad laugh, and then she just sighs an even sadder sigh. "If you're planning on asking me questions like this all night, I'd much rather you just fuck me."

I cover my mouth with my hand, absorbing her words like a knife to the chest. She seriously can't be this broken. No one can be this alone, can they?

"Have you ever loved *anyone*, Bridgette?"

Silence. Complete silence until her voice shatters it like glass. "It's hard to fall in love with assholes, Warren."

That's a comment from a girl who's been jaded way too many times. I stand up and slide the shower curtain open. She's standing beneath the stream of water. Mascara has streaked its way down her cheeks.

"Maybe you just haven't met the right asshole yet."

She immediately lets out a quick burst of laughter, along with a few tears. Her eyes are sad, and her smile is appreciative, and for the first time she's completely bare. It's as though she's holding her heart out to me, begging me not to break it. The vulnerability she's showing me right now is something I'm almost positive she's never shown anyone else. No other man, at least.

I step into the shower. She looks at me in shock as my clothes quickly become drenched. I take her face in my hands, and I kiss her.

I don't kiss her fast.

I don't kiss her rough.

I don't kiss her hard.

I press my lips to hers with such delicacy; I want her to feel everything she's ever deserved to feel at the hands of someone else. She deserves to feel beautiful. She deserves to feel important. She deserves to feel cared for. She deserves to feel respected. She deserves to feel like there's at least one other person in this world who accepts her for exactly who she is.

She deserves to know how *I* feel, because I feel all of those things. And maybe a little more.

Chapter Nine

Since that day in the shower, things have changed between us.

Not that she had this miraculous personality shift or that she's actually nice to me during the day. In fact, she's still pretty damn mean to me most of the time. She also still thinks Sydney is deaf, which is almost unbelievable that the prank has gone on for this long. So I can't even say that my excitement over pranking her has changed.

What *has* changed are our nights together.

The sex.

It's different now. Slower. Way more eye contact. Way more kissing. Way more buildup. Way more kissing. So much kissing, and not just on the mouth. She kisses me everywhere, and she takes her time when she does it. And she enjoys it.

She still isn't the type to want to cuddle afterward, and she always kicks me out of her bed before the sun comes up.

But still, it's different. That night in the shower tore a wall down between us. Because I know that every night when I have her in bed, she gives me a part of herself that no one else has ever seen. And that's enough to keep me happy for a long damn time.

I just hope today doesn't ruin that.

We both have the day off and that doesn't happen very often between both of our jobs and school. I have a few errands to run and I asked her to go with me, which might be a little strange. We've been sleeping together for a few months now, but this is the first time we've ever actually done anything that didn't involve sex.

Which also makes me wonder if I should ask her out on a date eventually. I know she's not a typical girl, but surely she likes some of the same things other girls do, like being taken out on dates. But she's never hinted that she wants me to take her on one, and frankly, I'm scared to ask her. I feel like our setup is perfect for both of us and if we start throwing dates into the mix, it'll screw it all up.

That includes daytime dates. Like today. Like what we're about to do.

Shit.

"So," Sydney says. She's seated on the couch next to me. I'm watching porn, naturally, because Bridgette still refuses to give me the name of the one she was in. Sydney doesn't mind it, though. She's focusing on her homework, oblivious to the fact that I'm kind of having a minor internal freak-out over the fact that I may or may not have just invited Bridgette on a daytime date to run errands.

"What's up with Bridgette?"

I glance at Sydney and she's still focusing on her textbook, making notes.

"What do you mean?"

Sydney shrugs. "She's just so . . . mean."

I laugh, because it's true. Bridgette can be awful. "She can't help it," I say. "She's had a rough life."

"So has Ridge," Sydney says, "but he doesn't bite people's heads off when they try to speak to him."

"That's because Ridge is deaf. He can't yell at people, it's physically impossible for him."

Sydney looks up at me and rolls her eyes, laughing. She elbows me in the ribs, just as Bridgette walks out of her bedroom. Bridgette glares at Sydney and I hate that she still assumes there could ever be something between Sydney and me. I like her, and I think she's cool, but I have a feeling Ridge would put a stop to that in a heartbeat.

Which isn't a good thing, considering Ridge has Maggie. But those are issues I don't feel like getting involved in at the moment, because *my* issue is glaring right at me. "Please don't tell me you invited your little girlfriend," Bridgette says, shifting her eyes toward Sydney.

Sydney is really good at this prank thing. She doesn't even bat an eye as Bridgette talks about her. She just goes on pretending she can't hear a word Bridgette says. I'm pretty sure Sydney has gone on this long with the prank because it's a whole lot easier than having to actually *speak* to Bridgette.

"She's not coming," I say, standing up. "She has plans."

Bridgette turns away, giving her attention to the purse she has just slung over her shoulder. I walk up to her and wrap my arms around her from behind. "I'm kidding," I whisper in her ear. "I didn't invite anyone else to run errands with me today but you."

Bridgette's hand meets my forehead, and she pushes me away from her. "I'll stay here if you expect today to be like this."

I take a step back. "Like what?"

She points at me. "You. Touching me. Kissing me. PDA.

Gross." She walks to the front door and I clutch my hand to my heart and wince at Sydney.

"Good luck," she mouths as I make my way to the door.

Once we're in my car and it's moving away from the apartment, Bridgette finally speaks. "So where are we going first? I need to go to Walgreens before we come back."

"First, we go to my sister's house, then we go to the bank, then we go to Walgreens, then we go eat lunch, then we go home."

Her hand flies up and she holds up a finger. "What did you just say?"

I repeat myself. "First we go to my sister's house, then we go to . . ."

"Why in the *hell* are you taking me to your sister's house? I don't want to meet your sister, Warren. We aren't that kind of couple."

I roll my eyes and grab the hand she's holding up in protest. "I'm not bringing you as my girlfriend. You can stay in the damn car for all I care. I just need to drop off a package at her house."

This actually eases her apprehension. She relaxes into the seat and flips her hand over so that I can slide my fingers through hers. I look down at our hands and seeing them linked together on the seat between us feels like I just went further with her than the night we first had sex.

She would have never let me hold her hand back then. Hell, she would have never let me hold her hand last month. But we're holding hands now.

Maybe I should ask her out on a date.

She pulls her hand from mine and I immediately glance

up at her. She's staring straight at me. "You were smiling too much," she says.

What?

I reach over and grab her hand again and pull it back to me. "I was smiling because I like holding your hand."

She yanks her hand back. "I know. That's why I don't want you to hold it."

Goddammit. She's not winning this one.

I reach across the seat again, swerving the car in the process. She tries to shove her hand beneath her legs so that I can't grasp it, so I pull at her wrist instead. I release the steering wheel and reach across with both hands now, steering with my knee. "Give me your hand," I say through clenched teeth. "I want to hold your damn hand." I have to grab the wheel to steer us back into our lane. Once we're no longer in danger of crashing, I slam on the brakes as I pull over to the side of the road. I throw the car in park and lock the doors so she can't run. I know how she works.

I lean across the seat and pry her hand away from being tucked against her chest. I grab her wrist with both hands and I pull her toward me. She's still trying to fight me by pulling her hand away, so I release her and look her directly in the eye. "Give. Me. Your. Hand."

I'm not sure if I just scared her a little, but she relaxes and allows me to grab her wrist. I put her wrist in my left hand and I hold up my right hand in front of hers. "Spread your fingers."

She makes a fist instead.

I pry open her fist, then force our fingers to intertwine. I hate that she's being so resistant. She's pissing me the hell off. All I want to do is hold her damn hand and she's making such a big deal out of it. We're doing everything backward in this relationship. Couples are supposed to start out holding hands and going on dates. Not us. We start out fighting, end up screwing, yet we apparently haven't even made it to the point where we can hold hands. If things continue at this rate, we'll probably move in together before we even go on our first date.

I squeeze her hand until I know she can't pull away from me. I scoot back to my seat and I put the car in drive with my left hand and then ease back onto the road.

We drive the next several miles in silence, and she occasionally tries to ease her hand from mine, but each time she does it I squeeze a little tighter and get even more agitated with her. She's gonna hold my damn hand whether she likes it or not.

We hit a red light and the lack of movement outside the car and the lack of conversation inside the car shifts the mood tremendously, thickening the air with tension and . . . *laughter?*

She's laughing at me.

Figures.

I slowly tilt my head in her direction, giving her a side-long glance. She's covering her mouth with her free hand, trying not to laugh, but she is. She's laughing so hard that her body is shaking.

I have no idea what she finds so funny, but I'm not laughing with her. And as much as I want to turn away and punch the steering wheel, I can't stop watching her. I watch the tears form at the corners of her eyes, and I watch her chest heave when she attempts to catch her breath. I watch her lick her lips as she tries to stop herself from smiling so much. I watch her run her free hand through her hair as she sighs, coming down from her fit of laughter.

She finally looks at me. She's no longer laughing, but the residue is still there. The smile is still on her mouth and her cheeks are still a shade pinker than normal, and her mascara is smudged at the corners of her eyes. She shakes her head, keeping her focus on me. "You're insane, Warren." She laughs again, but only for a second. The fact that I'm not smiling is making her uncomfortable.

"Why am I insane?"

"Because," she says. "Who throws that big a fit over holding someone's hand?"

I don't move a muscle. "*You* do, Bridgette."

The smile slowly leaves her face, because she knows I'm right. She knows that she's the one who made a big deal out of holding hands. It was me who wanted to show her how easy it was.

We both look down at our hands as I slowly pry my fingers away from hers and release my grip. The light turns green as I grab the steering wheel and press on the gas. "You sure do know how to make a guy feel like shit, Bridgette."

I give my full attention back to the road and rest my left elbow on the window. I cover my mouth with my hand, squeezing the stress out of my jaw.

We make it three blocks.

Three blocks is all it takes for her to do the most considerate thing she's ever done for me since the moment I met her.

She reaches to the steering wheel and takes my hand.

She pulls it to her lap and slides her fingers between mine. She doesn't stop there, though. Her right hand slides over the top of my hand and she strokes it. She strokes my fingers and the top of my hand and my wrist and back down to my fingers. She stares out her window the whole time, but I can feel her. I can feel her speaking to me and holding me and making love to me, all in the motion of her hands.

And I smile the entire way to my sister's house.

. . .

"Is she older or younger than you?" Bridgette asks when I turn off the ignition.

"Ten years older."

We both exit the car and begin walking toward the house. I didn't ask her to come with me, but the fact that she didn't wait in the car is proof that another wall has been torn down between us.

I walk up the steps, but before I knock on the door, I turn and face her. "What do you want me to introduce you as?" I ask her. "Roommate? Friend? Girlfriend?"

She glances away and shrugs. "I don't care, really. Just don't make it weird."

I smile and knock on the door. I immediately hear tiny footsteps and squealing and things falling and *shit, I forget how crazy it is over here.* I probably should have warned her.

The door swings open and my nephew, Brody, jumps up and down. "Uncle Warren!" he yells, clapping his hands. I open the screen door, set the package my mother sent for my sister on the floor and immediately swoop Brody up. "Where's your mom?"

He points across the living room. "In the kitchen," he says. His hand meets my cheek and he makes me face him. "Wanna play dead?"

I nod and set him down on the carpet. I motion for Bridgette to follow me inside, and then I fake stab Brody in the chest. He falls to the floor in a dramatic display of defeat.

Bridgette and I both stand over him as he writhes in pain. His body convulses a few times and then his head falls limp to the carpet.

"He dies better than any four-year-old I've ever seen," I say to Bridgette.

She nods, still staring down at him. "I'm in awe," she says.

"Brody!" my sister yells from the kitchen. "Is that Warren?"

I begin walking in the direction of the kitchen and Bridgette follows me. When I round the corner, Whitney has Conner on her hip and she's stirring something on the stove with her other arm.

"Brody's dead, but yeah, it's me," I say to her.

As soon as Whitney glances at me, cries come from the baby monitor next to the stove. She sighs, exasperated, and motions for me to come to the stove. I walk over to her and take the spoon from her hands. "It has to be stirred for at least another minute, then remove the burner from the pan."

"You mean remove the pan from the burner?"

"Whatever," she says. She pulls Conner off her hip and walks toward Bridgette. "Here, hold Conner. I'll be right back."

Bridgette instinctively holds out her hands and my sister

shoves Conner at her. Bridgette's arms are outstretched, as far from her body as she can get them. She's holding Conner under his armpits, staring at me wide-eyed.

"What do I do with it?" she whispers. Her eyes are filled with terror.

"Have you never held a kid before?" I ask in disbelief. Bridgette immediately shakes her head.

"I don't know any kids."

"Me a kid," Conner says.

Bridgette gasps and looks at Conner, who is staring right back at her with just as much terror and fascination. "It talked!" she exclaims. "Oh, my God, you talked!"

Conner grins.

"Say *cat*," Bridgette says.

"Cat," Conner repeats.

She laughs nervously, but is still holding him like he's a dirty towel. I remove the pot from the burner and turn it off, then walk over to her. "Conner's the easy one," I tell her. "Here, hold him like this." I pull him around to her hip and wrap her arm behind him, securing him against her waist. She's trading nervous glances between Conner and me.

"He won't shit on me, will he?"

I laugh and Conner giggles. He slaps her chest twice and kicks his legs. "Shit on me," he says, still laughing.

Bridgette's hand clamps over her mouth. "Oh, my God, he's just like a parrot," she says.

"Warren!" Whitney yells from the top of the stairs.

"I'll be right back."

Bridgette shakes her head and points to Conner. "But . . . but . . . *this* . . ." she stutters.

I pat her on top of her head. "You'll be fine. Just keep him alive for two minutes." I scale the steps and Whitney is standing in the doorway to the nursery. She's wiping her neck with a rag.

"He pissed in my face," she says. She looks so frazzled. I want to hug her, and I would if she weren't covered in infant piss. She hands me the baby. "Take him downstairs while I jump in the shower, please."

I lift him out of her hands. "No problem."

She begins to head to her room, but pauses right before I make it back to the stairs. "Hey," she says. I turn and face her. "Who's the girl?" she signs.

I love that she signs this, so Bridgette has no chance of hearing her ask. Having a family that is all fluent in sign language definitely comes in handy.

"Just my roommate," I sign back to her, shrugging it off. She smiles and walks into her room. I walk down the stairs holding the baby against my chest. I step over Brody, who is still playing dead on the floor. When I make it to the doorway in the kitchen, I pause. Bridgette has sat Conner on the kitchen island. She's standing right in front of him so that he doesn't fall and she's holding up her fingers, counting with him.

"Three. Can you count to three?"

Conner touches his finger to the tips of hers. "One. Two. Twee," he says. They both start clapping and he says, "Me now."

Bridgette begins to count his fingers this time. I lean my head against the doorframe and watch her interact with him.

I don't know why I've never spent time with her outside

of the bedroom before this. I could add up all the things she's done to me at night, and I'm positive I wouldn't trade today for all of that combined.

This is the Bridgette that *I* see. The part of her she gives to me. And now that I'm watching her, I see that she's very capable of giving it to others who deserve it.

"Do you stare at all your roommates like this?" Whitney whispers in my ear. I spin around, and she's standing behind me, watching me watch Bridgette. I shake my head and look back at Bridgette. "No. I don't."

As soon as I say it, I regret saying it. Whitney will be texting me within the hour, wanting to know all the details. How long I've known her, where she's from, if I'm in love with her.

Time to leave.

"Ready, Bridgette?" I ask, handing the baby back to Whitney.

Bridgette glances up at me and then back to Conner. She actually looks a little sad that she has to say goodbye.

"Bye, Bwidjet," Conner says to her with a wave. Bridgette gasps and turns to face me.

"Oh, my God! Warren, he said my name!"

She turns back to Conner, and he's still waving. "Shit on me," he says.

Bridgette immediately picks him up and sets him down on the floor. "Ready," she says quickly, walking away from him and toward the front door.

Whitney is pointing at Conner and looking at me, "Did he just say . . ."

I nod. "I think he did, Whit. You need to watch your

language around your kids." I give her a quick kiss on the cheek and head for the front door.

Bridgette is standing over Brody, looking down at him. "Seriously impressive."

He's in the exact same position we left him in. "I told you he dies better than anyone I know." I step over him and hold the front door open for her. We walk outside and she doesn't even flinch or pull away when I slide my hand through hers. I walk her to the passenger side door, but before I open it, I turn her to face me and I press her against the car. My hand touches her forehead and I wipe away a wisp of hair.

"I never thought I wanted kids," she says, glancing back at the house.

"But you do now?"

She shakes her head. "No, not really. But maybe if I could have Conner. At that age, for like a year, maybe two. Then I'd probably get tired of him and not want him anymore, but a year or two out of my life might be fun."

I laugh. "So why don't you kidnap him and bring him back when he's five?"

She faces me again. "But you would know it was me who took him."

I smile down at her. "I would never tell. I like you better than I like him."

She shakes her head. "You love your sister too much to do that to her. It would never work. We'd have to kidnap someone else's kid."

I sigh. "Yeah, you're probably right. Besides, we should probably kidnap a celebrity's kid. That way we could get ransom out of it and never have to work again. We could give the kid back, take the money, and spend the rest of our lives having sex all day."

Bridgette smiles. "You're so romantic, Warren. No other guy has ever promised me a kidnapping and ransom."

I tilt her chin up so that her mouth is positioned closer to mine. "Like I said, you just haven't met the right asshole." I press my lips to hers and kiss her, briefly. I keep it PG in case Brody has come back to life and is watching us.

I reach behind her and open the door. She walks around me to climb inside, but before she does, she stands on her tiptoes and kisses me on the cheek.

To Brody or anyone else watching, that was just a kiss on the cheek. But knowing Bridgette like I know her, that was a whole lot more than just a kiss. That was her saying she doesn't need anyone else.

That kiss on the cheek means we're official.

That kiss on the cheek means I have a girlfriend.

Chapter Ten

"So you think it's official because she kissed you on the cheek?" Sydney says, confused. She doesn't get it. She's like everyone else and sees Bridgette at face value, which is fine. Bridgette gives people a pretty rough face value, and that's Bridgette's right.

I stop trying to explain to Sydney my relationship with Bridgette. Besides, I kind of like that no one gets it. And even though we had this really crazy, nonsexual experience with the hand-holding and the cheek kissing the other day, it hasn't affected us in the bedroom. In fact, last night we moved past the slow and steady streak we've been on and played out a fantasy of mine that involved her Hooters uniform.

"You should try to get a job at Hooters," I tell Sydney. I know she's been looking for work, and even though it doesn't seem up her alley, the tips really are good.

"No, thanks," she says. "I wouldn't be caught dead in those shorts."

"They're actually very nice shorts. Soft. Stretchy. You'd be surprised. And last night when Bridgette was pretending she was serving me a platter of hot wings, I reached down and . . ."

"Warren," Sydney says. "Stop. I don't care. How many times do I have to tell you I don't care about your sex life?"

I frown. Ridge doesn't really like to hear about it, either, and I can't tell Bridgette because she's a part of the story and it would just be redundant. I miss Brennan. He always listened.

Bridgette's bedroom door opens, and I watch as her eyes search the living room for me. I can see a hint of a smile, but she's good at making sure I'm the only one who sees it.

"Good morning, Bridgette," I say to her. "Sleep well?"

Her eyes fall on Sydney, who's seated next to me on the couch again. She looks away, but not before I see a flash of hurt on her face.

"Screw you, Warren," Bridgette says, turning her attention toward the refrigerator.

Still, after holding hands and kissing my cheek, she thinks I'd ever mess with another girl?

I watch her as she slams stuff around in the kitchen, angrily. "I don't like how she's up your ass all the time," Bridgette says. I immediately turn to Sydney and laugh, because for one, she still thinks Sydney can't hear her, and two, I can't believe she just said that to me. If that isn't her laying claim to me, I don't know what is.

I love it.

"You think that's funny?" Bridgette says after spinning around. I quickly shake my head and lose my smile, but she throws her hand in Sydney's direction. "The girl obviously has it bad for you, and you can't even respect me enough to distance yourself from her until I'm out of the house?" She turns her back to us again. "First she gives Ridge some sob story so he'll let her move in, and now she's taking advantage of the fact that you know sign language so she can flirt with you."

I don't know who to feel worse for, Bridgette or Sydney. Or *myself.* "Bridgette, stop."

"*You* stop, Warren," she says, turning back around to face me. "Either stop crawling in bed with me at night or stop shacking up on the couch with *her* during the day."

I knew it was coming, but I hoped I wouldn't be here when it finally did.

Sydney reaches her breaking point and slaps her book against her thighs. "Bridgette, please!" she yells. "Shut up! Shut up, shut up, shut up! Christ! I don't know why you think I'm deaf, and I'm definitely not a whore and I'm not using sign language to flirt with Warren. I don't even know sign language. And from now on, please stop yelling when you speak to me!"

I'm scared to look at Bridgette. I feel torn, because I want to high-five Sydney for finally standing up for herself, but I want to hug Bridgette because I know this has to be hard for her. I suddenly feel like the prank was the worst prank in the history of pranks.

I glance up just in time to see a flood of hurt wash over Bridgette's face. She marches to her room and slams her door.

This is going to be impossible to fix. Sydney just single-handedly ruined my entire relationship with that outburst.

Okay, it wasn't all her. I played a huge part in it, too.

My chest hurts. I don't like this. I don't like the silence, and I don't like the fact that I'm about to have to go make this right. I put my hands on my knees and begin to stand. "Well, there goes my chance to act out all the role-playing scenes I've been imagining. Thanks a lot, Sydney."

She pushes her book off her lap and stands up. "Screw you, Warren."

Ouch. Double hurt.

Sydney walks over to Bridgette's bedroom door and knocks. After a few seconds, she cautiously slips inside and closes the door behind her.

If she somehow fixes this, I'll be indebted to her forever.

I sigh and run my hand through my hair, knowing this is my fault. I glance over at Ridge and he's staring at me. "What'd I miss?" he signs.

I slowly shake my head in shame. "Bridgette found out Sydney's not deaf and now Bridgette hates me. Sydney went to Bridgette's room to try and fix things because she feels guilty."

Confusion clouds Ridge's face. "Sydney?" he signs. "What does *she* have to feel guilty for?"

I shrug. "Going along with the prank, I guess. She feels bad that it embarrassed Bridgette."

Ridge shakes his head. "Bridgette deserved it. If anyone should be apologizing, it should be her. Not Sydney."

Why is he defending Sydney like he's her overprotective boyfriend? I glance at Bridgette's bedroom door, shocked that I actually hear a conversation going on in her room, rather than a catfight. Ridge waves his hand in the air to get my attention again.

"Bridgette isn't yelling at her, is she?" he signs. He looks worried, and frankly, that concerns me.

"You sure do seem to care a lot about Sydney's well-being," I sign.

His jaw tightens, and I know I probably shouldn't have

said anything. I can't help it, though. I've been through a lot with Ridge and Maggie, and I don't want him screwing things up just because he might find another girl attractive.

I can tell he doesn't want to take the conversation in that direction, so I redirect it back to me.

"No, neither of them are yelling," I sign. "But Bridgette *will* be as soon as she walks back out of her bedroom. She'll more than likely move out now, and I'll never be able to crawl out of bed again because . . ." I clasp my hand to my chest, "She's gonna take my heart with her."

He knows I'm being dramatic, so he rolls his eyes and laughs, turning to face his laptop again. The door to Bridgette's bedroom swings open, and she marches out.

I didn't prepare for this. I knew she'd be mad, but I'm not sure I can defend myself against her physically if we were in a real fight.

I sit up straight and watch in fear as she walks swiftly toward me. She kneels down onto the couch and slides her leg across my lap, straddling me.

I'm so confused.

Her hands meet my cheeks and she sighs. "I can't believe I'm falling in love with such a stupid, stupid asshole."

My heart wants to rejoice, but my mind is pulling on the reins.

Falling in love.

With an asshole.

A stupid, stupid asshole.

Holy shit! That's *me!*

I wrap my hands around her head and pull her mouth to mine at the same time that I stand up and begin making my way into my bedroom. I shut the door behind us and walk over to the bed and drop her on it. I take off my shirt and throw it on the floor.

"Say it again." I slide on top of her and she smiles, touching my face with the palms of her hands.

"I said I'm falling in love with you, Warren. I think. I'm pretty sure that's what this is."

I kiss her again, frantically. Those are the most beautiful words I've ever heard come out of another human. I pull back and look at her again. "But you wanted to kill me five minutes ago. What changed?" I lift up onto my hands. "Did Sydney pay you to say that? Is this a prank?" My heart stops. Bridgette shakes her head.

I would die. I would literally die if she took them back. I would die so much better than Brody dies, because my death would be *actual* death.

"I just . . ." Bridgette pauses, searching for the right words. "I've been thinking this whole time that maybe you were messing around with Sydney. But after talking to her, I know that's not true. And she also mentioned that one night when you were drunk, you said you might love me. And that just . . . I don't know, Warren."

God, I love this. I love her nervousness. I love her hesitation. I love that she's talking to me so openly. "Tell me, Bridgette," I say quietly, urging her to finish what she was saying. I roll onto my side and lift up onto my elbow. I brush the hair away from her forehead and lean forward to kiss it.

"When she said that, it made me feel . . . *happy*. And I realized that I'm never happy. I was an unhappy child and I'm an unhappy adult and nothing in my life makes me feel the way you do. So I just . . . I think that's what this feeling is. I think I'm falling in love with you."

A small droplet of a tear escapes from the corner of her eye, and as much as I want to bottle it up and save it for all of eternity, I pretend not to notice it, because I know that's what she would prefer. I kiss her lips again before pulling back and looking her directly in the eyes. "I'm falling in love with you, too."

She smiles and reaches her hand up to the back of my head, slowly pulling my mouth to hers. She kisses me softly and then gently pushes me onto my back. She eases herself on top of me and presses her hands against my chest.

"I think I should clarify that I never said I was *in* love with you. I just said I was *falling* in love with you. There's a difference."

I grab her by the hips and pull her closer. "The only difference between *falling* in love and *being* in love is that your heart already knows how you feel, but your mind is too stubborn to admit it." Then I whisper in her ear. "But take all the time you need. I have nothing but patience for you."

"Good, because I'm not telling you I love you yet. Because I don't. I might be on my way to that point, but anything could derail that."

I can't help but smile and kiss her after that little disclaimer.

After a few more minutes of kissing, she turns her head to the side and holds up a finger, silently asking me to stop. She pulls away and sits up on the bed, hugging her knees. She lays her head on her arms and squeezes her eyes shut.

She's quiet for several moments, and her reaction is unusual for her. She looks guilty. She doesn't ever look guilty because she's always too angry to feel any sense of guilt.

"What's the matter?" I ask her.

She quickly shakes her head. "I'm the worst person in the world," she whispers. She turns her head toward mine, slowly. I don't like the look on her face.

She begins to scoot off the bed and I feel my heart dragging behind her. "It was a prank, Warren," she says softly as she stands.

I rise up onto my elbows. "What do you mean?"

She turns to face me and her eyes are so full of shame, she can't even look at me without wincing. "I was trying to get back at you for letting me think Sydney was deaf." She opens the bathroom door and looks down at her feet. "I said all that because I was mad at you, not because it's really how I feel. I'm not falling in love with you, Warren."

I think you're standing on my heart, Bridgette.

She glances over her shoulder into the bathroom, and then back at me. "I didn't mean to take it that far. This is really awkward. I'm gonna go back to my room now." She closes the door behind her.

I'm too numb to feel. Too numb to move. Too numb to process the words that just came out of her mouth. My throat hurts, my stomach hurts, my chest hurts, even my fucking lungs hurt and *oh, my God*, it hurts so much.

I fall back to the bed and bring two fists to my forehead.

"Hey, Warren," she says from the doorway.

I look up at her and she still looks just as guilty. She waves her hand back and forth between us. "That whole thing that just happened? That was . . ." Her frown transforms into a shit-eating grin. "*That* was actually the prank!"

She runs and jumps on the bed, and begins dancing around me. "You should have seen your face!" She's laughing and jumping, bouncing every aching part of me up and down on the bed.

I want to kill her.

She falls to her knees and leans over me, pressing her lips to mine. When she pulls back, I don't want to kill her anymore. My whole body is miraculously healed by her smile. I feel better than I've ever felt. I feel stronger, more alive, happier, and somehow more in love with her than I was five minutes ago. I pull her against me. "That was a really good prank, Bridgette."

She laughs. "I know. It was the best."

I nod. "It really was."

I hold her for several quiet minutes, replaying the entire scene in my head. "God, you're such a bitch."

She laughs again. "I know. A bitch who finally met the right asshole."

Chapter Eleven

Guess who woke up in Bridgette's bed again this morning?

Me.

And guess who'll be falling asleep in Bridgette's bed tonight?

That's right. *Me.*

Both of those things are great, but not as great as this moment. Right now.

We're both seated on the couch, and she's lying between my legs with her head on my chest. We're watching a movie where the actors actually stay dressed for the entire film. But it's not really important what film it is, because Bridgette's cuddling with me.

This is a first, and it's incredible, and I love how she makes me appreciate such simple, mundane things.

Both of us glance at the door when we hear a key being inserted into the lock. The door opens and Brennan walks in. I immediately sit up on the couch, because he's supposed to be in Dallas tonight. He has a show tomorrow, and I'm positive I booked him a hotel for the right night.

Bridgette sits up on the couch and looks at him. He smiles at her, but it's a forced smile. He reaches for his back pocket and pulls out a sheet of paper. He holds it up. "This came today," he says.

Bridgette squeezes my hand and that's when I realize he's holding the test results. I've known Brennan long enough to know by his reaction that he's not happy about the results. I just don't know if that's a good thing or a bad thing for Bridgette.

"Just tell me," she whispers.

Brennan looks down at his feet and then up to me. The look in his eyes is enough for Bridgette to know that she's not any closer to figuring out who her real father is than she was a few months ago.

She inhales a deep breath, and then stands up. She mutters a "thank you" to Brennan and begins heading toward her bedroom, but he grabs her by the arm and pulls her to him. He wraps his arms around her and gives her a hug, but in true Bridgette fashion, she doesn't allow it to last more than two seconds. She begins to cry, and I know that Bridgette doesn't want anyone to see her cry. She ducks her head and rushes to her room.

Brennan tosses the paper on the counter and runs his hands through his hair. "This sucks, man," he says. "I felt like she really needed it to be true, and instead, it just adds to all the shit she's had to deal with her whole life."

I sigh and drop my head against the couch. "You sure about the results? There's no way they could have messed up?"

Brennan shakes his head. "She's not his daughter. And in a way, I'm happy for her because who would want him for a dad? But I know she liked the idea of finally having a little bit of closure."

I stand up and squeeze the back of my neck. "I don't think closure is the only thing she was hoping for." I point to her bedroom. "I'm gonna go check on her," I tell him. "Thanks for coming all this way to tell her."

Brennan nods, and I make my way into her bedroom. She's curled up on the far side of her bed, facing opposite from the door.

I'm not good at consoling, so I'm not sure what I can say to make her feel any better. Instead, I just climb onto the bed and scoot in behind her. I wrap my arm over her and grab her hand.

We lie like this for several minutes, and I let her get all her tears out. When it doesn't sound like she's crying anymore, I press a kiss into her hair.

"He would have been a horrible father, Bridgette."

She nods. "I know. I just . . ." She sucks in a rush of air. "I like it here. I feel like all of you accept me for who I am, and that's never happened before. And now that Brennan knows I'm not his sister, what happens now? Do I just leave?"

I squeeze her tighter, hating that she even thinks that's an option. "Over my and Brody's dead bodies. No way am I letting you go anywhere."

She laughs and wipes at her eyes. "You guys don't have to be nice to me out of pity."

I roll her onto her back and shake my head in confusion. "Pity? This isn't pity, Bridgette. I mean, yeah, I feel bad for you. Yeah, it might have been cool if you were their sister. But it doesn't change anything. The only thing those test results would have changed is that you'd go from not knowing who your real father is to having one of the worst fathers in the world." I kiss her on the forehead. "I don't care whose sister you are, I love you the same."

Her eyes widen, and I can feel her body stiffen in my arms. I didn't say I was falling in love this time.

I just told her I loved her. Like, actively. And yes, those three words could probably make her flip out more than any other three words in the English language, but I can't take it back. I *won't* take it back. I love her, and I've loved her for months now and I'm tired of being too scared of her reaction to say it.

She begins to shake her head. "Warren . . ."

"I know," I interject. "I said it. Get over it. I love you, Bridgette."

Her expression is void of any emotion right now. She's absorbing it. She's waiting to see how those words make her feel, because I'm not sure if she's ever heard them before.

Her jaw grows tense, and she places her hands against my chest. "You're a liar," she snaps, attempting to roll out from under me.

Here we go again.

I pull her back to the mattress while she attempts to squirm away. "You're exhausting, you know that?" I roll her onto her back and she begins to nod, frantically.

"That's right, Warren. I'm exhausting. I'm mean. I always see the glass half empty, and if you think telling me you love me will make me nicer and less exhausting, you're wrong. You can't change me. Everyone wants to change me, but I am who I am, and if you think me telling you that I love you, too, will make me shit out unicorns and rainbows, you're wrong. I *hate* unicorns and rainbows."

I drop my face to her neck and I start to laugh. "*Oh, my God*, I can't believe you're mine." I kiss her on the cheek, and then I kiss her on the forehead, and then her nose and her chin and her other cheek. I look back at her eyes full of confusion.

"I don't *want* you to change, Bridgette. I'm not in love with who you *could* be, or who you *used* to be, or who the world *says* you should be. I'm in love with *you*. Right now. Just like this."

She's still guarded and defensive, so I pull her closer to me and wrap my arms around her, hugging her tightly. "Stop," I whisper in her ear. "Stop telling yourself that you aren't lovable, because it's pissing me off. I don't care if you aren't ready to admit how you really feel about me yet, but don't you dare dismiss how I feel about you. Because I love you." I kiss her on the side of the head, and I say it again. It feels so good to finally say it. "I love you, Bridgette."

She pulls away just enough for me to see her face. Her eyes are rimmed with tears.

"Bridgette, I love you," I say again, this time looking her straight in the eyes. I can feel her struggling internally. Part of her wants to enjoy this moment, and part of her is trying to hold up that last wall that still stands between us.

"I love you," I whisper again.

One of the tears escapes from her eyes, and I'm afraid she's about to break and push me away like she always does. I press my lips against hers, and I inhale deeply. I touch her cheek and wipe away her tear with my thumb.

"You're the most genuine person I know, Bridgette. So whether you think you deserve love or not, it doesn't matter, because I can't help it. I fell in love with you, and I'm not sorry for it."

Another tear falls from her eyes.

A smile forms on her lips.

A laugh escapes her mouth, and her chest begins to shake because she's laughing and crying and kissing me. And I kiss her right back, crashing right through the last wall that stood between us.

She wraps her hands in my hair and rolls me onto my back, still with her lips pressed to mine. I open my eyes and she backs away from my mouth, still smiling. She begins to shake her head in slow disbelief. "I can't believe I'm in love with such a stupid, stupid asshole."

I'm not sure this sentence could mean more to any other man in the world.

"I love you, Warren."

I can't even tell her I love her back, because hearing those words come out of her mouth has left me completely speechless. But I don't think she cares, because her lips are on mine so hard and fast, I wouldn't be able to speak anyway.

I'm in love with Bridgette.

Bridgette is in love with me.

All is finally right in the world.

We continue to kiss while we remove each other's clothes. Neither one of us is in control this time. She makes love to me at the same time I make love to her, and no one is in charge. No one is calling the shots. It's completely equal now. She feels about me how I feel about her and when we're finished, she whispers, "I love you, Warren."

And I say, "I love you, Bridgette."

And no one argues.

She lies peacefully in my arms and doesn't try to kick me

out of her bed. Just the thought of having to go back to my room and sleep alone seems ridiculous, and I'm not sure I ever want to sleep alone again.

I stroke her arm with my fingers. "I have an idea," I whisper against her hair.

She shakes her head. "I'm not doing anal."

I laugh and pull back. "*What?* No. Not that. Not yet, anyway." I push her off me and sit up, pulling her to a seated position. I take both of her hands in mine, and I look her very seriously in the eyes. "I think we should move in together."

Her eyes widen in shock and she's looking at me like I've lost my mind. Maybe I have. "We already live together, dumbass. And we hardly have to pay rent. We'd be broke if we got our own place."

I dismiss her concerns with a shake of my head. "I don't mean into a new apartment. Move into my bedroom with me. We're together every night anyway."

She's still shaking her head. "Why would I want to do that?"

"Because," I say to her, brushing her hair behind her ear. "It's romantic."

"No, Warren, it's dumb."

I fall back onto the bed, frustrated. She drops to my side and glares down at me. "Why would I want to move all my clothes into your tiny closet? That's so stupid. I have way too much closet stuff."

"Fine," I tell her. "You can keep all your clothes in your own closet, but move everything else into my room."

She drops her forehead to my chest. "I don't *have* any other stuff. I have a bed. That's it."

I tuck my finger under her chin and lift her eyes to mine. "Exactly. Move your bed to my room. We both have full-size beds. Putting them together would be like having a king, and we'd have more room to have sex, and when we're finished you can roll over to your side of the bed and I can watch you sleep."

She considers my proposal for several quiet moments, and then smiles. "This is so dumb."

I sit up and pull her off the bed. "And romantic. Come on, get dressed. I'll help you."

We put our clothes back on and begin tossing the blankets and pillows off her bed. We lift the mattress and begin scooting it out the door, into the living room, and toward my room. Ridge and Brennan are both sitting on the couch, staring at us.

"What the hell are you doing?" Brennan asks.

I press my hip against the mattress so I can sign back to them. "Bridgette and I are moving in together."

Ridge and Brennan look at each other, then back at me. "But . . . you already *live* together," Brennan says.

I dismiss them with a wave of my hand, and we finish moving Bridgette's mattress next to mine. Once her bed is remade, she falls onto hers and I onto mine. We roll until we're facing each other. She rests her head on her arm and sighs.

"We've lived together for two minutes, and I'm already sick of your face."

I laugh. "I think you should move out. We got along so much better before this."

She flips me off, so I grab her hand and link my fingers through hers. "I need to ask you something else."

She falls onto her back. "So help me God, Warren, if you ask me to marry you I'll cut your nuts off."

"I don't want to marry you," I say. "Yet. But . . ."

I crawl over to her part of our home and lie next to her. "Will you go on a date with me?"

She looks away from me and stares up at the ceiling. "Oh, my God," she whispers. "We've never been on a date before?"

"Not a real one."

She slaps a hand to her forehead. "I'm such a whore. I already moved in with you and we haven't even been on a date?"

"You're not a whore," I say to her with mock reassurance. "We haven't even had sex . . . *oh, wait.*" I grimace. "You *are* such a whore. A huge, slutty whore who wants me to try anal with her tonight."

She laughs and shoves me in the chest.

I shove her back.

She shoves me harder.

I push her until she's at the edge of her bed.

She lifts her legs to kick me.

I kick her back, pushing her off the bed until she's lying on the floor. After several quiet seconds, I scoot to the edge of the mattress and look down at her. She's still lying flat on her back in the same position she landed.

"You could give Brody a run for his money," I tell her. She reaches up a hand to hit me, but I grab it and pull it to my mouth. I kiss the top of it and hold her hand while I lock eyes with her.

She's in an unusually agreeable mood right now, which leads me to believe that maybe . . . *just maybe* . . .

"I have one more question, Bridgette."

She cocks an eyebrow and slowly shakes her head. "I'm not telling you the name of that porn."

I drop her hand and roll onto my back. "Fuck."

Maybe not.

Acknowledgments

A huge thank-you to so many people. First, my family. Without you I could never finish anything. To my publisher, Atria Books, and Judith Curr, for not saying no when I said, "I want to write a novella about Warren. And I want it to be a surprise!" A special thanks to my editor, Johanna Castillo, for being the absolute best! I say it with every book, but we really are a great team. To my brand-new publicist, Ariele, for being top-notch at her job. Yer er der berst, Erererl! And to my agent, Jane Dystel, and her team of amazing people. To Murphy and Stephanie for always keeping my head above water. And last but not least, my readers. Without you, none of the people just mentioned would have a job, including me. Your passion for reading gives us the ability to live our passion. For that, we ALL thank you!

Enjoy an excerpt from Colleen Hoover's
Maybe Someday, **the novel that inspired the**
characters in *Maybe Not*

prologue

Sydney

I just punched a girl in the face. Not just *any* girl. My best friend. My roommate.

Well, as of five minutes ago, I guess I should call her my *ex*-roommate.

Her nose began bleeding almost immediately, and for a second, I felt bad for hitting her. But then I remembered what a lying, betraying whore she is, and it made me want to punch her again. I would have if Hunter hadn't prevented it by stepping between us.

So instead, I punched *him*. I didn't do any damage to him, unfortunately. Not like the damage I'd done to my hand.

Punching someone hurts a lot worse than I imagined it would. Not that I spend an excessive amount of time imagining how it would feel to punch people. Although I am having that urge again as I stare down at my phone at the incoming text from Ridge. He's another one I'd like to get even with. I know he technically has nothing to do with my current predicament, but he could have given me a heads-up a little sooner. Therefore, I'd like to punch him, too.

Ridge: Are you OK? Do u want to come up until the rain stops?

Of course, I don't want to come up. My fist hurts enough as it is, and if I went up to Ridge's apartment, it would hurt a whole lot worse after I finished with him.

I turn around and look up at his balcony. He's leaning against his sliding-glass door; phone in hand, watching me. It's almost dark, but the lights from the courtyard illuminate his face. His dark eyes lock with mine, and the way his mouth curls up into a soft, regretful smile makes it hard to remember why I'm even upset with him in the first place. He runs a free hand through the hair hanging loosely over his forehead, revealing even more of the worry in his expression. Or maybe that's a look of regret. As it should be.

I decide not to reply and flip him off instead. He shakes his head and shrugs his shoulders, as if to say, *I tried*, and then he goes back inside his apartment and slides his door shut.

I put the phone back in my pocket before it gets wet, and I look around at the courtyard of the apartment complex where I've lived for two whole months. When we first moved in, the hot Texas summer was swallowing up the last traces of spring, but this courtyard seemed to somehow still cling to life. Vibrant blue and purple hydrangeas lined the walkways leading up to the staircases, and the fountain affixed in the center of the courtyard.

Now that summer has reached its most unattractive peak, the water in the fountain has long since evaporated. The hydrangeas are a sad, wilted reminder of the excitement

I felt when Tori and I first moved in here. Looking at the courtyard now, defeated by the season, is an eerie parallel to how I feel at the moment. Defeated and sad.

I'm sitting on the edge of the now empty cement fountain, my elbows propped up on the two suitcases that contain most of my belongings, waiting for a cab to pick me up. I have no idea where it's going to take me, but I know I'd rather be anywhere except where I am right now. Which is, well, homeless.

I could call my parents, but that would give them ammunition to start firing all the *We told you sos* at me.

We told you not to move so far away, Sydney.

We told you not to get serious with that guy.

We told you if you had chosen prelaw over music, we would have paid for it.

We told you to punch with your thumb on the outside *of your fist.*

Okay, maybe they never taught me the proper punching techniques, but if they're so right all the damn time, they *should* have.

I clench my fist, then spread out my fingers, then clench it again. My hand is surprisingly sore, and I'm pretty sure I should put ice on it. I feel sorry for guys. Punching sucks.

Know what else sucks? Rain. It always finds the most inappropriate time to fall, like right now, while I'm homeless.

The cab finally pulls up, and I stand and grab my suitcases. I roll them behind me as the cab driver gets out and pops open the trunk. Before I even hand him the first suitcase, my heart sinks as I suddenly realize that I don't even have my purse on me.

Shit.

I look around, back to where I was sitting on the suit-cases, then feel around my body as if my purse will magically appear across my shoulder. But I know exactly where my purse is. I pulled it off my shoulder and dropped it to the floor right before I punched Tori in her overpriced, Cameron Diaz nose.

I sigh. And I laugh. Of course, I left my purse. My first day of being homeless would have been way too easy if I'd had a purse with me.

"I'm sorry," I say to the cab driver, who is now loading my second piece of luggage. "I changed my mind. I don't need a cab right now."

I know there's a hotel about a half-mile from here. If I can just work up the courage to go back inside and get my purse, I'll walk there and get a room until I figure out what to do. It's not as if I can get any wetter.

The driver takes the suitcases back out of the cab, sets them on the curb in front of me, and walks back to the driver's side without ever making eye contact. He just gets into his car and drives away, as if my canceling is a relief.

Do I look that pathetic?

I take my suitcases and walk back to where I was seated before I realized I was purseless. I glance up to my apartment and wonder what would happen if I went back there to get my wallet. I sort of left things in a mess when I walked out the door. I guess I'd rather be homeless in the rain than go back up there.

I take a seat on my luggage again and contemplate my situation. I could pay someone to go upstairs for me. But who? No one's outside, and who's to say Hunter or Tori would even give the person my purse?

This really sucks. I know I'm going to have to end up calling one of my friends, but right now, I'm too embarrassed to tell anyone how clueless I've been for the last two years. I've been completely blindsided.

I already hate being twenty-two, and I still have 364 more days to go.

It sucks so bad that I'm . . . *crying*?

Great. I'm crying now. I'm a purseless, crying, violent, homeless girl. And as much as I don't want to admit it, I think I might also be heartbroken.

Yep. Sobbing now. Pretty sure this must be what it feels like to have your heart broken.

"It's raining. Hurry up."

I glance up to see a girl hovering over me. She's holding an umbrella over her head and looking down at me with agitation while she hops from one foot to the other, waiting for me to do something. "I'm getting soaked. *Hurry.*"

Her voice is a little demanding, as if she's doing me some sort of favor and I'm being ungrateful. I arch an eyebrow as I look up at her, shielding the rain from my eyes with my hand. I don't know why she's complaining about getting wet, when there isn't much clothing to *get* wet. She's wearing next to nothing. I glance at her shirt, which is missing its entire bottom half, and realize she's in a Hooters outfit.

Could this day get any weirder? I'm sitting on almost everything I own in a torrential downpour, being bossed around by a bitchy Hooters waitress.

I'm still staring at her shirt when she grabs my hand and

pulls me up in a huff. "Ridge said you would do this. I've got to get to work. Follow me, and I'll show you where the apartment is." She grabs one of my suitcases, pops the handle out, and shoves it at me. She takes the other and walks swiftly out of the courtyard. I follow her, for no other reason than the fact that she's taken one of my suitcases with her and I want it back.

She yells over her shoulder as she begins to ascend the stairwell. "I don't know how long you plan on staying, but I've only got one rule. Stay the hell out of my room."

She reaches an apartment and opens the door, never even looking back to see if I'm following her. Once I reach the top of the stairs, I pause outside the apartment and look down at the fern sitting unaffected by the heat in a planter outside the door. Its leaves are lush and green as if they're giving summer the middle finger with their refusal to succumb to the heat. I smile at the plant, somewhat proud of it. Then I frown with the realization that I'm envious of the resilience of a plant.

I shake my head, look away, then take a hesitant step inside the unfamiliar apartment. The layout is similar to my own apartment, only this one is a double split bedroom with four total bedrooms. My and Tori's apartment only had two bedrooms, but the living rooms are the same size.

The only other noticeable difference is that I don't see any lying, backstabbing, bloody-nosed whores standing in this one. Nor do I see any of Tori's dirty dishes or laundry lying around.

The girl sets my suitcase down beside the door, then steps aside and waits for me to . . . well, I don't know what she's waiting for me to do.

She rolls her eyes and grabs my arm, pulling me out of the doorway and further into the apartment. "What the hell is wrong with you? Do you even speak?" She begins to close the door behind her but pauses and turns around, wide-eyed. She holds her finger up in the air. "Wait," she says. "You're not . . ." She rolls her eyes and smacks herself in the forehead. "Oh, my God, you're deaf."

Huh? What the hell is wrong with this girl? I shake my head and start to answer her, but she interrupts me.

"God, Bridgette," she mumbles to herself. She rubs her hands down her face and groans, completely ignoring the fact that I'm shaking my head. "You're such an insensitive bitch sometimes."

Wow. This girl has some serious issues in the people-skills department. She's sort of a bitch, even though she's making an effort not to be one. Now that she thinks I'm deaf. I don't even know how to respond. She shakes her head as if she's disappointed in herself, then looks straight at me.

"I . . . HAVE . . . TO . . . GO . . . TO . . . WORK . . . NOW!" she yells very loudly and painfully slowly. I grimace and step back, which should be a huge clue that I can hear her practically yelling, but she doesn't notice. She points to a door at the end of the hallway. "RIDGE . . . IS . . . IN . . . HIS . . . ROOM!"

Before I have a chance to tell her she can stop yelling, she leaves the apartment and closes the door behind her.

I have no idea what to think. Or what to do now. I'm standing, soaking wet, in the middle of an unfamiliar apartment, and the only person besides Hunter and Tori whom I feel like punching is now just a few feet away in another room. And speaking of Ridge, why the hell did he send his psycho Hooters girlfriend to get me? I take out my phone and have begun to text him when his bedroom door opens.

He walks out into the hallway with an armful of blankets and a pillow. As soon as he makes eye contact with me, I gasp. I hope it's not a noticeable gasp. It's just that I've never actually seen him up close before, and he's even better-looking from just a few feet away than he is from across an apartment building's courtyard.

I don't think I've ever seen eyes that can actually speak. I'm not sure what I mean by that. It just seems as if he could shoot me the tiniest glance with those dark eyes of his, and I'd know exactly what they needed me to do. They're piercing and intense and—oh, my God, I'm staring.

The corner of his mouth tilts up in a knowing smile as he passes me and heads straight for the couch.

Despite his appealing and slightly innocent-looking face, I want to yell at him for being so deceitful. He shouldn't have waited more than two weeks to tell me. I would have had a chance to plan all this out a little better. I don't understand how we could have had two weeks' worth of conversations without his feeling the need to tell me that my boyfriend and my best friend were screwing.

Ridge throws the blankets and the pillow onto the couch.

"I'm not staying here, Ridge," I say, attempting to stop him from wasting time with his hospitality. I know he feels bad for me, but I hardly know him, and I'd feel a lot more comfortable in a hotel room than sleeping on a strange couch.

Then again, hotel rooms require money.

Something I don't have on me at the moment.

Something that's inside my purse, across the courtyard,

in an apartment with the only two people in the world I don't want to see right now.

Maybe a couch isn't such a bad idea after all.

He gets the couch made up and turns around, dropping his eyes to my soaking-wet clothes. I look down at the puddle of water I'm creating in the middle of his floor.

"Oh, sorry," I mutter. My hair is matted to my face; my shirt is now a see-through pathetic excuse for a barrier between the outside world and my very pink, very noticeable bra. "Where's your bathroom?"

He nods his head toward the bathroom door.

I turn around, unzip a suitcase, and begin to rummage through it while Ridge walks back into his bedroom. I'm glad he doesn't ask me questions about what happened after our conversation earlier. I'm not in the mood to talk about it.

I select a pair of yoga pants and a tank top, then grab my bag of toiletries and head to the bathroom. It disturbs me that everything about this apartment reminds me of my own, with just a few subtle differences. This is the same bathroom with the Jack-and-Jill doors on the left and right, leading to the two bedrooms that adjoin it. One is Ridge's, obviously. I'm curious about who the other bedroom belongs to but not curious enough to open it. The Hooters girl's one rule was to stay the hell out of her room, and she doesn't seem like the type to kid around.

I shut the door that leads to the living room and lock it, then check the locks on both doors to the bedrooms to make sure no one can walk in. I have no idea if anyone lives in this apartment other than Ridge and the Hooters girl, but I don't want to chance it.

I pull off my sopping clothes and throw them into the sink to avoid soaking the floor. I turn on the shower and wait until the water gets warm, then step in. I stand under the stream of water and close my eyes, thankful that I'm not still sitting outside in the rain. At the same time, I'm not really happy to be where I am, either.

I never expected my twenty-second birthday to end with me showering in a strange apartment and sleeping on a couch that belongs to a guy I've barely known for two weeks, all at the hands of the two people I cared about and trusted the most.

1.

Sydney

I slide open my balcony door and step outside, thankful that the sun has already dipped behind the building next door, cooling the air to what could pass as a perfect fall temperature. Almost on cue, the sound of his guitar floats across the courtyard as I take a seat and lean back into the patio lounger. I tell Tori I come out here to get homework done, because I don't want to admit that the guitar is the only reason I'm outside every night at eight, like clockwork.

For weeks now, the guy in the apartment across the courtyard has sat on his balcony and played for at least an hour. Every night, I sit outside and listen.

I've noticed a few other neighbors come out to their balconies when he's playing, but no one is as loyal as I am. I don't understand how someone could hear these songs and not crave them day after day. Then again, music has always been a passion of mine, so maybe I'm just a little more infatuated with his sound than other people are. I've played the piano for as long as I can remember, and although I've never shared it with anyone, I love writing music. I even switched my major to music education two years ago. My plan is to be an elementary music teacher, although if my father had his way, I'd still be prelaw.

"A life of mediocrity is a waste of a life," he said when I informed him that I was changing my major.

A life of mediocrity. I find that more amusing than insulting, since he seems to be the most dissatisfied person I've ever known. And he's a lawyer. Go figure.

One of the familiar songs ends and the guy with the guitar begins to play something he's never played before. I've grown accustomed to his unofficial playlist since he seems to practice the same songs in the same order night after night. However, I've never heard him play this particular song before. The way he's repeating the same chords makes me think he's creating the song right here on the spot. I like that I'm witnessing this, especially since after only a few chords, it's already my new favorite. All his songs sound like originals. I wonder if he performs them locally or if he just writes them for fun.

I lean forward in the chair, rest my arms on the edge of the balcony, and watch him. His balcony is directly across the courtyard, far enough away that I don't feel weird when I watch him but close enough that I make sure I'm never watching him when Hunter's around. I don't think Hunter would like the fact that I've developed a tiny crush on this guy's talent.

I can't deny it, though. Anyone who watches how passionately this guy plays would crush on his talent. The way he keeps his eyes closed the entire time, focusing intently on every stroke against every guitar string. I like it best when he sits cross-legged with the guitar upright between his legs. He pulls it against his chest and plays it like a stand-up bass, keeping his eyes closed the whole time. It's so mesmerizing to watch him that sometimes I catch myself holding my breath, and I don't even realize I'm doing it until I'm gasping for air.

It also doesn't help that he's cute. At least, he seems cute from here. His light brown hair is unruly and moves with him, falling across his forehead every time he looks down at his guitar. He's too far away to distinguish eye color or distinct features, but the details don't matter when coupled with the passion he has for his music. There's a confidence to him that I find compelling. I've always admired musicians who are able to tune out everyone and everything around them and pour all of their focus into their music. To be able to shut the world off and allow yourself to be completely swept away is something I've always wanted the confidence to do, but I just don't have it.

This guy has it. He's confident and talented. I've always been a sucker for musicians, but more in a fantasy way. They're a different breed. A breed that rarely makes for good boyfriends.

He glances at me as if he can hear my thoughts, and then a slow grin appears across his face. He never once pauses the song while he continues to watch me. The eye contact makes me blush, so I drop my arms and pull my notebook back onto my lap and look down at it. I hate that he just caught me staring so hard. Not that I was doing anything wrong; it just feels odd for him to know I was watching him. I glance up again, and he's still watching me, but he's not smiling anymore. The way he's staring causes my heart to speed up, so I look away and focus on my notebook.

Way to be a creeper, Sydney.

"There's my girl," a comforting voice says from behind me. I lean my head back and tilt my eyes upward to watch Hunter as he makes his way onto the balcony. I try to hide the fact that I'm shocked to see him, because I'm pretty sure I was supposed to remember he was coming.

On the off chance that Guitar Boy is still watching, I make it a point to seem really into Hunter's hello kiss so that maybe I'll seem less like a creepy stalker and more like someone just casually relaxing on her balcony. I run my hand up Hunter's neck as he leans over the back of my chair and kisses me upside down.

"Scoot up," Hunter says, pushing on my shoulders. I do what he asks and slide forward in the seat as he lifts his leg over the chair and slips in behind me. He pulls my back against his chest and wraps his arms around me.

My eyes betray me when the sound of the guitar stops abruptly, and I glance across the courtyard once more. Guitar Boy is eyeing us hard as he stands, then goes back inside his apartment. His expression is odd. Almost angry.

"How was school?" Hunter asks.

"Too boring to talk about. What about you? How was work?"

"Interesting," he says, brushing my hair away from my neck with his hand. He presses his lips to my neck and kisses his way down my collarbone.

"What was so interesting?"

He tightens his hold on me, then rests his chin on my

shoulder and pulls me back in the chair with him. "The oddest thing happened at lunch," he says. "I was with one of the guys at this Italian restaurant. We were eating out on the patio, and I had just asked the waiter what he recommended for dessert, when a police car rounded the corner. They stopped right in front of the restaurant, and two officers jumped out with their guns drawn. They began barking orders toward us when our waiter mumbled, 'Shit.' He slowly raised his hands, and the police jumped the barrier to the patio, rushed toward him, threw him to the ground, and cuffed him right at our feet. After they read him his rights, they pulled him to his feet and escorted him toward the cop car. The waiter glanced back at me and yelled, 'The tiramisu is really good!' Then they put him in the car and drove away."

I tilt my head back and look up at him. "Seriously? That really happened?"

He nods, laughing. "I swear, Syd. It was crazy."

"Well? Did you try the tiramisu?"

"Hell, yeah, we did. It was the best tiramisu I've ever had." He kisses me on the cheek and pushes me forward. "Speaking of food, I'm starving." He stands up and holds out his hand to me. "Did you cook tonight?"

I take his hand and let him pull me up. "We just had salad, but I can make you one."

Once we're inside, Hunter takes a seat on the couch next to Tori. She's got a textbook spread open across her lap as she halfheartedly focuses on both homework and TV at the same time. I take out the containers from the fridge and make his salad. I feel a little guilty that I forgot tonight was one of the nights he said he was coming. I usually have something cooked when I know he'll be here.

We've been dating for almost two years now. I met him during my sophomore year in college, when he was a senior. He and Tori had been friends for years. After she moved into my dorm and we became friends, she insisted I meet him. She said we'd hit it off, and she was right. We made it official after only two dates, and things have been wonderful since.

Of course, we have our ups and downs, especially since he moved more than an hour away. When he landed the job in the accounting firm last semester, he suggested I move with him. I told him no, that I really wanted to finish my under-grad before taking such a huge step. In all honesty, I'm just scared.

The thought of moving in with him seems so final, as if I would be sealing my fate. I know that once we take that step, the next step is marriage, and then I'd be looking at never having the chance to live alone. I've always had a roommate, and until I can afford my own place, I'll be sharing an apart-ment with Tori. I haven't told Hunter yet, but I really want to live alone for a year. It's something I promised myself I would do before I got married. I don't even turn twenty-two for a couple of weeks, so it's not as if I'm in any hurry.

I take Hunter's food to him in the living room.

"Why do you watch this?" he says to Tori. "All these women do is talk shit about each other and flip tables."

"That's exactly why I watch it," Tori says, without taking her eyes off the TV.

Hunter winks at me and takes his food, then props his feet up on the coffee table. "Thanks, babe." He turns toward the TV and begins eating. "Can you grab me a beer?"

I nod and walk back into the kitchen. I open the refrigerator door and look on the shelf where he always keeps his extra beer. I realize as I'm staring at "his" shelf that this is probably how it begins. First, he has a shelf in the refrigerator. Then he'll have a toothbrush in the bathroom, a drawer in my dresser, and eventually his stuff will infiltrate mine in so many ways it'll be impossible for me ever to be on my own.

I run my hands up my arms, rubbing away the sudden onset of discomfort washing over me. I feel as if I'm watching my future play out in front of me. I'm not so sure I like what I'm imagining.

Am I ready for this?

Am I ready for this guy to be the guy I bring dinner to every night when he gets home from work?

Am I ready to fall into this comfortable life with him? One where I teach all day and he does people's taxes, and then we come home and I cook dinner and I "grab him beers" while he props his feet up and calls me *babe*, and then we go to our bed and make love at approximately nine P.M. so we won't be tired the next day, in order to wake up and get dressed and go to work and do it all over again?

"Earth to Sydney," Hunter says. I hear him snap his fingers twice. "Beer? Please, babe?"

I quickly grab his beer, give it to him, then head straight to my bathroom. I turn the water on in the shower, but I don't get in. Instead, I lock the door and sink to the floor.

We have a good relationship. He's good to me, and I know he loves me. I just don't understand why every time I think about a future with him, it's not an exciting thought.

Ridge

Maggie leans forward and kisses my forehead. "I need to go."

I'm on my back with my head and shoulders partially propped against my headboard. She's straddling my lap and looking down at me regretfully. I hate that we live so far apart now, but it makes the time we do spend together a lot more meaningful. I take her hands so she'll shut up, and I pull her to me, hoping to persuade her not to leave just yet.

She laughs and shakes her head. She kisses me, but only briefly, and then she pulls away again. She slides off my lap, but I don't let her make it very far before I lunge forward and pin her to the mattress. I point to her chest.

"You"—I lean in and kiss the tip of her nose—"need to stay one more night."

"I can't. I have class."

I grab her wrists and pin her arms above her head, then press my lips to hers. I know she won't stay another night. She's never missed a day of class in her life, unless she was too sick to move. I sort of wish she was feeling a little sick right now, so I could make her stay in bed with me.

I slide my hands from her wrists, delicately up her arms until I'm cupping her face. Then I give her one final kiss before I reluctantly pull away from her. "Go. And be careful. Let me know when you make it home."

She nods and pushes herself off the bed. She reaches

across me and grabs her shirt, then pulls it on over her head. I watch her as she walks around the room and gathers the clothes I pulled off her in a hurry.

After five years of dating, most couples would have moved in together by now. However, most peoples' other halves aren't Maggie. She's so fiercely independent it's almost intimidating. But it's understandable, considering how her life has gone. She's been caring for her grandfather since I met her. Before that, she spent the majority of her teenage years helping him care for her grandmother, who died when Maggie was sixteen. Now that her grandfather is in a nursing home, she finally has a chance to live alone while finishing school, and as much as I want her here with me, I also know how important this internship is for her. So for the next year, I'll suck it up while she's in San Antonio and I'm here in Austin. I'll be damned if I ever move out of Austin, especially for San Antonio.

Unless she asked, of course.

"Tell your brother I said good luck." She's standing in my bedroom doorway, poised to leave. "And you need to quit beating yourself up, Ridge. Musicians have blocks, just like writers do. You'll find your muse again. I love you."

"I love you, too."

She smiles and backs out of my bedroom. I groan, knowing she's trying to be positive with the whole writer's block thing, but I can't stop stressing about it. I don't know if it's because Brennan has so much riding on these songs now or if it's because I'm completely tapped out, but the words just aren't coming. Without lyrics I'm confident in, it's hard to feel good about the actual musical aspect of writing.

My phone vibrates. It's a text from Brennan, which only makes me feel worse about the fact that I'm stuck.

Brennan: It's been weeks. Please tell me you have something.

Me: Working on it. How's the tour?

Brennan: Good, but remind me not to allow Warren to schedule this many gigs on the next leg.

Me: Gigs are what gets your name out there.

Brennan: OUR name. I'm not telling you again to stop acting like you aren't half of this.

Me: I won't be half if I can't work through this damn block.

Brennan: Maybe you should get out more. Cause some unnecessary drama in your life. Break up with Maggie for the sake of art. She'll understand. Heartache helps with lyrical inspiration. Don't you ever listen to country?

Me: Good idea. I'll tell Maggie you suggested that.

Brennan: Nothing I say or do could ever make Maggie hate me. Give her a kiss for me, and get to writing. Our careers are resting squarely on your shoulders.

Me: Asshole.

Brennan: Ah! Is that anger I detect in your text? Use it. Go write an angry song about how much you hate your little brother, then send it to me. ;)

Me: Yeah. I'll give it to you after you finally get your shit out of your old bedroom. Bridgette's sister might move in next month.

Brennan: Have you ever met Brandi?

Me: No. Do I want to?

Brennan: Only if you want to live with two Bridgettes.

Me: Oh, shit.

Brennan: Exactly. TTYL.

I close out the text to Brennan and open up a text to Warren.

Me: We're good to go on the roommate search. Brennan says hell no to Brandi. I'll let you break the news to Bridgette, since you two get along so well.

Warren: Well, motherfucker.

I laugh and hop off the bed, then head to the patio with my guitar. It's almost eight, and I know she'll be on her balcony. I don't know how weird my actions are about to seem to her, but all I can do is try. I've got nothing to lose.

About the Author

COLLEEN HOOVER is the #1 *New York Times* bestselling author of *Slammed*, *Point of Retreat*, *This Girl*, *Hopeless*, *Losing Hope*, *Finding Cinderella*, *Maybe Someday*, and *Ugly Love*. She lives in Texas with her husband and their three boys. Please visit ColleenHoover.com.

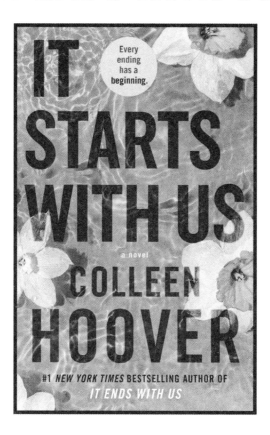

Maybe Now

Also by Colleen Hoover

SLAMMED SERIES
Slammed
Point of Retreat
This Girl

HOPELESS SERIES
Hopeless
Losing Hope
Finding Cinderella
Finding Perfect

MAYBE SOMEDAY SERIES
Maybe Someday
Maybe Not
Maybe Now

IT ENDS WITH US SERIES
It Ends with Us
It Starts with Us

STAND-ALONES
Ugly Love
Confess
November 9
Without Merit
All Your Perfects
Too Late
Regretting You
Heart Bones
Layla
Verity
Reminders of Him

ALSO BY COLLEEN HOOVER AND TARRYN FISHER
Never Never: The Complete Series

Maybe Now

A Novel

Colleen Hoover

ATRIA PAPERBACK

NEW YORK   LONDON   TORONTO   SYDNEY   NEW DELHI

An Imprint of Simon & Schuster, Inc.
1230 Avenue of the Americas
New York, NY 10020

This Atria Paperback edition September 2022

ATRIA PAPERBACK and colophon are trademarks of
Simon & Schuster, Inc.

For information about special discounts for bulk purchases, please contact Simon & Schuster Special Sales at 1-866-506-1949 or business@simonandschuster.com.

The Simon & Schuster Speakers Bureau can bring authors to your live event. For more information or to book an event, contact the Simon & Schuster Speakers Bureau at 1-866-248-3049 or visit our website at www.simonspeakers.com.

Interior design by Erika R. Genova

Manufactured in China

3 5 7 9 10 8 6 4 2

Library of Congress Control Number: 2022941207

ISBN 978-1-6680-1334-2
ISBN 978-1-6680-1335-9 (ebook)

This book is for every single member of
Colleen Hoover's CoHorts.

Except the murderers.
This book isn't for those two.

Maybe Now

Prologue

Maggie

I set the pen down on the paper. My hand is shaking too much to finish filling it out, so I inhale a few quick breaths in an attempt to calm my nerves.

You can do this, Maggie.

I pick up the pen again, but I think my hand is shaking worse than before I put it down.

"Let me help you with that."

I look up to see the tandem instructor smiling at me. He grabs the pen and picks up the clipboard, then takes a seat in the chair to my right. "We get a lot of nervous first-timers. It's easier if you just let me fill out the paperwork because your handwriting probably won't be legible," he says. "You act like you're about to jump out of an airplane or something."

I'm immediately put at ease by his lazy smile, but

become nervous all over again when I realize I'm a horrible liar. Lying on the medical section would have been a lot easier if I were filling it out myself. I'm not sure I can lie out loud to this guy.

"Thanks, but I can do it." I try to take back the clipboard, but he pulls it out of my reach.

"Not so fast"—he quickly glances down at my form—"Maggie Carson." He holds out his hand, still holding the clipboard out of my reach with his other hand. "I'm Jake, and if you're planning on jumping out of a plane at ten thousand feet while at my mercy, the least I can do is finish your paperwork."

I shake his hand, impressed with the strength behind his grip. Knowing these are the hands I'm about to entrust my life to eases my mind a tiny fraction.

"How many tandem jumps have you completed?" I ask him.

He grins, then returns his attention to my paperwork. He begins flipping through the pages. "You'll be my five hundredth."

"Really? Five hundred sounds like a big deal. Shouldn't you be celebrating?"

He brings his eyes back to mine and loses his smile. "You asked how many tandem jumps I've completed. I don't want to celebrate prematurely."

I gulp.

He laughs and nudges my shoulder. "I'm kidding, Maggie. Relax. You're in good hands."

I smile at the same time I inhale a deep breath.

He begins to scroll through the form.

"Any medical conditions?" he asks, already pressing his pen to the box marked *no*. I don't answer him. My silence prompts him to look up at me and repeat his question. "Medical conditions? Recent illnesses? Any crazy ex-boyfriends I should be aware of?"

I smile at his last comment and shake my head. "No crazy exes. Just one really great one."

He nods slowly. "What about the other part of the question? Medical conditions?" He waits for my answer, but I fail to give him anything other than a nervous pause. His eyes narrow and he leans forward a little bit more, eyeing me carefully. He's looking at me like he's trying to figure out answers to more than just what's on the questionnaire he's holding. "Is it terminal?"

I try to hold my resolve. "Not really. Not yet."

He leans in even closer, looking at me with an expression full of sincerity. "What is it, then, Maggie Carson?"

I don't even know him, but there's something calming about him that makes me want to tell him. But I don't. I look at my hands, folded together in my lap. "You might not let me jump if I tell you."

He leans into me until his ear is close to my mouth. "If you say it quietly enough, there's a good chance I might not even hear it," he says in a hushed voice. A wave of his breath caresses my collarbone, and I'm immediately covered in chills. He pulls back slightly and eyes me as he waits for my response.

"CF," I say. I'm not sure he'll even know what CF means, but if I keep it simple he might not ask me to elaborate.

"How are your O$_2$ levels?"

Maybe he does know what it means. "So far so good."

"Do you have a doctor's release?"

I shake my head. "Last-minute decision. I tend to be a little impulsive at times."

He grins, then looks back to the form and checks no on medical conditions. He glances at me. "Well, you're lucky, because I happen to be a doctor. But if you die today, I'm telling everyone you lied on this questionnaire."

I laugh and nod in agreement, appreciative he's willing to shrug it off. I know what a big deal that is. "Thank you."

He looks at the questionnaire and says, "Why are you thanking me? I didn't do anything." His denial makes me smile. He continues to scroll down the list of questions, and I answer them honestly until we finally make it to the last page. "Okay, last question," he says. "Why do you want to skydive?"

I lean over him to glance at the form. "Is that really a question?"

He points to the question. "Yep. Right here."

I read the question, then give him a blunt answer. "I guess because I'm dying. I have a long bucket list of things I've always wanted to do."

His eyes harden a little, almost as if my answer upset him. He returns his attention to the form, so I tilt my head and lean over his shoulder again and watch as he writes down an answer that isn't at all the one I gave him.

"I want to skydive because I want to experience life to the fullest."

He hands me the form and the pen. "Sign here," he says, pointing to the bottom of the page. After I sign the form and give it back to him, he stands up and reaches out for my hand. "Let's go pack our chutes, Five Hundred."

● ● ●

"Are you really a doctor?" I yell over the roar of the engines. We're seated directly across from each other in the small airplane. His smile is huge and full of teeth so straight and white, I would bet money he's actually a dentist.

"Cardiologist!" he yells. He waves a hand around the interior of the airplane. "I do this for fun!"

A cardiologist who skydives in his spare time? Impressive.

"Your wife doesn't get upset that you're so busy all the time?" I yell. *Oh, God. That was such an obvious, cheesy question.* I cringe that I even asked that out loud. I've never been good at flirting.

He leans forward and yells, "What?"

He's really going to make me repeat myself? "I asked if your wife gets upset that you're so busy all the time!"

He shakes his head and unbuckles his safety harness,

then moves to the seat next to me. "It's too loud in here!" he yells, waving his hand around the interior of the airplane. "Say it one more time!"

I roll my eyes and begin to ask him again. "Does . . . your . . . wife . . ."

He laughs and presses a finger to my lips, but only briefly. He pulls his hand away and leans toward me. My heart reacts more to this quick movement of his than it does to the fact that I'm about to jump out of this airplane.

"I'm kidding," he says. "You looked so embarrassed after the first time you said it, I wanted to make you say it again."

I slap him on the arm. "Asshole!"

He laughs and stands up, then reaches for my safety harness and presses the release latch. He pulls me up. "You ready for this?"

I nod, but it's a lie. I am absolutely terrified, and if it weren't for the fact that this guy is a doctor and he does things like this for fun—and he's really hot—I'd probably be backing out right about now.

He turns me until my back is to his chest and connects our safety harnesses together until I'm securely fastened to him. My eyes are closed when I feel him pull my goggles on. After several minutes of waiting for him to finish prepping us, he walks me forward toward the opening of the airplane and presses his hands against either side of the opening. I am literally staring down at clouds.

I squeeze my eyes shut again, just as he brings his mouth close to my ear. "I don't have a wife, Maggie. The only thing I'm in love with is my life."

I'm somehow smiling during one of the scariest moments of my life. His comment makes the question worth the three times he had me repeat it. I tighten my grip around my safety harness. He reaches around me and takes both of my hands, then lowers them to my side. "Sixty more seconds," he says. "Can you do me a favor?"

I nod, too scared to disagree with him right now since I've practically placed my fate in his hands.

"If we make it to the ground alive, will you let me take you to dinner? To celebrate being my five hundredth time?"

I laugh at the sexual undertone in his question and look over my shoulder. "Are tandem instructors allowed to date their students?"

"I don't know," he says with a laugh. "Most of my students are men, and I've never had the desire to ask one of them out."

I stare straight ahead again. "I'll let you know my answer when we land safely."

"Fair enough." He pushes me a step forward, then intertwines his fingers with mine, spreading our arms out. "This is it, Five Hundred. You ready?"

I nod as my pulse somehow begins to beat even more rapidly than before, and my chest tightens with the fear consuming me, knowing what I'm about to willingly do. I feel his breath and the wind against my neck as he inches us to the very edge of the plane's opening.

"I know you said you want to skydive because you're dying," he says, squeezing my hands. "But this isn't dying, Maggie! This is living!"

With that, he shoves us both forward . . . and we jump.

Chapter One

Sydney

As soon as I open my eyes, I immediately roll over to find the other side of my bed empty. I grab the pillow Ridge slept on and pull it to me. It still smells like him.

It wasn't a dream. Thank God.

I still can't wrap my head around last night. The concert he orchestrated with Brennan and Warren. The songs he wrote for me. That we were finally able to tell each other how we really felt without guilt being attached to those feelings.

Maybe that's where this new sense of peace comes from—the absence of all the guilt I've always felt in his presence. It was hard falling in love with someone who was committed to someone else. It was even harder trying to prevent it from happening.

I roll out of bed and scan the room. Ridge's shirt is next to mine on the floor, so that means he's still here. I'm a little nervous to walk out of my bedroom and see him. I don't know why. Maybe because he's my boyfriend now, and I've barely had twelve hours to adjust to it all. It's so . . . official. I have no idea what it will be like. What our lives together will be like. But it's an excited nervous.

I reach down and grab his T-shirt, then pull it over my head. I make a detour to the bathroom to brush my teeth and wash my face. I debate fixing my hair before I walk into the living room, but Ridge has seen me in worse conditions than the present one. We used to be roommates. He's seen me in *way* worse conditions.

When I open the door to the living room, he's there, seated at the table with a notebook and my laptop. I lean against the doorframe and watch him for a while. I'm not sure how he feels about it, but I love that I can watch him unabashedly without him hearing me enter the room.

He pulls a frustrated hand through his hair at one point, and I can tell by the stiffness of his shoulders that he's stressed. Work stuff, I assume.

He eventually catches sight of me, and that seeing me in the doorway seems to ease his stress completely erases all my nervous energy. He stares for a moment and then drops his pen on the notebook. He smiles and scoots his chair back to stand, then makes his way across the living room. When he reaches me, he grabs me and pulls me against him, pressing his lips against the side of my head.

"Good morning," he says, pulling back.

I will never grow tired of hearing him speak. I smile at him and sign, "Good morning."

He looks at my hands and then back at me. "That is so damn sexy."

I grin. "You speaking is so damn sexy."

He kisses me, then pulls away and heads to the table. He grabs his phone and texts me.

Ridge: I have a ton of work to catch up on today and I really need my own laptop. I'm going to head back to my apartment so you can get ready for work. Want me to come over tonight?

Sydney: I drive by your place on my way home from work. I'll just stop by on my way home.

Ridge nods and picks up the notebook he was writing in. He closes my laptop and walks back to me. He wraps his arm around my waist and pulls me against him, pressing his mouth to mine. I kiss him back, and we don't stop, even when I hear him toss the notebook on the bar. He lifts me up with both arms, and a few seconds later, we're across the living room and he's lowering me onto the couch, and then he's on top of me and I'm pretty sure I'm going to get fired this week. There's no way I can tell him I'm already late for work when I'd rather be fired than have to stop kissing him.

I'm being dramatic. I don't want to get fired. But I've waited so long for this and don't want him to leave. I start counting to ten, promising myself that I'll stop kissing him and get ready for work when I reach ten. But I make it all the way to twenty-five before I finally press against his chest.

He pulls back, smiling down at me. "I know," he says. "Work."

I nod and do my best to sign what I'm saying. I know I'm not getting it all right, but I spell out the words I don't know yet. "You should have chosen this coming weekend to sweep me off my feet rather than a work night."

Ridge smiles. "I couldn't wait that long." He kisses my neck and then starts to roll off me so I can get up, but he pauses and stares at me appreciatively for a moment.

"Syd," he says. "Do you . . . feel . . ." He pauses, then pulls out his cell phone. We still have a huge communication barrier in that he doesn't feel completely comfortable speaking full conversations out loud yet, and I don't know enough sign language to hold a full conversation at a decent pace. I'm sure until we both get better, texting will remain our primary form of communication. I watch him text for a moment, and then my phone pings.

Ridge: How do you feel now that we're finally together?

Sydney: Incredible. How do you feel?

Ridge: Incredible. And . . . free? Is that the word I'm looking for?

I'm still reading and rereading his text when he immediately begins typing out another one. He's shaking his head, like he doesn't want me to take his previous text the wrong way.

Ridge: I don't mean free in the sense that we weren't free before we reunited last night. Or that I felt tied down when I was with Maggie. It's just . . .

He pauses for a moment, but I respond to him before

he replies because I'm pretty sure I know what he's trying to say.

Sydney: You've been living a life for others since you were a kid. And choosing to be with me was kind of a selfish choice. You never do things for yourself. Sometimes putting yourself first can feel freeing.

He reads my text, and as soon as his eyes flick to mine, I can see we're on the same page.

Ridge: Exactly. Being with you is the first decision I've made simply because I wanted it for myself. I don't know, I guess I feel like I shouldn't feel this good about it. But I do. This feels good.

Even though he's saying all of this like he's relieved he finally made a selfish choice, there's still a wrinkle between his furrowed brows, like his feelings are also accompanied by guilt. I reach my hand up and smooth it out, then cup his face. "Don't feel guilty. Everyone wants you to be happy, Ridge. Especially Maggie."

He nods a little, then kisses the inside of my palm. "I love you."

He said those words numerous times last night, but hearing them again this morning still feels like he's saying them for the first time. I smile and pull my hand from his so I can sign, "I love you, too."

This all feels so surreal—him actually being here with me after so many months of wishing it could be this way. And he's right. It felt so stifling being apart from him, yet feels liberating now that he's here. And I know he isn't saying all of what he just said because he felt like his life with

Maggie was in any way something he didn't want. He loved her. Loves her. What he's feeling is the result of spending an entire life making decisions that were in the best interest of others and not himself. And I don't think he regrets any of it. It's just who he is. And even though I was a selfish decision he finally made for himself, I know he's still the same selfless person he's always been, so there's going to be some residual guilt there. But people need to put themselves first sometimes. If you aren't living your best life for yourself, you can't be your best self for those in your life.

"What are you thinking?" he asks, brushing my hair back.

I shake my head. "Nothing. Just . . ." I don't know how to sign what I want to say, so I grab my phone again.

Sydney: This all feels surreal. I'm still trying to soak it all in. Last night was completely unexpected. I was starting to convince myself that you were getting to a point where you didn't think we could be together.

Ridge's eyes shoot to mine, and he laughs a little, like my text was completely absurd. Then he leans forward and gives me the softest, sweetest kiss before replying.

Ridge: I haven't been able to sleep for three months. Warren forced me to eat because I was anxious all the time. I've thought about you every minute of every day, but I kept my distance because you said we needed time apart. And even though it killed me, I knew you were right. Since I couldn't be with you, I forced myself to write music about you.

Sydney: Are there any songs I haven't heard yet?

Ridge: I played all my new songs for you last night. But I've been working on one. I've been stuck because the lyrics didn't feel quite right. But last night after you fell asleep, the lyrics started flowing like water. I wrote them down and sent them to Brennan as soon as I got them down on paper.

He wrote an entire song after I fell asleep last night? I narrow my eyes at him and then reply.

Sydney: Have you even slept yet?

He shrugs. "I'll nap later," he says, brushing his thumb over my bottom lip. "Keep an eye on your email today," he says as he leans in for another kiss.

I love it when Brennan makes rough cuts of the songs Ridge writes. I don't think I'll ever get tired of dating a musician.

Ridge rolls off the couch and then pulls me up with him. "I'll leave so you can get ready for work."

I nod and kiss him goodbye, but when I try to walk to my bedroom, he doesn't release his grip on my hand. I turn around, and he's looking at me expectantly.

"What?"

He points to the shirt I have on. *His* shirt. "I need that."

I look at his T-shirt and laugh. Then I pull the shirt off—slowly—and hand it to him. He's eyeing me up and down as he takes his shirt and pulls it over his head. "What time did you say you're coming over tonight?" He's still staring at my chest when he asks this question, completely unable to look me in the eyes.

I laugh and push him toward the door. He opens it and slips out of my apartment, but not before stealing another quick kiss. I close the door behind him and realize for the first time since the day I moved out of my old apartment, I finally feel like I'm no longer resentful for the turmoil Hunter and Tori caused.

I am absolutely, without a doubt, so grateful for Hunter and Tori. I would live through the Tori/Hunter heartache a million times over if Ridge was always my final result.

• • •

A few hours later, I get an email from Brennan. I duck into a bathroom stall at work with my headphones and click on the email with the subject line, "Set Me Free." I lean against the wall, press play on my phone, and close my eyes.

"Set Me Free"

I've been running 'round
I've been laying down
I've been underground with the devil
You've been saving me like a ship at sea
Saying follow me to the light now

So here we go
A little more
Something I've been waiting for

Here we go
A little more

You set me free
Shook the dust right off me
Locked up tight you found the key
And now I see
Ain't no place I'd rather be
I got you and you got me
You set me free

Hard to know the cost of it
But when you've lost something
Then you know there's a price tag
Think you might have been born to
Be my come through when
I can't keep it all together

So here we go
A little more
Something I've been waiting for
Here we go
A little more

You set me free
Shook the dust right off me
Locked up tight you found the key
And now I see

Ain't no place I'd rather be
I got you and you got me
You set me free

I was sitting low
I didn't know where I could go
Thought the bottom was the ceiling
No remedy to heal it
A Hail Mary to a sin
A new start to an end

You set me free
Shook the dust right off me
Locked up tight you found the key
And now I see
Ain't no place I'd rather be
I got you and you got me
You set me free

I stand completely silent after the song ends. There are tears running down my cheeks, and it isn't even a sad song. But the meaning behind the lyrics Ridge wrote after falling asleep next to me last night mean more to me than any other lyrics he's ever written. And even though I understood what he was saying this morning when he said he feels free for the first time, I didn't realize just how much I identified with what he was feeling.

You set me free, too, Ridge.

I pull the headphones out of my ears, even though I want to put the song on repeat and listen to it for the rest of the day. On my way out of the bathroom, I catch myself singing the song out loud in the empty hallway with a ridiculous smile on my face.

"Ain't no place I'd rather be. I got you and you got me . . ."

Chapter Two

Maggie

I think about death every minute of every hour of every day of my life. I'm almost positive I think about death more than the average person. It's hard not to when you know you've been given a fraction of the time almost everyone else on earth has been given.

I was twelve when I started to research my diagnosis. No one had ever really sat me down and explained to me that cystic fibrosis came with an expiration date. Not an expiration date on the illness, but an expiration date on my life.

Since that day, at only twelve years old, I look at life completely differently than I looked at it before. For example, when I'm in the cosmetics section of a store, I look at the age cream and know that I'll never need it. I'll be lucky if my skin even starts to wrinkle before I die.

I can be in the grocery section, and I'll look at the expiration dates on food and wonder which one of us will last longer, me or the mustard?

Sometimes I receive invitations in the mail for a wedding that's still a year out, and I'll circle the date on the calendar and wonder if my life will last longer than the couple's engagement.

I even look at newborn babies and think of death. Knowing that I'll never live to see a child of my own grow into adulthood has erased any desire to ever have a child.

I'm not a depressed person. I'm not even sad about my fate. I accepted it a long time ago.

Most people live their lives as if they'll live until they're one hundred years old. They plan their careers and their families and their vacations and their futures as if they'll be around for all of it. But my thoughts work differently from most people's, knowing that I don't have the option to pretend I'll live until I'm one hundred years old. Because I won't. Based on the current state of my health, I'll be lucky to live another ten years. And that's precisely why I think about death every minute of every hour of every day of my life.

Until today.

Until the moment I jumped out of the plane and I looked down on an earth that seemed so insignificant that I couldn't help but laugh. And I couldn't stop laughing. The entire time we were falling, I laughed hysterically until I started crying because the experience was beautiful and exhilarating and far exceeded my expectations. The entire time I was plummeting toward the earth at over one hundred miles per hour, I didn't once think about death. I could only think of how lucky I was to be able to feel that alive.

Jake's words kept repeating in my head as I was pushing against the wind. *This is living!*

He's right. This is the most I've ever lived, and I want to do it again. We've only been on the ground for all of a minute. Jake's landing was impeccable, but I'm still harnessed to him and we're sitting on the ground, my feet out in front of me as I try to catch my breath. I appreciate that he's given me a quiet moment to soak it all in.

He begins to unlatch us and stands up. I'm still sitting when he walks around in front of me and blocks the sun with his height. I look at him and am slightly embarrassed that I'm still crying, but not enough to try to hide it.

"Well?" he says, holding out his hand. "How was it?" I take his hand, and he pulls me up as I use my other hand to wipe the tears away from my cheeks. I sniff and then laugh. "I want to do it again."

He laughs. "Right now?"

I nod vigorously. "Yeah. That was incredible. Can we do it again?"

He shakes his head. "The plane is booked for the rest of the afternoon. But I can put you on the schedule for my next day here."

I smile. "I would love that."

Jake helps me remove my harness, and I hand him my

helmet and goggles. We go inside, and I change out of my gear. When I make it back to the front counter, Jake has printed out pictures and downloaded a video of the skydive for me.

"I sent it to the email address you have on file," he says, handing me a folder with the pictures inside it. "Is the address on your form your correct home address?"

I nod. "Yeah. Should I be expecting something in the mail?"

He glances up from the computer and smiles at me. "No, but you can expect me at your front door tonight at seven."

Oh. He was serious about celebrating tonight. Okay, then. I just got super nervous all of a sudden. I don't react, though. I smile at him and say, "Will this be a casual or formal celebration?"

He laughs. "I could make a reservation somewhere, but honestly, I'm more of a pizza-and-beer kind of guy. Or burgers or tacos or anything that doesn't require me to wear a tie."

I smile, relieved. "Perfect," I say, backing away from the counter. "See you at seven. Try not to be late."

I turn and walk toward the door, but before I exit, he says, "I won't be late. In fact, I want to show up early."

• • •

Ridge and I dated for so long, that I don't even remember the last time I've stressed over what to wear on a date. Aside from his infatuation with front-clasping bras, I don't even think Ridge paid attention to what underwear I wore. But here I am, digging through my dresser, trying to search for anything that matches or doesn't have holes or isn't tailored to fit a grandmother.

I can't believe I don't have any cute panties.

I open my bottom drawer full of stuff that, for whatever reason, I'd convinced myself I'd never wear. I sift through unmatched socks and gag-gift crotchless panties until I come across something that makes me forget about my search altogether.

It's a folded sheet of paper. I don't have to open it to know what it is, but I walk to my bed and open it anyway. I sit and stare at the list I started writing over ten years ago, back when I was only fourteen.

It's a bucket list of sorts, although back then I didn't know what the term "bucket list" meant. Which is why I titled it *Things I Want to Do Before I Turn Eighteen.* The *Before I Turn Eighteen* part of the title is marked out because I spent my eighteenth birthday in the hospital. When I got home, I was bitter at the whole world, and that I hadn't marked anything off my list. So I scribbled out the end of the title and changed it to *Things I Want to Do. Maybe One of These Days . . .*

There are only nine things on the list.

1) Drive a race car.
2) Skydive.

3)   See the Northern Lights.

4)   Eat spaghetti in Italy.

5)   Lose $5,000 in Vegas.

6)   Visit the caves in Carlsbad Caverns.

7)   Bungee jump.

8)   Have a one-night stand.

9)   Visit the Eiffel Tower in Paris.

I look over the list and realize that out of the nine things I hoped for as a teenager, I have only done one. I went sky-diving. And I didn't even do that until today, yet it ended up being the best moment of my life.

I reach to my nightstand and grab a pen. I cross out the second item on my list.

Eight more things remain on my bucket list. And honestly, they're all doable. Maybe. If I can somehow prevent myself from catching an illness while I travel, every single thing on this list is doable. Number eight might even be doable tonight.

I don't know how Jake would feel about being checked off as an item on my bucket list, but I don't think he'd complain too much about being the other half of my one-night stand. It's not like I'm going to let anything come of this date tonight, anyway. The last thing I want is another situation where I'll feel like I'm a burden to someone. The thought of being someone's irresistible one-night stand has me way more excited than the prospect of being someone's terminally ill girlfriend.

I fold the list and put it in the drawer of my night-stand. I walk over to my dresser and grab a random pair of panties. I don't even care what they look like. If all goes as planned, I won't even be wearing them long enough for Jake to care what they look like. I'm pulling on my jeans when I receive a text.

Ridge: Mission successful.

I smile when I read the text. It's been several months since we ended things, but Ridge and I still text occasion-ally. As hard as it was to see our relationship come to such an unexpected end, it would be even harder to lose his friendship. He and Warren are the only two friends I've had for the past six years of my life. I'm grateful that even though our relationship didn't work out that it doesn't mean our friendship can't. And yes, it's weird discussing Sydney with him, but Warren has been keeping me up to date on all things Ridge, even in the areas I don't care to be up to date on. In all honesty, I want Ridge to be happy. And as angry as I was when I found out he'd kissed Sydney, I still like the girl. It's not like she showed up with evil inten-tions and tried to steal him from me. She and I actually got along, and I know they both tried to do the right thing. I'm not sure we'll ever get to a point where we'll all hang out as friends. That would be too weird. But I can be happy that Ridge is happy. And since Warren filled me in on their plan to trick Sydney into going to a bar last night so Ridge could convince her to be with him, I've been curious how it would all turn out. I told Ridge to text me if their plan was successful last night, but I don't think I want the details. I can accept that she's a part of his life now, and I really am happy for him. I just don't think I'll ever be in the position to want the details.

Maggie: That's great, Ridge!

Ridge: Yeah, that's all we'll say about that because it's still too weird discussing it with you. Any word on the thesis yet?

I'm glad we're on the same page. And I can't believe I forgot to tell him the good news.

Maggie: Yes! Found out yesterday. Got a 5!

Before he responds, there's a knock at my front door. I look at the time on my phone and it's only 6:30. I toss the phone on my bed, walk to the living room, and look through the peephole. Jake wasn't kidding when he said he might show up early. I haven't even finished getting ready.

I back up to the mirror in my hallway and yell, "Just a sec," while I check my reflection. Then I rush back and look through the peephole again. Jake is standing with his hands in the pockets of his jeans, looking out over my front yard as he waits for me to open the door. It's honestly a bit surreal, knowing I'm about to go on a date with this guy. He's a freaking doctor! Why is he even single? He's really cute. And so tall. And successful. And . . . is that a . . .

I swing open the door and step outside. "Holy shit, Jake. Is that a Tesla?" I don't mean to be rude, but I brush right past him and walk straight to his car. I hear him laugh behind me as he follows me to the driveway.

I'm not a car fanatic by any means, but one of my neighbors dates a guy who drives a Tesla, and I'd be lying if I said I wasn't a tad bit obsessed with these cars. But I don't know my neighbor well enough to go ask her if I can go for a ride in her boyfriend's car.

I run my hand over the sleek black hood. "Is it true they don't have engines?" I spin around, and Jake is watching me with amusement as I ogle his car instead of him.

He nods. "Want to see under the hood?"

"Yes."

He pops the hood with his key fob and then steps next to me to open it. There's nothing but an empty trunk inside, lined with carpet. No engine. No transmission. There's just . . . nothing.

"So there's no engine at all in these cars? You never have to fill up with gas?"

He shakes his head. "Nope. There's not even oil that needs changing. Only upkeep is the brakes and tires, really."

"How do you keep it charged?"

"I have a charger in my garage."

"You just plug it in at night like you're charging a phone?"

"Basically."

I turn back toward the car, admiring it. I can't believe I get to ride in a Tesla tonight. I've been wanting to ride in one for two years. If I had updated my bucket list at all in the past few years, this would definitely be something I'd be crossing off it tonight.

"They're really good for the environment," he says, leaning against the hood. "No emissions."

I roll my eyes. "Yeah, yeah, that's nice. But how fast does it go?"

He laughs and crosses his feet at the ankles. His voice is intentionally low and sexy when he raises a brow and says, "Zero to sixty . . . in 2.5 seconds."

"Oh my God."

He nods at the car. "You want to drive it?"

I glance at the car and then back at him. "Really?"

His smile is sweet. "Actually . . . let me make a phone call," he says, pulling out his phone. "I might can get us in over at Harris Hill."

"What's Harris Hill?"

He raises the phone to his ear. "A public racetrack in San Marcos."

I cover my mouth with my hand, trying to hide my excitement. What are the chances that I'll mark a third of my bucket list off in one day? Skydiving, race-car driving, *and* a possible one-night stand?

Chapter Three

Ridge

I open my eyes and stare at the ceiling. My first thought is of Sydney. My second thought is that I can't believe I fell asleep on the couch in the middle of the afternoon.

I barely slept last night, though. Actually, I've barely slept for the entire past week. I was so anxious leading up to the show I had planned for Sydney last night, not knowing how she would react to it. And then, after she reacted better than I ever imagined and we ended up at her place, I still couldn't sleep because I couldn't stop texting Brennan lyrics. He's probably got enough material from last night alone to make three songs out of.

When I left Sydney's apartment this morning, my plan was to come home and catch up on work, but I couldn't concentrate on anything because I was so exhausted. I finally lay down on the couch and turned on *Game of*

Thrones. I'm probably the last person to start the series, but Warren has been trying to get me to catch up to him for months. He's on season three, and I made it through the first three episodes of season one today before I passed out.

I wonder if Sydney has watched it. If not, I'd much rather start it over and watch it with her.

I pick up my phone and have two unread texts from Warren, one from Maggie, one from Brennan, and one from Sydney. I go straight to Sydney's text first.

Sydney: I listened to the song. It made me cry. It's really good, Ridge.

Ridge: I think you're just partial because you're in love with me.

She texts back immediately.

Sydney: Nope. I'd love the song even if I didn't know you.

Ridge: You're not good for my ego. What time will you be here?

Sydney: On my way now. Will Warren and Bridgette be there?

Ridge: Pretty sure they both work tonight.

Sydney: Perfect. See you soon.

I close out my texts to Sydney and open Warren's text.

Warren: Brennan sent me the new song. I like it.

Ridge: Thanks. Started Game of Thrones today. I like it.

Warren: IT'S ABOUT DAMN TIME! Have you made it to the episode where they decapitate Stark in front of his daughters yet?

I press my phone to my chest and close my eyes. I hate him sometimes. Like really hate him.

Ridge: You are a fucking asshole.

Warren: Dude, it's the best episode!

I toss my phone on the coffee table and stand up. I walk to the kitchen and open the refrigerator to search for a way to get revenge on him. I hope Warren is kidding. Ned Stark? Really, George?

There's a block of one of Bridgette's fancy cheeses in the drawer. I pull it out and open the packaging. It's some sort of white cheese with fancy pieces of spinach or something in it. Smells like shit, but it looks just like a bar of soap once the wrapping is removed. I take it to Warren's bathroom, remove his bar of soap from the shower, and replace it with the cheese.

Ned gets decapitated? I swear to God, if that actually happens, I'm throwing away my television.

When I walk back to the living room, my phone is lighting up on the coffee table. It's a text from Sydney, telling me she just parked. I walk to the door and open it, then make my way down the stairs. She's making her way up, and as soon as I see the smile on her face, I forget all about the decapitation I'm praying is a just a terrible prank Warren is pulling on me.

We meet in the middle of the staircase. She laughs at my eagerness when I push her against the railing and kiss her.

God, I love her. I swear, I don't know what I'd have done if she hadn't signed "when" last night. I'm sure I'd still be sitting on that stage, playing every sad song I could think of while I drank every last drop of alcohol in the bar. But not only did the worst-case scenario not happen—the best-case scenario happened. She loved it and she loves me and here we are, together, about to spend a perfect, boring night at my apartment doing nothing but eating takeout and watching television.

I pull away from her, and she reaches up to wipe lip gloss off my mouth.

"Have you ever watched *Game of Thrones*?" I ask her.

She shakes her head.

"Do you want to?"

She nods. I grab her hand and walk up the stairs with her. When we get inside, she goes to use the bathroom and I pick up my phone. I open the unread text from Maggie.

Maggie: Yes! Found out yesterday. Got a 5.

Ridge: Why am I not surprised? Congratulations! Hope you're doing something to celebrate.

Maggie: I did. Went skydiving.

Skydiving? I hope she's kidding. Skydiving is the last thing she should be doing. That can't be good for her lungs. I start to respond to her, but I pause in the middle of my text. This is the one thing she disliked the most about me. My constant worrying. I have to stop stressing about her doing things that might make her situation worse. It's her life, and she deserves to live it however she wants.

I delete my response to her. When I look up from my phone, Sydney is standing at the refrigerator, watching me. "You okay?" she asks.

I stand up straight and slide my phone into my pocket.

I don't want to talk about Maggie right now, so I smile and save it for another day. "Come here," I say to her.

She smiles and walks over to me, sliding her arms around my waist. I pull her to me. "How was your day?"

She grins. "Excellent. My boyfriend wrote me a song."

I press my lips to her forehead, then hook my thumb beneath her chin, tilting her face up to mine. As soon as I start to kiss her, she grabs my shirt and starts walking backward toward my bedroom. We don't break the kiss until she's falling onto my bed and I'm climbing on top of her.

We kiss for several minutes with our clothes on, which I would rectify, but it's nice. We didn't really fall in love in a typical way, so we went from a kiss that filled us with weeks of guilt, to a three-month stretch of not communicating at all, to a night of making up and making love. We were nothing at all and then suddenly all in. It's nice taking it slow right now. I want to spend the rest of the night kissing her because I've thought about kissing her like this for three months straight.

She rolls me onto my back and then slides on top of me, breaking our kiss. Her hair is falling around her face, so she moves it out of the way by sliding it over her shoulder. She kisses me softly on the mouth and then sits up, straddling me so she can sign.

"Last night feels like . . ." She pauses, struggling to sign the rest, so she speaks it. "It feels like forever ago."

I nod in agreement and then lift my hands to teach her

how to sign the word *forever*. I say it out loud as she signs it. When she gets it right, I nod and sign, "Good job."

She falls to my side and lifts up onto her elbow. "What's the sign for the word *deaf*?"

I make the motion for the word, sliding my hand across my jaw and toward my mouth.

She drags her thumb from her ear to her chin. "Like that?"

I shake my head to let her know she got it wrong. I lift up onto my elbow, then take her hand to tuck in her thumb and straighten out her index finger. I press it to her ear and slide it over her jaw, toward her mouth. "Like that," I tell her. She repeats the sign for *deaf* with perfection. It makes me smile. "Perfect."

She falls back onto her pillow and smiles up at me. I love that she studied sign language for the three months we were apart. As mad as I am at Warren for ruining *Game of Thrones* for me, I'll never be able to repay him for everything he's done to help Sydney and me learn to communicate without so many barriers. He really is a good friend . . . when he isn't being a complete asshole.

She's picked up ASL so fast. Every time she signs something, I'm impressed all over again. It makes me want her to sign everything from now on, and it makes me want to voice all the words I ever say to her.

"My turn," I say. "How do you make the sound a cat makes?"

There are so many words I still don't understand, and

animal sounds are a huge portion of that. Maybe I struggle with knowing how they should sound because it's impossible to read lips when the sound is coming from a cat or a dog.

"You mean meow?" she asks.

I nod and press my fingers against her throat so I can feel her voice when she says it. She repeats the word, and then I give it my best attempt. "Me . . . oh?"

She shakes her head. "First part sounds like . . ." She signs the word *me*.

"Me?"

She nods. "Second part . . ." She lifts her hand to sign the letters *Y, O,* and *W* while saying them out loud again. I keep my palm pressed against her throat.

"Again," I say.

She enunciates slowly. "Me . . . yow."

I love the way her lips form a circle at the end of the sound. I bend down and kiss her before trying to speak the sound again. "Me . . . yow."

She grins. "Better."

I say it faster. "Meow."

"Perfect."

I start to ask her why *meow* is used in certain instances, but I forget how new she is at signing, and her eyes grow big with her confusion as she tries to follow along with my hands. I lean over her and grab my phone and type out my question.

Ridge: Why is the word MEOW sometimes used to depict

when something is sexy? Does the word make a sexy sound when it's spoken?

She laughs and her cheeks blush a little when she says, "Very."

I find that interesting.

Ridge: Is it also sexy when a person barks like a dog?

She shakes her head. "No. Not at all."

The verbal form of the English language is so confusing. But I love learning more about it from her. It's the first thing that drew me to her beyond the physical attraction. Her patience with my inability to hear and her eagerness in wanting to know all about it. There aren't a lot of people like her in this world, and every single time she signs for me, it reminds me how lucky I am.

I pull her closer and lean toward her ear. "Meow." When I pull back, she's no longer smiling. She's looking at me like that was the sexiest thing she's ever heard. She confirms my thoughts by sliding her fingers through my hair and pulling my mouth to hers. I roll on top of her and part her lips with my tongue. Just as I start to give her a deeper kiss, I feel the vibration of her moan, and then I'm a goner.

And so are our clothes. So much for taking it slow tonight.

Chapter Four

Sydney

I follow the path of Ridge's finger with my eyes as he runs it back and forth over my stomach. We've been lying like this for five minutes now, him running his fingers in soft circles over my skin while he watches me. Every now and then, he kisses me, but we're both too exhausted for round two.

I don't even know how he's still awake. He barely slept last night at my house because he stayed up writing that song for me, and then as soon as I got here an hour and a half ago, we came straight to the bedroom and have stayed fairly busy. It's almost eight, and if I don't eat dinner soon, I'm going to fall asleep right here in his bed.

My stomach growls, and Ridge laughs, pressing his palm flat against my stomach. "You hungry?"

"You felt that?"

He nods. "Let me shower, and then I'll figure out dinner." He kisses me and rolls off the bed, heading for his bathroom. I find his T-shirt and pull it on before heading to the kitchen for something to drink. When I open the refrigerator, someone behind me says, "Hi."

I yelp, and then I swing the refrigerator door wide open and try to hide my undressed bottom half behind it. Brennan is sitting on the couch, grinning.

So are the other two guys from his band, whom I've still yet to be formally introduced to.

Brennan tilts his head. "The first night I met you, you weren't wearing a shirt. And now a shirt is all you're wearing."

I can't recall ever being this mortified in my life. I didn't even put my panties on, and even though Ridge's shirt covers my ass, I don't know how to make it from here all the way back to his bedroom without losing my last shred of dignity.

"Hi," I say, sticking my arm up over the door with a pathetic wave. "Do you guys mind looking away so I can find some jeans?"

All three of them laugh, but they look at the wall to spare me a few seconds to run back to Ridge's room. As soon as I start to swing the refrigerator door shut, the front door flies open, and Warren stomps into the apartment. I pull the refrigerator door open again to continue shielding myself.

Bridgette storms into the apartment behind Warren,

and then Warren slams the door. "Go!" he says, waving her away as she storms across the living room toward their bedroom. "Go hide in your room and give me the silent treatment like you always do!"

Bridgette slams their bedroom door. I look back at Warren, who is staring at Brennan and the other two guys on the couch. "Hey," he says, still not noticing me. "What's up?"

None of them are looking at Warren because I asked them to turn toward the wall, so Brennan is still staring at the wall when he says, "Hey, Warren."

"Why are you staring at the wall?"

Brennan points toward the refrigerator, but continues to stare at the wall. "Waiting for her to run back to Ridge's room so she can put some clothes on."

Warren swings his attention to me, and his eyes immediately light up. "Well, what a sight for sore eyes," he says, tossing his keys on the bar. "I know I see you all the time, but it's good to finally see you back in this apartment."

I swallow, doing my best to remain stoic. "It's . . . good to be back, Warren."

He points at the refrigerator door. "You really shouldn't stand there with the door open like that. Ridge makes me split the bills with him now, and you're wasting a lot of electricity."

I nod. "Yeah. Sorry. But I sort of don't have any pants on, and if you'd walk over there and stare at the wall with those guys, I'll shut the door and go back to Ridge's room."

Warren tilts his head and then takes two steps toward me and leans to the right like he's trying to look around the refrigerator door.

"See?" Bridgette yells from across the room, standing in Warren's now-open doorway. "This is exactly what I'm talking about, Warren! You flirt with everyone!" Their door slams again.

Warren rolls his head and sighs, then walks toward their bedroom. I use the opportunity to make a mad dash back to Ridge's bedroom. I shut the door and lean against it, covering my face with my hands.

I'm never going back out there.

I make my way toward Ridge's bathroom just as he opens the door. There's a towel wrapped around his waist, and he's drying his hair with another towel. I rush toward him and wrap my arms around him, burying my face against his chest as I squeeze my eyes shut. I just start shaking my head until he pulls me away from his chest so he can look at me. I can't even imagine what he's seeing because I'm groaning and frowning and laughing at my embarrassment.

"What happened?"

I point to the living room and then sign, "Your brother. Warren. The band. Here." Then I motion toward my half-naked body and the fact that my butt cheeks are practically hanging out of his T-shirt. He eyes me up and down and then glances toward the living room, then looks at me again, squinting like he's remembering something. "The first time you met Brennan . . . you were wearing just a bra. Now you're wearing—"

"I *know*," I groan, falling onto his bed. Ridge starts laughing while he pulls on his jeans. Then he leans forward, and I think he's going to kiss me, but instead he just slips his shirt over my head and pulls it off me. He's fully dressed, and I'm even more naked than I was when I walked into the living room. He hands me my clothes, and I know he wants to officially introduce me to the band, but I want to curl up into a ball and hide until everyone leaves.

I force myself to suck it up and get dressed because Ridge is smiling at me like this entire thing amuses him, and his smile makes me forget how embarrassed I am. The kiss he gives me when he pulls me toward the door makes me forget it even more.

When we walk back into the living room, Brennan is now sitting on the bar with his legs dangling, swinging back and forth. He grins at me, and it's unnerving how much he and Ridge look alike yet carry themselves so differently. Ridge walks me to the couch where the other two members of Sounds of Cedar are standing up to shake my hand.

"Spencer," the tall brunette one says. He's the drummer. I know this because I've seen them play. I've just never actually been introduced to them.

"Price," the other one says, shaking my hand. He plays lead guitar and sings backup vocals, and while the star of the band is definitely Brennan, I think Price gives him a run for his money. He's got the rock-star swagger down, even though their music isn't typically rock. It's got a more pop/alternative vibe. But he could probably pull off any sound because he's so charismatic onstage. Brennan sometimes takes a step back and lets him shine.

"I'm Sydney," I say, with a lot of forced confidence. "It's so good to finally meet you guys. I'm a huge fan of the band." I wave my arm across them and over to Brennan. "It's so impressive how fast you guys get stuff recorded."

Price laughs and says, "Sydney, we're all huge fans of yours. Ridge went through a pretty long dry spell until you came along."

My eyes widen, and I look over at Ridge, who is looking at Brennan, who is signing everything everyone is saying. Ridge immediately looks back at me, and then at Price.

"Dry spell?" Ridge says out loud.

"*Lyrical* dry spell," Price says, clarifying what he meant. "I meant lyrical." Now Price looks embarrassed.

God, this is so awkward.

"I'm hungry," Brennan says, slapping his hands on the bar on either side of him. "Has anyone eaten?"

"Chinese sounds good," I suggest.

Brennan picks up his phone and looks at it. "A girl who knows what she wants. I like it." He pulls the phone to his ear. "Chinese it is. I'll just order a shit-ton of everything."

I try not to stare at him too hard. I just can't get over how much he looks like Ridge physically, but with a completely different personality. Ridge is responsible and mature, and Brennan seems like he doesn't give a shit. About anything. It's like he doesn't have a single care, yet his older brother takes on the burden of caring about every single thing.

"So, Bridgette and I are fighting, if you didn't notice," Warren says, taking a seat on the couch and scrolling through his texts. He looks up at me. "She says I flirt with other people too much."

I laugh. "You do."

Warren rolls his eyes and mutters, "Traitor. You're supposed to be on my side."

"There are no sides when it's a discussion of facts," I say. "You flirt with me. You flirt with Bridgette. You flirt with the old lady who lives in my apartment building. Hell, you even flirt with her dog. You're a flirt, Warren."

"He flirts with me," Spencer says.

Warren is still scrolling through his texts when he reads something that makes him pause. He laughs a little and then looks over at Ridge and Brennan. "Maggie went skydiving today."

My breath catches at the mention of her name. Naturally, I look over at Ridge, who is leaning against the bar next to Brennan. Brennan covers his phone with his hand and says, "Good for her."

Ridge just nods, expressionless, and says, "I know. She told me earlier." He glances at me for a brief second and then looks down at his phone.

My mouth feels dry. I press my lips together. There was a moment earlier, when I came out of the bathroom and saw Ridge holding his phone with a torn expression. I had no idea what had caused him to react like he was. I assumed it was work.

But . . . it wasn't work. It was Maggie. He was worried about Maggie.

I don't like how I'm feeling right now. I pull my phone out of my pocket and try to busy myself, but I'm standing awkwardly in the middle of the living room. Brennan ends his call to the Chinese place, and Warren and Ridge are both looking at their phones. I suddenly feel out of place. Like I don't belong in this living room with these people in this apartment. Brennan signs something to Ridge without speaking, and then they start a silent conversation with Warren that's too fast for me to keep up with, which makes me think they don't want me to know what they're saying. I try to ignore them, but I can't help but look when Warren says, "You worry too much, man."

"Typical Ridge," Brennan says. As soon as he says that, Brennan looks at me and then at Ridge and then stiffens a little. "Sorry. Is that weird? We shouldn't talk about Maggie. That's weird." He looks over at Warren, who brought up the entire conversation. "Shut the fuck up, Warren."

Warren brushes off Brennan's comment with a flippant wave in my direction. "Sydney's cool. She's not a PSYCHOTIC JEALOUS GIRLFRIEND LIKE SOME PEOPLE!" he yells toward his bedroom.

Two seconds later, Bridgette swings open the door and says, "I'm not your girlfriend. I broke up with you."

Warren looks offended. And confused. He holds up his hands. "When?"

"Right now," Bridgette says. "I'm breaking up with you right now, asshole." She slams the door, and sadly, no one really pays it much attention. Some things haven't changed a bit around here. Warren doesn't even get up from the couch to chase after her.

I feel my phone vibrate, so I look at the text.

Ridge: Hi.

I glance over at him, and he's sitting on the bar now, next to Brennan. They're both swinging their legs, seated the same way, and Ridge looks completely adorable as he smiles at me. The looks he gives me are intoxicating. He motions for me to come stand with him, so I walk over to him. He spreads his legs wider, turning me until my back is against his chest. He kisses me on the side of my head and wraps his arms around my shoulders.

"Hey, Sydney," Brennan says. "Did Ridge play you the song Price wrote?"

I glance at Price and then back at Brennan. "No, which one is it?"

Brennan signs for Ridge to play me the song, so Ridge holds his phone in front of me and searches his files.

"'Even If Your Back Was Turned,'" Price says from the couch.

"We just recorded it last week," Brennan says. "I like it. I think it'll do well. Price wrote it for his mommy."

Price throws a pillow in Brennan's direction. "Fuck

you," he says. He looks at me and shrugs. "I am a momma's boy."

I laugh, because he doesn't look like your typical momma's boy.

Ridge finds the song and presses play. He sets the phone on his thigh and then wraps his arms around me again as I listen. Almost as soon as it starts to play, a text notification goes off on Ridge's phone. I look down at it.

Maggie: Guess what? I'm finally riding in a TESLA!!!

Ridge must see the text as soon as I hear it and read it, because his legs stop swinging and he stiffens. We're both looking at the phone, and I know he's waiting on my reaction, but I don't know how I should react. I don't even know what I'm supposed to be feeling right now. It's just all too weird. I reach over and swipe up on her text so it'll disappear. Then I pause the song and say to Price, "I'll listen to it later. It's too loud in here."

Ridge wraps his arm tighter around my waist as he picks up his phone and begins texting with one hand. I don't know if he's responding to her or not, but I guess it's not my business. Is it? I don't even know if I should be mad. I don't think I'm mad. *Confused* is a better word for it. Or maybe *uncomfortable* is the best way to describe what I'm feeling.

Ridge pulls on my hand so I'll turn and look at him. I'm still standing between his legs, but this time I'm facing him, looking at him, trying not to let him read my thoughts. He puts his phone in my hand, and when I look at it to read whatever he's written in his note app, he lowers his forehead to mine.

She's my friend, Sydney. We text sometimes.

As I'm reading the note on his phone, his hands are sliding softly down my arms in a comforting gesture. It's amazing how much more he can communicate nonverbally as a result of being so stifled by his verbal communication. By pressing his forehead to mine as I read what he typed, it's as if he's silently saying, *We're a team, Sydney. You and me.*

And the way he's sliding his hands down my arms is equivalent to a thousand verbal reassurances.

I expected that he still talks to Maggie. What I didn't expect was for it to bother me like it is. But it's not because I think Ridge and Maggie are in the wrong. It's because I feel like I'll always be the girl who came between them, no matter how friendly they remain. I can be friendly with every single friend Ridge ever has, but I'm not sure I could ever be friends with Maggie, so the fact that he *is* friends with her makes me feel like a third wheel to that friendship.

It's a strange feeling. And one I don't like, so I can't help but have a noticeable reaction. Especially to Ridge. He notices every nonverbal reaction I have because that's the focus of his communication.

I hand Ridge's phone back to him and force a smile, but I know my feelings are probably written all over my face. He pulls me in for a reassuring hug and then kisses the side of my head. I press my face against his neck and sigh.

"God, you two are so cute together," Brennan says.

"It makes me want a girlfriend. For like a whole week, maybe."

His comment makes me laugh. I pull away from Ridge and turn around, leaning my back into him again.

"You're about to have one for more than a week," Spencer says. "Sadie's opening for us for the next two months."

Brennan groans. "Don't remind me."

I welcome the distraction. "Who is Sadie?"

Brennan looks at me pointedly and says, "Sadie is Satan."

"Her name is Sadie Brennan," Warren says, standing up. "Not to be confused with Brennan Lawson. Coincidence that they share part of a name, and also a coincidence that Brennan thought she was a groupie the first time he met her."

Brennan grabs a roll of paper towels off the bar and throws them at Warren. "It was an honest mistake."

"I think this is a story I need to hear," I say.

"No," Brennan says firmly.

At the same time Brennan says *no*, Warren pipes up and says, "I'll tell it." He flips one of the table chairs around backward and sits down, facing us. "Brennan has a routine," Warren says and signs. "Sounds of Cedar isn't a widely known band, but locally, you know, they have a decent following. Quite a few fangirls who come to the meet and greets after the shows."

Warren is signing everything for Ridge, so it makes me laugh when Brennan's head falls back and he groans, then signs, "Shut up," at the same time he says it. It'll never get old that they sign everything for Ridge. It's like it's second nature, and they don't even realize they're doing it. That's my goal. I want to learn to communicate that way to the point where Ridge and I have absolutely no barriers.

"Sometimes after the shows, if Brennan thinks a girl is cute, he'll slip her a note with his hotel information, asking if she wants to chat in private. Five times out of ten, they show up an hour later at his hotel room door."

"Ten times out of ten," Brennan corrects.

God, he and Ridge are so different.

Warren rolls his eyes and continues, "Sadie happened to be one of the girls he slipped a note to. But what he didn't know was that she wasn't at his meet and greet as a fan. She was there looking to talk with him about a gig. And what she didn't know is that Brennan slips someone his number after every show with the intention of hooking up. She thought he slipped her a note because he wanted to chat with her about opening for the band on our upcoming tour. So when she showed up at his hotel room that night, let's just say there was a lot of confusion."

I look at Brennan, and he's running his hand down his face like he's embarrassed. "Dude, I hate this story."

He might hate it, but I'm enjoying the hell out of it. "What happened?"

Brennan groans. "Can't we just end the story here?"

"No," Warren says. "This is where it gets good."

Brennan looks so embarrassed, but he continues the story himself. "Let's just say it took her a few seconds to realize what I assumed she was there for, and it took me more than a few seconds to realize she wasn't there because she wanted me to take off her shirt."

"Oh no. That poor girl."

Brennan makes a face. "Poor girl, my ass. I told you she's Satan. She makes Bridgette look like an angel."

"I heard that," Bridgette yells from her room. Brennan shrugs. "It's true."

"She's not that bad," Price says to Brennan. "She just hates *you*."

"But . . . she's opening for you guys on the next tour? She must not hate you too much," I say.

Brennan shakes his head. "No, she definitely hates me. But she also has mad talent. That's the only reason why she got the gig."

"Do you have any of her songs?" I ask. "I want to hear one."

Brennan scoots closer to us and hands me his phone after pulling up a YouTube video. Ridge scoots me over and hops off the bar to set out plates for the Chinese food. I can't help but stare at the video on Brennan's phone in complete awe. The girl is really pretty. And she's super talented. I watch the first video, and then another, and then a third before I realize Brennan hasn't moved a muscle. He can pretend he isn't into her all he wants, but he holds his breath through every video, never taking his eyes off the screen.

We're watching the fourth video when the food arrives. We all make our plates and sit around the table. It's the first meal Ridge and I have eaten together as a couple.

He's sitting right next to me with his left hand on my thigh. We've eaten a lot of meals at this table together while forcing ourselves to sit as far apart from each other as we possibly could. It feels good to finally be able to touch him—sit close to him—and not fight everything inside me that was growing.

I like this.

The door to the bathroom between Warren and Bridgette's old bedroom swings open. Bridgette is standing in a towel, sopping wet from the shower. Her eyes scan the table until she finds Warren, and then she tosses something at him, hitting him in the chest. Whatever it is falls onto his plate. Then the door slams.

Everyone looks at Warren. He picks up the block of whatever she just threw at him and stares at it for a second. Then he sniffs it. His head slowly turns toward Ridge.

"Cheese? You put *cheese* in my shower?"

I look at Ridge, and he's attempting to force back a smile.

Warren sniffs the cheese again and then takes a small bite of it. I cover my mouth with my hand, trying not to gag. *Does he not realize that Bridgette had to rub that block of cheese on some part of her body before realizing it wasn't soap?*

Warren sets the cheese on his plate like he just received a free course with his meal.

As disgusting as some of them are, I've missed their pranks so much. I squeeze Ridge's leg to let him know that was a clever one.

When we finish eating, I text Ridge and tell him I should go. I have an early day tomorrow, and it'll be after ten by the time I get home. I tell all the guys goodbye, and Ridge walks me down. When we reach my car, he opens my door but doesn't kiss me goodbye. He waits for me to sit, and then he walks around to the passenger side and takes a seat.

He grabs my phone, which I just placed in the console, and hands it to me.

Ridge: You okay?

I nod, but he doesn't look convinced. I don't know how to say, *Stop having friends!* without feeling a little like Bridgette.

Ridge: Does it bother you?

He doesn't even have to specify what he's talking about. We both know. And I don't know how to answer him. I don't want to be that jealous girlfriend who takes issue with every single thing, but how can I not be jealous when there's still a part of me that's envious of Maggie?

Ridge: Please be honest, Syd. I want to know what you're thinking.

I sigh, thankful he cares enough to talk about it but also wishing we could brush it under the rug at the same time.

Sydney: It's uncomfortable. It bothered me that you seemed so worried about her. But it would also bother me if you didn't care. So it's just . . . weird. It's going to take time to get used to, I guess.

Ridge: I do worry about her. And I care about her. But I am not in love with her, Sydney. I'm in love with you.

When I finish reading his text, he leans across the seat and takes my face in his hands. "I love you."

The sincerity in his expression makes me smile. "I know you do. I love you, too."

He stares at me for a moment, searching for any remaining doubt in my expression. Then he kisses me goodnight. When he gets out of the car, he takes the stairs two at a time. He reaches the top and texts me again.

Ridge: Let me know when you make it home safe. And thank you.

Ridge: For being you.

When I look up, he smiles and then disappears inside his apartment. I watch his door for a moment and then drop my phone in my purse, just as someone knocks on my window. I jump and press my hand to my chest. When I look out my window, I roll my eyes.

You've got to be kidding me.

Hunter is standing at my driver's-side window, looking at me expectantly. I forgot he even frequented this apartment complex. I guess that means he's still with Tori. I stare at him for a moment and feel absolutely nothing. Not even anger.

I put my car in reverse and back up, pulling away from the complex without looking back. The only way to look now is forward.

• • •

Ridge: You asleep?

I look at the time stamp on his text. He just sent the message two minutes ago. I pull the towel off my head and run my fingers through my hair before I text him back.

Sydney: Nope. Just got out of the shower.

Ridge: Oh yeah? So you're naked?

Sydney: I have a towel on. And no, you aren't getting a pic.

Ridge: I don't want a pic. I want you to open your front door and let me in.

I glance toward the living room, then look back down at my phone. *He's here?* I only left his apartment an hour ago. I rush to the living room with worry in the pit of my stomach. I hope nothing is wrong. Surely Hunter didn't do anything stupid after I pulled away.

I look through the peephole, and there he is, staring at the door. I leave the living room light off since I'm opening the door with only a towel on. Ridge slips inside my apartment. I close the door. It's dark, and I'm suddenly no longer wearing a towel. Ridge's mouth is on mine, and my back is against the living room wall.

Ridge isn't really the type to just show up without telling me first, but I don't mind it.

I don't mind it *at all*.

What I do mind is that he's dressed and I'm not.

I pull off his shirt and unbutton his jeans. His mouth is everywhere, but his hands have me caged against the wall. He kicks off his pants and then picks me up, wrapping my legs around his waist. He starts toward the bedroom, but realizes we're way closer to the couch, so he turns and lowers me to the sofa.

We're still kissing when he lowers himself on top of me, and then he's inside me and it's incredible. I am so in love with this man.

He stops kissing me for a moment, so I let my head fall back onto the cushion, and I relax as he kisses my neck. When he reaches my mouth again, he pulls back and stares down at me. He brushes my hair back, and there's just enough light from the window shining down on us so that I can see every emotion in his eyes. He's looking at me with so much feeling when he says, "I love you, Sydney." He pauses above me so that I'm focused on his words and nothing else. "I love you more than I have ever loved anyone."

I close my eyes because the impact of his words hits me everywhere. I had no idea how much I wanted those words. *Needed* those words. And he knows I would never ask him to admit that or compare us to his last relationship, but here he is, wanting to diminish any shred of doubt I might have had while at his apartment tonight. I repeat his words silently, never wanting to forget this moment. This feeling. *I love you more than I have ever loved anyone.*

His warm mouth presses gently against mine, and his tongue slides past my lips, delicately searching for mine. When I kiss him back, I wrap my hand in his hair and pull him as close as I can. For the next several minutes, Ridge proves to me just how much I mean to him without speaking or signing another word.

Even when it's over, several minutes go by with our lips still connected. Every time he tries to stop kissing me, he can't. It's just one kiss after another after another. He eventually buries his face against my neck and sighs against my skin. "Can I spend the night with you?"

His question makes me laugh. I don't know why. It just feels like it's a given at this point. As soon as I nod, he grabs my arms and pulls me up with him, then lifts me and carries me to the bedroom. He lays me on the bed and then crawls under the covers with me, wrapping his bare legs around me. I love that neither of us are dressed. This is a first.

I kiss him on the nose and want to sign to him, but it's dark. He also can't read lips in the dark, so I grab my phone.

Sydney: That was completely unexpected.

Ridge: Do you prefer your boyfriend to be more predictable?

Sydney: I prefer my boyfriend to be you. That's really my only requirement. Just be Ridge Lawson and you can date me.

Ridge: I'm pretty good at being Ridge Lawson. You're in luck.

We are so cheesy. I hate us and love us.

Sydney: Unexpected or predictable, I like all the versions of you.

Ridge: I like all the versions of you, too. Even if the rest of our lives were predictable, I'd never get tired of you. We could live the same day over and over and I'd just ask for more.

Sydney: Like Groundhog Day. I feel the same way.

Ridge: You make routine something I actually look forward to. If you told me you wanted us to go wash dishes together right now, I'd get excited.

Sydney: What if I asked you to do laundry with me? Would that excite you?

The light from our phones makes it possible for me to see him when he looks at me. He nods slowly, like the thought of doing laundry with me turns him on. I grin and look back at my phone.

Sydney: Would you look forward to eating the same meal every single day?

Ridge: I would if I were eating it with you.

Sydney: Would you be able to drink the same drink every single day?

Ridge: If I were drinking it with you, I would still be thirsty for it on my deathbed.

Sydney: Oh, that's a good line. Keep going.

Ridge: If I could hear music, I would listen to the same song over and over and never tire of it as long as I was listening to it with you.

I laugh.

Sydney: I see you still have the same self-deprecating deaf jokes you've always had.

Ridge reaches out and touches my mouth. "And you have the same beautiful smile you've always had." His thumb runs over my bottom lip, but his eyes grow intense as he stares at my mouth. "Same smile . . . same laugh." He pulls his hand from my mouth and lifts up. "This feels like a song," he says. As soon as he says it, he rolls over and turns on the lamp. "Paper?" He opens my top drawer. He doesn't find paper, but he finds a pen. He faces me with a look of urgency. "I need paper."

I roll off the bed and walk to my desk. I grab a legal pad and a book for him to place it on. He grabs them out of my hands before I'm even seated back on the bed; then he starts writing lyrics. I've missed this so much. He writes a few sentences, and I lean over his shoulder and watch him.

Same seats on the couch
Same drinks when we go out
Same smile, same laugh
You know I'll never get enough of that

He pauses for a moment, then he looks at me. He smiles and hands me the pen. "Your turn." It feels like old times. I take the pen and the legal pad and think for a moment before adding my own lines.

Same clothes on the floor
Same dog at our door
Same room, same bed
I wouldn't wish for anything instead

He's staring at the lyrics when he hops off the bed and starts looking around the floor. "Jeans?" he says. I point to the living room. He nods, like he forgot we came to my bedroom naked. He points over his shoulder. "Guitar. My car." He rushes out of my room, and a minute later, I hear him walk out my front door. I look at the page and read through the lyrics again. I have two more sentences written when he makes it back to my bedroom with his guitar.

When everything is changing
Baby you're written in stone

He sets his guitar on the bed and looks over the lyrics, then motions for the pen. He tears out the lyrics and starts writing out chords and notes on another page. This is my favorite part. This is the magic—watching him hear a song that doesn't even have sound and doesn't even exist yet. The pen is flying over the paper frantically. He pulls the lyrics back in front of him and starts adding to them.

Feels like we made it
Got something of our own
Maybe it's predictable
But I can't complain
With you and me
All I need
Is more of the same
More of the same

He hands me the notepad and pen and picks up his guitar. He starts playing, and I'm reading the lyrics, wondering how he does this with such little effort. Just like that, he's created a new song. An entire song from nothing more than a few sentences and a little inspiration.

I begin to write another verse while he plays the chords.

Same songs in the car
We never need to go too far and I won't leave you alone
Just stay the same baby I've always known that
When everything is changing
Baby you're written in stone
Feels like we made it
Got something of our own
Maybe it's predictable
But I can't complain
With you and me
All I need is more of the same
More of the same

When I finish writing the chorus again, he reads it all. Then he hands me the lyrics and leans back against my headboard. He motions for me to sit between his legs, so I crawl over and turn my back toward him as he pulls me against him and wraps his guitar around us. He doesn't even have to ask me to sing the song. He starts playing, leaning his head against mine, and I start singing the song for him so that he can perfect it.

The first time he played for me, we were sitting like this. And just like that first day, I am completely in awe of him. His concentration is inspiring, and the way he creates such a pleasing sound that he can't even hear makes it hard for me to focus on the lyrics. I want to turn around and watch him play. But I also like that we're wrapped together on my bed and I'm caged against him by his guitar, and every now and then, he kisses the side of my head.

I could do this every night with him and still want more of the same.

We sing and play the song about three times, and he pauses to make notes between each run-through. After the fourth and final time, he tosses the pen on the floor and then pushes his guitar to the other side of the bed. Then he turns me around so I'm straddling his lap. We're both smiling.

It's one thing for a person to find their passion, but it's another thing entirely to be able to share that passion with the person you're passionate about.

It's fun and intense, and I think we're both realizing for the first time that we get to do this together all the time. Write songs, kiss, make love, be inspired to write more songs.

Ridge kisses me. "This is my new favorite song."

"Mine, too."

He slides both hands to my cheeks and bites his lip for a second. Then he clears his throat. "With you and me . . . all I need . . . is more of the same."

Oh my God. *He's singing.* Ridge Lawson is serenading me. And it's terrible because he's so out of tune, but a tear falls from my eye because it's the most beautiful thing I've ever witnessed or heard or felt.

He wipes my tear away with his thumb and smiles. "That bad, huh?"

I laugh and shake my head, and then I kiss him harder than I've ever kissed him because there is no way I can verbally express my love for him right now. Instead, I love him silently. He doesn't even break the kiss when he reaches behind him and turns off the lamp. He pulls the covers over us and then tucks my head under his chin as he wraps himself around me.

Neither of us says *I love you* before we fall asleep.

Sometimes two people share a silent moment that feels so deep and so powerful, a simple phrase such as *I love you* risks losing all prior meaning if spoken aloud.

Chapter Five

Maggie

I've only taken three bites of my burger, but I push the plate away from me and lean back. "I can't finish this," I mutter, letting my head fall back against the booth. "I'm sorry."

Jake laughs. "You jumped out of an airplane for the first time ever and then drove a car in circles for an hour straight. I'm surprised you're able to eat anything at all."

He says this with an empty plate sitting in front of him while scarfing down a milkshake. I guess when you're used to jumping out of planes and driving fast cars, the adrenaline doesn't jack with your equilibrium to the point that you feel like the world is spinning inside your stomach.

"It was fun, though," I say with a smile. "It's not every day I cross two things off my bucket list."

He scoots both of our plates to the edge of the table and leans forward. "What else is on your bucket list?"

"Vegas. The Northern Lights. Paris. The usual." I fail to tell him that he's who I hope will be number eight on my list. We've had so much fun tonight, I want to do it again. But I also don't, simply because we had so much fun tonight. I've spent the entirety of my adulthood in a relationship. I don't want that again. Even if he is too good to be true. "Why are you single?" I ask him.

He rolls his eyes like the question embarrasses him. He pulls his glass of water in front of him, sipping from it in order to avoid it for a few seconds longer. When he lets the straw fall away from his lips, he shrugs. "I'm usually not."

I laugh. That's expected, I suppose. A skydiving, Tesla-driving, good-looking cardiologist doesn't sit home every Friday night. "Are you a serial dater?"

He shakes his head. "The opposite, actually. I just got out of a relationship. A really long relationship."

I didn't expect that answer. "How long did you date her?"

"Twelve years."

I sputter a cough. "Twelve years? How old are you?"

"Twenty-nine. Started dating her in high school."

"Can I ask what ended it? Or do you want to change the subject?"

Jake shakes his head. "I don't mind talking about it. I moved out about six months ago. We were engaged, actually. I proposed four years ago. We never got around to planning the wedding because we were waiting until we finished our residencies."

"She's a doctor, too?"

"Oncologist."

Jeez. I suddenly feel so . . . young. I just barely finished my thesis, and here he is with an ex-fiancée who went through medical school with him and saves lives. I pull my drink to my lips and take a sip, attempting to wash down all my insecurities.

"Was it a mutual breakup?" I ask him.

He looks down at his hands briefly. A flash of guilt takes over his expression before he responds. "Not really. I realized about twelve years too late that I didn't want to spend the rest of my life with her. I know that sounds bad after being with her for so long. But for some reason, choosing to spend the rest of my life with her was a lot easier than breaking up with her."

Why am I feeling everything he's saying? I find myself wanting to raise my arm and say, *Amen*, like I'm in church. "I can absolutely relate to what a hard decision that must have been."

Jake leans forward, folding his arms on the table. He tilts his head in thought for a moment, then says, "I had a moment before I ended it. I remember asking myself what I would regret more. Ending something that was good so I didn't end up with regrets? Or spending the rest of my life regretting that I didn't have the courage to end something simply because I was afraid of regret? Either choice would have left me with some form of regret, so I chose to end it. And it was hard. But I'd rather regret ending something good than be what prevents her from finding something great."

I stare at him a moment, but I have to break my stare because I'm starting to have that feeling again. That I want him to be more than a one-night stand.

"How long were you and your boyfriend together?" he asks.

"Almost six years."

"Were you the one who ended it?"

I think about his question for a moment. From the outside looking in, I'd say I was. But being in it . . . I'm not so sure. "I don't know," I admit. "He fell in love with another girl. And it wasn't like it was some torrid, scandalous affair. He's a good person, and he would have chosen me in the end. But he would have chosen me for the wrong reasons."

Jake looks surprised. "He cheated on you?"

I hate that word. I find myself shaking my head, even though he did. Ridge cheated on me. It makes him sound malicious, which he is not. "*Cheating* is such an ugly term to describe what happened." I think about it for a moment as I stir my straw around in my glass. Then I look up at Jake and say, "He . . . connected with someone else on a deeper level, I think. To call him a cheater feels like an insult he doesn't deserve. He crossed a line with someone he connected with. We'll just leave it at that."

Jake watches me for a moment, reading my expression. "You don't have to talk about it if you don't want to. I just find it fascinating that you don't sound like you hate him."

I smile. "He's one of my best friends. And he tried to do the right thing. But sometimes the wrong thing is the right thing."

Jake fights a smile, like he's impressed with this conversation, but he doesn't want to show it. I like that. I like how interesting he is. And I like that he seems to find me interesting.

He's still staring, like he wants to hear more, so I continue. "Ridge writes lyrics for a band. About two years ago, the band released a new song, and I'll never forget the first time I heard it. Ridge always sent me the songs ahead of their release, but for some reason, he never sent me this particular song. After I downloaded it and listened to it, I immediately knew why he never sent it. It's because he wrote it about us."

"A love song?"

I shake my head. "No. It was kind of the opposite. Sort of a falling-out-of-love song, about a couple who needed to move on from each other but didn't know how. It wasn't until I heard that song that I realized he felt the same way I did. But neither of us was in a place to admit that to the other at the time."

"Did you ever ask him about it?"

"No. I didn't have to. I knew it was about me as soon as I heard the first line."

"What was the line?"

"'I keep on wondering why I can't say bye to you.'"

"Wow," Jake says, leaning back. "That's definitely telling."

I nod. "I don't know why we waited so long after that to end it. I guess it's like you said. Things between us were good, but I knew he'd found something great in another girl. And he deserved better than just good."

Jake's expression is stoic as he watches me silently for a few seconds. But then he smiles with a shake of his head. "How old are you?"

"Twenty-four."

He makes a face like he's impressed. "You're a little young to have life figured out so well."

His compliment makes me smile. "Yeah, well, I have a shorter life span than everyone else. I have to cram a lot into a smaller time frame."

I almost regret making a joke about having a terminal illness, but it doesn't dismay him at all. In fact, it makes him smile. *God, I hate how much I like him already.*

"Is this your first date since Ridge?" he asks. I nod, and he says, "Mine, too."

I think about that for a moment. If he hasn't dated since his breakup, that means he hasn't dated another girl since high school. And I probably shouldn't open my mouth, but the sentence is already coming out. "If you dated your ex for twelve years, that means you've only been with—"

"Her," he says, matter-of-fact. "That is correct."

And here we are, somehow discussing sexual partners over dinner on a first date. And somehow, the conversation isn't at all uncomfortable. Conversation with him has been great, actually. There hasn't been a lull all night. Not even while I was driving his car one hundred miles per hour in circles around a racetrack.

There also hasn't been a lull in our chemistry. There were a couple of times tonight when I thought he might kiss me—and I absolutely would have let him—but he'd grin and step away from me like he enjoys the feeling of torture. I guess that would make sense. He's an adrenaline junkie. Adrenaline and attraction feel very closely related.

He's staring at me right now, and I'm staring at him, and I don't know exactly what it is that's taken over me at the moment. A little bit of adrenaline. Attraction. Maybe even infatuation. Whatever it is, I have a bad feeling about it. I don't know Jake well enough, but I think the intense look on his face suggests he feels it, too.

I break eye contact with him and clear my throat. "Jake . . ." I lift my eyes, meeting his stare again. "I don't want a relationship. At all. Not even remotely."

My words have no visible impact on him. He simply presses his lips together and then, a moment later, asks, "What do you want?"

I lift my shoulders in a slow, unsure shrug. "I don't know," I say, dropping my shoulders again. "I wanted to have fun with you on our date. And I did. I am. But I'm not sure it's a good idea if we go out again."

I wish I could explain to him all the reasons why I don't want to go on another date with him. But there are way too many reasons not to go on another date, as opposed to only one reason why I should.

Jake squeezes the back of his neck and then leans forward, folding his arms over the table again. "Maggie," he says. "I've been out of practice when it comes to this whole dating thing. But . . . I feel like you like me. Do you like me? Or am I just blinded to your disinterest because I'm insanely attracted to you?"

Ugh. I can't help the smile that forces its way out. I can also feel myself blushing over the fact that he's insanely attracted to me. "I do like you. And . . ." This is so hard for me to say. Flirting is so foreign to me. "I'm insanely attracted to you, too. But I don't want to date you after tonight. It's nothing personal. I want to live in the moment, and right now, another serious relationship is not a part of my moment. I've been there, done that. I have other plans for my life."

Jake looks both intrigued and disappointed by my answer, if that's even possible to feel both things at once. He nods and says, "So this is it? I leave a tip on the table and then I drive you home and drop you off and we never see each other again?"

I bite my bottom lip, because knowing it's now or never makes me nervous. I either use this moment to mark off another item on my bucket list, or I wake up tomorrow regretting that I was too scared to ask him to come over.

I'm not scared. I can do this. I am Maggie fucking Carson. I am the girl who jumped out of an airplane and raced a sports car in the same day.

I swallow the last shred of shyness and look him in the eyes. "This date doesn't have to end when we pull into my driveway."

I can see the immediate change in his demeanor. I can see his intrigue and his attraction and his hope, all settled behind his eyes that are staring at my mouth. He lowers his voice a little and says, "When, exactly, does it have to end?"

Holy shit. This is actually happening. Bucket list item number eight, practically in the bag.

"How about we just live in the moment?" I suggest. "And then when that moment is over, you go home, and I fall asleep."

The corners of his mouth curl into a grin. Then he pulls out his wallet and lays a tip on the table. He stands up and offers me his hand. I slip my fingers through his, and we leave the restaurant, living in the moment and not a second beyond it.

Chapter Six

Maggie

I roll over to see if he's gone as soon as I open my eyes.

He is.

I run my hand over his pillow, wondering how someone can feel so full of emptiness.

Last night was . . . well . . . It was bucket-list-worthy, that's for sure. As soon as we left the restaurant, we headed to my house. He let me drive. We talked about cars, my thesis, that I want to try bungee jumping. He offered to take me, but realized he was essentially asking me out on another date, so he corrected himself and told me a place he thinks I should try. When we got to my house, we were both laughing as we walked inside because the sprinklers came on as soon as we got out of the car, the spray of water hitting us both right in the face. I walked to my kitchen and grabbed a hand towel to dry my face. Jake followed me, and when I handed him the towel to use, he tossed it over his shoulder and reached for me, kissing me like he'd been waiting to do it since the moment he'd laid eyes on me.

It was unexpected, but wanted, and even though I felt every single thing while his mouth was on mine, I was also full of uncertainty. I've only been with two people sexually in my life, and I was in love during both of those relationships. This was the first time I was about to have sex with someone I wasn't in love with. I wasn't sure what to expect, but knowing he didn't either made me feel more at ease. I kept reminding myself of that with every new part of my neck he kissed.

After about fifteen minutes of full-on making out with him, something switched in me. I don't know how he did it, but he was so attentive and into it that all my concerns and insecurities eventually fell away with my clothing. By the time we made it to the bedroom, I was all in. And then he was all in, in more ways than one.

It was everything. Afterward, we rolled onto our backs, and just when I thought he was getting ready to leave, he turned his head and looked at me. "Are there rules to one-night stands I'm not aware of? Are we only allowed to have sex once?"

I laughed, and then he was on top of me again, and as much fun as it was the first time, the second time was even better. It was intense. And slow. And perfection.

He didn't roll onto his back after the second time. He rolled onto his side and wrapped his arms around me and whispered, "Goodnight," before kissing me. I liked that he said *goodnight* instead of *goodbye*, because it took the focus off the fact that we both knew he'd be leaving before I woke up.

I just assumed I'd wake up in a state of euphoric bliss today. Not a state of melancholy.

Feeling a little down about it being over isn't necessarily a bad thing, though. It means I couldn't have chosen a better person to have my one-night stand with. Had it been anyone else, I don't think I would have enjoyed it as much as I did. And if I hadn't enjoyed it, I wouldn't feel like I'd have the right to cross it off my bucket list.

So yes, it sucks that I can't find anything wrong with him. But it would suck even more to fall back into something I'll just want out of eventually. I can't put myself in another position where someone will become obligated to take care of me.

It's not a good feeling, knowing someone has convinced themselves they're more in love with you than they are simply because you're dependent on them. I'd rather feel melancholic than pathetic.

I grab the pillow Jake slept on—the same pillow I was just rubbing in longing—and I throw it off my bed. I'll throw it in the trash later. I don't even want to smell him again.

I walk over to my dresser and grab my bucket list. I mark out number eight and then look over the list again. I suddenly feel accomplished, knowing number eight was probably the one thing on my bucket list I was certain I would never have the guts to do.

Maggie fucking Carson. You are a badass.

I fold the list and set it on top of my dresser. I open the second drawer, then grab a pair of panties and a tank top and pull them on. I need to go visit my grandfather today while I have the opportunity, but first I need waffles and a shower.

Waffles before shower. I'm way too excited for waffles after not having been able to eat much last night.

I might even go get a manicure today. I'm staring down at my nails when I walk into my living room. But then I freeze when I smell bacon. I slowly raise my head to find Jake standing at my kitchen stove.

Cooking.

He spins around to reach for a plate and sees me. He grins. "Morning."

I don't smile. I don't speak. I don't even nod a greeting in return. I stand there and stare at him and wonder how a twenty-nine-year-old man could honestly not understand the meaning behind one-night stand. *Night* being the key word. There's not supposed to be a morning included in that definition.

I look at my tank top and underwear and suddenly feel modest, even though he spent enough time on top of me last night that he probably has every inch of my body memorized. But still, I wrap my arms around myself.

"What are you doing?" I ask.

Jake is watching me, a little unsure of himself after seeing my reaction to him still being here. He looks at the stove and then at me, and I swear he deflates right in front of me.

"Oh," he says, suddenly seeming out of place. "You thought . . . Okay." He starts nodding and immediately reaches to the stove and turns off the burner. "My bad," he says, not looking at me. He grabs a glass that's next to the stove and takes a quick drink. When he faces me again, he can't even look at me. "This is awkward. I'll go. I just . . ." He finally makes eye contact with me. I wrap my arms around myself even tighter because I hate that I've created such an awkward moment when he was obviously trying to do something nice.

"I'm sorry I made this awkward," I say. "I just wasn't expecting you to still be here."

Jake nods, walking toward me to grab the shoes he kicked off next to the couch last night. "It's fine. I misread things, obviously. I know you made yourself clear last night. But that was before we . . . twice . . . and it was . . ."

I press my lips together.

His shoes are now on his feet, and he stands, eyeing me. "Wishful thinking, I guess." He points at my front door. "I'm gonna leave now."

I nod. It's probably for the best. I just ruined every good thing about last night.

Actually, *he* ruined every good thing about last night. I walked into my living room accepting that I'd never see him again, and he ruined it by assuming I wanted him to stay and cook me breakfast.

He reaches for the front door, but before he opens it, he pauses. When he turns around, he stares at me for a moment, then walks back over to me. He stops about two feet away and tilts his head. "Are you positive you don't want to see me again? There's no wiggle room for me to convince you to give this one more shot?"

I sigh. "I'll be dead in a few years, Jake."

He takes half a step back, but doesn't take his eyes off me. "Wow." He brings a hand to his mouth and runs it over his jaw. "You're really using that one?"

"It's not an excuse. It's a fact."

"A fact I'm very aware of," he says. His jaw is hard, and now he's mad. *See?* If he would have just left before I woke up, this would have ended perfectly! Now, when he leaves, we're both going to be frustrated and full of regret.

I take a step forward. "I'm dying, Jake. *Dying.* What's going to come of this? I don't ever want to get married. I don't want children. I have no desire for another relationship where I'll eventually become someone's burden. Yes, I like you. Yes, last night was incredible. And that's exactly why you should have left already. Because I have things I want to do, and falling in love and fighting with someone about how I live the last few years of my life is not something that's ever been on my bucket list. So thank you for last night. And thank you for attempting to cook me breakfast. But I need you to leave."

I blow out a frustrated breath and then immediately look at the floor because I hate the look in his eyes right now. Several seconds pass, and he doesn't respond. He stands there and soaks in everything I said. He eventually takes a step back, and then another. I look up, and he looks away, turning toward the front door. He opens it and steps outside, but before he closes it, he looks straight at me.

"For the record, Maggie. I was just making you breakfast. I wasn't proposing."

He shuts the door, and my house has never felt emptier than it does in this moment.

I hate this. I hate everything I just said to him. I hate how much I wish it weren't the truth.

I hate this stupid fucking illness.

And I hate that I said all that and made him leave before he could even finish cooking the damn bacon. I stare at the pan and then walk over to it and throw the entire pan in the trash.

I lean against the bar and can't help but pout. Is Jake ending a relationship twelve years too late better or worse than me ending a relationship completely and entirely too early? He's someone I could love. *If* I had the life to love him in.

I bring my hands up to the back of my head and press my elbows together, bending over. I try to stop myself from being so disappointed. But the fact that I'm disappointed over a guy I met twenty-four hours ago disappoints me even more. I take a few minutes to recover, then force myself upright.

I grab the box of waffles I had intended to have for breakfast from the freezer. Only now, I'm not nearly as excited to eat them.

Chapter Seven

Ridge

Sydney swings open my bedroom door. I'm sitting at my desk, finishing up a website for a client, when she goes straight to my bed and falls face-first onto the mattress.

Rough day, I guess.

It's probably my fault because I stayed another night at her house last night. Maybe I should give her a night to catch up on her sleep. Outside of her job, we've been together almost nonstop since Monday. I know it's only Friday, but we get exhausted being together. In the best way.

I'll make sure tonight is a little more relaxing than the last few nights. We can take the *chill* out of *Netflix and chill* and literally just watch TV shows all night. Then I'll let her sleep in as long as she wants tomorrow. Hell, I'll probably sleep in *with* her.

I walk over to the bed and lie down beside her. I brush

her hair out of her face, and she opens her eyes and grins at me, despite looking exhausted.

"Bad day?" I ask her.

She shakes her head and rolls over onto her back. She lifts her hands to sign, but whatever she wants to say, she doesn't know how to sign. "Midterms," she finally says.

I tilt my head. "Midterms?" She nods.

"You had midterms this week?"

She nods again.

Now I feel like an asshole. I grab my phone and text her.

Ridge: Why didn't you tell me? I wouldn't have stayed at your apartment.

Sydney: Mine were Monday, so no worries. Your timing Monday night was impeccable. It's just that I work at the library and it's insane during midterms. The students are insane. The professors are insane. I'm so happy it's Friday.

Ridge: Me too. Let's do nothing tonight but watch TV. I need to find out if Ned really gets decapitated.

Sydney: Who?

Shit. Warren is rubbing off on me. I don't want her to know I just spoiled season one of *Game of Thrones*.

Ridge: Oh, nothing. Talking about The Walking Dead.

Sydney stares at her phone for a second, confused.

Sydney: I don't remember that from The Walking Dead.

She watches *The Walking Dead*. Great. Now I want to have sex, and I already told her we'd be lazy tonight.

Sydney's attention moves away from me and toward my bedroom door. "Someone is knocking," she signs.

I climb off the bed and head to the living room. Through the peephole, I notice it's a girl with a FedEx uniform on. I open the door, and she hands me a package. Once I've signed for it, I walk the package to the bar and wait for Sydney as she walks into the kitchen. I read the label, and it's addressed to me, but there's no return address.

Sydney leans over me and then signs, "You got a present?"

I shrug. I'm not expecting anything that I can remember, but I open the package and there's another package inside of it. Knowing Warren, he probably sent me a roll of toilet paper with his face all over it. I start to pull the tape off, but I notice Sydney walk around me, toward the living room. When I glance up at her, she's holding her phone up, aiming her camera in my direction.

"Are you recording me?"

She nods and gives me a sweet smile. "The present is from me."

"You bought me something?"

Her shy smile is so fucking adorable. Every time I think I'm too exhausted to even think about picking her up and throwing her on my bed, she does something that completely reinvigorates me and makes me feel like I could run a marathon.

I look back down at the package and feel bad that she got me a gift. I suck at gifts. Shit, what if she's the type who gives the best gifts? I'm the guy who once bought his nine-year-old brother a hamster for Christmas, but didn't realize it had died in the box. Brennan opened it and cried the entire day.

And this beautiful girl has *me* as her boyfriend.

Although this gift is hard as shit to open. I set it on the bar and yank at the lid.

A sudden cloud of dust bursts out of the container and hits me in the face. It happens so fast, I can't even close my mouth in time. I step back from whatever the hell was in that container, and I start spitting. *What the hell just happened?*

I walk to the sink and run my hands under the water, then wet my face. When I pull my hands back, they're sparkling like a fucking unicorn.

Glitter. Everywhere.

On my arms, my shirt, my hands, the counter. In my mouth. I look over at Sydney and she's rolling on the floor with laughter. Tears are in her eyes, she's laughing so hard.

She glitter bombed me.

Wow.

I guess that means the prank war has recommenced.

I wash my mouth out and then calmly walk to the bar, where the explosion just happened. I scoop a handful of glitter into my palm. *Two can play this game.* Her laughter hasn't let up at all. I think she's laughing even harder now that she sees me up close. I'm sure I look fantastic in sparkles.

I've read the word *squeal* before and know that it's a form of laughter, but I have no idea what it sounds like at all. As soon as I tip my hand over and watch the glitter fall all over her, I'm almost positive that's what she's doing. *Squealing.*

She clutches her stomach and falls onto her back. A tear falls down her cheek.

My God. I'd give anything to be able to hear her right now. I spend so much time trying to imagine what her voice and her laughter and her sighs sound like, but there isn't enough imagination in one person to come close to what I know it probably sounds like.

She sees the look on my face and suddenly stops laughing. Her eyebrows pull together when she signs, "Are you angry?"

I smile and give my head a slight shake. "No. I just really wish I could hear you right now."

Her expression relaxes a little. Saddens, even. She pulls in her bottom lip for a second as she stares up at me. Then she reaches her hand up and grabs mine, pulling on it. I lower myself to the floor, sliding my knee between her legs.

I might not be able to hear her like I wish I could, but I can smell her and taste her and love her. I run my nose over her jaw until my lips reach hers. When I brush my lips against hers, her tongue slips into my mouth, soft and inviting. I return the action, searching her mouth for remnants of laughter.

She's an incredible communicator when it comes to her kiss. Her kiss sometimes says more to me than anything she could ever sign or text or speak. Which is why I immediately know when she's distracted. I don't even have to hear it. She hears it for me, and then I feel her reaction and I just know. I pull back and look down at her, just as her attention moves to Warren and Bridgette's bathroom door. I look up, and Bridgette is walking out of the bathroom. She pauses and looks at us, lying on the living room floor together, covered in glitter.

And then she does the unthinkable.

Bridgette smiles.

Then she steps over us and walks away. When she leaves the apartment, I look down at Sydney, wondering if she's just as shocked as I am by that exchange. Her eyes are wide as she looks back at me. She starts laughing again. I quickly press my ear to her chest, wanting to feel it, but her laughter fades too quickly. I bring my hand to her waist and start tickling her. I feel her start laughing again, so I keep tickling her because it's the closest I can get to hearing that laugh.

Her phone is next to me on the floor, so when it lights up, I naturally glance at it. I stop tickling her when I see the name and the message that appear on the screen.

Hunter: Thank you, Syd. You're the best.

She hasn't noticed her phone. She's still laughing and trying to squirm away from me, so I sit back on my knees and pick up her phone. I hand it to her as I'm standing up to walk away. I try to bite down my anger as I grab a rag and begin wiping the glitter off the bar. I glance at her to see her reaction, but she's sitting cross-legged now, responding to that fucker's text.

Why is she talking to him?

Why does it seem like they're somehow miraculously on good terms?

"Thank you, Syd"? Why is he calling her *Syd*, like he has any right to be that casual with her after what he did to her? And why is she sitting so casually like this is okay? I grab my phone.

Ridge: Let me know when you're finished chatting with your ex. I'll be in the shower.

I don't look at her as I head to my bedroom and then my bathroom. I pull open the shower curtain and turn on the water, and then take my shirt off. I swear, I just want to make loud noises. It's not very often I feel the need to be loud, but in situations like this, I know it probably feels good to be able to groan so that I can hear my frustrations leaving my body. Instead, I toss my shirt at the wall and unbutton my jeans with nowhere for my noise to go.

When the bathroom door opens, I regret not locking it because I really need a minute. Or two or three. I glance at Sydney, and she leans against the door frame and raises an eyebrow.

"Seriously?"

I stare at her expectantly. What does she want me to say? Does she expect me to be okay with this? Does she expect me to smile and ask her how Hunter is doing?

Sydney hands me her phone and scrolls up on her texts to Hunter so I can read them. I have no desire to read them, but she uses both of her hands to force mine around her phone, and then she motions for me to read them. I look down at the string of messages.

Hunter: I know you don't want to speak to me. I don't blame you for driving away the other night. And believe me, I would leave you alone, but I gave you all my financial forms to give to your dad to look over during our company's merger last year. It's almost April and I need them for taxes. I called his office and they said they sent them back with you a few months ago.

Sydney: They're in Tori's apartment in my old bedroom. Look in the red folder at the top of the closet.

Hunter: Found them!

Hunter: Thank you, Syd. You're the best.

Sydney: Can you delete my number now?

Hunter: Done.

I lean against the sink and rub a hand down my face. She immediately starts texting me when I hand her back her phone, so I check my phone.

Sydney: I realize my situation with Hunter is different from your situation with Maggie, but I have been extremely accommodating to the friendship you chose to keep, Ridge. EXTREMELY ACCOMODATING! But you are being a hypocritical tool right now. It's very unattractive.

I blow out a breath of mixed relief and regret. She is absolutely right. I'm a hypocritical tool.

Ridge: You're right. I'm sorry.

Sydney: I know I'm right. And that little apology doesn't really make me any less angry with you.

I glance at her and swallow because I haven't seen her this angry in a very long time. I've seen her upset and frustrated, but I don't think I've seen her this angry since the morning she woke up in my bed and found out I had a girlfriend.

Why did I have to react that way? She's right. She's been nothing but patient with me, and the first chance I have to show her the same trust and patience in return, I stomp out of the room in a tantrum.

Ridge: I was jealous and in the wrong. 100% wrong. Actually, I was so wrong, I think I stretched the limit of 100%. I was 101% wrong.

I look at her, and I'm thankful I can read her nonverbal cues so well. Even though she tries to hide it, I can see her relax a little with that text. So I send her another one. I'll text her apologies all night if I have to in order to get rid of this tension I caused.

Ridge: Remember when we used to tell each other our flaws so it would help fight our attraction for each other?

She nods.

Ridge: One of my flaws is that I never knew I had a jealous streak until I had you to be jealous over.

She doesn't smile, but she does lean against the counter next to me. Our shoulders touch, and it's such a subtle thing, but it means so much right now.

Sydney: My flaw is that I forgive too easily and I can't stay mad.

She may find that to be a flaw, but I couldn't be more grateful for that side of her. Especially right now. She lifts her eyes and shrugs a little, like she's already over it. I give her a quick kiss on her forehead.

Ridge: My flaw is that I'm covered in glitter. I somehow even got it . . .

I pull at the flap of my jeans. "Down there," I say. She starts laughing. And I smile because *fuck Hunter.*

I have the absolute best girlfriend there ever was to walk this earth.

Sydney: My flaw is that I kind of already forgot why we were fighting because you're so cute when you sparkle.

Ridge: We're fighting because you are perfect and I don't deserve you.

Sydney rolls her eyes and then sets down her phone. I stand up straight and place my phone on top of hers, pushing them to the back of the counter. I move in front of her, and she grips the counter at her sides, looking at me with glitter in her lashes and her hair. Such a beautiful girl. Inside and out. I lower my mouth to hers while bringing my hands to the front of her jeans. I unzip and unbutton them and then continue to kiss her as I undress her.

I pull her into the shower with me, and for the next half hour, I apologize profusely with my mouth.

Chapter Eight

Maggie

I've spent seventeen nights in the hospital this past year alone.

I've been to visit my doctor more times than that. Since the day I was born, I've been at appointments to check my health more times than I've gone grocery shopping.

And I'm sick of it.

Sometimes when I arrive at my doctor's office, I sit there and stare at the building, wondering what would happen if I drove away and never went back. What would happen if I stopped having tests administered? What would happen if I stopped receiving treatment for every single cold I'm afflicted with?

I'd get pneumonia. That's what would happen. Then I would die. At least I'd never have to go back to a doctor's office. The nurse takes the blood pressure cuff off my arm. "It's a tad high."

"I had a lot of sodium for breakfast." I pull my sleeve back down. My blood pressure is high because I'm here. At the doctor. They call it white-coat syndrome. Anytime I have my blood pressure checked inside a doctor's office, it's high because of nerves. But outside of a doctor's office, it's fine.

I lick my lips, trying to moisten them. My mouth is dry from the nervous energy of being here. I don't want to be here. But here I am. No turning back now.

The nurse hands me a gown and tells me I can change when she leaves the room. I look down at the gown and cringe.

"Is this necessary?" I ask, holding up the gown.

She nods. "It's a requirement. We'll probably run a few tests today, and your chest needs to be easily accessible."

I nod and watch as she slips my chart in the door slot and starts to pull it shut. She smiles reassuringly. "Doctor will be in shortly," she says. She has a look of pity about her, like she wants to hug me. I get that a lot. Especially from the really sweet nurses. I remind them of when they were in their formative years, young and vibrant and full of life. And they try to imagine themselves in my shoes at this age, and their eyes fill with pity for me. I'm used to it. Sometimes I even pity myself, but I don't think that's related to the illness. I think, as humans, we all have a degree of self-pity.

I blow out a breath, more nervous than I've ever been

to be in a doctor's office. My hands are shaking when I pull off my shirt. I hurry up and put on the gown and then sit on the exam table. It's cold in here, so I rub my hands over my arms, fighting the chills. I press my knees together and then squeeze them with my hands, trying my best not to think about the reason I'm here. I sweat when I'm nervous. I don't want to be sweaty.

I feel my chest tighten, and then my throat becomes itchy and I start to cough. I cough so hard, I have to stand up and walk over to the sink to balance myself. There's a knock on the door in the middle of one of my coughing fits, and I turn around to find the nurse peeking her head in.

"You okay?"

I nod, still coughing. She walks over to the sink and takes a cup and then fills it with water. But I don't need more liquid in my throat right now. I take the cup and thank her, but I wait until my coughing subsides before I take a sip. She leaves the room again. I walk back over to the exam table, and as soon as I sit, there's another knock at the door.

This is it.

The door begins to open and my heart starts to pound so hard; I'm relieved no one is checking my blood pressure at the moment. He flips my chart open before he looks up. He pauses as soon as he opens it, probably because he's shocked to see my name on the chart.

I knew he'd be surprised. Hell, *I'm* surprised I worked up the courage to come here.

Jake immediately lifts his head and looks at me. I realize there are probably much better ways to reach out to him, but I feel like my undeniable attraction should be just as dramatic as my denial of him was. I still feel a little guilty for how we left things a few days ago. But since he walked out my front door, I've done nothing but mope, because the time we spent together was so good. Fun. Easy. I haven't stopped thinking about him. Especially his parting words.

I was just making you breakfast. I wasn't proposing.

I've flip-flopped all week about this. Sure, he was just making me breakfast. But when a good-looking doctor cooks you breakfast, that breakfast turns into lunch and then dinner and then breakfast again, and then trips together on the weekends and then grocery shopping together, and then all that eventually turns into being the emergency contact at the hospital.

So yeah, he was just cooking me breakfast. But because of how much I like him, that's not where it would have ended. And the idea of him feeling forced to care for me makes me sad to think about.

But on the other hand, I can't stop thinking about him. And when I think about him, I get this empty pit in my stomach that distracts me and makes everything I want out of life seem to pale in comparison to the thought of spending time with him. But the idea of setting ourselves up for emotional investment just makes me sad since I know it won't end well. So what do I do? What choice do I make? Avoid him and be sad? Or embrace him and be sad?

Either way, I'll be sad.

So . . . here I am. Faking a need to see a cardiologist just so I can let him know I overreacted. And also to let him know that bungee jumping alone just sounds boring.

I can see the surprise on Jake's face, but he holds it in well. He glances at my chart again. "According to this, you're here because you're experiencing excessive heart palpitations."

I can see the grin he stifles before looking back at me.

I nod. "Something like that."

Jake's eyes scan me from head to toe for a moment, and then he sets the chart on the counter and pulls his stethoscope to his ears. He straddles a chair and sits, rolling toward me.

"Let's take a listen."

Oh, God. I'm not *really* having heart palpitations. He knows it was just an excuse to show up here. Now he's about to listen to my heart just to be an ass because he knows I'm nervous right now. And it's going to be beating stupid fast because he's even better-looking today with his white coat and stethoscope, straddling a rolling chair. If he actually listens to my heartbeat right now, he might call for a defibrillator.

He rolls his chair right up to the exam table. Right up to me. We're eye to eye now as he lifts the stethoscope and places it over my heart. He closes his eyes and lowers his head as if he's actually concentrating on my heartbeat.

I close my eyes because I have to calm down. Him listening to my heartbeat is making me completely transparent. I keep my eyes closed, even when he pulls the stethoscope away from me. There's a quiet pause, and then in a low voice, he says, "What are you doing here, Maggie?"

I glance at him, and his eyes are searching mine. I suck in a deep breath and then slowly release it before saying, "I'm trying to live in the moment."

He sighs, and he's so stoic right now, I can't tell if it's a good sigh. But then I feel his hand on my knee, his thumb brushing over the top of it. He searches my face and then reaches up and tucks a lock of hair behind my ear. "That's all I want," he says. "A few moments here and there. I'm not asking for your entire timeline."

I stare at him, completely infatuated with his mouth and his blue eyes and the words that he just said. I nod a little, but I don't really have anything to say. I just want him to kiss me. And so he does.

He takes my face in both of his huge, warm hands and presses his lips to mine as he stands, kicking the chair away from him. I sigh against his lips. I grip the collar of his white coat and take his tongue as he pushes my knees apart and slides in front of me. I'm so thankful I was forced to put this gown on. I wrap my legs tightly around his waist as he lowers me to the exam table and leans over me, kissing me with extreme urgency. But he breaks that kiss with the same urgency seconds later, breathing heavily, looking down on me with heated eyes. He shakes his head. "Not here."

I nod. I wasn't expecting this to happen here. I can tell

he's about to pull back, but then he pauses, looking at me with so much hunger, I can practically see his ethics melt right to the floor. He kisses me again, and the way his hand is sliding up my thigh has me forgetting that he's a doctor and we're in a clinic and I'm technically on record as his patient now. But none of that matters because his hands feel so good, and his mouth even better, and I've never had so much fun visiting a doctor before.

He's making his way to my neck when he pauses and glances at the door. He immediately pulls me up, giving my gown a quick tug over my thighs. He spins toward the sink and turns on the water.

The door opens, and I swing my head toward the nurse who is now standing in the doorway. Jake is casually washing his hands, trying to pretend he didn't just have his hand halfway up my thigh and his tongue all the way down my throat. I'm trying to catch my breath, but his hands and his kiss have left my already weak lungs aching for air. I'm practically gasping.

The nurse gives me another concerned, pitiful look. "You sure you're okay?"

After my coughing fit earlier and now this, she probably thinks I'm near my deathbed. I nod quickly. "I'm fine. Just . . . shitty lungs. Side effect of CF."

I hear Jake clear his throat, attempting to cover a laugh. He gives his full attention to the nurse.

"They need you in three," she says. "Kind of urgent."

Jake gives her a nod. "Thanks, Vicky. Be right there."

When she closes the door, Jake covers his face with his hand. When he looks up at me, he's grinning. He pushes off the counter and walks past but turns toward me. "Put your clothes back on, Maggie," he says, backing toward the door. "I'll come over tonight and take them right back off."

I'm smiling so stupidly when he leaves the room. I hop off the table and walk over to the chair to retrieve my clothes. Feeling another coughing fit coming on, I cover my mouth, still unable to stop smiling. I'm so glad I showed up here.

I clear my throat, but it doesn't help. Pressing my hand on the counter for more balance doesn't do anything, either, because here it is. *Hello, old friend.* I can feel it about to happen before it actually happens. I always do.

As soon as the room begins to spin, I allow my knees to buckle so the impact isn't as hard when I hit the floor.

Chapter Nine

Jake

My father took me to Puerto Vallarta when I was ten, just so I could jump out of an airplane.

I'd begged him to take me skydiving with him since I learned how to talk, but it's not so easy in Texas to give your child legal permission to jump out of an airplane.

He was an adrenaline junkie, just like the child he had created. Because of that, I basically lived at the jump zone where he spent all of his free time. Most dads golf on Sundays. My dad jumped out of airplanes.

By the time I graduated high school, I had already completed four hundred fifty of the five hundred jumps it took to qualify as a tandem instructor. But because of the turn my life took during my senior year, it was several years to finish those last fifty jumps. I finally became certified as a tandem instructor right out of med school. And even though Maggie was my five hundredth tandem jump, I've probably taken that leap at least three times that amount doing it solo since the age of ten.

Even with that much experience, that five hundredth tandem jump felt like the most terrifying jump I'd ever taken. I'd never been nervous to jump out of a plane before then. I've never worried that my chute wouldn't open. I've never once been concerned for my life until that moment. Because if that particular jump didn't end well, that meant dinner with Maggie was off the table. And I *really* wanted to take her to dinner. I'd planned to ask her out since the moment I laid eyes on her as I walked into the facility that day.

My immediate reaction to her surprised me. I can't even remember the last time I was attracted to someone like that. But the second I saw her, something in me woke up. Something I knew was there, but had never been rattled until then. I hadn't looked at a girl and felt that way in so long, I forgot how stupefying attraction could be.

She was standing at the counter, taking paperwork from Corey, who was on schedule to jump tandem with her. As soon as I realized she was there alone, I waited until she took a seat to fill out her paperwork, and then I begged Corey to let me take over and be the one to jump with her.

"Jake, you're barely here once a month. This isn't even your job," he said. "I'm here every day because I actually need the money."

"You can have the fee," I said. "I'll give you the credit. Just let me have this one."

When I told him he could keep the money for none of the work, he made a face like I was an idiot and then waved his hand toward Maggie. "All yours," he said, walking away.

I felt triumphant for a split second, until I looked back at her, sitting in the chair, all alone. Skydiving is such a monumental moment in the lives of most people who do it. Most first-timers never come alone. They almost always have people with them who are experiencing their own monumental moment by also jumping, or they have people with them waiting on the ground for when they survive the jump.

In all honesty, she was the first first-timer I'd ever seen show up completely alone, and her independence both intrigued and intimidated me. Since the moment I walked up to her and asked if she needed help filling out the forms, nothing has changed when it comes to the situation inside my chest. It's been days, and I'm still filled with that same nervous energy. I'm still intrigued. Still intimidated.

And I have no idea how to move forward.

That's why I'm stuck in this hallway, right outside the hospital room where they brought her two hours ago.

I was dealing with another patient when Vicky found Maggie and dealt with the entire situation without my even being aware. She didn't tell me until I finished up with two more patients and Maggie had already been gone for an hour.

Vicky said she noticed it was taking Maggie a while to get dressed and exit the room, so she went to check on her.

Maggie was on the floor, just recovering from a blackout. Vicky tested her sugar levels immediately and then sent staff with her over to the hospital. The clinic I work at is adjacent to our hospital, so we're used to having to transport patients. I'm just not used to the medical emergencies also feeling like a *personal* emergency.

Since the moment Vicky informed me of what happened, I haven't been able to concentrate. I finally had a colleague take over so I could come check on Maggie. Now that I'm in the hallway, standing in front of her room, I'm not sure how to feel or what to do or how to approach this entire situation. We've been on one date with the potential of another. But now she's in the hospital and in the exact vulnerable situation she was scared she'd be in when it came to us.

Her being constrained by her illness. Me being here to witness it.

I step aside when the door to her hospital room opens. A nurse walks out, heading for the nurse's station. I follow her. "Excuse me," I say, touching her shoulder. She pauses, and I point at Maggie's room. "Have you notified this patient's family yet?"

The nurse glances at the name on my coat and says, "Yes. Left a voice mail as soon as she was brought in." She looks down at the file. "I thought she was Dr. Kastner's patient."

"She is. I'm her cardiologist. She was at my clinic when her condition worsened, so I'm just checking in."

"You're from cardiology?" she asks without looking up from the file. "We're aware of the CFRD, but have nothing on file about heart issues."

"It was just a preventative checkup," I say, backing away before she gets too nosy about my nosiness. "I just wanted to make sure her family was notified. Is the patient alert?"

The nurse nods, but also makes a face like she's annoyed that I'm questioning her ability to do her job. I turn and walk back toward Maggie's room, pausing just outside the door. Once again, I fail to walk in because I don't know her well enough to know what kind of reaction she would prefer from me right now. If I walk in and try to pretend her passing out in my office wasn't a big deal, she might be put off by my casualness. If I walk in and act like I'm concerned, she might use that concern as a weapon against us.

I think if we were more than just one overnight date in, the next few minutes might not matter as much. But since we've only been on one date, I'm almost positive she's in there right now regretting showing up at my office and regretting that I'll see her in such a vulnerable state, and possibly even regretting that she even walked into my life on Tuesday. I feel like my next moves are extremely crucial to how all of this will turn out.

I don't think I've ever worried this much about how to act in front of someone. I normally have the attitude that if someone doesn't like me, that's not going to matter to me or my life, so I've always just done and said what I feel like doing and saying. But right now, with Maggie, I'd give anything to have a handbook.

I need to know what she needs from me in order for her not to push me away again.

I put my hand on the door, but my phone begins to ring as soon as I start to push it open. I quickly back up so she isn't aware I'm right outside her door. I walk a few feet down the hallway and pull my phone out of my pocket.

I smile when I see that it's Justice, trying to FaceTime me. I'm relieved to have a few minutes more to prepare before walking in to see Maggie.

I accept the call and wait the several seconds it usually takes for the FaceTime to connect us. When it finally does, it's not Justice's face I see on his phone. His screen is covered by a piece of paper. I squint to see it, but the grade is too blurry.

"It's too close to your phone," I tell him.

He pulls the paper back a few inches, and I can see the number eighty-five circled in the top right-hand corner.

"That's not too bad for a night of horror movies," I say.

Justice's face is on the screen now. He looks at me like I'm the child and he's the parent. "Dad, it's a B. My first B all year. You're supposed to yell at me so I'll never make another B again."

I laugh. He's looking at me so seriously, like he's more disappointed that I'm not furious with him than he is disappointed in getting his first B. "Listen," I tell him as I lean against the wall. "We both know you know the material. I'd be mad if you didn't study, but you did. The reason you got a B is because you went to bed too late. And I already yelled at you for that."

I woke up at three o'clock this morning and heard the television on in my living room. When I went to turn it off, Justice was on the couch with a bowl of popcorn, watching *The Visit*. He's obsessed with M. Night Shyamalan. His obsession is mostly my fault. It started when I let him watch *The Sixth Sense* when he was five. He's eleven now, and the obsession has only gotten worse.

What can I say? He takes after his father. But as much of me as he has in him, he's also very much his mother's child. She stressed over every paper and every homework assignment throughout high school and college. I once had to console her because she was crying over receiving a ninety-nine on a paper when she was aiming for a perfect score.

Justice has that overachieving side to him, but it's constantly warring with that side of him that wants to stay up late and watch scary movies when he isn't supposed to. When I dropped him off at school today, I had to wake him up when I pulled into the drop-off lane.

I knew his math test wasn't going to end well when he wiped the drool off his mouth, opened the door to get out of my car, and said, "Goodnight, Dad."

He thought I was dropping him off at his mother's house. I laughed when he got out of the car and realized it was a school day. He turned back to the car and tried to open the door. I locked it before he could climb back inside the car and beg me for a skip day.

I cracked the window, and he stuck his fingers inside and said, "Dad, please. I won't tell Mom. Just let me sleep today."

"Actions have consequences, Justice. Love you, good luck, and stay awake."

His fingers slipped out of the window, and he backed up, defeated as I drove away.

I watch my phone as he wads up the paper and tosses it over his shoulder. He rubs his eyes and says, "I'm going to ask Mr. Banks if I can get a redo."

I laugh. "Or just accept the eighty-five. It's not a terrible grade."

Justice shrugs and then scratches his cheek. "Mom went out with that guy again last night." He says it so casually, like the possibility of a stepdad doesn't deter him. That's a good thing, I guess.

"Oh yeah? Did he call you *squirt* and tousle your hair again?"

Justice rolls his eyes. "No, he wasn't so bad this time. I don't think he has kids, and Mom told him people don't call eleven-year-olds *squirts*. But anyway, she wanted me to ask you if you were busy tonight because they're going out again."

It's still a little weird, hearing about Chrissy's dates from the child we created together. This is new territory I don't know how to deal with, so I do my best to make it seem like it's not weird. It was my decision to end things with her, and it wasn't easy. Especially since we share a child. But knowing that Justice was the only reason we were still together just didn't seem fair to any of us. Chrissy took it hard in the beginning, but only because we were all comfortable with the life we shared. But there was a void, and she knew it.

When it comes to loving someone else, I've always believed there should be a level of madness buried in that love. An I-want-to-spend-every-minute-of-every-day-with-you madness. But Chrissy and I have never had that kind of love. Our love is built on responsibility and mutual respect. It's not a maddening, heart-stopping love.

When Justice was born, we felt that maddening love for him, and that was enough to hold us over through high school graduation, college, medical school, and most of our residencies. But when it came to what we felt for each other, it was the type of love that was too thin to attempt to stretch it out over an entire lifetime.

We separated over a year ago, but I didn't get my own place until about six months ago. I bought a house two streets away from the house we'd raised Justice in. The judge gave us joint custody with an outline of who gets him and when, but we haven't once stuck to that. Justice stays with both of us a fairly equal amount, but it's more on his terms than either of ours. With our houses being so close, he just goes back and forth whenever he feels like it. I actually prefer that. He's adjusted really well, and I think this way of letting him control most of the visitation has made our separation a smooth transition for him.

Sometimes *too* smooth.

Because, for some strange reason, he thinks I want to know about his mother's dating life, when I'd rather be kept in the dark. But he's only eleven. He's still innocent in almost every sense, so I like that he keeps me up to date on the half of his life I'm no longer a part of.

"Dad," Justice says. "Did you hear me? Can I stay at your house tonight?"

I nod. "Yeah. Of course."

I told Maggie I'd go to her place tonight, but that was before . . . *this*. I'm almost positive they'll keep her overnight for monitoring, so my Friday night is wide open. Even if it weren't, it would have become wide open for Justice. I work a lot, and I have a lot of hobbies, but that all comes second to him. Everything comes second to him.

"Where are you?" Justice leans in, squinting at the phone. "That doesn't look like your office."

I turn the phone and face it toward the empty hallway, angling it at Maggie's door. "I'm at the hospital visiting a sick friend." I face the phone back at myself. "If she wants to see me."

"Why wouldn't she?" Justice asks.

I stare at him a moment, then shake my head. I didn't mean to say that last part out loud. "It's not important."

"Is she mad at you?"

This is too weird, talking to him about a girl I went

on a date with who isn't his mother. As casual as he may be about it, I'm not sure I'll ever feel comfortable talking to him about my dating life. I pull the phone closer to my face and raise an eyebrow. "I'm not talking to you about my dating life."

Justice leans forward and mimics my expression. "I'll remember this conversation when I start dating."

I laugh. Hard. He's only eleven, and he's already got more wit than most adults. "Fine. If I tell you about her, will you promise you'll tell me the first time you kiss a girl?"

Justice nods. "Only if you don't tell Mom."

"Deal."

"Deal."

"Her name is Maggie," I say. "We went on a date Tuesday, and I'm pretty sure she likes me, but she didn't want to go out with me again because her life is hectic. But now she's in the hospital, and I'm about to go see her, but I have no idea how to act when I walk through that door."

"What do you mean you don't know how to act?" Justice asks. "You're not supposed to act or pretend around other people. You always tell me to be myself."

I love it when my parenting advice actually sinks in with him. Even if my own advice isn't sinking in with me. "You're right. I should just walk in there and be myself."

"Your *real* self. Not your doctor self."

I laugh. "What does that even mean?"

Justice cocks his head and makes a face at the phone that looks just like a face I probably make a lot of the time.

"You're a cool dad, but when you go into doctor mode, it's so boring. Don't talk about work or medical stuff if you like her."

Doctor mode? I laugh. "Any other advice before I go in there?"

"Take her a Twix bar."

"A Twix?"

Justice nods. "Yeah, if someone brought me a Twix, I'd want to be friends with them."

I nod. "Okay. Good advice. I'll see you tonight and let you know how it goes."

Justice waves and then ends the FaceTime.

I slide my phone into my pocket and walk toward Maggie's door. *Just be yourself.* I stand in front of the door and inhale a calming breath before knocking. I wait for her to say, "Come in," before I open the door. When I walk farther into the room, she's curled up on her side. She smiles when she sees me and lifts up onto her elbow.

That smile is everything I needed.

I walk over to her bed as she adjusts it, raising the head of it a little bit. I sit in the empty chair next to the bed. She tucks her arm under her head and rests on her pillow. I reach over and rest my hand on the side of her head, then lean in and give her a soft peck on the mouth. When I pull back, I have no idea what to say. I lay my chin on the bed rail and run my fingers through her hair while I stare at her.

I love how I feel when I'm near her. Full of adrenaline,

like I'm in the middle of a nighttime skydive. But even though I'm full of adrenaline and I'm touching her hair and she smiled at me when I walked in the door, I can see in her eyes that my chute is about to fail and I'm about to free-fall alone, with nothing ahead of me but an ugly impact.

Her gaze flits away for a moment. She pulls her oxygen mask to her mouth and inhales a cycle of air. When she pulls it away, she forces another smile. "How old is your child?"

I narrow my eyes, wondering how she knows that about me. But the quietness in the room reveals the answer. Everything happening outside this door can be heard very clearly.

I pull my hand from her hair and lower it to her hand that's resting on her pillow. I trace a soft circle around where the IV is taped to her skin. "He's eleven."

She smiles again. "I wasn't trying to eavesdrop."

I shake my head. "It's fine. I wasn't trying to hide that I have a kid. I just didn't know how to bring it up on a first date. I'm a little protective of him, so I feel like I should guard that part of my life until I'm positive it's something I want to share."

Maggie nods in understanding, flipping her hand over. She lets me trace the skin on her wrist for a moment. She watches my fingers as they trickle over her palm, down her wrist, until they reach the IV again. Then she looks back up at me again. "What's his name?"

"Justice."

"That's a great name."

I smile. "He's a great kid."

I continue touching her hand, but it's quiet for a while. I don't want to delve even deeper into this conversation because I know it's going to go where I don't want it to go. But at the same time, if I don't keep talking, she might take the floor and begin to tell me, once again, why she doesn't want any part of this.

"His mother's name is Chrissy," I say, filling the void. "We started dating because we had a lot in common. We both wanted to go to med school. We had both been accepted to UT. But then I got her pregnant senior year. She gave birth to Justice a week before our high school graduation."

I stop tracing her skin and slide my fingers through hers. I love that she lets me. I love the feel of her hand wrapped around mine.

"It's impressive that the two of you had a newborn in high school and still somehow managed to become doctors."

I appreciate that she recognizes how hard that was for us. "There was a stretch during her pregnancy where I looked into other careers. Easier ones. But the first time I laid eyes on him, I knew that I never wanted him to think he was a hindrance to our lives in any way, simply because we had him so young. We did everything we could to make sure we stuck to our goals. It was a challenge, two teenagers trying to make it through premed with an infant. But

Chrissy's mom was—*is*—a lifesaver. We couldn't have done it without her."

Maggie squeezes my hand a little when I finish talking. It's gentle and sweet, like she's silently saying, *Good job.* "What kind of father are you?"

No one's ever asked me to evaluate my own ability as a parent. I think about it for a moment and then answer the question with complete honesty. "An insecure one," I admit. "With most jobs, you know right away if you're going to be good at them or not. But with parenting, you don't really know if you're good at it until the child is grown. I'm constantly worried I'm doing everything wrong, and there's no way to know until it's too late."

"I think your worry about whether you're a good father is testament that you shouldn't worry."

I shrug. "Maybe so. But even still, I worry. Always will."

There's a moment of hesitation on her face when I mention how much I worry about him. I want to take it back. I don't want her to think I have too much on my plate. I want her to think about right now and right now only. Not tomorrow or next week or next year. But she is. I can see it in the way she's staring at me—wondering how she could possibly feel okay with fitting herself somewhere in my life. And I can see in the way she looks away from me and focuses on everything *but* me that she doesn't see herself fitting in at all.

She was already hesitant when she thought my biggest concern outside of work was if the weather was right for skydiving. And even though she showed up at my office today, ready to give it a chance, I can see that finding out about Justice has not only changed her mind, but filled her with even more resolve than she held as she was kicking me out of her house.

I release her hand and bring mine back up to the side of her head, running my thumb over her cheek in order to bring her attention back to me. When she finally looks up at me, her mind is made up. I can see it in all the pieces of broken hope that are floating around in her eyes. It's amazing how someone can convey so much in one look.

I sigh, sliding my thumb over her lips. "Don't ask me to leave."

Her eyebrows draw apart, and she looks absolutely torn between what she wants and what she knows she needs. "Jake," she says. She doesn't follow my name up with anything else. My name lingers in the air, heavy with weariness.

Not only do I know I can't change her mind, but I'm not sure I should even try to. As much as I want to see her again and as much as I want to get to know her better, it's not fair of me to beg. She knows her situation better than anyone. She knows what she's capable of, and she knows what she wants her life to look like. I can't argue all the reasons why she shouldn't push me away, because I'm almost positive I'd have the same outlook if our roles were reversed.

Maybe that's why we're both being so quiet. Because I understand her.

The mood is thick in the room. It's full of tension and attraction and disappointment. I try to imagine what it would be like to love her. Because if spending one night with her can fill a room with this much angst, I can only imagine that this is what the beginning of a maddening love would feel like.

I've finally found someone I think could one day fill the void in my life, but to her, she feels that by being in my life, her absence would one day *create* a void. It's ironic. *Maddening.*

"Have you seen Dr. Kastner yet?"

She nods but doesn't elaborate.

"Has anything changed with your condition?"

She shakes her head, and I can't tell if she's lying. She answers too quickly.

"I'm fine. I probably need to rest, though."

She's asking me to leave, but I want to tell her that even though I barely know her, I want to be here for her. I want to help her cross those last several items off her bucket list. I want to make sure she keeps living and doesn't continue to focus on the fact that she may not have as much time as everyone else.

But I say nothing, because who am I to assume she won't have a completely fulfilled life if she doesn't allow me to be a part of it? That's something only a narcissist would think. The girl in front of me right now is the same girl who showed up alone to skydive for the first time this week. So I will respect her choice and I will walk away for the exact same reason I was drawn to her in the first place. Because she's an independent badass who doesn't need me to fill a void. There are no voids in her life.

And here I am wanting to selfishly beg her to fill mine.

"You were on a roll with your bucket list," I say. "Promise me you'll knock off some more items."

She immediately begins to nod, and then a tear slips from her eye. She rolls her eyes like she's embarrassed. "I can't believe I'm crying. I barely know you." She laughs, squeezing her eyes shut, and opens them again. "I'm being so ridiculous."

I smile at her. "Nah. You're crying because you know if your situation were different, you'd be falling for me right about now."

She lets out a sad laugh. "If my situation were different, I would have started that free fall back on Tuesday."

I can't even follow that up with anything. I lift out of my chair and lean forward to kiss her. She kisses me back, holding on to my face with both hands. When I pull back, I press my forehead to hers and close my eyes.

"I almost wish I'd never met you."

She shakes her head. "Not me. I'm grateful I met you. You ended up fulfilling a third of my bucket list."

I lean away and smile at her, wishing more than anything that I was selfish enough to try to change her mind. But simply knowing the one day I spent with her meant something to her is enough for now. It has to be.

I kiss her one last time. "I can stay until your family gets here."

Something changes in her expression. She hardens a little. She shakes her head and pulls her hands from my head. "I'll be fine. You should go."

I nod, standing up. I don't even know anything about her family. I know nothing about her parents, or whether she has brothers and sisters. I sort of don't want to be here when they get here. I don't want to meet the most important people in her life if I don't have the chance to someday *be* one of them.

I squeeze her hand one more time, looking down on her while trying to hide my regret. "I should have brought you a Twix."

She makes a confused face, but I don't clarify. I step back, and she gives me a small wave. I wave back, but then I turn without saying goodbye. I walk out of the room as fast as I can.

As someone who has craved the feeling of adrenaline my entire life, I haven't always made the smartest decisions. Adrenaline makes you do stupid shit without putting too much thought into your actions.

It was stupid of me at thirteen to crash my first dirt bike because I wanted to know what it felt like to break a bone.

It was stupid of me at eighteen to have sex with Chrissy when we didn't have a condom, simply because it felt thrilling and we ignorantly assumed we were immune to the consequences.

It was stupid of me at twenty-three to jump backward off a cliff I wasn't familiar with in Cancún, relishing in the buzz of not knowing if there were rocks beneath the surface of the water.

And it would be stupid of me at twenty-nine to beg a girl to jump headfirst into a situation that might end up being that maddening love I've been craving my whole life. When a person sinks into a love that deep, they don't come back out of it, even when it ends. It's like quicksand. You're in it forever, no matter what.

I think Maggie knows that. And I'm positive that's why she's pushing me away again.

She wouldn't push someone away so adamantly if she weren't scared her death would also kill *them*. I can take that assumption with me as I go, at least. The assumption that she saw something in us that had enough potential that she felt the need to end it before we both sank.

Chapter Ten

Ridge

I'm at the sink straining pasta, watching Sydney walk around the kitchen and living room as she points at things and signs them. I correct her when she's wrong, but she's mostly been right. She points at the lamp and signs, "Lamp." Then the couch. The pillow, the table, the window. She points at the towel on her head and signs, "Towel."

When I nod, she grins and then pulls the towel off her head. Her damp hair falls around her shoulders, and I've imagined more times than I'd like to admit what her hair smells like fresh out of the shower. I walk over to her and wrap my arms around her, pressing my face against her head so I can inhale the scent of her.

Then I go back to the stove, leaving her standing in the living room, looking at me like I'm weird. I shrug as I pour the Alfredo sauce into the pan of noodles. Someone grips my shoulder from behind me, and I know immediately that it's Warren. I glance at him.

"Is there enough for me and Bridgette?"

I don't know why we didn't do this at Sydney's apartment. It's a lot more peaceful over there for me, and I can't even hear. I can only imagine how much more peaceful it is for Sydney.

"There's plenty," I sign, realizing just how much I need to take Sydney out on a real date. I need to get her out of this apartment. I will tomorrow. I'll take her on a twelve-hour date tomorrow. We'll eat lunch and then go to the movies and then dinner, and we won't have to see Warren and Bridgette at all.

I'm taking the garlic bread out of the oven when Sydney rushes to the bathroom. At first, it concerns me that she just ran to the bathroom, but then I remember our phones are still on the counter. She must have a phone call.

She returns a moment later to the kitchen with her phone to her ear. She's laughing as she talks to someone. Probably her mother.

I want to meet her parents. Sydney hasn't told me a whole lot about them, other than her father is a lawyer and her mother has always been a stay-at-home mom. But she doesn't seem put out when she speaks to them. The only people I've met in her life are Hunter and Tori—and I'd like to forget I ever met them—but her family is different. They're her people, so I want to know them, even if it's to tell them they've raised an exceptional woman who I love with all my heart.

Sydney smiles at me and signs, "Mom," as she points to her phone. Then she slides my phone across the bar to me. I press the home button and see that I have a missed call and a voice mail. It's rare that I get phone calls, because everyone who knows me knows I can't answer the phone. I usually only receive text messages.

I open my voice mail app to read the transcription, but it says, "Transcription not available." I put my phone in my pocket and wait for Sydney to finish her phone call. I'll just have her listen to the voice mail and let me know what it says.

I turn off the stove and the oven and set plates out at the table, along with the pans of food. Warren and Bridgette both magically appear as soon as dinner is ready. They're like clockwork. They disappear when it's time to clean or pay bills, but show up every time there's food to be eaten. If they ever move out, they're both going to starve.

Maybe *I* should move out. Let them have this apartment and see how fun it is having to pay bills on time. One of these days I will. I'll move in with Sydney, but not yet. Not until I've met everyone in her family and not until she's had the chance to live on her own for a while like she's always wanted.

Sydney ends her phone call and sits down at the table next to me. I slide my phone to her and point to the voice mail. "Can you listen to that?"

She asked me earlier this afternoon to start signing everything I say to her, so I do. It'll help her learn faster. I grab her plate as she listens to the voice mail, and I fill it with pasta. I throw a piece of garlic bread on it and set it in front of her, just as she pulls the phone away from her ear.

She stares at the screen for a second and then looks at Warren before looking at me. I've never seen this look on her face before. I'm not sure how to read it. She looks hesitant, worried, and somehow sick, and I don't like it.

"What is it?"

She slides my phone back to me and grabs the glass of water I poured for her. "Maggie," she says, forcing my heart to a stop. She says something else, but she doesn't sign it, and I'm not able to read her lips. I swing my eyes to Warren, and he signs what Sydney just said.

"It was the hospital. Maggie was admitted today."

Everything sort of just stops. I say *sort of* because Bridgette is still making her plate of food, ignoring everything happening. I glance at Sydney again, and she's taking a drink of her water, avoiding my gaze. I look at Warren, and he's staring at me like I should know what to do.

I don't know why he's acting like it's my choice to direct this scene. Maggie is his friend, too. I look at him expectantly and then say, "Call her."

Sydney looks at me, and I'm looking at her, and I have no fucking idea how to handle this situation. I don't want to seem too worried, but there's no way I can find out Maggie is in the hospital and not be worried. But I'm equally concerned about how this is making Sydney feel. I sigh and reach for Sydney's hand under the table while I wait for Warren to get in touch with Maggie. Sydney slides her fingers through mine, but then props her other arm on the table, covering her mouth with her hand. She turns her attention to Warren, just as he stands up and starts talking into the phone. I watch him and wait. Sydney watches him and waits. Bridgette scoops up a huge portion of pasta with her bread and takes a bite.

Sydney's leg is bouncing up and down. My pulse is pounding even faster than her leg. Warren's conversation is dragging, taking what feels like forever to finish. I don't know what is being said, but in the middle of the conversation, Sydney winces and then pulls her hand from mine and excuses herself from the table. I get up to follow her, just as Warren ends the call.

Now I'm standing in the middle of the living room about to rush after Sydney, but Warren starts to sign. "She passed out at a doctor's office today. They're keeping her overnight."

I blow out a breath of relief. The hospitalizations for her diabetes are the best-case scenarios. It's when she contracts a virus or a cold that it usually ends up taking weeks for her to recover.

I can tell by the look on Warren's face that he's not finished speaking yet. There's something he hasn't said. Something he said to Maggie that upset Sydney enough for her to walk away. "What else?" I ask him.

"She was crying," he says. "She sounded . . . scared. She needs our help, but she wouldn't tell me more than that. I told her we're on our way."

Maggie wants us there.

Maggie *never* wants us there. She always feels like she's inconveniencing us.

Something else must have happened.

I cover my mouth with my hand, my thoughts frozen.

I turn to walk toward my bedroom, but Sydney is standing in the doorway with her shoes on and her purse over her shoulder. She's leaving.

"I'm sorry," she says. "I'm not leaving because I'm mad. I just need to process all this." She waves her hand flippantly around the room, then drops it to her side. She doesn't leave, though. She simply stands there, confused.

I walk over to her and take her face in my hands because I'm confused, too. She just squeezes her eyes shut when I press my forehead to hers. I don't know how to handle this situation. I have so much to say to her, but texting isn't fast enough, and I'm not sure I can speak everything I want to say or that everything I say would even be understandable to her. I pull away from her and grab her hand, then walk her back to the table.

I motion for Warren to help us communicate if we need him. Sydney sits in her chair, and I scoot mine to where I'm right in front of her. "Are you okay?"

She seems at a loss for how to answer that question.

When she finally does, I can't understand her, so Warren signs for me. "I'm trying, Ridge. I really am."

Just seeing the pain when she speaks makes her my only focus. I can't leave her like this. I look at Warren. "Can you go by yourself?"

He looks disappointed by my question. "You expect me to know what to do?" He tosses his hands up in frustration. "You can't stop being there for her just because you have a new girlfriend. We're all Maggie has, and you know it."

I'm just as frustrated by Warren's answer as I am my own question. Of course I'm not going to stop being there for Maggie. But I don't know how to be there for both her and Sydney right now. I didn't really think ahead when Maggie and I split up. I doubt she thought ahead, either. But Warren is right. What kind of person would that make me if I just walked out on the girl who has depended solely on me for the past six years when it comes to her medical needs? Hell, I'm still her emergency contact. That shows how much of a support system she has in her life. And I can't send Warren alone. He can't even take care of himself, much less Maggie. I'm the only one who knows her medical needs. Her entire medical history. The medications she takes, the names of all her doctors, what to do in an emergency, how to operate her respiratory equipment at her house. Warren would be lost without me.

As if Sydney's thoughts are on the same track as mine, she speaks to Warren, and he signs for me. "What do you normally do when this happens?"

"Normally, when this happens, Ridge goes. Sometimes we both go. But Ridge always goes. We help her get home, pick up her prescriptions, make sure she's settled, she gets mad because she doesn't think she needs any help, and after a day or two, she usually forces us to go back home. The same routine we've had since her grandfather could no longer care for her."

"Does she not have anyone else?" Sydney asks. "Parents? Siblings? Cousins? Aunts, uncles, friends? A really reliable mailman?"

"She has relatives she doesn't know very well who live out of state. None that would drive to pick her up at the hospital. And none that know anything at all about how to handle her medical condition. Not like Ridge does."

Sydney looks exasperated. "She really has no one else?"

I shake my head. "She's spent all her time focusing on college, her grandparents, and her boyfriend for six years. We are literally all she has."

Sydney absorbs my answer and then nods slowly, like she's trying to be understanding. But I know it's a lot to take in. She's probably spent the last several months trying to convince herself that Maggie and I wouldn't get back together. I doubt she's even thought far enough ahead to realize that even though Maggie and I are no longer in a relationship, I'm still her primary caregiver when she's not in the position to care for herself.

I know she tolerates the occasional text messages, but

because Maggie hasn't had any episodes for the past several months, this part of Maggie's and my new friendship has yet to be navigated. I've been so focused on just getting Sydney to give me a chance, it hasn't occurred to me until this second that Sydney might not be okay with that.

The realization hits me with the weight of a thousand bricks. If Sydney isn't okay with this, where does that leave us? Will I be able to walk away from Maggie completely, knowing she has no one else? Would Sydney actually put me in a position to choose between her happiness and Maggie's health?

My hands start to shake. I feel the pressure coming at me from all sides. I grab Sydney's hand and lead her to my bedroom. When I close the door, I lean against it and pull her to my chest, squeezing her, scared to death that she's about to put me in an unthinkable situation. And I wouldn't blame her. Asking her to be supportive of such an unusual relationship with the girl I was in love with for years is basically asking her to be heroic.

"I love you," I say. It's the only thing I have the strength to say right now. I feel her sign the words back to me against my chest. She clings to me and I cling to her, and then I feel her start to cry in my arms. I press my cheek to the top of her head and hold her, wanting to take away every ounce of ache she's feeling in her heart right now. And I could. I could text Maggie right now and tell her it's too much for Sydney and that I can't be a part of her life anymore.

But what kind of person would that make me? Could

Sydney even love a guy who would completely cut someone out of his life like that?

And if Sydney asked me to do it—if she asked me never to speak to Maggie again—what kind of person would that make *her* if her jealousy won out over human decency?

She's not that type of person. And neither am I. That's why we're both standing in the dark, wrapped around each other while she cries. Because we know what will eventually happen tonight. I'll leave to take care of Maggie. And it won't be the last time, because Maggie will likely need me until Maggie doesn't need me anymore. And that's a thought I don't feel like processing right now.

I know I've tried to do right by them, but I haven't always *been* right. Part of me feels like this is Karma. I'm being forced to hurt Sydney because I hurt Maggie. And hurting either of them hurts me.

I lift her head from my chest and kiss her, holding her face in my hands. Her eyes are sad, and tears are staining her cheeks. I kiss her again and then say, "Come with me."

She sighs and shakes her head. "It's too soon for that. She wouldn't want me there."

I brush her hair back and kiss her twice on the forehead. She backs up a step and reaches into her pocket for her phone. She types out a text, but my phone is still on the table, so she hands me hers so I can read her text.

Sydney: If you go, I'm probably going to cry myself to sleep. But she's in the hospital, Ridge. And she's all alone. So if you don't go, she'll probably cry herself to sleep, too.

I type out a text to her in return.

Ridge: Your tears mean more to me, Sydney.

Sydney: I know. And as much as this situation sucks and as much as it hurts, the fact that you're torn right now because you don't want to abandon her makes me think more of you than I already do. So go, Ridge. Please. I'll be okay as long as you come back to me.

I hand her back her phone and then run my hands through my hair. I turn away from her and face the door, squeezing the back of my neck. I try to hold it in, but in all my twenty-four years, I have never felt this depth of love from anyone. Not Maggie. Certainly not my parents. And as much as I love Brennan, I'm not sure I've ever felt this depth of love from my own brother.

Sydney Blake, without a doubt, loves me harder than I've ever been loved. She loves me more than I deserve, and in this moment, more than I can even handle.

I wish there were a sign in ASL that could convey my need to hold her even more than a hug can, but there isn't. So I turn and hug her and press my face into her hair. "I don't deserve your compassion. Or your heart."

• • •

She helps me pack.

I let the moment sink in and respect it for what it is. My new girlfriend is helping me pack so that I can go make sure my ex-girlfriend isn't alone in the hospital tonight.

The entire time Sydney is replenishing items in my

duffel bag, I keep distracting her, pulling her to me, kissing her. I don't think I've ever loved her more than I do in this moment. And even though I won't be here tonight, I want her in my bed. I grab her phone and type out a message in the notes app.

Ridge: You should stay here tonight. I want to smell you on my pillow tomorrow.

Sydney: I planned on it. I still need to eat and then I'll clean up the kitchen.

Ridge: I can clean tomorrow. Eat, but leave the mess for me. Or maybe Bridgette will finally contribute.

She rolls her eyes with a laugh after that message. We both know what a stretch it is. We walk into the living room, and Warren and Bridgette are still at the table. Warren is scarfing down his food with a backpack hanging on his chair. Bridgette is sitting across from him, staring at her phone. When she looks up, she seems a little shocked that Sydney and I are walking out of the bedroom together. I guess she wasn't expecting this to end so amicably.

"Ready?" Warren signs.

I nod and walk to the table to grab my phone. Warren walks around the table to give Bridgette a kiss, but she turns her face so that he can only kiss her on the cheek. He rolls his eyes and stands up straight, grabbing his backpack as he walks away from the table.

"Is she mad at you?" I sign.

Warren looks confused. He looks back at Bridgette and then looks at me. "No. Why?"

"She refused to kiss you goodbye."

He laughs. "That's because she just *fucked* me goodbye."

I glance at Bridgette, who is still looking down at her phone. Then I look back at Warren. He smiles with a shrug. "We're quick."

Bridgette looks up from her phone and glares at Warren. He rolls his eyes and starts backing away from me, toward the door. "I have to learn how to stop speaking out loud when I sign to you." He glances at Sydney and gives her a once-over. "You okay with all this?" he asks.

Sydney nods, but then both of them look at Bridgette. Bridgette begins speaking—which is unusual—so I look back at Warren, and he signs everything Bridgette is saying.

"Take it from me, Sydney," she says. "Some men come with heavy baggage, like five kids and three different baby mommas. But Ridge and Warren's baggage is just an ex-girlfriend they sometimes have slumber parties with. Let them go play with their Barbie. We'll stay here and get drunk and order pizza with Warren's debit card. Ridge's pasta sucked, anyway."

Wow.

That's the most Bridgette has ever spoken at one time. Sydney looks at me, wide-eyed. I'm not sure if she's wide-eyed because Bridgette spoke so much or because she just invited Sydney to hang out with her. Either is unprecedented for Bridgette.

"Must be a full moon," Warren says. He walks to the

front door and opens it. I look down at Sydney and wrap my arm around her waist, pulling her against me. I dip my head and press my mouth to hers.

She kisses me back, pushing me toward the door. I tell her I love her three times before I'm finally able to close the door. And as soon as we get to Warren's car, I pull out my phone and text her as we're driving away.

Ridge: I love you, I FUCKING. LOVE. YOU. SYDNEY.

Chapter Eleven

Maggie

I am craving a Twix so bad right now. *Dammit*, Jake.

I couldn't hear the majority of his conversation with his son when he was out in the hallway earlier. I heard words here and there and could tell he was talking to a child, so when I heard the word *dad*, it all made sense.

I suddenly understood why he seemed so alpha male on the surface, but also somehow had an extremely adorable, romantic side to him. I knew he loved fast cars and extreme sports, but on our date, I couldn't help but wonder what must have forced him to settle down and take his career seriously like he had.

That something turned out to be Justice.

I still don't know why Jake made that Twix comment, but now the only things on my mind are the speed at which Jake rushed out of this hospital room . . . and Twix.

I reach over to my nightstand and grab my phone. I don't know which one of them is driving, so I open up a group text between the three of us.

Maggie: I really need a Twix.

Warren: A Twix? Like the candy bar?

Maggie: Yes. And a Dr Pepper, please.

Ridge: Warren, stop texting and driving.

Warren: It's cool, I'm invincible.

Ridge: But I'm not.

Maggie: Are you guys almost here?

Ridge: Five minutes away. We'll stop at the store before we get there, but we're only getting you a Diet Dr Pepper. You need to watch your blood sugar. Need anything else?

Maggie: I think we're way overdue for an AMA.

Ridge: Nope. I don't think so.

Warren: Did someone say AMA? (And I'll get you a Twix, Maggie.)

Ridge: No.

Warren: LET'S DO IT!!! Be out front in five minutes, Maggie!

Ridge: Don't, Maggie. We'll be up there in five minutes.

Warren: No, we'll be out front in five minutes.

I ignore Ridge's concern and choose to side with Warren. I throw the covers off me, feeling the first flicker of happiness since Jake walked into this room. God, I've missed them so much. I look around the room to make sure I won't be leaving anything behind. My doctor left about half an hour before Jake showed up, so I'm not due for another visit from her until morning. This is the perfect time to make my escape. I reach down to remove my IV, knowing exactly what Ridge is thinking right now.

AMA is the acronym for when a patient leaves a hospital Against Medical Advice. I've only been able to successfully sneak out of a hospital twice in all my years, but Warren and Ridge were there for both escapes. And it's not as irresponsible as Ridge is making it seem. I'm an expert when it comes to IVs and needles. And I know they're only keeping me overnight to be monitored. Not because I'm in any immediate danger. I have been more congested today than normal, but my blood sugars are stable now, and that's the only reason I'm here right now. Stable enough to eat at least a *bite* of a Twix bar. And the last thing I want to do is lie in a hospital bed all night while getting absolutely no sleep.

I'll contact the hospital in the morning and apologize, letting them know it was a family emergency. My doctor will be pissed, but I piss her off a lot. She's used to being irritated with me.

When she was here earlier, she started to get invasive about my "support system" since my health has been on somewhat of a decline this year. She's been my primary doctor for ten years now, so she knows everything about my situation. I was raised by my grandparents, who are no longer taking care of me. My grandmother passed away, and my grandfather was recently put in hospice. My doctor knows about Ridge and our recent breakup because he's almost always with me at my appointments and anytime

I'm in the hospital. But she's noticed his sudden absence in my life, because she asked about it during my last visit with her. And then today, she asked again because no one was with me in the hospital this time.

After hearing her concern today, for a split second it made me regret pushing Ridge away in the end. I'm not still in love with him, but I do love him. And part of me, when I start to worry about being alone, thinks maybe I made a mistake. Maybe I should have held on to his love and loyalty. But *most of me* knows that ending our relationship was the right thing to do. He would have conveniently remained in a mediocre relationship with me for the rest of my life if I hadn't forced him to look at our relationship through a magnifying glass instead of his rose-colored glasses.

Our relationship wasn't a healthy one. He was stifling me, wanting me to be someone I didn't want to be. I was growing resentful under the weight of his protection. And I always felt guilty. Every time he dropped everything he was doing for me, I felt guilty for pulling him away from his life.

Yet . . . here we are, in the same predicament.

I don't think I realized how alone I was outside of him while I was dating him. It was when we finally separated that I truly realized he and Warren were all I had. It's part of the reason I agreed they could come tonight. I think the three of us need to really sit down and have a heart-to-heart about this entire situation. I don't want Ridge to feel like he's all I have when I do have an emergency. But in reality . . . he *is* all I have. And I don't want that to hinder his relationship with

Sydney in any way. I mean, I know I have Warren, too. But I think Warren needs more care than even I do.

My life is starting to feel like a merry-go-round, and I'm the only one on the ride. Sometimes it's fun and exciting, but sometimes I feel like puking and I want it all to just stop. I realize I focus on all the negative way more than I should, but part of me wonders if it's because my situation is so unusual. Most people have huge support systems, so they can live normal lives with this illness. My support system was my family, and that's now nonexistent. Then my support system became Ridge. Now? It's still Ridge, but with different rules. The last few months of dissecting my situation have been eye-opening. And it puts me in weird funks. I used to feel stifled, but never alone.

I wish I could find a good mental balance. I want to do things, see things, live a normal life. And sometimes there are stretches where I do that and it's all fine. But then I have days or weeks where the illness reminds me that I'm not in full control.

Sometimes I feel like I'm two different people. I'm Maggie, the girl who chases down items on her bucket list at one hundred miles per hour, the girl who turns down hot doctors because she wants to be single, the girl who sneaks out of hospitals because she enjoys the thrill, the girl who broke up with her boyfriend of six years because she wants to live her life and not be held down.

The girl who feels full of life, despite her illness.

And then there's this quieter version of Maggie, who's

been looking back at me in the mirror these last few days. The Maggie who lets her worries consume her. The Maggie who thinks she's too much of a burden to date a man she's completely into. The Maggie who has moments of regret for ending a six-year relationship, even though it absolutely needed to end. The Maggie who allows her illness to make her feel like she's dying, despite her being very much alive. The Maggie whose doctor was so concerned about her today, she called in a prescription for antidepressants.

I don't like this version of myself. It's a much sadder, lonelier me, and luckily only appears once in a blue moon. The original version of myself is what I strive to be at all times. Most of the time that's who I am. But this week . . . not so much. Especially after the visit with my doctor today. She's never seemed as concerned for me as she was today. Which makes me more concerned than I've ever been. Which is why I just pulled out my IV, am changing out of this gown, and am about to sneak out of this hospital.

I need to feel like the original Maggie for a few hours. The other version is exhausting.

The walk out of my room and down the hallway is surprisingly uneventful. I even pass one of the shift nurses in the hospital, and she just smiles at me like she has no idea she refilled my IV solution an hour ago.

When I step off the elevator and into the lobby, I can see Warren's car idling outside. I'm instantly filled with adrenaline as I rush across the lobby and out the doors. Ridge steps out of the passenger seat and opens the door for me. He forces a smile, but I can see it all over his face. He's angry that I'm leaving before being discharged. He's angry that Warren is encouraging it. But unlike pre-breakup Ridge, he says nothing. He holds his tongue and holds the door as I climb quickly inside. He closes my door, and I'm putting on my seat belt when Warren leans across the seat and kisses me on the cheek.

"Missed you."

I smile, relieved to be in this car. Relieved to see both him and Ridge. Relieved to be getting the hell out of this hospital. Warren reaches between us and holds up a Twix and a Diet Dr Pepper. "We brought you dinner. King-size."

I immediately open the package and pull out one of the bars. I say, "Thank you," with a mouthful of chocolate. I hand Warren one of the four bars just as he hits the gas and drives away from the hospital. I turn around, and Ridge is sitting in the middle of the backseat, looking out the window.

His gaze meets mine, and I hand him one of the Twix bars. He takes it and smiles at me. "Thank you," he says.

My mouth falls open so far, chocolate almost falls out of it. I laugh and cover my mouth with my hand. "You"—I look at Warren—"He spoke." I look back at Ridge. "You're speaking?"

"Pretty cool, huh?" Warren says.

I'm dumbfounded. I have never heard him speak a single word. "How long have you been verbalizing?" I sign.

Ridge shrugs like it isn't a big deal. "A few months."

I shake my head, completely in shock. His words are exactly how I imagined they would sound. Our relationship with the deaf culture is what ultimately brought all of us together. Warren's parents. Mine and Ridge's hearing loss. But Ridge's hearing loss is much more profound. Mine is so mild, it doesn't even hinder my life in any way. Which is why, for years, when we were together, I did all of his speaking for him. Even though we could both communicate using ASL, I still wanted so badly for him to learn to speak out loud. I just never really pushed him because I don't know what it's like to have profound hearing loss, so I didn't know what it was that was holding him back.

I guess he figured it out, though. And I want to know every detail. I'm excited for him. This is huge! "How? Why? When? What was the first thing you said out loud?"

Something immediately changes in his expression. He becomes guarded, like it's not something he wants to talk to me about. I glance at Warren, who is staring straight at the road like he just purposefully checked out of this conversation. I look back at Ridge, but he's looking out the window again.

And then I get it.

Sydney.

She's why he's talking now.

I suddenly feel envious of them. Of her. It makes me wonder what it was about her that made him overcome whatever obstacle it was that had held him back. Why wasn't I enough of a motivator to ever make him want to say things to me out loud?

And here she is again: the insecure, depressing version of myself.

I grab the Diet Dr Pepper and take a drink, trying to drown this sudden onslaught of jealousy. I'm happy for him. And I'm proud of him. It shouldn't matter what spurred him to want to learn how to communicate in more ways. All that matters is that he is. And even though my chest still burns a little, I'm smiling. I turn back around and make sure he can see the pride in my expression.

"Have you cussed out loud yet?" I sign.

He laughs, wiping the corner of his mouth with his finger. "*Shit* was my first cuss word."

I laugh. Of course it was. He liked watching me say that word when I was angry. I realize speaking words out loud without being able to hear them probably isn't as satisfying as being able to hear your own voice, but it has to feel a little good, finally being able to cuss out loud.

"Call Warren an asshole," I say.

Ridge looks at the back of Warren's head. "You're an asshole."

I cover my mouth with my hand, completely in shock that Ridge Lawson is verbalizing. It's like he's this whole new person.

Warren looks over at me, taking the steering wheel with his knee so that he can sign what he's saying for Ridge. "He isn't a toddler. Or a parrot."

I punch Warren in the shoulder. "Shut up. Let me enjoy this." I look back at Ridge and rest my chin on the headrest. "Say fuck."

"Fuck," he says, laughing at my immaturity. "Anything else? Damn. Goddamn. Motherfucker. Hell. Son of a bitch. Bridgette."

I die with laughter as soon as he includes her name in his string of profanity. Warren flips him off. I turn around and face the road again, still laughing. I take another sip of my drink and then relax against the seat with a sigh.

"I've missed you guys," I say. Only Warren knows I've said it.

"We've missed you, too, Maggot."

I roll my eyes, hearing that nickname again. I look over at him but make sure my headrest is a barrier between me and Ridge so that he can't read my lips. "Is Sydney mad that he came?"

Warren glances over at me briefly and then stares back at the road. "*Mad* isn't the right word. She did react, but not like most people would have reacted." He pauses for a moment and then says, "She's good for him, Maggie. She's just . . . *good*. Period. And if this whole situation weren't so damn weird, I feel like you would really like her."

"I don't *dis*like her."

Warren looks at me out of the corner of his eye. He smirks. "Yeah, but you won't be getting manicures together and going on road trips with her anytime soon."

I laugh in agreement. "That's for damn sure."

Ridge leans forward between the seats and grips both the front headrests. He looks at me, and then he looks at Warren. "Rearview mirrors," he says. "It's like a sound system for deaf people." He leans back in his seat. "Stop talking about us like I'm not right here."

Warren laughs a little. I just sink into my seat, ruminating over that last sentence.

Stop talking about us like I'm not right here.

Stop talking about us . . .

Us.

He refers to himself and Sydney as an *us* now. And he speaks out loud. And . . . I take another sip of my drink because this isn't quite as easy to swallow as I assumed it would be.

Chapter Twelve

Sydney

I don't know what's more awkward: watching Ridge leave to go stay the night with his ex-girlfriend, or sitting in his apartment alone with Bridgette.

As soon as Warren and Ridge left, Bridgette's phone rang. She answered it and walked to her bedroom without acknowledging me. It sounded like she may have been talking to her sister, but that was an hour ago. Then I heard her shower start running.

Now, here I am, cleaning their kitchen and doing their dishes. I know Ridge told me not to worry about it, but I won't be able to sleep if I know there's food out all over the counter.

I'm loading the last of the silverware when Bridgette walks out of her room with pajamas on. Her phone is to her ear again, but this time she's looking at me. "You aren't, like, gluten-free or vegetarian, are you?"

Wow. We're really doing this. And wow. I'm actually a little bit excited. I shake my head. "I've never met a slice of pizza I didn't like."

Bridgette places the phone on the bar and puts it on speaker as she opens the refrigerator and pulls out a bottle of wine. She hands it to me, expecting me to open it, so I take it and look for the bottle opener.

"Pizza Shack," a guy says, answering her call. "Will this be carry-out or delivery?"

"Delivery."

"What can I get you?"

"Two large pizzas with everything. One thick crust, one thin."

I open the wine bottle while she continues to order. "Do you want all the meats?"

"Yeah," Bridgette says. "Everything."

"You also want feta cheese added?"

"I said I want everything."

There's a tapping sound, like fingers against keys, while the guy takes a moment to enter the order. "Do you want pineapple?"

Bridgette rolls her eyes. "I've said *everything* like three times. All the meats, all the vegetables, all the fruits. Whatever you have, just put it on there and bring us the damn pizza!"

I pause and glance over at her. She makes a face at me like she's on the phone with the biggest idiot in the world. Poor guy. He doesn't ask her any more questions. He takes her address, and she gives him Warren's debit card number before she ends the call.

I'm curious to see what kind of pizzas we're about to get. I pray that restaurant doesn't have sardines or anchovies. I pour two glasses of wine and hand Bridgette one. She takes a sip and then folds her arms over her chest, holding the wineglass to her lips as she looks me up and down.

She's very pretty, in a sexy way. I can see why Warren is so drawn to her. They really are the most interesting couple I've ever met. And when I say *interesting*, I don't necessarily mean that as a compliment.

"I used to hate you," Bridgette says, matter-of-fact. She leans against the bar and takes another drink of her wine.

So casual, like this is how people are supposed to interact with other people. She reminds me of one of my friends from childhood. Her name was Tasara, and she said anything and everything that was on her mind. I swear, she spent more days in detention than she did in class. I think that's why I was drawn to her, though. She was mean, but she was honest.

It's one thing when you're mean and you lie. But it's a lot more endearing when you're just brutally honest.

Bridgette doesn't seem like the type to waste time on lying, and for that reason, her comment doesn't offend me. And if I'm going to dissect her words, I have to acknowledge that her sentence was past tense. She *used* to hate me. That's probably the best compliment I'll ever get from her.

"You're starting to grow on me, too, Bridgette."

She rolls her eyes, then walks past me to the cabinet below the sink. She reaches for the Pine-Sol bottle that holds the liquor, and then grabs two shot glasses. *The wine isn't enough?*

She pours the shots and, as she hands me one, she says, "That wine isn't strong enough. I get really awkward when people are nice to me. I'm gonna need liquor for this."

I laugh and take the shot glass from her. We raise them at the same time, and I make a toast. "Cheers to women who don't need their boyfriends in order to have a good time." We clink our shot glasses together before downing the liquor. I don't even know what it is. Whiskey, maybe? Whatever. As long as it does the job.

She pours us another shot. "That toast was way too cheerful, Sydney." We hold up our glasses again, and she clears her throat before speaking. "Cheers to Maggie and her mad skills at remaining friends with both of her ex-boyfriends, to the point that they are somehow still at her beck and call, even when sex isn't involved."

I'm dumbfounded as she clinks her glass against mine and then downs her shot. I don't move my shot glass. When she sees her words have made me speechless, she pushes my shot glass toward my mouth and uses her fingers to tilt it up. I finally down it.

"Good girl," she says. She takes the shot glass from me and hands me my wineglass. She pulls herself up onto the bar and sits cross-legged. "So," she says. "What do girls do when they hang out like this?"

She is so unlike anyone I've ever spent time with as an adult. She's like an entirely different class of animal. There are amphibians, reptiles, mammals, birds, fish—and then there's Bridgette. I shrug and laugh a little, then pull myself up onto the kitchen bar across from her. "It's been a long time since I've had a girls' night, but I think we're supposed to bitch about our boyfriends while we talk about Jason Momoa."

She cocks her head. "Who is Jason Momoa?"

I laugh, but she looks at me like she's clueless. Oh my God. She's serious? She doesn't know who Jason Momoa is? "Oh, Bridgette," I say with pity. "Really?"

She still has no clue who I'm talking about. I grab my phone but don't feel like jumping off the bar to enlighten her. "I'll text you his picture."

I find a picture of him and text it to her. I've only ever sent her one text in the history of knowing her. Sending her a second one practically makes us best friends now.

When I've hit send, I go back to my messages and open up a missed text from Ridge. He sent it five minutes ago.

Ridge: Just letting you know that Maggie didn't want to stay at the hospital tonight so she talked Warren into helping her sneak out. We're taking her home and we'll probably stay there just to make sure she's fine. Are you okay with that? Also, are you having fun with Bridgette?

I read his text twice. I want to be casual about it all, despite my warring emotions, but I'm scared if I'm *too* casual, he'll run to her anytime she misses him. But if I'm not casual enough, I'll be disappointed in my inability to empathize with Maggie's situation. I don't know how to respond, so I do the unthinkable and look up at Bridgette.

"Ridge says they're taking Maggie home. She left before she was discharged. Now he and Warren are probably staying the night at her house."

Bridgette is staring at her phone. "That's shitty."

I agree. But I don't know which part she thinks is shitty. Maggie asking them to come when it doesn't seem like a medical emergency? Ridge saying they might stay the night? Or the entire situation as a whole?

"Does it ever bother you that she and Warren are so close?"

Bridgette immediately lifts her head. "Fuck yeah, it bothers me. Warren flirted with her every time she was here. But he also flirts with you and every other woman he comes across. So I don't know. For the most part, I trust him. Besides, my Hooters uniform would slide right off that shapeless figure of hers, and that uniform is Warren's favorite thing about me."

That explanation was going in such a good direction before it took a nosedive. I don't even know why I asked how she reacts to their situation, because theirs is so different from ours. Warren dating Maggie for a few weeks when she was seventeen hardly compares to Ridge spending six years of his life with her up until a few months ago.

Bridgette must see the worry in my expression while I stare back down at the text. "I really don't think you should stress about it," she says. "I've seen how Ridge is with Maggie, and I've seen how Ridge is with you. It's like comparing chopsticks and computers."

I look at her, confused. "Chopsticks and computers? How is that—"

"Exactly," she says. "You can't compare them because they're incomparable."

That . . . somehow . . . makes complete sense. And makes me feel so much better. I think about the glitter bomb and how Bridgette smiled at me and Ridge when we were laughing together on the floor. I can't believe I've never hung out with this girl before. She's actually not so mean when you peel back all the layers of . . . *mean.*

"Holy. Shit." Bridgette is staring at her phone, and based on how she says those two words, it can only mean one thing. She opened the pic I just sent. "Who is this exemplary specimen of man that has somehow never been introduced into my life?"

I laugh. "*That* is Jason Momoa."

Bridgette brings her phone up to her face and licks her phone screen.

I cringe and laugh at the same time. "You're as gross as Warren."

She holds up her hand. "Please don't mention his name while I stare at this man. It's ruining my moment."

I give her a moment to search him on Google Images while I finish off my glass of wine and reopen my text from Ridge. I type out a response to him and try to avoid the elephant in the room. Or would it be elephant in the *phone*, since Ridge and I aren't in the same room?

Yeah, okay, I think I might be a little buzzed.

Sydney: Glad Maggie is feeling okay. And Bridgette is not so bad, actually. It's weird. Like we're in another dimension.

Ridge: Wow. Is she having a legitimate conversation with you like a normal human?

Sydney: Normal is a stretch. But yeah. She's mostly giving me advice about you. ;)

Ridge: That's unsettling.

Sydney: Good. I want you to feel unsettled until I see you tomorrow.

Ridge: Don't worry, I do feel unsettled. I feel a lot of things. I feel guilty because I left you alone. Worried that you're sad. Lonely because I'm here and not with you. But mostly I feel grateful because you make difficult situations so much easier for everyone involved.

I bring my hand to my mouth and trace my smile. I love that he says exactly what I need to hear.

Sydney: I love you.

Bridgette: Tell Ridge goodbye. This is my time.

I glance up at Bridgette, who is looking at me with severe boredom. I laugh.

Sydney: Bridgette says I can't talk to you anymore.

Ridge: Better do what she says. No telling what the consequences are. I love you. Goodnight. I love you. Goodnight.

Sydney: You said that twice.

Ridge: I mean it even more than that.

I close out the texts, still smiling, and then place my phone facedown on the bar. Bridgette is pouring herself another glass of wine.

"Can I ask you a personal question?" she says.

"Sure." I hop off the bar and grab the wine from her, then turn and refill my glass.

"Does he . . . moan?"

I spin around at that question. "Excuse me?"

Bridgette waves her hand, dismissing my shock. "Just tell me. I've always wondered if he makes noises during sex since he can't hear anything."

I choke out a laugh. "You wonder what my boyfriend sounds like during sex?"

She tilts her head and glares at me, rolling her head. "Oh, come on. Lots of people wonder that about deaf people."

I shake my head. "No, I'm confident most people *don't* wonder that, Bridgette."

"Whatever. Just answer the question."

She's not going to stop. My face and neck feel flushed, but I don't know if it's because of all the alcohol or if it's because she just asked such a personal question. I take a long drink and then nod. "He does. He moans and grunts and sighs, and I don't know why, but the fact that he's deaf makes all his noises that much more of a turn-on."

Bridgette grins. "That is so hot."

"Don't call my boyfriend's sex noises *hot*."

She shrugs. "You shouldn't have made them sound so hot, then." She spends the next several minutes looking up images of Jason Mamoa. And even though I've seen them all, she holds up her phone and shows me each one like she's doing me a favor.

The doorbell eventually rings, and Bridgette suddenly looks happier than I've ever seen her look. She rushes toward the door with starved excitement, like she didn't just eat an entire plate of Alfredo pasta two hours ago. "Grab money for a tip, Syd. I don't have any."

She is perfect for Warren. Absolutely perfect.

Chapter Thirteen

Ridge

It's the first time I've been to Maggie's house since the night
we broke up. It's a little weird, but it could be worse. Warren
has always had this magical ability to make sure he's weirder
than any situation ever could be. And that's exactly what's
happening right now. He just raided Maggie's freezer and
refrigerator and is standing in her kitchen, dipping soggy
microwaved fish sticks into chocolate pudding.

"You eat some of the grossest stuff," Maggie says,
opening her dishwasher.

I'm sitting on Maggie's couch, watching them. They're
laughing, making jokes. Maggie is cleaning her kitchen
as Warren messes it up. I stare at Maggie's wrist—at the
hospital bracelet still attached to it—and try not to be upset
that I'm here. But I *am* upset. I'm annoyed. If she's well

enough to sneak out of a hospital and clean her kitchen, what am I even doing here?

Maggie grabs a paper towel and covers her mouth with it while Warren beats her on the back a few times. I noticed in the car that she was coughing a lot. Back when we were dating and I'd notice she was coughing, I would put my hand on her back or her chest to feel how bad of a cough it was. But I can't do that anymore. All I can do is ask her if she's okay and trust that she isn't downplaying her health.

This coughing fit lasts for an entire minute. She probably hasn't used her vest at all today, so I stand up and walk to her bedroom. It's on the chair by her bed. I grab the vest and the generator it's attached to, and walk it to the couch to hook it up in the living room.

She's supposed to use it two to three times a day to help break up the mucus in her lungs. When a person has cystic fibrosis, it causes their mucus to thicken, which then causes blockage to major organs. Before these vests were invented, patients relied on other people to do manual chest percussions, which meant beating on the back and chest several times a day to break up all the mucus.

The vests are a lifesaver. Especially for Maggie, because she lives alone and has no one to administer chest percussions. But she's never used it as much she should, and that used to be a huge point of contention between us. I guess it still is, because here I am, hooking it up, about to force her to use it.

After I get it hooked up, Maggie taps me on the shoulder. "It's broken."

I look back down at the generator and power it on. Nothing happens. "What's wrong with it?"

She shrugs. "It stopped working a couple of days ago. I'll take it in Monday and trade it in."

Monday? She can't go an entire weekend without it. Especially if she's already coughing like she is. I sit on the couch to try to figure out what's wrong with it. Maggie walks back into the kitchen and says something to Warren. I can tell by his body language and the way he looks over at me that she said something about me.

"What did she say?"

Warren looks at Maggie. "Ridge wants to know what you just said."

Maggie glances over her shoulder at me and laughs, then faces me. "I said you haven't changed."

"Yeah, well, neither have you."

She looks offended, but honestly, I don't care. She's always tried to make me feel guilty for worrying about her. Clearly, nothing has changed, and my concern still annoys her.

Maggie seems irritated by my response to her. "Yeah, it's kind of impossible to stop having cystic fibrosis."

I stare at her, wondering why she's in such a shit mood. Probably for the same reason I am. We're having the same arguments we've always had, only this time there isn't a relationship between us to fall back on and cushion our feelings.

I'm annoyed that she left the hospital, but now that she's so unappreciative of us being here trying to help her, my anger is starting to build. My girlfriend was crying because I was leaving her, concerned about us, and now Maggie's scolding—*mocking*—me even though I came. *For her.*

I can't sit here and have this conversation. I stand up and unplug the generator, then carry everything back to her bedroom. Maggie and Warren can eat their sacrilegious combination of fish sticks and chocolate pudding, and I'll be in the other room, continuing to try to repair a vest that literally aids in keeping her alive.

I'm not even all the way into her room when I turn around and see that she's following me. I set the generator on the table next to the chair and sit down, pulling the table closer. I turn on the lamp next to the chair. Maggie is still standing in the doorway.

"What is your problem, Ridge?"

I laugh, but not because anything about tonight is funny. "What did you eat this morning before you passed out from low blood sugar?" Maggie's eyes narrow. I'm asking her this because she probably can't even remember. Hell, she probably didn't even eat. "Have you even checked your glucose levels since you ate half of a king-size Twix bar?"

I can tell she's about to yell. When she's really angry at me, she signs and yells. It used to turn me on. Now I would just give anything to be able to yell back at her.

"You have no right to comment on the food I consume,

Ridge. In case you don't remember, I'm not your girlfriend anymore."

"If I don't get a say in how you take care of yourself, then why am I here?" I stand up and walk closer to her. "You don't take care of yourself and you end up in the hospital, and then you call Warren, crying and scared. We drop everything to be there for you, but as soon as we get there, you leave the hospital without being discharged! Forgive me if I have better things to do than come running every time you're irresponsible!"

"You didn't have to come, Ridge! I didn't even know the hospital called you guys. And I didn't cry to Warren on the phone or tell him I was scared! He asked if I wanted company, and I told him yes because I thought we could all figure this stupid situation out like grown adults! BUT I GUESS NOT!" She slams the door on her way out of her bedroom.

I pull it right back open. I don't do it to follow Maggie, though. I go straight to the kitchen and look at Warren. "Why did you tell me she cried and that she was scared?" Maggie is standing on the other side of me, her arms crossed, while she glares at Warren. He's holding a soda, looking back and forth at both of us. His eyes finally land on me.

"I exaggerated. It's not a big deal. You wouldn't have come otherwise."

I force myself to inhale a calming breath. It's either that or I'm going to punch him.

"It's a long drive from Austin to San Antonio," Warren says. Besides, we needed to be together. The three of us. We have to figure out how to deal with all of this going forward."

"All of this?" Maggie says. She motions to herself. "You mean me? We have to figure out how to deal with *me*? I guess this proves I really am nothing but a burden to you guys."

She isn't yelling anymore. She's only signing. But even though I can tell she's hurting and upset, I'm still not convinced things would be different if she would take all this a little more seriously like I've been trying to get her to do for the last six years.

"You're not a burden, Maggie," I sign. "You're selfish. If you took care of yourself and monitored your blood sugar and used your vest like you're supposed to and—I don't know—maybe didn't jump out of fucking *airplanes*, none of us would even be arguing. I've put Sydney in an awkward situation that she wouldn't be in right now if you'd just take better care of yourself."

Warren covers his face with his hand like I just screwed up.

Maggie rolls her eyes with exaggeration. "Poor Sydney. She really is the victim in all of this, isn't she? Gets the man of her dreams *and* she's healthy. Poor *fucking* Sydney!" She turns her attention on Warren. "Don't ever force him to come take care of me again! I don't need him to take care of me. I don't need either of you to take care of me!"

Warren raises an eyebrow, but remains stoic. "With all due respect, you kind of *do* need us, Maggie."

I squeeze my eyes shut and look down. I know that had to hurt her, and I don't want to watch the sting. When I open my eyes again, she's marching to her bedroom. She slams the door. Warren turns and punches the refrigerator. I walk to the table by the couch and grab Warren's car keys.

"I want to leave." I toss Warren his keys, but his eyes dart up to Maggie's bedroom door. He rushes across the living room and swings the door open. Naturally, I rush with him because I can't hear whatever it is he just heard.

Maggie is in her bathroom, hugging the toilet, vomiting. Warren grabs a washcloth and bends down next to her. I walk over and sit on the edge of the tub.

This happens when she has too much buildup in her lungs. I'm sure right now, it's a combination of that and not using her vest for several days, and all the yelling she just did. I reach over and pull her hair back until it stops. It's hard for me to be upset with her right now. She's crying, leaning against Warren.

I don't know what it's like to be the one with this illness, so I probably shouldn't be judging her actions so harshly. I only know what it's like to be the one to care for someone with this illness. I used to have to remind myself of that all the time: No matter how frustrated I get, it's nothing compared to what she must go through.

It looks like I still need that reminder.

Maggie won't even look at me the whole time we wait with her to see if her episode is over. She doesn't even look at me when we're convinced it is over and Warren helps her to her bedroom. It's her way of giving me the silent treatment. She used to refuse to look at me when she was mad because she didn't want to give me the chance to sign to her.

Warren gets her in the bed, and I take her generator back to the living room. Once Maggie is settled, Warren leaves her door halfway open while he comes back to the living room and takes a seat on the couch.

I'm still pissed that he lied about their phone call in order to guilt me into coming. But I also understand why he did it. The three of us do need to sit down and figure this out. Maggie doesn't want to be a burden, but until she buckles down and makes her health her primary focus, she'll never be as independent as she wishes she could be. And as long as she's dependent, it's the two of us who will be taking care of her.

I know we're all she has. And I know that Sydney understands that. I would never walk away from Maggie completely, knowing how much she needs someone in her corner. But when you do things that continue to belittle and even disrespect the efforts of those in your corner, eventually you're going to lose your team. And without your team, eventually you lose the fight.

I don't want her to lose the fight. None of us do. Which is why Warren and I stay, because she needs a treatment. And that can't happen until I repair her vest.

Warren watches TV for the next hour, getting up once to take Maggie a glass of water. When he comes back into the room, he waves his hand to get my attention.

"Her cough sounds bad," he says.

I just nod. I already know. It's why I'm still trying to work on this vest.

It's after two a.m. when I finally figure out the issue. I found an old generator she used to use in her hallway closet. I switch out the power cords and can get it to kick on, but it won't stay on unless I'm holding the cord with my fingers.

Warren is asleep on the couch when I take the vest to Maggie's bedroom. Her lamp is still on, so I can see that she's still wide awake. I walk over to her bed and plug in the generator and hand her the vest. She sits up and slips it on.

"There's a short. I have to hold the cord while it's powered on or it'll cut off."

She nods, but she doesn't say anything. We both know this routine. The machine runs for five minutes, and then she has to cough to clear out her lungs. I run it for another five minutes and then let her take another coughing break. The routine continues for half an hour.

When the treatment is over, she slips off the vest and continues to avoid eye contact with me as she rolls over. I lay it on the floor, but when I look back at her, I can tell by the movement in her shoulders that she's crying.

And now I feel like an asshole.

I know I get frustrated with her, but she isn't perfect. Neither am I. And as long as we're doing nothing but arguing and pointing out each other's shortcomings, we're never going to get her health on the right track.

I sit next to her on the bed and squeeze her shoulder.

It's what I used to do when I felt helpless to her situation. She reaches up and squeezes my hand, and just like that, the argument is over. She rolls over onto her back and looks up at me.

"I didn't tell Warren on the phone that I was scared."

I nod. "I know that now."

A tear falls from her eye and slides down into her hair. "But he's right, Ridge. I am scared."

I've never seen this look on her face before, and it completely guts me. I hate this for her. I really do. She starts crying harder and rolls away from me. And as much as I want to tell her it wouldn't be so scary if she'd stop acting like she was immune to the effects of her illness, I don't respond. I wrap my arm around her because she doesn't need a lecture right now.

She just needs a friend.

• • •

I made Maggie do a second treatment in the middle of the night last night. I'm pretty sure I fell asleep somewhere in the middle of her second treatment, because I woke up at eight o'clock this morning and realized I was on her bed. I know Sydney wouldn't be comfortable with that, so I moved to the couch. I'm still on the couch. Facedown. Trying to sleep, but Warren is shaking me.

I reach for my phone and look at the time, not expecting it to be noon. I sit up immediately, wondering why he let me sleep so long.

"Get up," he signs. "We need to get Maggie's car and drop it back off here before we head back to Austin."

I nod, rubbing the sleep from my eyes. "We need to go to the medical supply store first," I tell him. "I want to see if they can give her a generator until hers gets repaired."

Warren signs, "Okay," and walks to the bathroom.

I fall back against the couch and sigh. I hate how this whole trip has gone. It's left me with an unsettled feeling, which, funny enough, is exactly what Sydney was hoping for. I smile, knowing she got her way and she doesn't even realize it. I haven't spoken to her since all the fighting between me, Maggie, and Warren last night. I open my texts to her and notice she hasn't texted since we talked last night. I wonder how her night with Bridgette went.

Ridge: Heading back soon. How was your sleepover?

She begins texting back immediately. I watch the text bubbles appear and disappear several times until her text comes through.

Sydney: Apparently not as eventful as yours.

Her text confuses me. I look at Warren, who is walking out of the bathroom. "Did you tell Sydney about the argument last night?"

"Nope," Warren says. "I haven't talked to either one of them today. My guess is that they're hungover and still in bed."

My chest tightens because her text is unlike her.

Ridge: What do you mean?

Sydney: Check Instagram.

I immediately close out my texts to her and open Instagram. I scroll down until I see it.

Son of a bitch.

Maggie posted a picture of us. She's making a silly face up at the camera and I'm next to her. In her bed. Asleep. The caption reads, "Haven't missed his snoring."

I fist my phone in both hands and pull it to my forehead, squeezing my eyes shut. *This. This* is why I should have stayed home.

I stand up. "Where's Maggie?"

Warren nods toward the hallway and signs, "The laundry room."

I walk to her laundry room and find her casually hanging up a shirt like she didn't just try to sabotage my relationship with Sydney with her petty Instagram post. I hold up my phone. "What's this?"

"A picture of you," she says, matter-of-fact.

"I see that. But why?"

She finishes hanging up the shirt and then leans against her washing machine. "I also posted a picture of Warren. Why are you so mad?"

I roll my head and throw my hands up in frustration. I'm confused why she did it in the first place, and now I'm confused as to why she's acting like it isn't a big deal.

She pushes off her washing machine. "I didn't realize we had rules to this friendship. I've posted pictures of all of us for six years. Are we catering our lives to Sydney now?" She tries to walk toward the door, but I step in front of it.

"You could show a little respect for our situation."

Maggie's eyes narrow. "Are you serious right now? Did you really just ask me to show respect to the relationship you're in with the girl you *cheated* on me with?"

That is not fair. We're past that now. At least I *thought* we were. "You could have posted any picture of me, but you chose to post one of me in your bed. A bed I was in because I stayed up for hours to make sure you were okay. Using that as an opportunity to throw my mistake back in my face is not fair, Maggie."

Her jaw hardens. "You want to talk fair? How fair is it that you're the one who had an emotional affair, but I'm the one who has to be sensitive about what I post on Instagram? How fair is it that I'm the bad guy for eating a Twix? I wanted a fucking *Twix*, Ridge!" She pushes past me, so I follow her. She spins around when she reaches her living room. "I forgot how I'm never allowed to have any fun when you're around. Maybe you shouldn't come back, because this is the worst day I've had in months!"

In all my years of knowing her, I've never been this mad at her. I don't know why I thought this could work. "If you have an actual emergency, let me know, Maggie. I'll be here for you. But until then, I can't be friends with you." I walk to the front door and swing it open, then face Warren. "Let's go."

Warren is standing in the living room, frozen, at a complete loss as to what to say or do. "What about Maggie's car?"

"She can take an Uber." I walk out of Maggie's house and head for Warren's car.

It takes him a few minutes to finally walk outside. I'm sure he was reassuring Maggie. Let him. Maybe he can re-assure the unreasonable, but I sure can't.

When Warren finally makes it to his car, I open up my texts to Sydney. I don't even try to justify the picture with an excuse. I'll explain it all when we're face-to-face with her.

Ridge: I'm sorry she posted that, Sydney. I'm on my way back to my apartment now.

Sydney: No hurry. I won't even be at your apartment when you get here.

I get a separate text from Bridgette.

Bridgette: Dick. You're a dick. Dick, dick, dick.

Sydney: And don't bother coming to my apartment. Me and Bridgette are having another sleepover.

Bridgette: NO DICKS ALLOWED!

I close out the texts to both of them and lean my head against the seat. "Drive to Sydney's apartment first."

Chapter Fourteen

Maggie

I sit down on the couch after Warren closes the door. I stare at the floor.

I bury my face in my hands.

What is wrong with me?

I pushed Jake away. I pushed Ridge away. I even told Warren to get the hell out of my house when he stayed back and tried to get me to tell him why I was acting the way I was.

I don't know what's gotten into me this week. This isn't me. I, honest to God, don't want to be in a relationship with Ridge, but when I woke up this morning and saw him asleep next to me, it felt good to have him back. I've missed him. But not in a romantic way. I've just missed his company. And I started wondering if he missed my company, or if Sydney is all he needs now. Then I started feeling insecure again because he was here, even though he expressed just how much he didn't want to be here. And as I lay there and stared at him, I started thinking about the day I found all the messages between him and Sydney, and I got angry all over again.

I shouldn't have posted the picture. I know that. But I think I did it because I thought it would make me feel better in some twisted way. I missed him, I was angry at him, I was angry at myself. I feel like years of just trying to live despite this illness is catching up to me. Because Ridge is right. I don't take care of myself like I should, but it's because I'm sick of this illness, and sometimes I don't care if it wins. I really don't.

I pull out my phone and delete the picture; then I open a text to Ridge.

Maggie: It's been the shittiest week of my life. Tell Sydney I am so sorry. I deleted the picture.

I hit send and then power off my phone and lie down. I press my face into the couch and I cry.

The problem with hating yourself when you're all alone is that you have no one to remind you of any of your good qualities. Then you just hate yourself even more, until you sabotage anything good in your life and in yourself.

I'm at that point.

Maggie Carson. Not so much of a badass today.

Chapter Fifteen

Sydney

I had so much fun last night.

I ate Bridgette's disgusting pizza, and then she told me all about how she and Warren started dating. That only solidified my opinion of their weirdness. Then we watched *Justice League* and fast-forwarded through all the parts Jason Momoa wasn't in.

I don't remember much after that because we were several bottles of wine in. My sleep and my fun were both cut abruptly short today when Bridgette shook me awake and shoved Maggie's Instagram post in my face.

I'm more hurt than angry. I'm sure Ridge will have an excuse. He always does. But what's Maggie's excuse? I know, in a sense, I'm the other woman who came between them. I was the Tori in that situation. But I honestly thought we were all beyond that. From the way Warren and Ridge made it sound, she took it well and was even mature about it. But this feels so . . . *petty. Gross*, even.

I couldn't stand being in Ridge's apartment after seeing her post. The way I felt reminded me of the stark and pitiful misery I went through while I lived there. And the entire place smelled like pepperoni and anchovies. I told Bridgette I was going back to my place, and she went to her room to grab her stuff and told me she was going with me.

I think she might be just as upset as I am, because she brought another bottle of wine with her, and now we're drinking again, and it's barely two o'clock in the afternoon. But I don't mind that she's here. I actually prefer it, because I really don't want to be alone right now or I'll overanalyze this entire situation and come up with far-fetched reasons for him being on that bed before he can even explain himself.

Bridgette is sitting cross-legged on my bed. She reaches to the floor and grabs her purse, pulling her phone out of it. "That's it. I can't take it. I'm commenting on her Instagram post."

I try to pull her phone away. "Don't. I don't even want her to know I saw it. It'll serve her purpose."

Bridgette rolls onto her stomach to protect her phone from me. "That's why I said *I'll* comment. I'll say something to make her feel as insecure as she's trying to make you feel. I'll tell her she looks healthy. Everyone knows when you tell someone they look healthy, it really means fat."

"You can't say that to someone who is actually sick. And really skinny."

Bridgette groans and then rolls onto her back, tossing her phone aside. "She deleted it! Dammit!"

Thank God. I appreciate Bridgette's support, but I really don't need her wedging herself into Ridge's and my—and Maggie's—issues.

"You want me to call Warren and ask him what happened?" Bridgette sounds almost giddy. She would be one to thrive on drama.

And I'm not gonna lie. I've thought about calling Warren myself because I have so many questions. I know they're driving back right now and Ridge will probably come over and try to explain himself, but it would be nice to be a little enlightened beforehand so I know exactly how much and how loud I should yell at him when he arrives. Not that the decibel of my voice will matter in our argument, but it might make me feel better to scream at him.

Bridgette calls Warren and puts the phone on speaker.

"Hey, babe," he says as he answers.

"So, what the fuck happened last night?" Bridgette says.

Yeah, she doesn't know how to do anything with tact. Warren clears his throat, but before he starts speaking, I interrupt him.

"Are you signing this conversation for Ridge? I really don't want to talk to him right now."

"I'm driving," Warren says. "Kind of hard for me to drive, hold my phone, eat this cheeseburger, and sign everything I'm saying. Besides, he's staring out the passenger window, brooding."

Bridgette leans toward the phone. "Sydney and Ridge's relationship is in jeopardy, yet you guys had time to stop for burgers?"

"*I* stopped for a burger. Ridge won't eat until all is right in the world of Ridney."

I roll my eyes. "Well, then he's gonna be really hungry by tonight."

"He didn't do anything wrong, Sydney," Warren says. "I swear. That was all Maggie."

"He was asleep on her bed!" Bridgette says.

"Yeah, because he spent two hours repairing the generator to her vest and then had to hold the cord so she could use it. He didn't sleep all night, and when he finally did get a few hours of sleep, Maggie took a picture of him and went and pulled some really shady shit. I'm telling you, it was all Maggie. I've never seen her like this."

I glance up at Bridgette. I don't know if I can trust Warren. As if she can sense what I'm thinking, she says, "We're not stupid, Warren. Bros before hos. You would defend Ridge even if he murdered you."

"Hold on," Warren says. "I need to take a drink."

Bridgette and I wait and listen as he slurps down a drink. I fall back onto my bed, frustrated with Warren. With Ridge. With Maggie. But for once, I'm not at all frustrated with Bridgette.

"Okay," Warren says. "Here's what happened. After we left the hospital and got back to Maggie's house last night, it was an entire hour of them screaming at each other. It's like they both released years of aggression all at once, and there were so many insults coming from both sides. All of the—"

"Wait," Bridgette says. "Now I know for a fact you're lying."

"I'm not lying!" Warren says defensively.

"You said they were screaming at each other. Ridge can't scream, you idiot."

I press my hand to my forehead. "It's sort of a figure of speech in this situation, Bridgette. He was angry and he was signing. Warren refers to it as screaming." Bridgette shoots me a look of suspicion, like she still doesn't trust what Warren is saying. I give my attention back to the phone. "Why were they fighting?"

"Why *weren't* they fighting? Ridge was mad because he was there and she wasn't even that sick. He was mad she isn't taking her health seriously, and it's starting to inconvenience those around her. She was mad because he brought up the fact that she was inconveniencing you and putting a strain on your relationship with Ridge. I'm telling you, I've never seen them like this. And it wasn't the kind of fighting that me and Bridgette do, where we're just trying to get under each other's skin. This was legit *I'm fucking angry at you* fighting."

I close my eyes, hating the entire situation. I'm not pleased that they're fighting. That's helping no one. But it does explain why she posted that picture. It wasn't to get back at me. She was pissed at Ridge, and her best form of revenge on him is to involve me.

"And then they both got mad at me," he says. "All the yelling caused her to start vomiting, and then Ridge made her wear her vest, and he fell asleep on her bed during one of her treatments. As soon as he woke up, he went to the couch and slept for four hours until I woke him up and InstaGate happened. And that's the whole story."

I kick my legs on the mattress. "Ugh! I don't know who to be mad at! I just need to be mad at someone!"

Bridgette points to the phone and whispers, "Be mad at Warren. It's a great stress reliever." She raises her voice so he can hear her. "Why did they get mad at you?"

"Not important," Warren says. "We're pulling up to your apartment right now, Sydney. Let us in."

He ends the call, and I don't even know if I feel any better. I never thought Ridge was in Maggie's bed because he was cheating on me. I knew he probably had a valid excuse related to her health. But why couldn't they have been on the couch together, instead? Or the floor? Why did he have to fall asleep in a place where they've probably been intimate with each other for years?

I stand up. "I need more wine."

"Yep, yep. Wine," Bridgette says, following me to my kitchen.

When Ridge and Warren finally make it inside, I've just downed my second glass for the day. Warren walks in first, and then Ridge walks in. I hate how Ridge frantically searches for me and then looks relieved when he sees me. I just want to stay mad at him, but he makes it so hard with those kissable lips and apologetic eyes.

I know what I'll do. I just won't look at him. That way I won't succumb so easily to my forgiveness. I spin around so that I can't see Ridge or the door. I can only see Warren as he tries to hug Bridgette, but she pushes against his forehead.

Turning my back on Ridge doesn't do me any good, because he walks up behind me and wraps his arms around me, tucking his face into the space between my neck and shoulder. He kisses me softly on the neck and keeps his arms wrapped around me, apologizing without words.

I don't accept this apology. I'm still mad, so I remain stiff and don't react to his touch. Externally, anyway. Internally, I just combusted.

Bridgette downs the rest of her wine, then gives her attention to Warren. "Why were Ridge and Maggie mad at you?"

I want to hear Warren's answer, but Ridge releases me, turning me so that I'm face-to-face with him. He slides his hands to my cheeks and looks at me very seriously. "I'm sorry."

I shrug. "Still hurts."

Warren ignores Bridgette's question and walks toward me and Ridge. I glance over Ridge's shoulder as Warren touches his chest, looking somewhat guilty. "It was mostly my fault, Sydney. I'm really sorry."

"Figures," Bridgette says, walking to the kitchen for more

wine. She walks right between Ridge and me, separating us completely. "Just spill it, Warren."

Warren squeezes the back of his neck with his hand as he winces. "Well. Funny story . . ."

"I bet it's a riot," Bridgette deadpans.

Warren ignores her and continues, "I might have exaggerated about the phone call with Maggie. She wasn't crying, and she technically didn't beg us to come. I just knew if I didn't stretch the truth a little, Ridge wouldn't have gone."

Bridgette's mouth drops open. She makes a shocked sound and then looks at me, then back at Warren. "You wanted a sleepover with your ex-girlfriend, so you lied to everyone?"

"You're such an asshole, Warren," I say. Why would he lie and put Ridge in that situation yesterday? God, I am so angry at him. It feels good to finally have a solid target for my anger.

"Look," Warren says, throwing his hands up in the air. "Ridge and Maggie were way overdue for a conversation about this. I wasn't doing it to be malicious. I was trying to be helpful!"

"Yeah, sounds like the entire trip was a success," I say.

Warren shrugs, placing his hands on his hips. "There may not be a resolution yet, but Maggie needed to hear everything Ridge had to say. In fact, I think you'd be proud of him. After last night and everything he said to defend you, there isn't a doubt in my mind that he's one hundred percent aboard the Sydney train."

I fold my arms over my chest. "You mean you had doubts before last night?"

Warren looks up at the ceiling. "Not what I meant." He looks at Bridgette, and I can tell he's done with this day already. "Let's go. They need privacy. So do we."

Bridgette pulls out a chair at the bar and takes a seat. "No. I'm not finished with my wine."

Warren walks to the counter and grabs the bottle of wine. Then he takes her glass out of her hand and walks out the front door with it. Bridgette looks at the door and then at me. Then at the door and then at me again. Her eyes are full of panic. She points helplessly at the door. "Wine."

"Go," I say, walking around Ridge, toward the door. She rushes to the door, and I shut it behind her. When I turn back around, Ridge is leaning his head against the refrigerator, staring at me. I sigh and stare back at him, hating how tired he looks. As irritated as I am at Warren, I'm relieved he explained everything. I'm not as angry at Ridge.

Ridge pulls his phone out and starts to text me. I go to my room and get my phone and then head back to the kitchen as I read his text.

Ridge: I have no idea what's been happening for the last ten minutes. No one signed a single word of any of that and it's really hard to read lips when people are angry and moving around.

My shoulders drop when I read his text. I feel bad that we all just excluded him while we argued around him.

Sydney: To sum it up, Warren said you were innocent and he was guilty and Maggie was bitter and it was just a huge cluster-fuck of a slumber party.

Ridge reads the texts and then shrugs a shoulder.

Ridge: No matter the reason, I shouldn't have been on Maggie's bed without thinking about how that would make you feel. But for the record, I fell asleep during her treatment and then moved to the couch as soon as I woke up.

Sydney: Well, it wasn't soon enough. Because it bit you right in the ass.

Ridge: Whoever said Karma is a bitch must have never met her. Because Karma is very friendly and she follows me around everywhere I go. Everywhere. All the time.

I smile, but Ridge just looks so sad. I hate that we're in the position to have to make up after another argument, and we haven't even been together a week. I hope this isn't any indication of how the rest of our relationship is going to go. Of course, the first argument was all his fault, and he was being a tool. But this one . . .

I don't know. From what I gathered through Warren's explanation, Ridge really is making a huge attempt at putting me first. It's just hard when there are so many obstacles. *Oh man*. Did I just refer to Maggie as an obstacle? She's not an obstacle. Her recent *behavior* is the obstacle.

Ridge: Can I please kiss you? I need to. So bad.

I smile a little as I read his text. He must see it, because he doesn't even wait for me to look up and answer him. He just rushes toward me and lifts my face and then presses his mouth firmly to mine. He kisses me like he's starved for me. It's my favorite kind of kiss from him. It's so desperate and mostly one-sided from him that the strength behind his kiss ends up forcing me backward. He continues kissing me until my back is against the living room wall. But as desperate as it is, it's not a sensual kiss. It's just full of need. A need to feel me and know I'm not upset. A need for reassurance. A need for forgiveness.

After a good minute of him kissing me, he presses his forehead to mine. Still, even after I've let him kiss me, he seems distraught. I slide my hand up to his cheek and brush my thumb across it, bringing his eyes to mine.

"Are you okay?"

He inhales and then slowly exhales. He nods unconvincingly and then pulls me against him. I barely have time to wrap my arms around him when he bends down and slides an arm behind my knees and lifts me up. He carries me to the bedroom and lowers me to the bed.

Whatever is still bothering him can wait, because his mouth is on mine again. But this time his kiss isn't a need for my reassurance. It's just a need for me. He pulls his shirt over his head and then stands up and slides off my pajama bottoms. Then he's over me again, his tongue in my mouth, his hand sliding up my thigh, lifting my leg.

I want to hear him. Since the moment I described how hot his noises were last night, I've been craving them all. I unzip his jeans and slip my hand inside, pulling him out and guiding him inside of me.

His mouth is against my neck when I get his groan. It rumbles up his chest as he pushes into me, and then he sighs, softly, as he pulls out. He repeats the rhythm, and I close my eyes. The entire time he makes love to me, I remain quiet and listen to the sensual sounds of Ridge.

Chapter Sixteen

Ridge

There are three things that produce such beautiful sounds that countless poems have been written about them.

Oceans, waterfalls, and rain.

I've only been to the ocean once. Sounds of Cedar played a gig in Galveston two years ago, and I joined them for the trip. The morning after the concert, I walked to the beach. I took my shoes off and sat down in the sand and watched the sun rise.

I remember this feeling building inside me as I watched it. Almost like every negative emotion I've ever felt was evaporating with each new ray of sun that trickled out over the horizon.

It was a feeling of complete and utter awe, like nothing I had ever experienced. And as I sat there, I realized I was in awe of something that occurs every single day, and has occurred every single day since the very first sunrise. And I thought to myself, *How can something be so magnificent when it isn't even a thing of rarity?*

The sun and its rise and fall is the most expected, dependable, and repetitive natural occurrence known to mankind. Yet it is one of the few things that maintains a universal ability to render a man speechless.

In that moment, as I sat alone on the beach, my toes buried in the sand, my hands wrapped around my knees . . . I wondered, for the first time, if the sunrise made a sound. I was almost positive it didn't. If it did, I was sure I would have read about it. And I was sure there would be more poetry about the sound of the sunrise than there is about oceans or waterfalls or rain.

And then I wondered what that same sunrise must feel like to those who could hear the ocean as the sun broke itself free from the constraints of the horizon. If a soundless sunrise could mean so much to me, what must it mean to those who watch it as it's accompanied by the roll of the water?

I cried.

I cried . . . because I was deaf.

It's one of the few times I've ever felt resentful about this part of me that has limited my life so significantly. And it's the first and only time I've ever cried because of it. I still remember how I felt in that moment. I was angry. I was bitter. Upset that I had been cursed with this disability that hindered me in so many ways, even though most of my days were spent not even thinking about it.

But that day—that moment—gutted me. I wanted to feel the complete effect of that sunrise. I wanted to absorb every call of the seagulls flying overhead. I wanted the sound of the waves to enter my ears and trickle down my chest until I could feel them thrashing around in my stomach.

I cried because I felt sorry for myself. As soon as the sun had risen fully, I stood up and walked away from the beach, but I couldn't walk away from that feeling. The bitterness followed me throughout the entire day.

I haven't been back to the ocean since.

As I sit here with my hands pressed against the tile of the shower, the spray of the water beating down on my face, I can't help but think about that feeling. And how, until that moment, I never truly understood what Maggie probably feels on a daily basis. Bitter and hurt that she was dealt a hand in life that she's expected to accept with grace and ease.

It's easy for someone on the outside to look in and think that Maggie is being selfish. That she's not thinking about anyone's feelings but her own. Even I think that a lot of the time. But it wasn't until that day on the beach two years ago that I truly understood her with every part of my being.

My being deaf limits me very little. I'm still able to do every single other thing in the world besides hear.

But Maggie is limited in countless ways. Ways that I can't even fathom. My one bitter day on the beach alone when I truly felt the weight of my disability is probably how Maggie feels on a daily basis. Yet those on the outside of her illness would probably look at her pattern of behavior and say that she's ungrateful. Selfish. Despicable, even.

And they would be right. She is all those things. But the difference between Maggie and judgmental people who aren't Maggie is that she has every right in the world to be all those things.

Since the day I met her, she has been fiercely independent. She hates feeling as if she's hindering the lives of those around her. She dreams of traveling the world, of taking risks, of doing all the things her illness tells her she can't do. She wants to feel the stress of college and a career. She wants to revel in the independence the world doesn't think she deserves. She wants to break free of the chains that remind her of her illness.

And every time I want to scold her or point out everything she's doing wrong and all the ways she's hindering her own longevity, I only need to think back on that moment at the beach. That moment that I would have done whatever it took to be able to hear everything I was feeling.

I would have traded years of my life for just one minute of normalcy.

That's exactly what Maggie's doing. She just wants a minute of normalcy. And the only way she gets a moment of normalcy is when she ignores the weight of her reality.

If I could rewind the clock and start yesterday over again, I would do so many things differently. I would have included Sydney in that trip. I wouldn't have allowed Maggie to leave the hospital. And I would have sat down with her and explained to her that I want to help her. I want to be there for her. But I can't be there for her when she refuses to be there for herself.

Instead, I allowed every pent-up negative thought I've never said spill out all at once. It was truthful, yes, but the delivery was hurtful. There are much better ways to share your truth than to force it on someone so hard it injures them.

Maggie's feelings were hurt. Her pride was bruised. And while it's easy for me to say her actions warranted my reaction, it doesn't mean I don't regret that reaction.

I'm trying not to think about it, but it's consuming me. And I know the only thing that can alleviate everything I'm feeling is to talk to the one person in my life who understands my feelings more than anyone. But she's also the last person I want to subject to a discussion about Maggie.

I turn off the water in Sydney's shower. I've been in here for over half an hour, but I'm trying hard to figure out how to suppress everything I'm feeling right now. Sydney deserves a night untainted by my past relationship. This week has been tough, and she deserves one night of near perfection, where she is my sole focus and I am hers.

And I'm going to give her that.

I walk out of her bathroom in just a towel. Not because I'm trying to distract her from the homework she's currently doing on her bed, but because my pants are on her bedroom floor and I need them. When I drop the towel and pull on my jeans, she looks up from her homework with the tip of her pencil in her mouth, chewing on it with a grin.

I smile back at her because I can't help it. She pushes her books aside and pats the bed beside her. I sit down and lean back against the headboard. She slides her leg over me and straddles me, running her hands through my wet hair. She leans forward, kissing me on the forehead, and I'm not sure if she's ever done that before. I close my eyes as she plants soft kisses all over my face. She ends with a soft peck against my lips.

I just want to revel in this moment, so I pull her to me, not really interested in conversation or making out. I just want to hold her and keep my eyes closed and appreciate that she's mine. And she allows it for all of two minutes, but one of the advantages she holds over me is being able to hear the sighs I forget I'm even releasing.

This includes the heavy sigh that instantly causes her concern to resurface. She pulls back, holding my face with her hands. She narrows her eyes as if it's a warning that I better not lie to her.

"What is wrong with you? Be honest this time."

I'm not getting out of this without complete transparency. I slide my hands from her waist up to her shoulders. I squeeze them and then gently move her off me. "Laptops," I tell her.

We use our laptops for the serious conversations. The ones we know will require too much patience for signing or lipreading or text. I walk to her living room and grab my laptop out of my bag. When I make it back to her room, she's sitting against the headboard with her laptop, her eyes following me to my spot on the bed. I open up our messenger and begin the conversation.

Ridge: For the record, I wanted to avoid this conversation tonight. But I'm not sure there's a single emotion I can feel without you reading it.

Sydney: You're not as transparent as you seem to think you are.

Ridge: I only feel transparent to you.

Sydney: Well, let's see if you're right. I'm going to try and pinpoint what's bothering you.

Ridge: Okay. Are we taking bets? Because if you guess right, I'm taking you out on a date tonight. But if you guess wrong, you're going on a date with me tonight.

Sydney: ;) We've never been on a real date before.

Ridge: You better guess either right or wrong then, or we won't be going.

Sydney: Okay. I'm gonna take a stab at it, then. I can tell by your body language that your mind is somewhere else tonight. And based on the past twenty-four hours you've had, I'm going to assume your mind is on Maggie.

Ridge: I wish I could tell you you're wrong. But you're right. I just hope you know it's completely innocent. I just can't help but feel bad for everything I said to her.

Sydney: Have you spoken to her since you left her house today?

Ridge: She texted after I left and gave a two-sentence apology to both of us. But I didn't respond. I was too angry to respond. Now I don't know how to respond because I feel guilty, but also don't feel like she deserves any kind of apology from me. That's what confuses me. Why do I feel guilty if I don't feel like apologizing for what I did?

Sydney: Because. It bothers you that deep down inside, you know if you and Maggie were in any other situation, neither of you would speak again. You're both so different. If it weren't for her illness, the two of you probably would have ended your relationship long before y'all did. But that's not the situation, so she's probably having a hard time processing the fact that you're only in her life because you have to be.

I read her message, and I feel the truth dig straight into my bones. Sydney is right. Maggie's illness is the only reason we're still connected. As much as I know that, I haven't wanted to admit it. But there's me and there's Maggie and we're on opposite sides of the earth right now with this string called cystic fibrosis tying us together.

Ridge: You're right. But I wish you weren't.

Sydney: I'm sure she wishes it were different, too. How do you think that made her feel that you were at her house simply because you needed to be and not because you wanted to be?

Ridge: I'm sure that made her feel resentful.

Sydney: Exactly. And when people feel resentful, they act out. They say things they don't mean.

Ridge: Maybe so, but what was my excuse? I lashed out at her like I've never lashed out at anyone. And that's why I can't stop thinking about this situation, because I feel like I lost my patience with her.

Sydney: It sounds like you did. But I don't think you should regret it. Sometimes caring about someone means saying things you don't want to say, but that need to be said.

Ridge: Yeah. Maybe so.

Sydney: Your heart is my favorite thing about you, Ridge.

She really does love the side of me that Maggie never could. I think that's why it just works with Sydney and me. I finally have someone who is in love with the entirety of me.

Sydney: I won't lie, though. Sometimes your heart scares me.

Ridge: Why does it scare you?

Sydney: Because. I worry that Maggie is spiraling downward. And I know you worry about that, too. I'm scared your guilt and your worry are going to force you to get back together with her, just so you can fix her.

Ridge: Sydney . . .

Sydney: Hey, we're being uncomfortably honest right now.

I look at her, completely dumbfounded by that response. She looks up at me with a hint of fear in her expression, like she thinks I might actually agree with that asinine concern.

Ridge: Sydney, I would never leave you in order to fix her issues. I would be broken without you. Then who would fix me?

She reads my message, and I watch as she reaches a hand up to her laptop screen and runs her thumb over my words. Then she highlights the sentence and copies it. She opens a Word document and pastes it below a bunch of other messages.

I lean over to get a better view of her computer screen, but she hurries and closes out the Word program. I only got a half-second glance, but I could swear the title of the document said Things Ridge Says.

Ridge: Did that document have my name in the title?

Sydney: Maybe. Don't worry about it.

I glance down at her, and she's trying to stifle a smile. I shake my head, almost certain I know what she just did.

Ridge: Do you save things? Things I say to you? Like . . . you have an actual file of things I've said to you?

Sydney: Shut up. You act like that's weird. Lots of people have collections.

Ridge: Yeah, of tangible things, like coins or taxidermies. I don't think most people collect pieces of conversations.

Sydney: Fuck off.

I laugh and then highlight her sentence and copy it. I open a new Word file and paste it into the document, then save the file as Things Sydney Says.

She shoves me in the shoulder. I close my laptop and then shut hers, and slide them both to the other side of her. I wrap my arm around her and rest my chin on her chest, looking up at her. "I love you."

She raises an eyebrow. "Quick bean church."

I tilt my head. "Say that again. I'm pretty sure I misread your lips."

"Quit. Being. A. Jerk."

I grin at my bad lipreading and then kiss her chest. Then her neck. Then I peck her on the lips and pull her off the bed. "Time for our date. Let's get dressed."

She signs, "Where are we going?"

I shrug. "Where do you want to go?"

She grabs her phone while I'm putting on my shirt and she texts me.

Sydney: Would it be weird if we went back to that diner?

I try to recall a diner that we've been to, but the only one I can think of that she might be referring to is the one I took her to the first night we met in person. It was her birthday, and I felt bad that her day was so shitty, so I took her for cake.

Ridge: The one close to my apartment?

She nods.

Ridge: Why would that be weird?

Sydney: Because. It was the first night we met. And maybe going there on our first date would be sort of celebrating that moment.

Ridge: Sydney Blake. You have got to forgive yourself for falling in love with me. We've shared a lot of chapters that don't need to be torn out of our book simply because there are things in them you don't like. It's part of our story. Every single sentence counts toward our happy ending, good or bad.

Sydney reads my text and then slides her phone in her pocket like dinner is solidified thanks to that last text. She signs the next thing she says. "Thank you. That was beautiful. Bridge. Cloud. Pimple."

I laugh. "Was that supposed to be a real sentence?"

Sydney shakes her head. "I don't know how to sign a lot of words yet. I decided I'm just going to make random words up when I don't know how to sign what I really want to say."

I motion for her to get her phone out of her pocket.

Ridge: You said bridge, cloud, and pimple. LOL. What were you trying to sign?

Sydney: I didn't know how to sign that you are getting so lucky after this date tonight.

I laugh and wrap my arms around her, pulling her until her forehead meets my lips. Damn, I cannot get enough of my girl. I also can't get enough of the bridge, cloud, pimple.

• • •

We drove Sydney's car to my apartment because I didn't have my car, and we can't walk to the diner from her apartment like we could from mine. She insisted we walk like we did the last time we came here. Sydney ordered breakfast for dinner, but she also ate half my onion rings and three bites of my burger.

We decided to play twenty questions during dinner, so we used our phones instead of signing because it was hard to do that and eat at the same time. In the forty-five minutes we've been here, I haven't thought about my fight with Maggie. I haven't thought about how behind on work I am. I haven't even thought about that damn *Game of Thrones* spoiler. When I'm with Sydney like this, her presence absorbs all the bad parts of my day, and I find it so easy to concentrate on her and only her.

Until Brennan appears.

Now I'm concentrating on Brennan as he slides into the booth next to Sydney and reaches across the table for my last onion ring.

"Hi." He pops the onion ring into his mouth, and I lean

back in my seat, wondering what the hell he's doing here. Not that I mind. But it is our first official date, and I'm confused why he's crashing it.

"What are you doing here?" I sign.

Brennan shrugs. "I don't have anything scheduled tonight. I was bored and went to your apartment, but you weren't home."

"But how did you know we were here?"

"The app," he says, pulling my soda to him and taking a drink. I give him a look that lets him know I have no idea what he's talking about.

"You know," he says. "Those apps you can use to track people's phones. I track yours all the time."

What the hell? "But you have to set that app up with my phone."

Brennan nods. "I did like a year ago. I know where you are all the time."

That actually explains a lot. "That's weird, Brennan."

He leans back in his seat. "No, it isn't. You're my brother." He looks at Sydney. "Hi. Nice to see you fully clothed."

I kick him under the table, and he just laughs, then folds his arms over the table and speaks his next sentence. "You feel like writing something tonight?"

I shake my head. "I'm on a date with my girlfriend."

Brennan's shoulder's slump, and he falls back against the booth. Sydney looks back and forth between me and Brennan.

"A song?" she says. "You want to write a song tonight?"

Brennan shrugs. "Why not? I need more material, and I'm in the mood. My guitar is in my car."

Sydney perks up and starts nodding. "Please, Ridge? I want to watch you two write a song."

Brennan nods. "Please, Ridge?"

Brennan's begging does nothing to change my mind, but that's only because Sydney's begging already changed it. Besides, the whole time I've been on this date with Sydney, song lyrics have been swirling around in my head. Better to get them out now while I'm feeling it.

I pay the check, and we go outside to head back to the apartment, but Brennan points across the street at a park. He runs to his car and retrieves his guitar and stuff to write with. The three of us walk over to the park and find two benches across from each other. Brennan sits on one, and Sydney and I sit on the other.

Brennan turns his guitar over and presses the notepad to it. He writes on it for a few minutes and then hands it over to me. He's written out the music to a chorus he's working on, but there are no lyrics. I spend several minutes studying it. I can see Brennan and Sydney having a conversation while I look over the music and try to figure out how to add the first line of the chorus. He signs the first part of the conversation, but when he sees I'm not paying attention to either of them, he stops signing and they continue the conversation. I like that they're holding a conversation without me. It's not like the conversations people have where they forget to sign for me. It's just a conversation they're having because they know I need a while to focus on this song.

I think back to Sydney's and my conversation from earlier, and how she expressed a fear that I would someday take Maggie back because I want to fix everything going wrong in Maggie's life. I try to work that into a couple of sentences, but nothing sticks. I close my eyes and try to recall the exact words I said to her.

I would be broken without you. Then who would fix me?

I read that sentence over and over again. *Who would fix me?*

This is how I sometimes build a foundation for my lyrics. I think of a person. I think of a conversation with that person, or a thought I have about that person. And then I ask myself a question about that thought, then build a line of lyrics around the answer.

So . . . who *would* fix me? The only person who could mend my shattered heart would be Sydney.

I find my sweet spot in that answer and write down the lyric, "You're the only one who fixes me."

I tap my pencil on the page in the tempo of the music that Brennan wrote out for me. Brennan picks up his guitar and watches my pencil, then starts to play. I can see Sydney out of the corner of my eye as she pulls her knees up on the bench and wraps her arms around them, watching us. I look at her for a moment, waiting for thoughts of her to inspire another line. What do I want her to know when she hears this song?

I write down several sentences in no particular order,

and none of them rhyme, but they all remind me of Sydney. I'll build around them in a moment and make each of them into verses. I just need to get out the basic things I'm thinking.

There was a truth in you from the start.
I think you're pretty when you speak.
I bring the mess and you bring the clean.
Time will come and you will see.
You're the only one who fixes me.

I look up from the page, and Brennan is still playing, working through the tempo of the song that I just laid his chorus out to. Sydney is watching me, smiling. It's all I need to finish the lyrics. I move to the bench with Brennan and show him the lyrics, matched up with his chorus. He starts tweaking it while I finish the lyrics.

Almost an hour later, we have a complete song. It's the fastest the two of us have ever written together. Brennan hasn't sung any of the lyrics out loud yet for her, so I move to the bench with her and pull her against me before he plays her the full song. He begins strumming his guitar, and she wraps an arm around me, leaning her head against my shoulder.

Wake up early, go to bed late
That's what I do, that's my mistake
Tell me something and I forget
I'm not perfect, I'm far from it

I'm out the door fifteen too late
Thinking I'm early, but I make you wait
Don't wash my dishes for a week
But I think you're pretty when you speak

Ask around, you'll figure out
You're the one I'm thinking 'bout
Time will come and you will see
You're the only one who fixes me
You're the only one who fixes me

I bring the mess and you bring the clean
I think you're funny when you're mean
There was a truth in you from the start
And nothing can break this hold on my heart

Ask around, you'll figure out
You're the one I'm thinking 'bout
Time will come and you will see
You're the only one who fixes me
You're the only one who fixes me, yeah

Out of order, out of my mind
Had you waiting on a white lie
Took a minute but I finally found my way

Ask around, you'll figure out
You're the one I'm thinking 'bout

Time will come and you will see
You're the only one who fixes me

Ask around, you'll figure out
You're the one I'm thinking 'bout
Time will come and you will see
You're the only one who fixes me
You're the only one who fixes me, yeah

When Brennan finishes playing the song, Sydney doesn't move right away. She's curled up to me, her hand fisted in my shirt. I think she must need a moment to absorb that.

When she finally pulls away from my chest, there are tears in her eyes, and she wipes them away with her fingers. Brennan and I wait for her to say something, but she just shakes her head. "Don't make me talk right now. I can't."

Brennan smiles at me. "Speechless. Your girl approves." He stands up and says, "I'm gonna head to your apartment and get this one recorded on my phone while it's fresh in my head. Want a ride?"

Sydney nods and grabs my hand. "Yes. But we aren't staying at Ridge's. We have to go back to my apartment. It's important."

I give her a confused look.

She shoots me an adamant look in return. "Bridge, cloud, pimple. Now."

I smile as she pulls me toward Brennan's car.

I think she loved that song.

Chapter Seventeen

Sydney

Ridge and Brennan have both exited Brennan's car, but I'm still sitting in the front passenger seat, looking at the car parked next to ours. It's Hunter's car. But it's not Hunter shutting the back door. It's Tori. Which is why I'm frozen to my seat, because I wasn't expecting to see her, and I really don't want her to see me. I'm certain it won't end up with me punching her again, but I still have no desire to talk to her.

It's too late, though, because Ridge doesn't recognize her, and he opens my door so that we can move from Brennan's car to Ridge's right as she's walking by. She pauses in her tracks when our eyes meet.

Dammit.

I take Ridge's hand and slowly get out of the car. Tori looks like she's seen a ghost. But she doesn't run away like I wish she would. Instead, she walks the sacks of groceries she's carrying to the hood of her car and sets them down. Then she turns to me, hugging herself.

"Hi," she says. I can tell she wants to talk. And I just don't have it in me to be a complete dick to her.

I look at Ridge. "You go," I sign. "Two minutes."

Ridge glances at Tori and then at me. He nods and backs away, falling into step with Brennan as they head up to Ridge's apartment.

Tori looks good. She's always looked good. I find myself pulling at my ponytail and wiping a wisp of hair out of my face.

"Is that your boyfriend?" she asks.

I glance up at the top of the stairs. Ridge is walking into his apartment backward, looking down at us with concern. I give him a reassuring smile before he closes the door. I turn my attention back to Tori, folding my arms over my chest. "Yeah."

There's a knowing look in Tori's eye. "He's the guy from the balcony, right? The one you were writing lyrics for?"

I suddenly become protective of everything going on in my life, and I don't want to reveal anything to Tori. I don't even know why I'm out here right now. She just seemed like she really wanted me to stop and talk to her. Maybe so she can move past everything that happened between us.

I look behind her, at Hunter's car. There are FOR SALE signs posted in the side and back windows.

"Hunter is selling his car?"

Tori looks over her shoulder at it. "Yeah. We think it has water damage or something. It's been smelling weird for a while now."

I cover my mouth with my hand, ensuring she doesn't see my smile breaking through. When I'm certain I can hold it in, I move my hand and grip the strap of my purse. "That's too bad. I know he loves that car."

Tori's phone rings, and she glances down at it, then answers it, turning away from me a little. Almost as if she doesn't want me to be privy to her conversation.

"What?" she whispers. The way she answers the phone makes it seem like she's irritated with whoever is on the other line. She glances up at her apartment and says, "I still have another load of groceries to bring up. Give me a sec."

She ends the call and slides her phone into her pocket. She walks over to the hood of the car and starts grabbing the sacks of groceries. She stands in front of me, two sacks in each hand, arms down at her sides. "So, um . . ." She pauses and inhales a sharp breath, exhaling it just as quickly. "You wanna grab coffee sometime? I'd really like to catch up. Hear all about the new boyfriend."

I stare at her a moment, wondering why she would think I'm okay with that. I realize I was also a Tori at a very short point during mine and Ridge's friendship, but as mad as I am at Hunter and as mad as Maggie must have been at Ridge, there are few betrayals on earth that hurt worse than the betrayal of your very best friend. She's the person I shared my life with. A home with. All my secrets with. And the entire time we lived together, she was betraying me on a daily basis.

I don't want coffee with her. I don't even want to be outside chatting with her, acting like she didn't break my heart with ten times the strength that Hunter ever could.

I shake my head. "I don't think coffee is a good idea." I choose to walk around the back of her car so that I don't have to get even closer to her. Before I head for the stairs, I look at her. "You really hurt me, Tori. More than Hunter ever could have. But I still think you deserve better than a man who doesn't even bother to come down and help you carry up groceries."

I walk away and run up the stairs, away from her, away from that smelly car, and away from the sad reality that she still hasn't found happiness yet. I wonder if she ever will.

I walk inside the apartment, and Brennan is on the couch with his guitar. He nods his head toward Ridge's room. When I open the door to Ridge's bedroom, he's lying across the bed on his stomach, hugging a pillow. I walk over to him, but he's asleep. I know he's had a long twenty-four hours, so I don't bother waking him. I let him rest.

Brennan is at the table now, playing the song he and Ridge just wrote. I walk to the kitchen and pour myself a glass of wine. There's only enough left for one glass. Bridgette and I really tore through their stash. Ridge is probably going to start keeping the wine in a Windex bottle.

"Sydney?"

I turn toward Brennan, and he's hugging his guitar, his chin resting on it. "I'm really hungry. Do you think you can make me a grilled cheese?"

I laugh as soon as the question comes out of his mouth. But then I realize he's serious. "You're asking me to make you a sandwich?"

"It's been a long day, and I don't know how to cook. Ridge always cooks for me when I'm over here."

"Oh my God. How old are you? Twelve?"

"Transpose those numbers and you've got your answer."

I roll my eyes and open the refrigerator to take out the cheese. "I can't believe I'm making you a sandwich. I feel like I'm disappointing every female who has ever fought for our equality."

"It only counts against feminism when you make your man a sandwich. It doesn't count if it's just a friend."

"Well, we won't even be friends if you think you can ask me to cook for you every time you visit your brother."

Brennan smiles and turns back toward his guitar. He starts strumming it to a tune I haven't heard from him before. Then he starts to sing.

Cheddar, swiss, provolone. That is where I feel at home.
Slap that cheese on some bread. I like it more than getting head.
Grilled cheese,
Grilled cheese,
Grilled cheese from Sydney.
Blake. Not Australia.

I'm laughing at his impressive improv abilities, even though it was a terrible song. He's obviously just as talented as Ridge is. He just suppresses it for some reason.

He sets his guitar on the table and walks over to the bar. He grabs a paper towel and places it in front of him. I guess that's the extent of his sandwich prep.

"Do you even have trouble writing lyrics? Or do you pretend you can't write because of your guilt?"

"What would I have to feel guilty for?" Brennan asks, taking his seat at the bar.

"Just a hunch, but I think you hate that you were born with the ability to hear, and Ridge wasn't. So you pretend you need him more than you actually do. Because you love him." I flip the grilled cheese over. Brennan doesn't respond right away, so I know I have him pegged.

"Does Ridge think that, too?"

I face him full-on. "I don't think so. I think he loves writing lyrics for you. I'm not telling you to stop pretending you don't know how to write lyrics as well as he can. I'm just saying I understand why you do it."

Brennan smiles, relieved. "You're smart, Sydney. You really should consider doing more with your life than just making sandwiches for hungry men."

I laugh and pick up his sandwich with the spatula. I drop it on the paper towel in front of him. "You're right. I quit."

He takes a bite, right as the front door opens. Bridgette walks in holding a sack, wearing her Hooters uniform and a scowl. She sees us in the kitchen and nods, then walks to her room and slams the door. "Did she just nod her head at you?" Brennan asks. "That was an oddly nice gesture that didn't include a middle finger. Does she not hate you anymore?"

"Nah. We're practically best friends now." I start to clean the kitchen, but Bridgette yells my name from her bathroom. Brennan raises an eyebrow, like he's worried for me. I walk toward her bathroom and can hear a lot of commotion. When I open the door, she grabs my wrist and pulls me inside and then slams the door shut. She turns toward the counter and begins dumping out the contents of her sack into the sink.

My eyes go wide when I see five unopened boxes of pregnancy tests. Bridgette starts frantically ripping into one and hands me another. "Hurry," she says. "I have to get this over with before I freak out!" She pulls a stick out of the box and then grabs another one to open.

"I think one is enough to indicate if you're pregnant."

She shakes her head. "I have to be sure I'm not pregnant or I won't sleep until I have twelve periods."

I have two of the tests open, and she rips the last one open, then grabs a mouthwash cup from next to the sink and rinses it out. She pulls down her shorts and sits on the toilet.

"Did you even read the instructions? Are you supposed to pee in an unsanitized cup?"

She ignores me and begins peeing in the cup. When she's finished, she sets it on the counter. "Dip them!" she says.

I stare at her cup of pee and shake my head. "I don't want to."

She flushes the toilet and pulls her shorts up, then shoves me out of the way. She dips all five sticks into the cup at once and holds them there. Then she pulls them out and lays them all on a towel.

This is all happening so fast, I'm not sure I've had time to process the thought that we're about to find out if Bridgette is going to be a mother. Or whether Warren is going to be a father.

"Do either of you even want kids?" I ask.

Bridgette shakes her head adamantly. "Not even a little bit. If I'm pregnant, you can have it."

I don't want it. My idea of hell is having a child composed of pieces of Warren and Bridgette.

"Bridgette!" Warren yells, right before the front door slams shut. Bridgette cringes. The bathroom door swings open, and I suddenly don't feel like I should be in here anymore. "You can't text me something like that in the middle of my study group and then ignore me when I call you back!"

Warren . . . in *study* group? I laugh, but my laughter causes both of them to turn their glares on me. "Sorry. I just can't picture Warren in a study group."

He rolls his eyes. "It's a mandatory group project." He turns his attention back on Bridgette. "Why do you think you're pregnant? You're on the pill."

"Pickles," she says, as if that's a good explanation. "I

stole three pickles off my customers' plates tonight, and I hate pickles. But all I can think about are pickles!" She turns back toward the pregnancy tests and picks one up, but it hasn't been long enough yet.

"*Pickles?*" Warren says, flabbergasted. "Jesus Christ. I thought this was serious. So you craved a fucking pickle."

Warren is stuck on pickles, but I'm still stuck on the idea of Warren in a study group. "When do you graduate?" I ask him.

"Two months."

"Good," Bridgette says. "Because if I'm pregnant, you need to get a real job so you can raise this child."

"You aren't pregnant, Bridgette," Warren says, rolling his eyes. "You craved a pickle. You're so dramatic."

This entire conversation is making me want to ensure Ridge and I use double the protection from now on. I take my birth control religiously, but there's been a time or two that we haven't used a condom. Never again, though.

Bridgette picks up one of the pregnancy tests and presses her hand against her forehead. "Oh, fuck." She turns and tosses the stick toward Warren. It hits him in the cheek and then he fumbles as he tries to catch it.

"Is it positive?" I ask.

Bridgette nods, running her hands down her face. "There's a line! Shit, shit, shit, there's a really long, visible line! Fuck!"

I look at one of the boxes. "A line just means it's working. It doesn't mean you're pregnant."

Warren is holding the stick between two fingers when he drops it back on the towel. "That has your pee on it."

Bridgette rolls her eyes. "No shit, Sherlock. It's a pregnancy test."

"You *threw* it at me. There's pee on my face." He takes a hand towel and wets it under the faucet.

"You aren't pregnant," I reassure her. "It's not a plus sign."

She picks up another one of the tests and studies it, leaning against the counter. "You think?" She picks up one of the boxes and reads it, then sighs with relief. She pours the cup of urine out in the sink.

"Why didn't you pour that in the toilet?" Warren asks with a grossed-out look on his face. This, coming from the guy who ate a bar of cheese after Bridgette tried to wash herself with it.

"I don't know," Bridgette says, looking at the sink. She turns the water on to rinse it out. "I'm distressed. I wasn't thinking."

Warren slips in front of me and wraps his arms around Bridgette, bringing her head to his level. He brushes her hair back gently. "I'm not going to get you pregnant, Bridgette. After our first scare, I wrap my Jimmy Choo up hella tight every time."

I was on my way out of the bathroom to give them privacy, but I freeze when I hear Warren refer to his penis as a Jimmy Choo.

I turn back around. "Jimmy Choo?"

Warren looks at me through the reflection in the mirror. "Yeah, that's his name. Ridge doesn't nickname his penis after cool things?"

"Cool things?" I say. "Jimmy Choos are designer shoes."

"No," Warren says. "A Jimmy Choo is a rare Cuban cigar. Right, Bridgette?" he says, looking at her. "You're the one who named him."

Bridgette tries to keep a straight face, but she sputters laughter. She brushes past me and runs into the living room, but Warren is right on her heels. "You said Jimmy Choos were huge cigars!" They end up on the couch, Warren on top of her. They're both laughing, and it's the first time I've ever really seen them affectionate.

It's disturbing that a pregnancy scare is what brings out the best in them as a couple.

Warren kisses her on the cheek and then says, "We should go celebrate with breakfast tomorrow." He sits up and looks at me and Brennan. "All of us. Breakfast is on me."

Bridgette pushes Warren away from her and stands up. "I will if I wake up on time."

Warren follows her out of the living room and into their bedroom. "Girl, you aren't even sleeping tonight."

Their door closes.

I look at Brennan. He looks away from their door, toward me.

We both just shake our heads.

"I'm heading home," he says, standing up to pack his guitar. He grabs his keys and walks toward the door.

"Thanks for the sandwich, Sydney. Sorry I'm a brat. It's Ridge's fault for spoiling me for so long."

"That's actually good to know. If Ridge is the one who spoiled you, then I'm not going to have to break up with him for expecting me to make him sandwiches."

Brennan laughs. "Please don't break up with him. I think you might be the first thing that's ever made Ridge's life easier."

He closes the door behind him, and I can't help but smile at his parting words. He didn't have to say that, but the fact that he did makes me think Brennan and Ridge are more alike than I initially thought. Both thoughtful.

After Brennan leaves, I lock the front door. I hear a thumping sound behind me, so I spin around and listen for a few seconds to see where it's coming from.

Warren and Bridgette's bedroom.

Oh. *Gross.* Gross, gross, gross.

I rush to Ridge's bedroom and close the door, then crawl into bed with him. I wasn't planning on staying here tonight. I still have homework I haven't finished this weekend, and really do need to have some alone time in order to get it all done. Ridge is way too distracting.

"Syd," Ridge says, rolling toward me. His eyes are closed, and I think he might even still be asleep. "Don't . . . be scared . . . the chicken." He signs the last word.

He's talking and signing in his sleep. I grin at his non-sensical words. Did he talk in his sleep before he started verbalizing? Or is that something new?

I kiss him on the cheek and fold his arm over me as I snuggle against him. I wait to see if he speaks again, but he doesn't. He just sleeps.

• • •

I was awake by seven, but Ridge was still asleep. He woke up sometime in the middle of the night and took off his jeans and shoes, but then went right back to sleep.

I was making a pot of coffee when Warren walked out of his bedroom and told me to stop. "I'm treating you to breakfast, remember?" Then he went to wake up Ridge, but Ridge told him he needed two more hours of sleep.

"Let's let him sleep," I said. "Let me go change out of my pajamas and we can go."

Warren told me no, that the place we're going to eat actually requires pajamas.

I have no idea where we're going, but Bridgette wanted to sleep in, so now it's just me and Warren, going to breakfast in our pajamas to celebrate Bridgette's negative pregnancy test. *Without* Bridgette.

Nope. Not weird at all.

"Did this restaurant just open?" I ask Warren. "Is that why I've never heard of it?" He told me earlier it was called Fastbreak Breakfast, but it doesn't sound familiar.

"We're not going to a restaurant."

I glare at him from the passenger seat, just as he pulls into the parking lot of a hotel and drives around to the side of the building. "Wait here," he says, hopping out of the car. He takes his keys with him.

I sit and watch him as he stands next to the side entrance to the hotel. I start to text Ridge to ask him what the hell I've just gotten myself into, but before I can type out the text, a businessman walks out of the side door and doesn't even notice as Warren grabs the door handle and holds the door open. He waves me out of the car, so I get out and follow him inside, shaking my head. It's finally registered why he told me to wear pajamas. Because he wants it to look like we're guests here.

"Are you kidding me, Warren? We're sneaking into a free continental breakfast?"

He smiles. "Oh, it's not just any free breakfast, Sydney. They have Texas-shaped waffles here."

I can't believe this is his idea of treating people to breakfast. "This is stealing," I whisper, just as we walk into the breakfast area. He reaches for a plate and hands it to me, then grabs his own.

"Maybe so. But it doesn't count against your track record because I'm the one who brought you here."

We make our plates and take a seat at an area by the window that's not visible to the front desk. For the first ten minutes, Warren talks about school, since I was so intrigued by the idea of him actually sitting in a study group. He's majoring in management, which is something else that intrigues me. Baffles me, even. I can't imagine him in a position where he's in charge of other people, but I guess he does manage Sounds of Cedar pretty well.

I don't think I give Warren enough credit. He has a job, he goes to school full-time, he manages a successful local band, and he manages to keep Bridgette somewhat happy. I guess it's just his addiction to porn and his inability to clean up after himself that led me to assume he's got a lot of growing up to do.

When we're finished eating, Warren grabs a tray and piles muffins and juices on it, then brings it back to the table. "For Ridge and Bridgette," he says, covering the muffins with a napkin.

"How often do you come here? You seem to be experienced in the art of breakfast theft."

"Not very often. I have a few hotels around town that I frequent, but I try to mix it up every now and then. Don't want the desk clerks becoming suspicious."

I laugh, sipping the last of my orange juice.

"Ridge has never been on board. You know how he is, always trying to do the right thing. Maggie came with me a few times, though. She liked the thrill of possibly getting caught. She's actually why I call it Fastbreak Breakfast. We had to make a break for it once because a clerk walked around writing down room numbers and checking them to last names."

I look down when he says Maggie's name, not wanting to hear how good of friends he is with her. Not that I care if Warren and Maggie are friends. I just don't want to hear about it. Especially this early in the morning.

He notices my reaction, because he leans forward and

folds his arms over the table. He tilts his head in thought. "Our friendship with her really bothers you, huh?"

I shake my head. "Not as much as you probably think. What bothers me is how much Ridge stresses about it."

"Yeah, well, imagine how much Maggie stresses about it."

I roll my eyes. I know how much Maggie probably stresses about it. But just because she stresses more than I do doesn't mean I'm not allowed to stress. "I already told Ridge it's just going to take me a little time to get used to it."

Warren laughs under his breath. "Well, hurry up and get used to it, because I already told you once that he'll never leave her."

I remember that night very clearly. I don't need Warren to point it out again. It was when Ridge and I were hugging in the hallway. Warren walked inside the apartment and didn't like what he was seeing, because Ridge was dating Maggie at the time. Ridge didn't know Warren was in the apartment, but before Warren walked to his room, he made sure I was aware of his thoughts on our predicament. Warren's exact words were, *I'm only going to say this once, and I need you to listen. He will never leave her, Sydney.*

I lean back in my seat, growing defensive like I always do when Warren talks about Ridge's and my relationship. He always seems to take it a step too far, even though I feel like I've been more than accommodating and understanding when it comes to Ridge's friendship with Maggie. "You did say that," I agree. "But you were wrong, because they did break up."

Warren stands up and begins gathering trash from the

table. He shrugs. "They broke up, sure. But I didn't tell you they'd never break up. I told you he'd never *leave* her. And he won't. So maybe instead of trying to convince yourself that you just need time to warm up to the idea of her always being a part of his life, you should remind yourself that you already knew that. Long before you agreed to start a relationship with him."

I stare at him, dumbfounded, as he walks the trash to the trash can. He comes back to the table and reclaims his seat. I forget what a casual asshole he can be to everyone. I recall his words again, only this time they mean something completely different.

He will never leave her, Sydney.

This whole time, I thought Warren was saying Ridge would never break up with her, when all along, Warren just meant that Maggie would always be a part of Ridge's life.

"You know the one thing that could make this entire situation a little easier?" Warren asks.

I shake my head, unsure about anything anymore. He looks at me pointedly. "You."

What?

"Me? How could I make it easier? If you haven't noticed, I've worked really hard to try and have the patience of a freaking saint."

He nods in agreement. "I'm not talking about your patience," he says, leaning forward. "You have been patient. But what you *haven't* been is apologetic. There's a girl you seriously wronged, who is a huge part of Ridge's life. And even though she claims not to blame you, you probably still owe her an apology. Apologies shouldn't happen because of the response of the person who was wronged. Apologies should happen because of the wrong." He slaps his hands on the table like the conversation is over, and he stands up, grabbing the tray of food he made for Ridge and Bridgette.

My stomach turns at the thought of being face-to-face with Maggie after everything that has happened. And even though I don't take any responsibility for all the resentment she and Ridge have been building up toward each other over the years, I do take responsibility for the fact that I was a Tori for a hot minute and never once reached out to her to apologize.

"Come on," Warren says, pulling me up and out of my stupor. "There are worse things in life than having a boyfriend with a heart the size of an elephant's."

• • •

I'm completely silent on the ride home. Warren doesn't even try to get me to talk. When we get back to Ridge's apartment, Ridge is still asleep. I write him a note and leave it beside him on the bed.

> *Didn't want to wake you because you deserve the sleep. I've got a lot of homework to catch up on today, so maybe I can come over tomorrow night after work.*
>
> *I love you.*
> *Sydney.*

I feel bad lying to him, because I'm not going home to do homework. I'm going home to change clothes.

This drive to San Antonio is long overdue.

Chapter Eighteen

Maggie

My mother was a dramatic woman. Everything revolved around her, even when it wasn't about her. She was the type of person who, when someone close to her would experience something bad in their lives, would somehow relate it to her own life so that their tragedy could be her tragedy, too. Imagine what having a daughter with cystic fibrosis was like for her. It was her moment to soak up the sympathy—to make everyone feel sorry for her and the way her child had turned out. My illness became more of a problem for her than it was for me.

But it didn't last long, because she took a temporary position with her company in Paris, France, when I was three. She left me with my grandparents because it was "too cold" for me there, and it would be "too difficult" learning to navigate a new country with a sick child in tow. My father was never a part of my life, so that wasn't an option. But my mother always promised she would one day take me to Paris to live with her.

My grandparents had my mother at a very late age, and my mother had me in her late thirties. It was getting to the point that my grandparents could hardly care for themselves, much less a child. But my mother's temporary position became permanent, and every year when she would come home to visit, she would promise me she'd take me back with her when the time was right. But her Christmas visits would always end on New Year's Day, with her leaving to go back to Paris without me.

Maybe she did have intentions of taking me back with her, but after spending two weeks with me at my grandparents' every year at Christmas, she would be reminded of what a huge responsibility I would be in her life. I used to think it was because she didn't love me, but I remember the year I turned nine, I figured out that my illness was what she didn't love about me. It wasn't me.

I got the idea that if I could just convince her that I could take care of myself and that I didn't need her help, she would take me with her and we could finally be together. In the weeks leading up to Christmas the year I turned nine, I was extremely cautious. I consumed all the vitamins I could get my hands on so that I wouldn't catch a cold from my classmates. I used my vest twice as much as I was required to. I made sure I got eight hours of sleep every night. And even though Austin saw its first snow in years that winter,

I refused to go outside to experience it because I was afraid I'd catch a cold and end up in the hospital during my mother's visit.

When she arrived the week before Christmas, I was very careful never to cough in front of her. I wouldn't take my medications in front of her. I did everything I could to appear like a vibrant, healthy child so that she'd have no choice but to see me as the child she'd always wished I was and that she would take me back to Paris with her. But that didn't happen because on Christmas morning, I overheard her and my grandmother having an argument. My grandmother was telling my mother that she wanted her to move back to the States. She said she was concerned about what would happen to me when they died of old age. *What will Maggie do when we're gone if you're not around to care for her? You need to come back to the States and develop a better relationship with her.*

I will never forget the words my mother said to her in response.

You're worried about things that may never happen, Mother. Maggie will more than likely succumb to her illness before either of you succumb to old age.

I was so shattered by her response to my grandmother that I ran back to my bedroom and refused to speak to her for the rest of her trip. In fact, that was the last time I ever spoke to her. She cut her trip short and left the day after Christmas.

She sort of faded out of my life after that. She called

my grandmother to check in every month or so, but she never came back for Christmas, because every year I told my grandmother I didn't want to see her. Then, when I was fourteen, my mother passed away. She was traveling from France to Brussels on a train for a business trip and suffered a massive heart attack. No one on the train even noticed she had died until three stations past her stop.

When I found out about her death, I went to my bedroom and cried. But I didn't cry because she'd died. I cried because as dramatic as she was, she never made a dramatic attempt at winning my forgiveness. I think it's because it was easier for her to live a life without me while I was mad at her than when I was missing her.

Two years after her passing, my grandmother died. That was the hardest thing I've ever endured. I still don't think I've fully absorbed her passing. She loved me more than anyone had ever loved me, so when she died, I felt the absolute loss of that love.

And now my grandfather—the last of the people who raised me—has been put in hospice due to recently declined health, coupled with a case of pneumonia he's too weak to fight. My grandfather will pass away any day now, and because of my cystic fibrosis and the nature of his illness, I am not allowed to see him and tell him goodbye. He'll likely die sometime this week, and just like my grandmother feared, they'll all be gone and I'll be all alone.

I guess my mother was wrong about me succumbing to my illness before them. I'll outlive them all.

I know my experience with my mother hinders all my other relationships. It's hard for me to fathom that someone else could love me despite my illness, when my own mother wasn't even able to do that.

Ridge did, though. He was in it with me for the long haul. But I guess that was the problem. Ridge and I wouldn't have stayed together as long as we did if it weren't for my illness. We were too different. So I guess whatever end of the spectrum people are on—whether they are too selfish to take care of me or too selfless to stop—I'm going to resent them. Because for whatever reason, I seem to have lost a piece of myself to this illness.

I wake up thinking about this illness. I spend my days thinking about it. I fall asleep thinking about it. I even have nightmares about it. As much as I claim that I am not my illness, somewhere along the way, it has consumed me.

There are days I'm able to break out of this web, but there are more days that I'm not. It's why I never wanted Ridge to move in with me. I can lie to myself and lie to him and say that it's because I wanted to be independent, but in reality, it's because I didn't want him to see the dark side of me. The side that gives up more than it fights. The side that resents more than it appreciates. The side that wants to face all of this with dignity, when really, I can hardly even accept it with disdain.

I'm sure everyone who fights to live on a daily basis has moments where they give up every now and again. But these aren't just moments for me. Lately, they've become my norm.

I wish I could go back to Tuesday. Tuesday was great. Tuesday, I woke up wanting to conquer the world. And by Tuesday night, I sort of had.

But then Wednesday morning happened, when I overreacted and made Jake leave. Friday happened, when I finally swallowed my pride, but then ended up in the hospital, drowning in my own humiliation. Then Friday night happened, when I just wanted to forget the ups and downs of the past few days, but our fight was a new low for the week.

And if Friday night was my low, Saturday morning was my rock bottom.

Or maybe today is. I don't know. I'd say they've been equal.

I can't even focus on school. I have two months left, and I sometimes think Ridge was right. I've worked so hard on my graduate degree in order to begin work on my doctorate, only to feel like I accomplished something. But maybe I should have put all my energy into something more worthwhile, like making friends and building an actual life for myself outside of school and my illness.

I've worked at proving myself to no one but myself. In the end, it's left me with nothing but a graduate degree that no one really cares about but me.

I wish there were a magic pill that could get me out of this funk. I'm sure if Warren had his way, that magic pill would come in the form of an apology. He texted me this morning to let me know he was sorry for the stunt he pulled when he told Ridge I was upset, but then he scolded me for posting that picture of Ridge in my bed and told me I should apologize.

I didn't respond to him, because I wasn't in the mood for Righteous Warren this morning. I swear, every time there's a wrinkle in a scenario, he pulls out his iron and tries to smooth everything, while burning us all in the process. He's like a Sour Patch Kid. Sour and then sweet. Or sweet and then sour. There's no in between with Warren. He's completely transparent, and sometimes that's not a good thing.

But I've never had to wonder what Warren is thinking, nor have I ever worried about hurting his feelings. He's impenetrable, but I think because he's impenetrable, he assumes everyone else is, too. As much as I can appreciate him, it's not enough for me to respond to his texts from this morning with anything other than Don't want to talk about it yet. Text you tomorrow.

I knew if I didn't let him know I was okay, he'd show up at my front door to make sure nothing happened to me. Which is precisely why I texted him.

But . . . I don't think it worked. Because my doorbell is ringing. There's only a small chance that it's Warren, though. My bet is that it's my landlord. Since I informed her a few months ago that I'd be moving back to Austin soon to start my doctorate, she's brought me a loaf of banana bread every Sunday. I think she does it to make sure I'm still living here and that I haven't destroyed the house, but whether it's out of kindness or nosiness, I don't really care. It's damn good banana bread.

I open the door and force a smile, but my smile falls flat. It's not banana bread.

It's Sydney.

I am so confused. I glance behind her and look to see if she's here with Ridge, but Ridge isn't behind her. Nor is his car in the driveway. I look at her.

"It's just me," she says.

Why would Sydney show up at my house alone? I look her up and down, taking in her casual jeans and T-shirt, her flip-flops, her thick blond hair that's pulled up into a pony-tail. I don't know why she's here, but if any other girlfriend showed up at their boyfriend's ex-girlfriend's house, they wouldn't show up looking this casual, even if it were just to borrow a cup of sugar. Women like making other women jealous. They especially like making the women who have slept with the men they're in love with jealous. Most women would show up in their most flattering outfit with sculpted makeup and perfect hair.

Seeing Sydney at my front door is jarring enough for me to want to close it in her face, but seeing that her goal has nothing to do with making me envious of her is enough for me to step back and wave her inside.

There can only be one other reason she's here.

"Are you here about the Instagram post?" *She must be.* She's never been here before. In fact, we haven't spoken since the day I read all the messages between the two of them.

Sydney shakes her head as her eyes dart around the living room, taking in my home. She doesn't seem nervous, but she steps inside my house so cautiously that it makes her seem somewhat vulnerable. I wonder if Ridge knows she's here. It's not like him to allow his girlfriend to show up and fight his battles for him. And Sydney doesn't seem like the type who would fight his battles.

Which can only mean she's here to fight her own battle.

"Sorry to just show up like this," she says. "I would have texted you first, but I was worried you would tell me not to come."

She's right, but I don't admit that out loud. I watch her for a moment and then turn and walk to my kitchen. "You want something to drink?" I ask, looking back at her.

She nods. "Water would be nice."

I grab two bottles of water out of the refrigerator and motion her over to my dining room table. Something tells me this conversation is going to be more fitting for the table than a couch. We both take a seat across from each other. Sydney sets her phone and her keys beside her and opens the bottle of water. She takes a big swig and then puts the lid back on it, hugging the bottle to her as she leans forward on the table.

"What are you doing here?" I don't mean for my voice to sound so stiff, but this is all so weird.

She licks her lips to moisten them, which makes me think she is nervous. "I'm here to apologize to you," she says, matter-of-fact.

I narrow my eyes, trying to make sense of this. I spend

the night fighting with her boyfriend, then I post a picture on Instagram in a moment of selfish stupidity, yet she says she's here to apologize to me? There must be a catch.

"Apologize for what?"

She blows out a quick breath but holds eye contact with me. "For kissing Ridge when I knew he was dating you. I never apologized to you. It was shitty of me, and I'm sorry."

I shake my head, still confused why she drove all the way here for an apology I'm not even in need of. "I've never expected an apology from you, Sydney. You weren't the one in a relationship with me. Ridge was."

Sydney's mouth twitches a little, like she's relieved I'm not full of rage, but she knows the situation doesn't call for a smile of relief. She nods instead. "Even still. You didn't deserve what happened to you. I know what it feels like when someone you love betrays you. I once punched a girl in her face for sleeping with my boyfriend, and you didn't even yell at me for falling in love with yours."

I appreciate that she recognizes as much. "It was hard for me to figure out who to be angry at after reading all the messages," I admit. "You both seemed to try so hard to do the right thing. But from what Ridge told me about your last relationship, that experience was a lot different from what happened between you and Ridge. Your friend and boyfriend put your feelings last with their affair, but you and Ridge seemed to at least attempt to put my feelings first."

Sydney nods. "He cares about you," she says, her voice

barely above a whisper. "He worries a lot. Even still." She takes another sip from her water bottle.

Her words fill me with even more regret over what happened between Ridge and me this weekend. Because I know he worries. And I feel like it's my fault he still has to worry about me. Not only because I don't take care of myself in all the ways he would like, but because I put this on him to begin with. I allowed a relationship to start up with him, knowing if we didn't work out in the end, a part of him would always stay with me because that's just the type of human he is. I'm not in a situation where he can choose to walk away from me completely and feel okay with that choice. Which must affect Sydney somehow, knowing she'll never be rid of me until I make that final choice to cut my friendship off from Ridge completely. It's just impossible to cut me out of his life entirely when we'll still have a mutual friend.

I lean forward and fold my arms over the table, tugging at my shirtsleeve while I look down at it. "Is that why you're here?" I ask, looking up at her. "To tell me you want me out of the picture?"

I expect her to nod now that I've pegged the reason she drove all the way from Austin. She needed to clear her conscience before asking me politely to never speak to Ridge again. But she doesn't nod. She doesn't shake her head. She just stares at me as if she's trying to form an answer that won't offend me.

"Ridge will worry about you whether he's an active

part of your life or not. I'm here because I want to make sure you're okay. And if you aren't, I want to know what I can do to help get you there. Because if you're okay, Ridge won't worry as much. And then I won't have to worry about Ridge."

I don't know what to say to that. I'm not even sure if I should feel offended by it. She's here, not because she's worried about *me* but because she's worried about Ridge. Part of me wants to tell her to leave, but part of me is relieved she said that. Because if she pretended to be worried about me, I wouldn't believe her. She's a little like Warren in that respect—transparent to the point that it sometimes stings.

Sydney blows out a heavy breath and then says, "I've spent a lot of time trying to put myself in your shoes. Telling myself what I would do differently if I were you." She's not looking at me as she speaks. She's fidgeting with the label on her bottle of water, avoiding eye contact with me. "I tell myself that I would take better care of my health than you do. Or that I wouldn't make irresponsible choices, like leaving a hospital before I'm discharged. But those things are easy for me to say because I'm not actually in your shoes. I can't even fathom what you go through, Maggie. I don't know what it's like to have to take multiple medications every day, or to visit the doctor more than I visit my own parents. I don't have to worry about germs every time I step foot out my front door or every time someone touches me. I don't base my entire schedule around treatments I'm forced to give myself in order to simply take a breath. I don't have to base every life decision I make on the chance that I'll likely die sometime in the next decade. And I can't sit here and assume that if I were in your shoes, I wouldn't fault Ridge for caring too much about me. Because the only thing that ties him to me is his love. There are no other factors tying him to me, so I can see why you would grow to resent that about him. He tried to protect you, but you just wanted him to ignore your illness so that you could ignore it, too."

She finally looks up from her water bottle, and I swear there are tears in her eyes. "I know I don't know you very well at all," she says. "But I do know that Ridge would not be as upset as he is if there weren't a million qualities that he sees in you. I'm hoping one of those qualities is your ability to swallow your pride enough to realize that you should apologize to him for making him feel the way he felt after leaving your house Saturday. He deserves at least that much after how hard he's loved you, Maggie."

She swipes at a tear. I open my mouth to respond, but nothing comes out. I'm in shock, I think. I wasn't expecting her to be here because she wants me to contact Ridge.

"You may think you don't need him, and maybe that's true," she adds. "Maybe you don't. But Ridge needs you. He needs to know that you're taken care of and that you're safe, because if he doesn't at least have that reassurance, his worry and guilt are going to eat at him. And to answer your question from earlier . . . No. I don't want you out of the picture. This was your picture first. Yours and Warren's and Ridge's. But now that I'm a part of it, we all need to figure out how to fit in the frame."

I'm still at a loss for words. I take a sip of my water and then slowly screw the cap back on, staring down at it, avoiding Sydney's teary eyes. I'm trying to make sense of everything she just said without taking too much time before I respond. "That was a lot," I say. "I need a moment."

Sydney nods. We sit together in silence for a bit while I process everything. While I process her. I don't understand her. How can one person be this understanding? It would be so easy for her to be in Ridge's ear right now instead of mine, convincing him that I don't appreciate him and all that he's done for me. But instead, she's here. More than likely without his knowledge. She's not fighting to erase me from the picture—one I honestly no longer belong in. She's fighting to fit into a picture that already exists. To embrace its inhabitants. *To be included.*

"You're a better person than me," I finally say. "I can see now why he fell in love with you."

Sydney smiles a little. "He once fell in love with you, too, Maggie. I find it hard to believe he didn't have a million reasons for doing so."

I stare at her, wondering if that's actually true. I've always felt like my illness was the reason Ridge fell in love with me. I even said that to him once. My exact words were, *I think my illness is the thing you love the most about me.* I said it right here in the living room when we ended things for good.

But maybe that wasn't true. Maybe he loved me for me, and in doing so, he really did want the best for me because of me, and not because of his personality.

My God, my mother sure fucked me up. I guess that's expected, though. When you have a mother who can't love you, how are you supposed to believe anyone else could?

Sydney is right. Ridge deserves a lot more respect than what I've given him. He also deserves the girl sitting across from me right now, because this situation could have taken so many possible roads, but Sydney chose the high one. When a person takes the high road, it encourages those around them to do the same.

It might be a tight and awkward fit at first, but I'm glad she's now in our frame.

Chapter Nineteen

Ridge

I'm walking around my apartment on eggshells, afraid to open doors, afraid to eat food out of the refrigerator, afraid to go to sleep. It's Warren's turn to prank me, so I'm expecting it every hour and with everything I eat or drink. But it never comes. Which makes me even more paranoid.

Maybe not pranking me *is* the prank.

No, he's not that clever.

I wish I could stay over at Sydney's place tonight just to get rid of this paranoia, but she works at the library until close, so she won't even be home until after midnight. Then she has class at eight in the morning.

I haven't seen her since Saturday. Or Sunday, really, but I slept so hard I don't even remember her leaving for breakfast or writing me the note. But it's Tuesday now, and I'm going through Sydney withdrawals.

I'm finally caught up on work, though. And I've sent Brennan lyrics to a whole new song. Now I'm googling new ways to prank Warren because I feel like I need to stay a step ahead of him, but the best Google can come up with are the Post-it note pranks we refuse to stoop to. Everything else, we've tried.

I'm watching a video compilation on YouTube of roommates pranking each other when I feel my phone vibrate on my bed.

Sydney: I'm tired of restocking books. They really should have robots for this by now.

Ridge: But then you'd be out of a job.

Sydney: Unless I was an engineer. Then I could be in charge of the robot.

Ridge: Maybe you should switch your major.

Sydney: What are you doing right now?

Ridge: Googling ways to prank Warren. I'm out of ideas. You got any?

Sydney: You should fill a box with five kittens and put it in his bedroom. Because buying your friend one kitten is kind of sweet, but buying them five kittens is terrible.

Ridge: I'm not sure that would be funny for me because he'd probably keep all five of them and I'd end up having to pay five pet deposits.

Sydney: Yeah, that was a terrible prank idea.

Ridge: I see nothing has changed. I'm still the prank master.

Sydney: Says the guy who's experiencing a bad case of pranker's block.

Ridge: Touché. Hey, do you get a lunch break tonight?

Sydney: Just took it at six. :/

Ridge: Dammit. I guess I'll see you tomorrow afternoon. You want me to come to your place?

Sydney: Yes, please. I want you all to myself for the night.

Ridge: Then I am yours. I love you. See you tomorrow.

Sydney: Love you.

I close out our texts and open up the missed text from Bridgette I just received while I was saying goodbye to Sydney. Bridgette never texts me unless it's to tell me something in the apartment is broken. Not this time, though. Her text simply says, Someone is at the door, like she's too busy to get up and answer it. She never does answer the door, though. I wonder if that's because she doesn't really feel like this is her apartment.

I walk to my closet and grab a T-shirt, pulling it over my head as I make my way to the front door. I look through the peephole while my hand is turning the doorknob, but I stop turning it as soon as I recognize Maggie. She's standing in front of the door, hugging herself as the wind whips her hair around.

The next few seconds are a little bizarre for me. I watch her for a moment, wondering what she wants, but not wondering enough to open the door in a hurry. I turn around and face the living room, needing a second to focus on my next move. This is the first time she's shown up at my apartment as something other than my girlfriend. I've never opened the door for her and not immediately kissed her.

I've never opened the door for her without pulling her to my bedroom. I have no desire to do either of those things, nor do I feel a loss because it's no longer our routine. I just feel . . . different.

I turn and open the door, just as she gives up and walks toward the apartment stairs. She glances up at me and pauses her foot over the first step, then slowly turns around and faces me. Her expression is calm. She isn't looking at me like she can't stand me—like she was looking at me this past weekend. She lifts her hand and pushes her hair from her face, waiting for me to invite her in. There's an air of humility about her as she glances down at her feet for a few seconds. When our eyes meet again, I step back and hold the door open. She stares at her feet as she walks into the apartment.

I slide my phone out of my pocket as Maggie stands in the middle of the living room. I don't want this becoming anything it isn't, so I text Sydney.

Ridge: Maggie just showed up unannounced. Not sure what she's here for yet, but I wanted you to know.

I slide my phone back into my pocket and look up at Maggie. She motions to the refrigerator and asks if she can grab something to drink. It's odd, because she would never have asked before. She would have just grabbed a drink. I nod and say, "Of course."

She walks to the refrigerator and opens the door, but she just stares inside blankly for a moment. That's when I realize I don't have any Dr Pepper for her. I used to keep the refrigerator stocked with Dr Pepper for whenever she showed up, but it's been months since she's been here. I stopped buying Dr Pepper after we broke up. It was odd at first, not grabbing the usual twelve-pack I used to get every time I went grocery shopping, but I don't even think about it anymore. Now I just make sure I have water and tea.

She grabs two waters and hands me one of them. "Thank you," I say.

She points to the kitchen table and signs, "Do you have a minute?"

I nod, but am very aware my phone hasn't buzzed in my pocket. Either Sydney hasn't read my text yet, or she's upset that Maggie showed up here. I'm hoping it's the former. I'm sure it is. Sydney is the most reasonable person I've ever met. Even if it upset her that Maggie showed up here, she would still text me back.

We're both at the table now, me at the head of it and her in the chair to my right. She takes her jacket off and then folds her hands together in front of her, resting her elbows on the table. She's staring down at them, inhaling a calming breath. Her eyes swing in my direction when she begins to sign. "I would have come by sooner, but my grandfather died two days ago. Sunday night."

I immediately blow out a breath and grab her hand. I squeeze it, then pull her in for a hug. I feel like such an asshole right now. I knew he was sick. No matter how things were left between us Saturday morning, I should have checked in with her about her grandfather. He died two days ago, and I had no idea. Why wouldn't she at least tell Warren?

I pull back to ask her if she's okay, but she answers the question before I'm even able to ask it. "I'm okay," she signs. "You know it's been expected for a while now. My aunt flew in from Tennessee and helped with the arrangements today. We decided against a service."

Her eyes are red and a little puffy, like she's already cried enough about it. "That's not why I'm here, though. I was in Austin and wanted to stop by because . . ." She pauses to take a drink and to gather herself. It's a big jump going from the death of her grandfather to another subject entirely. She seems a little jarred, so I give her a minute. She wipes her mouth with her sleeve and then looks at me again. "I'm here because I have a lot to say, and I'd like the opportunity to get it all out before you interrupt me, okay? You know how hard it is for me to apologize."

She's here to *apologize*? Wow. This isn't what I was expecting, because she's right. It's very hard for her to apologize. It's one of the things that are so different about Maggie and Sydney; it's difficult getting used to. Sydney is quick to forgive and quick to ask for forgiveness, whereas with Maggie, everything needs a period of adjustment.

Like right now. She takes an entire minute to adjust to what she's about to say before she actually says it.

"You told me once that when you wore hearing aids, they were a constant reminder that you couldn't hear. And that when you didn't wear them, you didn't even think about it," she signs. "That's how I've always felt about my illness, Ridge. About doctors and hospitals and medications and my vest. It's all a constant reminder that I have this illness, but when I'm able to avoid those things, I don't even think about it. And it's nice, being able to have those moments of normalcy sometimes. And being with you in the beginning was part of my cherished moments of normalcy. We had just begun dating, and we couldn't get enough of each other. But the longer we were together, you started to notice that I would skip treatments or doctors' visits in favor of being with you."

She pauses a moment, like what she's trying to say is taking a huge amount of courage. And it is. So I wait patiently without interrupting like I promised her I would.

"After a while, you started to worry about me," she says. "You took over my schedule to make sure I was on time to every appointment. You texted me several times a day to tell me it was time for my treatments. I even caught you counting my pills once so you could be positive I was taking them like I was supposed to. And I know that every single one of those things was for my benefit, because you loved me. But I started lumping you in with all the things I wanted to avoid, like doctor's appointments and breathing treatments." She looks me in the eyes. "You became one of the constant reminders that I was living with this illness. And I didn't know how to deal with that."

A tear falls out of her eye, and she swipes it away with her sleeve.

"I know I sometimes didn't show it, but I did appreciate you. I do appreciate you. So much. It's just so confusing for me because I also resented you, but my resentment had everything to do with me and nothing at all to do with you. I know that everything you did for me is because you wanted the best for me. I know that you loved me. The things I said to you the other day came from a part of me that I'm not proud of. And . . ." Her lips are quivering, and tears are beginning to fall down her cheeks in pairs. "I'm sorry, Ridge. I really am. For everything."

I blow out a quick, shaky breath.

I need out of this chair.

I stand up and walk to the kitchen and grab her a napkin, then take it back to her. But I can't sit down. I wasn't expecting this, and I don't even know how to respond to her. Sometimes I don't say the right things to her, and it upsets her. She's already upset enough. I put my hands on the back of my neck and pace the living room a couple of times. I come to a pause when I feel my phone vibrate. I grab it.

Sydney: Thanks for letting me know. Be patient with her, Ridge. I'm sure it took a lot of courage for her to show up there.

I stare at Sydney's text and shake my head, wondering how in the hell she's more understanding of my own situation than even I am. I honestly don't know why she's majoring in music. Her real talent is psychology.

I slide the phone back into my pocket and look over at Maggie, who is still sitting at the table, dabbing at her tearful eyes. This had to be hard for her. Sydney is right. Being here and then saying everything she just said has to be taking a huge amount of courage.

I walk back to my seat, and I reach across the table and take her hand. I hold it between both of mine. "I'm sorry, too," I say, squeezing her hand so that she can feel the sincerity in that statement. "I should have been more of a boyfriend to you and less of a . . . dictator."

My word choice makes her laugh through her tears. She shakes her head. "You weren't a dictator," she signs. "Maybe more of a mild authoritarian."

I laugh with her. Which is something I never thought would happen again after leaving her house Saturday morning.

Maggie's head swings in the other direction, so I look up to see Bridgette. She's leaving for work, but pauses when she sees Maggie in our living room, sitting next to me at the table. She glances at Maggie for a moment, then at me. Her eyes narrow.

"Dick."

She marches to the front door, and I'm pretty sure she probably slams it when she leaves. I look back at Maggie, and she's staring at the door. "What was that all about?"

I shrug. "She's become oddly protective of Sydney now. It's been . . . interesting."

Maggie arches a brow. "Maybe you should text Sydney and let her know I'm here. Before Bridgette does."

I smile. "I already did."

Maggie nods knowingly. "Of course you did," she signs.

She's smiling now, and the tears are no longer invading her eyes. She takes another sip of water and then leans back in her chair. "So. Is Sydney the one?"

I don't respond for a moment, because it's odd. I don't want Maggie thinking she lacked anything, but it's simply different with Sydney. It's more. It's deeper and better, and I crave it like I've never craved anything, but how do I express that without being insensitive to what Maggie and I had? I nod slowly and sign, "She is definitely the last one."

Maggie nods, and a sadness enters her eyes. I hate it. But I can't do anything to change it. Things are how they're supposed to be now, even if Maggie might sometimes feel regret for that.

"I wish life came with a handbook," she says. "Seeing what you and Sydney have makes me realize what an idiot I am for pushing away a really great guy. I'm almost positive I ruined that chance for good."

I shift in my seat with those words. I don't even know what to say. Did she think coming here would open up an opportunity to get back together with me? If so, I've been treating this entire conversation as something it isn't. "Maggie. I'm not—*we're* not ever getting back together."

Maggie's eyes narrow, and she gives me one of the looks she used to give me when I was being an idiot. "I'm not talking about *you*, Ridge." She laughs. "I'm referring to my hot doctor–slash–skydiving instructor."

I tilt my head, feeling both relieved and embarrassed. "Oh. Well. That was awkward."

She starts to laugh again. She swings a finger back and forth between us. "You thought . . . When I said *great guy* . . . you immediately thought of yourself?" She's laughing even harder now. I'm trying not to crack a smile, but I can't help it. I love that she's laughing, and I love even more that she's talking about someone else.

This is good.

Maggie stands up. "Will Warren be here Saturday?" I nod and stand as well. "Yeah, he should be. Why?"

"I want us all to sit down together and talk. I feel like we need to map out a plan going forward."

"Yeah. Of course. I'd love it if we could do that. Do you mind if Sydney comes?"

Maggie puts on her jacket. "She already has it on her schedule," Maggie says, winking at me.

Okay, now I'm confused. "You've talked to Sydney?"

Maggie nods. "For some reason, she felt like she owed me an apology. And . . . I owed her one. We had a good chat." Maggie walks toward the door but pauses before opening it. "She's very . . . diplomatic."

I nod, but I'm still confused about when they had this chat. Or why I didn't know about it. "Yeah," I say. "She is definitely diplomatic."

Maggie opens the door. "Don't let Bridgette ruin her," she says. "See you Saturday."

"See you Saturday." I hold the door open for her. "And Maggie. I'm really sorry about your grandfather."

She smiles. "Thank you."

I watch as she walks down the stairs to her car. Once she pulls away, I don't close my door. I rush to my counter and grab my keys, then slip on my shoes.

I drive straight to the library.

• • •

I spot her in the back corner of the library. She's next to a cart, holding a marker in her hand, crossing things out on a list as she restocks the shelves from her library cart. Her back is to me, so I watch her for an entire minute as she works. The place is mostly empty, so I don't feel like anyone will notice that I'm staring at her. I just can't understand when or how she and Maggie would have had a conversation. Or why. I pull out my phone and I text her.

Ridge: You and Maggie had a conversation and you didn't tell me?

I watch her reaction as she reads the text. She freezes, staring down at the phone, and then she rubs her forehead. She leans against the library shelf and inhales a deep breath.

Sydney: Yes. I should have told you. I just wanted the two of you to have the chance to speak before I brought it up, but I drove to her house on Sunday. Not to start drama, I swear. I just had some things I needed to say to her. I'm sorry, Ridge.

I look back up at her, and everything about her is on edge now. She's worried, rubbing the back of her neck now, refusing to pull her eyes away from her phone until I text her back.

I hold up my phone and snap a picture of her, then text

it to her. It takes a moment for the picture to come through on her end, but as soon as it does, she spins around. Our eyes lock.

I shake my head, just barely, but not because I'm upset with her in any way, shape, or form. I shake my head in slight disbelief that this woman would take it upon herself to drive to my ex-girlfriend's house because she wanted to make things better between us.

I have never felt this amount of appreciation for anyone or anything in my entire life.

I begin to walk toward her. She pushes off the bookshelf when I get closer and stands, stiff, anticipating my next move. When I reach her, I don't say or sign a single word. I don't have to. She knows exactly what I'm thinking, because with Sydney, all she has to do is be near me for us to communicate. She looks up at me, and I look down at her, and as if we're in perfect sync, she takes two steps back and I take two steps forward, so that we're hidden between two walls of books.

I love you.

I don't say or sign those words. I only feel them, but she hears it.

I lift my hands and run my fingers down her cheeks. I try to touch her with the same softness that she uses to touch me. I drag my thumbs over her lips, admiring her mouth and every gentle word that comes out of it. I slide my hands down to her neck and press my thumbs against her throat. I can feel her rapid pulse beneath my fingertips.

I lower my forehead to hers, and I close my eyes. I just want to feel her heartbeat against my thumbs. I want to feel her breath against my lips. I take a moment and do these things while I silently thank her, our foreheads still pressed together.

I wish we weren't in public right now. I would thank her in so many more ways, and without using a single word.

I keep my hands on her throat and press myself against her to turn and position her against the bookshelves behind her. When her back meets the books, I keep her face tilted up toward mine, while drawing our mouths closer together, barely connecting mine to hers. I can feel her rapid breaths crashing against my lips, so I hold still and swallow a few of them before I slip my tongue inside her mouth and coax even more of those rapid breaths out of her. Her mouth is warmer and more inviting than it's ever been.

She brings her hands to my chest, slapping the paper and the marker against my shirt while she steadies herself. The paper falls to the floor. She tilts her head up to mine even more and opens her mouth a little wider, wanting more of our kiss. I curve my right hand around the back of her head as I close my mouth over hers and inhale.

I kiss her. I love her.

I love her. I kiss her.

I kiss her.

I am so very in love with her.

It's the hardest thing I've ever had to do when I pull away from her mouth. Her hands are clenched in fists around my shirt. Her eyes are still closed when I pull back, so I stare down at her for a moment, convinced that Karma might actually know what she's doing after all. Maybe there was a reason so many shitty things had to happen in my life. It wouldn't have been a balanced life if I'd had a beautiful childhood, only to grow up and share a life like the one I know I'm going to share with Sydney. I think my childhood was the balance I needed so that I could have her. She is so good and so perfect, maybe I was made to suffer first before earning a reward of this magnitude.

I slide my hands to hers, which are still clenching my shirt. The paper she was holding has long since fallen to the floor, but the marker is still in her fist. I pry it from her fingers and she opens her eyes, just as I slip my fingers beneath the collar of her shirt. I pull it down, exposing the skin over her heart. I pull the cap off the marker with my teeth and then press the marker to her chest. I write four letters directly over her heart.

MINE

I put the cap back on the marker, and then I kiss her one last time before I turn and walk away.

It's the most we've ever communicated and the least we've ever said.

Chapter Twenty

Sydney

I'm sitting in the passenger seat of Ridge's car, staring out the window. My right hand is touching my chest, lightly fingering the word he wrote over my heart Tuesday night. *MINE*. It's faded now because it's been four days since he wrote it, but luckily it was a permanent marker, and I've avoided scrubbing it off in the shower.

When he left the library Tuesday night, I immediately had to sit down. He had left me so breathless, I almost felt faint. He wasn't even there five minutes, and it was the most intense five minutes of my life. So much so, I convinced my coworker to stay for the rest of my shift, and then I drove straight to Ridge's apartment to finish what he'd started. Those five intense minutes in the library became two intense hours in his bed.

Since then, we've spent three of the last four nights together.

He told me all about his conversation with Maggie. I hate that her grandfather passed away just hours after I left her apartment on Sunday. But knowing she was dealing with all of that, yet still made the time to stop by Ridge's and apologize to him, made me appreciate her effort even more. And it really did make a huge difference in Ridge. It's like a heavy weight was lifted after their talk on Tuesday. The last four days with him have been the best four days I've spent with him since the day we met.

In the beginning of getting to know him, every conversation we had was encased in guilt because of Maggie. Then, after his and Maggie's fight last week, every conversation we had was laced with worry because of Maggie. But since Tuesday, every time we're alone, it finally feels like we're actually alone. Somehow, merging Maggie more into our lives seems to have removed her even more from our relationship. It shouldn't make sense, but it does. Putting more focus on their friendship than on the fact that she's his ex-girlfriend will be better for our relationship in the long run.

Hopefully, Bridgette will be able to realize that soon. Because right now, she's not happy. Warren and Bridgette are in the backseat. Ridge is driving. Bridgette hasn't said a single word on the way to Maggie's house, because she and Warren got into a fight right before we left. She demanded she come with him, but he told her he didn't want her there because she doesn't know how to be nice to Maggie. That pissed her off. They went to their room and fought while Ridge and I sat on the couch and waited.

Actually, we sat on the couch and made out, so we didn't really care how long their fight lasted. But it still hasn't ended because we're pulling into Maggie's driveway, and the only words Bridgette has spoken between Austin and this driveway are, "I have to pee." She says it as she gets out of the car and slams her door.

Bridgette isn't the most reasonable person. But I'm growing to really like her and even understand her. She wears her emotions on her sleeve. But she has a lot of emotions, so it's more like she wears her emotions on several long-sleeved shirts, layered on top of one another.

No one has to knock on the door, because Maggie opens it as we're walking up the driveway. Warren walks in first and gives her a hug. Bridgette passes right by her, but Ridge gives her a quick hug. I do, too, simply because I'd rather start this off with a good sentiment.

"Smells good," Ridge signs as he tosses his keys on the counter.

"Lasagna," Maggie says. "I'm reading this book where the characters make lasagna anytime they need to talk through something. Thought it was fitting for tonight." Maggie looks at me as she walks into her kitchen. "Do you like to read, Sydney?"

"Love to read," I say, taking off my cardigan. I set it over the back of one of the chairs. "I just don't have a lot of time. Which is sad, considering I work in a library."

Bridgette walks to the bathroom, and Warren tosses himself dramatically on the couch, facedown into a throw pillow. "Kill me now," he mutters.

"Trouble in paradise?" Maggie says.

Warren lifts his head and looks at her. "Paradise? When have Bridgette and I ever lived in paradise?"

"Trouble in Sheol?" Maggie corrects.

Warren sits up on the couch. "I don't even know what that means."

"It's another word for *hell*."

"Oh," Warren says. "You know not to use big words around me."

"It's only five letters long."

I'm watching them converse, my attention going back and forth between them. I finally focus on Ridge, who is standing in front of me now. "You thirsty?" he asks.

I nod. He walks to the kitchen and opens a cabinet, then begins getting us both something to drink. It's odd, watching him move his way around the kitchen like it's his kitchen. It makes me realize that in a way, it used to be. There's no telling how much time he spent here at her house. I guess this is one of those fairly awkward moments I'm going to have to get used to. Ridge brings me a glass of water, and then he takes a seat on the couch next to Warren.

I walk into the kitchen.

"You need any help?" I ask Maggie.

She shakes her head and opens the refrigerator, placing a salad inside. "No, thanks. Everything is finished except the lasagna." She looks at Ridge and Warren. "You guys ready to sit at the table and do this before we eat?"

Warren slaps his jeans. "Ready," he says, hopping up.

The four of us make our way to the kitchen table just as Bridgette walks out of the bathroom. Maggie is at the head of the table. I'm sitting next to Ridge, and Warren is seated next to an empty chair, but Bridgette chooses to claim the chair at the opposite head of the table so that there's an empty seat between Warren and her. He shakes his head, ignoring her.

Maggie opens up a folder and then sits up straight and signs everything as she begins to speak. I like watching her sign. I don't know why, but I find it a little easier to follow her than Ridge or Warren. Maybe because her hands are more delicate, but it seems like she signs a little slower and—if this even makes sense—with more enunciation.

She looks at all of us. "Thank you for agreeing to this." She directs her attention at me. "And thank *you*," she says, without being specific. I nod, but really, it's Warren she should be thanking. He's the one who gave me the kick in the rear I needed to finally make a forward move with Maggie.

"I've made a couple of decisions that I want to talk about first, because they affect the next year of my life. And, subsequently, yours." She nods her head toward her hallway. We all look at the hallway, and for the first time, I notice moving boxes. "My internship is over, and so is my thesis, so I've decided to move back to Austin. My landlord informed me on Wednesday that she was able to rent the house to someone else, so I have to be out by the end of the month."

I take her pause as an opportunity to interrupt with a question. "Isn't your doctor here in San Antonio?"

Maggie shakes her head. "She has a satellite office here one day a week. But she's based out of Austin, so it'll actually be easier for me."

"Have you found an apartment yet?" Warren asks. "The end of the month is just a few days away."

Maggie nods again. "I have, but it won't be ready until April fifth. The tenants just moved out, and they have to carpet and repaint."

"Is it the same complex as last time?" Warren asks.

Maggie's eyes flicker from Warren to Ridge. There's something unspoken there, even though she's shaking her head, giving them an answer. "They didn't have anything available. This one is in North Austin."

Warren leans forward and gives her a look that I don't understand. Ridge sighs heavily. I feel lost.

"What?" I ask. "What's wrong with North Austin?"

Maggie looks at me. "It's pretty far from you guys. Ridge and I . . . back when I had my apartment in Austin . . . we both chose complexes that were close to the hospital and my doctor. It made things easier."

"Have you checked our complex?" Warren asks. "I know there are units available."

Bridgette makes a noise of protest. She clears her throat and then plops her purse down on the table. She pulls out a nail file, leans back in her chair, and starts filing her fingernails.

I look back at Maggie, and she's looking at me. She shakes her head and says, "No, but North Austin should be fine. I've been here in San Antonio for a year now, and everything has been fine."

"I wouldn't say *fine*," Warren says.

"You know what I mean, Warren. I haven't had an emergency to the point that I would have died without you guys here. I think I'll be fine if I'm only on the other side of town."

Ridge shakes his head. "You would have died in my bathroom if Sydney hadn't found you. Just because you've been lucky doesn't mean it's been a smart move."

"Agreed," Warren says. "You live north of San Antonio. We live in South Austin. It takes forty-five minutes from our driveway to yours. But if you move to North Austin, with traffic, it'll take more than an hour to get to you. You might be moving to the same city, but it's farther away from us."

Maggie sighs. She looks down and lowers her voice a little. "I can't afford anything else right now. The only apartments near the hospital with any availability are too expensive for me."

"Why don't you get a job?" Bridgette asks.

We all turn our attention toward Bridgette. I don't think anyone was expecting anything to come out of her mouth. She's holding the nail file against her thumbnail, staring at Maggie.

"It's hard to hold a job when you're in the hospital on a regular basis," Maggie says. "I had to apply for disability three years ago just to be able to pay my rent." She's being a little defensive, but I get it. Bridgette doesn't seem to sugarcoat her questions around Maggie at all. Or anyone, for that matter.

Bridgette shrugs and goes back to filing her nails.

"Like I asked earlier, have you even checked availability in our complex?" Warren asks.

Again, Maggie's attention is on me when this is brought up. I glance at Ridge, and he looks at me. We read each other without saying a word.

I nod, even though it seems absurd if I give it too much thought. But for whatever reason, it doesn't feel absurd. Having her in the same complex as Ridge and Warren would make things easier on all of them. And I truly don't believe Ridge or Maggie want to go down a road they've already traveled, so I surprisingly don't feel at all threatened by the thought of it. Maybe I'm being naïve, but I have to go with my gut. And my gut is telling me that she needs to be closer to them rather than farther away.

"I don't mind if you live in the same complex as Ridge, if that's what's stopping you," I say. "My ex-boyfriend moved into the complex with my ex–best friend after I moved in with Ridge and Warren last year. We can see right into their living room from Ridge's balcony. Believe me, nothing can feel weirder than that."

Maggie smiles appreciatively at me and then looks

toward Bridgette across the table. Ridge puts his arm on the back of my chair and then leans over, quickly kissing the side of my head. I love his silent thank-yous.

Bridgette looks up, directly at Maggie. She doesn't look happy. She turns her attention toward Warren and leans forward. "Shit, Warren, why don't you just move her into one of the spare bedrooms? We can be one big happy family."

Warren rolls his eyes. "Bridgette, stop."

"No. Think about it. I moved in and you started sleeping with me. Sydney moved in and Ridge started messing around with her. It's only fair that Maggie gets a turn."

I close my eyes and drop my head, shaking it. Why did Bridgette have to go there? I glance at Maggie, and she's shooting daggers at Bridgette.

"I think you forget that I've already been with them both, Bridgette. I actually don't need a turn, but thank you for being considerate."

"Oh, fuck off," Bridgette says.

And . . . this just went from bad to worse. I don't even think Ridge knows what just happened. As soon as that sentence comes out of Bridgette's mouth, Maggie calmly scoots her chair back and stands up. She walks to her bedroom and closes the door. They both just took this way, way too far. My head is in my hands now, and all I can say is, "Bridgette. Why?"

Bridgette looks at me like I've betrayed her. She waves a hand toward Maggie's bedroom. "How can you be okay with this? She's ungrateful and always has been, and now she's moving herself into our complex and twisting it to make it look like your idea!"

For a second, I entertain her thoughts. But only for a second. After two seconds, I stand up and make my way to Maggie's bedroom. I honestly think Bridgette has her pegged wrong. I don't see Ridge loving someone who is that ungrateful and manipulative. I just don't.

I push open Maggie's bedroom door, and she's sitting cross-legged on her bed, wiping away a tear. I sit down on the bed next to her. Maggie lifts her head, looking at me with eyes full of guilt.

"I'm sorry. That was tacky. But Bridgette is wrong. I'm not trying to take over either of your lives," she whispers. I can tell by her voice that she's on the verge of more tears. "If it were up to me, I'd be so far out from under their thumbs, it would take hours for them to drive to me. But I'm trying to be more cooperative, Sydney. I'm trying to be more respectful of their time."

That I believe. I think Maggie would much rather live in a place where she could get away with being lax. "I believe you. And I agree," I say. "We're here because Warren and Ridge are going to be your primary caregivers when you're sick. I think we need to leave Bridgette's feelings out of it. And mine. And honestly, even yours. This is about how we can make things easier on Warren and Ridge, and you living in the same complex as them will definitely make things easier on them."

Maggie nods. "I know. But I don't want to cause trouble between Warren and Bridgette. I think it should ultimately be Bridgette's and your decision, but I don't think she'll ever agree to it. I honestly don't blame her."

She's right. It should be something we all agree to. I turn my head toward the door and yell, "Bridgette!"

I hear a chair scoot across the floor, followed by dramatic stomps heading in the direction of Maggie's bedroom. Bridgette finally opens the door, but she leans against the door frame and folds her arms across her chest.

I pat the bed. "Come here, Bridgette."

"I'm fine right here."

I look at her like I would look at an ornery child. "Get your ass over here right now."

Bridgette stomps to the bed and throws herself across the foot of it. She's being just as dramatic as Warren was being when he threw himself on Maggie's couch earlier. Their intense similarities make me want to laugh. Bridgette stares at me and avoids eye contact with Maggie.

I lean back against the headboard and tilt my head as I look at her. "What are you feeling, Bridgette?"

She rolls her eyes and lifts up onto her elbow. "Well, Dr. Blake," she says sarcastically, "I feel like the ex-girlfriend of both of our boyfriends is about to move into the same apartment complex as us, and I don't like it."

"You think I do?" Maggie says.

Bridgette looks at her. There is absolutely no love between the two of them. At all.

"How long have you two known each other?" I ask.

"She moved in with Ridge and Warren a few months before you did," Maggie says, talking about her like she's not on the same bed. "And I tried being nice to her at first, but you know how that goes."

"I think the three of us just need to get drunk together," I suggest. It worked for Bridgette and me. Maybe it could work for Bridgette and Maggie.

Maggie looks at me like I've lost my mind. "That sounds like an absolute nightmare."

Bridgette nods in agreement. "Alcohol can't erase years of history between her and Warren."

Maggie laughs, addressing Bridgette directly now. "Do you really think there's a chance in hell I would ever be romantically interested in Warren again? That's absurd."

Bridgette rolls onto her back and looks up at the ceiling. "I'm not worried about you falling for him. I'm worried about him falling for you. You're really pretty, and Warren is shallow."

Maggie and I both look at each other. Then we both start laughing. I shake my head, completely taken aback by Bridgette's insecurity. "Do you not realize what a knockout you are? Warren could be as shallow as a desert and he'd still be head over heels for you."

"I don't really want to compliment you because you're mean to me," Maggie says to Bridgette. "But Sydney is right. Have you seen your ass? It looks like two Pringles hugging."

What the hell does that even mean? Maggie's comment makes Bridgette laugh, even though she tries to hide it.

"You work at Hooters, for Christ's sake," Maggie adds. "If I showed up at Hooters, they'd turn me away, thinking I was a twelve-year-old boy."

Bridgette turns her head toward Maggie. "Go on . . ." she says, urging us to continue with the compliments.

I roll my eyes and stretch my legs out, kicking her playfully in the thigh. "Warren loves you. Get over your weird insecurities. You're lucky you have a man who has a heart big enough to want to care for one of his best friends."

Maggie nods. "It's true. He's a good guy. A really shallow, somewhat conceited, extremely perverted good guy."

Bridgette groans and then sits up on the bed. She looks at me, and then she looks at Maggie. She doesn't say it's okay for Maggie to move into the same complex, but she also isn't protesting anymore, so I'll take this as a victory. She stands up and walks toward the door, but pauses in front of Maggie's floor-length mirror. She turns around and looks at herself over her shoulder, cupping her butt with both hands. "You really think it looks like two Pringles hugging?"

Maggie reaches behind her and grabs a pillow, then throws it at Bridgette. Bridgette pats her own ass and then leaves the bedroom.

Maggie falls onto her bed and groans into her mattress, then sits back up and looks at me, her head tilted to the side. "Thank you. I've never known how to deal with her. She terrifies me."

I nod. "Me too."

Bridgette and I may get along now, but I'm still scared to death of her wrath.

Maggie slides off the bed and walks back toward the living room. I follow her. Once we're all seated at the table, she pulls her folder in front of her. I look at Ridge, and he smiles at me. *I love you*, he mouths.

He says it all the time to me, so I don't know why it makes me blush this time.

"They have two available units," Warren says, sliding his phone toward Maggie. "One up, one down. The one downstairs is at the other end of the complex, but I think you should be downstairs."

Maggie looks at his phone. "It says it isn't available until the third. I can call in the morning and reserve it, then just get a hotel for a few days between apartments."

"That's a waste of money," Bridgette says. "It's only a few days. Just stay in my old bedroom. Or Brennan's. They're both empty." She's filing her nails again, but the words that just came out of her mouth are monumental. It's the closest she could come to an apology without actually saying to Maggie, *I was rude. I'm sorry.*

Ridge looks at me and squeezes my hand under the table, then texts me.

Ridge: I'll stay at your place while she's at ours, if it's okay.

I nod. I would probably have made him, even if he hadn't suggested it.

I don't even know that I could disagree with her staying

there for a few days at this point because everything going on with the people at this table has long since passed the definition of normal. Warren once said to me, *Welcome to the weirdest place you'll ever live.*

I get it now. I don't even live with them anymore, but that apartment and the rotating door attached to it defy every boundary ever put into place.

Warren scoots his chair back and stands up, then claims the empty chair next to Bridgette. He reaches over and grabs her nail file, then tosses it into the living room. He pulls her chair closer to his and kisses her.

And Bridgette actually lets him for a good five seconds. It's both adorable and highly uncomfortable.

Maggie rolls her eyes and then pushes her folder in front of Ridge. "I've made a list of compromises. There are things I still want to do that I'm going to need you to be okay with. And in return, I promise I'm going to take better care of myself. But you can't be bossy with me until you've given me a little time to adjust. I'm a hot mess, and it's going to take some time to improve that part of my personality."

Ridge looks over the list for a moment, but looks up at her and signs something I don't recognize. Maggie nods. "Yes. I'm going bungee jumping, and you can't tell me no. We're compromising."

Ridge sighs and then pushes the list back in front of Maggie. "Fine. But you're joining a support group."

Maggie laughs, but Ridge doesn't.

"That's not a compromise," Maggie says. "That's torture."

Ridge shrugs. "We're compromising," he says. "If you hate it, you can stop. But I think it'll be good for you. I don't think any of us truly knows what you're going through, and I think it'll be good for you to talk with people who do."

Maggie groans and drops her head on the table, hitting it three times against the wood. She scoots back from her chair and looks at me. "You're going with me," she says, walking toward the kitchen.

"To your support group?" I ask, confused. I don't know why I'm suddenly being tortured in this compromise.

"Nope," Maggie says. "Not to support group. CF support groups are only online. You're going bungee jumping with me."

Bungee jumping. *Hmm.* My boyfriend's ex-girlfriend wants me to jump off a bridge. Kind of ironic when you think about it. I look over at Ridge and grin. I've always wanted to bungee jump. He just shakes his head and smiles back at me, like he was just defeated.

"I've always wondered something," Bridgette says, looking across the room at Maggie. Warren is in the living room retrieving Bridgette's nail file. "Why don't you just get a lung transplant? Won't that cure the disease?"

I've wondered that, too, but haven't brought it up to Ridge yet.

"It's not that easy," Warren says, handing Bridgette the nail file. "Cystic fibrosis doesn't just affect the lungs, so new lungs won't cure someone of the disease completely."

"Also, I'm not in that predicament yet," Maggie says. "In order to get new lungs, you have to have a really grim prognosis, but without being too sick to receive a lung transplant. Luckily, I'm too healthy to be a candidate right now. It's a tricky position to be in. New lungs would be nice, but I don't really want to be in the position to be a candidate because it means my health would have to decline first. And a transplant could prolong someone's life by a few years, but it could also cut it short. Way short. Not something I'm hoping for anytime soon, to be honest."

"New advancements happen every day, though," Warren adds. "Which is why we're really only discussing the near future tonight, not a long-term plan. If we try to plan too far ahead, it might discourage other possibilities. Maggie doesn't want to hinder our lives, and we don't want to hinder hers, so right now, the best scenario is to just tackle things a few months at a time with the tools we have to tackle them."

Ridge nods, but then responds to Warren. "Sometimes I feel like your brain is on a power reserve. It's off most of the time, but the few times you do turn it on, it's at high power."

Warren smiles at him. "Why, thank you, Ridge."

Maggie laughs. "I'm not sure that was a compliment, Warren."

"Sure it was," Warren says.

I think it was both an insult and a compliment, which makes me laugh.

We spend the next half hour eating the lasagna Maggie prepared and working out more compromises. Bridgette doesn't say much, but she's also not rude at all, which is a huge improvement from when we walked through the front door.

After we tell Maggie goodnight, Ridge grabs my hand and leads me to the backseat of the car. He forces Warren to drive home since he drove here, which is fine with me because I really want to share the backseat with Ridge on the ride home.

He reaches across the seat and slides his fingers through mine as we're pulling out of Maggie's driveway. He pulls out his phone and texts me one-handed.

Ridge: You're like the Bridgette whisperer. I don't know how you do it.

Sydney: She's not that bad. I think she's always so defensive because no one has ever really made any effort to break through that defensiveness.

Ridge: Exactly. It says something that you made the effort.

Sydney: So did Warren.

Ridge: Only because he wanted to sleep with her. I don't think he ever expected to fall in love with her. That was a surprise to everyone. Especially him.

Sydney: You have unique friends. I like them.

Ridge: They're your friends now, too.

He squeezes my hand after I read his text. Then he reaches over and unbuckles my seat belt, pulling me closer to him. Once I'm in the middle of the backseat, he refastens the middle seat belt around me, pulling me against him. "Better," he says, wrapping his arm around me.

His thumb is grazing my shoulder, but his hand eventually makes its way down, just far enough so that he can trace the faded letters he wrote over my heart. He presses his mouth against my ear. "Mine," he says quietly.

I smile and place my hand over his heart. "Mine," I whisper.

Ridge presses his mouth to mine, and I smile through the whole kiss. I can't help it. When he pulls back, he leans against the door, pulling me even closer. I lift my legs onto the seat and curl them under me as I snuggle against him.

This feels right. Finally. It used to feel so wrong, but nothing about us feels wrong anymore. I owe a lot of that to Maggie's willingness to forgive and move forward and even accept me into her life after everything that happened.

So much has changed in the past year. The day I turned twenty-two, I thought it was going to be the worst year of my life. But little did I know, a boy on a balcony with his guitar would change all of that.

Now I'm here in his arms, unable and unwilling to wipe the smile off my face because his heart is mine.

MINE.

Chapter Twenty-One

Ridge

It's really hard to tell Warren everything he's doing wrong when my hands are full with the mattress we're carrying upstairs and his headphones on. I'd really hate to see him try to maneuver a boat or back up a trailer if he can't even walk forward up the damn stairs while pushing a mattress.

I also don't understand why we're even moving Maggie's mattress upstairs. Her apartment will be ready in four days, and there's a couch, plus Brennan's bed is empty. But I'm not arguing, because if she's going to be in my apartment, I'd rather her be in the farthest bedroom from mine just so this will feel less awkward, even though I'll be staying the night at Sydney's this week.

Warren stops three steps from the top to take a break. He leans his arm on the railing and pulls his headphones off. "This is the only thing we're moving, right? Everything else stays in the U-Haul?"

I nod and sign for him to pick up the mattress again. He rolls his eyes and readjusts his grip, pushing it toward me.

Maggie's new apartment is on the other side of the complex. Close to Sydney's old apartment, actually. Maggie has tried to back out several times and find somewhere else to stay because she's worried it'll be too much, living so close. But this will honestly be better for everyone. She gets sick so often, and for the past year I've had to spend a huge chunk of my nights in San Antonio. Even if she's only a few miles away, her being in another complex would require me or Warren to stay overnight when she's sick because she gets so weak, she can't even get out of bed.

With her being in the same complex, it'll make everything easier. I won't have to spend uncomfortable nights in the same apartment as her, but she'll be close enough that Warren or I can run over there and check on her every hour. I honestly think that's why Sydney was so agreeable to it. She's seen Maggie during the sicker times, and Sydney knows that when Maggie's down for the count, even a glass of water is impossible for her to get on her own. Not to mention administering her medications, making sure she's doing her breathing treatments while she's weak and recovering from an illness, and ensuring her sugar levels are good every few hours. If she weren't in the same complex, her care would require a car to get to her, and leaving her alone wouldn't be possible. But being in the same complex, it actually requires less of my time and less of my presence and, in the end, will make Maggie feel more independent. Which is what she wants.

We're leaving everything else in the U-Haul because one of Warren's coworkers also works part-time for the company that is renting it to us. They're allowing us to keep it for the week for just nineteen dollars a day, so it'll remain full of Maggie's stuff and parked in the parking lot until she moves into her place.

Maggie is still down at the U-Haul, gathering what she'll need to get her through the next four days. Sydney went to pick Bridgette up from work. Warren and I finally get the mattress into the bedroom and plop it flat on the floor. Warren is breathing heavily with his hands on his hips. He looks over at me. "Why aren't you out of breath?"

"We went up a flight of stairs. Once. And I work out."

"No, you don't."

"Yes, I do. In my room. Every day."

He glares at me like my admitting that I work out daily is some type of betrayal. He stares back down at the mattress. "Is this weird?"

I look down at Maggie's mattress, finally inside the same apartment as me. I used to hate that she would never agree to move in with me, and now she kind of is for a few days, and not a single part of me wants it to happen the way that I used to. That's weird for me. For all these years, I assumed Maggie and I would end up living in this apartment together and that we'd eventually be married. I never imagined my life taking the turn it did, but now I couldn't imagine it any differently.

So, yes. To answer Warren's question, it *is* weird, so I nod. But it's only weird because it all seems to be working out. I'm just waiting for the other shoe to drop. Whether that's Maggie's or Bridgette's or Warren's shoe, I don't know. But I highly doubt it'll be Sydney's. She's handled this better than anyone, and she has the most reasons not to.

"What if Sydney and Bridgette lived together and they decided to move in some dude who they had both dated in the past? Do you think we'd be cool with it?"

I shrug. "Guess it depends on the situation."

"No, it doesn't," Warren signs. "You'd be pissed. You'd hate it. You'd act like a whiny little bitch, just like I would, and then we'd all break up."

I don't want to think I'd be like that. "More reason to let them know how much we appreciate them."

Warren kicks at a leaf on Maggie's mattress and then bends to pick it up. "I let Bridgette know how much I appreciate her all night last night." He grins, and I take that as my cue to head back down to the U-Haul.

On my way down the stairs, I receive a text. I look at my phone and pause on the steps when I see that it's from Sydney. It's a group text with Warren and me.

Sydney: At the DQ drive-thru down the road. Anyone want a Blizzard?

Warren: Does a one-legged dog swim in a circle? I'll take a Reese's.

Ridge: M&M please.

I look down at the U-Haul in the parking lot and watch Maggie walk up the ramp and disappear inside of it. This is one of the weird moments we're going to have to learn to navigate. I need to remind Sydney that Maggie is here and she might want one. But it feels weird to remind Sydney to include her. It's probably not as weird as anything else that's happened in the last two weeks of us dating. And part of me struggles with what to say to Maggie and whether I should even offer her ice cream, knowing she isn't supposed to have a lot of sugar. But I don't want to be the one to bring up her health right now. I'm trying to keep my distance with the hope that she's stepping up and taking control on her own.

Right in the middle of my internal struggle, Maggie sends a text through to the group.

Maggie: I'll take a large Diet Dr Pepper. Thanks!

I didn't even realize Sydney had included her in the group text. But of course she had. Every time any of this starts to feel awkward, Sydney somehow alleviates that awkwardness before it's even able to fully set in.

I walk to the U-Haul, and Maggie is all the way inside of it, digging in her top dresser drawer. She's throwing stuff on top of the dresser, in search of something. She finds the shirt that she's looking for and stuffs it in a bag. She looks up and sees me standing at the opening of the U-Haul.

"Can you grab this suitcase and bring it up?"

I nod and she signs, "Thank you," then walks out of the U-Haul and heads toward the stairs to the apartment. I walk over to the dresser to grab the suitcase from on top of it, but I pause when I see a sheet of paper on the floor of the U-Haul. I bend to pick it up. I don't want to be invasive, so I set it on top of the dresser, but it's unfolded, and I can see that it's a list. At the top, it says, *Things I Want to Do*, but the title next to it is scratched out and written over. I pick it up, even though I probably shouldn't.

There are three out of the nine things on the list scratched out: *skydive*, *drive a race car*, and have a *one-night stand*.

I know she went skydiving, but when did she race a car? And when did she have a . . .

Never mind. Not my business.

I read the rest of the items on the list, remembering how she used to talk about some of these things to me. I always hated that she had so many things she was so adamant about doing, because I always felt like I had to be the voice of reason and it would put her in a bad mood.

I lean against the dresser, staring down at it. We planned on a trip to Europe once. It was right after I finished my second year in college, about four years ago. I was terrified for her to go because even being in such close quarters with strangers on an international flight for ten hours was enough to put her health at risk. Not to mention the change in oxygen levels and atmosphere and being in a touristy area and in a country with hospitals that aren't familiar with her medical history. I tried so hard to talk her out of it, but she got her way because I honestly couldn't blame her for wanting to see the world. And I didn't want to be that one thing that was holding her back.

But in the end, it wasn't me who held her back from actually going. It was a lung infection she contracted that landed her in the hospital for seventeen days. It was the sickest I'd ever seen her, and the entire time she was in the hospital, I couldn't help but feel nothing but relief that she hadn't come down with the illness in Europe.

After that, I wouldn't even entertain the idea of an international trip. Maybe I should have. I realize that now, after knowing how much she resented my caution. And honestly, I don't blame her. Her life is not my life, and even though my only goal was to give her life more length, all she's ever wanted was a life with more substance.

I can see movement out of the corner of my eye, so I turn and look up, just as Sydney makes her way up the ramp to the U-Haul with two Blizzards in her hands. She's wearing one of my Sounds of Cedar T-shirts, and it's hanging off her shoulder because it's too big for her. If I had my way, she'd wear one of my shirts every day for the rest of our lives. I love this effortless look on her.

She smiles and hands me one of the Blizzards. She pulls the spoon out of hers and licks ice cream from it, then closes her mouth over the spoon.

I grin. "I think I like yours better, and I don't even know what flavor you got."

She smiles and stands on her tiptoes, kissing me briefly on the lips. "Oreo," she says. She pokes at her ice cream with her spoon and nods her head toward the sheet of paper I'm still holding. "What's that?"

I look down at the list, wondering if it's my place to even share something like this with her since it isn't mine.

"Maggie's bucket list. It was on the floor." I set it down on the dresser and grab the suitcase. "Thank you for the ice cream." I kiss her on the cheek and make my way out of the U-Haul. When I turn around to see if she's following me, she isn't.

She's picking up the sheet of paper.

Chapter Twenty-Two

Sydney

When I was eight years old, we went on a road trip to California. My father stopped at Carlsbad Caverns National Park just in time for the bat flight. I was scared to death and hated every second of it.

When I was eleven, we spent two weeks on a train tour of Europe. We saw the Eiffel Tower, we went to Rome, we visited London. I have the picture of my mother and me on my refrigerator that my father took of us in front of Big Ben.

I've been to Vegas once with Tori. We went for my twenty-first birthday and stayed one night because we couldn't afford more than that, and Hunter was upset that I was gone on my birthday.

I've done several things that are on Maggie's bucket list, and while I didn't take the trips for granted, I certainly don't think I appreciated them enough. I've never thought about writing a bucket list or what would even be on it if I did. I don't plan that far ahead.

That's just the thing, though. Neither does Maggie. But far ahead for her and far ahead for me have two completely different meanings.

I set my Blizzard on top of the dresser and stare at number seven on the list. *Bungee jump.*

I've never been bungee jumping. I can't say that it would have been a bucket list item for me, but the fact that it's a bucket list item for Maggie and she asked me to join her gives the entire sentiment a whole new meaning.

I fold the list and grab my ice cream, then make my way out of the U-Haul and up to Ridge's apartment. Ridge is in the kitchen with Warren. They're leaning against the counter, finishing their ice cream. Bridgette is probably taking a shower because she smelled like chicken wings. I walk to Maggie's bedroom, and she's kneeling in front of her suitcase, rifling through it. She looks up to see me standing in the doorway.

"Can I come in?"

She nods, so I walk in and sit on her mattress. I set my cup on the floor next to the mattress and unfold her list. "Found this," I say, holding it up for her to see. She's just a few feet away, so she reaches over and grabs it, then glances down at it. She makes a face like it's as useless as trash and then tosses it on the bed.

"I was a big dreamer." She gives her full attention back to her suitcase.

"This might make you think less of me," I say, "but I've been to Paris, and I probably shouldn't admit this, but the Eiffel Tower looks just like a really big transmission tower. It's kind of underwhelming."

Maggie laughs. "Yeah, you definitely shouldn't admit that to anyone else." She folds the top of her suitcase shut and then moves to the bed, lying down on her stomach. She grabs the list and pulls it in front of her. "I crossed off three of these in one day."

I remember the day she went skydiving because it wasn't that long ago. Which means . . . the one-night stand wasn't that long ago, either. I'm curious about it, but I'm not sure we're at a point where I want to ask about her sex life.

"Most of the other ones I wrote down are a little far-fetched. I get sick too easily and too often to travel internationally."

I look at the Vegas one. "Why would you want to lose five grand instead of win five grand?"

She rolls onto her back and looks up at me. "If I had five grand to lose, it means I'd be rich. Being rich is an inadvertent item on my bucket list."

I laugh. "Do you plan on doing anything else on the list other than bungee jump?"

She shakes her head. "It's really hard for me to travel. I've tried it a couple of times and never made it very far. I have too much medical equipment. Too many medications to worry about. It's really not all that fun for me, but I didn't realize it when I wrote the list."

I hate that for her. I almost want to alter a couple of these just so she can mark more of them out. "How far are you able to travel without it being an inconvenience?"

She shrugs. "Day trips are cool. And I could probably go somewhere for a couple of nights, but there's nowhere around here I haven't already been. Why?"

"One sec." I stand up and walk to the living room and grab a pen and spiral notebook off the table. I go back to Maggie's room, feeling Ridge and Warren watching me the whole time. I turn around and smile at them before walking back to Maggie's bed. I place her bucket list on the spiral notebook. "I think with a little modification, these are all doable."

Maggie lifts up onto her elbow, curious as to what I'm doing. "What kind of modification?"

I scroll down the list. I stop on Carlsbad Caverns. "What interests you about Carlsbad? The bats or the caves?"

"The caves," she says. "I've seen the bat flights here in Austin a dozen times."

"Okay," I say, drawing an open parenthesis next to Carlsbad Caverns on the list. "You could go to the Inner Space Cavern in Georgetown. Probably not nearly as cool as Carlsbad, but it's definitely a cave."

Maggie stares at the list for a moment. I'm not sure if she thinks I'm crossing a line by writing on her bucket list. I almost hand her back the list and apologize, but she leans over and points at the Eiffel Tower. "There's a mock Eiffel Tower in Paris, Texas."

I smile when she says that, because it means we're on the same page. I write *Eiffel tower in Paris, Texas* next to number nine.

I scroll the list again with the pen and then pause at number three. *See the Northern Lights.* "Have you ever heard of the Marfa Lights in West Texas?"

Maggie shakes her head.

"Doubt it's even remotely the same, but I've heard you can camp out there and watch them."

"Interesting," Maggie says. "Write it down." I write *Marfa Lights* in parentheses next to *Northern Lights.* She points to number four. *Eat spaghetti in Italy.* "Isn't there a town somewhere in Texas called Italy?"

"Yeah, but it's really small. Not even sure they'd have an Italian restaurant, but it's close to Corsicana, so you could get spaghetti to go and take it to a park in Italy."

Maggie laughs. "That sounds really pathetic, but definitely doable."

"What else?" I ask, scrolling the list. She's already apparently driven a race car and had a one-night stand, which we've successfully avoided discussing. The only thing left that we haven't modified is Vegas. I point to it with the pen. "There are casinos right outside of Paris, Texas. Technically, you could just go there after visiting the fake Eiffel Tower. And maybe you should"—I scratch out two of the zeros—"only lose fifty dollars instead of five grand."

"There are casinos in Oklahoma?" she asks.

"Huge ones."

Maggie pulls the list from me and looks it over. She smiles while she reads it, then pulls the notebook and pen from my hands. She places the list on top of the notebook. At the top of the list, it reads, *Things I Want to Do. Maybe One of These Days* . . .

Maggie scratches out part of the title so that the list reads, *Things I Want to Do. Maybe Now.*

Chapter Twenty-Three

Maggie

I was scolded today.

It's the first time I've seen my doctor since she walked out of my hospital room—right before I bailed. The first half of my appointment today was spent apologizing to her and promising to take things more seriously from now on. The second half of my appointment was spent with different specialists. When you have cystic fibrosis, your team comes to you in one central location, as it's not safe to sit in the different waiting rooms for each specialist. It's one of the things I love about my doctor that I didn't get the full benefits of while living in San Antonio. I really do feel like my health will be easier to maintain now that I'm back in Austin. I just have to quit letting my frustration over this illness win out over my will. Which is hard, because I'm very easily frustrated.

I've been gone most of the day, but when I pull back up to the apartment, I'm surprised to see Ridge's car here. He's been staying at Sydney's the majority of the week. Today is Friday, and I was supposed to move tomorrow, but it's been pushed back to Sunday. I'm sure Ridge will be happy to have his own bed again.

Or not. I doubt he's all that upset about spending so much time at Sydney's.

When I open the living room door, they're both on the couch. Ridge is holding a book in front of him, his feet propped up on the coffee table. Sydney is leaning against him, looking at the words on the pages as he reads aloud.

Ridge is reading. Out loud.

I stare at them for a moment. He struggles with a word, and Sydney makes him look at her as she sounds it out for him. She's helping him pronounce the words out loud. It's such an intimate moment, I want to be anywhere else when I close the door and gain Sydney's attention. She looks up and then sits up straight, putting a little distance between herself and Ridge. I notice. So does he, because he stops reading and follows Sydney's gaze until he sees me.

"Hey." I smile and set my purse on the bar.

"Hi," Sydney says. "How was the appointment?"

I shrug. "Overall, it was good. But I spent most of it being scolded." I grab a water out of the refrigerator and then head toward the bedroom I'm staying in. "I deserved it, though." I walk to my room and close the door. I fall down onto the bed because it's the only thing in here. There isn't even a dresser or a TV or a chair. Just me and a bed, and a living room I feel slightly uncomfortable in.

Not because Ridge is in there with Sydney. I honestly don't mind seeing them together. The only thing that bothers me about it is that seeing them together reminds me of Jake, and I feel a sting of jealousy that it's not me and Jake cuddled together on a couch somewhere. I feel like Ridge and Sydney fit together in a way that's similar to how Jake and I fit together. Or *could have* fit together.

It's interesting to me, looking back, just how wrong Ridge and I were for each other. And it isn't at all because anything is necessarily wrong with us as individuals. We just didn't bring out the best sides of each other. Not like Sydney does with him. I mean, he's sitting on a couch, reading to her. And he's doing it because it's his way of perfecting his speaking voice. That's not a side of him I ever brought out. Or even encouraged. We had conversations in the past about why he didn't verbalize, but he always just shrugged it off and said he didn't like doing it. I never asked for a deeper explanation than that.

I remember the day I was in the hospital and found all the messages between him and Sydney. I didn't read them all in that moment because I honestly didn't want to. I was hurt and a little blindsided. But once I made it home, I read every word. More than once. And the conversation that hurt me the most was when Ridge explained to Sydney where the band Sounds of Cedar got its name.

The reason it hurt so much is because I realized, in all

the years we'd been dating, I'd never once asked Ridge where the band name came from. And because of that, I'd never known exactly how much he'd done for Brennan when they were younger.

There was a lot I read that I once wished I'd never read between the two of them. Between all the iMessages and Facebook messages, I sat there for hours reading. But reading all of it also made something very clear to me: There was so much more to Ridge than I was aware of. There were things he shared with Sydney over a short period of knowing her that he never once shared with me over a six-year stretch. And that wasn't because Ridge was hiding anything from me about himself or his past, or lying in any way. There were just things about both of us we never dug deep enough to figure out. It occurred to me that maybe we didn't share those things because they were sacred to us. And you only share the really sacred stuff with the people who reach you on that deep of a level.

I didn't reach Ridge on the level that Sydney did. And Ridge didn't reach me.

I ultimately decided to end our relationship because of their connection. Not because they had formed it . . . but because Ridge and I never had.

People are supposed to bring out the best in each other. I didn't bring out the best in Ridge. He didn't bring out the best in me. But seeing Sydney on the couch with him just now, helping him . . . She brings out the best in him.

I noticed how she pulled away from him a little when

she realized I was in the room with them. It bothers me that she felt she needed to do that. I want her to know that their physical affection is not something they should feel obligated to hide on my account. I actually, in a weird way, like seeing how much they like each other. It gives me even more reassurance that I made the right choice by not allowing Ridge to use my illness as a reason to stay with me.

I stand up and make my way back to the living room. The only thing that's going to alleviate the awkwardness when we're all in a room together is to force us all to be in a room together even more. Me hiding in my bedroom isn't going to get us anywhere.

Sadly, Ridge is no longer on the couch with Sydney when I walk back into the living room. She's in the kitchen, rummaging through a cabinet. Ridge is no longer in the room.

I walk to the bar and take a seat, watching Sydney. "What are you guys doing tomorrow?" I ask her.

She spins around and her hand is over her heart. "You scared me." She laughs and closes the cabinet. "I think we all planned to help you move tomorrow, so the day is open now that you aren't moving until Sunday."

"What do you mean *we all*? Is Warren off tomorrow, too?"

She nods. "Bridgette, too. Although I don't think she was actually going to help with the move."

I laugh. "I would have been shocked if she did."

"True. Why are you asking?" Sydney says. "Do you have something in mind?"

I shrug. "Nothing specific. I just thought . . . I don't know. Maybe it would be good for all of us if we spent more time together. Now that . . . well . . ."

Sydney nods, like she's been thinking the same thing. "Now that the dynamics have changed and it's hella awkward?"

"Yep. That."

Sydney laughs and then leans forward on the counter in thought. "Maybe we could do the cave thing. In Georgetown."

"I was thinking more along the lines of lunch," I admit. "I don't expect you guys to spend your entire Saturday with me."

"The caves sound really fun, though."

I tilt my head, watching her for a sign that she's just saying that to be polite. Sometimes she seems too nice and too accommodating, to the point that it makes me suspicious. But I also get nothing but an authentic vibe from her. Maybe some people just don't stoop to the same levels of jealousy that others do. As if Sydney can sense the suspicion in my expression, she continues speaking.

"Remember the night of Warren's birthday party?"

I nod. "You mean the night I thought your bra was cute and stupidly wanted Ridge to see it?"

Sydney cringes a little. "That's the night," she confirms. She looks down at her hands, clasped together on the counter in front of her. "I had a lot of fun with you that night, Maggie. I really did. At the time, I thought there was a chance we'd end up becoming friends, and it excited me because I really needed a friend after what Tori did to me. But then I kind of ruined that opportunity when I broke girl code and kissed your boyfriend." She looks up at me. "I've always hated that I ruined what I really do think could have been a good friendship between us. And now, months later, here we are again. And for whatever reason, you're extending an olive branch. So, yes, lunch tomorrow sounds good. But I also really want to see the caves, so if you can find it in yourself to extend an entire olive *tree*, then I think it'll be fun."

She looks nervous as she waits for my answer. I don't make her wait long, because I don't want her to feel nervous. Or awkward or guilty or anything else this girl doesn't deserve to feel. I smile at her. "You didn't ruin anything by breaking girl code, Sydney."

My words make her smile. "Bet you don't bring guys around me ever again, though. And I would completely understand."

"I'm done with guys," I say with a laugh. "Especially after what I did to the last one."

Sydney's eyebrow rises in curiosity, and I suddenly realize I spoke more than I should have. I don't want to talk about Jake, but based on the look she's giving me right now, she wants details.

"Is this your one-night stand?"

I nod. I was honestly surprised she didn't ask me about it when she was modifying my bucket list the other day. "Yeah. His name is Jake. I freaked out on him."

"Why?"

"He cooked me breakfast."

Sydney shoots me a look of mock horror. "Oh, how *dare* he," she says.

I laugh at her sarcasm and then cover my face with my hands. "I know. I *know*, Sydney. And I tried to rectify it a couple of days later but then ended up in the hospital and found out he has a kid, and I don't know . . . it just felt stupid of me to try and pursue him at that point."

"Why? Because you hate kids?"

"No. No, not at all. I was in my hospital room, and I could hear him outside talking to his son on the phone, and it all just felt so real in that moment. Like not only would this guy—who is really awesome and smart and funny—be entering my life, but so would his kid, who sounded like a great kid, and I just . . . I got scared."

"Of what?"

I sigh. That's a good question, because even I'm confused as to why I kept pushing him away. "I think my fears flipped on me somewhere along the way. I told myself that I didn't want to break his heart or become his burden. But in all honesty, I'm more scared that he'll break mine. It hit me when I realized how much I liked him that maybe most people aren't as committed as Ridge and aren't willing to put up with what a relationship with me could entail.

I became terrified that he would end up being the one to walk away, so I did it first. Maybe I didn't want things with him to end badly. I don't know. I question my choice every single day."

Sydney regards me silently for a moment. "If you had the chance, knowing Ridge's and your relationship came to an end, would you take back the six years you spent with him?"

I don't even need a second to answer her. I shake my head. "No. Of course not."

Sydney lifts her shoulder in a knowing shrug. "If things ended badly between you and this Jake guy, I doubt you would take back the time you spent with him, either. We shouldn't revolve our lives around their possible endings. We should revolve our lives around the experiences that *lead* to the endings."

It's quiet for a while.

Her words stick with me. Cling to me. Absorb into my skin.

She's right. And while it's been my goal to try to live life without focusing on the ending, that's exactly what I keep reverting to. Especially when it comes to Jake. I don't know why I've been telling myself that I can't do both—experience my life to the fullest *and* allow myself to experience another relationship. It's not like I can only have one and not the other.

"Maybe you should give him another chance," Sydney suggests.

I let my head fall back with a sigh. "This poor guy," I say. "I'm gonna give him whiplash with as much as I've gone back and forth with him."

Sydney laughs. "Well, make sure you only go forth with him from now on, and not back."

I take a deep breath and then stand up. "Okay. I'm going to call him."

Sydney smiles, and I try to ignore my nerves as I walk back to my bedroom. I pull out my phone and open up my contacts. My hand begins to shake as I select his contact. I lean against my bedroom door and close my eyes after I press his number and put the phone on speaker.

It rings twice and then is immediately pushed through to voice mail.

He just pushed me through to voice mail.

It's a crushing blow, but one I probably deserve. I wait for his voice.

"Hi, you've reached Dr. Jacob Griffin. Please leave a detailed message and I'll return your call as soon as I'm available."

I wait for the beep. And then I stutter my way through. "Hey, Jake. It's Maggie. Carson. Um . . . call me if you can. Or if you want, rather. If not, I understand. I just . . . yeah. Okay. Bye."

As soon as I hang up, I groan and then fall onto my mattress. I can't believe he pushed me through to voice mail. But then again, I can. And now the only thing he has that could change his mind is a nervous, embarrassing voice mail he's probably listening to right now.

I wallow in self-pity for a few moments, but then I push myself off the bed and walk to the living room. Sydney is still at the bar, but Ridge is now back in the room. He's showing her something on his phone, but Sydney gives her attention to me as soon as I walk out of my bedroom. I wave off her curiosity.

"He pushed me through to voice mail."

She makes a face. "Oh. Maybe he's busy?"

I shake my head and fall down onto the sofa, staring up at the ceiling. "Or maybe he realizes what a psycho I am for kicking him out of my house before he even finished cooking the bacon."

"Yeah, that could be a possibility as well," Sydney says.

I throw my arm over my face and try to come up with all the reasons why Jake isn't worthy of this much regret.

I come up with nothing. He is absolutely worthy of my regret.

• • •

It's been two hours. I've showered, put on my pajamas, and looked at my phone five thousand times. Ridge left to go pick up dinner for everyone. Bridgette and Warren are here now and are actually sitting on the couch with me. Warren is in the middle, and Bridgette is on the other side of Warren. I'm playing Toy Blast on my phone, but not because I'm interested in the game. I'm just obsessed with staring at my phone screen now. Waiting. Hoping.

"*Lesbian Libidos*?" Warren asks.

"Not even close," Bridgette says.

I glance over at him, wondering why the hell he keeps spouting off weird titles that sound like porn. He's scrolling through a list on his phone.

"*Babes in Bali*?"

Bridgette actually laughs at that one. "If I got to go to Bali to film a porn, I wouldn't be working at Hooters."

Warren turns to her. "Wait," he says. "How long have you worked at Hooters? Is it a Hooters-related porn?"

Okay, now I'm staring at both of them. *What in the hell are they talking about?*

Sydney is at the kitchen table doing homework. Apparently, she senses my confusion, because she offers up an explanation. "Bridgette kissed a girl in a porn film, and she refuses to tell Warren the name of it so that he can watch it. It's become his life's mission."

Wow. "That explains so much," I say.

Warren looks at me. "How many porn movies do you think are filmed every year?"

I shrug. "I wouldn't even know how to make a guess."

"A fucking lot. That's how many."

I nod and then give my complete focus back to Toy Blast. I don't even want to think about how much porn Warren feels forced to watch.

There's a quick knock at the front door before it swings

open. Brennan walks in, and I immediately jump up, excited to see him. I don't think I've seen him since Warren's birthday party.

"Maggie?" He immediately wraps his arms around me and hugs me, then puts his hands on my shoulders, holding me at arm's length. "What are you doing here?"

I wave my hand toward Bridgette's old bedroom. "I'm staying a few days until my apartment is ready."

He shakes his head. "Apartment? Where? *Here*?" His confusion is genuine. It surprises me Ridge hasn't mentioned it to him. He glances over at the table and sees Sydney. He releases my shoulders and takes a step back, eyeing me. Then he looks around the room. "Where's Ridge?"

"He went to grab dinner," Warren says. "Tacos. Nom nom."

I walk back to the couch to reclaim my seat and immediately check my phone for missed calls, even though the ringer is on. Nothing. I look back up at Brennan, who is scratching his head in confusion. He's literally scratching his head. It makes me laugh.

"You're moving into the same complex as Ridge?" he asks. Then he looks at Sydney. "And you're okay with that?" He looks back at me. "What is happening?"

I look at Sydney, and she's fighting a smile. "Welcome to maturity, Brennan," Sydney says.

"*Breasts of Burden?*" Warren asks Bridgette. We all look at him. He shrugs innocently. "Hey, I'm not the mature one. Don't look at me."

Ridge walks through the door with tacos, and Brennan immediately forgets about the odd arrangement that just threw him for a loop, and Warren is off the couch with a one-track mind that has nothing to do with porn movies.

Tacos can alleviate pretty much any issue. I'm convinced of that now.

I'm making my plate when my phone starts to ring. "Oh my God," I whisper.

Sydney is standing next to me. "Oh my God," she says.

I rush to the living room. Jake's name is flashing across the screen. I look at Sydney, wide-eyed. "It's him."

"Answer it!" she yells.

I look down at the phone.

"Who is it?" Bridgette asks.

"A guy Maggie likes. She didn't think he'd call back."

I look at Bridgette, and she's looking at me expectantly now. "Well, answer it," she says, waving at my phone, annoyed with me.

"Maggie, answer it!" Sydney says. I love how she sounds just as nervous as I am.

I swallow my nerves, clear my throat, and then slide my finger across the screen.

I walk toward the bedroom, slip inside, and close the door. "Hello?" It doesn't matter that I cleared my throat before I said that. My voice still shakes with my nerves.

"Hi."

I let my head fall back against the bedroom door when I hear his voice. I feel it in every part of me.

"Sorry I put you through to voice mail earlier," he says. "I was in a meeting. Forgot to silence my phone."

His admission makes me smile. At least it wasn't because he was annoyed that I'd called.

"It's okay," I say. "How have you been?"

He sighs. "Good. I'm good. You?"

"Also good. I moved to Austin a few days ago, so I've been busy."

"You moved?" he asks, not expecting that response from me. "That's . . . unfortunate."

I walk over to my bed and sit down. "Not really. I have a rule against dating anyone in the same zip code, so it's a good thing. Keeps things from becoming overwhelming."

He laughs. "Maggie, I'm too busy to be overwhelming, even if we lived on the same street."

"I don't think you can help but be a little overwhelming, Jake. We've had sex. You're hardly *under*whelming."

I expect him to laugh, but he doesn't. His voice is quiet when he says, "I'm glad you called."

"Me too." I lie back on my bed, pressing a hand to my stomach. I haven't been this nervous talking to a guy . . . ever. I don't know how to process all the things his voice does to my stomach, so I just press my hand against it as if that will somehow calm the storm brewing inside me.

"I can't talk long," he says. "I'm still at work. But I want to say something before I go."

I blow out a quiet breath, preparing for the impact of his rejection. "Okay," I whisper.

He sighs heavily. "I feel like you don't know what you want. You agree to go out with me, but you tell me on our date you don't want to see me for a second time. But then we have an entire night of incredible sex. Then you kick me out the next morning before I'm even finished cooking breakfast. A few days later, you show up at my office, then you shoot me down the same day at the hospital. Now you're leaving me a voice mail. I'm not asking for anything other than a little consistency. Even if that consistency is agreeing to never speak again. I just . . . I need consistency."

I close my eyes, nodding to myself. He's right. He's so right, I'm surprised he even called me back. "I can respect that. And I can give you that."

He doesn't say anything for a moment. I like the quiet. It's almost as if I can feel him more in the quiet. Almost half a minute goes by without either of us saying a word. "I've wanted to call you every day."

Those words make me frown more than smile because I know exactly what he's been feeling, and I don't feel good for making him feel that way. "I've wanted to apologize to you every day," I admit.

"You don't need to apologize for anything," he says. "You're a woman who was certain you didn't want a relationship with anyone. But then you met me and we had such a great night together that your feelings confused you. I like that I was the guy who put a wrinkle in your plan."

I laugh. "You have a really unique way of looking at my extreme indecisiveness. I like it."

"I figured you would. Listen, I have to go," he says. "Want me to call you tonight?"

"Actually . . . are you busy tomorrow?"

"I have a lecture at the hospital I have to attend tomorrow. From eight to ten. But I'm free after that."

"You're free the whole day?"

"The whole day," he says.

I don't know that I've ever asked a guy on a date before. This might be a first. "I'm going with some friends to Georgetown tomorrow. To Inner Space Cavern. You can come if you want. Or we could just do something after if you think going to look at caves with people you've never met before is a little weird."

"Won't be weird if you're there. I can be in Austin by noon at the latest."

I'm smiling like an idiot. "Okay. I'll text you the address."

"Okay," he says. I can almost hear the smile in his voice, too. "See you tomorrow, Five Hundred."

I stare at the phone after he ends the call, fingering my smile. How does he fill me so full of feels, even over the phone?

They all look at me as I get to the living room, and Sydney pauses midchew. After I grab two tacos out of the sack in the kitchen, I say, "We might have to take two cars tomorrow so we'll all fit."

It's all I say, but when I look over at Sydney, she's smiling.

So is Bridgette, but her smile is a little more sinister. "This should be fun. A shiny new toy for Warren to break in."

I look at Warren. Then back at Bridgette. Jake is going to spend the day with these two tomorrow. The entire day.

What was I thinking?

Chapter Twenty-Four

Ridge

It's been a good week. *Finally.* I've stayed at Sydney's the last few nights, and honestly . . . I don't want to leave. I love sleeping next to her. I love waking up next to her. I love doing absolutely nothing with her. But I also know that this is a very new relationship that already seems to be moving at warp speed, so the last thing we need to do is live together.

Tomorrow night will be the last night I stay here before going back to my own apartment. I'm bummed because I'd much rather be here with Syd than in an apartment with Warren and Bridgette. But that's what's going to happen because I'm not speeding this relationship up even faster. Once we move in together, we'll live together forever. I want to wait until Sydney has experienced life on her own before making that kind of commitment.

I finish brushing my teeth, and then head to the living room. Sydney is on the couch with her computer in her lap. She sees me walk into the room, and she makes room for me on the couch next to her. Like a fluid dance, I sit and she moves and then we're effortlessly situated in what's become our standard positions on the couch this week. Me in a half-seated, half-lying pose against the arm of the couch while she lies with her back against my chest and my arm wrapped around her.

We can't communicate this way very well since we aren't facing each other, so we usually chat on messenger. Her with her laptop, me using my phone. It feels natural, though. And I like it in the evenings when we spend time together like this because she wears headphones and listens to music on her laptop while we chat. I like it when she listens to music. I like watching her feet sway with the music. I like feeling her voice against my chest when she sings along to some of the lyrics. She's singing right now as she scrolls through iTunes on her computer. She has the newest Sounds of Cedar album pulled up. They released it as an indie album a couple of weeks after Sydney moved in with us, so none of the stuff she helped me write is on the album she's browsing. The songs I wrote with Sydney haven't officially been released yet.

That's not to say none of the songs on the album she's browsing were inspired by her. She just doesn't know that. I watch as she opens her messenger app and types me a message.

Sydney: Can I ask you a question?

Ridge: Didn't I tell you once to never propose a question by asking if you can propose a question?

Sydney: I just called you a dickhead out loud.

I laugh.

Sydney: The song called "Blind." Did you write that about Maggie?

I look away from my phone and down at her. She tilts her head and looks back at me, her eyes full of genuine curiosity. I nod and look back down at my phone, not really wanting to discuss the songs I wrote about Maggie.

Ridge: Yes.

Sydney: Did it make her mad?

Ridge: I don't think so. Why?

Sydney: The lyrics. Specifically the part you wrote that says, "A hundred reasons for the pain and only one on my mind. When did looking out for you make me go blind?"

Sydney: I just feel like if she listened to that, she would have understood what you meant by it and it might have hurt her feelings.

Sometimes I think Sydney understands my lyrics better than I do.

Ridge: If Maggie took those lyrics literally, she never made it seem that way. I write very honestly. You know that. But I don't think Maggie knows that. She didn't think everything I wrote was really how I felt. Even though it is, in some form or another.

Sydney: Is that going to be an issue going forward with us? Because I'll be dissecting every single word of every lyric. Just so you know.

I laugh at her comment.

Ridge: That's the beauty of lyrics. They can be interpreted many different ways. I could write a song and you might not even know it was inspired by you.

She shakes her head.

Sydney: I would know.

I smile. Because she's wrong.

Ridge: Play the third song on that album called "For a Little While."

Sydney presses play on the song and then sends me a message.

Sydney: I know this song by heart.

Ridge: And you think you know what it's about?

Sydney: Yes. It's about you wanting to escape for a little while with Maggie. Like maybe it's a song about her illness and how you wish you could get her away from it all.

Ridge: You're wrong. This song was inspired by you.

She pauses and then tilts her head, looking up at me. She looks confused, and rightfully so. This song was released shortly after she moved in with me, which probably made her think none of these songs were related to her in any way. Her fingers start tapping at her keyboard as she writes a response.

Sydney: How is this song about me? You would have had to have written it before I even moved in with you. They were already cutting this album when I moved in.

Ridge: Technically, the song isn't about you. It was just inspired by you. The song is more about me, and how sometimes being outside on that balcony, playing music for the girl across the courtyard, was my escape. It was the little bit of time I got every day where I didn't feel so stressed. Or worried. I didn't know you. You didn't know me. But we were both helping each other escape our worlds for a little while every night. That's what the song is about.

Sydney immediately stops the song and restarts it from the beginning. She pulls up the lyrics on Google and reads along as the song plays.

"For a Little While"

I don't know what you want but you do
If you told me I would make it true
Oh, for a little while
Oh, for a little while

Something changes when the sunlight shines
Shadows fall out of my worried mind
Things go right and then I feel just fine
You and me will be just one tonight
Oh, for a little while
Oh, for a little while

You know for a little while
Oh, for a little while

For a little while I feel okay
For a little while I float away

For a little while I can stay
For a little while I'm on my way

For a little while I'll be all right
For a little while I'll be outside
For a little while I'll be okay

I'll be okay
For a little while
For a little while
For a little while

When the song ends, she closes out the lyrics and lifts a hand to her eye, presumably to wipe away a tear. I stroke her hair with my fingers while she types.

Sydney: Why have you never told me this song is about us?

I inhale a breath and release it, pulling my hand from her hair so I can respond to her.

Ridge: It's the first song that was inspired by you while I was still with Maggie. It was innocent between us because we had never even spoken at the time, but the sentiment still made me feel guilty. This song was my truth and I think I tried to hide it, even from myself.

Sydney: I can understand that. In a way, the song kind of makes me sad for you. Like you were living a life you needed a break from.

Ridge: Almost everyone needs a break from their real life

every now and then. I was content with my life before I met you. You know that.

Sydney: Are you still content with your life?

Ridge: No. I was content before I met you. But now I'm deliriously happy with my life.

I lean forward and press a kiss into Sydney's hair. She leans back and gives me access to her lips, but from an upside-down angle. I kiss her, and she laughs against my mouth before lifting her head and returning her attention to her keyboard.

Sydney: My father used to say, "A life of mediocrity is a waste of a life." I used to hate that he would say that because he only said it to prove a point to me about how he didn't think I should become a music teacher. But I think I get it now. I'll be content with becoming a music teacher. But he wanted me to be passionate about my career. I always thought that was enough—to just be content. But now I'm scared it's not.

Ridge: Are you thinking about changing your major?

Sydney nods, but she doesn't type her response.

Ridge: To what?

Sydney: I've been thinking lately about going into psychology. Or counseling of some form. I'm just so far into my degree that I would practically have to start over.

Ridge: People's passions change. It happens. I think if you really see yourself in a different line of work other than being a music teacher, it's better it happens now than ten years into the future. And . . . for what it's worth . . . I think you would be an amazing psychologist. You're good with music, no doubt. But you're incredible with people. You could even combine the two majors and do music therapy.

Sydney: Thank you. But I don't know. Starting over just seems so daunting, especially because I'll need to get my master's degree. Which means I'll be struggling financially for another five years. Which will become your issue, too, if we ever move in together. I won't have much money to contribute to the bills. It's just a lot to think about. If I stick with my current major, I'll be done in less than a year.

Ridge: We don't need much to get by. I think it's more important that you do what your heart is telling you to. As long as you're doing what you really want, I'll do whatever I need in order to help you see it through to the end. Whether that's next year with a teaching degree or ten years and a doctorate from now.

Sydney: I'm adding that to my Things Ridge Says folder. In case I have to refer back to it in the future. Because if I change majors, I'm going to be really broke. So broke, I won't even be able to buy new clothes. I'll be wearing this same shirt five years from now.

Ridge: Even if your clothes are faded, they'll always look new on you.

I feel her laugh.

Sydney: Oh, that's a good line. You should put that in a song.

Ridge: I will. I promise.

She slides her laptop off her lap and flips over, climbing up me. She kisses me. "Do you want some ice cream? I want dessert."

I shake my head. "I'll just take a bite of yours."

She kisses me again and then stands and walks to the kitchen. I readjust myself on the couch and open up a text to Warren.

Ridge: What time are we leaving tomorrow?

Warren: I dunno. Let me open up a group text and ask Maggie.

Warren: Maggot, what time are we leaving for the caves tomorrow?

Maggie: Call me that again and I'll use all the hot water tonight. I don't know. It'll be after lunch. Jake can't be here until noon.

Ridge: Are we doing lunch on the way or should we eat before?

Maggie: Let's eat on the way. I'll feel bad if he gets here and hasn't eaten.

Warren: Okay. Lunch. Be hungry. Got it. Ridge, you and Syd meeting us here or do we need to pick you up?

Ridge: We can meet you guys there.

Maggie: Can I ask a favor? And this is mostly of Warren.

Warren: I'M GOING TO BE NICE TO HIM! STOP WORRYING, MAGGIE!

Maggie: I know you'll be nice. I don't worry about that. I worry about you being completely inappropriate.

Warren: Oh. Well, yeah. You should definitely worry about that.

I laugh and set my phone down because Sydney is walking back to the couch with a spoonful of ice cream in her mouth, and I don't want to think about anything else right now. As if she can see my thoughts, she grins a little, pulling the spoon out of her mouth.

"You want a bite?"

I nod.

She doesn't sit next to me on the couch to share it with me. She straddles me, holding the bowl of ice cream between us as she adjusts her legs on either side of me. She scoops a small spoon of the ice cream and gives me a bite. I swallow it, and then she dips her head and kisses me. Her mouth tastes like vanilla. Her tongue is cold as it slides against mine.

I pull her closer, but the bowl of ice cream between us is hindering me. I grab the bowl and set it aside on the table next to her and then pull her to me. I kiss her as I slowly lower her to the couch.

She's about to melt, just like her bowl of ice cream.

Chapter Twenty-Five

Maggie

Last night I dreamt Jake showed up with a date. A tall redhead with a French accent and black Louboutin heels.

Who goes to explore caves in high heels?

Or . . . better yet . . . *who shows up for a date with a date?* I was covered in sweat when I woke up, but I'm not sure if it was because Jake showed up in my dream with a date or because Warren and Bridgette shared one body with two heads. Both aspects of my dream were equally disturbing.

I don't know if it's my dream that has me so shaken, or if it's the fact that I've yet to have a conversation with Jake about the dynamics of our group, but I'm standing at the bathroom sink trying to brush my teeth, and my hand is visibly shaking.

I want to be able to talk to Jake before he meets everyone, but he'll be here in half an hour, and I can't very well call him minutes before he arrives and say, *Oh, by the way, you're about to hang out with my ex-boyfriend today. Both my ex-boyfriends, actually. It'll be fun!*

I should have canceled.

I almost did when I woke up after the nightmare I had last night. I had an excuse all typed out in a text to him about why I needed to cancel, but I was too scared to send it. He'd see right through it. I've been unreliable one too many times with him, and pushing him away again would probably be the last contact he'd have with me. Besides, in our conversation last night, he said he wants consistency. I don't want our consistency to be me pushing him away. I want it to be me following through with him. I just have to get him alone somehow before he meets Warren or Ridge. He deserves to know what he's getting into before he walks into this apartment.

If I could get him from the front door to my bedroom without him meeting anyone, it would give us a few minutes alone to reacquaint ourselves without standing in the danger zone that is the communal living room of this apartment.

That's what I'll do. I'll somehow drag him to my room before introductions.

As soon as I finish brushing my teeth, I dry my mouth with a hand towel and stare at my reflection. Other than the absolute fear in my eyes, I look like I usually do. I return my toothbrush to my toiletry bag, just as Bridgette swings open the bathroom door that leads to their room. She pauses when she sees me. I pause when I see her.

It's always been awkward between us, but we've never had to share a bathroom before, so the fact that she's in her barely there underwear takes awkward to a whole new level. For me, anyway. She doesn't seem bothered that I'm seeing her nearly nude, because she walks straight to the toilet and pulls down her panties to pee.

She's just as uninhibited as Warren.

"So," Bridgette says, unrolling toilet paper into her hand, "does this guy realize what he's getting into?"

"What do you mean?"

She waves a hand in a circle. "You know. This whole group he's about to spend the day with. Does he know the history?"

I close my eyes for a second, breathing in steadily. "Not yet," I say, exhaling.

Bridgette does something she rarely does. She grins.

No . . . she *smiles*. A huge, excited smile that reveals all her perfect white teeth. She should smile more often. She has a great smile, although it's appearing at an odd moment.

"Why do you look so happy?" I ask with caution.

"It's just been so long since I've been this excited about something."

I look away from her without responding and glance back at my own reflection. I look pale. I can't tell if it's because I'm nervous or if my blood sugar levels are off. Sometimes it's hard to tell the difference between low blood sugar, high blood sugar, or the onset of a panic attack.

I leave the bathroom and walk to the kitchen. My purse

is on the counter, so I dig through it until I find my glucose monitor kit. I lean against the counter while I check my blood sugar. As soon as I insert the test strip into the monitor, the front door begins to open.

Ridge and Sydney walk into the apartment, hand in hand. Sydney greets me, and Ridge nods, then signs to Sydney that he's going to shower. On his way to his bedroom, though, he does a double take when he sees the testing kit in my hands. His forehead naturally creases with worry.

"I'm fine," I sign. "Just wanted to check it before we leave to be safe."

Relief floods his expression. "How long before we leave?"

I shrug. "No rush. Jake isn't even here yet."

He nods and heads to his bedroom. Sydney sets her purse on the bar next to mine and opens a cabinet, grabbing a bag of tortilla chips.

My glucose levels are in the normal range. I sigh, relieved, then put the kit back in my purse. I grab my phone and open up my texts with Jake. We had a quick conversation this morning. I sent him the address to our apartment, and half an hour later he responded with a text that said, Conference over. On my way.

That was almost an hour ago. Which means he'll be knocking on the door any minute now.

"You okay?" Sydney asks.

I look up from my phone. She's leaning against the

counter, staring at me with concern as she munches on chips. "You look a little nervous," she adds.

Is it that obvious? "I do?"

She nods softly, as if she's trying not to offend me with her observation.

I wasn't even this nervous when I woke up this morning from my nightmare. But as the hours progress, so does my regret. I wring my hands together as I glance toward Ridge's and Warren's bedroom doors to make sure they're closed. I look back at Sydney once I'm positive she's the only one in my vicinity. "I've picked up my phone to cancel at least three times this morning, but I was never able to hit send on the texts. I just know there's no way he could possibly enjoy today. I don't even know why I invited him. I was so flustered when he called back yesterday that I didn't think any of this through."

Sydney tilts her head and smiles at me reassuringly. "It'll be fine, Maggie. He obviously likes you, or he wouldn't have agreed to drive all the way here and spend time with people he doesn't even know."

"That's the problem," I say. "He *does* like me. But he likes a version of me that's confident and independent and has one-night stands. He hasn't hung out with the insecure version of me who is living on a mattress on the floor of the spare bedroom of my ex-boyfriend's apartment."

Sydney dismisses my comment with a flippant wave of her hand. "For one more day. You're moving out tomorrow, and you'll be independent and in your own place again."

I shrug. "Even still. It doesn't change the fact that I've been an emotional toddler for most of the past couple of weeks." I let my head fall back, and I groan. "I've been so hot and cold with him. He probably only agreed to today because he's hoping I'll impress him enough so that he can forget about all the times I was *un*impressive."

Sydney sets down the bag of chips. She rolls her eyes and walks up to me, placing her hands on my shoulders. She backs me up against a barstool, keeping her hands on my shoulders as she forces me to sit. "Do you know what I did for the first two weeks of living here?"

I shake my head.

"I cried every day. I cried because my life was shit, and I cried because I got fired from the library for having an emotional breakdown and throwing books at the wall. And, sure, I got better for a while. But a few months later, when I moved out and got my own place, I cried every day for weeks again."

I raise an eyebrow. "Why are you telling me this?"

"Because," she says, releasing my shoulders and standing up straight. "I was all over the place with my emotions for months on end. But every time I saw you, you were the epitome of strength. Even the day you found out about me and Ridge, I was so intimidated by your resolve. And . . . maybe even a little impressed. But you seem to be forgetting about all of that, and instead, you're focusing on a few bad days you've had." She reaches down and grabs my hands, looking at me with an expression full of sincerity. "No one is the best version of themselves all the time, Maggie. But what creates the difference between confidence and insecurity are the moments in our past that we choose to obsess over. You're obsessing over your shittiest moments when you should be obsessing over the better ones."

I haven't been around her a whole lot, but when I am around her, she impresses me more and more with how right she always is. I put a lot of weight on that as I cycle through a couple of breaths. I begin to nod. I've definitely had some unpleasant moments. So has she. So has Ridge. So have Warren and Bridgette. And . . . even though he seems perfect . . . Jake has had moments in his past when he hasn't been perfect. And I'm sure if I knew about his imperfect moments, I wouldn't hold them against him for a second. Which means he probably doesn't hold my indecisiveness against me like I've been worried he might. Otherwise, he wouldn't be knocking on the door right now.

Oh, God. He's knocking.

"Oh, God," I say out loud.

Sydney glances at the door and then back at me. "You want me to answer it?"

I shake my head. "No. I'll do it."

She waits for me to stand, but I don't. I just stare at the door, unmoving.

"Maggie."

"I know. I just . . . I don't think I'm ready for introductions yet. Can you . . ."

She nods, pulling me out of my chair. "I'll disappear," she agrees. "You answer the door."

Sydney gives me a quick shove toward the door as she rushes off toward Ridge's bedroom. Jake knocks again, and I'm scared if I don't open the door right away, Warren will walk out of his bedroom to answer the door. Or worse . . . Bridgette.

That thought swings me into action. I open the front door, and Jake is here, standing right in front of me. He's taller than I remember. Cuter. I suck in a breath at the sight of him, but I don't give myself time to give him a once-over. I grab his hand and pull him inside the apartment and across the living room. I don't release his hand until we're safely alone in my bedroom. I turn and shut the door behind us, leaning my forehead against it. I blow out a breath, still facing the door. I'm slightly more at ease now that we're out of the danger zone, but still nervous as hell as I slowly turn and face him.

He's standing a couple of feet in front of me, looking down at me like he's trying not to laugh.

God, he's cute. He's wearing jeans and a navy-blue graphic T-shirt with an anatomically correct heart on the front of it. *Funny.* I stare at the shirt for a moment, admiring how good he looks in it. Then I look him in the eye and stand up a little straighter. I clear my throat.

"Hi," I say.

He tilts his head a bit, curiosity clouding his expression. He's probably wondering why I rushed him into this room like there were zombies chasing us. "Hello, Maggie." I can see all the questions he isn't asking as he narrows his eyes, lifting a brow.

"Sorry. I just wanted a minute alone with you before introductions."

He smiles, and I just want to sink to the floor. Not because his smile melts me, but because I'm so embarrassed about the conversation I'm about to have with him. I'm embarrassed by the condition of this bedroom. I'm embarrassed that he's a doctor who seems to have all his shit together, whereas my life is currently akin to a broke college coed's, living in a sparse dorm room.

Jake's hands slide into his back pockets and he glances around the room—at the mattress on the floor. He looks back at me. "Is this your bedroom?"

"Just until tomorrow. All my stuff is in a U-Haul downstairs. I'm moving to another unit in the complex."

He laughs a little, like he's relieved to know I own more than just a pathetic mattress pushed against the wall of an empty room. He's a few feet away from me, but I still have to look up at him. I suck in a shaky breath after I respond to him. He notices.

"You seem nervous," he says.

"I am," I admit.

He smiles at my honesty. "Me too."

"Why?" I blurt out.

He shrugs. "Same reasons you are, I assume."

I know for a fact we aren't nervous for the same reasons.

"Please," I say, rolling my eyes with a laugh. "You're a cardiologist raising a half-grown child. I'm just a college student with roommates, sleeping on a mattress on the floor of an empty room. I can assure you we are not nervous for the same reasons."

Jake stares at me a moment, contemplating my words. "Are you saying you feel inferior to me?"

I nod. "Just a little," I lie. Because I feel a *lot* inferior to him.

He releases a quick laugh, but he doesn't respond. He just takes a step away from me and looks around the room again, turning his back to me. His focus falls on my mattress for a moment. He looks back at me over his shoulder and then half turns, reaching out his hand.

I look down at his hand, beckoning for mine. I slide my hand into his, admiring the strength behind his grip as he closes his fingers around mine. He pulls me with him, walking toward the mattress.

He sits down, scooting to the middle of the mattress, resting his back against the wall. He still has a grip on my hand, so he pulls on it, urging me to follow suit. As soon as I begin to kneel, he pulls one of my legs over his lap so that I'm straddling him.

Not what I was expecting.

We're almost eye to eye, but I haven't relaxed yet, so I'm slightly taller than him in this position. He leans his head back against the wall, looking up at me.

"There," he says, smiling gently. "Now, you're in

a position of control. It should make you a little less nervous."

He rests his hands on my waist. I feel some of the tension leave my shoulders when I realize what he just did. I smile as I'm reminded how patient and kind he is. He returns my smile, and I suddenly feel like melting to the floor again, but not out of embarrassment. This time I want to melt because he's so damn perfect, and it's making me blush.

Also, I can't help but be relieved that he didn't show up with a high-heeled French redhead. I exhale. "Thank you. This helps."

He breaks eye contact and finds my hands, threading his fingers through them. "You're welcome."

Now that I've relaxed a little, I lower my legs until our thighs are flush together. We're eye to eye now, and I feel stupid for how nervous I've been. I forgot how everything about him is so calming. He's been a calming presence since the moment we met and I was scared to death to skydive until he sat down next to me to fill out my paperwork. His presence is like a sedative, flowing through my veins, taming my thoughts and my worries. In a matter of minutes, the fear in my eyes has been subdued, and now I'm forcing myself not to grin. He makes me feel somewhat giddy, but I don't want him to know that.

"How was your lecture this morning?" I ask, hoping to direct the subject toward him.

Jake laughs a little. "Justice told me I shouldn't go into

doctor mode when I'm around you. He says I'm boring when I talk about medical stuff."

That couldn't be further from the truth. "Our medical talk was the highlight of our date for me. It's the first time anyone has ever been that interested in the details of my thesis."

Jake narrows his eyes. "Really?"

I nod. "Yes, really. You probably shouldn't take dating advice from an eleven-year-old."

Jake laughs at that. "Yeah, you're probably right." He brings my hands to his chest and places them there, moving his own hands to the tops of my thighs. "We had a speaker who is about to have a new study published in the *Journal of Medical Science*. He presented about communication signals between the brain and the heart and what happens when those signals are severed."

Yeah, Justice is definitely wrong. I absolutely want to hear this. "And?"

Jake leans his head back against the wall again, relaxing a little. He lifts one of my hands off his chest and brings it up between us. "In ancient times, humans believed the heart was at the center of all thought process and that the brain and heart didn't communicate at all." He touches my wrist with two gentle fingers. "They believed this because when you feel an attraction to someone, your brain doesn't respond in a noticeable way that would suddenly make you aware of that attraction. But the rest of the body does." Jake begins to move his fingers in a delicate circle over my wrist.

I swallow heavily, hoping he doesn't notice what it's doing to my pulse.

"The heart is what makes a person most aware of physical attraction. It increases in speed. It begins to beat harder against the walls of the chest. It creates an erratic pulse whenever you're around the person you're attracted to."

It's quiet as he presses his fingers firmly against my wrist, waiting several seconds before he begins to speak. He grins a little, and I know it's because my pulse has changed so much since we started this particular conversation.

"It doesn't feel like that attraction is being manifested in the brain," he says, pressing his other hand right over my heart. "It feels like it's developing right here. Right behind the walls of your chest, in the very core of the organ that goes haywire."

Jesus Christ. He pulls his hand from my chest and releases my wrist. He lowers his hands to my waist, gripping gently.

"We're aware the heart doesn't retain or produce actual emotion. The heart is simply a messenger, receiving signals directly from the brain that let the heart know when an attraction is present. The heart and the brain are in sync because they are both vital and they work as a team. When the heart begins to die, a flurry of signals is sent from the brain, which ultimately causes the demise of the heart. And in turn, lack of oxygen from the heart is ultimately what causes the demise of the brain. One organ cannot survive without the other." He grins. "Or so we thought. In today's lecture, we learned that a new study proves that if communication between the heart and brain is severed in the minutes before death, an animal lives up to three times as long as those whose heart-brain connection is still left intact. Which, if proven correct, means that when the chemical connection is severed between the two organs, one doesn't immediately know when the other begins to die because they're unable to communicate. Therefore . . . if the heart begins to die and the brain is unaware, it gives doctors more time to save the heart before the brain begins to shut down. And vice versa."

I could honestly listen to him talk like this all day. "Are you saying that the heart and the brain might actually be detrimental to one another?"

He nods once. "Yep. It's almost as if they communicate *too* well. The study suggested that if we can make one organ temporarily oblivious to the failing of the other organ, we may be able to save them both."

"Wow," I say. "That's . . . fascinating."

Jake smiles. "It is. I thought about it the entire drive over. Essentially, if we could figure out how to sever some of the communication between the heart and brain in *non-*life-or-death situations, we could likely make it so that attraction wouldn't manifest physically in a person."

I shake my head. "But . . . why would a person not want to feel the full extent of an attraction?"

"Because," he says, matter-of-fact, "that way when a doctor develops an intense attraction to a girl he meets while skydiving, his mind won't be completely distracted for every minute of the two weeks that follow, and he might actually be able to focus on his job instead of thoughts of her."

His words make me blush so heavily, I immediately lean forward and lower my head to his shoulder so that he can't see my reaction. He laughs at my response, running a hand up my back and into my hair. He presses a quick kiss to the side of my head.

I eventually pull back and look at him. Everything he just said makes me want to lower my head again, but this time I want to lower it so that my mouth is positioned right against his. I refrain, though. Somehow.

He inhales and loses some of the smile in his eyes, trading it for a more serious expression. His hands slide up and then back down my arms. "I came back to the hospital to see you Saturday, but you were already gone," he admits.

I close my eyes briefly. I wondered if he showed back up.

I don't want to admit to him that I left before I should have. But I don't want to lie to him, or even omit the truth. "I left Friday night. Before they discharged me." I look him in the eyes, needing to explain myself before he passes judgment. "I know you're a doctor and you're going to tell me it was a stupid move, but I already know that. I just couldn't take being there for another second."

He stares back at me for a quiet moment, but he doesn't look angry or annoyed. He just shakes his head softly. "I get it. I have patients who practically live in hospitals, and I know how draining it is, both emotionally and physically.

Sometimes I want to look the other way and tell them to run because I know how much they don't want to be there."

I have no immediate reply to that because it's not a reaction I'm used to. I love that he didn't scold me just now. But I'm sure he sees patients with all different levels of frustration, so it would make sense that he'd be more empathetic than disapproving.

Jake lifts a hand to my hair and twists his fingers in a few strands of it. He stares at my hair as it slides through his fingers. When our eyes meet again, I can tell he's about to kiss me. His eyes drop briefly to my mouth. But I can't allow that until I explain to him the real reason for most of my nerves today.

"I need to tell you something," I say. I'm hesitant to bring it up, but he's here, and he's about to meet everyone, and he needs to know what he's getting into. He looks back at me patiently as I continue. "This is Ridge's apartment. My ex-boyfriend that I told you about on our date?"

Jake gives no hint of a response in his expression, so I continue, glancing away from him and down at our hands. I lace our fingers together. "Ridge and his girlfriend, Sydney, are going with us today. So are Warren and Bridgette, who are the other two roommates here. You'll meet them all in a little while. I just . . . It's why I wanted you to come to my room before meeting them, so if our history is brought up today, you won't be caught off guard." I make eye contact with him again, releasing a pent-up breath. "Does that bother you?"

Jake doesn't answer right away. I don't blame him, so I give him a moment to process everything I just said. It's a weird situation that I probably shouldn't have put him in.

"Does it bother *you*?" he asks, squeezing my hands.

I shake my head. "We're friends now. I really like Sydney. I feel like all of us are exactly where we need to be, but after I invited you here, I became paranoid that maybe I shouldn't have. I don't want it to be awkward."

Jake lifts a hand, sliding it against my cheek. His fingers graze the back of my head as he looks at me intently. "If it doesn't bother you, then it doesn't bother me," he says with finality.

His quick acceptance makes me smile with relief, even though I fail to tell him that it is *very* awkward for me.

Sydney is wrong. Some people are the best versions of themselves all the time.

That thought fills me with immediate guilt, because there's so much more to the situation than what I just admitted to Jake. He has no idea that Warren and Ridge are basically the only family I have. But I don't want to put too much on him at once. Not until we know for sure that this thing between us might actually go somewhere beyond today. I honestly don't know that I want it to until he has a clear idea of who I am, but I have no idea where to start. He spent one of my better days with me, but he hasn't gotten to know all of me yet. He knows I'm spontaneous and indecisive, but what else does he actually know?

"I'm fickle," I blurt out. "And sometimes I can be selfish." I know I should shut up, but the blunt honesty feels warranted. He needs to know exactly what he's dealing with. I don't want to experience another relationship with someone I'm not completely up front and open with. "I have a rebellious streak that I'm really trying to work on. I sometimes spend entire days binge-watching Netflix in my underwear. I've lived alone most of my adult life, so I eat ice cream out of the tub and drink straight out of the milk carton. I've never wanted children of my own. I kind of want a cat, but I'm too scared of the responsibility. I love show tunes and Hallmark Christmas movies, and I absolutely hate Austin traffic. And I know none of that really matters because we aren't even dating, but I feel like you should know all those things about me up front." When I'm finished, I bite my bottom lip nervously, waiting for him to either laugh at me or run. I'd completely understand either reaction.

He reacts in a completely different way than what I expect. He sighs and tilts his head a little, pulling our hands to his chest. His thumbs brush back and forth over mine.

"I internalize everything negative that happens at work," he says. "I need solitude on the really bad days. Sometimes even from Justice. And . . . I'm messy. I haven't done dishes in four days or laundry in two weeks. Most doctors are organized, and their houses are spotless, but mine is chaotic most of the time. And I probably shouldn't admit this because I'm a cardiologist, but I love fried food. I've watched every episode of *Grey's Anatomy*, although I'll deny it if you ever repeat that. And . . . I've only been with two women, so I don't even know that I'm all that impressive in bed."

The fact that he just admitted all that makes me feel like I might get a little emotional, but luckily, the last part of his admission makes me laugh. "You're impressive, Jake. Trust me."

He arches a brow. "Am I?"

I nod, feeling the heat rise to my cheeks just thinking about it.

"Can you be more specific?" he teases. "What was your favorite part?"

I think back on our night together, and honestly, all of it was great. But if I had to narrow it down to a favorite moment, I know exactly which one it is. "The second time. When you kept your eyes open and watched me while we . . ." My voice trails off. I can't even finish that sentence. Jake stares at me very seriously for a moment. His hands cover mine completely. "That was my favorite part, too."

I duck my head a little, breaking eye contact with him. Not because I'm nervous anymore, but because I'm trying to prevent myself from kissing him.

He reaches out and slides his hand to the nape of my neck, pulling my gaze back to his. His other hand slides around to my lower back, pulling me closer. "There were a lot of parts I liked about that night." He smiles as he inches his mouth closer to mine. "I liked undressing you as we stood next to your bed," he whispers, right before he presses his lips to mine.

I close my eyes, completely weakened by his kiss, but he pulls back.

"And I liked it when I lowered you to the bed." His lips lightly feather mine, and I feel him shift as he leans forward and lowers me to the mattress. I'm no longer in the position of control, but I don't mind it. My eyes feel heavy when I open them, looking up at him while he hovers over me. "And I really liked it the next morning when I woke up and you were wrapped around me so tight, it took me ten minutes to sneak out of the bed without waking you."

I open my mouth slightly, preparing a response, but he doesn't allow it. He dips his head and kisses me. As soon as his lips close over mine, I'm reminded of everything I felt the first time he kissed me. I don't know how I was able to deny him even once, much less twice.

Sometimes I'm impressed by my own strength, because right now, there's no way I could choose anything else over this kiss. I don't even care if we leave this room today, because his tongue has found mine and my hands are sliding through his hair, and *why can't I be in my own apartment already?* I'm conscious of every noise I want to make right now.

Luckily, he stops it before more parts of us get involved in this make-out session than simply our mouths. He kisses me softly, twice, before pressing his cheek to mine and releasing a heavy sigh into my hair.

I sigh right along with him, realizing that we're going to have to leave this room at some point. "I guess I should introduce you to my roommates now."

His gaze scrolls my face for a moment. "Yeah. I guess so."

I swallow, feeling the nerves start to build as I think about him meeting everyone. Specifically Warren. "Can you promise me something?"

Jake nods.

"Don't judge me too harshly based on a couple of my roommates. Warren's sole purpose today will be to embarrass me as much as he possibly can."

Jake's mouth breaks out into a devilish grin. "Oh, I can't wait to meet him now."

I roll my eyes and push against his chest. Jake rolls off me and onto his back. I stand up and straighten out my shirt, but he remains on the bed, staring up at me with an unusual expression.

"What?" I ask, wondering why he looks so . . . satiated.

He stares for a moment longer, then shakes his head and pushes off the mattress. He stands up, pressing a quick kiss to my forehead. "You're so fucking pretty," he mutters, almost in passing, as he grabs my hand and walks me toward my bedroom door.

That one comment completely eviscerates every hesitant, nervous feeling that remained from before he arrived. If he weren't pulling me out of the bedroom right now to go and meet everyone, I would make him wait so that I could find a pen and add another line to my bucket list. It would only be two words.

Jake. Griffin.

It wouldn't say, *Make love to Jake Griffin* or *Marry Jake Griffin*.

The entire tenth item on my bucket list would simply be his name, almost as if I could somehow accomplish him as a whole.

Item number ten to accomplish:

Jake Griffin.

Chapter Twenty-Six

Jake

When people ask me why I became a doctor, which is quite a common question, I give them the quintessential answer: I want to save lives. I want to make a difference. I like helping people.

It's all bullshit.

I became a doctor because I love adrenaline.

Of course, the other answers are true as well. But the main reason is adrenaline. I love being the difference in a life-or-death situation. I love the rush I get when my skills are put to the test against a rapidly failing organ. I love the satisfaction I get when I win.

I was born competitive.

But there's a difference between being competitive and being in competition with someone else. I'm not competitive against other doctors or other people. I'm only competitive against myself. I'm in a constant battle to improve my own skill set in everything I do, whether that's in the operating room, jumping out of an airplane, or being the absolute best father I can be to Justice. I'm always on a quest to be a better me tomorrow than I was yesterday. It's never been about competing with anyone other than myself.

Until this moment. Because in this particular moment, I find myself hoping Ridge doesn't measure up to me. I haven't even met him yet, but I've never been in a situation where I'm about to meet the ex-boyfriend of the girl I'm interested in. It's not something I was prepared to do today. *Or ever.* When I started dating Chrissy in high school, I was her first legitimate boyfriend. I was her first kiss. Her first date. Her first everything. And considering we spent more than ten years together after that, I've never had to deal with feeling competitive with another man.

I'm not sure I like it.

When Maggie mentioned Ridge for the first time on our date, she talked about how he'd met someone else while he was dating her, which was ultimately what led to their breakup. I don't know the guy, but that was an automatic strike against him in my book. She also mentioned he writes music for a band, which is another strike against him. Not that being in a band is a bad thing, but it's hard to compete with a musician, even when you're a doctor.

What little she did say about Ridge gave me the impression that she doesn't regret the demise of their relationship. But it's still slightly uncomfortable knowing this is his apartment. Maggie is his ex. I'm about to spend the day with his friends. I can't imagine many guys being okay with their ex bringing along a new guy, so unless he's some kind of saint, I probably have good reason to suddenly be on edge. I don't like that I'm experiencing jealousy over a girl for the first time, and I haven't even met the guy who is the cause of my irrational jealousy.

But that's about to change because we're walking out of Maggie's bedroom now, specifically for introductions. I open the door and step aside so that Maggie can walk out of her bedroom first. She looks up at me as she passes, and she smiles with a hint of calm appreciation in her eyes, despite her own nervousness.

It's the same look she gave me when I was helping her with her skydiving paperwork the first day we met. She was a ball of nervous energy—enough for me to have felt it from all the way across the room. But as soon as I sat down next to her, she somehow smiled at me with an appreciative look in her eyes that made me feel as though I were in the process of jumping out of that plane with her. She says a lot without saying anything. I've never met anyone else whose expressions hold entire conversations.

Right now, her expression is saying, *This is awkward, I know. But it'll be fine.*

She leaves her bedroom door open and walks ahead of me across the living room. There's a guy standing in the kitchen with his back to us. I can't tell from this view, but it looks like he may be on his phone. There's a blond girl standing near the bar, slipping into a pair of shoes. She glances up as soon as she hears us exiting Maggie's bedroom. Her whole face lights up when she sees me next to Maggie.

Maggie waves her hand toward her. "Jake, this is Sydney."

Sydney continues twisting her shoe into the carpet to get it on her foot. Once she does, she walks over to me, half hopping as she extends her hand. "It's so good to meet you," she says, pulling on the other shoe.

I return her handshake. "You too."

Maggie mentioned Sydney's name to me earlier, and that she's Ridge's current girlfriend. I'm not sure how this scenario played out, but Maggie and Sydney seem to get along, which says a lot about them as individuals. And there's something about Sydney that feels genuine. I like her almost immediately.

I can't say the same for the guy behind her in the kitchen with his back still to us. He's obviously completely uninterested in introductions. I can only assume this is Ridge, but before I can put too much thought into what his reaction means and how this is definitely a competitive move on his part, two people walk out of one of the other rooms.

Based on Maggie's passing, almost agitated look as she turns to face them, I can only assume the guy walking toward me is Warren. The gleam in his eyes screams *mischief*, and Maggie did mention Warren's sole purpose today is to embarrass her.

He's holding his arms out as he makes his way over to

me. He pulls me in for a hug. I reluctantly hug him back. I'm not sure I've been greeted with a hug from another guy in years. In my occupation, it's handshakes and professional introductions and inquiries about which golf course you prefer to frequent on Sundays.

It isn't bear hugs and pats on the cheeks. This guy is *actually patting my cheeks.*

"Wow," he says. "You are really good-looking." He glances at Maggie. "Good job, Maggot. He looks like Captain America."

I laugh and back up a step, not sure if embarrassing Maggie is his sole intention. I think he wants to embarrass both of us.

"Warren, this is Jake," Maggie says, already appearing exhausted with him.

Warren salutes me. "Good to meet you, Jake."

With as much enthusiasm as Warren is showing, the other guy is still showing none. He continues to ignore the situation, completely uninterested that I'm here. Maybe this is why Maggie warned me. Because I'm not exactly welcome by everyone.

I give my full attention back to Warren. "Good to meet you, too."

Warren points at the brunette standing next to him. "This is my girlfriend, Bridgette."

She doesn't say anything to me. She just nods and walks to the refrigerator.

Warren points at Ridge. "Did you meet Ridge already?"

I shake my head. "Not yet." I'm not sure I *want* to meet Ridge at this point. He obviously has no interest in meeting me.

Warren closes the distance between himself and the kitchen and taps Ridge on the shoulder. When Ridge turns, Warren begins to sign at the same time he says, "Jake is here." Ridge spins around fully and finally makes eye contact with me.

I always teach Justice not to make assumptions about people. Yet here I am . . . being an assumptive asshole. Ridge isn't bothered that I'm here. He didn't *know* I was here.

He walks around the bar, closing the distance between us. "Hi," he says, shaking my hand. "Ridge Lawson." His voice is a clear indicator that he wasn't intentionally ignoring me and that I am, in fact, an assumptive asshole.

I return his handshake with relief. "Jake Griffin."

I don't know if Maggie intentionally left out that Ridge is deaf, or if his deafness is their norm and she just didn't think to mention it. Either way, I'm relieved by it, because five seconds ago I was ready to call it a day when I assumed I was intruding, but now his genuine welcome is as comforting as Sydney's.

I no longer harbor the competitive, jealous feelings I was attempting to suppress on the way out of Maggie's bedroom. I don't know the history between these people beyond what Maggie has shared, which isn't much, but there doesn't seem to be any ill will between any of them.

Although I still haven't spoken to Warren's girlfriend. Maybe she's just shy.

The next few seconds are a flurry of activity. Ridge is putting on his shoes, Sydney is pulling on a jacket, Warren walks over to the girl who just shut the fridge . . . *Bridgette* . . . and tries to kiss her, but she pushes him away.

I glance over at Maggie, and she smiles at me. "Let me grab my sweater." She walks back to her bedroom. I look around at the apartment and notice there are several doors leading to other rooms. Maggie mentioned how she and Ridge know each other, but I still don't know the connection between everyone else.

"Are you all roommates?" I ask, looking around at the four of them. "Is that how you all know each other?"

Bridgette is in the middle of sipping from a bottle of water, but she perks up at my question, just as Maggie reappears from her bedroom with a sweater. "Oh, I'll happily explain how we all know each other," Bridgette says, screwing the cap on her water bottle.

Maggie says her name in what appears to be an attempt to stop Bridgette from speaking, but Bridgette ignores her.

"Warren and Ridge have been best friends for years," Bridgette explains, pointing between Warren and Ridge with the water bottle. She then points it in Maggie's direction. "Warren used to date Maggie, but they didn't last very long before Ridge swooped in and claimed her."

Wait. *Both* of these guys used to date Maggie?

"Maggie and Ridge dated for six years, but that ended when Sydney moved in last year. Now *Sydney* is dating Ridge, but she doesn't actually live here with us anymore. Maggie does, though. Until her new apartment is ready, which is here in the same complex as both of her ex-boyfriends." Bridgette looks at me. "And no, none of this is weird. At all. Especially right now as we all pretend we're best friends and we spend the whole day doing best-friend stuff together. *Yay.*"

Bridgette says the last word of that sentence with absolutely zero enthusiasm.

I guess I had her pegged wrong, too. She isn't shy at all.

The next ten seconds are quiet. Quieter than any ten seconds have ever been. I glance at Maggie, and she has a look of horror on her face. Sydney glares at Bridgette, silently scolding her. Bridgette looks at Sydney and shrugs like she did nothing wrong.

Then my phone rings.

The interruption is an immediate excuse for everyone to scatter. Everyone but Maggie, who is watching me, waiting for my next move.

I pull my phone out of my pocket, knowing by the distinct ring that it's Chrissy. She never calls unless it's important. Long gone are the days when we called each other just to chat. I swipe my finger across the screen and then pull the phone to my ear as I point toward Maggie's bedroom, letting her know I'm heading in there to take the call in private. I close the door partially as I walk into the room.

"Hey."

"Hey," Chrissy says, breathless. I can tell she's rushing, probably pulling on her scrubs. "Got called in. Can I drop Justice off with you?"

I close my eyes. He's almost twelve. We leave him alone on occasion, but not when I'm more than a block away. "I'm in Austin." I squeeze the back of my neck. "It'll take me an hour to get back."

"Austin?" she says. "Oh. Okay. I would send him to Cody's house for the day, but he woke up in the middle of the night with a stomach bug. Should I call my mom?"

I glance at Maggie's bedroom door. "No. No, I'm on my way. I'll pick him up and take him over to my place for the night."

Chrissy thanks me and ends the call. I stare down at the phone, wondering how Maggie will take this. I sort of wish she'd heard the entire conversation so she doesn't think I'm making up an excuse to get out of today after Bridgette's spiel.

I slide the phone into my pocket and walk toward Maggie's door. When I open it, she glances at me from the kitchen, where she's talking with Sydney.

"Can we chat?" I point back toward her room to indicate I'd like to do it in private. She nods and then shares a quick glance with Sydney before walking back to her room. She closes the door once we're both inside.

"I'm sorry," she says. "Bridgette made it all seem so weird, but I swear—"

I hold up my hand, interrupting her. "Maggie, it's fine. I know you wouldn't have invited me here if you were still hung up on someone else."

She looks relieved by my comment.

"My timing couldn't be shittier," I say. "But Chrissy, my ex-wife, just called. Justice is sick, and she got called in to work. I have to head back home."

There isn't a single shred of doubt in Maggie's expression. Only concern. "Is he okay?"

"Yeah, it's just a stomach bug."

She nods, but I can tell she's somewhat disappointed that I'm leaving. So am I, though. I pull her to me to give her a hug goodbye. She molds to my chest, making it difficult to want to release her.

"Downfall of two doctors sharing a child," I say. "You're on call even on the weekends you aren't on call."

She pulls back and looks up at me. I slide my hands to her cheeks and bend down to give her a kiss. I can't help but notice that our physical interaction is way ahead of our relationship. We aren't even dating, but the way I hug her and kiss her and respond to her would indicate otherwise. It's why I make sure our kiss goodbye is nothing more than a peck. The last thing I want to do is overwhelm her again. "Have fun today."

She smiles. "I will. I hope Justice feels better soon."

"Thank you. And send me some pictures of the caves. I'll call you tonight after you're back if it's not too late."

"I would like that," she says. "Want me to walk you out?"

"I would like that."

•   •   •

One would think that a man who regularly slices through people's chests wouldn't be bothered by a little vomit.

Not the case with me.

I'm convinced Justice has vomited more today than he did the first five years of his life. Or maybe it just seems that way because he's older and bigger and produces more vomit, but fuck, there was so much vomit. I couldn't be happier that it's over. For now. There can't possibly be anything left in the poor kid to even puke up.

When I'm finished scrubbing the bathroom, showering, and checking on Justice, I finally settle into the couch to catch up on my conversation with Maggie. They returned from the caves a little over an hour ago, and she sent me a few pictures. I told her I'd FaceTime with her as soon as I got Justice to bed.

She answers almost immediately. The smile on her face disappoints me, but only because I'm not seeing it in person.

"How is Justice?"

I love that she asks this before we even say hello.

"Asleep. And empty. I think he's expelled everything he's eaten since January."

She makes a face. "Poor kid."

She's lying on her bed, her hair spread out over the pillow. She's holding the phone above her. It's the same view I had of her earlier today as I was hovering over her, preparing to kiss her. I force the thought out of my head before she sees through me. "Was the trip as fun as your pictures made it seem?"

She nods. "It was. Well, mostly." She pushes the hair away from her forehead to reveal a small bandage near her temple. "Warren thought it would be a good idea to hide from us and then scare us. I turned really fast, and me and Bridgette butted heads." She laughs, smoothing her hair back in place. "Warren felt so bad, he bought us all dinner. I mean, it was Taco Bell, but still. Warren never pays for anything ever."

I smile. I like that she seems to have had fun. Happiness looks really good on her. "You ready for the big move tomorrow?"

She nods, rolling onto her side as she lowers the phone. "I'm ready to have my own bathroom again."

"I'd offer to come help, but Chrissy is on call until Monday. I should probably keep Justice at my place until he's feeling better so there isn't a lot of back-and-forth."

"We have plenty of help. I don't have a whole lot to move, anyway. But I'll FaceTime you tomorrow night and show you my new place after we're finished."

"I'd like it better if I could see it in person."

She grins. "When's your next day off?"

"I have an early day on Wednesday. I could drive to

you . . . We could order takeout. Can't spend the night this time, but I could stay a few hours."

"That sounds good. I'll cook for you," she says.

"Do you know how long it's been since I've had a home-cooked meal?"

She smiles again and then follows her smile up with a sigh. I open my mouth to tell her how pretty she looks, but I'm interrupted when Justice walks into the room. "Hey, buddy," I say, looking up from my phone. "You feeling okay?"

Justice nods but doesn't look at me. He walks to the kitchen and opens the refrigerator.

"I'll let you go," Maggie whispers, pulling my attention back to my phone.

I smile appreciatively at her. "Call me tomorrow when you're all settled."

"I will. Goodnight."

I stare at her a moment, not quite ready to end my conversation with her. But I also don't want to be on the phone with her while Justice is in the room. "Goodnight, Maggie," I whisper. She waves and then ends the call. I toss my phone on the couch and then walk into the kitchen with Justice.

He's standing with the refrigerator door open, and he's opening a slice of American cheese. He takes a bite out of it, leaving the slice dangling from his mouth while he grabs the deli meat. He pulls out a slice of ham and shoves it in his mouth, along with the rest of the slice of cheese.

"It would be easier if you just let me make you a sandwich," I offer.

Justice grabs the bag of ham and closes the fridge. "I can't wait that long. I feel like I might die of starvation." He grabs a bag of chips and sits down at the bar with the ham in front of him. He opens the bag of chips and puts a few in his mouth. "Who were you talking to?"

"I take it you're feeling better."

"If you count starving to death as feeling better. Who were you talking to?" he repeats.

"Maggie."

"The same girl you went to see in the hospital?"

This is why I didn't want to be on the phone with her while he was in the room. He doesn't shy away from anything. And I'm a big believer in being honest with him, so I nod. "Same one."

"Why was she in the hospital?"

"She has cystic fibrosis."

"That sounds serious."

"It is. You should research it."

Justice rolls his eyes because he knows I'm being serious. Every time he asks a question that I tell him to research, I always follow up with him the next day to make sure he did. Then I correct him on anything he learned that was inaccurate. That's the downside of Google. There's a lot of information, but you have to know how to weed through the bullshit. I think that's really why I always have him research answers to a lot of his questions—so that he can learn how to properly navigate the bullshit.

"Is Maggie your girlfriend?"

I shake my head. "Nope."

"But you've had sex with her?"

The combination of my eleven-year-old asking if I've had sex with someone while chewing on a mouthful of ham is both odd and entertaining. *"What?"*

"You mentioned something about not being able to spend the night with her again. Which means you've spent the night with her before. Which probably means you've had sex with her because Cody says that's what adults do when they spend the night with each other."

"Cody is eleven. He isn't always right."

"So that's a no?"

I feel guilty because I'm currently wishing Justice were still in bed sick. "Can we put this conversation on pause until you're about fourteen?"

Justice rolls his eyes. "You say you like that I'm a curious kid, but then you never want to feed my curiosity."

"I like that you're curious. I like feeding your curiosity. But sometimes you're too hungry." I open the refrigerator and grab him a water. "Drink this. You haven't had enough liquid today."

Justice grabs the water from me. "Fine. But on my fourteenth birthday, be prepared to revisit this conversation."

I laugh. *God, I love this kid.* But at this rate, I'm not sure

I'll make it until he's fourteen. His curiosity is going to kill the cat. I'm the cat.

"You want me to make you something else to eat?"

Justice nods and closes the deli meat. "I'll take some cinnamon toast. Can we watch *Signs*?"

I want to tell him no because the idea of watching one of his favorite movies for the twentieth time sounds excruciating. But I know before long, the last thing he'll want to do is watch movies with his dad. As a father, I've learned to take what I can get while I can get it, because none of the phases a child goes through last forever. Eventually, the things you once found repetitive and irritating become the very things you'd give anything to repeat.

"Yeah, we can watch *Signs*. Get it started while I make your toast."

Chapter Twenty-Seven

Sydney

I scan the radio stations in search of a song I can sing to. I'm in the mood to sing. My windows are down, the weather is gorgeous, and it occurred to me on my way home from work that I haven't been in the mood to sing at the top of my lungs in my car in a long time. I don't know if it's because of the trajectory my life took over the past year, or if it's college, or a combination of both. But something shifted this past week. It's as if my life were a roller coaster, speeding through dark tunnels and spinning through loops with my entire body being jerked left to right and front to back and then . . . *whoosh*. The emotional roller coaster is coming to a smooth, slow, comforting part of the ride where I can just release a breath and know that I'm safe and everything inside of me is beginning to settle.

That's what this feels like. My life is finally beginning to feel settled.

After helping move Maggie in on Sunday, we were all exhausted. We sprawled out on her living room furniture, me and Ridge on one couch, Maggie and Bridgette on the other, and Warren on the floor. We all watched the season finale of *The Bachelor*—a show none of us has seen a single episode of all season, but we couldn't find the remote, and no one felt like changing the channel. Warren got really into it and started arguing with the TV when he felt the guy picked the girl Warren would have bet against if Warren had money.

When it was over, Ridge and I walked back to his apartment and crashed for the night. I was too exhausted to drive home, and we were both too exhausted to even shower. We walked straight to the bed and fell on top of it. We must have fallen asleep right away without even removing our clothes, because I woke up in the middle of the night to him slipping off my shoes and pulling the covers over me.

It's been three days since then, and it's all just felt so right. So good. It's strange how I don't even have my shit together yet, being a college student living paycheck to paycheck. But I feel like I would be happy with my life if it stayed this way forever. It goes to show that a person really doesn't need much if they're surrounded by the right people. Loved by the right people.

If I could bottle up the love I have for my life today, I would. It's a love worth saving.

I pull into my complex and grab my phone to check it as I exit my car. There's still no text from Ridge. He told me he'd text when he finished up with work today, but it's after seven, and I haven't heard from him.

Sydney: You coming over tonight?

Ridge: Do you want me to?

Sydney: I always want you to.

I insert my key into the lock and open my apartment door. I'm staring down at my phone as I walk inside, waiting for Ridge to text me back, when someone grabs me from behind. I scream, but realize almost immediately that it's Ridge, just by the feel of his arms wrapped around me. I spin in his arms, and he's smiling down at me.

"I'm glad you didn't say no, because I'm already here."

I laugh. My heartbeat is erratic. I wasn't expecting anyone to be here, but I couldn't be happier to see him right now. He kisses me, and it somehow makes this day even better.

I can't even stand myself right now. I don't recall ever being this in love with my life before today, and I don't know how to get used to this new version of myself. I got so used to being so full of gloom for so long, it's like I'm discovering a part of me that didn't exist before this month.

Or maybe it always existed . . . I just never had anyone who could pull out the best parts of me like Ridge does.

I stand on my tiptoes and kiss him. His hands cradle my cheeks, and he kisses me back, walking me until my back meets the counter. We kiss for a good minute before I recognize that my entire apartment smells like a restaurant. I pull away from him and turn around to find dinner prepared on the stove. When I look back at Ridge, he's smiling at me. "Surprise. I cooked."

"What's the special occasion?"

"There doesn't need to be a special occasion for me to want to make you happy. I'll be treating you like this for the rest of your life."

I like the sound of that.

Ridge leans in and plants quick kisses down my neck before pulling away and walking to the stove. "It'll be ready in five minutes if you want to change."

I smile on my way to my bedroom. He knows me too well. He knows that no matter what time of day it is, as soon as I walk through the door, I like to be comfortable. That means getting rid of my bra the minute I get home. It means getting out of my jeans and pulling on a pair of pajama pants and one of his T-shirts. It means pulling my hair up in a knot and having absolutely zero care about anything but being as comfortable as I can possibly be.

I love that he loves that about me.

When I walk back into the kitchen, he's setting the table. He made baked chicken and vegetables with a side of risotto. I honestly don't know that my kitchen has ever experienced this kind of meal before. I rarely cook full meals because it's just me. Sometimes Ridge and me. But it's rare that we go all out and do something as drastic as use the oven. Microwave, sure. Stovetop, maybe. But the oven means a serious meal, and we haven't had much time for that. I sign and tell him it looks delicious, and then proceed to eat half of it without stopping. It tastes even better than it looks.

"Seriously, Ridge. It's delicious."

"Thank you."

"I can't cook like this."

"Yes, you can. It just tastes better to you because you didn't make it. That's how cooking works."

I laugh. Hopefully that's true. "How was work today?"

He shrugs. "Played catch-up. But Brennan texted and said he needs me to play a show with him because they're short a guitarist next weekend."

"Where at?"

"Dallas. You want to come? Make a weekend of it?"

I nod. Watching Ridge onstage is my favorite thing. "Absolutely. Will Sadie be there?"

Ridge gives me a look to let me know he doesn't know who I'm talking about.

"Sadie the singer," I clarify. "The girl who started opening for Brennan. I think he likes her."

"Oh yeah. I'm sure she will be." He grins. "That should be interesting."

From what I've learned about Brennan, he doesn't get crushes on girls very often, which makes me invested in seeing how this turns out. I hope I get to meet her.

That thought leads me to my next thought. I can't visit Dallas without stopping to see my parents. "Since we'll be in Dallas . . . do you want to have dinner with my parents?"

Ridge answers immediately. "I would love to meet your parents, Sydney."

I don't know why, but that sentence makes my heart melt a little. I smile and take a drink.

"Have you told your parents about me?" he asks.

"I told my mother I have a boyfriend. She asked me twenty questions."

He grins. "Only twenty?"

"Maybe twenty-five."

"What did you say? How did you describe me?"

"I said you're very talented. And very cute. And good at pranks. And good in bed."

Ridge laughs. "I'm sure you did." He leans back in his chair, casually bumping my knee with his. He's staring at his plate, scooting around the rest of his risotto. "Did you tell them I'm deaf?"

I didn't tell them, but for no other reason than it just didn't come up, and I honestly didn't think about it. "Should I have?"

Ridge shrugs. "Might be worth mentioning. I don't like to catch people off guard if I can avoid it. I like for them to have a heads-up."

"You didn't give me a heads-up."

"It was different with you."

"How?"

He tilts his head and contemplates his answer. Then he

picks up his phone, which means he wants to explain something that he feels he can get across better in text than if he were to verbalize.

Ridge: In most cases, I like to warn people before we meet. It makes for less of an uncomfortable moment when they find out. I didn't warn you because it felt like . . . I don't know. It was just different with you.

Sydney: A good different?

Ridge: The best kind of different there can possibly be. My whole life I've been the deaf guy. It comes first with every person I ever meet. Being deaf and how a person will react to that is my first thought in every new conversation I have. It's most likely the first thought of the person I'm having the conversation with. It defines how they treat me, how they react to me, and how I react to them. But with you, I sometimes forget that part of myself. With you, I forget the one thing that defines me to everyone else. With you . . . I'm just me.

I'm glad he texted all that, because it's one more thing he's said to me that I want to keep track of and remember forever.

"My parents are going to love you just as much as I do."

Ridge smiles for a moment, but the smile is fleeting. He tries to hide it as he reaches for his drink, but I saw the split-second conflict in his eyes. It makes me wonder if he's only agreeing to meet them to appease me. What if he isn't ready to take that step? It's not like we've been dating long at all.

"You okay?" I sign.

He nods, reaching for my hand. He rests his on top of mine on the table, brushing his thumb across it. "I'm good," he says. "It's just that sometimes you make me wish I had better parents. Parents who could meet you and know you're perfect for me. Parents who could love you."

His words make my heart ache for him. "You have Brennan. He loves that you're happy."

"Yeah," he says, smiling. "And Warren."

"And Bridgette."

Ridge makes a face. "Oddly enough."

"Right? I really like her," I say with a laugh. "If someone would have told me six months ago that me and Bridgette would eventually be good friends, I would have bet my life savings against it. It's only five hundred dollars, but still."

Ridge laughs. "If you would have told me six months ago that me and you would be dating and spending an entire day helping Maggie move into my complex, I would have bet your life savings against it, too."

"Life is strange, isn't it?"

Ridge nods. "Beautifully strange."

I smile at him, and we finish eating in comfortable silence. I clear the table and load the dishes into the dishwasher. Ridge hooks his phone up to the Bluetooth on my stereo and turns on one of my Spotify playlists.

This is how I know he truly loves me. He does things that don't have an impact on him at all, like making sure there's always music playing, even though he can't hear it. He knows I like it, so he does it to make me happy. It reminds me of the first time he did this. We were in his car, driving home from the club, and he turned on his car radio for me.

It's the small things people do for others that define the largest parts of them.

Ridge folds his arms over the bar and leans forward, smiling at me. "I got you a present."

I grin as I turn on the dishwasher. "You did?"

He reaches out for my hand. "It's in your bedroom."

I have no idea what it is, but I grab his hand with both of mine and pull him to the bedroom because I'm excited. He pulls me back so he can walk through the door first. He lets go of my hands so he can sign what he's speaking. "We were writing a song together once when you mentioned how you wish you had one of these."

He pushes open the door and walks to my bed, then pulls a huge box out from beneath it. It's an electric keyboard, complete with a stand and a stool. I recognize the brand immediately. It's the same one I use in my music classes, so I know exactly how much he spent on this gift, and I immediately want to tell him I can't accept it. But at the same time, I'm so excited about it, I rush over to it and run my hand over the box.

I throw my arms around him and kiss him all over his face. "Thank you, thank you, thank you!"

He laughs, knowing how happy he just made me. "Is it the right one?"

I nod. "It's perfect."

I had a piano growing up at my parents' house, but it's too big to travel with. I grew up playing it, which started my love for music. I've slowly been integrating other instruments, but the piano is where my heart is. Ridge sets the keyboard up against the wall. I sit down and start playing a song, and Ridge sits down on the bed. He watches my hands with the same appreciation as someone who would be able to hear what they're creating.

When I finish playing the song, I run my hand appreciatively over the keys. I can't believe he remembered one comment I made a long time ago about wishing I had a piano like the ones we use at school. "Why did you get me this?"

"Because. You're good at songwriting, Syd. Really good. You deserve an instrument that can help you create music."

I crinkle up my nose at him because he knows I'm weird with compliments. Just like he is, I guess. I crawl onto the bed with him and wrap my arms around him, looking him in the eyes. "Thank you."

He brushes my hair back, sliding his hand to the side of my head. "You're welcome."

I'm inspired. By him, by his gift, by the feeling I had on my way home, when the windows were down and the music was blaring. "Let's write a song right now. I got an idea on the way home from work." I lean over to the nightstand and grab the pad of paper and pens. We both sit up against my headboard, but the guitar he leaves here is against the wall. He doesn't retrieve it, and instead, we decide to start with lyrics first.

On the way home, I had the thought that I wanted things

to feel this way forever. I wanted to bottle up his love and save it forever. As soon as I had that thought, I knew I wanted to write a song that revolved around that feeling. At the top of the page, I write the potential title, "Love Worth Saving." I write the first few lines of lyrics as they come to me.

Got a little money
Enough to get us by
Our house ain't pretty, honey
But baby, it keeps us dry

Our friends ain't rich or famous
But we pretend on the weekend

I tap the page as I move my fingers across the lyrics to give Ridge an idea of the pacing of the song. He pats his hand on his knee in time with mine and then reaches for the pen and writes, "Chorus," then follows that up with a few lines of his own.

Even if our clothes are fading
They'll always look new on you
Even when the times are changing
Nothing's gonna change my view on you
You know we got a love worth saving

As soon as I see the lines, *Even if our clothes are fading, they'll always look new on you*, I smile. Last week we were having a conversation about my possibly changing degree paths. I still don't know what I want to do, but he is supportive of whatever I decide, even if it means we'll struggle financially a little longer. He said those words to me, that clothes would look new on me, even if they're faded, and I told him he better put it in a song. It's almost as if he's been waiting for this moment and already had those lyrics prepared. It's incredible how seamlessly we work together. Writing music is such a solitary thing, much like how I assume writing a book would be. But when we're together, it just works. It's like we're better together than we are alone.

He's tapping through the beat of the chorus, but I'm still stuck on the lyrics he wrote. I draw a heart next to them to let him know I love them. Then I pause for a moment until I can come up with the next few lines of lyrics.

Don't need no gold or diamonds
Got the glow right in your eyes
If it's your love you're selling
You know I'm gon' keep on buyin'
We can make something outta nothing
Just keep that feel-good coming

Ridge hops off the bed and grabs his guitar. I decide to use the record feature on the keyboard, so I move over to the bench and he sits on the bed. He spends the next fifteen minutes working out the song on his guitar, and I use what he's creating on the guitar to match it with the piano.

He adds a few more lyrics and another chorus, and within an hour, the song is mostly worked out. We just need to give it to Brennan for a rough recording this week to see how it sounds. This was one of the easier ones we've written together. I record us playing through it again and then hit play on the keyboard so I can listen to it. It's more upbeat than most of the songs we write together.

I love writing with two instruments. The options to add more variations using the keyboard makes the song sound more polished than ones we've sent Brennan in the past just using Ridge's guitar. I'm so excited about the song and the gift Ridge gave me that it makes me want to dance as it's playing back.

Ridge sets his guitar aside and watches me dance around the room as the song plays. I laugh every time our eyes meet because I'm in such a good mood. At one point, when I glance at him, he's not smiling. I pause, wondering what just changed in him.

He signs, "I wish I could dance with you."

"You can. You have."

He shakes his head. "Not to a slow song where I just stand there. I mean like this." He waves his hand toward me. "To a faster rhythm."

My chest tightens with his words. I step toward him and grab his hand, pulling him up. "Ridge Lawson, you can do anything you want."

I wrap one hand around his neck, and he places his hands on my waist. I start tapping my other hand against his chest along with the beat of the song. I move left to right to the rhythm, and he starts to follow my lead. I sing the lyrics so he can watch my mouth and know where we are in the song. When the song ends, I reach over and hit play again so we can keep going.

Ridge starts to fall in line with the rhythm, and I laugh when it finally happens. He laughs, too, as he starts to take over and keep up with a beat he can't even hear. He leads me around the room as I sing and tap against him. At the end of the final chorus, he spins me and then pulls me against his chest as we both come to a slow stop.

He holds me there, staring down at me as I look up at him. We're both smiling. Looking in his eyes, I can see the complete appreciation he has for me like I've never seen before. Like I just gave him something he thought he would never experience.

For me, it was a simple dance—something I do all the time and take for granted. For him, it was a breakthrough. Something he's never done before that he believed he couldn't do.

How he's probably feeling right now is how he makes me feel every time he turns on the stereo for me. It's the little things like these that create the biggest moments between us.

He takes my face in his hands, preparing to say something to me. But instead of speaking or signing, he just drags in a speechless breath as he stares silently at me. He lowers his mouth to mine, kissing me gently on the lips. Then he meets my eyes, conveying more with one look than he's ever conveyed through any other form of our communication.

"Sydney," he says quietly. "Everything we've gone through to get here. Right here. It was all worth it."

There isn't a thing I could signs or words I could say that could top the meaning in what he just spoke to me.

I reach over and hit play on our song again. He grins as I clasp my hands behind his neck. He presses his forehead to mine, and we dance.

Chapter Twenty-Eight

Ridge

I wanted to send Brennan a rough cut of the song Sydney and I wrote tonight, but I needed my laptop to do it. Which is why we just showed up at my apartment and placed ourselves in this horrible predicament.

Us, standing at the door.

Warren's ass, staring back at us from the couch.

It's so . . . *pale.*

Sydney spins around as soon as we walk through the apartment door. She's covering her eyes, even though she's not facing the direction of Warren's ass anymore. She's shaking her head like she wishes she could unsee what she just saw. I wish that, too.

I think Bridgette might be yelling now. Thank God I can't hear it. All I see is Warren covering her up with the throw blanket from the back of the couch. *Mental note to wash that blanket tomorrow.*

Warren covers his junk with a throw pillow. *Wash the pillow, too.*

"Knock much?" he signs.

"Lock doors much?" I sign back. I grab Sydney's hand and pull her to my bedroom. When we're safe from Warren's nudity, she finally opens her eyes.

"I'm never sitting on that couch again," she says, walking to my dresser. She kicks off her flip-flops. I point to the restroom, and she nods. Right before I walk away, she says, "I'm gonna borrow sunblock."

I'm in the bathroom with the door shut before I realize what she said didn't make sense. Or at least I didn't read her lips right. Sunblock? It's nighttime. She doesn't need sunblock. What did she say if she didn't say sunblock?

Some *socks.*

She's gonna borrow some socks.

Shit! The ring!

I swing open the bathroom door, but it's too late. The sock drawer is open. The box is in her hands. The box is open, and she's looking down at the engagement ring with a hand covering her mouth.

Chapter Twenty-Nine

Maggie

My old landlord texted me this morning and said she had some of my mail, so I decided to drive to San Antonio to meet up with Jake rather than have him drive to Austin. I texted him after I picked up my mail to let him know he didn't have to come to me for dinner. He responded almost immediately with his address. That text was followed by another that read, Key under the rock next to the grill on the back patio. I'll be there in a couple of hours.

That was seven hours ago.

He's texted several times since then, apologizing profusely. He got called into an emergency surgery. I keep reassuring him that it's fine. I even offered to come back another time, but he made me swear I wouldn't leave before he got home.

So . . . in an attempt to make hanging out for seven

hours in the home of a guy I'm not officially dating a little less strange, I've kept myself busy. I think I underestimated Jake's honesty when he said he was a messy person. Because . . . even after a trip to the store for cleaning supplies and hours of straight work . . . this place still isn't spotless. I've done four loads of laundry, two loads of dishes, made his bed for what I'm sure is the first time ever, scrubbed both bathrooms, and now I'm prepping dinner.

I came to his house prepared to stay the night. I'm not sure if that's something he'll ask me to do, but just in case, I brought my medications, an extra set of clothes, and my respiratory vest. The thought of using it in front of him is embarrassing, but the thought of avoiding my responsibilities and ending up sick again would be even more embarrassing.

I do get the feeling he'll want me to stay the night. Our texts started getting flirty a couple of hours ago. The last text I sent him was a picture of my hand touching his sparkling clean kitchen sink, and he responded with, That is the sexiest fucking picture I've ever seen.

I'm layering the cheese on the pizza when I hear his key in the front door. When he opens it, I get this tiny little quiver inside my stomach. It's so dumb, but I like him so much. It helps that he's fun to look at. He's wearing a pair of faded jeans and a light blue shirt with a black tie. And a smile. He tries to take in his kitchen as he walks closer to me, but his eyes keep falling back to mine. I can tell by the way he's looking at me that he's been waiting for this moment all day.

"Do you wear scrubs at work?"

He tosses his keys on the counter. "Yes. Most days, but I keep them at work. Sterilization purposes." He begins to undo his tie while he stares at me. "You should move in with me."

I laugh at his deadpan humor. "No, thank you. I have no plans to be your maid." I face the counter again and finish putting the toppings on the pizza.

Jake walks up behind me and wraps his arms around me. I lean into him, missing the way he feels and smells. He lowers his mouth to my ear. "If you were my maid, I could pay you in orgasms."

"After today, I think I'm already due one or two."

He laughs against my neck. "Considering the pristine condition of my kitchen, I owe you quite a few."

I toss the chopped onion onto the the pizza and wash my hands. He's still behind me, his arms around me. "Are you spending the night?" He sounds hopeful.

I don't want to seem desperate, so I fail to admit my change of clothes is already in his bedroom in my backpack. "We'll play it by ear," I tease.

I feel him shake his head, and then he spins me so that I'm facing him. "No, I say we go ahead and call it now. Stay the night."

"Okay." *I'm way too easy.* I move around him and slide the pizza onto the oven rack.

"How long does that take to cook?"

I close the oven door and turn around and face him. "About as long as it would take you to pay back one of the orgasms you owe me."

Finally, he kisses me. Then he lifts me, carries me to his bedroom, and lays me on his perfectly made bed. He looks around for a moment when he realizes I also cleaned his bedroom. Then he leaves me lying on his bed while he walks to his bathroom. When he sees his spotless bathroom, he then walks toward his laundry room.

He eventually makes it back to the bed, where he crawls on top of me. "Maggie Carson."

That's all he says. Just my name, with a smile. And then he disappears from my line of sight as he makes his way down my body, to the button on my jeans.

He thanks me, and when he's done, we still have five minutes to spare before the pizza's ready.

Chapter Thirty

Sydney

"It's not what you think," Ridge says.

I lift my gaze and drop my hand from my mouth. "I think it's an engagement ring. Is it not?"

Ridge shakes his head as he walks over to me and says, "No. *Yes.* I mean . . . it is, but it isn't. It is an engagement ring . . . but . . . it isn't yours."

He's treading very carefully, so it takes me a moment to realize why there's nothing but a cautious, regretful look in his eyes. I look back down at the ring that isn't meant for me. "Oh," I say. "I didn't know you ever proposed to her."

He shakes his head, almost adamantly. "I didn't."

The poor guy looks terrified of my potential reaction. What he can't see is how fucking *relieved* I am. We haven't even been officially dating for a whole month yet. If he had already bought me a ring with the intention of proposing,

I probably would have cried, but not from feelings of joy. I'm pretty sure, based on how I'm feeling right now, I would have been scared. Which is weird. I love Ridge more than I could ever love anyone, and I would love to be his wife. I would love to be married to him. But I want to enjoy the stages of our relationship for as long as we can.

I would love to be his fiancée, but I love being his girlfriend just as much. I want more of the boyfriend/girlfriend thing before we move it to the next level.

I laugh, clutching my chest. My heart is beating so fast. "My God, Ridge. I thought you were about to propose to me." I sit on the bed, still clutching the box. "I love you, but . . . too soon."

All the tension in his neck and jaw eases with my response. "Oh, thank God," he says, running a hand down his face. But then he tries to quickly recover. "Not that I don't want to propose to you. Just . . . yeah. Someday."

He sits down next to me on the bed, and I bump him with my shoulder as I grin at him. "Maybe someday."

He smiles back. "Maybe someday."

I look back down at the ring and run my finger over it. It looks like an antique. "It's a beautiful ring."

He picks up his phone and begins texting me. I pull out my phone to read it.

Ridge: It belonged to Maggie's grandmother. Her grandfather gave it to me while she and I were dating, but I never got around to asking her. I've been meaning to give it back to her since our breakup, but the timing was always weird. She doesn't know I have it.

Sydney: You keep it in your sock drawer. That's the most obvious place for a ring to be hidden. She's more than likely seen this.

Ridge: It's been in my closet for three years. I just moved it to the sock drawer two weeks ago to remind myself to give it to her.

Sydney: You've had it for three years and never proposed? What was stopping you?

Ridge shrugs and then says, "It never felt right."

I want to smile, but I don't. It's just that hearing him say it never felt right makes me feel good. Should it? Who knows? I'm honestly tired of second-guessing my reactions to every little thing I feel. From now on, I just want to feel. Unabashedly. Without guilt. And right now, I feel relieved. Relieved that the ring isn't for me, but also relieved that he never gave it to Maggie.

"I'll give it back to her tomorrow." He reaches for it, but I pull it away from him.

"No," I say. "I think you should wait."

"Wait? Why?"

I text him my lengthy response because it's too much to try to sign for me and too much for him to try to understand.

Sydney: I think this ring would mean a lot to Maggie. And I know it's still new between them, but I think Jake means a lot to her, too. Maybe you should wait and see how things go with the two of them. If they fall in love, I think you should give the ring to Jake. Not Maggie.

Ridge smiles after he reads my text. Then he looks at me appreciatively. "Okay."

I hand him the ring, and he walks it back to the drawer. He slides his hands into his pockets. "What do you want to do for the rest of the night?"

I shrug. "Seeing Warren's ass got me out of the mood for round two."

Ridge laughs and drops down on the bed next to me. "We could go watch a movie."

"Nope," I say, shaking my head immediately. "Not sitting on that couch ever again."

"No, I mean at a theater."

"But . . . how would that be fun for you? There aren't any captions."

"Then take your earplugs and we'll deaf-watch it together."

I stand up, eager and ready. A date. I may not be in the mood for sex right now, thanks to Warren, but I am so in the mood for a date with my boyfriend of less than a month, whom I love with all my soul, but do not want an engagement ring from quite yet.

Chapter Thirty-One

Jake

When I woke up this morning, I made her breakfast. Bacon, eggs, biscuits. The works. And just as I had hoped, the outcome was the complete opposite from when I made her breakfast at her place, after the first night we spent together. She walked over to me, wearing nothing but a bra and the shirt I came home from work in yesterday. Unbuttoned. I couldn't stop staring at her; I almost burned the eggs.

She kissed me on my cheek and then made herself something to drink. I was already running late, but I didn't care. I wanted to eat breakfast with her, so I stayed another half hour. When I started to leave for work, she was getting dressed. The thought of not seeing her again for another week or two was not a thought I wanted to entertain.

"Stay," I said, pulling her to me before I walked out the door.

She smiled up at me. "Why? So I can clean the kitchen you just destroyed while cooking for me?"

I'm still so embarrassed she cleaned my house yesterday.

Appreciative, yes. But it was in the worst condition it's ever been in. I've worked so much over the last couple of weeks, all I can do is crash when I get home. And Justice was sick, so his chores weren't getting done. I'm a messy person, but I've never been as messy as what she walked into yesterday.

"Stay and be lazy. Watch Netflix. I have chocolate in the pantry."

She grinned. "What kind of chocolate?"

"Reese's. Maybe some Twix."

Her nose scrunched up. "Sounds tempting, but I need to watch my sugar."

"There's sugar-free chocolate, too."

"Ugh," she said, letting her head fall back in defeat. "I can't say no to that. Or you. What time will you be back?"

"I don't know. I'll try to move around some afternoon appointments."

"Okay. But I'm taking your advice and not cleaning." She gave me a peck on the lips and then dropped down onto the couch. "I'm staying right here. All day."

"Good." I leaned over her and gave her a kiss. A good kiss. No, a *great* kiss. One that stayed with me all day. One I can't wait to get back home to repeat.

I was able to move around my last three appointments today. It's the second time in two weeks I've done this. It's out of the norm for me, so my nurse, Vicky, knew something was up. When I was on my way out the door, she said, "Have fun on your date."

I paused and turned around to look at her. She shot me a knowing look and walked back down the hallway.

I didn't think I was being transparent, but it's hard to hide this kind of euphoria. I'm not sure I've ever known this side of a relationship. With Chrissy, we became parents so early on in our relationship. Before that, we were just kids. Between medical school and raising Justice, we never really took the time to just enjoy each other.

I like it.

I'm really enjoying Maggie's company. I hate the idea that she'll probably leave tonight or in the morning, but I've also vowed not to beg her to stay like I did this morning. Weak moment. I need to remember this is the same girl who freaked out on me twice already. I'm new at getting back into the dating game and don't want to scare her away again.

• • •

Yeah, that promise I made to myself earlier lasted three hours.

We just got back from dinner, and she's shoving her things into her backpack.

"Leave in the morning," I say.

She laughs and shakes her head. "Jake, I can't. There has to be some rule that says you can't stay two nights in a row with someone you aren't even officially dating."

"Then let's make it official. Be my girlfriend. Spend the night."

She looks at me funny.

"Oh, was that not a hint that you wanted to make it official?"

"No, I only said that because it's a concern. I don't want to smother you."

I brush her hair out of her face. "I wouldn't mind that."

She drops her forehead against my chest and groans, then takes a step away from me. "We have responsibilities. I have three weeks left of school. You have to work tomorrow. We can't just pretend this is how it's going to be. Some blissful, romantic whirlwind of a relationship."

"Who's pretending?"

She raises an eyebrow like maybe I'm about to freak her out again. I can see her guard going up. I wrap my hand around her wrist and pull her back to me. "You know what?"

"What?"

"I am not your ex."

"I'm very much aware of that," she says.

"But just because I haven't been around for most of your past doesn't mean I'm not aware of our present. And all the things that might or might not happen in the future. Stop pretending we need to be more responsible than we are just because you're scared of where this whirlwind takes us."

"That was deep."

"I'm trying to be shallow. I don't want you to think about responsibilities or illnesses or what the rules of relationships should be tonight. I want you to drop your bag, kiss me, and stop worrying so much." I press my forehead to hers. "Live in the moment, Maggie."

Her eyes are closed, but I can see the smile spread across her face as she drops her backpack to the floor. "You are so good for me, Jake Griffin. But also kind of bad." She kisses my chin and then lifts up and kisses me on the mouth. Her arms find the hem of my shirt, and she slips her hands beneath it and slides them up my back.

I help her out of her shirt and then walk her to the bedroom. Counting our one-night stand, this is our fifth time to have sex. I wonder when I'll stop counting.

We spend the next half hour living in the moment. Me on top, then her, then me again. When the moment is over, I roll onto my back to catch my breath. She lays her head on my chest and moves with my breaths.

God, I could get used to this. I run my fingers through her hair, wondering if we made it official. I don't think she objected, but she also didn't agree.

"Maggie?"

She lifts her head and rests her chin on my chest, looking up at me. "Yes?"

"Are we official?"

She nods. "After that round? *Very* official."

I smile, but my smile is smacked right off my face when I hear the front door open.

"Dad?"

"Shit!" I roll off the bed and grab my jeans.

Maggie stands up and grabs hers. "What do I do?" she whispers. "Do you want me to hide somewhere?"

I rush to my closet door. "Yeah, hide in here."

She makes her way to my closet without question. I can't help but laugh. I grab her wrist right as she reaches the door. "I was kidding, Maggie." I try to stifle my laughter, but *she was really about to hide in the closet.* "He already knows about you. Get dressed and come meet him."

She stares at me a moment, then slaps me in the chest. "Ass."

I'm still laughing as I grab my shirt from the floor. "Dad?" Justice calls out.

"Coming!" I say.

When I'm dressed, I give Maggie a quick kiss and then leave her to finish dressing in the bedroom. Justice is standing in the kitchen with his friend Cody.

"What's up?" I say, as casually as possible.

Justice turns around. "Not much, Dad. What's up with *you?*"

I pause. He knows something. He's smirking.

His friend Cody holds up Maggie's shirt. "Whose shirt is this?"

They both start laughing. I grab the shirt and walk it back to my bedroom. I open the door and toss Maggie her shirt, then wait for her to put it on. "Thanks," she says. "I was worried they would see it."

I fail to tell her they did. She pulls it on and follows me out of the bedroom. When we walk into the kitchen,

Cody's jaw drops when he sees Maggie. He nudges Justice with his elbow.

"Dude," Cody says to Justice. "Your new stepmom is hot."

Justice rolls his eyes. "Not awkward at all."

Maggie just laughs. *Thank God.*

I introduce them. "Maggie, this is my son, Justice." Justice waves at her. "And his best friend, Cody."

Maggie smiles at them. "Hi. I'm . . . *not* anyone's stepmom."

"Even better," Cody says. I glare at him, and he wipes the smirk off his face.

The microwave dings, and Justice pulls a bag of popcorn out of it. "Mom got called in. She told me to call first and make sure it was okay that I came over."

"And why didn't you call first?"

Justice smiles and says, "Because then you'd know I was coming." Justice looks at Maggie. "Do you know who M. Night Shyamalan is?"

"The director? Of course."

Justice shoots me a look of approval, and then looks back at Maggie. "What's your favorite movie of his?"

She makes her way over to the bar and takes a seat. She seems comfortable. I'm glad. I didn't want this to be weird, but I also wasn't planning on introducing them so soon. But hiding her would have been even weirder.

"Hard to say," she says. "*Signs*, obviously, but *The Sixth Sense* will always hold a special place in my heart."

"What's your stance on *The Happening*?" Justice asks.

"I've never seen it."

Cody opens the bag of popcorn and says, "Well, Maggie, *who is not a stepmom*, tonight is your lucky night."

Justice pours the popcorn into two bowls and hands one to Maggie. She pops a piece in her mouth as Justice and Cody make their way to the living room.

I blow out a breath, although I'm not sure why. They're eleven years old. Not sure why all of that just made me nervous.

"I like him," she says.

"I told you he was great."

She stands up and puts a piece of popcorn in my mouth. "I might even like him more than I like you." She walks past me, spinning to face me as she goes. "Nobody puts Maggie in a closet."

I laugh. "Clever." She walks away, into the living room. I follow her, because that's what boyfriends do, right?

Justice and Cody have taken the main sofa directly in front of the TV. Maggie and I sit on the love seat. She leans against me, positioning herself lengthwise so she can see the TV better. She props her feet up on the arm of the couch.

Justice starts the movie, and I'm not even disappointed that I've seen it four times. I'm just happy this is how the night has ended up.

Tomorrow, that thought might scare me, knowing what I'm getting my heart into with this girl.

But right now, I just want to live in the moment.

Chapter Thirty-Two

Three months later

Sydney

I've been trying to get Bridgette to warm up to Maggie since Maggie moved into their complex several months ago. As it stands, Bridgette is still pretty cold.

She's sitting on Maggie's bed while I help Maggie pick out an outfit for tonight, so we're making progress. She hasn't been over here since Maggie moved in, other than one time when Maggie had to stay a few nights in the hospital for an illness. Bridgette came to get some clothes for her, but only because Warren made her.

"I think the black shirt would look better with these," Maggie says. "I'm gonna try it on." She grabs the shirt I brought over and takes it to her bathroom, closing the door behind her. I look at Bridgette. She's on her back, staring up at the ceiling, yawning. I pull out my phone and text her because I don't want Maggie hearing our conversation.

Sydney: You're making this uncomfortable.

Bridgette reads the text and then looks at me, holding up a frustrated hand.

Bridgette: What?! I'm just being me.

Sydney: Yeah, no offense, but that's the issue. Sometimes people have to make an effort NOT to be themselves in order to make situations around them a little more tolerable. You haven't said a word to her. Make an effort. Ask her questions.

Bridgette: I AM making an effort. I'm here. Besides, I don't have any questions for her. What would I even say? I don't know how to do fake.

Sydney: Ask her about her graduation. Ask her about when we went bungee jumping. Ask her how she and Jake are doing. Lots of potential conversation starters if you just try.

Maggie walks out of the bathroom just as Bridgette drops her phone onto the bed and rolls her eyes.

"I like that shirt on you," I say to Maggie. She's turning back and forth in the mirror.

I look at Bridgette and make a face. Bridgette sits up dramatically, slapping her palms against the bed. She clears her throat.

"So . . . *Maggie*. How are . . . you and *Jake* doing? Well? I hope?" She forces a smile but sounds like a stiff robot.

Maybe this was a bad idea. I glance over at Maggie, and she's just standing there, staring at Bridgette with her head tilted.

I glance back at Bridgette and shake my head. "Wow. You really don't know how to talk to people."

Bridgette throws her hands up and says, "I *told* you!"

Maggie looks at me. "Did you make her ask me that?"

I shrug. "I'm just trying to teach her how to interact with humans in a normal way."

Looking back at Bridgette, Maggie says, "It doesn't suit you."

"See?" Bridgette falls back on the bed. "I should just be me. I'm good at being me."

"Fine. I'm sorry I tried." I give my attention back to Maggie. "But how *are* you and Jake doing?"

Bridgette sits up on the bed again and throws a hand out toward me. "Why does it sound so normal when *you* say it?"

Maggie and I both laugh. She looks in the mirror and fingers her hair. "We're good," she says, smiling into the mirror. "It's all been so easy with him. He's just . . . simple. He likes to have fun, doesn't take anything too seriously. Until he needs to."

"But is he good in bed?" Bridgette asks.

I see a pattern here. The only conversations that come naturally to Bridgette always have to do with sex. *Does Ridge moan during sex? Is Jake good in bed?*

"He's *very* good," Maggie says without hesitation.

"Who is better?" Bridgette asks her. "Ridge or Jake? Or *Warren*? Wow, you've slept with all three of our boyfriends."

I slap a hand to my forehead. She's a lost cause.

Luckily, Maggie just laughs it off. "Yeah, Bridgette, let's just not do the whole conversation thing, okay?"

Bridgette pouts. "But I actually want to know the answer to this question. I bet it was Warren."

Maggie looks at me and scrunches up her nose while shaking her head. *It wasn't*, she mouths.

Bridgette mutters something about wanting a snack, so she heads to the kitchen. I hand Maggie a purple button-up shirt. "Try this one on. I think you'll like it better than the black one."

"What's it even matter? Jake is on call all weekend, so he won't be there." Maggie goes back to the bathroom just as Bridgette walks back into the bedroom, crunching on chips. She looks at herself in the mirror, turning so she can see her ass. She holds up a Pringle and positions it so that it covers her butt in the mirror.

"What are you *doing*?" I ask her, just as Maggie comes out in the purple shirt. "Definitely that shirt. It's perfect."

"Maggie," Bridgette says, still looking at herself in the mirror. "When you said my ass looked like two Pringles hugging, was that a compliment?"

Maggie laughs. "Have you *seen* your ass? Of course it was."

"I don't see it." Bridgette pulls another Pringle out of the can and holds both chips back to back so that they're curved away from each other. "This is not attractive."

Maggie walks over and grabs the two Pringles, turning them inward. "Like this."

Bridgette stares at the chips and nods, like it finally clicks. "Oh. Yeah, it kind of *does* look like that."

• • •

Ridge and Warren have been at the venue helping the band set up for the show, so Maggie and I rode with Bridgette. Ridge isn't playing tonight, though. He said sometimes he just likes being a spectator.

Maggie has a smile on her face as we get out of the car, but I can tell it's strained. She pauses as she looks up at the building. "I wish Jake could have made it," she says quietly.

I grab her hand. "He can come to the next one. Just try to have fun."

I'm anxious to get inside, so I pull her after me and text Ridge to let him know we're at the back door. A moment later, the door opens and Ridge walks out. He's followed by Warren. I feel bad because Ridge is giving me a hug, and Warren is giving Bridgette a hug, and Maggie is just standing there, awkward and alone.

It won't last long, though.

Just when the door slams shut, it's pushed open from the inside. Jake walks out.

It's been hell keeping it from her, but he really wanted to surprise her. He was able to switch his on-call weekends, but he didn't want her to know. He's planning on staying with her until Monday morning.

As soon as she realizes he's actually here and she's not seeing things, she lights up all over and runs at him. She jumps on him and wraps herself around him like a spider monkey, her feet locked around his back, her wrists locked behind his neck. He's holding her with little effort, and it makes me envious that I can't jump on Ridge like that. I mean, I guess I could. But I'm not as tiny as Maggie. We'd need to plan it. We'd need a spotter. And a mattress for when we fell.

They're so in love. It's so adorable.

Ridge leans into my ear and says, "You look beautiful." His comment gets him a kiss. *We're so adorable.*

Warren opens the back door and holds it for everyone as we all shuffle inside. I feel my phone vibrate, so I look back at Ridge and he indicates he just texted me something.

Ridge: I gave Jake the ring.

Sydney: You did? Did it freak him out? Or did he seem appreciative?

Ridge: He thanked me like five times and kept staring at it on the drive over. I doubt he waits long.

That makes me smile. I know marriage wasn't an item on Maggie's bucket list, but I think she's at a point in her life where she wants to add more to the list. And Jake isn't going anywhere. I can see that just by the way they look at each other.

The room is packed when we get out to the floor. Luckily, one of the crew members saved an area up front for us. *Perks of writing music for the band.*

Jake and Maggie stand next to us. He's standing behind her with his arms wrapped around her. When Brennan and the band walk onstage, Maggie separates herself from him and starts clapping and jumping. I have no idea how long it's been since she's seen them play, but she's genuinely stoked to hear them. It makes me think about everyone's dynamic and how she's been a part of these people's lives since right after they started the band. I'm sure Brennan and everyone onstage mean more to her than I ever realized.

It makes me appreciate what we had to go through to get here even more. Had we all not figured out a way to co-exist, she would have had to give up huge pieces of her life. I never would have felt right about that.

I look over at Warren and Bridgette, and even she's smiling and clapping as Brennan introduces the band to the audience. Warren has his hands cupped around his mouth as he yells for the band. Then he drops his arm and wraps it around Bridgette's waist. She looks up at him and he smiles down at her, then gives her a quick kiss. It's so odd to see them in moments like this, but when I do get glimpses of it, it's beautiful. They love each other, even if they do it differently from everyone else.

That's the beauty of love, isn't it? It comes in so many different forms, shapes, sizes, textures. And it's ever changing. Like the love Ridge held for Maggie. It's still there . . . It's just a different form. And that's what I love the most about him. He never stopped loving her. He never stopped caring for her. And now that she's one of my closest friends, I can't help but love that for her, because she deserves it. She deserved his love then as his girlfriend, and she deserves his love now as one of his best friends.

Ridge moves closer behind me and wraps his arms around me, lifting one hand to my chest. He rests his palm at the base of my throat and presses his head to the side of mine. He wants to hear the concert through me, so I start singing along to the music. And I don't realize it until halfway through the song, but I'm crying.

I don't even know why.

I just love him so much. And I love being here with him. And I love his friends.

I just . . . *love.*

Chapter Thirty-Three

Ridge

She knows every word to every song. I'm not sure when she learned all the songs that were written before I met her, but it makes me wonder if she learned them for me. For these moments when we're watching the band onstage, so she can sing them to me.

When the song ends and she starts clapping, I notice tears are falling down her cheeks. I wipe one of them away and then lean in and kiss her briefly before walking away. She tries to grasp at my shirt, but I disappear into the crowd before making my way onstage. Brennan told me to come up after the first song to perform the one I wrote for her, but I didn't tell Sydney I wrote a new song for her.

When I get up on the stage, I can feel the excitement of the room, even though I can't hear it. The looks on their faces, the people in the front few rows jumping up and down, the heat from the lights, the smile on Sydney's face when I finally find her in the crowd. I lean in to the microphone and sign while I tell her out loud why I wrote the song.

"Sydney." *She's grinning so wide right now, it makes me smile.* "I wrote a happy song for you this time. Because . . . well . . . you make me happy. No matter what happens or where we go . . . we're in it together. And that makes me so fucking happy."

She laughs and wipes at a tear, then signs, "You make me happy, too."

I take the guitar Brennan hands me and wait for his cue. Then I close my eyes and start playing the chords, repeating the lyrics quietly in my head while Brennan uses his voice to sing them out loud.

Well, maybe we can be
Somewhere where the land and the water meet
Somewhere where the worry just can't be
Only got enough room for you and me

Well, maybe the sun will rise
And peek through the pulled-down bamboo blinds
Shine across your slept-on perfect hair
And we won't care
No, we won't care

Cuz we got everything, everything we need right here
The world can try to make it all disappear

But let me tell you something that I happen to know
It's gonna feel like this wherever we go
Wherever we go

Well, what if all we saw
Was the rain dancing off the roof as it falls
Swaying in the leaves at the top of the tree
Water washing sand right from our feet

Well, what if all we knew
Was right from wrong with no point of view
The day can go off the tracks, up in the air
And we won't care
No, we won't care

Cuz we got everything, everything we need right here
The world can try and make it all disappear
But let me tell you something that I happen to know
It's gonna feel like this wherever we go
Wherever we go

You know we'll be here for a while
I think we better do it with a little style
So we make the most of every day like it's faded away
We'll be all right

Cuz we got everything, everything we need right here
The world can try and make it all disappear

But let me tell you something that I happen to know
It's gonna feel like this wherever we go
Wherever we go

When the song is over, I hand the guitar to Brennan and make my way back down to the floor. I find Warren and Bridgette. I see Maggie and Jake. I spin around, but there's no Sydney. I look at Maggie and sign, "Where did she go?"

Maggie points to the stage.

I spin around and look at where I was just performing. *Why is Sydney onstage?*

Brennan is saying something to her as she takes a seat on the barstool. He looks out at the crowd and says something into the microphone, then signs it for me. "This is Sydney Blake. She's one of our songwriters, and this is her first time onstage. Give her a round of applause."

She looks nervous, but I don't think she's as nervous as I am for her. I had no idea she was doing this.

Brennan starts to play, and I move closer to the stage to see which chords he's playing . . . which song. And I realize almost immediately that it's "Maybe Someday"—our song. I look at Sydney, just as the lyrics are about to start, but there's no microphone in front of her.

That's when she starts to sign the words.

Holy shit. She's signing the song for me.

Fuck. How am I supposed to just stand here and not get emotional?

I shake my head when she makes eye contact with me.

I'm in complete disbelief as I watch her sign the lyrics to a song she's completely rewritten into a new song.

"Maybe ~~Someday~~ Now"

I am right in front of you, here to stay
Breathe a little easier every day
Now that I'm yours, and you are mine
You ask me what I'll want someday
It's the same as yesterday
All I want . . . is you

With you I'm at my best
Someday has been laid to rest
I am ready to make that a vow
Maybe tomorrow
Maybe now

When you speak, I listen close
Hear all the words you say in prose
We're only silent when we kiss

I smell my perfume in your bed
Thoughts of you invade my head
Truths were written, now they're said

With you I'm at my best
Someday has been laid to rest

I am ready to make that a vow
Maybe tomorrow
Maybe now

You hear my heartbeat every night
Life with you, it feels so right
We are endless, like our song
Only good can come this way
Nights with you turn into day
Forever yours, forever mine

With you I'm at my best
Someday has been laid to rest
I am ready to make that a vow
Maybe tomorrow
Or maybe now

I don't remember when the song ended or when she walked off the stage or when she appeared right in front of me. I just know that in one moment, I was watching her onstage, and the next moment, I was kissing her. I can feel the music to the next song playing, and I'm still kissing her. My hands are in her hair when I finally pull back and press my forehead to hers. "I love you," I whisper.

I do. I love her so damn much.

•   •   •

I'm not even sure what other songs were played after that. I couldn't focus on anything other than Sydney. After the show, everyone met with the band backstage to figure out where we were going for dinner. While they chatted, Sydney and I stayed out in the hallway and made out. We're at dinner now, and it's torture keeping my hands off of her.

Brennan and the guys needed to get on the road, so it's Syd and me, Maggie and Jake, and Warren and Bridgette. I'm not sure why we even got a communal table, because none of us couples are paying attention to each other.

Well . . . we weren't. But Warren has turned his attention on Sydney now.

"Settle something for us," he says, referring to Bridgette and him.

"What's up?" Sydney says.

"So . . . in the song you rewrote . . . you mentioned vows. Was that a hint that you want to get married?"

Sydney laughs and then looks at me. She looks back at Warren and shakes her head. "We talked about how we weren't ready a few months ago. When I was rewriting the song, I realized maybe I am. I mean . . ." She looks at me. "Did you take it that way? I wasn't saying I expect a proposal. I just meant whenever you're ready . . . *I'm ready.*"

Yeah, I'm ready. But I don't tell her that. She deserves a more thought-out proposal.

"Hold up," Warren says before I can even respond. "Slow down. Bridgette and I have been together the longest. We should get married first."

"No," Bridgette says. "I think Jake and Maggie should get married first. She has less time."

I was hoping I misread her lips, but she just made Sydney spew out her drink, so I guess I understood what Bridgette said just fine. Bridgette is lucky that Maggie is laughing at her right now, rather than choking her.

"*What?*" Bridgette says innocently. "It's true." She looks at Maggie. "I'm not trying to be mean. But seriously, you should try to do as much as you can as fast as you can. It makes sense. Add marriage to your bucket list and get it over with."

Maggie's cheeks are a shade darker than they were before all the attention was on her. Bridgette doesn't seem to care that she's embarrassing her. Or maybe she just doesn't notice.

"We aren't getting married," Maggie says. "We've only known each other for a few months. Statistically speaking, the less time you date someone before you marry them, the greater your chances of it ending in divorce."

Warren leans forward, holding up a finger in thought. It always makes me nervous when he tries to impart wisdom on other people. "Maybe so," he says. "But wouldn't adding marriage to your bucket list be worth the risk? You and Jake can date like this forever and you'll never know what it's like to get married. Or you can risk it and possibly experience marriage *and* divorce before you die."

Jake cocks an eyebrow and glances at Maggie. "Sounds like a win-win to me."

Maggie's eyes widen. Jake smiles at her while he takes

a sip of his drink. And then he says, "It makes sense if you think about it. At the risk of sounding like a medical professional, your life expectancy isn't as long as mine. So . . . I'm ready when you're ready."

Maggie stares at him blankly. We all do, actually. I don't think anyone was expecting him to *agree* with Warren.

"I hope that wasn't a proposal," Maggie says to Jake. "It didn't even come with an *I love you*. Or an engagement ring."

Jake stares back at Maggie for a moment. Then he reaches his hand out across the table. "Give me your keys, Ridge."

I don't even hesitate. I give him my keys, and Maggie watches him in bewilderment as he leaves the restaurant. "What is he doing?" she says. "Is it something I said?"

Warren is shaking his head. "Fucker is gonna beat me to it."

"To what?" Maggie says.

She seems confused, so none of us gives her any hints that we know what's happening. When Jake walks back into the restaurant, he approaches the table with purpose. He's holding the ring I gave him earlier, but before he opens the box, he stands at the head of the table and looks at Maggie. Warren signs everything he says.

"Maggie . . . I know it's only been a few months. But it's been the best few months of my life. From the moment I first saw you, I have been absolutely consumed by you. I wish I had this speech and this moment planned out, but we both like spontaneous." He gets down on one knee and opens the box. None of us can tell what Maggie's thinking. This could go one of two ways, and I'm not so sure it's going to go the way Jake wants it to.

He opens the box. "This ring belonged to your grandmother. And I wish more than anything that I could have known her, because I would have thanked her for raising such an amazing, independent, perfect woman. And the perfect woman for me. Whether you marry me or not, this ring is yours." He pulls it out and lifts her hand, then slips the ring onto her trembling finger. "But I would really love it if you would take the biggest risk you've ever taken and marry me, despite knowing very little about me or if we're even compatible for a lifetime or—"

Maggie interrupts him by nodding her head and kissing him.

Holy shit. He did it.

Sydney is crying. Even Bridgette wipes away a tear.

Warren stands up, grabbing his wine glass to make a toast. "Congratulations, you two," he says toward Maggie and Jake, even though they're still kissing and not paying attention to him. "But this also kind of sucks because tonight was supposed to be my night."

To everyone's shock, Warren pulls a box out of his pocket. He opens it and turns toward Bridgette. "Bridgette, I wanted to propose tonight. I still do, even though I'm irritated that Jake did it first. So, before Sydney and Ridge steal the rest of my thunder, will you please marry me?"

Bridgette is looking at him like he's crazy. Because he is.

"You didn't get down on one knee," she says.

"Oh." Warren drops to his knee. "Will you marry me? Is that better?"

Bridgette nods. "Yes."

"Yes what?" Warren says. "Yes, that's better? Or yes, you'll marry me?"

She shrugs. "Both, I guess."

Holy shit.

What in the hell is happening tonight?

We sat down to dinner as three couples who were dating. Now four of the six of us are engaged. I look at Sydney, and she looks radiant . . . smiling as always as she watches everyone else. Jake and Maggie and Sydney are all clapping for Warren and Bridgette.

Warren pulls away from Bridgette and looks over at Jake and Maggie. "Congrats. You might have been engaged longer than us, but we're getting married first."

Maggie laughs. "You go right ahead, Mr. Competitive."

"Or . . ." Warren says, turning to look at me. "Maybe we should just do this right now. Ridge, ask Sydney to marry you. Then let's all go to Vegas."

I laugh. If there's anything in our relationship I want to be taken more seriously than anything else, it's the moment I ask Sydney to marry me. I have it all planned out already. I'm writing a song for it. I'm going to perform it onstage at one of Brennan's concerts. Sydney deserves more than a spontaneous proposal.

"Oh, come on," Warren says. "What are you waiting for? You gonna write her a love song and play it onstage like you've already done twice before?"

That fucker. "I mean . . . that was the plan," I sign, defeated.

"Well, it's predictable. And lame. But six best friends getting married all at once is memorable and fucking *epic*. Let's all go to Vegas and *do* this shit!"

Bridgette is looking at me with her hands beneath her chin, mouthing, *Please, please, please, please.*

My heart is beating twice as fast as it was two minutes ago. I turn to look at Sydney—to gauge her response—and she smiles. "Just say when," she signs.

"When," I say. I blurt it out faster than I would have been able to sign it.

Sydney's mouth is on mine, and we're both laughing. And . . . *I think we just got engaged.*

Holy shit.

"I'll buy you a ring tomorrow. Whatever you want."

She shakes her head. "I don't want a ring. Let's get tattoos."

"In Vegas," Warren says, pulling out his phone. "I'll look up flights."

"I'm already on it," Jake says, looking down at his phone. "We have to keep Maggie's health in mind, so I'd like to get the shortest flight. And as soon as we land, I want to set her up an appointment with a colleague of mine as a precaution. Then after that we can do the whole wedding thing."

That's something I would have never entertained—going to Vegas with Maggie. I would have been adamantly against it. He really is better for her than I was. He's throwing caution to the wind . . . while somehow still being cautious. My eyes move from Jake to Maggie. She's staring at her ring with tears in her eyes. When she catches me staring, she just smiles and mouths, *Thank you.* Because she knows how Jake got the ring. I smile back at her, glad that I'm here to see this moment. I've always wanted the best for her, and now that she's found it, I couldn't be happier.

I honestly couldn't.

This . . . right now. Everyone I love is exactly where they belong. My crazy best friend with the only girl on the planet I would say is perfect for him. My amazing, incredible ex-girlfriend about to experience life with a guy who is a better balance for her than I could have ever been.

And Sydney. The girl on the balcony I tried so hard not to fall in love with.

The girl I fell in love with anyway.

The girl I am confident I will *stay* madly in love with far beyond my last breath.

I take her hand and bring it to my mouth, kissing her ring finger, which won't be bare for long. "We're getting married," I say.

She nods, smiling up at me. "This better not be one of Warren's and your pranks."

I laugh. I laugh hard. And then I pull her to me and

whisper in her ear, "My love for you is forever off-limits to our pranks. Tomorrow, you'll be my wife."

I wrap my arms around her and bury my face in her hair. Maybe Warren was right. Maybe predictable isn't always preferable. Because I can't imagine this happening any other way than it did. I saw three people I love most in my life get everything they deserve and more.

As for me and Sydney . . . our *maybe someday* just became our *absolutely forever.*

Epilogue

Sydney

Dear Baby Lawson,

You're due in twenty-seven days. I can't begin to tell you how excited your daddy and I are to meet you.

Everyone is so excited to meet you. Your uncle Warren has been trying out nicknames for you since we found out I was pregnant. So far, he's called you Bean, Tomato, Sausage Patty, and, most recently, Silly Putty. I hope none of the nicknames stick; I've hated them all so far. But I've got your back. I'll make sure whatever he calls you, it'll be something that won't be too embarrassing.

Your aunt Bridgette is even more excited to meet you than Warren is. He's hoping for a niece, but she's hoping you're a boy, so they've got a five-hundred-dollar wager going. Bridgette says she wants a nephew because she gets along better with boys than girls, but I'd beg to differ. She gets along great with anyone who has the patience to truly get to know her.

I'm just excited things have gone well with the pregnancy so far, and that you're healthy and growing like you should. Hopefully you'll look like your father and have his talent.

Your father listens to you a lot. You'll learn as you grow up that your father can't necessarily hear things in a traditional way, but he's the best listener I've ever met. He sleeps with his hand on my stomach every night, wanting to feel you move around and kick and roll over. I don't think I've seen him this excited since we got married in Vegas four years ago and he went to his first Cirque du Soleil show.

He was so entranced by everything going on—the lights, the movement, the vibrations, the vibe. We ended up seeing every Cirque show they offered that weekend, and we've been back to two new ones since then. I'm sure it will be something he takes you to experience with him as soon as you're old enough to appreciate it. We go back to Vegas every year to celebrate our anniversary, and I don't think we'll stop once you're born. We're just going to take you with us and celebrate our anniversary with an extra person we love in attendance.

I think some people assume a quick Vegas wedding might be a little tacky, but it was honestly the best weekend of our lives. I don't regret it for a single second. Your father and I exchanged vows with each other alongside your aunt Maggie and uncle Jake, and your aunt Bridgette and uncle Warren. I know they aren't your legitimate aunts and uncles, but I can promise you they'll be there for you in a heartbeat, just like your uncle Brennan, for the rest of your life.

You're going to go through a lot of friends in your lifetime, but when you find the loyal ones, hold on to them. There's something magical about being able to choose the people you keep in your life. No matter how lonely you may feel at times, because all of us do at points in our lives, you're never alone when you surround yourself with the right people.

I sometimes want to tell you all about how I met your father and how I met his friends, but these aren't things I've ever asked my own parents about themselves, so would you even want to know? I still have twenty-seven days before I get to meet you, so maybe I'll write down everything I can about the times your father and I had together before you came along. Maybe that's something you'll want to know someday. It's definitely an interesting story, but probably not one I want to share in my first letter to you.

What I will tell you is that everything about our relationship is unusual, from the way we met right down to the wedding. We didn't plan the wedding—it just sort of happened, which is why we got married in Vegas on a whim.

We decided to do it because it was just one of those perfect moments spent with our friends, when we all decided we were with our forever partners, and we were all so happy, we wanted to celebrate that happiness with each other. After a quick conversation about it, we all decided to head to Vegas and get married.

It was a triple wedding. Your uncle Warren and aunt Bridgette argued the entire way there over whether we'd get married by an Elvis impersonator. But I'm sure you'll come to realize that when the two of them argue, it's always in fun. Your father and I didn't care whether Elvis married us or not, and neither did Maggie or Jake. Bridgette was adamant she didn't want to get married by a singer whose music she didn't know, but Warren wanted to have the most typical, cheesy Vegas wedding he could.

They finally came to a compromise, and Warren agreed not to get married by an Elvis impersonator if Bridgette would share the name of a movie he'd been searching for for over two years.

Needless to say, after their agreement, we did not get married by an Elvis impersonator. Instead, we got married in a twenty-four-hour chapel, and I don't even remember the name of who married us. All I remember is that it was somehow the most nontraditional triple wedding I never dreamed of, but that I wouldn't have wanted any other way. To share that day with our friends was a dream, but to be able to sign my vows to your father while he spoke his back to me was magical. And the three days we all spent in Vegas after the wedding were three of the best days of my life. I'm positive those days will be easily overshadowed on the day we get to meet you, but knowing there are multiple days in my life I'd give anything to relive again is a testament that I am certainly where I need to be and with who I need to be with.

The journey here wasn't always easy, though. I was at a lonely point in my life when I met your father and his friends, and the road was bumpy, but I learned so many lessons along the way.

Many of them I learned through the patience and love your father has for others. I know as you grow up, you'll see exactly what I mean. He's unlike any other man I've ever met, and I am so glad I get to love him. I'm even luckier that I ended up being someone he wants to love in return for the rest of his life.

You and I are very lucky to be loved by a man with a heart like his. I can honestly say I've never met another person like him. And even though we don't know you yet, your father and I are very lucky to be blessed with raising you together. We can't wait to meet you. We can't wait to hold you. We can't wait for you to cry and laugh and walk and talk and sing.

But just be warned. The people in your life love to play pranks on each other, but I'm getting really good at it, and I'm more than willing to teach you all my tricks, as long as you don't share them with your father.

I don't know who you'll be yet, or what we're even going to name you, but I already love you so much more than I thought one heart was capable of. Whether you're a girl or a boy, or someday decide to identify as neither, we are more than ready to support you and love you. Unconditionally. Forever.

Love,
Your mother, Sydney Lawson

Acknowledgments

I miss them already! This series holds a huge place in my heart, and I'm not sure I would feel that way if it weren't for you. The readers. Especially those of you who followed along as I was writing this on Wattpad. Your excitement, anger, and joy over the characters is what prompted me to write this and (finally) finish it.

When *Maybe Someday* ended, I felt as though Ridge and Sydney's story was over. But I always had Maggie in the back of my mind, knowing her story didn't get tied up with a pretty pink bow. I felt I owed it to her to dive back into the lives of these characters and figure out how they were going to fit everyone in the same frame. I hope you guys enjoyed exploring that as much as I enjoyed writing it.

And now for the thank-yous.

This book was written in real time, uploaded chapter by chapter, so I wanted to preserve the feel of that and not send it through heavy rounds of rewrites and editing. Murphy Rae and Marion Archer, thank you for the quick turnarounds and the insightful comments. Murphy is always a little bit meaner than Marion, but that's what sisters are for.

CoHorts, as always, you complete me.

To the members of the Maybe Now discussion group. I'm sorry I had to leave the group in order to finish the project, but your passion fueled me all the way to the end. I want to thank each and every one of you for your help. And, of course, the admins of the group: Tasara Vega, Laurie Darter, Anjanette Guerrero, Paula Vaughn, and Jaci Chaney. Your messages gave me life.

Thank you to Sean Fallon for being Griffin's Stephanie. If you don't know what that means, Sean, just know that it's the highest compliment I can give you.

And last but certainly not least, I want to thank Griffin Peterson. It doesn't matter if it's the middle of the night or first thing in the morning or if I need something yesterday, you are always on top of it with the best attitude. Collaborating with you on this series and combining book tours with concerts has been one of the best experiences of my life. I appreciate your talent, but even more, I appreciate you as a human. #GriffinIsLegit

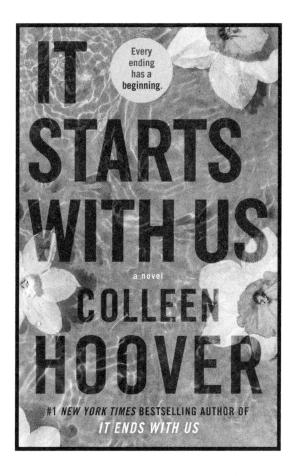

maybe someday

By Colleen Hoover

maybe someday

a novel

Colleen Hoover

ATRIA PAPERBACK

NEW YORK   LONDON   TORONTO   SYDNEY   NEW DELHI

ATRIA
PAPERBACK

A Division of Simon & Schuster, Inc.
1230 Avenue of the Americas
New York, NY 10020

First Atria Paperback edition March 2014

ATRIA PAPERBACK and colophon are trademarks of Simon & Schuster, Inc.

For information about special discounts for bulk purchases, please contact Simon & Schuster Special Sales at 1-866-506-1949 or business@simonandschuster.com.

The Simon & Schuster Speakers Bureau can bring authors to your live event. For more information or to book an event, contact the Simon & Schuster Speakers Bureau at 1-866-248-3049 or visit our website at www.simonspeakers.com.

Manufactured in China

25   27   29   30   28   26

ISBN 978-1-4767-5316-4
ISBN 978-1-4767-5317-1 (ebook)

For Carol Keith McWilliams

Special Content

Dear Reader,

Maybe Someday is more than just a story. It's more than just a book. It's an experience, and one that we are excited and grateful to share with you.

I had the pleasure of collaborating with musician Griffin Peterson in order to provide an original sound track to accompany this novel. Griffin and I worked closely together to bring these characters and their lyrics to life so that you will be provided with the ultimate reading experience.

It is recommended these songs be heard in the order they appear throughout the novel. Please scan the QR code below to experience the *Maybe Someday* sound track. This gives you access to the songs and also to bonus material, should you wish to learn more behind the collaboration and implementation of this project.

Thank you for being a part of our project. It has been incredible for us to create, and we hope it will be just as incredible for you to enjoy.

Colleen Hoover and Griffin Peterson

To listen to the songs, please scan the QR code above. To do so, download the free Microsoft Tag app. Then hold your phone's camera a few inches away from the tag, and enjoy what comes next.

You may also visit the website at www.maybesomeday soundtrack.com to access this content.

maybe someday

prologue

Sydney

I just punched a girl in the face. Not just *any* girl. My best friend. My roommate.

Well, as of five minutes ago, I guess I should call her my *ex*-roommate.

Her nose began bleeding almost immediately, and for a second, I felt bad for hitting her. But then I remembered what a lying, betraying whore she is, and it made me want to punch her again. I would have if Hunter hadn't prevented it by stepping between us.

So instead, I punched *him*. I didn't do any damage to him, unfortunately. Not like the damage I'd done to my hand.

Punching someone hurts a lot worse than I imagined it would. Not that I spend an excessive amount of time imagining how it would feel to punch people. Although I am having that urge again as I stare down at my phone at the incoming text from Ridge. He's another one I'd like to get even with. I know he technically has nothing to do with my current predicament, but he could have given me a heads-up a little sooner. Therefore, I'd like to punch him, too.

Ridge: Are you OK? Do u want to come up until the rain stops?

Of course, I don't want to come up. My fist hurts enough as it is, and if I went up to Ridge's apartment, it would hurt a whole lot worse after I finished with him.

1

I turn around and look up at his balcony. He's leaning against his sliding-glass door; phone in hand, watching me. It's almost dark, but the lights from the courtyard illuminate his face. His dark eyes lock with mine and the way his mouth curls up into a soft, regretful smile makes it hard to remember why I'm even upset with him in the first place. He runs a free hand through the hair hanging loosely over his forehead, revealing even more of the worry in his expression. Or maybe that's a look of regret. As it should be.

I decide not to reply and flip him off instead. He shakes his head and shrugs his shoulders, as if to say, *I tried*, and then he goes back inside his apartment and slides his door shut.

I put the phone back in my pocket before it gets wet, and I look around at the courtyard of the apartment complex where I've lived for two whole months. When we first moved in, the hot Texas summer was swallowing up the last traces of spring, but this courtyard seemed to somehow still cling to life. Vibrant blue and purple hydrangeas lined the walkways leading up to the staircases and the fountain affixed in the center of the courtyard.

Now that summer has reached its most unattractive peak, the water in the fountain has long since evaporated. The hydrangeas are a sad, wilted reminder of the excitement I felt when Tori and I first moved in here. Looking at the courtyard now, defeated by the season, is an eerie parallel to how I feel at the moment. Defeated and sad.

I'm sitting on the edge of the now empty cement fountain, my elbows propped up on the two suitcases that contain most of my belongings, waiting for a cab to pick me up. I have no idea where it's going to take me, but I know I'd rather be anywhere except where I am right now. Which is, well, homeless.

I could call my parents, but that would give them ammunition to start firing all the *We told you so's* at me.

We told you not to move so far away, Sydney.

We told you not to get serious with that guy.

We told you if you had chosen prelaw over music, we would have paid for it.

We told you to punch with your thumb on the outside *of your fist.*

Okay, maybe they never taught me the proper punching techniques, but if they're so right all the damn time, they *should* have.

I clench my fist, then spread out my fingers, then clench it again. My hand is surprisingly sore, and I'm pretty sure I should put ice on it. I feel sorry for guys. Punching sucks.

Know what else sucks? Rain. It always finds the most inappropriate time to fall, like right now, while I'm homeless.

The cab finally pulls up, and I stand and grab my suitcases. I roll them behind me as the cab driver gets out and pops open the trunk. Before I even hand him the first suitcase, my heart sinks as I suddenly realize that I don't even have my purse on me.

Shit.

I look around, back to where I was sitting on the suitcases, then feel around my body as if my purse will magically appear across my shoulder. But I know exactly where my purse is. I pulled it off my shoulder and dropped it to the floor right before I punched Tori in her overpriced, Cameron Diaz nose.

I sigh. And I laugh. Of course, I left my purse. My first day of being homeless would have been way too easy if I'd had a purse with me.

"I'm sorry," I say to the cab driver, who is now loading my second piece of luggage. "I changed my mind. I don't need a cab right now."

I know there's a hotel about a half-mile from here. If I can just work up the courage to go back inside and get my purse, I'll walk there and get a room until I figure out what to do. It's not as if I can get any wetter.

The driver takes the suitcases back out of the cab, sets them on the curb in front of me, and walks back to the driver's side without ever making eye contact. He just gets into his car and drives away, as if my canceling is a relief.

Do I look that pathetic?

I take my suitcases and walk back to where I was seated before I realized I was purseless. I glance up to my apartment and wonder what would happen if I went back there to get my wallet. I sort of left things in a mess when I walked out the door. I guess I'd rather be homeless in the rain than go back up there.

I take a seat on my luggage again and contemplate my situation. I could pay someone to go upstairs for me. But who? No one's outside, and who's to say Hunter or Tori would even give the person my purse?

This really sucks. I know I'm going to have to end up calling one of my friends, but right now, I'm too embarrassed to tell anyone how clueless I've been for the last two years. I've been completely blindsided.

I already hate being twenty-two, and I still have 364 more days to go.

It sucks so bad that I'm . . . *crying*?

Great. I'm crying now. I'm a purseless, crying, violent, homeless girl. And as much as I don't want to admit it, I think I might also be heartbroken.

Yep. Sobbing now. Pretty sure this must be what it feels like to have your heart broken.

"It's raining. Hurry up."

I glance up to see a girl hovering over me. She's holding an umbrella over her head and looking down at me with agitation while she hops from one foot to the other, waiting for me to do something. "I'm getting soaked. *Hurry.*"

Her voice is a little demanding, as if she's doing me some sort of favor and I'm being ungrateful. I arch an eyebrow as I look up at her, shielding the rain from my eyes with my hand.

I don't know why she's complaining about getting wet, when there isn't much clothing to *get* wet. She's wearing next to nothing. I glance at her shirt, which is missing its entire bottom half, and realize she's in a Hooters outfit.

Could this day get any weirder? I'm sitting on almost everything I own in a torrential downpour, being bossed around by a bitchy Hooters waitress.

I'm still staring at her shirt when she grabs my hand and pulls me up in a huff. "Ridge said you would do this. I've got to get to work. Follow me, and I'll show you where the apartment is." She grabs one of my suitcases, pops the handle out, and shoves it at me. She takes the other and walks swiftly out of the courtyard. I follow her, for no other reason than the fact that she's taken one of my suitcases with her and I want it back.

She yells over her shoulder as she begins to ascend the stairwell. "I don't know how long you plan on staying, but I've only got one rule. Stay the hell out of my room."

She reaches an apartment and opens the door, never even looking back to see if I'm following her. Once I reach the top of the stairs, I pause outside the apartment and look down at the fern sitting unaffected by the heat in a planter outside the door. Its leaves are lush and green as if they're giving summer the middle finger with their refusal to succumb to the heat. I smile at the plant, somewhat proud of it. Then I frown with the realization that I'm envious of the resilience of a plant.

I shake my head, look away, then take a hesitant step inside the unfamiliar apartment. The layout is similar to my own apartment, only this one is a double split bedroom with four total bedrooms. My and Tori's apartment only had two bedrooms, but the living rooms are the same size.

The only other noticeable difference is that I don't see any lying, backstabbing, bloody-nosed whores standing in this one. Nor do I see any of Tori's dirty dishes or laundry lying around.

The girl sets my suitcase down beside the door, then steps

aside and waits for me to . . . well, I don't know what she's waiting for me to do.

She rolls her eyes and grabs my arm, pulling me out of the doorway and further into the apartment. "What the hell is wrong with you? Do you even speak?" She begins to close the door behind her but pauses and turns around, wide-eyed. She holds her finger up in the air. "Wait," she says. "You're not . . ." She rolls her eyes and smacks herself in the forehead. "Oh, my God, you're deaf."

Huh? What the hell is wrong with this girl? I shake my head and start to answer her, but she interrupts me.

"God, Bridgette," she mumbles to herself. She rubs her hands down her face and groans, completely ignoring the fact that I'm shaking my head. "You're such an insensitive bitch sometimes."

Wow. This girl has some serious issues in the people-skills department. She's sort of a bitch, even though she's making an effort not to be one. Now that she thinks I'm deaf. I don't even know how to respond. She shakes her head as if she's disappointed in herself, then looks straight at me.

"I . . . HAVE . . . TO . . . GO . . . TO . . . WORK . . . NOW!" she yells very loudly and painfully slowly. I grimace and step back, which should be a huge clue that I can hear her practically yelling, but she doesn't notice. She points to a door at the end of the hallway. "RIDGE . . . IS . . . IN . . . HIS . . . ROOM!"

Before I have a chance to tell her she can stop yelling, she leaves the apartment and closes the door behind her.

I have no idea what to think. Or what to do now. I'm standing, soaking wet, in the middle of an unfamiliar apartment, and the only person besides Hunter and Tori whom I feel like punching is now just a few feet away in another room. And speaking of Ridge, why the hell did he send his psycho Hooters girlfriend to get me? I take out my phone and have begun to text him when his bedroom door opens.

He walks out into the hallway with an armful of blankets and a pillow. As soon as he makes eye contact with me, I gasp. I hope it's not a noticeable gasp. It's just that I've never actually seen him up close before, and he's even better-looking from just a few feet away than he is from across an apartment courtyard.

I don't think I've ever seen eyes that can actually speak. I'm not sure what I mean by that. It just seems as if he could shoot me the tiniest glance with those dark eyes of his, and I'd know exactly what they needed me to do. They're piercing and intense and—oh, my God, I'm staring.

The corner of his mouth tilts up in a knowing smile as he passes me and heads straight for the couch.

Despite his appealing and slightly innocent-looking face, I want to yell at him for being so deceitful. He shouldn't have waited more than two weeks to tell me. I would have had a chance to plan all this out a little better. I don't understand how we could have had two weeks' worth of conversations without his feeling the need to tell me that my boyfriend and my best friend were screwing.

Ridge throws the blankets and the pillow onto the couch.

"I'm not staying here, Ridge," I say, attempting to stop him from wasting time with his hospitality. I know he feels bad for me, but I hardly know him, and I'd feel a lot more comfortable in a hotel room than sleeping on a strange couch.

Then again, hotel rooms require money.

Something I don't have on me at the moment.

Something that's inside my purse, across the courtyard, in an apartment with the only two people in the world I don't want to see right now.

Maybe a couch isn't such a bad idea after all.

He gets the couch made up and turns around, dropping his eyes to my soaking-wet clothes. I look down at the puddle of water I'm creating in the middle of his floor.

"Oh, sorry," I mutter. My hair is matted to my face; my

shirt is now a see-through pathetic excuse for a barrier between the outside world and my very pink, very noticeable bra.
"Where's your bathroom?"

He nods his head toward the bathroom door.

I turn around, unzip a suitcase, and begin to rummage
through it while Ridge walks back into his bedroom. I'm glad
he doesn't ask me questions about what happened after our conversation earlier. I'm not in the mood to talk about it.

I select a pair of yoga pants and a tank top, then grab my
bag of toiletries and head to the bathroom. It disturbs me that
everything about this apartment reminds me of my own, with
just a few subtle differences. This is the same bathroom with
the Jack-and-Jill doors on the left and right, leading to the two
bedrooms that adjoin it. One is Ridge's, obviously. I'm curious about who the other bedroom belongs to but not curious
enough to open it. The Hooters girl's one rule was to stay the
hell out of her room, and she doesn't seem like the type to kid
around.

I shut the door that leads to the living room and lock it,
then check the locks on both doors to the bedrooms to make
sure no one can walk in. I have no idea if anyone lives in this
apartment other than Ridge and the Hooters girl, but I don't
want to chance it.

I pull off my sopping clothes and throw them into the sink
to avoid soaking the floor. I turn on the shower and wait until
the water gets warm, then step in. I stand under the stream
of water and close my eyes, thankful that I'm not still sitting
outside in the rain. At the same time, I'm not really happy to be
where I am, either.

I never expected my twenty-second birthday to end with
me showering in a strange apartment and sleeping on a couch
that belongs to a guy I've barely known for two weeks, all at
the hands of the two people I cared about and trusted the most.

1.

Sydney

I slide open my balcony door and step outside, thankful that the sun has already dipped behind the building next door, cooling the air to what could pass as a perfect fall temperature. Almost on cue, the sound of his guitar floats across the courtyard as I take a seat and lean back into the patio lounger. I tell Tori I come out here to get homework done, because I don't want to admit that the guitar is the only reason I'm outside every night at eight, like clockwork.

For weeks now, the guy in the apartment across the courtyard has sat on his balcony and played for at least an hour. Every night, I sit outside and listen.

I've noticed a few other neighbors come out to their balconies when he's playing, but no one is as loyal as I am. I don't understand how someone could hear these songs and not crave them day after day. Then again, music has always been a passion of mine, so maybe I'm just a little more infatuated with his sound than other people are. I've played the piano for as long as I can remember, and although I've never shared it with anyone, I love writing music. I even switched my major to music education two years ago. My plan is to be an elementary music teacher, although if my father had his way, I'd still be prelaw.

"A life of mediocrity is a waste of a life," he said when I informed him that I was changing my major.

A life of mediocrity. I find that more amusing than insulting, since he seems to be the most dissatisfied person I've ever known. And he's a lawyer. Go figure.

One of the familiar songs ends and the guy with the guitar begins to play something he's never played before. I've grown accustomed to his unofficial playlist since he seems to practice the same songs in the same order night after night. However, I've never heard him play this particular song before. The way he's repeating the same chords makes me think he's creating the song right here on the spot. I like that I'm witnessing this, especially since after only a few chords, it's already my new favorite. All his songs sound like originals. I wonder if he performs them locally or if he just writes them for fun.

I lean forward in the chair, rest my arms on the edge of the balcony, and watch him. His balcony is directly across the courtyard, far enough away that I don't feel weird when I watch him but close enough that I make sure I'm never watching him when Hunter's around. I don't think Hunter would like the fact that I've developed a tiny crush on this guy's talent.

I can't deny it, though. Anyone who watches how passionately this guy plays would crush on his talent. The way he keeps his eyes closed the entire time, focusing intently on every stroke against every guitar string. I like it best when he sits cross-legged with the guitar upright between his legs. He pulls it against his chest and plays it like a stand-up bass, keeping his eyes closed the whole time. It's so mesmerizing to watch him that sometimes I catch myself holding my breath, and I don't even realize I'm doing it until I'm gasping for air.

It also doesn't help that he's cute. At least, he seems cute from here. His light brown hair is unruly and moves with him, falling across his forehead every time he looks down at his guitar. He's too far away to distinguish eye color or distinct features, but the details don't matter when coupled with the passion he has for his music. There's a confidence to him that

I find compelling. I've always admired musicians who are able to tune out everyone and everything around them and pour all of their focus into their music. To be able to shut the world off and allow yourself to be completely swept away is something I've always wanted the confidence to do, but I just don't have it.

This guy has it. He's confident and talented. I've always been a sucker for musicians, but more in a fantasy way. They're a different breed. A breed that rarely makes for good boyfriends.

He glances at me as if he can hear my thoughts, and then a slow grin appears across his face. He never once pauses the song while he continues to watch me. The eye contact makes me blush, so I drop my arms and pull my notebook back onto my lap and look down at it. I hate that he just caught me staring so hard. Not that I was doing anything wrong; it just feels odd for him to know I was watching him. I glance up again, and he's still watching me, but he's not smiling anymore. The way he's staring causes my heart to speed up, so I look away and focus on my notebook.

Way to be a creeper, Sydney.

"There's my girl," a comforting voice says from behind me. I lean my head back and tilt my eyes upward to watch Hunter as he makes his way onto the balcony. I try to hide the fact that I'm shocked to see him, because I'm pretty sure I was supposed to remember he was coming.

On the off chance that Guitar Boy is still watching, I make it a point to seem really into Hunter's hello kiss so that maybe I'll seem less like a creepy stalker and more like someone just casually relaxing on her balcony. I run my hand up Hunter's neck as he leans over the back of my chair and kisses me upside down.

"Scoot up," Hunter says, pushing on my shoulders. I do what he asks and slide forward in the seat as he lifts his leg over the chair and slips in behind me. He pulls my back against his chest and wraps his arms around me.

My eyes betray me when the sound of the guitar stops

abruptly, and I glance across the courtyard once more. Guitar Boy is eyeing us hard as he stands, then goes back inside his apartment. His expression is odd. Almost angry.

"How was school?" Hunter asks.

"Too boring to talk about. What about you? How was work?"

"Interesting," he says, brushing my hair away from my neck with his hand. He presses his lips to my neck and kisses his way down my collarbone.

"What was so interesting?"

He tightens his hold on me, then rests his chin on my shoulder and pulls me back in the chair with him. "The oddest thing happened at lunch," he says. "I was with one of the guys at this Italian restaurant. We were eating out on the patio, and I had just asked the waiter what he recommended for dessert, when a police car rounded the corner. They stopped right in front of the restaurant, and two officers jumped out with their guns drawn. They began barking orders toward us when our waiter mumbled, 'Shit.' He slowly raised his hands, and the police jumped the barrier to the patio, rushed toward him, threw him to the ground, and cuffed him right at our feet. After they read him his rights, they pulled him to his feet and escorted him toward the cop car. The waiter glanced back at me and yelled, 'The tiramisu is really good!' Then they put him in the car and drove away."

I tilt my head back and look up at him. "Seriously? That really happened?"

He nods, laughing. "I swear, Syd. It was crazy."

"Well? Did you try the tiramisu?"

"Hell, yeah, we did. It was the best tiramisu I've ever had." He kisses me on the cheek and pushes me forward. "Speaking of food, I'm starving." He stands up and holds out his hand to me. "Did you cook tonight?"

I take his hand and let him pull me up. "We just had salad, but I can make you one."

Once we're inside, Hunter takes a seat on the couch next

to Tori. She's got a textbook spread open across her lap as she halfheartedly focuses on both homework and TV at the same time. I take out the containers from the fridge and make his salad. I feel a little guilty that I forgot tonight was one of the nights he said he was coming. I usually have something cooked when I know he'll be here.

We've been dating for almost two years now. I met him during my sophomore year in college, when he was a senior. He and Tori had been friends for years. After she moved into my dorm and we became friends, she insisted I meet him. She said we'd hit it off, and she was right. We made it official after only two dates, and things have been wonderful since.

Of course, we have our ups and downs, especially since he moved more than an hour away. When he landed the job in the accounting firm last semester, he suggested I move with him. I told him no, that I really wanted to finish my undergrad before taking such a huge step. In all honesty, I'm just scared.

The thought of moving in with him seems so final, as if I would be sealing my fate. I know that once we take that step, the next step is marriage, and then I'd be looking at never having the chance to live alone. I've always had a roommate, and until I can afford my own place, I'll be sharing an apartment with Tori. I haven't told Hunter yet, but I really want to live alone for a year. It's something I promised myself I would do before I got married. I don't even turn twenty-two for a couple of weeks, so it's not as if I'm in any hurry.

I take Hunter's food to him in the living room.

"Why do you watch this?" he says to Tori. "All these women do is talk shit about each other and flip tables."

"That's exactly why I watch it," Tori says, without taking her eyes off the TV.

Hunter winks at me and takes his food, then props his feet up on the coffee table. "Thanks, babe." He turns toward the TV and begins eating. "Can you grab me a beer?"

I nod and walk back into the kitchen. I open the refrigerator door and look on the shelf where he always keeps his extra beer. I realize as I'm staring at "his" shelf that this is probably how it begins. First, he has a shelf in the refrigerator. Then he'll have a toothbrush in the bathroom, a drawer in my dresser, and eventually, his stuff will infiltrate mine in so many ways it'll be impossible for me ever to be on my own.

I run my hands up my arms, rubbing away the sudden onset of discomfort washing over me. I feel as if I'm watching my future play out in front of me. I'm not so sure I like what I'm imagining.

Am I ready for this?

Am I ready for this guy to be the guy I bring dinner to every night when he gets home from work?

Am I ready to fall into this comfortable life with him? One where I teach all day and he does people's taxes, and then we come home and I cook dinner and I "grab him beers" while he props his feet up and calls me *babe*, and then we go to our bed and make love at approximately nine P.M. so we won't be tired the next day, in order to wake up and get dressed and go to work and do it all over again?

"Earth to Sydney," Hunter says. I hear him snap his fingers twice. "Beer? Please, babe?"

I quickly grab his beer, give it to him, then head straight to my bathroom. I turn the water on in the shower, but I don't get in. Instead, I lock the door and sink to the floor.

We have a good relationship. He's good to me, and I know he loves me. I just don't understand why every time I think about a future with him, it's not an exciting thought.

Ridge

Maggie leans forward and kisses my forehead. "I need to go."

I'm on my back with my head and shoulders partially propped against my headboard. She's straddling my lap and looking down at me regretfully. I hate that we live so far apart now, but it makes the time we do spend together a lot more meaningful. I take her hands so she'll shut up, and I pull her to me, hoping to persuade her not to leave just yet.

She laughs and shakes her head. She kisses me, but only briefly, and then she pulls away again. She slides off my lap, but I don't let her make it very far before I lunge forward and pin her to the mattress. I point to her chest.

"You"—I lean in and kiss the tip of her nose—"need to stay one more night."

"I can't. I have class."

I grab her wrists and pin her arms above her head, then press my lips to hers. I know she won't stay another night. She's never missed a day of class in her life, unless she was too sick to move. I sort of wish she was feeling a little sick right now, so I could make her stay in bed with me.

I slide my hands from her wrists, delicately up her arms until I'm cupping her face. Then I give her one final kiss before I reluctantly pull away from her. "Go. And be careful. Let me know when you make it home."

She nods and pushes herself off the bed. She reaches across me and grabs her shirt, then pulls it on over her head. I watch her as she walks around the room and gathers the clothes I pulled off her in a hurry.

After five years of dating, most couples would have moved

in together by now. However, most peoples' other halves aren't Maggie. She's so fiercely independent it's almost intimidating. But it's understandable, considering how her life has gone. She's been caring for her grandfather since I met her. Before that, she spent the majority of her teenage years helping him care for her grandmother, who died when Maggie was sixteen. Now that her grandfather is in a nursing home, she finally has a chance to live alone while finishing school, and as much as I want her here with me, I also know how important this internship is for her. So for the next year, I'll suck it up while she's in San Antonio and I'm here in Austin. I'll be damned if I ever move out of Austin, especially for San Antonio.

Unless she asked, of course.

"Tell your brother I said good luck." She's standing in my bedroom doorway, poised to leave. "And you need to quit beating yourself up, Ridge. Musicians have blocks, just like writers do. You'll find your muse again. I love you."

"I love you, too."

She smiles and backs out of my bedroom. I groan, knowing she's trying to be positive with the whole writer's block thing, but I can't stop stressing about it. I don't know if it's because Brennan has so much riding on these songs now or if it's because I'm completely tapped out, but the words just aren't coming. Without lyrics I'm confident in, it's hard to feel good about the actual musical aspect of writing.

My phone vibrates. It's a text from Brennan, which only makes me feel worse about the fact that I'm stuck.

Brennan: It's been weeks. Please tell me you have something.

Me: Working on it. How's the tour?

Brennan: Good, but remind me not to allow Warren to schedule this many gigs on the next leg.

Me: Gigs are what gets your name out there.

Brennan: OUR name. I'm not telling you again to stop acting like you aren't half of this.

Me: I won't be half if I can't work through this damn block.

Brennan: Maybe you should get out more. Cause some unnecessary drama in your life. Break up with Maggie for the sake of art. She'll understand. Heartache helps with lyrical inspiration. Don't you ever listen to country?

Me: Good idea. I'll tell Maggie you suggested that.

Brennan: Nothing I say or do could ever make Maggie hate me. Give her a kiss for me, and get to writing. Our careers are resting squarely on your shoulders.

Me: Asshole.

Brennan: Ah! Is that anger I detect in your text? Use it. Go write an angry song about how much you hate your little brother, then send it to me. ;)

Me: Yeah. I'll give it to you after you finally get your shit out of your old bedroom. Bridgette's sister might move in next month.

Brennan: Have you ever met Brandi?

Me: No. Do I want to?

Brennan: Only if you want to live with two Bridgettes.

Me: Oh, shit.

Brennan: Exactly. TTYL.

I close out the text to Brennan and open up a text to Warren.

Me: We're good to go on the roommate search. Brennan says hell no to Brandi. I'll let you break the news to Bridgette, since you two get along so well.

Warren: Well, motherfucker.

I laugh and hop off the bed, then head to the patio with my guitar. It's almost eight, and I know she'll be on her balcony. I don't know how weird my actions are about to seem to her, but all I can do is try. I've got nothing to lose.

2.

Sydney

I'm mindlessly tapping my feet and singing along to his music with my made-up lyrics when he stops playing mid-song. He never stops mid-song, so naturally, I glance in his direction. He's leaning forward, staring right at me. He holds up his index finger, as if to say, *Hold on*, and he sets his guitar beside him and runs into his apartment.

What the hell is he doing?

And oh, my God, why does the fact that he's acknowledging me make me so nervous?

He comes back outside with paper and a marker in his hands.

He's writing. What the hell is he writing?

He holds up two sheets of paper, and I squint to get a good look at what he's written.

A phone number.

Shit. His phone number?

When I don't move for several seconds, he shakes the papers and points at them, then points back to me.

He's insane. I'm not calling him. I can't call him. I can't do that to Hunter.

The guy shakes his head, then grabs a fresh sheet of paper and writes something else on it, then holds it up.

Text me.

When I still don't move, he flips the paper over and writes again.

I have a ?

A question. A text. Seems harmless enough. When he holds up the papers with his phone number again, I pull out my phone and enter his phone number. I stare at the screen for a few seconds, not really knowing what to say in the text, so I go with:

Me: What's your question?

He looks down at his phone, and I can see him smile when he receives my text. He drops the paper and leans back in his chair, typing. When my phone vibrates, I hesitate a second before looking down at it.

Him: Do you sing in the shower?

I shake my head, confirming my initial suspicion. He's a flirt. Of course he is, he's a musician.

Me: I don't know what kind of question that is, but if this is your attempt at flirting, I've got a boyfriend. Don't waste your time.

I hit send and watch him read the text. He laughs, and this irritates me. Mostly because his smile is so . . . *smiley.* Is that even a word? I don't know how else to describe it. It's as if his whole face smiles right along with his mouth. I wonder what that smile looks like up close.

Him: Believe me, I know you have a boyfriend, and this is definitely not how I flirt. I just want to know if you sing in the shower. I happen to think highly of people who sing in the shower and need to know the answer to that question in order to decide if I want to ask you my next question.

I read the lengthy text, admiring his fast typing. Guys aren't normally as skilled as girls when it comes to speed-texting, but his replies are almost instantaneous.

Me: Yes, I sing in the shower. Do you sing in the shower?

Him: No, I don't.

Me: How can you think highly of people who sing in the shower if you don't sing in the shower?

Him: Maybe the fact that I don't sing in the shower is why I think highly of people who do sing in the shower.

This conversation isn't going anywhere.

Me: Why did you need this vital piece of information from me?

He stretches his legs out and props his feet up on the edge of the patio, then stares at me for a few seconds before returning his attention to his phone.

Him: I want to know how you're singing lyrics to my songs when I haven't even added lyrics to them yet.

My cheeks instantly heat from embarrassment. Busted.

I stare at his text, then glance up at him. He's watching me, expressionless.

Why the hell didn't I think that he could see me sitting out here? I never thought he would notice me singing along to his music. Hell, until last night, I never thought he even noticed me. I inhale, wishing I'd never made eye contact with him to begin with. I don't know why I find this embarrassing, but I do. It seems as if I've invaded his privacy in some way, and I hate that.

Me: I tend to favor songs with lyrics, and I was tired of wondering what the lyrics to your songs were, so I guess I made up a few of my own.

He reads the text, then glances up at me without a hint of his infectious smile. I don't like his serious glances. I don't like what they do to my stomach. I also don't like what his smiley smile does to my stomach. I wish he would stick to a simple, unattractive, emotionless expression, but I'm not sure he's capable of that.

Him: Will you send them to me?

Oh, God. Hell, no.

Me: Hell, no.

Him: Please?

Me: No.

Him: Pretty please?

Me: No, thank you.

Him: What's your name?

Me: Sydney. Yours?

Him: Ridge.

Ridge. That fits him. Musical-artisty-moody type.

Me: Well, Ridge, I'm sorry, but I don't write lyrics that anyone
would want to hear. Do you not write lyrics to your own songs?

He begins to text, and it's a really long text. His fingers
move swiftly over his phone while he types. I'm afraid I'm
about to receive an entire novel from him. He looks up at me
just as my phone vibrates.

Ridge: I guess you could say I'm having a bad case of writer's
block. Which is why I really, really wish you would just send me
the lyrics you sing while I'm playing. Even if you think they're
stupid, I want to read them. You somehow know every single
song I play, even though I've never played them for anyone
except when I practice out here.

How does he know I know all his songs? I bring a hand up
to my cheek when I feel it flush, knowing he's been watching
me a lot longer than I initially thought. I swear, I have to be
the most unintuitive person in this entire world. I glance up at
him and he's continuing with another text, so I look back to my
phone and wait for it.

Ridge: I can see it in the way your whole body responds to
the guitar. You tap your feet, you move your head. And I've
even tried to test you by slowing down the song every once
in a while to see if you would notice, and you always do. Your
body stops responding when I change something up. So just
by watching you, I can tell you have an ear for music. And
since you sing in the shower, it probably means you're an okay
singer. Which also means that maybe there's a chance you
have a talent for writing lyrics. So, Sydney, I want to know what
your lyrics are.

I'm still reading when another text comes through.

Ridge: Please. I'm desperate.

I inhale a deep breath, wishing more than anything that this conversation had never started. I don't know how in the hell he can come to all these conclusions without my ever having noticed him watching me. In a way, it eases my embarrassment over the fact that he saw me watching *him*. But now that he wants to know what lyrics I made up, I'm embarrassed for an entirely different reason. I do sing, but not well enough to do anything with it professionally. My passion is mostly for music itself, not at all for performing it. And as much as I do love writing lyrics, I've never shared anything I've written. It seems too intimate. I'd almost rather he had sent me a vulgar, flirtatious come-on.

I jump when my phone vibrates again.

Ridge: Okay, we'll make a deal. Pick one song of mine, and send me the lyrics to just that one song. Then I'll leave you alone. Especially if they're stupid.

I laugh. And cringe. He's not going to let up. I'm going to have to change my number.

Ridge: I know your phone number now, Sydney. I'm not giving up until you send me lyrics to at least one song.

Jesus. He's not going away.

Ridge: And I also know where you live. I'm not above begging on my knees at your front door.

Ugh!

Me: Fine. Stop with the creepy threats. One song. But I'll have to write the lyrics down while you play it first, because I've never written them out before.

Ridge: Deal. Which song? I'll play it right now.

Me: How would I tell you which song, Ridge? I don't know the names of any of them.

Ridge: Yeah, me, neither. Hold up your hand when I get to the one you want me to play.

He puts down his phone and picks up his guitar, then begins playing one of the songs. It's not the one I want him to play, though, so I shake my head. He switches to another song, and I continue to shake my head until the familiar chords to one of my favorites meets my ears. I hold up my hand, and he grins, then starts the song over from the beginning. I pull my notebook in front of me and pick up my pen, then begin to write down the lyrics I've put to it.

He has to play the song three times before I finally get them all out. It's almost dark now, and it's hard to see, so I pick up my phone.

Me: It's too dark to read. I'll go inside and text them to you, but you have to promise you'll never ask me to do this again.

The light from his phone illuminates his smile, and he nods at me, then picks up his guitar and walks back inside his apartment.

I go to my room and sit on the bed, wondering if it's too late to change my mind. I feel as if this whole conversation just ruined my eight o'clock patio time. I can't go back outside and listen to him ever again. I liked it better when I thought he didn't know I was there. It was like my own personal space with my own personal concert. Now I'll be way too aware of him to actually enjoy listening, and I curse him for ruining that.

I regretfully text him my lyrics, then turn my phone on silent and leave it on my bed as I go into the living room and try to forget this ever happened.

Ridge

Holy shit. She's good. Really good. Brennan is going to love this. I know if he agrees to use them, we'll need her to sign a release, and we'll have to pay her something. But it's worth it, especially if the rest of her lyrics are as good as these.

But the question is, will she be willing to help out? She obviously doesn't have much confidence in her talent, but that's the least of my worries. The biggest worry is how I'll persuade her to send me more lyrics. Or how to get her to write *with* me. I doubt her boyfriend would go for that. He has to be the biggest jerk I've ever laid eyes on. I can't believe the balls of that guy, especially after watching him last night. He comes outside on the patio and kisses Sydney, cuddling up to her in the chair like the most attentive boyfriend in the world. Then, the second she turns her back, he's out on the patio with the other chick. Sydney must have been in the shower, because the two of them rushed outside as if they were on a timer, and the chick had her legs wrapped around his waist and her mouth on his faster than I could even blink. And it wasn't a first-time occurrence. I've seen it happen so many times I've lost count.

It's really not my place to inform Sydney that the guy she's dating is screwing her roommate. I especially can't tell her through a text. But if Maggie were cheating on me, I'd sure as hell want to know about it. I just don't know Sydney well enough to tell her something like that. Usually, the person to break the news is the one to catch all the blame, anyway. Especially if the person being cheated on doesn't want to believe it. I could send her an anonymous note, but the douchebag boyfriend would more than likely be able to talk his way out of it.

I won't do anything for now. It's not my place, and until I get to know her better, I'm not in a position for her to trust me. My phone vibrates in my pocket, and I pull it out, hoping Sydney decided to send me more lyrics, but the text is from Maggie.

Maggie: Almost home. See you in two weeks.

Me: I didn't say text me when you're almost home. I said text me when you're home. Now, stop texting and driving.

Maggie: Okay.

Me: Stop!

Maggie: Okay!

I toss the phone onto the bed and refuse to text her back. I'm not giving her a reason to text me again until she makes it home. I walk to the kitchen for a beer, then take a seat next to a passed-out Warren on the couch. I grab the remote and hit info to see what he's watching.

Porn.

Figures. The guy can't watch anything without nudity. I start to change the channel, but he snatches the remote out of my hands. "It's my night."

I don't know if it was Warren or Bridgette who decided we should divvy up the TV, but it was the worst idea ever. Especially since I'm still not sure which night is actually mine, even though, technically, this is my apartment. I'm lucky if either of them pays rent on a quarterly basis. I put up with it because Warren has been my best friend since high school, and Bridgette is . . . well, she's too mean for me to even want to strike up a conversation with her. I've avoided that since Brennan let her move in six months ago. I really don't have to worry about money right now, thanks to my job and the cut Brennan gives me, so I just leave it alone. I still don't know how Brennan met Bridgette or how they're involved, but even though their relationship isn't sexual, he obviously cares about her. I have no idea how or why, since she doesn't have any noticeable redeeming qualities other than how she looks in her Hooters uniform.

And of course, the second that thought passes through my head, so do the words Maggie said when she found out Bridgette was moving in with us.

"I don't care if she moves in. The worst thing that could happen would be for you to cheat on me. Then I'd have to break up with you, then your heart would shatter, and we'd both be miserable for life, and you would be so depressed you'd never be able to get it up again. So make sure if you do cheat, it's the best sex you ever have, because it'll also be the last sex you ever have."

She doesn't have to worry about my cheating on her, but the scenario she painted was enough to ensure that I don't even look at Bridgette in her uniform.

How in the hell did my thoughts wander this far?

This is why I'm having writer's block; I can't seem to focus on anything important lately. I go back to my room to transfer the lyrics Sydney sent onto paper, and I begin to work out how to add them to the music. I want to text Sydney to tell her what I think about them, but I don't. I should leave her hanging a little while longer. I know how nerve-racking it is to send someone a piece of yourself and then have to sit back and wait for it to be judged. If I make her wait long enough, maybe once I tell her how brilliant she is, she'll have developed a craving to send me more.

It might be a little cruel, but she has no idea how much I need her. Now that I'm pretty sure I've found my muse, I have to work it just right so she doesn't slip away.

3.

Sydney

If he hated them, the least he could have done was send a thank you. I know it shouldn't bother me, but it does. Especially because I never wanted to send them to him in the first place. I wasn't expecting him to praise me, but the fact that he begged so hard for them and then just ignored them sort of irritates me.

And he hasn't been outside at his usual time in almost a week. I've wanted to text him about it so many times, but if I do, then it'll seem as if I care what he thinks of the lyrics. I don't want to care. But I can tell by how disappointed I feel that I do care. I hate that I want him to like my lyrics. But the thought of actually having a hand in a song is a little bit exciting.

"Food should be here in a little while. I'm going to get the clothes out of the dryer," Tori says. She opens the front door, and I perk up on the couch when I hear the familiar sound of the guitar from outside. She closes the door behind her, and as much as I want to ignore it, I rush to my room and quietly slide out onto the balcony, books in hand. If I sink far enough into my chair, he might not notice I'm out here.

But he's looking straight at my balcony when I step outside. He doesn't acknowledge me with a smile or even a nod of his head when I take my seat. He just continues playing, and it makes me curious to see if he's just going to pretend our conversation last week never happened. I sort of hope so, because *I'd* like to pretend it never happened.

He plays the familiar songs, and it doesn't take me long to let go of my embarrassment over the fact that he thought my lyrics were stupid. I tried to warn him.

I finish up my homework while he's still playing, close my books and lean back, and close my eyes. It's quiet for a minute, and then he begins playing the song I sent him lyrics for. In the middle of the song, the guitar pauses for several seconds, but I refuse to open my eyes. He continues playing just as my phone vibrates with an incoming text.

Ridge: You're not singing.

I glance at him, and he's staring at me with a grin. He looks back down at his guitar and watches his hands as he finishes the song. Then he picks up his phone and sends another text.

Ridge: Do you want to know what I thought of the lyrics?

Me: No, I'm pretty positive I know what you thought. It's been a week since I sent them to you. No worries. I told you they were stupid.

Ridge: Yeah, sorry about the silence. I had to leave town for a few days. Family emergency.

I don't know if he's telling the truth, but the fact that he claims he's been out of town eases my fear that he hasn't been out on his balcony because of me.

Me: Everything okay?

Ridge: Yep.

Me: Good.

Ridge: I'm only going to say this once, Sydney. Are you ready?

Me: Oh, God. No. I'm turning off my phone.

Ridge: I know where you live.

Me: Fine.

Ridge: You're incredible. Those lyrics. I can't even describe to you how perfect they are for the song. How in the hell does that come out of you? And why can't you see that you need to LET it come out of you? Don't hold it in. You're doing the world a huge disservice with your modesty. I know I agreed not to ask you for more, but that was because I really didn't expect to get what I got from you. I need more. Give me, give me, give me.

I let out a huge breath. Until this moment, I didn't realize exactly how much his opinion mattered. I can't look up at him yet. I continue to stare at my phone for much longer than it takes me to read the text. I don't even text him back, because I'm still relishing the compliment. If he said he loved it, I would have accepted his opinion with relief, and I would have moved on. But the words he just texted were like stairs stacked one on top of the other, and each compliment was like me running up each step until I reached the top of the damn world.

Holy crap. I think this one text just gave me enough confidence to send him another song. I never would have predicted this. I never imagined I would be excited.

"Food's here," Tori says. "You want to eat out here?"

I tear my gaze away from the phone and look at her. "Uh. Yeah. Sure."

Tori brings the food out to the balcony. "I've never really looked at that guy before, but *damn*," she says, staring hard at

Ridge while he plays his guitar. "He's really hot, and I don't even *like* blonds."

"His hair isn't blond. It's brown."

"No, that's blond," she says. "But it's dark blond, so that's okay, I guess. Almost brown, maybe. I like the messy shag, and that body makes up for the fact that his hair isn't black." Tori takes a drink and leans back in her chair, still staring at him. "Maybe I'm being too picky. What do I care what color his hair is? It'll be dark when I have my hands in it, anyway."

I shake my head. "He's really talented," I say. I still haven't responded to his text, but he doesn't seem to be waiting around. He's watching his hands as he plays, not paying a bit of attention to us.

"I wonder if he's single," Tori says. "I'd like to see what other talents he has."

I have no idea if he's single, but the way Tori is thinking about him makes my stomach turn. Tori is incredibly cute, and I know she could find out if he had other talents if she really wanted to. She tends to get whomever she wants in the guy department. I've never really minded until now.

"You don't want to be involved with a musician," I say, as if I have any experience that would qualify me to give her advice. "Besides, I'm pretty sure Ridge does have a girlfriend. I saw a girl on his patio with him a few weeks ago." That's technically not a lie. I did see one once.

Tori glances at me. "You know his name? How do you know his name?"

I shrug as if it's no big deal. Because, honestly, it *is* no big deal. "He needed help with lyrics last week, so I texted him some."

She sits up in her chair. "You know his *phone* number?"

I suddenly become defensive, not liking the accusatory tone in her voice. "Calm down, Tori. I don't even know him. All I did was text him a few lyrics."

She laughs. "I'm not judging, Syd," she says, holding up her hands in defense. "I don't care how much you love Hunter, if you have an opening with *that*"—she flicks her hand in Ridge's direction—"I'd be livid if you *didn't* take advantage of it."

I roll my eyes. "You know I'd never do that to Hunter."

She sighs and leans back in her chair. "Yeah. I know."

We're both looking at Ridge when he finishes the song. He picks up his phone and types something, then picks up his guitar just as my phone vibrates and he begins to play another song.

Tori reaches for my phone, but I grab it first and hold it out of her reach. "That's from him, isn't it?" she says. I read the text.

Ridge: When Barbie goes away, I want more.

I cringe, because there's no way I'm letting Tori read this text. For one thing, he insulted her. Also, the second part of his text would have an entirely different meaning if she read it. I hit delete and press the power button down to lock my phone in case she snatches it away from me.

"You're flirting," she says teasingly. She picks up her empty plate and stands up. "Have fun with your sexting."

Ugh. I hate that she thinks I'd ever do that to Hunter. I'll worry about setting her straight later, though. In the meantime, I take out my notebook and find the page with the lyrics I wrote to the song he's currently playing. I transfer them to a text, hit send, and hurry back inside.

"That was so good," I say as I place my plate in the sink. "That's probably my favorite Italian restaurant in all of Austin." I walk to the couch and fall down next to Tori, trying to appear casual about the fact that she thinks I'm cheating on Hunter. The more defensive I get about it, the less likely she'll be to believe me when I try to deny it.

"Oh, my God, that reminds me," she says. "The funniest thing happened a couple of weeks ago at this Italian restaurant. I was eating lunch with . . . my mom, and we were out on the patio. Our waiter was telling us about dessert, when all of a sudden, this cop car comes screeching around the corner, sirens blaring . . ."

I'm holding my breath, scared to hear the rest of her story.

What the hell? Hunter said he was with a coworker. The odds of them both being at the same restaurant, without being there together, is way more than coincidental.

But why would they lie about being together?

My heart is folding in on itself. I think I'm gonna be sick.

How could they . . .

"Syd? Are you okay?" Tori is looking at me with genuine concern. "You look like you're about to be sick."

I put my hand over my mouth, because I'm afraid she might be right. I can't answer her right away. I can't even work up the strength to look at her. I try to still my hand, but I can feel it trembling against my mouth.

Why would they be together and not tell me? They're never together without me. They'd have no reason to be together unless they were planning something.

Planning something.

Oh.

Wait a second.

I press my palm against my forehead and shake my head back and forth. I feel as if I'm in the midst of the stupidest moment in all of my nearly twenty-two years of existence. Of *course* they were together. Of *course* they're hiding something. It's my birthday next Saturday.

Not only do I feel incredibly stupid for having believed they would do something like that to me, but I feel unforgivably guilty.

"You okay?" Tori says.

I nod. "Yeah." I decide not to mention the fact that I know she was with Hunter. I would feel even worse if I ruined their surprise. "I think the Italian food is just making me a little nauseated. I'll be right back." I stand and walk to my bedroom, then sit on the edge of my bed in order to regain my bearings. I'm filled with a mixture of doubt and guilt. Doubt, because I know neither of them would do what I briefly thought they had done. Guilt, because for a brief moment, I actually believed they were capable of it.

Ridge

I was hoping the first set of lyrics wasn't a fluke, but after seeing the second set she sent me and adding them to the music, I text Brennan. I can't not tell him about her any longer.

Me: I'm about to send you two songs. I don't even need you to tell me what you think of them, because I know you'll love them. So let's move past that, because I need you to solve a dilemma for me.

Brennan: Oh, shit. I was just kidding about the Maggie thing. You didn't really dump her for inspiration did you?

Me: I'm being serious. I found a girl who I'm positive was brought to this earth specifically for us.

Brennan: Sorry, man. I'm not into that shit. I mean, maybe if you weren't my brother, but still.

Me: Stop with the horseshit, Brennan. Her lyrics. They're perfect. And they come so effortlessly to her. I think we need her. I haven't been able to write songs like these since . . . well, ever. Her lyrics are perfect, and you need to take a look at them, because I sort of need you to love them and agree to buy them from her.

Brennan: What the hell, Ridge? We can't hire someone to write lyrics for us. She'll want a percentage of the royalties, and between the two of us and the guys in the band, it won't be worth it.

Me: I'm going to ignore that until you check the e-mail I just sent you.

I put my phone down and pace the room, giving him time to take a look at what I just sent him. My heart is pounding, and I'm sweating, even though it's not at all hot in this room. I just can't take his telling me no, because I'm scared that if we can't use her, I'll be facing another six months of a concrete wall.

After several minutes, my phone vibrates. I drop to my bed and pick it up.

Brennan: Okay. See what she's willing to take, and let me know.

I smile and toss the phone into the air and feel like yelling. After I calm down enough to text her, I pick up my phone and think. I don't want to freak her out, because I know she's completely new to this kind of thing.

Me: I was wondering if we could talk sometime soon? I have a proposition for you. And get your mind out of the gutter, it's completely music-related.

Sydney: Okay. I can't say I'm looking forward to it, because it makes me nervous. You want me to call you when I get off work?

Me: You work?

Sydney: Yes. Campus library. Morning shift mostly, except for this weekend.

Me: Oh. I guess that's why I never noticed. I don't usually get out of bed until after lunch.

Sydney: So do you want me to call you after I get home?

Me: Just text me. You think we can meet up sometime this weekend?

Sydney: Probably, but I'd have to talk to my boyfriend. Don't want him to find out and think you're using me for more than my lyrics.

Me: K. Sounds good.

Sydney: If you want, you could come to my birthday party tomorrow night. Might be easier, because he'll be here.

Me: It's your birthday tomorrow? Happy early birthday. And that sounds good. What time?

Sydney: Not sure. I'm not supposed to know about it. I'll just text you tomorrow night once I find out more.

Me: K.

Honestly, I don't like the fact that her boyfriend might be there. I want to talk to her about it alone, because I still haven't decided what to do about what I know is going on between that asshole and her roommate. But I need her to agree to help me before her heart gets shattered, so maybe my silence has been a little selfish. I do admire the fact that she wants to be honest with him, even though he doesn't deserve it. Which makes me think maybe this is something I should bring up to Maggie, even though it never occurred to me before that it might even remotely be an issue.

Me: Hey. How's my girl?

Maggie: Busy. This thesis is kicking my ass. How's my guy?

Me: Good. Really good. I think Brennan and I found someone who's willing to write lyrics with us. She's really good, and I've already finished almost two songs since you left last weekend.

Maggie: Ridge, that's great! I can't wait to read them. Maybe next weekend?

Me: You coming here, or am I going to you?

Maggie: I'll come there. I need to spend some time at the nursing home. Love you.

Me: Love you. Don't forget our video chat tonight.

Maggie: You know I won't. Already have my outfit picked out.

Me: That better be a cruel joke. You know I don't care to see clothes.

Maggie: ;)

Eight more hours.

I'm hungry.

I toss the phone aside. I pull open my bedroom door and take a step back when the shit that's been piled up on the other side begins to fall in on me. First it's the lamp, then the end table it was resting on, then the end table the lamp and the other end table were piled on top of.

Dammit, Warren.

These pranks are starting to get out of hand. I press my arm into the couch that's been shoved up against my bedroom door. I push it back out into the living room and jump over it, then head toward the kitchen.

• • •

I carefully spoon toothpaste onto an Oreo, then replace the top of the cookie and gently squeeze it. I put it back into the package with the rest of Warren's Oreos and seal the package shut, just as my phone vibrates.

Sydney: Can you do me a favor?

She has no idea how many favors I'd do for her right now. I'm pretty much at her mercy.

Me: What's up?

Sydney: Can you look out your balcony door and tell me if you see anything suspicious going on at my apartment?

Shit. Does she know? What does she want me to tell her? I know it's selfish, but I really don't want to tell her about her boyfriend until after I have the chance to talk to her about the lyrics.

Me: Okay. Hold on.

I walk to my balcony and glance across the courtyard. I don't see anything out of the ordinary. It's almost dark, though, so I can't see much. I'm not sure what she wants me to find, so I choose not to be too descriptive when I respond.

Me: Looks quiet.

Sydney: Really? Are the blinds open? You don't see people?

I look again. The blinds are open, but the only thing I can see from here is the glare from the TV.

Me: Doesn't look like anyone's home. Aren't you having a birthday party later tonight?

Sydney: I thought so. I'm really confused.

There's movement in one of the windows, and I see her roommate going into the living room. Sydney's boyfriend follows closely behind her, and they both sit on the couch, but all I can see is their feet.

Me: Wait. Your boyfriend and your roommate just sat on the couch.

Sydney: Okay. Sorry to bother you.

Me: Wait. What about tonight? Are you still having a birthday party?

Sydney: I don't know. Hunter says he's taking me out to eat as soon as I get home from work, but I sort of thought it was a lie. I know he and Tori had lunch together a couple of weeks ago, but they don't know I know. They were obviously planning something, and I assumed it was a surprise party, but tonight's the only night that could happen.

I wince. She actually caught them in a lie, and she thought they were together because they were planning something nice for her. Christ. I don't even know the guy, and I have a huge urge to walk over there and beat the shit out of him.

It's her birthday. I can't tell her on her birthday. I take a deep breath, then decide to text Maggie for advice.

Me: Question. You busy?

Maggie: Nope. Shoot.

Me: If it was your birthday and someone you knew found out I was cheating on you, would you want to know right then? Or would you hope that person would wait to tell you until it was no longer your birthday?

Maggie: If this is a hypothetical question, I'm going to kill you for this heart attack. If it's not hypothetical, I'm going to kill you for this heart attack.

Me: You know it's not me. It's not your birthday. ;)

Maggie: Who's cheating on whom?

Me: It's Sydney's birthday today. The girl I was telling you about who writes the lyrics. I happen to know her boyfriend is cheating on her, and I'm kind of in a position where I should tell her because she's becoming suspicious.

Maggie: Jesus. I'd hate to be you right now. But if she's suspicious and you know for a fact that he's cheating, you need to tell her, Ridge. If you don't say anything, you're inadvertently lying.

Me: Ugh! That's what I thought you'd say.

Maggie: Good luck. I'm still going to kill you for the heart attack next weekend.

I sit on the bed, then start a text to Sydney.

Me: I'm not sure how to say this, Sydney. You're not driving right now, are you?

Sydney: Oh, jeez. There are people there, aren't there? Lots of them?

Me: No, there isn't anyone there but the two of them. First, I need to apologize for not telling you this sooner. I didn't know how, because we don't know each other that well. Second, I'm sorry for doing it on your birthday, of all days, but I feel like an ass for even waiting this long. And third, I'm sorry you have to find out via text, but I don't want you to have to walk back into your apartment without knowing the truth first.

Sydney: You're scaring me, Ridge.

Me: I'm just going to rip the Band-Aid off, okay? Something has been going on between your roommate and your boyfriend for a while.

I hit send and close my eyes, knowing I'm completely ruin-ing her birthday. If not pretty much every day after today, too.

Sydney: Ridge, they've been friends for longer than I've even known Hunter. I think you've misinterpreted everything.

Me: If sticking your tongue down someone's throat while straddling him is friendship, then I'm sorry. But I'm positive I'm not misinterpreting anything. It's been going on for weeks. I'm assuming they come out to the patio while you're in the shower, because they're never out there long. But it happens a lot.

Sydney: If you're being honest, why didn't you tell me when we first started talking?

Me: How does one comfortably say this to another person, Sydney? When is there ever an appropriate time? I'm telling you now because you're becoming suspicious, and it's as appropriate a time as it can be.

Sydney: Please tell me you have a warped sense of humor, because you have no idea what you're doing to my heart right now.

Me: I'm sorry, Sydney. Really.

I wait patiently for a response. She doesn't text me back. I contemplate texting her, but I know she needs time to absorb this.

Dammit, I'm such an asshole. Now she'll probably be pissed at me, but I can't blame her. I guess I can kiss the lyrics good-bye.

My door swings open, and Warren barges in, then hurls a cookie straight at me. I duck, and it hits the headboard behind me.

"Asshole!" Warren yells. He turns and marches back out of the bedroom and slams the door.

4.

Sydney

I must be in shock. How the hell did the day turn out like this? How does one girl go from having a best friend, a boyfriend, a purse, and a roof over her head to being heartbroken and naked, standing frozen in a strange shower, staring at the wall for half an hour straight? I swear to God, if this is some huge elaborate birthday hoax at my expense, I'm never speaking to anyone. Ever again. Ever.

However, I know it's not a hoax. A hoax is just wishful thinking. I knew the second I walked through the front door and headed straight for Hunter that everything Ridge had said was true. I flat-out asked Hunter if he was sleeping with Tori, and the looks on both of their faces would have been comical if they didn't completely crush my heart and deplete my trust in one fell swoop. I wanted to sink to the floor and cry when he couldn't deny it. Instead, I walked calmly to my bedroom and began packing my things.

Tori came into the room, crying. She tried to tell me it meant nothing, that sex had always been a casual thing between them, even before they met me. Hearing her say it meant nothing to them hurt worse than anything. If it meant something to either of them, at least I could vaguely understand their betrayal. But the fact that she was claiming it meant nothing, yet it still happened, hurt me more than anything else she could have possibly said at that moment. I'm pretty sure that's when I punched her.

It doesn't help matters that I lost my job just minutes after Ridge told me about Hunter and Tori. I think it's frowned upon in most libraries when student workers begin crying and throwing books at the wall in the middle of their shift. But I can't help the fact that I happened to be stocking the romance section the second I found out my boyfriend of two years was sleeping with my roommate. The sappy, romantic covers on the cart in front of me just really pissed me off.

I turn the water off in Ridge's shower and step out, then get dressed.

I feel better physically after finally getting into dry clothes, but my heart is growing heavier and heavier with each passing minute. The more time that passes by, the more my reality begins to sink in. In the course of just two hours, I've lost the entire last two years of my life.

That's a lot of time to invest in two people who were supposed to be the most trusted people in my life. I'm not sure if I would have ended up marrying Hunter or if he would have been the father of any future children of mine, but it hurts to know that I trusted him enough to possibly fill those roles, and he ended up being the opposite of who I thought he was.

I think the fact that I misjudged him pisses me off more than the fact that he cheated on me. If I can't even accurately judge the people closest to me, then I can't trust *anyone*. Ever. I hate them for taking that away from me. Now, no matter who comes into my life after this, I'll always be skeptical.

I walk back into the living room, and all the lights are out except for a lamp beside the couch. I look at my phone, and it's barely after nine. Several texts came through while I was in the shower, so I take a seat on the couch and scroll through them.

Hunter: Please call me. We need to talk.

Tori: I'm not mad at you for hitting me. Please call me.

Hunter: I'm worried about you. Where are you?

Ridge: I'm sorry I didn't tell you sooner. Are you okay?

Hunter: I'll bring your purse to you. Just tell me where you are.

I drop the phone onto the coffee table and sink back onto the couch. I have no idea what I'm going to do. Of course, I never want to speak to either of them again, but where does that put me? I can't afford my own apartment right now, since financial aid doesn't come in for another month. I don't have enough money in savings to put down a deposit plus get all the utilities turned on until then. The majority of the friends I've made since I've been going to school here still live in dorms, so staying with them is out of the question. I'm basically left with two options: Call my parents, or enter into some odd plural relationship with Hunter and Tori in order to save money.

Neither option is one I'm willing to entertain tonight. I'm just thankful that Ridge allowed me to stay at his place. At least I'm saving money on a hotel room. I have no idea where I'll go when I wake up in the morning, but that's still a good twelve hours away. Until then, I'll just continue to hate the entire universe while I feel sorry for myself.

And what better way to feel sorry for myself than while getting drunk?

I need alcohol. Bad.

I walk to the kitchen and begin to scan the cabinets. I hear the door to Ridge's bedroom open. I glance over my shoulder at him as he comes out of his room.

His hair is definitely light brown. Take that, Tori.

He's in a faded T-shirt and jeans, and he's barefoot, eyeing me inquisitively as he makes his way into the kitchen. I feel a little embarrassed for being caught rummaging through his cabinets, so I turn away from him before he sees me blush.

"I need a drink," I say. "You got any alcohol?"

He's staring down at his phone, texting again. He either can't do two things at once, or he's upset because I had an attitude with him today.

"I'm sorry if I was a bitch to you, Ridge, but you have to admit, my response was a little justified considering the day I've had."

He casually slips his phone into his pocket and looks at me from across the bar, but he chooses not to respond to my half-assed apology. He purses his lips and cocks an eyebrow.

I'd like to smack that cocky eyebrow back down where it belongs. What the hell is his problem? The worst thing I did to him was flip him off.

I roll my eyes and shut the last cabinet, then walk back to the couch. He's really being a jerk, considering my situation. From the little time I've known him, I was under the impression that he was actually a nice guy, but I'd almost rather go back to my own apartment with Tori and Hunter.

I pick up my phone, expecting another text from Hunter, but it's from Ridge.

Ridge: If you aren't going to look at me when you speak, you might want to stick to texting.

I read the text several times, trying to make sense of it, but no matter how many times I read it, I don't understand it. I grow concerned that maybe he's a little weird and I need to leave. I look at him, and he's watching me. He can see the confusion on my face, but he still doesn't explain himself. Instead, he resumes texting. When my phone receives another message, I look at the screen.

Ridge: I'm deaf, Sydney.

Deaf?

Oh.

Wait. *Deaf?*

But how? We've had so many conversations.

The last few weeks of knowing him and talking to him flash through my memory, and I can't recall a single time I've actually heard him speak.

Is that why Bridgette thought *I* was deaf?

I stare at my phone, sinking into a heap of embarrassment. I'm not sure how to feel about this. I'm sure that feeling betrayed isn't a fair response, but I can't help it. I feel I need to tack this onto the "Ways the world can betray Sydney on her birthday" list. Not only did he not tell me he knew my boyfriend was screwing around on me, but he also failed to mention that he's deaf?

Not that being deaf is something he should feel obliged to tell me. I just . . . I don't know. I feel a little hurt that he didn't share that fact with me.

Me: Why didn't you tell me you were deaf?

Ridge: Why didn't you tell me you could hear?

I tilt my head as I read his text and flood with even more humiliation. He makes a very good point.

Oh, well. At least he won't hear me cry myself to sleep tonight.

Me: Do you have any alcohol?

Ridge reads my text and laughs, then nods. He walks to the cabinet below the sink and pulls out a container of Pine-Sol. He takes two glasses out of the cabinet, then proceeds to fill them with . . . cleaning liquid?

"What the hell are you doing?" I ask.

When he doesn't turn around, I slap myself in the forehead, remembering he can't hear me. This will take some getting used to. I walk to where he's standing. When he sets the Pine-Sol down on the counter and picks up both glasses, I grab the bottle of cleaning solution and read it, then arch an eyebrow. He laughs and hands me a glass. He sniffs his drink, then motions for me to do the same. I hesitantly bring it to my nose and am met with the burning scent of whiskey. He holds the glass out, clinks it to mine, and we both down our shots. I'm still recovering from the awful taste when he picks up his phone and texts me again.

Ridge: Our other roommate has an issue with alcohol, so we have to hide it from him.

Me: Is his issue that he hates it?

Ridge: His issue is that he doesn't like to pay for it himself and he drinks everyone else's.

I nod, set my phone back down, grab the container, and pour us each another shot. We repeat the motions, downing the second one. I grimace as the burn spreads its way down my throat and through my chest. I shake my head, then open my eyes.

"Can you read lips?" I ask.

He shrugs, then grabs a piece of paper and a pen conveniently placed on the counter next to him. *Depends on the lips.*

I guess that makes sense. "Can you read mine?"

He nods and takes the pen again. *Mostly. I've learned to anticipate what people are going to say more than anything. I take most of my cues from body language and the situations I'm in.*

"What do you mean?" I ask, pushing on the counter with my palms and hopping up onto the bar. I've never met anyone who couldn't hear before. I didn't realize I was full of so many questions. It could be that I'm already feeling a buzz or I just don't want him to go back to his room yet. I don't want to be left alone to think about Hunter and Tori.

Ridge sets the notepad down and picks up my phone, then tosses it to me. He pulls one of the bar stools out and sits on it next to where I'm seated on the counter.

Ridge: If I'm at the store and a cashier speaks to me, I can mostly guess what they're asking. Same thing with a waitress at a restaurant. It's pretty simple to gather what people are saying when it's a routine conversation.

Me: But what about right now? This isn't routine. I doubt you have many homeless girls spend the night on your couch, so how do you know what I'm saying?

Ridge: Because you're basically asking me the same questions as anyone else who initially finds out I can't hear. It's the same conversation, just different people.

This comment bothers me, because I don't want to seem like those kinds of people at all. It has to get old, having to field the same questions over and over.

Me: Well, I don't really want to know about it, then. Let's change the subject.

Ridge looks up at me and smiles.

Damn. I don't know if it's the whiskey or the fact that I've been single for two hours, but that smile does some serious flirting with my stomach.

Ridge: Let's talk about music.

"Okay," I say with a nod.

Ridge: I wanted to talk to you about this tonight. You know, before I ruined your life and all that. I want you to write lyrics for my band. For the songs I have written and maybe some future songs if you're up for it.

I pause before responding to him. My initial response is to ask him about his band, because I've been dying to see this guy perform. My second response is to ask him how the hell he can play a guitar if he can't hear, but again, I don't want to be one of "those people." My third response is to automatically say no, because agreeing to give someone lyrics is a lot of pressure. Pressure I don't really want right now, since my life has pretty much taken a nosedive today.

I shake my head. "No. I don't think I want to do that."

Ridge: We would pay you.

That gets my attention. I suddenly feel an option three making its way into the picture.

Me: What kind of pay are we talking about? I still think you're insane for wanting me to help you write lyrics, but you may have caught me at a very desperate and destitute moment, being as though I'm homeless and could use some extra money.

Ridge: Why do you keep referring to yourself as homeless? Do you not have a place to stay?

Me: Well, I could stay with my parents, but that would mean I'd have to transfer schools my senior year, and it would put me about two semesters behind. I could also stay with my roommate, but I don't know how much I'd like to hear her screwing my boyfriend of two years at night while I try to sleep.

Ridge: You're a smartass.

Me: Yeah, I guess I've got that going for me.

Ridge: You can stay here. We're kind of in search of a fourth roommate. If it means you'll help us with the songs, you can stay for free until you get back on your feet.

I read the text twice, slowly. I shake my head.

Ridge: Just until you can get your own place.

Me: No. I don't even know you. Besides, your Hooters girlfriend already hates me.

Ridge laughs at that comment.

Ridge: Bridgette is not my girlfriend. And she's hardly ever here, so you don't have to worry about her.

Me: This is too weird.

Ridge: What other option do you have? I saw you didn't even have cab fare earlier. You're pretty much at my mercy.

Me: I have cab fare. I left my purse in my apartment, and I didn't want to go back up to get it, so I didn't have a way to pay the driver.

Ridge frowns when he reads my text.

Ridge: I'll go with you to get it if you need it.

I look up at him. "Are you sure?" I ask.
He smiles and walks toward the front door, so I follow him.

Ridge

It's still raining out, and I know she just put on dry clothes after her shower, so once we reach the bottom of the stairwell, I pull my phone out and text her.

Me: Wait here so you don't get wet again. I'll go get it myself.

She reads the text and shakes her head, then looks back up at me. "No. I'm going with you."

I can't help but appreciate the fact that she doesn't respond to my being deaf the way I expect her to. Most people become uneasy once they aren't sure how to communicate with me. The majority of them raise their voices and talk slowly, sort of like Bridgette. I guess they think being louder will somehow miraculously make me hear again. However, it does nothing but force me to contain my laughter while they talk to me as if I'm an idiot. Granted, I know people don't do it to be disrespectful. It's just simple ignorance, and that's fine. I'm so used to it I don't even notice anymore.

However, I did notice Sydney's reaction . . . because there really wasn't one. As soon as she found out, she just propped herself up on the counter and continued talking to me, even though she moved from speaking to texting. And it helps that she's a fast texter.

We run across the courtyard until we reach the base of the stairs that lead up to her apartment. I begin walking up and notice that she's frozen at the bottom of the stairs. The look in her eyes is nervous, and I instantly feel bad for not realizing how hard this must be for her. I know she's probably hurting a lot more than she's letting on. Learning that your best friend and your boyfriend have betrayed you has to be difficult, and it hasn't even been a day since she found out. I walk back down the stairs and grab her hand, then smile at her reassuringly. I tug on her hand; she takes a deep breath and walks with me up the stairs. She taps me on the shoulder before we reach her door, and I turn around.

"Can I wait here?" she says. "I don't want to see them."

I nod, relieved that her lips are easy to read.

"But cow well you ass therefore my bird?" she says.

Or I *think* that's what she said. I laugh, knowing I more than likely completely misread her lips. She says it again when she sees the confusion on my face, but I still don't understand her. I hold up my phone so she can text me.

Sydney: But how will you ask them for my purse?

Yeah. I was a little off on that one.

Me: I'll get your purse, Sydney. Wait here.

She nods. I type out a text as I walk to the front door and knock. A minute passes, and no one comes to the door, so I knock again, with more force, thinking maybe my first knock was too soft to be heard. The doorknob turns, and Sydney's friend appears in the doorway. She eyes me curiously for a second, then glances behind her. The door opens wider, and Hunter appears, eyeing me suspiciously. He says something that looks like "Can I help you?" I hold up the text that says I'm here for Sydney's purse, and he looks down and reads it, then shakes his head.

"Who the hell are you?" he says, apparently not liking the fact that I'm here on Sydney's behalf. The girl disappears from the doorway, and he opens the door even farther, then folds his arms over his chest and glares at me. I motion to my ear and shake my head, letting him know that I can't hear what he's saying.

He pauses, then throws his head back and laughs and disappears from the doorway. I glance to Sydney, who is standing nervously at the top of the stairs, watching me. Her face is pale, and I give her a wink, letting her know everything is okay. Hunter comes back, slaps a piece of paper against the door, and writes on it. He holds the paper up for me to read.

Are you fucking her?

Jesus, what a prick. I motion for the pen and paper, and he hands them to me. I write my response and hand it back to him. He looks down at the paper, and his jaw tightens. He crumples up the paper, drops it to the floor, and then, before I can react, his fist is coming at me.

I accept the hit, knowing I should have been prepared for it. The girl reappears, and I can tell she's screaming, although I have no idea whom she's screaming at or what she's saying. As soon as I take a step back from the doorway, Sydney is in front of me, rushing into the apartment. My eyes follow her as she runs down the hallway, disappears into a room, and comes back out clutching a purse. The girl steps in front of her and places her hands on Sydney's shoulders, but Sydney pulls her arm back, makes a fist, and punches the girl in the face.

Hunter tries to step in front of Sydney to block her from leaving, so I tap him on the shoulder. When he turns around, I punch him square in the nose, and he stumbles back. Sydney's eyes go wide, and she looks back at me. I grab her hand and pull her out of the apartment, toward the stairs.

Luckily, the rain has finally stopped, so we both break into a run back toward my apartment. I glance behind me a couple of times to make sure neither of them is following us. Once we make it back across the courtyard and up my stairs, I swing open the door and step aside so she can run in. I shut the door behind us and bend over, clasping my knees with my hands to catch my breath.

What an asshole. I'm not sure what Sydney saw in him, but the fact that she dated him makes me question her judgment a little bit.

I glance up at her, expecting to see her in tears, but instead, she's laughing. She's sitting on the floor, attempting to catch her breath, laughing hysterically. I can't help but smile, seeing her reaction. And the fact that she punched that girl right in the face without a moment's hesitation? I've got to hand it to her, she's tougher than I first thought.

She looks up at me and inhales a calming breath, then mouths the words *thank you*, while holding up her purse. She stands up and brushes the wet hair out of her face, then walks to the kitchen and opens a few drawers until she finds a dishtowel and pulls it out. She wets it under the faucet, turns around, and motions me over. When I reach her, I lean against the counter while she takes my chin and angles my face to the left. She presses the towel to my lip, and I wince. I didn't even realize it was hurting until she touched it. She pulls the rag back, and there's blood on it, so she rinses it under the faucet and puts it back up to my mouth. I notice that her own hand is red. I take it and inspect it. It's already swelling.

I pull the rag from her hand and wipe the rest of the blood off my face, then grab a ziplock bag out of the cabinet, go to the freezer, and fill it with ice. I take her hand and press the ice onto it, letting her know she needs to keep it there. I lean against the counter next to her and pull my phone out.

Me: You hit her good. Your hand is already swelling.

She texts me with one hand, keeping the ice on top of the other as she rests it on the counter.

Sydney: It could be because that wasn't the first time I've punched her today. Or it could also be swollen because you aren't the first one to punch Hunter today.

Me: Wow. I'm impressed. Or terrified. Is three punches your daily average?

Sydney: Three punches is now my lifetime average.

I laugh.

She shrugs and sets her phone down, then pulls the ice off her hand and brings it back up to my mouth. "Your lip is swelling," she says.

My hands are clenching the countertop behind me. I become increasingly uneasy with how comfortable she is with all this. Thoughts of Maggie flash through my head, and I can't help but wonder if she'd be okay with this scenario if she were to walk through the front door right now.

I need a distraction.

Me: You want birthday cake?

She smiles and nods.

Me: I probably shouldn't drive, since you've turned me into a raging alcoholic tonight, but if you feel like walking, Park's Diner makes a damn good dessert, and it's less than a mile from here. Pretty sure the rain is over.

"Let me change," she says, motioning to her clothes. She pulls clothes from her suitcase, then heads to the bathroom. I put the top on the Pine-Sol and hide it back under the cabinet.

5.

Sydney

We don't interact much while we eat. We're both sitting in the
booth with our backs to the wall and our legs stretched out in
front of us on the seats. We're quietly watching the restaurant
crowd, and I can't stop wondering what it's like for him, not being
able to hear anything going on around us. I'm probably too blunt
for my own good, but I have to ask him what's on my mind.

> Me: What's being deaf like? Do you feel like you're in on a
> secret that no one else knows about? Like you have a leg
> up on everyone because the fact that you can't hear has
> magnified all your other senses and you've got superhuman
> powers and no one can tell just by looking at you?

He almost spits out his drink while reading my text. He
laughs, and it occurs to me that his laugh is the only sound I've
heard him make. I know that some people who can't hear can
still talk, but I haven't heard him say a single word all night.
Not even to the waitress. He either points to what he wants on
the menu or writes it down.

> Ridge: I can honestly say I've never thought about it like that
> before. I kind of like it that you think of it that way, though. To
> be honest, I don't think about it at all. It's normal to me. I have
> nothing to compare it to, because it's all I've ever known.

Me: I'm sorry. I'm being one of those people again, aren't I? I guess me asking you to compare being deaf to not being deaf is like you asking me to compare being a girl to being a boy.

Ridge: Don't apologize. I like that you're interested enough to ask me about it. Most people are a little weirded out by it, so they don't say anything at all. I've noticed it's kind of hard to make friends, but that's also a good thing. The few friends I do have are genuine, so I look at it as an easy way of weeding out all the shallow, ignorant assholes.

Me: Good to know I'm not a shallow, ignorant asshole.

Ridge: Wish I could say the same about your ex.

I sigh. Ridge is right, but damn if it doesn't sting to know I couldn't see through Hunter's bullshit.

I put my phone down and eat the last of my cake. "Thank you," I say as I put my fork down. I honestly forgot for a while that today was my birthday until he offered to take me out for cake.

He shrugs as if it isn't a big deal, but it *is* a big deal. I can't believe after the day I've had that I'm actually in a semidecent mood. Ridge can take credit for that, because if it weren't for him, I don't know where I'd be tonight or what kind of emotional state I'd be in.

He takes a drink of his soda, then sits upright in the booth. He nods his head to the door, and I agree that I'm ready to go.

The buzz from the alcohol has worn off, and as we make our way out of the restaurant and back into the dark, I can feel myself beginning to succumb to the heartache again. I guess Ridge sees the look on my face, because he puts his arm around me and briefly squeezes my shoulders. He drops his arm and pulls his phone out.

Ridge: For what it's worth, he doesn't deserve you.

Me: I know. But it still hurts that I ever thought he deserved me. And honestly, I'm more hurt about Tori than I am about what happened with Hunter. I'm mostly just pissed at Hunter.

Ridge: Yeah, I don't even know the guy, and I've been pretty pissed at him. I can't imagine how you must feel. I'm surprised you haven't retaliated with some evil revenge plot yet.

Me: I'm not that clever. I wish I were, because I'd be all about revenge right now.

Ridge stops walking and turns to face me. He cocks an eyebrow, and a slightly wicked grin appears. It makes me laugh, because I can tell by his smile that he's mapping out a plan.

"Okay," I say, nodding my head without even knowing what he's about to propose. "As long as it doesn't land us in jail."

Ridge: Do you know if he leaves his car unlocked?

•   •   •

"Fish?" I ask, crinkling my nose in disgust. We've made a pit stop at a local grocery store next to the apartment complex, and he's buying a huge, scaly whole fish. I'm assuming this has to be part of his elaborate revenge scheme, but he could just be hungry.

Ridge: We need duct tape.

I follow him to the hardware aisle, where he grabs a roll of heavy-duty duct tape.

Fresh fish and duct tape.

I'm still not sure what he has planned, but I sort of like where this is headed.

• • •

When we're back at the apartment, I point out Hunter's car. I run up to the apartment to grab his spare car key out of my purse, where I still have it, while Ridge wraps the fish with duct tape. I come back downstairs and hand him the key.

Me: So what exactly are we about to do with this fish?

Ridge: Watch and learn, Sydney.

We walk to Hunter's car, and Ridge unlocks the passenger door. He has me tear off several pieces of duct tape while he reaches under the passenger seat. I'm watching closely—in case I need to seek revenge against anyone in the future—and he presses it against the underside of the seat. I hand him several more pieces of duct tape, trying to contain my laughter while he secures the raw fish with it. After he's sure it won't come loose, he slides out of the car and closes the door, looking around innocently. My hand is over my mouth, stifling my laughter, and he's as cool and composed as can be.

We casually walk away from the car, and once we're on the stairs to the apartment, we begin laughing.

Ridge: His car is going to smell like death in a matter of twenty-four hours. He'll never find it.

Me: You're kind of evil. If I didn't know better, I'd think you've done this before.

He laughs as we make our way back inside. We kick off our shoes at the door, and he tosses the duct tape onto the counter. I use the bathroom and make sure to unlock the door to his bedroom before I walk back out. In the living room, all the lights are out, except for the lamp by the couch. I lie down and check my phone one last time before turning it on silent.

Ridge: Good night. Sorry your birthday sucked.

Me: Thanks to you, it was better than it could have been.

I place the phone under my pillow and cover up. I close my eyes, and my smile immediately fades when the silence takes over. I can feel the tears coming, so I cover my head with the blanket and brace myself for a long night of heartache. The respite with Ridge was nice, but I have nothing to distract me now from the fact that I'm having the worst day of my life. I can't understand how Tori could do something like this to me. We've been best friends for almost three years. I told her everything. I trusted her with everything. I told her things I would never dream of telling Hunter.

Why would she risk our friendship for sex?

I've never felt this hurt. I pull the blanket over my eyes and begin to sob.

Happy birthday to me.

•   •   •

I have the pillow pulled tightly over my head, but it doesn't drown out the sound of gravel crunching beneath shoes. Why is someone walking on a driveway so noisily? And why can I even hear it?

Wait. Where am I?

Did yesterday really happen?

I reluctantly open my eyes, and I'm met with sunlight, so I pull the pillow tighter over my face and give myself a minute to adjust. The sound seems to get louder, so I lift the pillow from my face and peer out with one eye open. The first thing I see is a kitchen that isn't mine.

Oh, yeah. That's right. I'm on Ridge's couch, and twenty-two is the worst age ever.

I lift the pillow all the way off my head and groan as I squeeze my eyes shut again.

"Who are you and why are you sleeping on my couch?"

My body jumps, and my eyes flick open at the deep voice that can't be more than a foot away. Two eyes peer down at me. I pull my head back against the couch to put more space between me and the curious eyes to get a better look at who they're attached to.

It's a guy. A guy I've never seen before. He's sitting on the floor directly in front of the couch, and he's holding a bowl. He dips a spoon into the bowl and shoves it into his mouth, then begins the loud crunching again. I'm guessing that's not gravel he's eating.

"Are you the new roommate?" he says with his mouth full.

I shake my head. "No," I mutter. "I'm a friend of Ridge's."

He cocks his head and looks at me suspiciously. "Ridge only has one friend," the guy says. "Me." He shoves another spoonful of cereal into his mouth and fails to back out of my personal space.

I push my palms into the couch and sit up so that he's not right in my face. "Jealous?" I ask.

The guy continues to stare at me. "What's his last name?"

"Whose last name?"

"Your very good friend, Ridge," he says cockily.

I roll my eyes and drop my head against the back of the couch. I don't know who the hell this guy is, but I really don't care to compete over our levels of friendship with Ridge. "I don't know Ridge's last name. I don't know his middle name. The only thing I know about him is that he's got a mean right hook. And I'm only sleeping on your couch because my boyfriend of two years decided it would be fun to screw my roommate and I really didn't want to stick around to watch."

He nods, then swallows. "It's Lawson. And he doesn't have a middle name."

As if the morning could get any worse, Bridgette appears from the hallway and walks into the kitchen.

The guy on the floor takes another spoonful of cereal and looks at Bridgette, finally breaking his uncomfortable lock on me. "Good morning, Bridgette," he says with an odd, sarcastic tone to his voice. "Sleep well?"

She looks at him briefly and rolls her eyes. "Screw you, Warren," she snaps.

He turns his gaze back to mine with a mischievous grin. "That's Bridgette," he whispers. "She pretends to hate me during the day, but at night, she *loves* me."

I laugh, not really trusting that Bridgette is capable of loving anyone.

"Shit!" she yells, catching herself on the bar before she trips. "Jesus Christ!" She kicks one of my suitcases, still on the floor next to the bar. "Tell your little friend if she's staying here, she needs to take her shit to her room!"

Warren makes a face as if he's scared for me, then turns his head toward Bridgette. "What am I, your bitch? Tell her yourself."

Bridgette points to the suitcase she almost tripped over. "GET . . . YOUR . . . SHIT . . . OUT . . . OF . . . THE . . . KITCHEN!" she says, before marching back to her bedroom.

Warren slowly turns his head back to face me and laughs. "Why does she think you're deaf?"

I shrug. "I have no idea. She came to that conclusion last night, and I failed to correct her."

He laughs again, much louder. "Oh, this is classic," he says. "Do you have any pets?"

I shake my head.

"Are you opposed to porn?"

I don't know how we just began playing Twenty Questions,

but I answer him anyway. "Not opposed to the principle of porn but opposed to being featured in one."

He nods, contemplating my answer for a beat too long. "Do you have annoying friends?"

I shake my head. "My best friend is a backstabbing whore, and I'm no longer speaking to her."

"What are your showering habits?"

I laugh. "Once a day, with a skipped day every now and then. No more than fifteen minutes."

"Do you cook?"

"Only when I'm hungry."

"Do you clean up after yourself?"

"Probably better than you," I say, taking in the fact that he's used his shirt for a napkin no fewer than three times during this conversation.

"Do you listen to disco?"

"I'd rather eat barbed wire."

"All right, then," he says. "I guess you can stay."

I pull my feet up and sit cross-legged. "I didn't realize I was being interviewed."

He glances at my suitcases, then back to me. "It's obvious you need a place to stay, and we've got an empty room. If you don't take it, Bridgette wants to move her sister in next month, and that's the last thing Ridge and I need."

"I can't stay here," I say.

"Why not? From the sound of it, you're about to spend the day searching for an apartment anyway. What's wrong with this one? You won't even have to walk very far to get here."

I want to say that Ridge is the problem. He's been nice, but I think that might be the issue. I've been single for less than twenty-four hours, and I don't like the fact that although I should have been consumed with nightmares about Hunter and Tori all night, instead, I had a slightly disturbing dream involving an extremely accommodating Ridge.

I don't tell Warren that Ridge is why I can't stay here, though. Partly because that would give Warren more ammunition for questions and partly because Ridge just walked into the kitchen and is looking at us.

Warren winks at me, then stands up and walks with his bowl to the sink. He looks at Ridge. "Have you met our new roommate?" Warren asks.

Ridge signs something to him. Warren shakes his head and signs back. I sit on the couch and watch their silent conversation, slightly in awe that Warren knows sign language. I wonder if he's learned it for Ridge's benefit. Maybe they're brothers? Warren laughs, and Ridge glances in my direction before walking back to his bedroom.

"What did he say?" I ask, suddenly worried that Ridge no longer wants me here.

Warren shrugs and begins walking back toward his bedroom. "Exactly what I thought he'd say." He walks into his room, then comes back out with a cap on and keys in his hand. "He said you two already worked out a deal." Warren slips a pair of shoes on by the front door. "Heading to work now. That's your room if you want to put your stuff in it. You might have to throw all of Brennan's shit in the corner, though." He opens the door and steps outside, then turns back around. "Oh. What's your name?"

"Sydney."

"Well, Sydney. Welcome to the weirdest place you'll ever live." He shuts the door behind him.

I'm not sure I'm comfortable with this, but what other choice do I have? I pull my phone out from under my pillow. I start to text Ridge, because I don't recall closing a deal last night regarding my living arrangements. Before I finish the text, he sends me one first.

Ridge: Are you okay with this?

Me: Are you?

Ridge: I asked you first.

Me: I guess. But only if you are.

Ridge: Well, then, I guess that means we're roommates.

Me: If we're roommates, can you do me a favor?

Ridge: What's that?

Me: If I ever start dating again, don't be like Tori and sleep with my boyfriend, okay?

Ridge: I can't make any promises.

A few seconds later, he walks out of his bedroom and goes straight to my suitcases. He picks them up and carries them through the other bedroom door. He opens it and nods his head toward the room, indicating that I should come with him. I stand up and follow him into the bedroom. He lays the suitcases on the bed, then pulls his phone out again.

Ridge: Brennan still has a lot of stuff in here. I'll box it up and put it in the corner until he can get it all. Other than that, you might want to change the sheets.

He shoots me a wary look regarding the condition of the sheets, and I laugh. He points to the bathroom.

Ridge: We share the bathroom. Just lock the main door to the hallway and both doors to the bedrooms when you're in there. I obviously won't know when you're in the shower, so unless you want me barging in on you, make sure to lock up.

He walks to the bathroom and flips a light switch on the outside of the door, which turns the lights on and off inside the bathroom, then turns his attention back to the phone.

Ridge: I added switches on the outside because it's an easy way for someone to get my attention, since I can't hear a knock. Just flip the switch if you need to come into the bathroom so I'll know. The whole apartment is set up this way. There's a switch outside my bedroom door that turns my lights on and off if you need me. But I usually have my phone on me, so there's always texting.

He shows me where clean sheets are and then cleans out what's left in the dresser while I put the new sheets on the bed.
"Do I need furniture?"
Ridge shakes his head.

Ridge: He's leaving it. You can use what's here.

I nod, taking in the bedroom that has unexpectedly just become my new home. I smile at Ridge to let him know I appreciate his help. "Thank you."
He smiles back.

Ridge: I'll be in my room working for the next few hours if you need anything. I have to go to the store this afternoon. You can go with me and get what you need for the apartment.

He backs out of the bedroom and gives me a salute. I sit down on the edge of the bed and salute him back as he shuts the door. I fall back onto the bed and let out a huge sigh of relief.
Now that I have a place to live, all I need is a job. And maybe a car, since Tori and I mostly shared hers. Then maybe I'll call my parents and tell them I moved.

Or maybe not. I'll give this place a couple of weeks in order to see how things turn out.

Ridge: Oh, and btw, I didn't write that on your forehead.

What?

I run to the dresser and look in the mirror for the first time today. Written across my forehead in black ink, it says: *Someone wrote on your forehead.*

Ridge

Me: Morning. How's the thesis coming along?

Maggie: Do you want me to sugarcoat it, or are you honestly giving me an opening to vent?

Me: Wide open. Vent away.

Maggie: I'm miserable, Ridge. I hate it. I work on it for hours every day, and I just want to take a bat to my computer and go all *Office Space* on it. If this thesis were a child, I'd put it up for adoption and not even think twice about it. If this thesis were a cute, fuzzy puppy, I'd drop it off in the middle of a busy intersection and speed away.

Me: And then you would do a U-turn and go back and pick it up and play with it all night.

Maggie: I'm serious, Ridge. I think I'm losing my mind.

Me: Well, you already know what I think.

Maggie: Yes, I know what you think. Let's not get into that right now.

Me: You're the one who wanted to vent. You don't need this kind of stress.

Maggie: Stop.

Me: I can't, Maggie. You know how I feel, and I'm not keeping my opinion to myself when we both know I'm right.

Maggie: This is exactly why I never whine to you about it, because it always comes back to this same thing. I asked you to stop. Please, Ridge. Stop.

Me: Okay.

Me: I'm sorry.

Me: Now is when you return a text that says, "It's okay, Ridge. I love you."

Me: Hello?

Me: Don't do this, Maggie.

Maggie: Give a girl a minute to pee! Dang. I'm not mad. I just don't want to talk about it anymore. How are you?

Me: Phew. Good. We got a new roommate.

Maggie: I thought she wasn't moving in until next month.

Me: No, it's not Bridgette's sister. It's Sydney. The one I was telling you about a few days ago? After I decided to break the news to her about her boyfriend, it left her with nowhere to go. Warren and I are letting her stay here until she finds her own place. You'll like her.

Maggie: So I guess she believed you about her boyfriend?

Me: Yeah. She was pretty pissed at first that I didn't tell her sooner, but she's had a few days to let it sink in, so I think she gets it. So what time will you be here Friday?

Maggie: Not sure. I would say it depends on whether I get enough work done on my thesis, but I'm not mentioning my thesis to you ever again. I guess I'll get there when I get there.

Me: Well, then, I guess I'll see you when I see you. Love you. Let me know when you're on your way.

Maggie: Love you, too. And I know you're just concerned. I don't expect you to agree with my decisions, but I do want you to understand them.

Me: I do understand, babe. I do. I love you.

Maggie: Love you, too.

I drop my head forcefully against the headboard and rub my palms up and down my face out of sheer frustration. Of course, I understand her decision, but I'll never feel good about it. She's so frustratingly determined I seriously don't see how I'll ever get through to her.

I stand up and put my phone into my back pocket, then walk to my bedroom door. When I swing it open, I'm met with a smell that I'm positive is exactly what heaven will smell like.

Bacon.

Warren looks up at me from the dining-room table and grins, pointing to his plate full of food. "She's a keeper," he signs. "The eggs suck, though. I'm only eating them because I don't want to complain, or she might never cook for us again. Everything else is great." He signs everything he's saying without verbalizing it. Warren usually verbalizes all of his signed communication, out of respect for others around us. When he doesn't verbalize, I know he wants our conversation to remain between the two of us.

Like the silent one we're having right now while Sydney's in the kitchen.

"And she even asked how we liked our coffee," he signs.

I glance into the kitchen. Sydney smiles, so I smile back. I'm shocked to see her in a good mood today. After we got back from our trip to the store a few days ago, she's been spending most of the time in her room. At one point yesterday, Warren went in to ask her if she wanted any dinner, and he said she was on her bed crying, so he backed out and left her alone. I've wanted to check on her, but there isn't really anything I can do to make her feel better. All she can do is give it time, so I'm glad she's at least out of bed today.

"And don't look right now, Ridge. But did you see what she's wearing? Did you see that dress?" He bites the knuckles on his fist and winces, as if simply looking at her is causing him actual physical pain.

I shake my head and take a seat across from him. "I'll look later."

He grins. "I'm so glad her boyfriend cheated on her. Otherwise, I'd be eating leftover toothpaste-filled Oreos for breakfast."

I laugh. "At least you wouldn't have to brush your teeth."

"This was the best decision we've ever made," he says. "Maybe later we can talk her into vacuuming in that dress while we sit on the couch and watch."

Warren laughs at his own comment, but I don't crack a smile. I don't think he realizes he signed *and* spoke that last sentence. Before I can tell him, a biscuit comes hurtling past my head and smacks him in the face. He jumps back in shock and looks at Sydney. She's walking to the table with a *Don't mess with me* look on her face. She hands me a plate of food, then sets her own plate down in front of her and takes a seat.

"I said that out loud, didn't I?" Warren asks. I nod. He looks at Sydney, and she's still glaring at him. "At least I was complimenting you," he says with a shrug.

She laughs and nods once, as if he just made a good point. She picks up her phone and begins to text. She glances at me briefly, giving her head a slight shake when my phone vibrates in my pocket. She texted me something but apparently doesn't want me to make it obvious. I casually slide my hand into my pocket and pull my phone out, then read her text under the table.

Sydney: Don't eat the eggs.

I look at her and arch an eyebrow, wondering what the hell is wrong with the eggs. She casually sends another text while she holds a conversation with Warren.

Sydney: I poured dish soap and baby powder in them. It'll teach him not to write on my forehead again.

Me: WTH? When are you going to tell him?

Sydney: I'm not.

Warren: What are you and Sydney texting about?

I look up to see Warren holding his phone, staring at me. He picks up his fork and takes another bite of the eggs, and the sight makes me laugh. He lunges across the table and grabs my phone out of my hands, then begins scrolling through the texts. I try to grab it back from him, but he pulls his arm out of my reach. He pauses for a few seconds as he reads, then immediately spits his mouthful back onto his plate. He tosses me back my phone and reaches for his glass. He calmly takes a drink, sets it back down on the table, then pushes his chair back and stands up.

He points to Sydney. "You just messed up, little girl," he says. "This means war."

Sydney is smirking at him with a challenging gleam in her eye. Once Warren walks back to his bedroom and shuts his door, she loses the confident smirk and turns to me, wide-eyed.

Sydney: Help me! I need ideas. I suck at pranks!

Me: Yeah, you do. Dish soap and baby powder? You need serious help. Good thing you have the master on your side.

She grins, then begins eating her breakfast.

I don't even get my first bite down before Bridgette walks out of her room, sans smile. She walks straight to the kitchen and proceeds to make herself a plate of food. Warren returns from his room and sits back down at the table.

"I walked away for dramatic effect," he says. "I wasn't finished eating yet."

Bridgette sits, takes a bite of bacon, then looks over at Sydney. "DID . . . YOU . . . MAKE . . . THIS?" she says, pointing at the food dramatically. I cock my head, because she's talking to Sydney the same way she talks to me. As if she's deaf.

I look over at Sydney, who nods a response to Bridgette. I look back at Bridgette, and she says, "THANK . . . YOU!" She takes a bite of the eggs.

And she spits them right back out onto her plate.

She coughs and rushes to take a drink, then pushes away from the table. She looks back at Sydney. "I . . . CAN'T . . . EAT . . . THIS . . . SHIT!" She walks back to the kitchen, drops her food in the trash, and heads back to her bedroom.

The three of us break out into laughter after her door closes. When the laughter subsides, I turn to Warren.

"Why does Bridgette think Sydney is deaf?"

Warren laughs. "We don't know," he says. "But we don't feel like correcting her just yet."

I laugh on the outside, but inside I'm a little confused. I don't know when Warren began referring to himself and Sydney as *we*, but I'm not sure I like it.

●　　●　　●

My bedroom light flicks on and off, so I close my laptop and walk to the door. I open it, and Sydney is standing in the hallway, holding her laptop. She hands me a piece of paper.

I already finished my homework for the rest of the week. I even cleaned the entire apartment, excluding Bridgette's room, of course. Warren won't let me watch TV because it's not my night, whatever that means. So I was hoping I could hang out with you for a little while? I have to keep my mind busy, or I'll start thinking about Hunter again, and then I'll start feeling sorry for myself, and then I'll want Pine-Sol, and I really don't want to have any Pine-Sol, because I don't want to become a raging alcoholic like you.

I smile, step aside, and motion her into my bedroom. She looks around. The only place to sit is my bed, so I point to it, then take a seat and pull my laptop onto my lap. She sits on the other side of the bed and does the same.

"Thanks," she says with a smile. She opens her laptop and drops her eyes to the screen.

I tried not to take Warren's advice this morning about admiring the dress she had on today, but it was hard not to look, especially when he so blatantly pointed it out. I'm not sure what kind of weird thing he and Bridgette have going on, but it rubs me the wrong way that he and Sydney seem to have hit it off so well.

And it really rubs me the wrong way that it rubs me the wrong way. I don't look at her like that, so I don't understand why I'm sitting here thinking about it. And if she were standing next to Maggie, there wouldn't be a doubt in my mind that Maggie is more physically my type. Maggie is petite, with dark eyes and straight black hair. Sydney is the complete opposite. She's taller than Maggie—pretty average height—but her body is a lot more defined and curvy than Maggie's. Sydney definitely fills out the dress well, which is why Warren liked it. At least she changed into shorts before showing up at my bedroom door. That helps a little. The tops she wears are usually way too big for her, and they hang off her shoulders, which makes me think she took a lot of Hunter's T-shirts with her when she packed her bags.

Maggie's hair is always straight, whereas Sydney's is hard to figure out. It seems to change with the weather, but that's not necessarily a bad thing. The first time I saw her sitting on her balcony, I thought she had brown hair, but it turns out her hair was just wet. After playing guitar for about an hour that night, I looked at her as she was walking back inside her apartment, and her hair had dried completely and was in piles of blond waves that fell past her shoulders. Today it's curly and pulled up into a messy knot on top of her head.

Sydney: Stop staring at me.

Shit.

I laugh and attempt to brush away whatever the hell that internal detour was I just took.

Me: You look sad.

The first night she showed up here, she seemed happier than she does right now. Maybe it just took time for reality to sink in.

Sydney: Is there a way we can chat on the computer? It's a lot easier for me than texting.

Me: Sure. What's your last name? I'll friend you on Facebook.

Sydney: Blake.

I open my laptop and search her name. When I find her profile, I send her a friend request. She accepts it almost instantly, then shoots me a message.

Sydney: Hello, Ridge Lawson.

Me: Hello, Sydney Blake. Better?

She nods.

Sydney: You're a computer programmer?

Me: Already stalking my profile? And yes. I work from home. Graduated two years ago with a degree in computer engineering.

Sydney: How old are you?

Me: 24.

Sydney: Please tell me 24 is a lot better than 22.

Me: 22 will be good for you. Maybe not this week or next week, but it'll get better.

She sighs and puts one of her hands up to the back of her neck and rubs it, then begins typing again.

Sydney: I miss him. Is that crazy? I miss Tori, too. I still hate them and want to see them suffer, but I miss what I had with him. It's really starting to hurt. When it first happened, I thought maybe I was better off without him, but now I just feel lost.

I don't want to be harsh in my response, but at the same time, I'm not a girl, so I'm not about to tell her that what she's feeling is normal. Because to me, it's *not* normal.

Me: You only miss the idea of him. You weren't happy with him even before you found out he was cheating. You were only with him because it was comfortable. You just miss the relationship, but you don't miss Hunter.

She looks up at me and cocks her head, narrowing her eyes in my direction for a few seconds before dropping them back to the computer.

Sydney: How can you say I wasn't happy with him? I was. Until I found out what he was doing, I honestly thought he was the one.

Me: No. You didn't. You wanted him to be, but that's not how you really felt.

Sydney: You're kind of being a jerk right now, you know that?

I set my laptop beside me and walk to my desk. I pick up my notebook and a pen and go back to the bed and take a seat next to her. I flip open my notebook to the first set of lyrics she sent me.

Read these, I write at the top of the page. I set the notebook in her lap.

She looks down at the lyrics, then takes the pen. *I don't need to read them*, she writes. *I wrote them.*

I scoot closer to her and put the notebook in my lap, then

circle a few lines of her chorus. I point to them again. *Read these as if you weren't the one who wrote them.*

She reluctantly looks down at the notebook and reads the chorus.

> *You don't know me like you think you do*
> *I pour me one, when I really want two*
> *Oh, you're living a lie*
> *Living a lie*
>
> *You think we're good, but we're really not*
> *You coulda fixed things, but you missed your shot*
> *You're living a lie*
> *Living a lie*

When I'm certain she's had time to read them, I pick up the pen and write: *These words came from somewhere inside you, Sydney. You can tell yourself you were better off with him, but read the lyrics you wrote. Go back to what you were feeling when you wrote them.* I circle several lines, then read her words along with her.

> *With a right turn, the tires start to burn*
> *I see your smile, it's been hiding for a while*
> *For a while*
>
> *Your foot pushes down against the ground*
> *The world starts to blur, can't remember who you were*
> *Who you were*

I look at her, and she's still staring at the paper. A single tear trickles down her cheek, and she quickly wipes it away.

She picks up the pen and begins writing. *They're just words, Ridge.*

I reply, *They're* your *words, Sydney. Words that came from you. You say you feel lost without him, but you felt lost even when you were* with *him. Read the rest.*

She inhales a deep breath, then looks down at the paper again.

> *I yell, slow down, we're almost out of town*
> *The road gets rough, have you had enough*
> *Enough*
>
> *You look at me, start heading for a tree*
> *I open up the door, can't take any more*
> *Any more*
>
> *Then I say,*
>
> *You don't know me like you think you do*
> *I pour me one, when I really want two*
> *Oh, you're living a lie*
> *Living a lie*
>
> *You think we're good, but we're really not*
> *You coulda fixed things, but you missed your shot*
> *You're living a lie*
> *Living a lie*

6.

Sydney

I continue to stare at the words in the notebook.

Is he right? Did I write them because that's how I really feel?

I never give it much thought when I write lyrics, because I've always felt no one would read them, so it doesn't matter what the meaning is behind the words. But now that I think about it, maybe the fact that I don't give them much thought proves that they really are a reflection of how I feel. To me, lyrics are harder to write when you have to invent the feelings behind them. That's when lyrics take a lot of thought, when they aren't genuine.

Oh, wow. Ridge is absolutely right. I wrote these lyrics weeks ago, long before I knew about Hunter and Tori.

I lean back against the headboard and open my laptop again.

Me: Okay, you win.

Ridge: It's not a competition. Just trying to help you see that maybe this breakup is exactly what you needed. I don't know you very well, but based on the lyrics you wrote, I'm guessing you've been craving the chance to be on your own for a while now.

Me: Well you claim not to know me very well, but you seem to know me better than I know myself.

Ridge: I only know what you told me in those lyrics. Speaking of which, you feel like running through them? I was about to compile them with the music to send to Brennan and could use your ears. Pun intended.

I laugh and elbow him.

Me: Sure. What do I do?

He stands and picks up his guitar, then nods his head toward the balcony. I don't want to go out on that balcony. I don't care if I was ready to leave Hunter, I sure wasn't ready to leave Tori. And being out there will be too much of a distraction.

I crinkle my nose and shake my head. He glances across the courtyard at my apartment, then pulls his lips into a tight, thin line and slowly nods his head in understanding. He walks over to the bed and sits on the mattress next to me.

Ridge: I want you to sing the lyrics while I play. I'll watch you so I can make sure we're on the same page with where they need to be placed on the sheet music.

Me: No. I'm not singing in front of you.

He huffs and rolls his eyes.

Ridge: Are you afraid I'll laugh at how awful you sound? I can't HEAR YOU, SYDNEY!

He's smiling his irritating smile at me.

Me: Shut up. Fine.

He sets the phone down and begins playing the song. When the lyrics are supposed to come in, he looks up, and I freeze. Not because I'm nervous, though. I freeze because I'm doing that thing again where I'm holding my breath because seeing him play is just . . . he's incredible.

He doesn't miss a beat when I skip my intro. He just starts over from the beginning and plays the opening again. I shake myself out of my pathetic awe and begin singing the words. I would probably never be singing lyrics in front of anyone one-on-one like this, but it helps that he can't hear me. He does stare pretty hard, though, which is a little unnerving.

He pauses after every stanza and makes notes on a page. I lean over and look at what he's writing. He's putting musical notes on blank sheet-music paper, along with the lyrics.

He points to one of the lines, then grabs his phone.

Ridge: What key do you sing this line in?

Me: B.

Ridge: Do you think it would sound better if you took it a little higher?

Me: I don't know. I guess we could try.

He plays the second part of the song again, and I take his advice and sing in a higher key. Surprisingly, he's right. It does sound better.

"How did you know that?" I ask.

He shrugs.

Ridge: I just do.

Me: But how? If you can't hear, how do you know what sounds good and what doesn't?

Ridge: I don't need to hear it. I feel it.

I shake my head, not understanding. I can maybe understand how he's taught himself to play a guitar. With enough practice and a good teacher and maybe a ton of studying, it's possible for him to play as he does. But that doesn't explain how he can know which key a voice should be in and especially which key *sounds* better.

Ridge: What's wrong? You look confused.

Me: I AM confused. I don't understand how you can differentiate between vibrations or however you say you feel it. I'm beginning to think you and Warren are trying to pull off the ultimate prank and you're only pretending to be deaf.

Ridge laughs, then scoots back on the bed until his back meets the headboard. He sits up straight and holds his guitar to his side. He spreads his legs, then pats the empty spot between them.

What the hell? I hope my eyes aren't open as wide as I think they are. There's no way I'm sitting that close to him. I shake my head.

He rolls his eyes and picks up his phone.

Ridge: Come here. I want to show you how I feel it. Get over yourself, and stop thinking I'm trying to seduce you.

I hesitate a few more seconds, but the agitation on his face makes me think I'm being a little immature. I crawl forward, then turn around and carefully sit in front of him with my back to his chest but with several inches between us. He pulls the guitar in front of me and wraps his other arm around me until he's holding it in position. He pulls it closer, which pushes me flush against him. Ridge reaches down to his side and picks up his phone.

Ridge: I'm going to play a chord, and I want you to tell me where you feel it.

I nod, and he brings his hand back to the guitar. He plays a chord and repeats it a few times, then pauses. I grab my phone.

Me: I felt it in your guitar.

He shakes his head and picks up his phone again.

Ridge: I know you felt it in the guitar, dummy. But where in your body did you feel it?

Me: Play it again.

I close my eyes this time and try to take this seriously. I've asked him how he feels it, and he's trying to show me, so the least I can do is try to understand. He plays the chord a few times, and I'm really trying hard to concentrate, but I feel the vibration everywhere, especially in the guitar pressed against my chest.

Me: It's hard for me, Ridge. It just feels like it's everywhere.

He pushes me forward, and I scoot up. He sets the guitar down, stands up, and walks out of the bedroom. I wait for him, curious about what he's doing. When he comes back, he's holding something in his fist. He holds his fist out, so I hold up my palm.

Earplugs.

He slides in behind me, and I scoot back against his chest again, then put the earplugs in. I close my eyes and lean my head back against his shoulder. He wraps his arms around me and picks up his guitar, pulling it against my chest. I can feel his head rest lightly against mine, and the intimate way we're seated suddenly registers. I've never sat like this with someone I wasn't seriously dating.

It's odd, because it seems so natural with him. Not at all as if he's got anything other than music on his mind. I like that about him, because if I were pressed up against Warren like this, I'm positive his hands wouldn't be on the guitar.

I can feel his arms moving slightly, so I know he's playing, even though I can't hear it. I concentrate on the vibration and focus all my attention on the movement inside my chest. When I'm able to pinpoint exactly where I feel it, I bring my hand to my chest and pat it. I can feel him nod his head, and then he continues playing.

I can still feel it in my chest, but it's much lower this time. I move my hand down, and he nods again.

I pull away from him and turn around to face him.
"Wow."
He lifts his shoulders and smiles shyly. It's adorable.

Me: This is crazy. I still don't understand how you can play an instrument like this, but I know how you feel it now.

He shrugs off my compliment, and I love how modest he is, because he clearly has more talent than anyone I've ever met.
"Wow," I say again, shaking my head.

Ridge: Stop. I don't like compliments. It's awkward.

I set down my phone and we both move back to the laptops.

Me: Well, you shouldn't be so impressive, then. I don't think you realize what an incredible gift you have, Ridge. I know you say you work hard at it, but so do thousands of people who can hear, and they can't put together songs like you can. I mean, I can maybe understand the whole guitar thing now that you've explained it, but what about the voices? How in the heck can you know what a voice sounds like and what key it needs to be in?

Ridge: Actually, I can't differentiate the sounds of a voice. I've never felt a person sing the way I "listen" to a guitar. I can place vocals to a song and develop melodies because I've studied a lot of songs and have learned which keys match up to which notes, based on the written form of music. It doesn't just come naturally. I work hard at this. I love the idea of music, and even though I can't hear it, I've learned to understand and appreciate it in a different way. I've had to work harder at the melodies. There are times I'll write a song, and Brennan will tell me we can't use it because it either sounds too much like an existing song or it doesn't actually sound good to hearing ears like I assumed it would.

He can downplay this all he wants, but I'm convinced I'm sitting next to a musical genius. I hate that he thinks his ability comes from working so hard at it. I mean, I'm sure it helps, because all talents have to be nurtured in order to excel, even for the gifted. But his talent is mind-blowing. It makes me hurt for him, knowing what he could do with his gift if he could hear.

Me: Can you hear anything? At all?

He shakes his head.

Ridge: I've worn hearing aids before, but they were more inconvenient than helpful. I have profound hearing loss, so they didn't help at all when it came to hearing voices or my guitar. When I used them, I could tell there were noises, but I couldn't decipher them. In all honesty, hearing aids were a constant reminder that I couldn't hear. Without them, I don't even think about it.

Me: What made you want to learn guitar, knowing you would never be able to hear it?

Ridge: Brennan. He wanted to learn when we were kids, so we learned together.

Me: The guy who used to live here? How long have you known him?

Ridge: 21 years. He's my little brother.

Me: Is he in your band?

Ridge glances at me in confusion.

Ridge: Have I not told you about our band?

I shake my head.

Ridge: He's the singer. He also plays guitar.

Me: When do you play next? I want to watch.

He laughs.

Ridge: I don't play. It's kind of complicated. Brennan insists that I have as much stake in the ownership of the band as he does because I write the majority of the music, which is why I refer to myself as being part of the band sometimes. I think it's ridiculous, but he's convinced we wouldn't be where we are at this point without me, so I agree to it for now. But with the success I think he's about to have, I'll make him renegotiate eventually. I don't like feeling as though I'm taking advantage of him.

Me: If he doesn't feel that way, then you definitely shouldn't feel that way. And why don't you play with them?

Ridge: I have a few times. It's kind of difficult, not being able to hear everything else going on with the band during a song, so I feel like I throw them off when I play with them. Besides, they're on tour right now, and I can't travel, so I've just been sending him the stuff I write.

Me: Why can't you tour with them? Don't you work from home?

Ridge: Other obligations. But next time they're in Austin, I'll take you.

I'll take you. I think I like that part of his message a little too much.

Me: What's the name of the band?

Ridge: Sounds of Cedar.

I slam my laptop shut and swing my eyes to his. "Shut up!" He nods, then reaches down and opens my laptop again.

Ridge: You've heard of us?

Me: Yes. Everyone on campus has heard of your band, considering they played almost every single weekend last year. Hunter loves you guys.

Ridge: Ah. Well, this is the first time I've ever wished we had one less fan. So you've seen Brennan play?

Me: I only went with Hunter once, and it was one of the last shows, but yes. I think I may have most of the songs on my phone, actually.

Ridge: Wow. Small world. We are close to a record deal. That's why I've been stressing so much about these songs. And why you need to help me.

Me: OMG! I just realized I'm writing lyrics for SOUNDS OF CEDAR!!!

I slide my laptop over, then roll onto my stomach and squeal into the mattress while I kick my legs up and down.

Holy crap! This is too cool.

I compose myself, ignoring Ridge's laughter, then sit up straight again and grab my laptop.

Me: So you wrote most of those songs?

He nods.

Me: Did you write the lyrics to the song "Something"?

He nods again. I seriously can't believe this is happening right now. Knowing he wrote those lyrics and now I'm sitting here next to him is exciting me way too much.

Me: I'm about to listen to your song. Since you get to decipher my lyrics, it's my turn to decipher yours.

Ridge: I wrote that song two years ago.

Me: Still. It came from you. From somewhere inside you, Ridge. ;)

He picks up a pillow and throws it at my head. I laugh and scroll through the music folder on my phone until I find the song, and I hit play.

SOMETHING

I keep on wondering why
I can't say 'bye to you
And the only thing I can
think of is the truth

It's hard to start over
Keep checkin' that rearview, too
But something's coming
Something right for you
Just wait a bit longer

You'll find something you wanted
Something you needed
Something you want to have repeated
Oh, that feeling's all right

You'll find that if you listen
Between all the kissing
What made it work
Wound up missing
Oh, that seems about right

I guess I thought that we would
Always stay the same
And I can tell that you find
Somebody to blame

And I know in my heart,
In my mind, it's all a game
Our hopes and wishes

Won't relight the flame
Just wait a bit longer

You'll find something you wanted
Something you needed
Something you want to have repeated
Oh, that feeling's all right

You'll find that if you listen
Between all the kissing
What made it work
Wound up missing
Oh, that seems about right

You don't ever have to wonder
'Cause you will always know
That what we had was for sure
For sure
Now that thing is no more
No more

You'll find what you wanted
You'll find what you needed
You'll find what you wanted
You'll find what you needed
You'll find what you needed

When the song ends, I sit back up on the bed. I would ask him about the lyrics and the meaning behind them right now, but I'm not sure I want to. I want to listen to it again without him watching me, because it's really hard to concentrate when he's staring at me. He's resting his chin in his hands, casually watching me. I try to hide my grin, but it's hard. I see a smile spread across his lips before he looks down at his phone.

Ridge: Why do I feel like you're fangirling right now?

Probably because I am.

Me: I'm not fangirling. Don't flatter yourself. I've witnessed how evil you can be with your revenge schemes, and I've been exposed to your severe alcoholism, so I'm not as enamored with you as I could be.

Ridge: My father was a severe alcoholic. Your jokes are a little off-putting.

I look up at him apologetically and with a hint of embarrassment. "I'm sorry. I was kidding."

Ridge: I'm kidding, too.

I kick him in the knee and glare at him.

Ridge: Well, sort of kidding. My father really is a raging alcoholic, but I don't give a shit if you joke about it.

Me: I can't now. You ruined the fun.

He laughs, and it's followed by an awkward moment of silence. I grin and drop my eyes back to my phone.

Me: OMG. Can I have your autograph?

He rolls his eyes.

Me: Please? And can I have my picture taken with you? OMG, I'm in Ridge Lawson's bed!

I'm laughing, but Ridge isn't finding me amusing.

Me: Ridge Lawson, will you sign my boobs?

He puts his laptop down beside him, leans over to his nightstand and picks up a marker, then turns back to me.

I don't *really* want his autograph. Surely he knows I'm kidding.

He pulls the lid off the marker, swiftly lunges across the bed, and knocks me onto my back, bringing the marker to my forehead.

He's trying to sign my *face*?

I lift my legs and create a barrier with my knees as I try to force his hands away.

Dammit, he's strong.

He puts one of my hands under his knee and locks my arm to the bed. His other arm grabs my arm that's pushing his face away, and he pushes that hand to the bed, too. I'm screaming and laughing and trying to turn my face away from him, but every time I move, the marker moves over my face while he tries to sign his name.

I'm unable to overpower him, so I eventually sigh and hold my head still so he'll stop drawing all over my face.

He hops up, puts the lid back on the marker, and smirks at me.

I reach over to my laptop.

Me: You are no longer my prank master. This has officially turned into a three-way war. Excuse me while I go Google my revenge.

I fold up my laptop and walk quietly out of the room while he laughs at me. As I head through the living room toward my bedroom, Warren glances at me. Twice.

"Should have stayed in here and watched porn with me," he says, taking in the marker all over my face.

I ignore his comment. "Ridge and I just finished discussing TV rules," I lie. "I get Thursdays."

"No, you don't," Warren says. "Tomorrow is Thursday. I watch Thursday-night porn on Thursday."

"Not anymore you don't. Guess you should have asked about my television habits when you were interviewing me."

He groans. "Fine. You can have Thursdays, but only if you wear that dress you had on earlier."

I laugh. "I'm burning that dress."

Ridge

"Why'd you give Sydney the TV tonight?" Warren signs. He drops onto the couch next to me. "You know I love Thursday night. I'm off work on Fridays."

"I never talked to Sydney about TV nights."

He glances toward Sydney's bedroom door with a scowl on his face. "What a little liar. How did you meet her, anyway?"

"Music-related. She's writing lyrics for the band."

Warren's eyes bulge, and he straightens up on the couch, turning to look at me as if I've just betrayed him.

"Don't you think this is something your manager should know about?"

I laugh and sign back to him. "Good point. Hey, Warren, Sydney is officially writing lyrics for us."

He frowns. "And don't you think your manager should have discussed a financial arrangement with her? What percentage are we giving her?"

"We're not. She feels guilty taking a percentage while she's not paying rent, so we're good for now."

He's standing now, glaring down at me. "How do you know you can trust her? And what if something happens with a song she helped write? What if it makes the cut on the album and she suddenly decides she wants a percentage? And why the hell aren't *you* writing the lyrics anymore?"

I sigh. We've been over this so many times it's making my head hurt. "I can't. You know I can't. It's just for a little while, until I get over my block. And calm down, she's agreed to sign over anything she helps with."

He drops back onto the couch, frustrated. "Just don't add

any more people to our band without consulting me first, okay? I feel like I'm being shut out when you don't include me." He folds his arms across his chest and pouts.

"Is sweet little Warren pouting?" I lean forward and wrap my arms around him, and he tries to shove me off. I climb on top of him and kiss his cheek, and he starts hitting me in the arm, trying to pull away from my grasp. I laugh and let go of his face, then look up at Sydney, who just walked into the room. She's staring at us. Warren slides his hand up my thigh and lays his head on my shoulder. I reach up and pat his cheek while we both stare up at her, straight-faced. She shakes her head slowly and walks back into her bedroom.

As soon as her bedroom door closes, we separate.

"I wish I hated Bridgette a little more than I do at night, because Sydney definitely needs me," Warren signs.

I laugh, knowing Sydney is more than likely swearing off guys based on the week she's had. "That girl doesn't need anything other than the opportunity to be alone for a while."

Warren shakes his head. "No, that girl definitely needs me. I wonder how I can pull off an elaborate prank that involves her agreeing to have sex with me."

"Bridgette," I remind him. I don't know why I remind him. I never remind him about Bridgette when he talks about other girls.

"You're a dream crusher," he signs, falling back against the couch at the same moment I receive a text.

Sydney: Can I ask you a question?

Me: As long as you promise never again to start a question off with whether or not you can propose a question.

Sydney: Okay, asshole. I know I shouldn't be thinking about him at all, but I'm curious. What did he write on that paper

when we went to get my purse? And what did you write back
that made him hit you?

Me: I agree that you shouldn't be thinking about him at all, but
I'm honestly shocked it's taken you this long to ask me about it.

Sydney: Well?

Ugh. I hate writing it verbatim, but she wants to know,
so . . .

Me: He wrote, "Are you fucking her?"

Sydney: OMG! What a prick!

Me: Yep.

Sydney: So what did you say back to him that made him punch
you?

Me: I wrote, "Why do you think I'm here for her purse? I gave
her a hundred for tonight, and now she owes me change."

I reread the text, and I'm not so sure it sounds as funny as
I thought it did.

My eyes dart up to her bedroom door, which is now swinging open. She runs into the living room, directly toward the
couch. I don't know if it's the look on her face or the hands that
are coming at me, but I immediately cover my head and duck
behind Warren. He doesn't really like being used as a human
shield, though, so he jumps off the couch. She continues slapping at my arms until I'm curled up in a fetal position on the
couch. I'm trying not to laugh, but she hits like a girl. This is
nothing compared to what I saw her do to Tori.

She backs away, and I reluctantly uncover my head. She marches back to her room, and I watch as she slams her door.

Warren is now standing next to the couch with his hands on his hips. He looks at me, then looks back at Sydney's door. He puts his palms up and shakes his head, then retreats into his bedroom.

I should probably apologize to her. It was just a joke, but I guess I can see how it would piss her off. I knock on her door a couple of times. She doesn't open it, so I text her.

Me: Can I come in?

Sydney: That depends. Do you have any bills smaller than a hundred this time?

Me: It seemed funny at the time. I'm sorry.

A few seconds pass, and then her door opens and she steps aside. I raise my eyebrows and smile, attempting to look innocent. She shoots me a dirty look and walks back to her bed.

Sydney: It wasn't what I would have wanted you to say, but I can see why you said it. He's a jerk, and I probably would have wanted to piss him off in that moment, too.

Me: He is a jerk, but I probably should have responded differently. I'm sorry.

Sydney: Yes, you should have. Maybe instead of insinuating that I was a whore, you could have gone with "If I could only be so lucky."

I laugh at her comment, then offer up another alternative answer.

Me: I could have gone with "Only when you're being faithful to her. Which is never."

Sydney: Or you could have said, "No, I'm not. I'm madly in love with Warren."

At least she's making jokes about it. I really do feel sort of bad for saying that to him, but it felt oddly appropriate at the time.

Me: We didn't really get any work done last night. Are you in the mood to make beautiful music together?

7.

Sydney

Ridge puts down his guitar for the first time in more than an hour. We haven't texted at all, because we've been on a roll. It's pretty cool how well we seem to work together. He plays a song over and over while I lie across his bed with a notebook in front of me. I write down the lyrics as they come to me, most of the time crumpling up the paper, chucking it across the room, and starting over. But I've finished lyrics for almost an entire song tonight, and he's only crossed out two lines he didn't like. I'd say that's progress.

There's something about these moments when we're writing music that I absolutely love. All my worries and thoughts about everything wrong in my life seem to go away for the short times we write together. It's nice.

Ridge: Let's do the whole song now. Sit up so I can watch you sing it. I want to make sure we have it perfect before I send it to Brennan.

He starts playing the song, so I begin singing. He's watching me closely, and the way his eyes seem to read my every movement makes me uneasy. Maybe it's because he can't express words through speaking, but everything else about him seems to make up for that.

As easy as he is to read, it's only that way when he *wants* to be read. Most of the time, he's able to hold back his expressions, and I don't know what the hell he's thinking. He holds the crown in the nonverbal department. I'm pretty sure that with the looks he gives, if he *could* speak, he'd never even have to.

I feel uncomfortable watching him watch me sing, so I close my eyes and try to recall the lyrics as he continues to play the song. It's awkward singing them with him only a few feet away. When I wrote the lyrics the first time, he was playing his guitar but was a good two hundred yards away on his balcony. Still, though, as much as I tried to pretend I was writing them about Hunter at the time, I knew I was imagining Ridge singing them all along.

A LITTLE BIT MORE
Why don't you let me
Take you away
We can live like you wanted
From place to place

I'll be your home
We can make our own
'Cause together makes it pretty hard
to be alone

We can have everything we ever wanted
And just a little bit more
Just a little bit more

His guitar stops, so naturally, *I* stop. I open my eyes, and he's watching me with one of his expressionless expressions.

I take that back. This expression isn't expressionless at all. He's thinking. I can tell by the squint in his eyes that he's coming up with an idea.

He glances away in order to pick up his phone.

Ridge: Do you mind if I try something?

Me: As long as you promise never again to propose a question by asking if I mind if you can try something.

Ridge: Nice try, but that made no sense.

I laugh, then look up at him. I nod softly, scared of what he's about to "try." He sits up on his knees and leans forward, placing both hands on my shoulders. I attempt to hold in my gasp, but it's a failed attempt. I don't know what he's doing or why he's getting so close to me, but holy crap.

Holy crap.

Why is my heart spazzing out right now?

He pushes me until I'm flat on his mattress. He reaches behind him and picks up his guitar, then lays it on the other side of me. He lies down next to me.

Calm down, heart. Please. Ridge has supersonic senses, and he'll feel you beating through the vibrations of the mattress.

Ridge scoots closer to me and by the way he's hesitating, it makes me think he's unsure if I'll allow him any closer.

I will. I absolutely will.

He's staring at me now, contemplating his next move. I can tell he's not about to make a pass at me. Whatever he's about to do is making him way more apprehensive than if he were just planning to kiss me. He's eyeing my neck and chest as if he's searching for a particular part of me. His eyes stop on my abdomen, pause, then fall back to his phone.

Oh, Lord. What is he about to do? Put his hands on me? Does he want to feel me sing this song? Feeling requires touching, and touching requires hands. *His* hands. Feeling *me*.

Ridge: Do you trust me?

Me: I don't trust anyone anymore. My trust has been completely depleted this week.

Ridge: Can you replenish your trust for about five minutes? I want to feel your voice.

I inhale, then look at him—lying next to me—and I nod. He sets down his phone without breaking my gaze. He's watching me as if he's warning me to stay calm, but it's having the exact opposite effect. I'm sort of panicked right now.

He scoots closer and slides his arm under the back of my neck.

Oh.

Now he's even closer.

Now his face is hovering over mine. He reaches across my body and pulls the guitar flush against my side, bringing it closer to us. He's still eyeing me with a look that seems intended to produce a calming effect.

It doesn't. It doesn't calm me down at *all*.

He lowers his head to my chest, then presses his cheek against my shirt.

Oh, this is great. Now he definitely feels how spastic my heart is beating right now. I close my eyes and want to die of embarrassment, but I don't have time for that, because he begins strumming the strings of the guitar next to me. I realize he's playing with both hands, one from underneath my head and one over me. His head is against my chest, and I can feel his hair brush my neck. He's pretty much sprawled across me in order to reach his guitar with both arms.

Oh, my dear sweet baby Jesus in a wicker basket.

How does he expect me to *sing*?

I try to calm down by regulating my breathing, but it's hard when we're positioned like this. As usual when I miss an intro, he seamlessly starts the song over again from the beginning. When he reaches the point where I come in, I begin singing. Sort of. It's really quiet, because I'm still waiting for air to find its way back into my lungs.

After the first few lines, I find a steadiness to my voice. I close my eyes and do my best to imagine I'm simply sitting up on his bed right now the way I have been for the last hour.

I'll bring my suitcase
You bring that old map
We can live by the book
Or we can never go back

Feeling the breeze
Never felt so right
We'll watch the stars
Until they fade into light

We can have everything we ever wanted
And just a little bit more
Just a little bit more

He finishes the last chord but doesn't move. His hands remain stilled on his guitar. His ear remains firmly pressed against my chest. My breaths are heavier now that I've just sung an entire song, and his head rises with each intake of air.

He sighs a deep sigh, then lifts his head and rolls onto his back without making eye contact with me. We lie in silence for a few minutes. I'm not sure why he's being so unresponsive, but I'm too nervous to make any sudden movements. His arm is still underneath me, and he's making no effort to remove it, so I'm not even sure if he's finished with this little experiment yet.

I'm also not sure I'd even be able to move.

Sydney, Sydney, Sydney. What are you doing?

I absolutely, positively, do *not* want to be having this reaction right now. It's been a week since I broke up with Hunter. The very last thing I want—or even need—is to develop a crush on this guy.

However, I'm thinking that may have happened *before* this week.

Crap.

I tilt my head and look at him. He's watching me, but I can't tell what his face is trying to convey. If I had to guess, I'd say he's thinking, *Oh, hey, Sydney. Our mouths sure are close together. Let's do them a favor and close this gap.*

His eyes drop to my mouth, and I'm incredibly impressed with my telepathic abilities. His full lips are slightly parted as he quietly takes in several slow, deep breaths.

I can actually hear him breathing, which surprises me, because that's another of his sounds that he keeps complete and total control over. I like that he can't seem to control it right now. As much as I claim to want to be unattached from guys and independent and strong, the only thing I'm thinking is how much I wish he would take complete and total control over me. I want him to dominate this situation by rolling on top of me and forcing that incredible mouth onto mine, rendering me completely dependent on him for breath.

My phone receives a text, interrupting my clearly overactive imagination. Ridge closes his eyes and turns to face the opposite direction. I sigh, knowing he didn't even hear the text, so turning away was of his own accord. Which means I'm feeling pretty awkward right now for just having that rich internal dialogue sweep through my mind. I reach behind my head and feel around until I find my phone.

Hunter: Are you ready to talk yet?

I roll my eyes. *Way to ruin the moment, Hunter.* I was hoping that after days of avoiding his texts and phone calls, he would finally get a clue. I shake my head and text him back.

Me: Your behavior is bordering on harassment. Stop contacting me. We're done.

Ridge

Stop with the guilt trip, Ridge. You didn't do anything wrong. You aren't doing anything wrong. Your heart is beating like this simply because you've never felt anyone sing before. It was overwhelming. You had a normal reaction to an overwhelming event. That's all.

My eyes are still closed, and my arm is still underneath her. I should move it, but I'm still trying to recover.

And I *really* want to hear another song.

This might be making her uncomfortable, but I have to get her to push through her discomfort, because I can't think of any other situation where I'll be able to do this.

Me: Can I play another one?

She's holding her phone, texting someone who's not me. I wonder if she's texting Hunter, but I don't peek at her phone, as much as I want to.

Sydney: Okay. The first one didn't do anything for you?

I laugh. I think it did a little too much, in more ways than I'd like to admit. I'm almost positive it was also obvious to her by the end of the song, with the way I was pressed against her. But feeling her voice and what it was doing to all the other parts of me was way more important than what *she* was doing to me.

Me: I've never "listened" to anyone like that before. It was incredible. I don't even know how to describe it. I mean, you were here, and you were the one singing, so I guess you don't really need me to describe it. But I don't know. I wish you could have felt that.

Sydney: You're welcome, I guess. I'm not really doing anything profound here.

Me: I've always wanted to feel someone sing one of my songs, but it would be a little awkward doing this with one of the guys in the band. Know what I mean?

She laughs, then nods.

Me: I'll play the one we practiced last night, and then I want to play this last one again. Are you okay? If you're tired of singing, just tell me.

Sydney: I'm good.

She lays down her phone, and I reposition myself against her chest. My entire body is battling itself. My left brain is telling me this is somehow wrong, my right brain is wanting to hear her sing again, my stomach is nowhere to be found, and my heart is punching itself in the face with one arm and hugging itself with the other.

I might never have this opportunity again, so I wrap my arm over her and begin playing. I close my eyes and search for the beat of her heart, which has slowed down some since the first song. The vibration of her voice meets my cheek, and I swear my heart flinches. She feels the way I imagined a voice would feel during a song but multiplied by a thousand. I focus on how her voice blends with the vibration of the guitar, and I'm in complete awe.

I want to feel the range of her voice, but it's hard without using my hands to feel it. I pull my hand away from the guitar and stop playing. Just like that, she stops singing. I shake my head no and motion a circle in the air with my finger, wanting her to keep singing even though I'm no longer playing the chords.

Her voice picks back up, and I keep my ear pressed firmly to her chest while I lay my palm flat against her stomach. Her muscles clench beneath my hand, but she doesn't stop singing. I can feel her voice everywhere. I can feel it in my head, in my chest, against my hand.

I relax against her and listen to the sound of a voice for the very first time.

•   •   •

I wrap my arm around Maggie's waist and pull her in closer. I can feel her struggling beneath me, so I pull her even tighter. I'm not ready for her to go home yet. Her hand smacks my forehead, and she's lifting me off her chest as she attempts to wiggle out from beneath me.

I roll onto my back to let her off the bed, but instead, she's slapping my cheeks. I open my eyes and look up to see Sydney hovering over me. Her mouth is moving, but my vision is too fogged over to see what she's trying to say. Not to mention that the strobe light isn't helping.

Wait. I don't have a strobe light.

I sit straight up on the bed. Sydney hands me my phone and begins to text me, but my phone is dead. Did we fall asleep?

The lights. The lights are going on and off.

I grab Sydney's phone out of her hand and check the time: 8:15 A.M. I also read the text she just tried to send me.

Sydney: Someone's at your bedroom door.

Warren wouldn't be up this early on a Friday. It's his day off.

Friday.

Maggie.

SHIT!

I hurriedly jump off the bed and grab Sydney's wrists, then swing her to her feet. She looks shocked that I'm panicking, but she needs to get the hell back to her room. I open the bathroom door and motion for her to take that route. She walks into the bathroom, then turns and heads back into my bedroom. I grab her by the shoulders and force her back into the bathroom. She slaps my hands away and points into my bedroom.

"I want my phone!" she says, pointing toward my bed. I retrieve her phone, but before I hand it to her, I type a text on it.

Me: I'm sorry, but I think that's Maggie. You can't be in here, or she'll get the wrong idea.

I hand her the phone, and she reads the text, then looks back up at me. "Who's Maggie?"

Who's Maggie? How the hell can she not remember . . .

Oh.

Is it possible I've never mentioned Maggie to her before?

I grab her phone again.

Me: My girlfriend.

She looks at the text, and her jaw tightens. She slowly brings her eyes back to mine, and she snatches the phone out of my hand, grabs the doorknob, and steps back into the bathroom. The door closes in my face.

So was not expecting that reaction.

But I don't have time to respond, because my light is still flickering. I head straight to the bedroom door and unlock it, then open it.

Warren is standing in the doorway with his arm pressed against the frame. There's no sign of Maggie.

My panic instantly subsides as I walk backward and fall onto my bed. That could have been ugly. I glance up at Warren, because he's obviously here for something.

"Why aren't you answering my texts?" he signs from the doorway.

"My phone died." I reach over to my phone and place it on the charging base on the nightstand.

"But you never let your phone die."

"First time for everything," I sign.

He nods his head, but it's an annoying, suspicious, *You're hiding something* kind of nod.

Or maybe I'm just being paranoid.

"You're hiding something," he signs.

Or maybe I'm *not* being paranoid.

"And I just checked Sydney's room." He arches a suspicious brow. "She wasn't in there."

I glance to the bathroom, then look back at Warren, wondering if I should even lie about it. All we did was fall asleep. "I know. She was in here."

He holds his stern expression. "All night?"

I nod casually. "We were working on lyrics. I guess we fell asleep."

He's acting strange. If I didn't know him better, I'd think he was jealous. Wait. I *do* know him better. He *is* jealous.

"Does this bother you, Warren?"

He shrugs and signs back. "Yeah. A little."

"Why? You spend almost every night in Bridgette's bed."

He shakes his head. "It's not that."

"What is it, then?"

He breaks his gaze, and I can see the discomfort cross his face before he exhales. He makes the sign that indicates Maggie's name. He brings his eyes back to mine. "You can't do this,

Ridge. You made this choice for yourself years ago, and I tried to tell you then what I thought about it. But you're in it now, and if I have to be the annoying friend to remind you of that, so be it."

I wince, because it kind of pisses me off how he's referring to my and Maggie's relationship. "Don't refer to my relationship with Maggie as being 'in it' ever again."

His expression grows apologetic. "You know what I mean, Ridge."

I stand and walk toward him. "How long have we been best friends?"

He shrugs. "That's all I am to you? A best friend? Ridge, I thought we were so much more than that." He smirks as if he's trying to be funny, but I don't laugh. When he sees how much his remarks have bothered me, his expression quickly sobers. "Ten years."

"Ten. Ten years. You know me better than that, Warren."

He nods, but his face is still full of doubt.

"Good-bye," I sign. "Shut the door on your way out." I turn and walk back to my bed, and when I face the door again, he's gone.

8.

Sydney

Why am I so pissed? We didn't do anything.

Did we?

I can't even tell what the hell happened last night before we fell asleep. Technically, it wasn't anything, but then again, it was, which is probably why I'm so pissed, because I'm so freaking confused.

First he doesn't tell me about Hunter for two solid weeks. Then he fails to mention that he's deaf, although I really have no right to be upset about that. That's not something I should feel obligated to have been told.

But Maggie?

Girlfriend?

How could he fail to mention in the three weeks I've been talking to him that he has a girlfriend?

He's just like Hunter. He has a dick and two balls and no heart, and that makes him Hunter's twin. I should probably just start calling him Hunter. I should just call them *all* Hunter. From here on out, all men shall be referred to as Hunter.

My father should be thanking the high heavens that I'm not in law school, because I am by far the absolute worst judge of character who has ever walked the planet.

Ridge: False alarm. It was just Warren. Sorry about that.

Me: SCREW. YOU.

Ridge: ???

Me: Don't even.

A few seconds pass with me staring at my silent phone, and then a knock comes from the bathroom. Ridge swings the door open and enters my room, holding his hands with his palms up in the air as if he has no idea why I'm upset. I laugh, but it isn't a happy laugh at all.

Me: This conversation will require a laptop. I have a lot to say.

I open my computer as he makes his way back to his room. I give him a minute to log on, then I open our chat.

Ridge: Can you please explain why you're so pissed?

Me: Hmm. Let me count the ways. (1) You have a girlfriend. (2) You have a girlfriend. (3) Why, if you have a girlfriend, was I even in your BEDROOM? (4) You have a girlfriend!

Ridge: I have a girlfriend. Yes. And you were in my room because we agreed to work on lyrics together. I don't recall anything happening between us last night to warrant this reaction from you. Or am I mistaken?

Me: Ridge, it's been three weeks! I've known you for three weeks now, and you've never ONCE mentioned that you have a girlfriend. And speaking of Maggie, does she even know I moved in?

Ridge: Yes. I tell her everything. Look, it wasn't an intentional omission, I swear. You and I have just never had a conversation where she came up.

Me: Okay, I'll let it go that you failed to mention her, but I'm not about to let everything else slide.

Ridge: And this is where I'm confused, because I'm not clear on what you think we did.

Me: You're such a guy.

Ridge: Ouch? I guess.

Me: Can you honestly say that your reaction to the possibility of her being at your door earlier was a normal, innocent reaction? You were freaking out that she would see me with you, which means you were doing something you wouldn't want her to see. I know all we did was fall asleep, but what about the WAY we fell asleep? Do you think she would have been okay with the fact that you had your arms around me all night and your face was practically glued to my chest? And not only that, but what about the fact that I sat between your legs the other night? Would she have smiled and kissed you hello if she had walked in right then? I doubt it. I'm fairly certain that would have ended with me being punched.

Ugh! Why is this upsetting me so much? I bang my head lightly against the headboard out of frustration.

Moments later, Ridge appears in the doorway between our bathroom and my bedroom. He's chewing on the corner of his bottom lip. His features are a lot calmer than when he was in here just a few minutes ago. He walks slowly into my room, then sits on the edge of my bed with his laptop on his knees.

Ridge: I'm sorry.

Me: Yeah. Good. Whatever. Go away.

Ridge: Really, Sydney. I haven't been looking at it like that at all. The last thing I want is for things to be weird between us. I like you. I have fun with you. But if for one second I led you to believe that something was going to happen between us, I am so, so sorry.

I sigh and attempt to blink the tears away.

Me: I'm not upset because I thought something was going to happen between us, Ridge. I don't WANT anything to happen between us. I haven't even been single for a whole week yet. I'm upset because I feel like there was a moment, or maybe two, when—as much as neither of us wants to cross that line— we almost did. And you can deal with your actions on your own, but the fact that I was unaware that you had a girlfriend was really unfair to me. I feel like—

I lean my head back against the headboard and squeeze my eyes shut, long enough to force back the tears once more.

Ridge: You feel like what?

Me: I feel like you almost made me a Tori. I absolutely would have kissed you last night, and the fact that I didn't know you were involved with someone would have made me a Tori. I don't want to be a Tori, Ridge. I can't tell you how much their betrayal hurts me, and I will never, ever do that to another girl. So that's why I'm upset. I don't even know Maggie, yet you made me feel like I've already betrayed her. And as innocent as you may be, I'm blaming you for that one.

Ridge finishes reading my message, then calmly lies back on the bed. He brings his palms to his forehead and inhales a deep breath. We both remain still as we think about the situation. After several quiet minutes, he sits back up.

Ridge: I don't even know what to say right now other than I'm sorry. You're right. Even though I thought you knew about Maggie, I can absolutely see what you're saying. But I also need you to know that I would never do something like that to her. Granted, what happened between us last night is not something I would ever want Maggie to see, but that's mostly because Maggie doesn't understand the process of writing music. It's a very intimate thing, and because I can't hear, I do have to use my hands or my ears to understand things that come naturally to others. That's all it was. I wasn't trying to cause anything to happen between us. I was just curious. I was intrigued. And I was wrong.

Me: I understand. I never thought for a second that your intentions weren't genuine when you asked me to sing for you. Everything just happened so fast earlier, and I was still trying to recover from the fact that I woke up in your bed and the lights were flickering. Then you go and flash the word "girlfriend" in my face. It's a lot to process. And I believe you when you say you thought I knew about her.

Ridge: Thank you.

Me: Just promise me one thing. Promise me you will never be a Hunter, and I will never, ever be a Tori.

Ridge: I promise. And that's impossible, because we're so much more talented than they are.

He glances up and smiles his smiley smile at me, which makes me automatically smile in return.

> Me: Now, get out of here. I'm going back to sleep, because someone spent the whole night drooling on my boobs and snoring way too loud.

Ridge laughs, but before he leaves, he messages me one last time.

> Ridge: I'm excited for you to meet her. I really think you'll like her.

He closes his laptop, stands, and walks back to his room.
I close my laptop and pull the covers over my head.
I hate that my heart is wishing so bad that he didn't have a girlfriend.

· · ·

"No, she already moved in," Bridgette says. Her cell phone is propped up on her shoulder, and from the sound of it, she just broke the news to her sister that I've taken the empty bedroom. Bridgette completely ignores that I'm even in the same room with her and continues talking about me.

I know the fact that I haven't clarified that I'm not deaf is a little mean, but who is she to assume I can't read lips?

"I don't know; she's a friend of Ridge's. I should have ignored him when he asked if I would go—in the *rain*, mind you—and bring her up to the apartment. Apparently, her boyfriend dumped her, and she had nowhere else to go."

She pulls a seat out at the bar and sits with her back facing me. She laughs at something the person on the other end of the line says. "Tell me about it. He seems to enjoy taking in strays, doesn't he?"

I grip the remote in my hand and hold it tightly in an attempt to keep from hurling it at the back of her head.

"I told you not to ask about Warren," she says with a sigh. "You know he irritates the hell out of me, but I just . . . *dammit*, I just can't stay away."

Wait. Did I just hear that correctly? Might Bridgette have . . . *feelings*?

She's lucky I like Warren, or the remote would be greeting her pretty little head right now. She's also lucky someone is knocking at the door loudly enough to distract me from hurting her.

Bridgette stands up and turns to face me, pointing at the front door. "SOMEONE'S . . . AT . . . THE . . . DOOR!" Rather than answer it, she walks to her bedroom and closes her door.

So hospitable, that one.

I stand and make my way to the front door, knowing it's more than likely Maggie. I place my hand on the doorknob and inhale a steady breath.

Here we go.

I open the door, and standing in front of me is one of the most beautiful women I've ever laid eyes on. Her hair is straight and jet-black, and it falls around two naturally tanned shoulders. Her face is smiling. Her whole, entire face is beaming. She's nothing but a face full of beautiful white teeth, and they're smiling at me, and it's making me smile back, even though I really don't want to.

I was really hoping she was ugly. I don't know why.

"Sydney?" she says. It's just one word, but I can tell by her voice that she's deaf, like Ridge. But, unlike Ridge, she speaks. And she enunciates really well.

"You must be the girlfriend!" I say with feigned excitement. *Is* it feigned? Maybe not. Her entire demeanor is making me feel sunny and happy, and maybe I am a tiny bit excited to meet her?

Weird.

She steps forward and gives me a hug. I close the door behind us, and she slips off her shoes and heads to the refrigerator.

"Ridge has told me a lot about you," she says as she pops open a soda, then walks to the cabinet for a glass. "I think it's great that you're helping him through his writer's block. Poor guy has been stressing for months now." She fills her cup with ice and soda. "So how are you fitting in? I see you've survived Bridgette. And Warren has to be a pain in the ass." She looks at me expectantly, but I'm still loving the fact that she's so . . . Pleasant? Likable? Cheerful?

I smile back at her and lean against the counter. I'm trying to figure out exactly how to respond to her. She's speaking to me as if she can hear me, so I reply the same way.

"I like it," I say. "I've never lived with this many people before, so it's taking some getting used to."

She smiles and tucks a lock of her hair behind her ear.

Ugh. Even her ears are pretty.

"Good," she says. "Ridge told me about your shitty birthday last weekend and how he took you out for cake, but it didn't make up for you never having the chance to celebrate."

I have to be honest. It bothers me that he told her he took me out for cake. It bothers me, because maybe he's right and he does tell her everything. And it also bothers me because he seems to tell me nothing. Not that I've earned that right from him.

God, I hate feelings. Or I hate my conscience. The two are constantly at war, and I'm not sure which one I'd rather turn off.

"So," she says, "we're going out tonight to celebrate."

I pause. "We?"

She nods. "Yeah. Me, you, Ridge, Warren, if he's not busy. We can invite Bridgette, but that's laughable." She walks past me toward Ridge's bedroom, then turns to face me again. "Can you be ready in an hour?"

"Um." I shrug. "Okay."

She opens Ridge's bedroom door and slips inside. I stand frozen, listening. Why am I listening?

I hear Maggie giggling behind the closed door, and it makes me wince.

Oh, *yay*. This should be *fun*.

Ridge

"Are you sure you don't want to stay in tonight?"

Maggie shakes her head. "That poor girl needs to have some fun, with the week she's had. And I've been so overwhelmed with my internship and the T word. I need a night out." She leans forward and kisses me on the chin. "Do you want to get a cab so you can drink, or do you want to drive?"

She knows I won't drink around her. I don't know why she always tries her reverse psychology on me. "Nice try," I sign. "I'll drive."

She laughs. "I have to change and get ready. We're leaving in an hour." She tries to slide off me, but I grip her waist and roll her onto her back. I know for a fact that it never takes her more than half an hour to get ready. That leaves a good thirty minutes.

"Allow me to help you out of your clothes, then." I pull her shirt off over her head, and my eyes drop to the very thin, intricately laced bra she has on. I grin. "Is this new?"

She nods and smiles her sexy smile. "I bought it for you. Front clasp, just how you like it."

I pinch the clasp and undo it. "Thank you. I can't wait to try it on."

She laughs and slaps my arm. I take off her bra, then lower myself on top of her and drop my mouth to hers.

I spend the next half hour reminding myself how much I've missed her. I remind myself how much I love her. I remind myself how good it feels when we're together. I keep reminding myself over and over, because for the past week, it felt as if I was starting to forget.

• • •

Me: Be ready in thirty minutes. We're going out.

Warren: I don't want to go, have an early shift tomorrow.

No. He has to go. I can't go out with Maggie and Sydney by myself.

Me: No, you're going. Be ready in thirty minutes.

Warren: No, I'm not. Have fun.

Me: You're going. 30.

Warren: Not going.

Me: Going.

Warren: Not.

Me: Yes.

Warren: No.

Me: Please? You owe me.

Warren: What the hell do I owe you for?

Me: Let's see, about a year's worth of rent, for one.

Warren: Low blow, man. Fine.

Thank God. I don't know what Sydney gets like when she drinks, but if she's a lightweight like Maggie is, I don't think I can handle the two of them on my own.

I walk to the kitchen, and Maggie is at the sink, pulling out the bottle of Pine-Sol. She holds it up to ask if I want any, and I shake my head.

"Figured I'd save money if I downed a couple of shots here first. You think Sydney wants any?"

I shrug but pull out my phone to ask her.

Me: You want a shot before we go?

Sydney: No, thank you. Not sure I feel like drinking tonight, but you go right ahead.

"She doesn't want any," I sign to Maggie. Warren walks out of his bedroom and sees Maggie pouring a shot from the Pine-Sol container.

Shit. There goes the hiding spot.

He doesn't even blink when he sees her filling her shot glass. "Make it two," he says to her. "If Ridge is forcing me to go out tonight, I'm getting so wasted he'll regret it."

I cock my head. "How long have you known that wasn't cleaning solution?"

He shrugs. "You're deaf, Ridge. You would be surprised how many times I'm behind you and you don't even know it." He picks up the shot Maggie poured, and they both turn their attention to something behind me. Their shocked expressions force me to turn around and see what they're looking at.

Oh, wow.

I shouldn't have turned around.

Sydney is walking out of her bedroom, but I'm not sure if it's really Sydney. This girl isn't wearing baggy shirts or walking around with her hair pulled up and a naked face. This girl is wearing a strapless black dress that's anything but simple. Her blond hair is down and thick, and I'm thinking it probably smells as incredible as it looks. She smiles past me and says

"Thanks" to either Maggie or Warren, one of whom more than likely just told her how great she looks. She's smiling at them, but then she holds her hands up and yells, "No!" just as a mist of liquid rains down on me from behind.

I spin around, and Warren and Maggie are both coughing and spitting into the sink. Warren is sipping straight from the faucet, making a face that says he didn't enjoy whatever just went down his throat.

"What the hell?" Maggie says, scrunching up her face and wiping her mouth.

Sydney runs into the kitchen with her hand over her mouth. She's shaking her head, trying not to laugh, but she looks apologetic at the same time. "I'm sorry," she keeps saying over and over.

What the hell just happened?

Warren composes himself, then turns to Sydney. He speaks and signs at the same time, which I appreciate. He can't know how isolating it feels when you're in a group of people who hear, but no matter what, he always signs when I'm in the room with him. "Did we actually just almost drink an entire shot of Pine-Sol?"

He's eyeing Sydney hard. She answers him, and he signs her response for my benefit. She says, "You two weren't supposed to drink it. It was supposed to be Ridge. And no, I didn't actually put Pine-Sol in there, idiot. I'm not trying to kill the guy. It was apple juice and vinegar."

She tried to prank me.

And she failed.

I start laughing and text her.

Me: Nice try. That was a valiant effort, although it backfired.

She flips me off.

I look at Maggie; luckily, she's laughing about it. "There is no way I could live here," she says. She walks to the refrigerator and pulls out the milk, then makes herself and Warren a quick drink to wash away the aftertaste.

"Let's go," Warren says after he downs the milk and tosses his cup into the sink. "Ridge is driving cuz I won't be able to walk in three hours."

9.

Sydney

I have no idea where we're going, but I'm doing my best to appear engaged. I'm in the backseat with Warren, and he's talking to me about the band, explaining his involvement in it. I ask the appropriate questions and nod at the appropriate moments, but my mind isn't here at all.

I know I can't expect the hurt and heartache to go away this quickly, but today has been the worst day so far since my actual birthday. I realize that all the pain I've been feeling hasn't been quite as bad because I've had Ridge this week. I don't know if it's the way he brings comedic relief when he's around or if it's because I really was developing a crush on him, but the times I've spent with him were the only times I felt remotely happy. They were the only times I wasn't thinking about what Hunter and Tori did to me.

But now, watching him in the front seat with his hand clasping Maggie's . . . I don't like it. I don't like how his thumb occasionally sweeps back and forth. I don't like the way she looks at him. I especially don't like the way he looks at her. I didn't like how he slipped his fingers through hers when we reached the bottom of the apartment stairs. I didn't like how he opened her door, then placed his hand on her lower back while she climbed inside the car. I didn't like how they had a silent conversation while he was putting the car in reverse. I didn't like how he laughed at whatever she said and then pulled her to him so he could kiss her forehead. I don't like how all of these things make me feel as though the only good moments I've had since last week are now over.

Nothing has changed. Nothing significant happened between the two of us, and I know we'll continue with the way things have been. We'll still write lyrics together. He might still listen to me sing. We'll still continue to interact the way we've done since I met him, so this situation shouldn't be bothering me.

I know in my heart that I didn't want anything to happen with him, especially at this point in my life. I know I need to be on my own. I *want* to be on my own. But I also know that the reason I'm feeling so conflicted by this entire situation is that I did have a little hope. Although I wasn't ready for anything right now, I thought the possibility would be there. I assumed that maybe someday, when I was ready, things could have developed between us.

However, now that Maggie is in the picture, I realize there can't be a *maybe someday* between us. There will never be a *maybe someday*. He loves her, and she obviously loves him, and I can't blame them, because whatever they have is beautiful. The way they look at each other and interact and obviously care about each other is something I didn't realize was missing between Hunter and me.

Maybe someday I'll have that, but it won't be with Ridge, and knowing that diminishes whatever ray of hope shone through the storm of my week.

Jesus, I'm so depressed.

I hate Hunter.

I really hate Tori.

And right now, I'm so pathetically miserable, I even hate myself.

"Are you crying?" Warren asks.

"No."

He nods. "Yes, you are. You're crying."

I shake my head. "I am not."

"You were about to," he says, looking at me sympatheti-cally. He puts his arm around my shoulder and pulls me against him. "Chin up, little girl. Maybe tonight we can find someone who will screw the thought of that jerkoff ex right out of that pretty little head of yours."

I laugh and slap him in the chest.

"I would volunteer to do it, but Bridgette doesn't like to share," he says. "She's kind of a bitch like that, if you haven't noticed."

I laugh again, but when my eyes meet Ridge's in the rear-view mirror, my smile fades. His jaw is firm, and his eyes lock with mine for a few seconds before he refocuses on the road in front of him.

He's unreadable most of the time, but I could swear I saw a small flash of jealousy behind those eyes. And I don't like how seeing him jealous that I'm leaning against Warren actu-ally feels good.

Turning twenty-two has rotted my soul. Who am I, and why am I having these awful reactions?

We pull into the parking lot of a club. I've been here a few times with Tori, so I'm relieved that it won't be completely un-familiar. Warren takes my hand and helps me out of the car, then puts an arm around my shoulders and walks with me to-ward the entrance.

"I'll make you a deal," he says. "I'll keep my hands off you tonight so guys won't assume you're madly in love with me. I hate cock blockers, and I refuse to be one. But if anyone makes you uncomfortable, just look at me and give me a signal so I can swoop in and pull you out of the situation."

I nod. "Sounds like a plan. What kind of signal do I give you?"

"I don't know. You can lick your lips seductively. Maybe squeeze your breasts together."

I elbow him in the side. "Or maybe I can just scratch my nose?"

He shrugs. "That works, too, I guess." He opens the door, and we all make our way inside. The music is overwhelming, and the second the doors close behind us, Warren leans in to shout into my ear. "There are usually booths open on the balcony level. Let's go there!" He tightens his grip on my hand, then turns to Ridge and Maggie and motions for them to follow.

•   •   •

I haven't had to use the secret code Warren and I agreed on, and we've been here more than two hours now. I've danced with several people, but as soon as the song ends, I make it a point to smile politely and head back to the booth. Warren and Maggie seem to have made a nice dent in the liquor stock, but Ridge hasn't had a drop. Other than a shot Warren persuaded me to take when we first arrived, I haven't had anything to drink, either.

"My feet hurt," I say.

Maggie and Ridge have danced a couple of times but that was to slow songs, so I made it a point not to watch them.

"No!" Warren says, attempting to pull me back up. "I want to dance!"

I shake my head. He's drunk and loud, and every time I try to dance with him, he ends up butchering my feet almost as badly as he butchers the moves.

"I'll dance with you," Maggie says to him. She climbs over Ridge in the booth, and Warren takes her hand. They head down to the lower level to dance, and it's the first time Ridge and I have been alone in the booth.

I don't like it.

I like it.

I don't.

I do.

See? Rotten soul. Corrupted, rotten soul.

Ridge: Having fun?

I'm not really, but I nod, because I don't want to be that annoying, brokenhearted girl who wants everyone around her to feel how miserable she is.

Ridge: I need to say something, and I may be way off base here, but I'm attempting to improve on how I unintentionally omit things from you.

I look up at him and nod again.

Ridge: Warren is in love with Bridgette.

I read his text twice. Why would he need to say that to me? Unless he thinks I like Warren.

Ridge: He's always been a flirt, so I just wanted to clear that up. I don't want to see you get hurt again. That's all.

Me: Appreciate your concern, but it's unnecessary. Really. Have no interest there.

He smiles.

Me: You were right. I like Maggie.

Ridge: I knew you would. Everyone likes Maggie. She's very likable.

I lift my eyes and look around when a Sounds of Cedar song begins to play. I scoot to the back of the booth and look over the railing. Warren and Maggie are standing by the DJ's table, and Warren is interacting with the DJ while Maggie dances around next to him.

Me: They're playing one of your songs.

Ridge: Yeah? That always happens when Warren's around. Are they playing "Getaway"?

Me: Yeah. How'd you know?

Ridge presses a flat palm to his chest and smiles.

Me: Wow. You can differentiate your songs like that?

He nods.

Me: What's Maggie's story? She communicates really well. She seems to dance really well. Does she have a different level of hearing loss from yours?

Ridge: Yes, she has mild hearing loss. She hears most things with hearing aids, which is why she also speaks so well. And she does dance well. I stick to slow songs when she wants me to dance with her, since I can't hear them.

Me: Is that why Maggie speaks out loud and you don't? Because she can hear?

His eyes swing up to mine for a few seconds, and then he looks back at his phone.

Ridge: No. I could speak if I wanted to.

I should stop. I know he's probably annoyed by these questions, but I'm too curious.

Me: Why don't you, then?

He shrugs but doesn't text me back.

Me: No, I want to know. There has to be a reason. It seems like it would make things a lot easier for you.

Ridge: I just don't. I get along fine with how I do things now.

Me: Yes, especially when Maggie and Warren are around. Why would you need to talk when they can do it for you?

I hit send before I realize I probably shouldn't have said that. I have noticed Maggie and Warren do a lot of his talking for him, though. They've ordered for him every time the waitress has come by the booth, and I've noticed Warren do it several times this week in different situations.

Ridge reads my text, then looks back up at me. It seems I made him uncomfortable, and I immediately regret saying what I did.

Me: I'm sorry. I didn't mean for that to come out how it probably sounded. I just meant you seem to let them do things for you that they wouldn't necessarily have to do if you would speak for yourself.

My explanation seems to bother him even more than the initial text. I feel as if I'm digging myself a hole.

Me: Sorry. I'll stop. It's not my place to judge your situation, because I obviously can't put myself in your shoes. I was just trying to understand.

He looks at me and pulls the corner of his bottom lip into his mouth. I've noticed he does this when he's thinking hard about something. The way he continues to stare at me makes my throat go dry. I break his gaze, pull the straw into my mouth, and take a sip of my soda. When I look back at him, he's texting again.

Ridge: I was nine when I stopped verbalizing.

His text does more to my stomach than his stare did. I don't know why.

Me: You used to talk? Why did you stop?

Ridge: It might take me a while to text the explanation.

Me: It's fine. You can tell me about it at home when we have our laptops.

He scoots to the edge of the booth and peers over the balcony. I follow his gaze down to Maggie and Warren, who are still both hovering around the DJ booth. When he sees that they're still occupied, he moves away from the railing and leans forward across the table, resting his elbows in front of him as he begins to text.

Ridge: They don't look like they're ready to leave, so I guess we have time now. Brennan and I didn't luck out in the parent department. They both had issues with addiction. They might still have them, but we wouldn't know, because we haven't spoken to either of them in years. My mother spent most of our childhood in bed, doped up on pain pills. Our father spent most of our childhood in bars. When I was five, I was enrolled in a school for the deaf. That's where I learned sign language. I would come home and teach Brennan, because neither of my parents knew ASL. I taught him because I was five years old and had never had a conversation with anyone before. I was so desperate to communicate I was forcing my two-year-old brother to learn signs like "cookie" and "window" just so I would have someone to talk to.

My heart sinks to my stomach. I look up at him, but he's still texting.

Ridge: Imagine walking into your first day of school to the realization that there is actually a way to communicate. When I saw kids having conversations with their hands, I was amazed. I lived the first five years of my life never knowing what it was like to communicate. The school began teaching me how to form words using my voice, how to read, how to sign. I spent the next few years practicing everything I learned on Brennan. He became just as fluent in ASL as I was. I wanted him to know it, but I also didn't want to use him as my way to communicate with my parents. So when I would talk to them, I would always speak my words. I couldn't hear my own voice, of course, and I know it sounds different when deaf people speak, but I wanted a way to communicate with them since they didn't know ASL. One day, when I was talking to my father, he told Brennan to tell me to shut up, then had Brennan speak for me. I didn't understand why, but he was angry. Every time I would try to talk to my father after that, the same thing would happen, and he would tell Brennan to tell me to stop voicing my words. Brennan would translate what my father wanted him to say back to me. I finally realized my father didn't want me to talk because he didn't like the way my voice sounded. It embarrassed him that I couldn't hear. He didn't like for me to speak when we were in public, because people would know I was deaf, so he would tell me to shut up every time I did it. One day at home, he became so angry that I was still doing it that he started yelling at Brennan. He assumed that since I continued speaking my words, Brennan wasn't relaying the fact that he didn't want me to speak. He was really drunk that day and took his anger too far, which wasn't uncommon. But he hit Brennan so hard upside the head it knocked him out.

Tears begin to well in my eyes, and I have to inhale a calming breath.

Ridge: He was only six years old, Sydney. Six. I never wanted to give my father another reason to hit him, so that was the last day I ever spoke out loud. I guess it just became habit after that.

He lays his phone on the table and folds his arms in front of him. He doesn't seem to be waiting for a response from me. He may not even want one. He watches me, and I know he sees the tears falling down my cheeks, but he doesn't react to them. I take a deep breath, then reach over and pick up a napkin and wipe my eyes. I wish he wouldn't see me responding like this but I can't hold it back. He smiles softly and begins to reach across the table for my hand, and then Warren and Maggie reappear at the booth.

Ridge pulls his hand back and looks up at them. Maggie's arms are draped across Warren's shoulders, and she's laughing at nothing in particular. Warren keeps trying to grab the back of the booth—it looks as if he's about to need support, too, but he can't seem to grasp anything. Ridge and I both stand up and assist them. Ridge pulls Maggie off Warren, and I wrap Warren's arm around my shoulders. He presses his forehead to mine.

"Syd, I'm so happy you got cheated on. I'm so happy you moved in."

I laugh and push his face away from mine. Ridge nods his

head toward the exit, and I nod in agreement. Another drink, and we would probably have to carry these two out.

"I like that dress you wear, Syd. That blue one? But please don't wear it again." Warren is leaning his head against mine as we make our way toward the stairs. "I don't like your ass in it, because I think I might love Bridgette, and your dress makes me love your ass."

Wow. He's really drunk if he's admitting that he might love Bridgette.

"I already told you I was burning that dress," I say, laughing.

"Good," he says with a sigh.

We reach the exit, and I notice Ridge is carrying Maggie now. Her arms are draped around his neck, and her eyes are closed. Once we reach the car, she opens her eyes as Ridge tries to stand her up. She attempts to take a step but ends up stumbling. Ridge opens the back door, and she practically falls inside. He scoots her to the other side of the seat, and she falls against the door, closing her eyes again. Ridge steps out of the way and motions for Warren to climb in. Warren steps forward and reaches up to Ridge's face. He pats Ridge's cheek and says, "I feel bad for you, buddy. I bet it's really hard not to kiss Sydney, cuz it's hard for me, and I don't even like her like you do."

Warren climbs inside the car and falls against Maggie. I'm thankful that he was too drunk to sign any of that, because I know that Ridge didn't understand what he said. I can tell by the confused look Ridge is giving me. He laughs and bends down, lifting Warren's leg, which is still hanging out of the car. He pushes it inside the car and closes the door, and my mind is still stuck on Warren's words.

Ridge reaches in front of me and pulls on the handle of the front passenger door, then opens it. I step forward, but the second Ridge's hand rests against my lower back, I pause.

I glance up at him, and he's looking straight down at me. His hand remains on my lower back as I force myself to slowly close the gap between myself and the car. The second I begin to lower myself into the seat, his hand slips away, and he waits until I'm all the way inside the car, then closes the door.

I lean my head back into the seat and close my eyes, terrified of what that simple gesture just did to me.

I hear him take his position behind the wheel, and the car cranks, but I continue to keep my eyes closed. I don't want to look at him. I don't want to feel what I feel when I look at him. I don't like how every minute I spend with him, I feel more and more like a Tori.

My phone receives a text, so I'm forced to open my eyes. Ridge is holding his phone, watching me.

Ridge: She doesn't do this a lot. Probably not even three times a year. She's been under a lot of stress lately, and she likes to go out. It helps.

Me: I wasn't judging her.

Ridge: I know. I just wanted you to know she's not a raging alcoholic like I am.

He winks at me, and I laugh. I glance into the backseat, where Warren is draped across Maggie. They're both out cold. I turn back around in my seat and text him again.

Me: Thank you for telling me all that earlier. You didn't have to, and I know you probably didn't want to, but thank you.

He gives me a sideways glance, then returns his attention to his phone.

Ridge: I've never told anyone that story. Not even Brennan. He was probably too young to even remember it.

He sets his phone down and puts the car in reverse, then begins to back out.

Why is it that the only question I wish I could ask him right now is the most inappropriate one? I want to ask him if he's ever told Maggie, but his answer shouldn't matter to me. It shouldn't matter at all, but it does.

He begins to drive, and he reaches down and turns on the radio, which confuses me. He can't hear it, so I don't understand why he would care if it was on or off.

But then I realize he didn't do it for himself.

He turned it on for me.

Ridge

After stopping at a drive-thru for food, we pull up to the apartment complex. I put the car in park.

> Me: Take the food up and unlock the door while I wake them up.

She picks up our two drinks and the bag of food. She heads up to the apartment, and I walk to the back door and open it. I shake Warren awake and help him out of the car. Then I wake Maggie up and help her out. She's still too out of it to walk, so I pick her up and shut the door behind me. I make sure Warren walks ahead of me up the stairs, because I'm not positive he won't fall down them.

When we make it inside, Warren stumbles to his bedroom, and I walk Maggie into my room. I lay her on the bed and take off her shoes, then her clothes. I pull the covers over her, then head back into the dining room, where Sydney has laid out our food. It's almost midnight, and we haven't eaten since lunch. I take a seat in front of her.

> Me: So now that you know one of my deep, dark secrets, I want to know one of yours.

We both have our phones out on the table while we eat. She smiles and begins to text me back.

> Sydney: You have more than one deep, dark secret?

Me: We're talking about you right now. If we're going to be working together, I need to know what I'm getting myself into. Tell me about your family. Any raging alcoholics?

Sydney: No, just raging assholes. My father is a lawyer, and he hates that I'm not going to law school. My mother stays home. She's never worked a day in her life. She's a great mom, but she's also one of those perfect moms, you know? Think *Leave It to Beaver* meets *Stepford Wives*.

Me: Siblings?

Sydney: Nope. Only child.

Me: I wouldn't have pegged you as an only child. Nor would I have guessed you were a lawyer's daughter.

Sydney: Why? Because I'm not pretentious and spoiled?

I smile at her and nod.

Sydney: Well, thanks. I try.

Me: I don't mean for this to come off as insensitive, but if your father is a lawyer and you still have a relationship with your parents, why did you not call them last week? When you had nowhere to go?

Sydney: The primary thing my mother instilled in me was the fact that she didn't want me to be her. She had no education and has always been completely dependent on my father. She raised me to be very independent and financially responsible, so I've always taken pride in not asking for their help. It's hard sometimes, especially when I really need their help, but I always get by. I also don't ask for their help because my father would point out in a not-so-nice way that if I were in law school, he'd be paying for it.

Me: Wait. You're paying for school on your own? But if you changed your major to prelaw, your father would pay for it?

She nods.

Me: That's not really fair.

Sydney: Like I said, my father is an asshole. But I don't go around blaming my parents for everything. I have a lot to be thankful for. I've grown up in a relatively normal household, both of my parents are alive and well, and they support me to an extent. They're better than most, just worse than some. I hate it when people spend their entire lives blaming their parents for every bad thing that happens to them.

Me: Yeah. I completely agree, which is why I was emancipated at sixteen. Decided to take my life into my own hands.

Sydney: Really? What about Brennan?

Me: I took him with me. The courts thought he stayed with my parents, but he moved in with me. Well, with Warren. We've been friends since we were fourteen. Both of his parents are deaf, which is how he knows ASL. Once I became emancipated, they allowed me and Brennan to stay with them. My parents still had guardianship over Brennan, but as far as they were concerned, I did them a huge favor by taking him off their hands.

Sydney: Well, that was incredibly considerate of Warren's parents.

Me: Yes, they're great people. Not sure why Warren turned out the way he did, though.

She laughs.

Sydney: Did they continue to raise Brennan after you left for college?

Me: No, we actually only stayed with them for seven months. When I turned seventeen, I moved us into an apartment. I dropped out of school and got a GED so I could start college sooner.

Sydney: Wow. So you raised your brother?

Me: Hardly. Brennan lived with me, but he was never the type who could be raised. He was fourteen when we got our own place. I was only seventeen. As much as I'd like to say I was the responsible, mature adult, I was quite the opposite. Our apartment became the hangout for everyone who knew us, and Brennan partied just as hard as I did.

Sydney: That shocks me. You seem so responsible.

Me: I wasn't as wild as I probably could have been, being on my own at that young an age. Luckily, all our money went to bills and rent, so I never got into any bad habits. We just liked to have fun. Our band was formed when Brennan was sixteen and I was nineteen, so that took up a lot of our time. That's also the year I started dating Maggie, and I calmed down a lot after that.

Sydney: You've been with Maggie since you were nineteen?

I nod but don't text her back. My food has hardly been touched from all the texting, so I pick up my burger. She does the same, and we eat until both of us are finished. We stand up and clear off the table. Then she gives me a wave and heads off to her room. I sit on the couch and turn on the TV. After about fifteen minutes of channel surfing, I finally stop on a movie channel. The captioning has been turned off on the TV, but I don't bother turning it back on. I'm too tired to read and follow along with the movie, anyway.

The door to Sydney's bedroom opens, and she walks out, looking slightly startled when she sees I'm still awake. She's in one of her baggy shirts again, and her hair is wet. She walks back to her room, then comes out with her phone and sits on the couch with me.

Sydney: I'm not tired. What are you watching?

Me: I don't know, but it just started.

She pulls her feet up and rests her head on the arm of the couch. Her eyes are on the TV, but my eyes are on her. I have to admit, the Sydney who went out tonight is a completely different Sydney from the one lying here. Her makeup is gone, her hair is no longer perfect, her clothes even have holes in them, and I can't help but laugh just looking at her. If I were Hunter, I'd be punching myself in the face right now.

She's beginning to lean forward for her phone when she cuts her eyes in my direction. I want to look back at the TV and pretend she didn't just catch me staring at her, but that would make this even more awkward. Luckily, she doesn't seem to care that I was looking at her, because she gives her attention to her phone.

Sydney: How are you watching this without captions?

Me: Too tired to read along right now. Sometimes I just like to watch movies without captions and try to guess what they're saying.

Sydney: I want to try it. Put it on mute, and we'll deaf-watch it together.

I laugh. Deaf-watch? That's a new one. I point the remote to the TV and press the mute button. She turns her attention back to the TV, but once again, I fail to look away from her.

I don't understand my sudden obsession with staring at her, but I can't seem to stop. She's several feet away. We aren't touching. We aren't speaking. She isn't even looking at me. Yet the simple fact that I'm staring at her makes me feel incredibly guilty, as if I'm doing something wrong. Staring is harmless, so why do I feel so guilty?

I attempt to talk myself out of the feelings of guilt, but deep down, I know exactly what's happening.

I don't feel guilty simply because I'm staring at her. I feel guilty for how it's making me feel.

•   •   •

This makes twice in a row I've been woken up like this. I push away the hand that's slapping me and open my eyes. Warren is standing over me. He slaps a piece of paper on my chest, then whacks his hand against the side of my head. He walks to the front door and grabs his keys, then leaves for work.

Why is he going to work this early?

I pick up my phone, and it says 6:00 A.M. I guess he's *not* leaving early.

I sit up on the couch and see Sydney still curled up at the

other end, sound asleep. I pull the paper from Warren off my chest and look down at it.

How about you go to your room and sleep in the bed with your girlfriend!

I wad up the note and stand, then take it to the trash can and bury it. I go back to the couch, put my hand on Sydney's shoulder, and shake her awake. She rolls onto her back and rubs her eyes, then looks up at me.

She smiles when she sees me. That's it. All she did just now was smile, but all of a sudden, my chest is on fire, and it feels as if a wave of heat just rolled down the entire length of my body. I recognize this feeling, and it's not good. It's not good at all. I haven't felt this way since I was nineteen.

Since I first began developing feelings for Maggie.

I point to Sydney's room to let her know she should go to bed, then quickly turn around and head into my bedroom. I pull off my jeans and T-shirt and softly slide into bed next to Maggie. I wrap my arms around her, pull her against my chest, and spend the next half hour falling asleep to a broken record of reminders.

You're in love with Maggie.
Maggie's perfect for you.
You're perfect for her.
She needs you.
You're happy when you're with her.
You're with the one and only girl you're meant to be with.

10.

Sydney

It's been two weeks since Ridge and I have worked on lyrics together. A few days after Maggie went home, Ridge ended up leaving for six days because of a family emergency. He was vague about what the emergency was, but it reminded me of when I still lived with Tori and he was absent from his balcony for several days. A family emergency was his excuse then, too.

Based on conversations I've heard Warren have on the phone with Brennan, I know it didn't have anything to do with Brennan. But he's never mentioned having family other than Brennan. When Ridge returned a few days ago, I asked him if everything was okay and he said things were fine. He didn't seem to want to share any details, and I'm trying to remind myself that his personal life is none of my concern.

I've immersed myself in school, and every now and then, I'll attempt to write lyrics on my own, but it isn't the same when I don't have the music to go along with it. Ridge has been home for a few days now, but he's spent most of his time in his room catching up on work, and I can't help but wonder if he's kept his distance for other reasons.

I've been hanging out with Warren a lot and have learned more about his relationship with Bridgette. I haven't had any more interactions with her, so as far as I know, she still assumes I'm deaf.

Based on what Warren has told me, their relationship is

anything but typical. Warren never met Bridgette before she moved in six months ago, but she's a longtime friend of Brennan's. Warren says that he and Bridgette don't get along at all, and during the day, they live separate lives. But at night, it's a completely different story. He has tried to go into more detail than I care to hear, so I force him to shut up when he begins to overshare.

I'm really wishing he would shut up right now, because he's in the midst of one of his oversharing moments. I have to leave for class in half an hour, and I'm trying to finish reading a last-minute chapter, but he's intent on telling me all about last night and how he wouldn't let her take her Hooters uniform off because he likes to role-play, and oh, my God, why does he think I care to hear this?

Luckily, Bridgette walks out of her room, and it's more than likely the first time I've ever been happy to see her.

"Good morning, Bridgette," Warren says, his eyes following her across the living room. "Sleep well?"

"Screw you, Warren," she says in return.

I'm beginning to understand that this is their typical morning greeting. She walks into the kitchen and glances at me, then at Warren seated next to me on the couch. She narrows her eyes at him and turns toward the refrigerator. Ridge is at the dining-room table, concentrating on his laptop.

"I don't like how she's up your ass all the time," Bridgette says with her back to me.

Warren looks at me and laughs. Apparently, Bridgette still assumes I can't hear her, but I'm not finding much humor in the fact that she's talking shit about me.

She spins around and eyes Warren. "You think that's funny?" she says to him. "The girl obviously has it bad for you, and you can't even respect me enough to distance yourself from her until I'm out of the house?" She turns her back to us again. "First she gives Ridge some sob story so he'll let her move in,

maybe someday | 151

and now she's taking advantage of the fact that you know sign language so she can flirt with you."

"Bridgette, stop." Warren isn't laughing anymore, because he can see how white my knuckles are, clasped around my book. I think he's afraid Bridgette's about to get hit upside the head with a hardback. He's right to be afraid.

"*You* stop, Warren," she says, turning back around to face him. "Either stop crawling into bed with me at night or stop shacking up on the couch with *her* during the day."

I drop my book onto my lap with a loud slap, then kick my feet up and down against the floor out of frustration, anger, and flat-out annoyance. I can't put up with this girl for another second.

"Bridgette, please!" I yell. "Shut up! Shut up, shut up, shut *up*! Christ! I don't know why you think I'm deaf, and I'm definitely *not* a whore, and I'm not using sign language to flirt with Warren. I don't even *know* sign language. And from now on, please stop yelling when you speak to me!"

Bridgette cocks her pretty little head, and her mouth hangs open in shock. She silently stares at me for several seconds. No one in the room makes a move. She turns her attention to Warren, and the anger in her eyes is replaced with hurt. She immediately looks away once the hurt takes over, and she heads straight back to her room.

I glance over to see Ridge staring at me, more than likely wondering what the hell just happened. I lean my head back against the couch and sigh.

I was hoping that would feel good, but it didn't feel good at all.

"Well," Warren says, "there goes my chance to act out all the role-playing scenes I've been imagining. Thanks a lot, Sydney."

"Screw you, Warren," I say, understanding a little bit where Bridgette's attitude comes from.

I slide my book off my lap and stand up, then walk to

Bridgette's door. I knock, but she doesn't open it. I knock again, turn the knob, and push the door slightly open to peek inside.

"Bridgette?"

A pillow meets the back of the door with a thud. "Get the hell out of my room!"

I ignore her and open the door a little further until I can see her. She's sitting on her bed, with her knees pulled up to her chest. When she sees me coming into her room, she quickly wipes her eyes, then turns the other way.

She's crying, and now I really feel shitty. I walk to her bed and sit on the edge of it, as far out of her reach as possible. I may feel bad, but I'm still scared to death of her.

"I'm sorry," I say.

She rolls her eyes and falls back onto the bed in a huff. "You are not," she says. "I don't blame you. I deserved it."

I tilt my head. Did she really just admit that she deserved it? "I'm not gonna lie, Bridgette. You are kind of a bitch."

She laughs softly, then folds her arm over her eyes. "God, I know. I just get so annoyed with people, but I can't help it. It's not like it's my goal in life to be a bitch."

I lie back on the bed with her. "So don't be one, then. It takes way more effort to be a bitch than it does to not be one."

She shakes her head. "You can say that because you're not a bitch."

I sigh. She may not think I'm a bitch, but I sure have been feeling like one lately. "For what it's worth, I'm more evil than you might think. I may not express my feelings in quite the same fashion as you, but I definitely have evil thoughts. And lately, evil intentions. I'm beginning to think I'm not as nice as I always thought I was."

Bridgette doesn't respond to my admission for a few quiet moments. She finally sighs heavily and sits up on the bed. "Can I ask you something? Now that I know you can actually answer me?"

I sit up, too, and nod.

"Are you and Warren . . ." She pauses. "You guys seem to get along really well, and I was curious if . . ."

I smile, because I know where she's going with this, and I interrupt her string of thought. "Warren and I are friends, and we could never be more than friends. He's sort of oddly infatuated with this bitchy Hooters waitress he knows."

Bridgette smiles, but then she quickly stops smiling and looks straight at me. "How long has Warren known that I thought you were deaf?"

I think back on the past few weeks. "Since the morning after I moved in?" I wince, knowing Warren's about to experience the side of Bridgette we all know too well. "But please go easy on him, Bridgette. As strangely as you two show it, he really does like you. He might even love you, but he was drunk when he said that, so I don't know for sure."

If it's possible to hear a heart stop, I just heard hers come to a screeching halt. "He said that?"

I nod. "A couple of weeks ago. We were leaving the club, and he was wasted, but he said something about how he's pretty sure he might love you. I probably shouldn't be telling you this, though."

She drops her eyes to the floor and is quiet for several seconds, then looks back up at me. "You know, most things people say when they're drunk are more accurate and honest than the things they say when they're sober."

I nod, unsure if that's a true fact or just a Bridgette fact. She stands up and walks swiftly to the door, then swings it open.

Oh, no.

She's about to kill Warren, and it's partly my fault. I stand up and rush to the door, prepared to catch the blame for telling her what Warren said. However, once I reach the living room, she's swinging her leg over his, sliding onto his lap. Warren's eyes are wide, and he's looking at her in fear, which tells me this isn't one of her usual moves.

Bridgette takes Warren's face in her hands, and he hesitantly brings his hands to her lower back. She sighs, staring him hard in the eyes. "I can't believe I'm falling in love with such a stupid, stupid asshole," she says to him.

He stares at her for several seconds while her comment registers, and then his hands fly up to the back of her head and he crashes their lips together. He scoots forward and stands with Bridgette wrapped around him. Then, without breaking for air, he takes her directly to his bedroom, where the door shuts behind them.

I'm smiling, because Bridgette is more than likely the only girl in existence who could pull off calling someone an asshole and in the same breath confess her love. And oddly enough, Warren is probably one of the few guys who would find that appealing.

They're perfect for each other.

Ridge: How in the hell did you pull that one off? I was waiting for her to come out here and strangle him. You spend two minutes with her, and she's all over him.

Me: She's actually not as bad as she seems.

Ridge: Really?

Me: Well, maybe she is. But I guess I admire that about her. She's true to herself.

Ridge smiles, sets his phone down, and drops his eyes back to his laptop. There's something different about him now. I can't pinpoint exactly what it is, but I can see it in his eyes. He looks distraught. Or sad. Or maybe just tired?

He actually looks like a little bit of all three, and it makes me hurt for him. When I first met him, he seemed to have everything together. Now that I've gotten to know him better, I'm beginning to think that's not the case. The guy standing in front of me right now looks as if his life is a mess, and I haven't even begun to scratch the surface.

Ridge: I'm still a little behind on work, but I should be caught up by tonight. If you feel like running through a new song, you know where to find me.

Me: Sounds good. I have an afternoon study group, but I'll be back by seven.

He smiles halfheartedly and heads to his room. I know I'm beginning to understand most of his expressions. The one he just shot me was definitely a look of nervousness.

Ridge

I assumed she didn't feel like writing tonight when she didn't show, and I told myself I was okay with that.

However, it's a few minutes past eight, and my light just flickered. I can't ignore the rush of adrenaline pumping through me. I tell myself my body is having the reaction it's having because I'm passionate about writing music, but if that were the case, why don't I get this excited when I write alone? Or with Brennan?

I close my eyes and gently lay my guitar next to me while inhaling a steady breath. It's been weeks since we've done this. Since the night she let me hear her sing and it completely changed the dynamic of our working relationship.

That's not her fault, though. I'm not even sure if it's my fault. It's nature's fault, because attraction is an ugly beast, and I'll be damned if I don't conquer it.

I can do this.

I open the door to my bedroom and step aside while she comes in with her notebook and her laptop. She walks confidently toward the bed and drops down onto it, then opens her laptop. I sit back down and open mine.

Sydney: I couldn't pay attention in class today, because all I wanted to do was write lyrics. I wouldn't let myself write any, though, because it comes so much better when you play. I've missed this. I didn't think I would like it at first, and it made me nervous, but I love writing lyrics. Love, love, love it. Let's go, I'm ready.

She's smiling at me and giddily patting her palms against the mattress.

I smile back as I lean against the headboard and begin playing the opening to a new song I've been working on. I haven't finished it yet, but I'm hoping that with her help, we'll make some headway tonight.

I play the song several times, and she watches me some of the time, then writes some of the time. She uses her hands to tell me to pause or back up or move on to the next chorus or to restart the song altogether. I keep a close eye on her while I play, and we continue this dance for more than an hour. She does a lot of scratching out and makes a heck of a lot of faces that I'm not sure convey that she's having any fun.

She eventually sits up and tears the paper out of the notebook, then wads it up and tosses it into the trash can. She slaps her notebook shut and shakes her head.

Sydney: I'm sorry, Ridge. Maybe I'm just exhausted, but it's not clicking right now. Can we try this again tomorrow night?

I nod, doing my best to hide my disappointment. I don't like seeing her frustrated. She takes her laptop and notebook and starts to walk back toward her bedroom. She turns back around and mouths, "Good night."

As soon as she disappears, I'm off the bed and digging through the trash can. I pull out her wadded-up sheet of paper and take it back to my bed and unfold it.

> *Watching him from here*
> *So far away*
> *Want him closer than my heart can take*
> *I want him here ~~I want~~*
> *Maybe ~~one of these days~~ Someday*

There are random sentences, some marked out, some not. I read all of them, attempting to work my way around them.

> I'd run for ~~him~~ you, if I could stand
> But I can't make that demand
> I can't be his right now
> ~~Why can't he take me away~~

Reading her words feels like an invasion of her privacy. But is it? Technically, we're in this together, so I should be able to read what she's writing as she writes it.

But there's something different about this song. It's different because this song doesn't sound like it's about Hunter.

This song sounds a little like it could be about me.

I shouldn't be doing this. I should not be picking up my phone right now, and I should definitely not be contemplating how to persuade her to help me finish this song tonight.

Me: Don't be mad, but I'm reading your lyrics. I think I know where your frustration is coming from.

Sydney: Could it be coming from the fact that I suck at writing lyrics and a few songs is all I had in me?

I pick up my guitar and head to her bedroom. I knock and open her door, assuming she's still decent since she just left my room two minutes ago. I walk to her bed and sit, then grab her notebook and pen and place her lyrics on top of the notebook. I write a note and hand it to her.

You have to remember the band you're writing lyrics for is all guys. I know it's hard to write from a male point of view, since you're obviously not male. If you stop writing this song from your own point of view and try to feel it from a different point of view, the lyrics might come. Maybe it's been hard because you know a guy will be singing it, but the feelings are coming from you. Just flip it around and see what happens.

She reads my note, then picks up the pen and shifts back on her bed. She looks at me and nods her head toward my guitar, indicating that she'll give it a try. I scoot off the bed and onto the floor, then stand my guitar upright and pull it against my chest. When I'm working out chords to a new song, it helps to play this way sometimes so I can feel the vibrations more clearly.

I close my eyes, lean my head against the guitar, and begin playing.

11.

Sydney

Oh, God. He's doing that thing again. The mesmerizing thing.

When I've seen him play his guitar like this in the past, it was before I knew he couldn't hear himself play. I thought maybe he just played this way to get a different angle on the strings, but now I know he does it so he can feel the music better. I don't know why, but knowing this makes me love watching him even more.

I should probably be working on the lyrics, but I watch him play the entire song without once opening his eyes. When he finishes, I quickly glance down to my notebook, because I know he's about to open his eyes and look up at me. I pretend I'm writing, and he flips his guitar around the correct way, then leans back against my dresser and begins playing the song again.

I focus on the lyrics and think about what he said. Ridge was right. I wasn't thinking about the fact that a guy would be singing them. I was focused on pouring my feelings onto paper. I close my eyes and try to picture Ridge singing the song.

I try to imagine what it would be like to be honest about what I'm feeling for him and use that to take the lyrics a little further. I open my eyes and cross out the first line of the song, then begin rewriting the first verse.

> ~~Watching him from here~~
> *Seeing something from so far away*

Get a little closer every day
Thinking that I want to make it mine

I think the real reason I'm not able to write tonight is that every line that ends up on paper is about Ridge, and I know Ridge will be able to see through it. He pulled the lyrics out of the trash and already read through them, so he has to have an idea. Still . . . he's here, wanting me to finish the song. I focus on the second verse and try to keep his advice in mind.

I'd run for ~~him~~ you if I could stand
~~But I can't make that demand~~
What I want I can't demand
'Cause what I want is you

I continue to go through the lyrics on the page, crossing out the old lines and changing them up as Ridge plays the song several times.

~~If I could be his, I would wait~~
And if I can't be yours now
I'll wait here on this ground
Till you come, till you take me away
Maybe someday
Maybe someday

The page becomes messy and hard to read, so I set it aside and open my notebook to rewrite everything. Ridge stops playing for a few minutes while I transfer everything onto the new page. When I look up at him, he points to the page, wanting to read what I've written. I nod.

He walks to the bed and sits next to me, leaning in toward me to read what I've got so far.

I'm extremely aware that he might see right through the lyrics and know they have more to do with him than with Hunter, which causes panic to course through my veins. He pulls the notebook closer to him, but it's still on my lap. His shoulder is pressed to mine, and his face is so close he could probably feel my breath against his cheek . . . if I were breathing. I force my eyes to fall where his have, onto the lyrics rewritten across the page on my lap.

> *I try to ignore what you say*
> *You turn to me*
> *I turn away*

Ridge picks up the pen and marks through the last line, then tilts his head to face me. He points the pen at himself and makes a writing motion in the air, indicating that he wants to change something.

I nod, full of nerves and fear that he doesn't like it. He presses his pen to the paper, next to the lyrics he crossed out. He pauses for a few seconds before writing and slowly turns to face me again. His expression is full of trepidation, and I'm curious about what's causing it. His eyes fall from mine, slowly grazing over me until his attention is back on the page. He inhales and carefully exhales, then begins writing the new lyrics. I watch him write out the lyrics to the entire song as I follow closely along, deciphering the new lyrics he adds in himself.

> MAYBE SOMEDAY
>
> *Seeing something from so far away*
> *Get a little closer every day*
> *Thinking that I want to make it mine*
>
> *I'd run for you if I could stand*
> *But what I want I can't demand*
> *'Cause what I want is you*

Chorus:
And if I can't be yours now
I'll wait here on this ground
Till you come
Till you take me away
Maybe Someday
Maybe Someday

I try to ignore what you say
You turn to me, I turn away
But Cupid must have shot me twice

I smell your perfume on my bed
Thoughts of you invade my head
Truths are written, never said

Repeat Chorus

You say it's wrong, but it feels right
You cut me loose, then hold on tight
Words unfinished, like our song

Nothing good can come this way
Lines are drawn, but then they fade
For her I bend, for you I break

Repeat Chorus

When he's finished writing, he sets the pen down across the paper. His eyes turn to mine again, and I don't know if he's expecting me to respond to what he just wrote, but I can't. I'm trying not to allow myself to feel as if there's any truth behind his lyrics, but his words from the first night we wrote together flash through my head.

"They're your words, Sydney. Words that came from you."

He was telling me then that lyrics have truth behind them, because they come from somewhere inside the person who wrote them. I look back down at the page.

For her I bend, for you I break

Oh, my God, I can't. I didn't ask for this. I don't *want* this.

But it feels so good. His words feel good, his closeness feels good, his eyes searching mine make my heart go haywire, and for the life of me, I can't figure out how something that feels like this can be so wrong.

I'm not a bad person.

Ridge isn't a bad person.

How can two good people who both have such good intentions end up with feelings, derived from all the goodness, that are so incredibly bad?

Ridge's expression grows more concerned, and he pulls his gaze away from mine and picks up his phone.

Ridge: Are you okay?

Ha. Am I okay? Yeah. That's why my palms are sweating and my chest is heaving and I'm clenching the sheet beside me on the bed so I don't do something to him with these hands that I'll never forgive myself for.

I nod, then gently push him aside as I stand up and walk to the bathroom. I shut the door behind me and lean against it, closing my eyes and silently repeating the mantra in my head that I've been repeating for weeks now.

Maggie, Maggie, Maggie, Maggie, Maggie.

Ridge

After several minutes, she finally walks back into her bedroom. She smiles at me, walks to the bed, and picks up her phone.

Sydney: Sorry. I felt sick.

Me: You okay?

Sydney: Yeah. Just needed water, I guess. I love the lyrics, Ridge. They're perfect. Do we need to run through them again, or can we call it a night?

I really would like to run through them again, but she looks tired. I'd also give anything to feel her sing them again, but I'm not sure that's a good idea. I already beat up my conscience enough while I was writing the rest of the lyrics down. However, the fact that I was more than likely writing about her didn't seem to stop me, because the only thing on my mind was the simple fact that I was actually *writing*. I haven't been able to write lyrics in months, and in just a matter of minutes, it was as if a fog lifted and the words began to flow effortlessly. I would have kept going if I didn't feel I'd already gone way too far.

Me: We'll call it a night. I'm really happy with this one, Syd.

She smiles, and I pick up my guitar and head to my room.

I spend the next several minutes transferring her lyrics into the music program on my laptop, and filling in the guitar chords. Once it's all entered, I hit send, close it out, and text Brennan.

> Me: Just sent you a very rough draft with lyrics. I really want Sydney to hear this one, so if you have time this week to work up a rough acoustic, send it over. I think it'll be good for her to finally be able to hear something she created come to life.

> Brennan: Looking at it now. I hate to admit this, but I think you were right about her. She really was sent to earth just for us.

> Me: Starting to seem that way.

> Brennan: Give me an hour. Not busy, so I'll see what we can work up.

An hour? He's sending it tonight? I immediately text Sydney.

> Me: Try not to fall asleep. I might have a little surprise for you after a while.

> Sydney: Um, . . . okay?

•   •   •

Forty-five minutes later, I get an e-mail with an attachment from Brennan that says, *Rough cut, Maybe Someday.* I open it on my phone, find a set of earbuds in the kitchen drawer, and head to Sydney's room. She opens the door after I knock and lets me into her room. I walk over to sit on her bed and motion to the spot on the mattress beside me. She looks at me questioningly but walks to the bed. I hand her the earbuds and pat her pillow, so she lies down and places them in her ears. She continues to watch me warily, as if I'm about to pull an elaborate prank on her.

I scoot down next to her and prop myself up on my elbow, then hit play. I set the phone down between us and watch her.

A few seconds pass, and her head swings in my direction. An "Oh, my God" passes her lips, and she's looking at me as if I've just given her the world.

And it feels pretty damn good.

She smiles and puts her hand over her mouth as her eyes fill with tears. She tilts her face back up to the ceiling, more than likely because she's embarrassed by her emotional reaction. She shouldn't be. It's exactly what I was hoping to see.

I continue to watch her as she listens, and her face conveys a mixture of emotions. She smiles, then exhales, then closes her eyes. When the song ends, she looks at me and mouths, "Again."

I smile and hit play on my phone again. I continue to watch her, but the second her lips begin moving and I realize she's singing along to the song, my smile is washed away by a sudden emotion I didn't expect to feel at all.

Jealousy.

Never in all my life and in all my years of living in a world of silence have I wanted to hear something as much as I want to hear her sing right now. I want to hear her so bad it physically hurts. The walls of my chest feel as if they're closing in on my heart, and I don't even realize that my hand has moved to her chest until she turns to me, startled. I shake my head, not wanting her to stop. She nods slightly, but the beat of her heart against my hand is increasing by the second. I can feel the vibration of her voice against my palm, but the material between my hand and her skin hinders my ability to feel her the way I want to. I move my hand upward, until it's at the base of her throat, and then I slide it up even farther, until my fingers and palm are flush against her neck. I scoot closer to her so that my chest is pressed against her side, because the overwhelming need to hear her has completely taken over, and

I don't allow myself to think about where the invisible lines are drawn.

The vibration of her voice stops, and I feel her swallow as she looks up at me with the exact emotions that inspired most of the lines in this song.

Say it's wrong, but it feels right.

There's no other way to describe how I feel. I know that the way I think about her and feel about her is wrong, but I struggle so much with how *right* it feels when I'm with her.

She's no longer singing. My hand is still wrapped around her throat, and her face is tilted toward mine. I slide my hand a little higher until it's grazing her jaw. I run my finger around the cord to the earbuds and pull them away from her. I return my fingers to her jaw, slowly slipping my hand behind her neck. My palm conforms so perfectly to the back of her head it's as if my hands were made to hold her like this. I gently pull her toward me, and she turns her body slightly toward mine. Our chests meet, and it creates a force so powerful that every other part of me is demanding to be pressed against every other part of her.

She reaches her hands up to my neck and lightly places her palms against my skin, then slowly eases her fingers up and into my hair. Having her so close feels as though we've created our own personal space, and nothing from outside our world can make its way in, and nothing from inside our world can make its way out.

Her breaths fall in waves against my lips, and although I can't hear them, I imagine they sound like how a heartbeat feels. I let my forehead fall against hers, and I feel a rumble from deep within my chest rise up my throat. The sound I feel pass my lips causes her mouth to open in a gasp, and the way her lips are slightly parted causes my mouth to immediately connect with hers in search of the relief I desperately need.

Relief is exactly what I find the second our lips meet. It's as if every pent-up, denied feeling I've held toward her is suddenly uncaged, and I'm able to breathe for the first time since I met her.

Her fingers continue to sift through my hair, and my grip tightens against the back of her head, pulling her closer. She allows my tongue to slip inside and find hers. She's warm and soft, and the vibrations from her moans begin to leave her mouth and flow straight into mine.

My lips softly close over hers, and then I part them, and we do it all over again, but with less hesitation and more desperation. Her hands are now running down my back, and my hand is slipping to her waist, and my tongue is exploring the incredible way hers dances against mine to a song only our mouths can hear. The desperation and speed at which we're escalating this kiss make it apparent that we're both attempting to get as much out of each other as we can before the moment ends.

Because we both know it has to end.

I grip her waist tightly as my heart begins to tear in two, half of it remaining where it's always been, with Maggie, and the other half being pulled to the girl beneath me.

Nothing in my life has ever felt so good yet hurt so achingly *bad*.

I tear my mouth away from hers, and we both gasp for breath as the desperate grip she has on me keeps me locked against her. I refuse to allow our mouths to reconnect as I struggle to figure out which half of my heart I want to save.

I press my forehead to hers and keep my eyes closed, inhaling and exhaling in rapid succession. She doesn't attempt to kiss me again, but I can feel her chest as her movements change from begging for breath to fighting back tears. I pull back and open my eyes, looking down on her.

Her eyes are shut tightly, but the tears are beginning to fall. She turns her face and covers her mouth with her hand as she tries to roll onto her side, away from me. I lift up onto my hands and look down at what I've done to her.

I've done the one thing I promised her I would never do.

I just made her a Tori.

I wince and drop my forehead to the side of her head and press my lips against her ear. I find her hand and reach for the pen beside us on the nightstand. I turn her hand over and press the tip of the pen to her palm.

I'm so sorry.

I kiss her palm, then crawl off the bed and back away. She opens her eyes long enough to look at her hand. She makes a tight fist and pulls her hand to her chest, then begins to sob into her pillow. I take my guitar, my phone, and my shame . . . and I leave her completely alone.

12.

Sydney

I don't want to get out of bed. I don't want to go to class. I definitely don't want to go job hunting again. I don't want to do anything but keep this pillow pulled over my eyes, because it's creating a nice barrier between myself and every mirror in this apartment.

I don't want to look in the mirror, because I'm scared I'll see myself for who I really am this time. A girl with no morals or respect for other people's relationships.

I can't believe I kissed him last night.

I can't believe he kissed *me*.

I can't believe I broke into tears the second he pulled away from me and I saw the look on his face. I didn't think it was possible to cram so much regret and sorrow into one expression. Seeing how much he regretted being in that moment with me was one of the biggest blows my heart has ever taken. It hurt worse than what Hunter did to me. It hurt worse than what Tori did to me.

But as much as it hurt seeing the regret on his face, it was nothing compared to the guilt and shame I felt when I thought of what I had done to Maggie. What *he* had done to Maggie.

I knew the moment he put his hand on my chest and moved closer to me that I should have flown off the bed and made him leave the room.

But I didn't. I *couldn't*.

The closer he moved and the longer we stared at each other, the more my body was consumed by need. It wasn't a basic need, like a need for water when I'm thirsty or a need for food when I'm hungry. It was an insatiable need for relief. Relief from the want and desire that had been pent up for so long.

I never realized how powerful desire could be. It consumes every part of you, enhancing your senses by a million. When you're in the moment, it enhances your sense of sight, and all you can do is focus on the person in front of you. It enhances your sense of smell, and suddenly, you're aware of the fact that his hair has just been washed and his shirt is fresh out of the dryer. It enhances your sense of touch and makes your skin prickle and your fingertips tingle, and it leaves you craving to *be* touched. It enhances your sense of taste, and your mouth becomes hungry and wanting, and the only thing that can satisfy it is the relief of another mouth in search of the same.

But the sense my desire enhanced the most?

Hearing.

As soon as Ridge placed the headphones in my ears and the music began to play, the hair on my arms rose, chills erupted from my skin, and it felt as if my heart rate slowly conformed to the beat of the song.

As much as Ridge craved that sense, too, he couldn't experience it. In that moment, all of his other senses combined failed to make up for the one sense he desired the most. He wanted to hear me just as much as I wanted him to hear me.

What happened between us didn't happen because we were weak. Ridge didn't run his hand up my jaw and around to the back of my head simply because I was in front of him and he was in the mood to make out. He didn't press his body against mine because he thinks I'm attractive and knew it would feel good. He didn't part my lips with his because he enjoys kissing and knew he wouldn't get caught.

Despite how hard we tried to fight it, all of those things happened between us because our feelings for each other are becoming so much stronger than our desire. Desire is easy to fight. Especially when the only weapon desire possesses is attraction.

It's not so easy when you're trying to win a war against the heart.

• • •

The house has been quiet since I woke up more than an hour ago. The more I lie here and allow myself to think about what happened, the less I want to face him. I know if we don't get it over with, the confrontation will only be harder the longer we wait.

I reluctantly get dressed and head to the bathroom to brush my teeth. His bedroom is quiet, and he usually has late nights that result in late mornings, so I decide to let him sleep. I'll wait it out in the living room. I hope Warren and Bridgette are either occupied with each other in a bed somewhere or still asleep, because I don't know if I can take either of them this morning.

I open the door and walk into the living room.

I pause.

Turn around, Sydney. Turn around and go back to your room.

Ridge is standing at the bar. However, it isn't the sight of Ridge that's rendered me completely immobile. It's the girl he has his arms around. It's the girl he's pressed against. It's the girl he's looking directly at, as if she's the only thing that has, does, and will ever matter to him. It's the girl who planted herself between me and my *maybe someday.*

Warren exits his bedroom and sees them standing together in the kitchen. "Hey, Maggie. I thought you weren't coming for a couple more weeks."

Maggie spins around at the sound of Warren's voice. Ridge's eyes move from Maggie over to me. His body tenses, and he stands up straighter, putting a slight distance between the two of them.

I'm still immobile, or I'd be putting distance between myself and all three of them.

"I'm about to leave," Maggie says, and signs simultaneously, facing Warren. Ridge steps away from her, then quickly breaks his gaze from mine and refocuses his attention on Maggie. "My grandfather was admitted to the hospital yesterday. I got here last night." She turns and gives Ridge a light peck on the lips, then heads for the front door. "It's nothing serious, but I'm staying with him until they release him tomorrow."

"Oh, man. Sorry about that," Warren says. "But you'll be here the weekend of my party, right?"

Party?

Maggie nods and takes a step back toward Ridge. She circles her arms around his neck, and he wraps his arms around her waist—two simple movements that completely shatter entire sections of my heart.

He rests his mouth against hers and closes his eyes. He brings his hands to her face, then pulls back and leans in again to kiss her on the tip of her nose.

Ouch.

Maggie exits the apartment without ever having noticed that I was standing here. Ridge closes the door behind her, turns around, and brings his eyes back to mine with an unreadable expression.

"What are we doing today?" Warren asks, moving his head back and forth between Ridge and me. Neither of us breaks our stare to respond to him. After several seconds, Ridge makes the slightest movement with his eyes, motioning toward his bedroom. He turns to Warren and signs something, and I walk back to my room.

It's amazing how many reminders I've had to give my organs in the last three minutes that should be basic, common knowledge.

Breathe in, breathe out.

Contract, expand.

Beat, beat, pause. Beat, beat, pause.

Inhale, exhale.

I walk to the bathroom and head for Ridge's bedroom. It was obvious he wants to talk, and I still think confronting it now is better than waiting. It's definitely better than not confronting it at all.

The journey across the bathroom is only a few feet and should take no longer than a few seconds, but I somehow stretch it out for five whole minutes. I place a nervous hand on his doorknob, then open it and walk into his room.

He's walking in at the same time as I'm closing the door to the bathroom. We pause and stare at each other. These stare-downs are going to have to end, because my heart can't take much more.

We both walk to his bed, but I pause before sitting down. I assume we're about to do some serious talking, so I hold up my finger and turn to get my laptop out of my room.

He's sitting on his bed with his laptop when I return, so I sit, lean against the headboard, and open mine. He hasn't messaged me yet, so I type something to him first.

Me: Are you okay?

I hit send, and after he reads my question, he turns his face toward mine and appears slightly puzzled. He turns back to his computer and begins typing.

Ridge: In what sense?

Me: All of them, I guess. I know it was probably difficult seeing Maggie after what happened between us, so I just wanted to know if you were okay.

Ridge: I think I'm a little confused right now. Are you not pissed at me?

Me: Should I be?

Ridge: Considering what happened last night, I would say so.

Me: I have no more of a right to be mad at you than you do to be mad at me. I'm not saying I'm not upset, but how will being mad at you help us work through this?

He reads my message and expels a huge breath, leaning his head back against the headboard. He closes his eyes for a moment before lifting his head and responding to me.

Ridge: Maggie showed up last night an hour after I got back to my room. I was convinced you were going to barge in and tell her what a jerk I am for kissing you. Then, in the kitchen earlier, when I saw you standing outside your door, I was bracing myself.

Me: I would never tell her, Ridge.

Ridge: Thank you for that. So what now?

Me: I don't know.

Ridge: Can we not do the thing where we brush it under the rug and act like it never happened, because I don't think that's going to work with us. I have a lot I need to say, and I'm scared if I don't say it right now, I'll never say it.

Me: I have a lot to say, too.

Ridge: You first.

Me: No, you first.

Ridge: How about we go at the same time? When we're both finished typing, we'll hit send together.

Me: Deal.

I have no idea what he's about to say to me, but I don't let it influence what I need to say to him. I tell him exactly what I want him to know, then I pause and wait for him to finish typing. When he finally stops, we look at each other, and he nods, and we both hit enter.

Me: I think what happened between us happened for a lot of reasons. We're obviously attracted to each other, we have a lot in common, and under any other circumstance, I honestly believe we'd be good for each other. I could see myself with you, Ridge. You're smart, talented, funny, compassionate, sincere, and a little bit evil, which I like. ;) And last night—I can't even describe it. It is by far the most I've ever felt while kissing someone. Although the feelings aren't all good. There's a lot of guilt mixed in there, too.

So as much as the thought of us being together makes sense, it also makes no sense whatsoever. I can't leave a relationship with as much hurt as I did and expect to find happiness within a few short weeks. It's too fast, and I still want to be on my own, no matter how right something might feel.

I don't know where your head is, and honestly, I'm scared to hit enter on this message, because I want us to be on the same page. I want us to work together to try to push past whatever it is we're feeling so we can continue to make music and be friends and pull ridiculous pranks on Warren. I'm not ready for that to end, but if my being here is too hard or makes you feel guilty when you're with Maggie, I'll leave. Just say the word, and I'll go. Well, I guess you can't really SAY the word. You could TYPE the word, and I'll go. (Sorry for the lame joke at your expense, but there's just too much seriousness going on right now.)

Ridge: First and foremost, I'm sorry. I'm sorry I put you in that position. I'm sorry I couldn't be stronger in that moment. I'm sorry I broke my promise to you about never becoming a Hunter. But I'm mostly sorry for leaving you crying on your bed last night. Walking out and leaving that whole situation unresolved was the worst move I could have made.

I wanted to come back and talk to you, but when I finally worked up the courage, Maggie showed up. If I knew she was coming, I would have warned you. After what I did to you last night and then seeing the look on your face when you saw us together this morning, I knew it was one of the most hurtful things I could have done.

I have no idea what's going through your head, but I have to say this, Sydney. No matter how I feel about you or how much I think we could work, I will never, ever leave her. I love her. I've loved her since the moment I met her, and I'll love her until the moment I die.

But please don't let that take away from how I feel about you. I never thought it was possible to have honest feelings for more than one person, but you've convinced me of how incredibly wrong I was. I'm not going to lie to myself and say I don't care about you, and I'm definitely not going to lie to you. I just hope you understand where I'm coming from and that you will give us a chance to navigate through this, because I believe we can. If there are two people in this world capable of figuring out how to be friends, it's us.

We read through each other's messages. I read his more than once. I didn't expect him to be so forthcoming and honest, especially about the fact that he cares about me. I never for one second expected him to contemplate leaving Maggie for me. That would be the worst outcome of all of this. If he left her and we attempted to build a relationship from that, it would never work. The entire relationship would be built on betrayal and deceit, and those two things have never made and will never make for a good foundation.

Ridge: Wow. I'm impressed with us. We're both so mature.

His comment makes me laugh.

Me: Yes, we are.

Ridge: Sydney, I can't tell you what your message just did for me. Seriously. I feel like the weight of all nine planets (because yes, Pluto will always be a planet to me) has been crushing my chest since the moment I walked away from you last night. But knowing that you don't hate me and that you're not mad and that you aren't concocting an evil revenge scheme feels so damn good right now. Thank you for that.

Me: Hold on. I never said I wasn't concocting an evil revenge scheme. ;) Also, while we're being so blunt, can I ask you a question?

Ridge: What did I tell you about initiating a question with whether or not you can propose a question?

Me: Oh, my God, I can't believe I ever kissed you. You're so ANNOYING!

Ridge. LOL. What's your question?

Me: I'm concerned. We obviously have an issue with the fact that we're attracted to each other. How do we get past that? I want to write music with you, but I also know that the few moments we've had that wouldn't make Maggie very happy have all been while we're writing music. I think I'm just too desirable when I'm being creative, and I want to know what I need to do to lessen my attractiveness. If that's even possible.

Ridge: Keep up the egotism. It's very unattractive, and if it continues, I won't even be able to look at you in a week's time.

Me: Deal. But what do I do about my attraction to YOU? Tell me some personal flaws that I can engrave into my memory.

He laughs.

Ridge: I sleep so late on Sundays I don't even brush my teeth until Monday.

Me: That's a start. I need a few more.

Ridge: Let's see. Once, when Warren and I were fifteen, I had a crush on a girl. Warren didn't know I liked her, and he asked me if I would ask her out for him. I did, and she agreed, because apparently, she had a crush on Warren in return. I told him she said no.

Me: Ridge! That's terrible!

Ridge: I know. I need a flaw from you now.

Me: When I was eight, we went to Coney Island. I wanted an ice cream, and my parents wouldn't buy me one because I was wearing a new shirt that "June Cleaver" didn't want me to get dirty. We were walking by a trash can, and there was a melted ice cream cone in it, so when my parents turned around, I picked it up and started eating it.

Ridge: Yeah, that's pretty gross. But you were only eight, so it really doesn't count. I need something more recent. High school? College?

Me: Oh! One time in high school, I spent the night at a girl's house who I didn't know very well. We made out. I wasn't into it, and it was really gross, but I was seventeen and curious.

Ridge: No. That does NOT count as a flaw, Sydney. Jesus Christ, work with me here.

Me: I like the smell of puppy breath.

Ridge: Better. I can't hear my own farts, so sometimes I'll forget that other people can hear them.

Me: Oh, my God. Yes, this is the type of thing that definitely sheds a different light on you. I think I'll be good for a while.

Ridge: One more from you, and then I think we'll be equally repulsed.

Me: A few days ago, when I was getting off the campus bus, I noticed Tori's car was gone. I used my extra key to let myself into her apartment, because I needed a few things I had forgotten. Before I left, I opened all her bottles of liquor and spit in them.

Ridge: For real?

I nod, because I'm too ashamed to type the word *yes*.
He laughs.

Ridge: Okay. I think we're good. Meet me here at eight tonight,
and we'll see if we can navigate through a song. If we need
to take breaks from the music every now and then in order to
replenish our repulsiveness with a few more flaws, just let me
know.

Me: Deal.

I close my laptop and begin to slide off the bed, but he
grabs my wrist. I turn around, and he's looking at me with a
serious expression. He leans over and grabs a pen, then picks up
my hand and writes: *Thank you.*

I press my lips together and nod. He releases my hand, and
I walk back to my room, attempting to ignore the fact that all
the repulsive details in the world couldn't stop my heart from
reacting to that simple gesture. I look down at my chest.

Hey, heart. Are you listening? You and I are officially at war.

Ridge

As soon as she's out of my bedroom and the door shuts behind her, I close my eyes and exhale.

I'm thankful that she isn't angry. I'm thankful that she isn't vindictive. I'm thankful that she's reasonable.

I'm also thankful that she appears to have more willpower than I do, because whenever I'm around her, I've never felt so weak.

13.

Sydney

Not much has changed in the way we practice together, other than the fact that we now practice five feet apart from each other. We've completed a couple of songs since "the kiss," and although the first night was a little awkward, we seem to have found our groove. We haven't talked about the kiss, and we haven't talked about Maggie, and we haven't discussed why he plays on the floor and why I write alone on the bed. There's no reason to discuss it, because we're both very aware of all of it.

The fact that we've admitted our attraction to each other doesn't seem to have eliminated it the way we'd hoped. For me, it's like a huge elephant in the room. It feels as if it takes up so much space when I'm with him that it presses me against the wall, squeezing the last traces of breath out of me. I keep telling myself it'll get better, but it's been almost two weeks since the kiss, and it hasn't gotten easier at all.

Luckily, I have two interviews next week, and if I get hired, at least it'll get me out of the house more. Warren and Bridgette both work and go to school, so they're not here a whole lot. Ridge works from home, so the fact that we're both here alone the majority of the day is always at the front of my mind.

Out of all the hours in the day, though, the hour I hate the most is when Ridge is in the shower. Which means I really hate this hour, since that's where he is right now. I hate where my thoughts go when I know he's one wall away from me, completely unclothed.

Jesus, Sydney.

I hear the water turn off and the shower curtain slide open, and I squeeze my eyes shut, trying once again not to picture him. This would probably be a good time of day to turn on some music to drown out my thoughts.

As soon as the door closes between the bathroom and his bedroom, there's a knock at the front door. I gladly jump off the bed and head toward the living room to get my mind off the fact that I know Ridge is in his room getting dressed right now.

I don't even bother looking through the peephole, which is a very bad oversight on my part. I swing open the door to find Hunter standing sheepishly at the top of the stairs. He eyes me, his expression apologetic and nervous. My heart drops to my stomach at the mere sight of him. It's been weeks since I last laid eyes on him. I was beginning to forget what he looked like.

His dark hair is longer since I last saw him, and it reminds me that I'm always the one to schedule his hair appointments. The fact that he hasn't even bothered to make his own appointment makes him that much more pathetic to me.

"Should I give Tori the number for your barber? Your hair looks awful."

The mention of Tori's name makes him grimace. Or maybe it's the fact that I'm not jumping back into his arms that's causing that regretful expression on his face.

"You look good," he says, capping his words off with a smile.

"I *am* good," I say, not sure if I'm lying to him or not.

He runs a free hand over his jaw and turns away from me, appearing to regret the fact that he's here.

How *is* he here? How does he even know where I live?

"How did you know where to find me?" I ask, tilting my head in curiosity.

I see the split-second shift of his eyes as they glance across the courtyard toward Tori's apartment. It's obvious he doesn't want me to notice what's going on in his mind, because it would only shed light on the fact that he's still visiting Tori on a regular basis.

"Can we talk?" he asks, his voice void of the confidence I've always known him to have.

"If I let you in and convince you it's over, will you promise to stop texting me?"

He barely nods his head, so I step aside, and he walks into the living room. I walk to the dining-room table and pull out a chair, making it obvious that he's not making himself comfortable by sitting on the couch. He walks toward the table as his eyes work their way around the room, more than likely in search of information on who lives here with me.

He grips the back of the chair and pulls it out slowly while his eyes focus on a pair of Ridge's shoes tucked beside the couch. I like that he noticed them.

"Are you living here now?" he asks, his voice tight and controlled.

"For now," I say, my voice even more controlled. I'm proud of myself for keeping calm, because I'm not going to lie and say it doesn't hurt to see him. I gave him two years of my life, and all the things I felt for him can't just be cut off at once. Feelings take time to disappear, so they're still here. They're just mixed and swirled together with a hell of a lot of hatred now. It's confusing to feel this way when I see him, because I never thought I could dislike the man in front of me. I never thought he would betray me the way he did.

"Do you think that's safe? Just moving in with some strange guy you barely know?" He's eyeing me disapprovingly as he takes his seat, as if he has the right to judge any part of my life.

"You and Tori didn't leave me much choice, did you? I found myself screwed over and homeless on my birthday. If anything,

I would think you should be congratulating me for handling it all so well. You sure as hell can't sit here and judge me."

He huffs, then leans forward over the table and closes his eyes, pressing the palms of his hands against his forehead. "Sydney, please. I didn't come here to fight or make excuses. I came here to tell you how sorry I am."

If there's one thing I'd like to hear from him, it's an apology. If there are *two* things I'd like to hear, it's an apology followed by a good-bye.

"Well, you're here now," I say quietly. "Have at it. Tell me how sorry you are." My voice isn't confident anymore. In fact, I want to punch myself, because it sounds really sad and heartbroken, and that's the last thing I want him to think I feel.

"I'm sorry, Sydney," he says, spitting the words out fast and desperately. "I'm so, so sorry. I know it won't make it better, but things have always been different between Tori and me. We've known each other for years, and I know it's not an excuse, but our relationship was sexual before you even met us. But that's all it was. It was just sex, and once you were in the picture, neither of us could figure out how to just put a stop to something that had been going on between us for years. I know this doesn't make sense, but what I had with her was completely separate from what I had with you. I love you. If you'll just give me one more chance to prove myself, I'll never speak to Tori again."

My heart is pounding as hard as it was the moment I found out they were sleeping together. I'm inhaling controlled breaths in an effort not to climb across the table and beat the shit out of him. I'm also clenching my fists in an effort not to climb across the table and kiss him. I would never take him back, but my head is so damned confused right now, because I miss what we had so much. It was simple and good, and my heart never ached the way it's been aching these past few weeks.

What's confusing me the most is the fact that my heart

hasn't been aching like this because I can't be with Hunter. It's aching because I can't be with Ridge.

I realize as I'm sitting here that I'm more upset that Ridge came into my life than I am that Hunter left it. How screwed up is that?

Before I can respond, Ridge's bedroom door opens, and he walks out. He's in jeans and nothing else, and I tense from the way my body responds to his presence. However, I love the fact that Hunter is about to turn around and witness Ridge looking like this.

Ridge pauses just feet from the table when he sees Hunter sitting across from me. He glances from Hunter to me, just as Hunter turns to see who I'm looking at. I can see the concern wash over Ridge's face, along with a flash of anger. He eyes me hard, and I know exactly what's going through his head right now. He's wondering what the hell Hunter is doing here, just as I am. I nod in reassurance, letting Ridge know I'm fine. I shift my eyes to his bedroom and silently tell him that Hunter and I need privacy.

Ridge doesn't move. He doesn't like that I just told him to go back to his bedroom. From the looks of it, he doesn't really trust Hunter alone with me. Maybe it's the fact that he wouldn't be able to hear me if I needed him to return for any reason. Whatever it is, I just made him completely uncomfortable with my request. Regardless, he nods and turns back toward his room, but not before eyeing Hunter with a warning shot.

Hunter faces me again, but his expression is no longer apologetic.

"What the hell was that?" he asks, his voice dripping in jealousy.

"That was Ridge," I reply firmly. "I believe the two of you have already met."

"Are the two of you . . . like . . . ?"

Before I answer him, Ridge walks back into the room with his laptop and heads straight to the couch. He drops down onto the sofa, eyeing Hunter the entire time while he opens his laptop and props his feet up on the coffee table in front of him.

The fact that Ridge refuses to leave me alone with Hunter pleases me way too much.

"Not that it's any of your business," I say, "but no, we aren't dating. He has a girlfriend."

Hunter returns his attention to me and laughs under his breath. I have no idea what he just found funny, but it pisses me off. I fold my arms while I glare at him and lean back against my seat.

Hunter leans forward and looks straight into my eyes. "Please tell me you see the irony in this, Sydney."

I shake my head, absolutely not seeing any irony in this situation.

My lack of comprehension makes him laugh again. "I'm trying to explain to you that what happened between Tori and me was strictly physical. It meant nothing to either of us, but you won't even try to understand my side of it. Yet you're practically eye-fucking your roommate who happens to be in love with another woman, and you don't see the hypocrisy in your actions? You can't tell me you haven't slept with him in the two months you've been here. How can you not see that what the two of you are doing isn't any different from what Tori and I did? You can't justify your own actions without forgiving mine."

I'm trying to keep my jaw off the floor. I'm trying to keep my anger subdued. I'm trying to keep myself from reaching across this table and punching him square between his accusing eyes, but I've learned the hard way that punching isn't all it's cracked up to be.

I allow myself several moments to calm down before I respond. I glance at Ridge, who is still eyeing me. He knows by the look on my face that Hunter just crossed the line. Ridge's hands are gripping the screen of his laptop, prepared to shove it aside if I need him.

I don't need him. I've got this.

I square up with Hunter, pulling my gaze off Ridge and focusing on the eyes I so desperately want to rip out of Hunter's head.

"Ridge has an amazing girlfriend who doesn't deserve to be cheated on, and luckily for her, he's the type of guy who realizes her worth. With that said, you're wrong about the fact that I'm sleeping with him, because I'm not. We both know how unfair it would be to his girlfriend, so we don't act on our attraction. You should take note that simply because a girl makes your dick hard, that doesn't mean you have to go *shove it inside her*!"

I push myself away from the table at the same time as Ridge sets his laptop aside and stands.

"Go, Hunter. Just go," I say, unable to look at him for another second. The simple fact that he thought he had Ridge pegged as being anything like him pisses me off, and he'd be smart to leave.

He stands up and walks straight to the door. He opens it and leaves without even looking back. I'm not sure if his exit was so simple because he finally understands that I'm not willing to take him back or if it's because Ridge looked as if he was about to kick his ass.

I have a good feeling I won't be hearing from Hunter anymore.

I'm still staring at the door when my phone sounds off. I take it out of my pocket and turn to Ridge. He's holding his phone, looking at me with concern.

Ridge: Why was he here?

Me: He wanted to talk.

Ridge: Did you know he was coming over?

I look up at Ridge after reading his text, and for the first time, I notice his jaw is tense and he doesn't look very happy. I'd almost label his reaction as slightly jealous, but I don't want to admit that.

Me: No.

Ridge: Why did you let him in?

Me: I wanted to hear him apologize.

Ridge: Did he?

Me: Yes.

Ridge: Don't let him in here again.

Me: I wasn't planning on it. BTW, you're kind of being a jerk right now.

He glances up at me and shrugs.

Ridge: It's my apartment, and I don't want him here. Don't let him in again.

I don't like his attitude right now, and to be honest, the fact that he just referred to this as his apartment doesn't sit right with me. It feels like a low blow to remind me that I'm at his mercy. I don't bother responding. In fact, I toss the phone onto the couch so he can't text me, and I head toward my room.

When I reach my bedroom door, my emotions catch up with me. I'm not sure if it's seeing Hunter again and having all of those hurtful feelings resurface or if it's the fact that Ridge is being an asshole. Whatever it is, the tears begin to well in my eyes, and I hate that I'm letting either of them get to me in the first place.

Ridge grabs my shoulder and turns me around to face him, but I keep my eyes trained on the wall behind him. I don't even want to look him in the eye. He puts my phone back in my hand, wanting me to read whatever he just texted, but I still don't want to. I throw the phone toward the couch again, but he intercepts it, then tries to force it back into my hand. I take it this time, but I press the power button down until the phone shuts off, and then I toss it onto the couch again. I look him in the eye now, and his expression is angry. He takes two steps toward the coffee table, grabs a pen out of the drawer, and walks back to me. He takes my hand, but I pull it from him, still not wanting to know what he has to say to me. I've had enough apologies for tonight. I try to turn away from him, but he grabs my arm and presses it against the door, holding it forcefully while he writes on it. When he's finished writing, I pull my arm away and watch as he tosses his pen onto the couch, then walks back to his bedroom. I look down at my arm.

Let him in next time if he's really what you want.

My barrier completely breaks. Reading his angry words depletes me of whatever strength I had left to hold back my tears. I rush through my bedroom door and straight into the bathroom. I turn on the faucet and squirt soap into my hands, then begin scrubbing his words off my arm while I cry. I don't even look up when the door to his bedroom opens, but I see him out of my peripheral vision as he closes the door behind him and slowly walks toward me. I'm still scrubbing the ink off my arm and sniffling back the tears when he reaches across me for the soap.

He dispenses some onto the palm of his hand, then wraps his fingers around my wrist. The tenderness in his touch lashes out and scars my heart. He runs the soap up my wrist where the words begin and lathers my skin as I drop my other hand away and grip the edge of the sink, allowing him to wash his words away.

He's apologizing.

He massages his thumbs into the words, rubbing them away with the water.

I'm still staring down at my arm, but I can feel his gaze directly on me. I'm aware of the exaggerated breaths I have to take in now that he's next to me, so I attempt to slow them down until there are no longer traces of ink on my skin.

He grabs a hand towel and dries my arm, then releases me. I bring my arm to my chest and hold it with my other hand, not knowing what move to make now. I finally bring my eyes to meet his, and I instantaneously forget why I'm even upset with him in the first place.

His expression is reassuring and apologetic and maybe even a little longing. He turns and walks out of the bathroom, then returns seconds later with my phone. He powers it on and hands it to me while he leans against the counter, still looking at me regretfully.

Ridge: I'm sorry. I didn't mean what I said. I thought maybe you were entertaining the thought of accepting his apology, and it upset me. You deserve better than him.

Me: He showed up unannounced. I would never take him back, Ridge. I was just hoping an apology from him would help me move on from the betrayal a little quicker.

Ridge: Did it help at all?

Me: Not really. I feel even more pissed than before he showed up.

As Ridge reads my text, I notice the tension ease in his expression. His reaction to my situation with Hunter borders on jealousy, and I hate that this makes me feel good. I hate that every time something Ridge-related makes me feel good, it's immediately followed up with guilt. Why do things between the two of us have to be so complicated?

I wish we could keep things simple, but I have no idea how to do that.

> Ridge: Let's go write an angry song about him. That might help.

He looks at me with a sly grin, and it makes my insides swirl and melt. Then I freeze just as fast from the guilt of those feelings.

For once, it would be nice not to be consumed with shame.

I nod and follow him to his room.

Ridge

I'm sitting on the floor again. It's not the most comfortable place to play, but it's much better than being on the bed next to her. I can never seem to focus on the actual music when I'm in her personal space and she's in mine.

She requested that I play one of the songs I used to play when I sat out on my balcony to practice, so we've been working through it. She's lying on her stomach, writing on her notepad. Erasing and writing, erasing and writing. I'm sitting here on the floor, not even playing. I've played the song enough for her to know the melody by now, so I'm just waiting while I watch her.

I love how she focuses so intently on the lyrics, as if she's in her own world and I'm just a lucky observer. Every now and then, she'll tuck behind her ear the hair that keeps spilling in front of her face. My favorite thing to watch her do is erase her words. Every time the eraser meets the paper, she pulls her top lip in with her bottom teeth and chews on it.

I hate that it's my favorite thing to watch her do, because it shouldn't be. It triggers all these *what-ifs* in my head, and my mind begins imagining things it shouldn't be imagining. I begin to picture myself lying next to her on the bed while she writes. I imagine her lip being tucked in while I'm just inches from her, looking down on the words she's written. I imagine her glancing up at me, noticing what she's doing to me with her small, innocent gestures. I imagine her rolling onto her back, welcoming me to create secrets with her that'll never leave this room.

I close my eyes, wanting to do whatever I can to stop the thoughts. They make me feel just as guilty as if I were to act on them. Sort of similar to how I felt a couple of hours ago when I thought there was a chance she was getting back together with Hunter.

I was pissed.

I was jealous.

I was having thoughts and feelings I knew I shouldn't be having, and it was scaring the shit out of me. I've never had an issue with jealousy until now, and I don't like the person it's turning me into. Especially when the jealousy I'm feeling has nothing to do with the girl I'm in an actual relationship with.

I flinch when something hits me on the forehead. I immediately open my eyes and look at Sydney. She's on the bed, laughing, pointing at my phone. I pick it up and read her text.

Sydney: Are you falling asleep? We aren't finished.

Me: No. Just thinking.

She moves over on the bed to make more room and pats the spot next to her.

Sydney: Come think right here so you can read these. I have most of the lyrics down, but I'm hung up on the chorus. I'm not sure what you want.

We haven't openly discussed the fact that we don't write on the bed together anymore. She's focused on the lyrics, though, so I need to pull my shit together and focus on them, too. I set my guitar down and pull myself up, then walk to the bed and lie beside her. I take the notebook out of her hands and pull it in front of me to read what she's written so far.

She smells good.

Damn.

I try to block off my senses somehow, but I know it's a wasted effort. Instead, I focus on the words she's written, quickly impressed at how effortlessly they come to her.

Why don't we keep
Keep it simple
You talk to your friends
And I'll be here to mingle

But you know that I
I want to be
Right by your side
Where I ought to be

And you know that I
That I can see
The way that your eyes
Seem to follow me

After reading what she's written, I hand her back the notebook and pick up my phone. I'm confused about the lyrics, because they aren't at all what I was expecting. I'm not sure I like them.

Me: I thought we were writing an angry song about Hunter.

She shrugs, then begins texting me back.

Sydney: I tried. The subject of Hunter doesn't really inspire me anymore. You don't have to use them if you don't like them. I can try something different.

I stare at her text, not sure how to respond. I don't like the lyrics, but not because they aren't good. It's because the words she's written down make me think she's somehow able to read my mind.

Me: I love them.

She smiles and says, "Thank you." She flips onto her back, and I catch myself appreciating this moment and this night and her low-cut dress way more than I probably should. When my eyes make their way back to hers, she's watching me, plainly aware of what's going through my head. Eyes don't lie, unfortunately.

When neither of us breaks our gaze, I'm forced to swallow the huge lump in my throat.

Don't get yourself in trouble, Ridge.

Thank God she sits up when she does.

Sydney: I'm not sure where you want the chorus to come in. This song is a little more upbeat than the ones I'm used to. I've written three different ones, but I don't like how any of them sound. I'm stuck.

Me: Let me watch you sing it one more time.

I roll off the bed and grab the guitar, then take it back to the bed but sit on the edge this time. We turn to face each other, and I play while she sings. When we make it to the chorus, she stops singing and shrugs, letting me know this is where she's stuck. I take her notebook and read the lyrics over a few times. I glance up at her without being too obvious about it and write the first thing that comes to mind.

> *And I must confess*
> *My interest*
> *The way that you move*
> *When you're in that dress*
>
> *It's making me feel*
> *Like I want to be*
> *The only man*
> *That you ever see*

I pause from writing and look up at her again, feeling every bit of the words in this chorus. I think we both know the words we write have to do with each other, but that doesn't seem to stop us at all. If we keep having moments like these with words that are way too honest, we'll *both* end up in trouble. I quickly look back down at the paper as more lyrics begin to enter my head.

> *Whoa, oh, oh, oh*
> *I'm in trouble, trouble*
> *Whoa, oh, oh, oh*
> *I'm in trouble now*

I refuse to look up at her again while I write. I keep my mind focused on the words that somehow seem to flow from my fingertips every time we're together. I don't question what's inspiring me or what they mean.

I don't question it . . . because it's obvious.

But it's art. Art is just an expression. An expression isn't the same as an act, as much as it sometimes feels that way. Writing lyrics isn't the same as directly informing someone of your feelings.

Is it?

I keep my eyes on the paper and continue to write the words I honestly wish I didn't feel.

The second I'm finished writing, I'm so worked up I don't allow myself to witness her reaction to the words. I quickly hand her back the notebook and pull my guitar around and begin playing so she can work through the chorus.

14.

Sydney

He's not looking at me. He doesn't even know I'm not singing the lyrics. I *can't* sing them. I've listened to him play this song dozens of times from his balcony, yet it never held emotion or meaning until this moment.

The fact that he can't even look at me makes the song feel way too personal. It feels as if this song somehow just became his song to me. I turn the notebook over, not wanting to read the words anymore. This song is just one more thing that never should have happened, even though I'm positive it's my new favorite.

> Me: Do you think Brennan can make a rough cut of this one? I want to hear it.

I nudge him with my foot after I send the text, then nod toward his phone when he looks at me. He picks it up to read the text and nods. He doesn't reply or make eye contact with me, though. I glance back down to my phone as the room grows quiet in the absence of the sound of his guitar. I don't like how awkward things just got between us, so I attempt to make small talk to fill the void. I roll onto my back and type out a question that's been on my mind for a while to break up the stillness around us.

> Me: Why don't you ever practice on your balcony like you used to?

This question gets me immediate eye contact from him, but it doesn't last. His eyes flicker across my face, down my body, and finally back to his phone.

Ridge: Why would I? You're not out there anymore.

And just like that, my defenses are down, and my willpower is shot to hell with his honest reply. I nervously pull my bottom lip in and chew on it, then slowly raise my eyes back to his. He's looking at me as if he wishes he were a guy like Hunter who cared only about himself.

He's not the only one wishing that.

I want to be Tori right now so much it hurts. I want to be just like her and not give a shit about my self-respect or about Maggie for just a few minutes. Long enough to allow him to do everything his lyrics make clear he wants to do.

His eyes fall to my lips, and my mouth runs dry.

His eyes fall to my chest, and it begins to heave deeper than it already was.

His eyes fall to my legs, and I have to cross them, because the way his gaze penetrates my body makes it seem as though he can see right through this dress I'm wearing.

His eyes close tightly, and knowing the effect I'm having on him makes me feel as if there might be a lot more truth to his lyrics than he'd like there to be.

It's making me feel like I want to be the only man that you ever see.

Ridge suddenly stands and drops his phone onto the bed, then walks straight into the bathroom and slams the door. I listen as the shower curtain slides open and the water kicks on.

I roll onto my back and release all my pent-up breaths. I'm flustered and confused and angry. I don't like the situation we've put ourselves in, and I know for a fact that even though we haven't acted on it again, nothing about this is innocent.

I sit up on the bed, then quickly stand. I need to get out of his room before it completely closes in on me. Just as I'm walking away from the bed, Ridge's phone vibrates on the mattress. I look down at it.

Maggie: I'm missing you extra hard today. When you're finished writing with Sydney, can we video chat? I need to see you. ;)

I stare at her text.
I hate her text.
I hate that she knows we were just writing together.
I hate that he tells her everything.
I want these moments to belong to me and Ridge and no one else.

• • •

It's been two hours since he got out of the shower, and I can't bring myself to leave my bedroom. I'm starving, though, and really want to go to the kitchen. I just don't want to see him, because I hate how we left things. I don't like that we both know we almost crossed a line tonight.

Actually, I don't like that we *did* cross a line tonight. Although we aren't verbalizing what we're thinking and feeling, writing it in lyrics isn't any less harmful.

There's a knock on my door, and knowing that it's more than likely Ridge causes my heart to betray me by dancing rapidly in my chest. I don't bother getting up to open the door, because he nudges it open right after knocking. He holds up a set of headphones and his cell phone, indicating that he has something he wants me to hear. I nod, and he walks over to the bed and hands them to me. He hits play but takes a seat on the floor while I scoot back onto the bed. The song begins to play, and I spend the next three minutes barely breathing. Ridge and I never once break our stare throughout the duration of the song.

I'M IN TROUBLE

Why don't we keep
Keep it simple
You talk to your friends
And I'll be here to mingle

But you know that I
I want to be
Right by your side
Where I ought to be

And you know that I
That I can see
The way that your eyes
Seem to follow me

And I must confess
My interest
The way that you move
When you're in that dress

It's making me feel
Like I want to be
The only man
That you ever see

Whoa oh, oh, oh
I'm in trouble, trouble
Whoa oh, oh, oh
I'm in trouble, trouble
Whoa oh, oh, oh
I'm in trouble now

I see you some places
from time to time
You keep to your business
and I keep to mine

But you know that I
I want to be
Right by your side
Where I ought to be

And you know that I
That I can see
The way that your eyes
Seem to follow me

And I must confess
My interest
The way that you move
When you're in that dress

It's making me feel
Like I want to be
The only man
That you ever see

Whoa oh, oh, oh
I'm in trouble, trouble
Whoa oh, oh, oh
I'm in trouble, trouble
Whoa oh, oh, oh
I'm in trouble now

Ridge

Maggie: Guess who gets to see me tomorrow?

Me: Kurt Vonnegut?

Maggie: Guess again.

Me: Anderson Cooper?

Maggie: No, but close.

Me: Amanda Bynes?

Maggie: You're so random. YOU get to see me tomorrow, and you get to spend a whole two days with me, and I know I'm trying to save money, but I bought you two new bras.

Me: How did I ever get so lucky to find the one and only girl who supports and encourages my transvestite tendencies?

Maggie: I ask myself that same question every day.

Me: What time do I get to see you?

Maggie: Well, it all depends on the dreaded T word again.

Me: Ah. Yes. Well, we shall discuss it no further. Try to be here by six, at least. Warren's birthday party is tomorrow night, and

I want to spend time with you before all his crazy friends get here.

Maggie: Thank you for reminding me! What should I get him?

Me: Nothing. Sydney and I are pulling the ultimate prank. We told everyone to donate to charity in lieu of gifts. He'll be pissed when people start handing him all the donation cards in his honor.

Maggie: You two are evil. Should I bring something? A cake, maybe?

Me: Nope, we got it. We felt bad for the "no gifts" prank, so we're about to bake him five different flavored cakes to make up for it.

Maggie: Make sure one of them is German chocolate.

Me: Already got you covered, babe. I love you.

Maggie: Love you, too.

I close out our texts and open up the unread one I have from Sydney.

Sydney: You forgot vanilla extract, dumbass. It was on the list. Item 5. Now you have to go back to the store.

Me: Maybe next time you should write more legibly and return my texts when I'm at the grocery store, attempting to decipher item 5. I'll be back in 20. Preheat the oven, and text me if you think of anything else.

I laugh, put my phone into my pocket, grab my keys, and head to the store. Again.

•　　•　　•

We're on cake number three. I'm beginning to believe that those who are musically gifted seriously lack talent in the kitchen-skills department. Sydney and I work really well together when it comes to writing music, but our lack of finesse and knowledge when it comes to mixing a few ingredients together is a little pathetic.

She insisted that we bake the cakes from scratch, whereas I would have grabbed the boxed mixes. But it's been kind of fun, so I'm not complaining.

She places the third cake in the oven and sets the timer. She turns around and mouths "thirty minutes," then pushes herself up onto the counter.

Sydney: Is your little brother coming tomorrow?

Me: They're gonna try. They open for a band in San Antonio at seven tomorrow night, so as long as they get loaded up on time, they should be here by ten.

Sydney: The whole band? I get to meet the whole band?

Me: Yep. And I bet they'll even sign your boobs.

Sydney: SQUEEEE!

Me: If those letters really make up a sound, I am so, so glad I can't hear it.

She laughs.

Sydney: How did y'all come up with the band name Sounds of Cedar?

Any time anyone's asked how I came up with the name of the band, I just say I thought it sounded cool. But I can't lie to Sydney. There's something about her that pulls stories about my childhood out of me that I've never told anyone. Not even Maggie.

Maggie has asked in the past why I never speak out loud and where I came up with the name of the band, but I don't like to bring up anything negative that might cause her even the smallest amount of concern. She's got enough to deal with in her own life. She doesn't need to add my childhood issues to that. They're in the past and there's no need to bring them up.

However, Sydney's a different story. She seems so curious about me, about life, about people in general. It's easy to tell her things.

Sydney: Uh-oh. Looks like I need to prepare myself for a good story, because you look like you don't want to answer that.

I turn around until my back is pressed against the countertop she's sitting on, and I lean against it.

Me: You just love the heart-wrenching stuff, huh?

Sydney: Yep. Give it to me.

Maggie, Maggie, Maggie.
I often find myself repeating Maggie's name when I'm with Sydney. Especially when Sydney says things like "Give it to me."

The last couple of weeks have been okay since our talk. We've definitely had our moments, but one of us is usually quick to begin pointing out flaws and repulsive personality traits to get us back on track.

Aside from a couple of weeks ago, when our writing session ended with me having to take a cold shower, two nights ago was probably the hardest time of all for me. I don't know what it is about the way she sings. I can simply be watching her, and I get the same feeling I get when I press my ear to her chest or rest my hand against her throat. She closes her eyes and starts singing the words, and the passion and feelings that pour from her are so powerful I sometimes forget I can't even hear her.

This particular night, we were writing a song from scratch, and we couldn't communicate well enough to understand it. I needed to hear her, and although we were both reluctant, it ended with my head pressed to her chest and my hand resting against her throat. While she was singing, she casually brought her hand to my hair and was twirling her fingers around.

I could have stayed in that position with her all night.

I would have, if every touch of her hand didn't make me crave a little bit more. I finally had to tear myself away from her, but just being on the floor wasn't enough separation. I wanted her so bad; it was all I could think about. I ended up asking her to tell me one of her flaws, and instead of giving me one, she stood up and left my bedroom.

The way she had been touching my hair was a very natural thing for her to do, considering the way we were positioned. It's what a guy would do to his girlfriend if he were holding her against his chest, and it's what a girl would do to her boyfriend if he were wrapped around her. But we aren't those things.

The relationship we have is different from anything I've experienced. Mostly because we do have a lot of physical closeness based on the nature of writing music together and the fact that I have to use my sense of touch to replace my sense of hearing in some situations. So while we're in those situations, the lines become muddy, and reactions become unintentional.

As much as I wish I could admit we've moved past our attraction for each other, I can't deny that I feel mine growing with each day that passes. Being around her isn't necessarily hard all the time, though. Just most of the time.

Whatever is going on between us, I know Maggie wouldn't approve, and I try to do right by my relationship with her. However, since I can't really define where the line is drawn between inappropriate and appropriate, it makes it hard to stay on the right side sometimes.

Like right now.

I'm staring down at my phone, about to text her, and she's leaning behind me, both of her hands kneading the tension out of my shoulders. With as much writing as we've been doing and the fact that I sit on the floor now instead of the bed, I've had a few issues with my back. It's become natural for her to rub it when she knows it's hurting.

Would I let her do this when Maggie was in the room? Hell, no. Do I stop her? No. Should I? Absolutely.

I know without a doubt that I don't want to cheat on Maggie. I've never been that type of guy, and I don't ever want to be that type of guy. The problem is, I'm not thinking about Maggie when I'm with Sydney. The times I spend with Sydney are spent with Sydney, and nothing else crosses my mind. But the times I spend with Maggie are spent with Maggie. I don't think about Sydney.

It's as though times with Maggie and times with Sydney occur on two different planets. Planets that don't intersect and in time zones that don't overlap.

Until tomorrow, anyway.

We've all spent time together in the past, but not since I've been honest with myself about how I feel for Sydney. And although I would never want Maggie to know I've developed feelings for someone else, I'm worried she'll be able to tell.

I tell myself that with enough effort, I can learn to control my feelings. But then Sydney will do or say something or give me a look, and I can literally feel the part of my heart that belongs to her getting fuller. As much as I want it to empty. I'm worried that feelings are the one thing in our lives that we have absolutely no control over.

15.

Sydney

Me: What's taking you so long? Are you writing a damn book?

I don't know if my rubbing his shoulders is putting him to sleep, but he's been staring at his phone for five solid minutes.

Ridge: Sorry. Lost in thought.

Me: I can see that. So, Sounds of Cedar?

Ridge: It's kind of a long story. Let me grab my laptop.

I open up our Facebook messages on my phone. When he returns, he leans against a counter several feet away from me. I'm aware of the fact that he's put space between us, and it makes me feel somewhat uncomfortable, because I know I shouldn't have been rubbing his shoulders. It's too much, considering what's happened between us in the past, but I feel as if it's my fault his shoulders hurt in the first place.

He doesn't really complain about what playing on the floor is doing to him, but I can tell it hurts sometimes. Especially after nights like last night, when we wrote for three hours straight. I asked him to start playing on the floor to help with the fact that things seem to be more difficult when he's on the bed. If I didn't still have such a huge crush on his guitar playing, it might not be as big a problem.

But I do still have a definite crush on his guitar playing. And I would say I have a definite crush on *him*, but crush doesn't even begin to define it. I'm not even going to try to define how I feel about him, because I refuse to let my thoughts go there. Not now and not ever.

Ridge: We had all been playing together for fun for about six months before we got our first real gig at a local restaurant. They needed us to give them the name of our band so they could put us on the schedule. We had never really considered ourselves an actual band before that, since it was all in fun, but that night, we agreed that maybe for local things like the restaurant, it would be good to have a name. We all took turns throwing out suggestions, but we couldn't seem to agree on anything. At one point, Brennan suggested we call ourselves Freak Frogs. I laughed. I told him it sounded like a punk band, that we needed a title with more of an acoustic sound. He got upset and said I shouldn't really be allowed to comment on how music or titles sound, since, well, yay for lame deaf jokes from sixteen-year-old little brothers.

Anyway, Warren didn't like how cocky Brennan was back then, so he said I should choose the name and everyone had to agree on it. Brennan got pissed and walked off, said he didn't want to be in the band anyway. I knew he was just having a Brennan tantrum. He didn't have them often, but when he did have them, I understood. I mean, the kid had virtually no parents, and he was raising himself, so I thought he was pretty damn mature despite the sporadic tantrums. I told the guys I wanted to think on it for a while. I tried to come up with names that I thought would mean something to everyone, but mostly to Brennan. I thought back on what got me into listening to music in the first place.

Brennan was around two years old, and I was five. I've already shared to you all the qualities my parents possessed, so I won't go back into that. But in addition to all their addictions, they also liked to party. They would send us to our rooms at night once all their friends began to arrive. I noticed that Brennan was always wearing the same diapers when he woke up that he wore to bed. They never checked on him. Never fed him at night or changed him or even checked to see if he was breathing. This is probably something that had been occurring since he was an infant, but I didn't really notice until I started school, because I think I was just too young. We weren't allowed to leave our rooms at night. I don't remember why I was too scared to leave my room, but I'm sure I'd been punished for it before, or it wouldn't have bothered me. I would wait until the parties were over and my parents went to bed before I could leave my room and go check on Brennan. The problem with this was that I couldn't hear, so I never knew when the music would stop, and I never knew if they had gone to their bedroom, because I wasn't allowed to open my door. Instead of risking being caught, I would just press my ear to the floor and feel the vibrations of the music. Every night, I would lie there for no telling how long, just waiting for the music to stop. I began to recognize the songs based on how they felt through the floor, and I learned how to predict which songs were coming next, since they played the same albums night after night. I even began to learn how to tap along with the rhythm. After the music would finally stop, I would keep my ear pressed to the floor and wait for my parents' footsteps to indicate that they had gone to their bedroom. Once I knew the coast was clear, I would go to Brennan's room and bring him back to bed with me. That way, when he woke up crying, I could help him.

Which brings me back to the point of this story, how I came up with the band name. I learned how to differentiate chords and sounds through all the nights my body and my ears were pressed against the cedar floor. Hence Sounds of Cedar.

Inhale, exhale.
Beat, beat, pause.
Contract, expand.

I don't even realize how on edge I am until I see the white in my knuckles as I grip my phone. We both remain still for several moments while I attempt to get the image of the five-year-old Ridge out of my head.

It's gut-wrenching.

Me: I guess that explains how you can differentiate vibrations so well. And I guess Brennan agreed once you told him the name, because how could he not appreciate that?

Ridge: Brennan doesn't know that story. Once again, you're the first person I've ever shared it with.

I lift my eyes back to his and inhale, but for the life of me, I can't remember how to exhale. He's a good three feet away, but I feel as if every single part of me that his eyes fall on is being directly touched by him. For the first time in a while, the fear etches its way back into my heart. Fear that one of these moments will be one neither of us can resist.

He sets his laptop on the counter and folds his arms across his chest. Before his eyes meet mine, his gaze falls on my legs, and then he slowly works his eyes up the entire length of my body. His eyes are narrow and focused. The way he's looking at me makes me want to lunge for the freezer and crawl inside.

His eyes are fixed on my mouth, and he quietly swallows, then reaches beside him and picks up his phone.

Ridge: Hurry, Syd. I need a serious flaw, and I need it now.

I force a smile, although my insides are screaming for me not to text him back a flaw. It's as if my fingers are fighting with themselves as they fly over the screen in front of me.

Me: Sometimes when I'm frustrated with you, I wait until you look away, and then I yell mean things at you.

He laughs, then looks back up at me. "Thank you," he silently mouths.

It's the first time he's ever mouthed words, and if he weren't walking away from me right now, I'd be begging for him to do it again.

Heart 1.

Sydney 0.

• • •

It's after midnight, but we finally finish adding icing to the fifth and final cake. He cleans the last of the ingredients off the counter while I secure the Saran wrap around the cake pan and slide it next to the other four pans.

Ridge: Do I finally get to meet the raging alcoholic side of you tomorrow night?

Me: I'm thinking you just might.

He grins and flips off the kitchen light. I walk to the living room to power off the TV. Warren and Bridgette should come home sometime in the next hour, so I leave the lamp on in the living room.

Ridge: Will it be weird for you?

Me: Being drunk? Nope. I'm pretty good at it.

Ridge: No. I mean Maggie.

I look up at him where he's standing in front of his bedroom door, watching his phone, not making eye contact with me. He looks nervous that he even asked the question.

Me: Don't worry about me, Ridge.

Ridge: Can't help it. I feel like I've put you in an awkward situation.

Me: You haven't. I mean, don't get me wrong, it would help if you weren't so attractive, but I'm hoping Brennan looks a lot like you. That way, when you're shacking up with Maggie tomorrow night, I can have drunk, wild fun with your little brother.

I hit send, then immediately gasp. What the hell was I thinking? That wasn't funny. It was *supposed* to be funny, but it's after midnight, and I'm never funny after midnight.

Shit.

Ridge is still looking down at the screen on his phone. His jaw twitches, and he shakes his head slightly, then looks up at me as if I've just shot him through the heart. He drops his arm and runs his free hand through his hair, then turns to walk to his room.

I. Suck.

I rush to him and put my hand on his shoulder, urging him to turn back around. He rolls his shoulder to brush my hand off but pauses, only partially turning to face me with a guarded expression. I step around to his front so he's forced to look at me.

"I was kidding," I say, slowly and very seriously. "I'm sorry."

His face is still tense and hard and even a little disappointed, but he lifts his phone and begins texting again.

Ridge: And therein lies the problem, Sydney. You should be able to screw whoever you want to screw, and I shouldn't give a shit.

I suck in a breath. At first, it pisses me off, but then I focus in on the one word that reveals the entire truth behind his statement.

Shouldn't.

He didn't say, "I don't give a shit." He said, "I shouldn't give a shit."

I look up at him, and his face is so full of pain it's heartbreaking.

He doesn't want to feel like this. *I* don't want him to feel like this.

What the hell am I doing to him?

He runs both of his hands through his hair, looks up at the ceiling, and squeezes his eyes shut. He stands like this for a while, then exhales and drops his hands to his hips, lowering his eyes to the floor.

He feels so guilty he can't even look at me.

Without making eye contact, he lifts an arm and grabs my wrist, then pulls me toward him. He crushes me to his chest, wraps one arm around my back, and curves his other hand against the back of my head. My arms are folded up and tucked between us while his cheek rests against the top of my head. He sighs heavily.

I don't pull away from him in order to text him a flaw, because I don't think he's in need of one right now. The way he's holding me is different, unlike all the times in the past few weeks when we've had to separate ourselves in order to breathe.

He's holding me now as if I'm a part of him—a wounded

extension of his heart—and he's realizing just how much that extension needs to be severed.

We stand like this for several minutes, and I begin to get lost in the way he's wrapped himself around me. The way he's holding me gives me a glimpse of what things could be like between us. I try to push those two little words into the back of my head, the two words that always inch their way forward when we're together.

Maybe someday.

The sound of keys hitting a counter behind me jerks me to attention. I pull back, and Ridge does the same as soon as he feels my body flinch against his. He looks over my shoulder and toward the kitchen, so I spin around. Warren has just walked through the front door. His back is toward us, and he's slipping off his shoes.

"I'm only going to say this once, and I need you to listen," Warren says. He still isn't facing us, but I'm the only one in the apartment who can hear him, so I know he's directing his comment to me. "He will never leave her, Sydney."

He walks to his bedroom without once looking over his shoulder, leaving Ridge to believe he never even saw us. The door to Warren's bedroom closes, and I turn back to face Ridge. His eyes are still on Warren's door. When they flick back to mine, they're full of so many things I know he wishes he could say.

But he doesn't. He just turns and walks into his room, closing the door behind him.

I remain completely motionless as two huge tears spill from my eyes, scarring their way down my cheeks in a trail of shame.

Ridge

Brennan: Gotta love rain. Looks like I'll be there early. I'm coming alone, though. The guys can't make it.

Me: See you when you get here. Oh, and before you leave tomorrow, make sure you get all your shit out of Sydney's room.

Brennan: Will she be there? Do I finally get to meet the girl who was brought to this earth for us?

Me: Yeah, she'll be here.

Brennan: I can't believe I've never asked this, but is she hot?

Oh, no.

Me: Don't even think about it. She's been through too much shit to be added to your list of concubines.

Brennan: Territorial, are we?

I toss my phone onto the bed and don't even bother with a reply. If I make her too off-limits to him, it'll just make him try that much harder with her.

When she made the joke last night about screwing him, she was just trying to add humor to the seriousness of the situation, but the way her text made me feel terrified me.

It wasn't the fact that she texted about hooking up with someone. What terrified me was my knee-jerk reaction. I wanted to throw my phone against the wall and smash it into a million pieces, then throw *her* against the wall and show her all the ways I could ensure that she never thinks about another man again.

I didn't like feeling that way. I probably should encourage Brennan. Maybe it would be better for my relationship with Maggie if Sydney actually started dating someone else.

Whoa.

The wave of jealousy that just rolled over me felt more like a tsunami.

I walk out of my bedroom and head to the kitchen to help Sydney get things together for dinner before everyone gets here. I pause when I see her bent over, rummaging through the contents of the refrigerator. She's wearing the blue dress again.

I hate it when Warren is right. My eyes slowly scroll from the dress, down her tanned legs, and back up again. I exhale and contemplate asking her to go change. I'm not sure I can deal with this tonight. Especially when Maggie gets here.

Sydney straightens up, pulls away from the refrigerator, and turns toward the counter. I notice she's talking, but she isn't talking to me. She pulls a bowl out of the refrigerator, and her mouth is still moving, so naturally, my eyes scan the rest of the apartment to see who it is she's talking to.

And that's when both halves of my heart—which were somehow still connected by a small, invisible fiber—snap apart and separate completely.

Maggie is standing in front of the bathroom door, eyeing me hard. I can't read her expression, because it's not one I've ever been exposed to before. The half of my heart that belongs to her immediately begins to panic.

Look innocent, Ridge. Look innocent. All you did was look at her.

I smile. "There's my girl," I sign as I walk to her. The fact that I'm somehow able to hide my guilt seems to ease her concern. She smiles back and wraps her arms around my neck when

I reach her. I slip my arms around her waist and kiss her for the first time in two weeks.

God, I've missed her. She feels so good. So familiar.

She smells good, she tastes good, she *is* good. I've missed her so damn much. I kiss her cheek and her chin and her forehead, and I love that I'm so relieved to have her here. For the past few days, I began to fear that I wouldn't have this reaction the next time I saw her.

"I have to go really bad. Long drive." She winces and points to the door behind her, and I give her another quick kiss. Once she's inside the bathroom, I slowly turn back around to gauge Sydney's reaction.

I've been as upfront and honest with Sydney as I can possibly be about my feelings for Maggie, but I know it's not easy for her to see me with Maggie. There's just no way around it. Do I compromise my relationship with Maggie to spare Sydney's feelings? Or do I compromise Sydney's feelings to spare my relationship with Maggie? Unfortunately, there's no middle ground. No right choice. My actions are becoming split directly down the middle, just like my heart.

I face her, and our eyes meet briefly. She refocuses her attention down to the cake in front of her and inserts candles. When she finishes, she smiles and looks back up at me. She sees the concern in my expression, so she pats her chest and makes the *"okay"* sign with her hand.

She's reassuring me that she's fine. I practically have to pry myself away from her every night, and then I maul my girlfriend right in front of her—and she's reassuring *me?*

Her patience and understanding with this whole screwed-up situation should make me happy, but they have the opposite effect. They disappoint me, because they make me like her that much more.

I can't win for losing.

• • •

Oddly enough, Maggie and Sydney seem to be having fun together in the kitchen, prepping ingredients for a pot of chili. I couldn't hang, so I retreated to my room and claimed I had a lot of work to catch up on. As good as Sydney is with this, I'm not as skilled. It was awkward for me every time Maggie would kiss me or sit on my lap or trail her fingers seductively up my chest. Which, come to think of it, was a bit odd. She's never really all that touchy-feely when we're hanging out, so she's either feeling a tad bit territorial, or she and Sydney have already been hitting the Pine-Sol.

Maggie comes into the bedroom just as I'm shutting the laptop. She kneels down on the edge of the bed, leans forward, and inches her way toward me. She's looking up at me with a flirtatious smile, so I set the laptop aside and smile back at her.

She crawls her way up my body until she's face-to-face with me, and then she sits back on her heels, straddling me. She cocks an eyebrow and tilts her head. "You were checking out her ass."

Shit.

I was hoping that moment had come and gone.

I laugh and cup my hands around Maggie's backside and scoot her a little closer. I let go and bring my hands back around in front of her and answer her. "I walked out of my room to a rear end pointed toward my bedroom door. I'm a guy. Guys notice things like that, unfortunately." I kiss her mouth, then pull back.

She's not smiling. "She's really nice," Maggie signs. "And pretty. And funny. And talented. And . . ."

The insecurity in her words makes me feel like a jerk, so I grab her hands and still them. "She's not you," I tell her. "No one can ever be you, Maggie. Ever."

She smiles halfheartedly and places her palms on the sides of my face and slowly runs them down to my neck. She leans forward and presses her mouth to mine with so much force I can feel the fear rolling off of her.

Fear that I put there.

I grab her face and kiss her with everything I have, doing all I can to erase her worries. The last thing this girl needs is something else to stress her out.

When she breaks apart from me, her features are still full of every single negative emotion I've spent the past five years helping her drown out.

"Ridge?" She pauses, then drops her eyes while she blows out a long, controlled breath. The nervousness in her demeanor twists around my heart and squeezes it. She brings her eyes carefully back to mine. "Did you tell her about me? Does she know?" Her eyes search mine for an answer to the question she should never even feel the need to ask.

Does she not know me by now?

"No. *God*, no, Maggie. Why would I do that? That's always been your story to tell, not mine. I would never do that."

Her eyes fill with tears, and she tries to blink them away. I let my head fall back against the headboard. This girl still has no idea how far I'll go for her.

I lift my head away from the headboard and look her hard in the eyes. "To the ends of the earth, Maggie," I sign, repeating our phrase to her.

She forces a sad smile. "And back."

16.

Sydney

Someone is removing my clothes. Who in the hell is removing my clothes?

I begin slapping away the hand that's pulling my shorts down past my knees. I try to remember where I am, why I'm here, and how I got here.

Party.

Cake.

Pine-Sol.

Spilling Pine-Sol on my dress.

Changing.

Drinking more Pine-Sol.

Lots of Pine-Sol.

Watching Ridge love Maggie.

God, he loves her so much. I saw it in the way he watches her from across the room. I saw it in the way he touches her. In the way he communicates with her.

I can still smell the alcohol. I can still taste it as I slide my tongue over my lips.

I danced . . .

I drank more Pine-Sol . . .

Oh! The drinking game. I invented my own solitary drinking game, where every time I saw how much Ridge loved Maggie, I downed a shot. Unfortunately, that made for a hell of a lot of shots.

Who in the hell is pulling off my shorts?

I try to open my eyes, but I can't tell if it's working. They feel open, but it's still dark inside my head.

Oh, my God. I'm drunk, and someone is undressing me.

I'm about to be raped!

I start kicking at the hands that are yanking the shorts from my feet.

"Sydney!" a girl yells. "Stop!" She's laughing. I focus for a few seconds and can tell the voice belongs to Maggie.

"Maggie?"

She comes closer, and a soft hand brushes back my hair as the bed dips down next to me. I squeeze my eyes shut, then force them wide open several times, until I finally begin to adjust to the dark. She puts her hands on my shirt and attempts to unbutton it.

Why in the hell is she still taking off my clothes?

Oh, my God! Maggie wants to rape me!

I slap at her hand, and she grips my wrist. "Sydney!" She laughs. "You're covered in puke. I'm trying to help you."

Puke? *Covered* in it?

That explains the massive headache. But . . . it doesn't explain why I'm laughing. Why am I laughing? Am I still drunk? "What time is it?" I ask her.

"I don't know. Tonight, I think. Like, midnight?"

"That's it?"

She nods, then starts laughing with me. "You threw up on Brennan."

Brennan? I met Brennan?

It looks as if her eyes are trying hard to focus on my face. "Can I tell you a secret?" she says.

I nod. "Okay, but I probably won't remember it, because I think I'm still drunk."

She smiles and leans forward. She's so pretty. Maggie is really, really pretty. "I can't stand Bridgette," she says quietly.

I laugh.

Maggie starts laughing again, too, and tries to pull my shirt off, but she's laughing too hard and keeps having to pause for deep breaths.

"Are you drunk, too?" I ask her.

She inhales again, attempting to pause her laughter, and then she exhales. "*So* drunk. I thought I took your shirt off already, but your shirt keeps coming back on, and I don't know how many shirts you have, but"—she lifts the edge of my shirt sleeve, which is still on my arm, and looks at it in confusion—"oh, my God, I really thought I took it off already, and here it is *again.*"

I lift myself up on the bed, then help her pull my shirt off. "Why am I already in bed if it's only midnight?"

She shrugs. "I have no idea what you just said."

She's funny. I reach to the nightstand and turn on the lamp. Maggie scoots off the bed and lowers herself to the floor. She lies flat on her stomach with a sigh and begins moving her arms, making snow angels against the carpet.

"I don't want to go to bed yet," I tell her.

She flips over onto her back and looks up at me. "Then don't. I told Ridge to let you stay up and play because we were having so much fun, but you threw up in Brennan's lap, so he made you go to bed." She sits up. "Let's go play some more. I want more cake." She pushes up on her hands and stands, then reaches for my hands and pulls me off the bed.

I look down at myself. "But you took off my clothes," I say, pouting.

She looks at my bra and underwear. "Where'd you get that bra? It's so cute."

"JCPenney."

"Oh. Ridge likes the kind that clasp in the front, but yours is really cute. I want one."

"You should get one," I say, smiling. "We could be bra twins."

She pulls me toward the door. "Let's go see if Ridge likes it. I want him to buy me one."

I smile. I hope he likes it. "Okay."

Maggie opens the door to my room and pulls me behind her into the living room. "Ridge!" she yells. I laugh, because I don't know why she's yelling for him. He can't hear her.

"Hey, Warren," I say, grinning when I see him on the couch. "Happy Birthday." Bridgette is seated next to him, glaring at me. She's looking me up and down, probably jealous because my bra really is cute.

Warren shakes his head and laughs. "That's only the fiftieth time you've said that tonight, although it's a little more fitting now that you're practically in your birthday suit."

Ridge is sitting on the other side of Bridgette. He's shaking his head like Warren. "Maggie wants to know if you like my bra," I say to Ridge. I pull on Maggie's hand so she'll turn around and sign to him.

"It's a very nice bra," Ridge says, staring at it with a cocked eyebrow.

I smile. Then I frown.

Did he just . . .? I yank my hand out of Maggie's and turn back toward Ridge. "Did you just *speak?*"

He laughs. "Did you not just ask me a question?"

I glare at him hard, especially when Warren bursts out into a fit of laughter.

Oh.

My.

God.

He's not deaf?

This whole time, he's been lying to me? It's been a prank?

I instantly want to strangle him. *Both* of them. Tears sting at my eyes, and the second I lunge forward, a strong hand grips my wrist and yanks my arm back. I turn and look up at . . . *Ridge?*

I turn back to the couch and look at . . . *Ridge?*

Warren is doubled over Bridgette's lap now, he's laughing so hard. Ridge Number 1 is laughing now, too. His whole face doesn't laugh when he laughs, like Ridge Number 2's face does.

And his hair is shorter than Ridge Number 2's hair. And darker.

Ridge Number 2 has his arm wrapped around my waist, and he's picking me up.

Now I'm upside down.

Not good for my stomach.

My face is toward his back, and my stomach is slumped over his shoulder as he carries me back toward my bedroom. I look at Warren and the guy I now realize is Brennan, and then I squeeze my eyes shut, because I think I'm about to throw up all over Ridge Number 2.

I'm being seated on something cold. A floor.

As soon as my mind comprehends where he's put me, my hands reach forward until I grasp the toilet, and then it suddenly feels as if I've eaten Italian food all over again. He holds my hair back while the toilet fills with Pine-Sol.

I wish it really *were* Pine-Sol. I wouldn't have to clean it.

"Don't you love her bra?" Maggie says from behind me, giggling. "I know it's a back clasp, but look at how cute the straps are!"

I feel a hand on one of my bra straps. I can feel Ridge pull her hand away. His arm moves, and I know he's signing something.

Maggie huffs. "I don't want to go to bed yet."

He signs something else, and then she sighs and walks into his bedroom.

When I'm finished, Ridge wipes my face with a rag. I allow my back to fall against the wall of the tub, and I look up at him.

He doesn't look very happy. In fact, he looks a little angry.

"It's a *party*, Ridge," I mumble, and close my eyes again.

His hands are under my arms, and I'm being carried again. He makes his way into . . . *his* room? He lowers me onto his bed, and I roll over and open my eyes. Maggie is grinning at me from the pillow next to me.

"Yay. A sleepover," she says with a groggy smile. She grabs my hand and holds it.

"Yay," I say, smiling.

Covers are pulled over both of us, and I close my eyes.

Ridge

"How did you get yourself into this mess?"

Warren and I are both standing at the edge of my bed, staring down at Maggie and Sydney. They're asleep. Sydney is spooning Maggie on the left side of the bed, because the right side of the bed is now covered in Maggie's puke.

I sigh. "This has been the longest twelve hours of my life."

Warren nods, then pats me heavily on the back. "Well," he signs, "I wish I could stay and help you nurse them back to health, but I'd rather pretend I have something better to do and leave." He turns and walks out of my room as Brennan makes his way in.

"I'm headed out," he signs. "Got my stuff out of Sydney's room."

I nod and watch as his eyes fall on Sydney and Maggie.

"I wish I could say it was fun getting to know Sydney, but I have a feeling I didn't even meet the real Sydney."

I laugh. "Believe me, you didn't. Maybe next time."

He waves and walks out of my bedroom.

I turn and look at them, at both halves of my heart, cuddled tightly together in a bed of irony.

• • •

I spent the entire morning assisting them as they alternated between the trash can and the bathroom. By lunch, Sydney's vomiting had subsided, and she made her way back to her own room. It's late afternoon now, and I'm spoon-feeding Maggie liquids and forcing her to down medicine.

"I just need sleep," she signs. "I'll be fine." She rolls over and pulls the covers up to her chin.

I tuck a lock of hair behind her ear, then run my hand down to her shoulder, where I trace circles with my thumb. Her eyes are now closed, and she's curled up in a fetal position. She looks so fragile right now, and I wish I could wrap myself around her like a cocoon and shield her from every single thing this world has left to throw at her.

I look over at the nightstand when the screen on my phone lights up. I tuck the covers more securely around Maggie and bend forward and kiss her cheek, then reach for my phone.

Sydney: Not that you haven't done enough, but could you please tell Warren to turn the volume down on the porn?

I laugh and text Warren.

Me: Turn the porn down. It's so loud even *I* can hear it.

I stand and walk into Sydney's room to check on her. She's flat on her back, staring up at the ceiling. I sit on the edge of her bed, reach to her face, and brush back a strand of hair from her forehead.

She tilts her face toward me and smiles, then picks up her phone. Her body is so weak she makes it look as if the phone weighs fifty pounds when she tries to text me.

I take the phone from her and shake my head, letting her know she just needs to rest. I set the phone on her nightstand and bring my attention back to her. Her head is relaxed against the pillow. Her hair is in waves, trailing down her shoulders. I run my fingers over a section of her sun-kissed hair, admiring how soft it is. She tilts her face toward my hand until her cheek is resting flush against it. I brush across her cheekbone with my thumb and watch as her eyes fall closed. The lyrics I wrote about her flash through my mind: *Lines are drawn, but then they fade. For her I bend, for you I break.*

What kind of man does that make me? If I can't prevent myself from falling for another girl, do I even deserve Maggie? I refuse to answer that, because I know that if I don't deserve Maggie, I also don't deserve Sydney. The thought of losing either of them, much less both of them, is something I can't bring myself to entertain. I lift my hand and trace the edge of Sydney's face with my fingertips, running them across her hairline, down her jaw, and up her chin, until my fingers reach her lips. I slowly trace the shape of her mouth, feeling the warm waves of breath pass her lips each time I circle around them. She opens her eyes, and the familiar pool of pain floats behind them.

She lifts a hand to my fingers. She pulls them firmly to her mouth and kisses them, then pulls our hands away, bringing them to rest on her stomach.

I'm looking at our hands now. She opens a flat palm, and I do the same, and we press them together.

I don't know a lot about the human body, but I would be willing to bet there's a nerve that runs directly from the palm of the hand, straight to the heart.

Our fingers are outstretched until she laces them together, squeezing gently when our hands connect completely, weaving together.

It's the first time I've ever held her hand.

We stare at our hands for what feels like an eternity. Every feeling and every nerve are centered in our palms, in our fingers, in our thumbs, occasionally brushing back and forth over one another.

Our hands mold together perfectly, just like the two of us. Sydney and me.

I'm convinced that people come across others in life whose souls are completely compatible with their own. Some refer to them as soul mates. Some refer to it as true love. Some people believe their souls are compatible with more than one person, and I'm beginning to understand how true that might be. I've known since the moment I met Maggie years ago that our souls were compatible, and they are. That's not even a question.

However, I also know that my soul is compatible with Sydney's, but it's also so much more than that. Our souls aren't just compatible—they're perfectly attuned. I feel everything she feels. I understand things she never even has to say. I know that what she needs is exactly what I could give her, and what she's wishing she could give me is something I never even knew I needed.

She understands me. She respects me. She astounds me. She predicts me. She's never once, since the second I met her, made me feel as if my inability to hear is even an inability at all.

I can also tell just by looking at her that she's falling in love with me. It serves as further proof that I need to do what should have been done a long time ago.

I very reluctantly lean forward, reach over to her nightstand, and grab a pen. I pull my fingers from hers and open her palm to write on it: *I need you to move out.*

I close her fingers over her palm so she doesn't read it while I'm watching her, and I walk away, leaving behind an entire half of my heart as I go.

17.

Sydney

I watch as he closes the door behind him. I'm clutching my hand to my chest, terrified to read what he wrote.

I saw the look in his eyes.

I saw the heartache, the regret, the fear . . . the *love*.

I keep my hand clutched tightly to my chest without reading it. I refuse to accept that whatever words are written on my palm will obliterate what little hope I had for our *maybe someday*.

• • •

My body flinches, and my eyes flick open.

I don't know what just woke me up, but I was in the middle of a dead sleep. It's dark. I sit up on the bed and press my hand to my forehead, wincing from the pain. I don't feel nauseated anymore, but I've never in my life been this thirsty. I need water.

I stand up and stretch my arms above my head, then glance down to the alarm clock: 2:45 A.M.

Thank God. I could still use about three more days of sleep to recover from this hangover.

I'm walking toward Ridge's bathroom when an unfamiliar feeling washes over me. I pause before reaching the door. I'm not sure why I pause, but I suddenly feel out of place.

It feels strange, walking toward this bathroom right now.

It doesn't feel as if I'm walking toward *my* bathroom. It doesn't feel as if it belongs to me at all, unlike how my bathroom felt in my last apartment. That bathroom felt like *my* bathroom. As if it belonged partly to me. That apartment felt like *my* apartment. All the furniture in it felt like *my* furniture.

Nothing about this place feels like me. Other than the belongings that were contained in the two suitcases I brought with me that first night, nothing else here feels even remotely like mine.

The dresser? Borrowed.

The bed? Borrowed.

Thursday-night TV? Borrowed.

The kitchen, the living room, my entire bedroom. They all belong to other people. I feel as if I'm just borrowing this life until I find a better one of my own. I've felt as if I've been borrowing everything since the day I moved in here.

Hell, I'm even borrowing boyfriends. Ridge isn't mine. He'll never be mine. As much as that hurts to accept, I'm so sick of this constant, ongoing battle with my heart. I can't take this anymore. I don't deserve this kind of self-torture.

In fact, I think I need to move out.

I do.

Moving out is the only thing that can start the healing, because I can't be around Ridge anymore. Not with what his presence does to me.

You hear that, heart? We're even now.

I smile at the realization that I'm finally about to experience life on my own. I'm consumed with a sense of accomplishment. I open the bathroom door and flip on the light . . . then immediately fall to my knees.

Oh, God.

Oh, no.

No, no, no, no, no!

I grab her by the shoulders and turn her over, but her whole body is limp. Her eyes are rolled back in her head, and her face is pale.

Oh, my God! "Ridge!" I crawl over her and reach for the door to his bedroom. I'm screaming his name so loudly my throat feels as if it's ripping apart. I attempt to turn the doorknob several times, but my hand keeps slipping.

She begins to convulse, so I lunge over her and lift her head, then drop my ear to her mouth to make sure she's breathing. I'm sobbing, screaming his name over and over. I know he can't hear me, but I'm scared to let go of her head.

"Maggie!" I cry.

What am I doing? I don't know what to do.

Do something, Sydney.

I lower her head carefully back to the floor and spin around. I grip the doorknob more firmly and pull myself to my feet. I swing his bedroom door open and rush toward the bed, then jump on it and climb over to where he's lying.

"Ridge!" I scream, shaking his shoulder. He lifts an elbow in defense as he rolls over, then lowers it when he sees me hovering over him.

"Maggie!" I yell hysterically, pointing to the bathroom. His eyes flash to the empty spot on his bed, and his focus shoots up to the open bathroom door. He's off the bed and on the bathroom floor on his knees in seconds. Before I even make it back to the bathroom, he's got her head cradled in his arms, and he's pulling her onto his lap.

He turns his head to look at me and signs something. I shake my head as the tears continue to flow down my cheeks. I have no idea what he's trying to say to me. He signs again and points toward his bed. I look at the bed, then look back at him helplessly. His expression is growing more frustrated by the second.

"Ridge, I don't know what you're asking me!"

He slams his fist against the bathroom cabinet out of frustration, then holds his hand up to his ear as if he's holding a phone.

He needs his phone.

I rush to the bed and search for it, my hands flying frantically over the bed, the covers, the nightstand. I finally find it under his pillow and run it back to him. He enters his password to unlock it, then hands it back to me. I dial 911, put the phone to my ear, and wait for it to ring while I drop to my knees next to them.

His eyes are full of fear as he continues to hold her head against his chest. He's watching me, nervously waiting for the call to connect. He intermittently presses his lips into her hair as he continues to try to get her to open her eyes.

As soon as the operator answers, I'm bombarded with a list of questions that I don't know the answers to. I give her the address, because it's the only thing I know, and she begins firing more questions I don't know how to communicate to him.

"Is she allergic to anything?" I say to Ridge, repeating what the operator is asking.

He shrugs and shakes his head, not understanding me.

"Does she have any preexisting conditions?"

He shakes his head again to tell me he has no idea what I'm asking him.

"Is she diabetic?"

I ask Ridge the questions over and over, but he can't understand me. The operator is firing questions at me, and I'm firing them at Ridge, and we're both too frantic for him even to read my lips. I'm crying. We're both terrified. We're both frustrated with the fact that we can't communicate.

"Is she wearing a medical bracelet?" the operator asks.

I lift both of her wrists. "No, she doesn't have anything on her."

I look up to the ceiling and close my eyes, knowing that I'm not helping a damn bit.

"Warren!" I yell.

I'm off my feet and out of the bathroom, making my way to Warren's bedroom. I swing open his door. "Warren!" I run to his bed and shake him while I hold the phone in my hand. "Warren! We need your help! It's Maggie!"

His eyes open wide, and he throws off his covers, springing into action. I push the phone toward him. "It's 911, and I can't understand anything Ridge is trying to tell me!"

He grabs the phone and puts it to his ear. "She has CFRD," he yells hastily into the phone. "Stage two CF."

CFRD?

I follow him to the bathroom and watch as he signs to Ridge while holding the phone in the palm of his hand, away from his ear. Ridge signs something back, and Warren runs into the kitchen. He opens the refrigerator, reaches toward the back of the second shelf, and pulls out a bag. He runs with it to the bathroom and drops to his knees next to Ridge. He lets the phone fall to the floor and shoves it aside with his knee.

"Warren, she has questions!" I yell, confused about why he tossed the phone aside.

"We know what to do until they get here, Syd," he says. He pulls a syringe from the bag and hands it to Ridge. Ridge pulls the lid off of it and injects Maggie in the stomach.

"Is she diabetic?" I ask, watching helplessly as Warren and Ridge silently converse. I'm ignored, but I don't expect anything different. They're in what looks like familiar territory for both of them, and I'm too confused to keep watching. I turn around and lean against the wall, then squeeze my eyes shut in an attempt to calm myself. A few silent moments pass, and then there's banging at the door.

Warren is running toward the door before I can even react. He lets the paramedics inside, and I step out of the way, watching as everyone in the room around me seems to know what the hell is going on.

I continue to back out of everyone's way until my calves meet the couch, and I fall down onto it.

They lift Maggie onto the gurney and begin pushing her toward the front door. Ridge walks swiftly behind them. Warren comes from Ridge's bedroom and tosses him a pair of shoes. Ridge puts them on, then signs something else to Warren and slips out the door behind the gurney.

I watch as Warren rushes to his room. He reemerges with a shirt and shoes on and his baseball cap in hand. He grabs his keys off the bar and heads back into Ridge's bedroom. He comes back out with a bag of Ridge's things and heads for the front door.

"Wait!" I yell. Warren turns to look at me. "His phone. He'll need his phone." I rush to the bathroom, grab Ridge's phone from the floor, and take it back to Warren.

"I'm coming with you," I say, slipping my foot into a shoe by the front door.

"No, you're not."

I look up at him, somewhat in shock at the harshness of his voice as I slip my other shoe on. He begins to pull the door shut on me, and I slap a palm against it.

"I'm coming with you!" I say again, more determined this time.

He turns and looks at me with hardened eyes. "He doesn't need you there, Sydney."

I have no idea what he means by that, but his tone pisses me off. I push against his chest and step outside with him. "I'm *coming*," I say with finality.

I walk down the stairs just as the ambulance begins to pull away. Ridge is standing with his hands clasped behind his head, watching as it leaves. Warren makes it to the bottom of the stairs, and as soon as Ridge sees him, they both rush toward Ridge's car. I follow them.

Warren climbs into the driver's seat, Ridge into the passenger seat. I open the door to the backseat and pull it shut behind me.

Warren pulls out of the parking lot and speeds until we're caught up to the ambulance.

Ridge is terrified. I can see it in the way his arms are wrapped around himself and he's shaking his knee, fidgeting with the sleeve of his shirt, chewing on the corner of his bottom lip.

I still have no idea what's wrong with Maggie, and I'm scared that she might not be okay. It still doesn't feel like my business, and I'm definitely not about to ask Warren what's going on.

The nervousness seeping from Ridge is making my heart ache for him. I move to the edge of the backseat and reach forward, placing a comforting hand on his shoulder. He lifts his hand to mine and grabs it, then squeezes it tightly.

I want to help him, but I can't. I don't know how. All I can think about is how completely helpless I feel, how much he's hurting, and how scared I am that he might lose Maggie, because it's so painfully obvious how that would kill him.

He brings his other hand up to mine, which is still gripping his shoulder. He squeezes both of his hands around mine desperately, then tilts his face toward his shoulder. He kisses the top of my hand, and I feel a tear fall against my skin.

I close my eyes and press my forehead against the back of his seat, and I cry.

•   •   •

We're in the waiting room.

Well, Warren and I are in the waiting room. Ridge has been with Maggie since we arrived an hour ago, and Warren hasn't spoken a single word to me.

Which is why I'm not speaking to *him*. He obviously has an issue, and I'm not really in the mood to defend myself, because I've done absolutely nothing to Warren that should even require defending.

I slouch back in my chair and pull up the search browser on my phone, curious to know about what Warren said to the 911 operator.

I type *CFRD* into the search box and hit enter. My eyes are pulled to the very first result: *Managing cystic fibrosis–related diabetes.*

I click on the link, and it explains the different types of diabetes but doesn't explain much more. I've heard of cystic fibrosis but don't know enough about it to know how it affects Maggie. I click a link on the left of the page that says, *What is cystic fibrosis?* My heart begins to pound and my tears are flowing as I take in the same words that stick out on every single page, no matter how many pages I click.

Genetic disorder of the lungs.

Life-threatening.

Shortened life expectancy.

No known cure.

Survival rates into mid- and upper thirties.

I can't read any more through all the tears I'm crying for Maggie. For Ridge.

I close the browser on my phone, and my eyes are pulled to my hand. I take in the unread words in Ridge's handwriting across my palm.

I need you to move out.

Ridge

Both Warren and Sydney spring to their feet when I round the corner to the waiting room.

"How is she?" Warren signs.

"Better. She's awake now."

Warren nods, and Sydney is looking back and forth between us.

"The doctor says the alcohol and dehydration probably caused her . . ." I stop signing, because Warren's lips are pressed into a firm line as he watches my explanation.

"Verbalize for her," I sign, nodding my head toward Sydney.

Warren turns and looks at Sydney, then refocuses his attention on me. "This doesn't concern her," he signs silently.

What the hell is his problem?

"She's worried about Maggie, Warren. It does concern her. Now, verbalize what I'm saying for her."

Warren shakes his head. "She's not here for Maggie, Ridge. She doesn't care how Maggie's doing. She's only worried about you."

I bury my anger, then slowly step forward and stand directly in front of him. "Verbalize for her. *Now.*"

Warren sighs but doesn't turn toward Sydney. He stares straight at me as he both signs and verbalizes for us. "Ridge says Maggie's okay. She's awake."

Sydney's entire body relaxes as her hands go to the back of her head and relief washes over her. She says something to him, and he closes his eyes, takes a quick breath, then opens them.

"Sydney wants to know if either of you need anything. From the apartment."

I look at Sydney and shake my head. "They're keeping her overnight to monitor her blood sugar. I'll come by tomorrow if we need anything. I'm staying a few days at her house."

Warren verbalizes again, and Sydney nods.

"You two head back and get some rest."

Warren nods. Sydney steps forward and gives me a tight hug, then backs away.

Warren begins to turn toward the exit, but I grab his arm and make him look at me again. "I don't know why you're upset with her, Warren, but please don't be a jerk to her. I've done that enough already."

He nods, and they turn to leave. Sydney looks back over her shoulder and smiles a painful smile. I turn and walk back to Maggie's room.

The head of her bed is slightly raised now, and she looks up at me. There's an IV drip in her arm, replenishing her fluids. Her head slowly rolls across her pillow as her eyes follow me across the room.

"I'm sorry," she signs.

I shake my head, not even remotely wanting or needing any type of apology from her. "Stop. Don't feel bad. Like you always say, you're young. Young people do crazy things like get drunk and have hangovers and puke for twelve hours straight."

She laughs. "Yes, but like *you* always say, probably not young people with life-threatening conditions."

I smile as I reach her bed, then scoot a chair close to it and take a seat. "I'm going back to San Antonio with you. I'll stay a few days until I feel better about leaving you alone."

She sighs and turns her head, looking straight up to the ceiling. "I'm *fine*. It was just an insulin issue." She turns back to face me. "You can't baby me every time this happens, Ridge."

My jaw clenches at "baby me." "I'm not *babying* you, Maggie. I'm *loving* you. I'm *taking care* of you. There's a difference."

She closes her eyes and shakes her head. "I'm so tired of having this same conversation over and over."

Yeah. So am I.

I lean back in my chair and fold my arms over my chest while I stare at her. Her refusal of help has been understandable up to this point, but she's not a teenager anymore, and I can't understand why she won't allow things to progress with us.

I lean forward, touching her arm so she'll look at me and listen. "You need to stop being so hell-bent and determined to have your independence. If you don't take better care of yourself, these brief one-night hospital stays will be a thing of the past, Maggie. Let me take care of you. Let me be there for you. I constantly worry myself sick. Your internship is causing you so much stress, not to mention the thesis. I understand why you want to live a normal life and do all the things other people our age do, like go to college and have a career." I pause to run my hands through my hair and focus on the point I want to make. "If we lived together, I could do so much more for you. Things would be easier for both of us. And when things like this happen, I'll be there to help you so you don't convulse alone on the bathroom floor until you die!"

Breathe, Ridge.

Okay, that was harsh. Way too harsh.

I roll my neck and look down at the floor, because I'm not ready for her to respond yet. I close my eyes and try to hold back my frustration. "Maggie," I sign, looking at her tear-soaked eyes. "I . . . love . . . you. And I am so scared that one of these days, I won't be able to walk out of the hospital with you still in my arms. And it'll be my own fault for allowing you to continue to refuse my help."

Her bottom lip is quivering, so she tucks it into her mouth and bites it. "Sometime in the next ten or fifteen years, Ridge, that *will* be your reality. You *are* going to walk out of the hospital without me, because no matter how much you want to be my hero, I can't be saved. You can't save me from this. We both know you're one of the few people I have in this world, so until the day comes when I can absolutely no longer take care of myself, I refuse to become your burden. Do you know what that does to me? To know that I've put that much pressure on you? I'm not living alone simply because I crave independence, Ridge. I want to live alone because . . ."

Tears are streaming down her cheeks, and she pauses to wipe them away. "I want to live alone because I just want to be the girl you're in love with . . . for as long as we can draw that out. I don't want to be your burden or your responsibility or your obligation. The only thing I want is to be the love of your life. That's *all*. Please, just let that be enough for now. Let it be enough until the time comes when you really do have to go to the ends of the earth for me."

A sob breaks free from my chest, and I reach forward and press my lips to hers. I grip her face desperately between my hands and lift my leg onto the bed. She wraps her arms around me as I pull the rest of my body on top of hers and do whatever I can to shield her from the unfairness of this evil, goddamned world.

18.

Sydney

I close the door to Ridge's car and follow Warren up the stairs toward the apartment. Neither of us said a word to each other on the drive home from the hospital. The rigidness in his jaw said all he needed to say, which was, more or less, *Don't speak to me.* I spent the drive with my focus out the window and my questions lodged in my throat.

We walk into the apartment, and he tosses his keys onto the bar as I shut the door behind me. He doesn't even turn around to look at me as he stalks off toward his bedroom.

"Good *night*," I say. I might have said it with a little bit of sarcastic bite, but at least I'm not screaming, "Screw you, Warren!" which is kind of what I feel like saying.

He pauses, then turns around to face me. I watch him nervously, because whatever he's about to say to me isn't "good night." His eyes narrow as he tilts his head, shaking it slowly. "Can I ask you a question?" he finally says, eyeing me with curiosity.

"As long as you promise never again to begin a question by asking whether or not you can propose a question."

I want to laugh at my use of Ridge's comment, but Warren doesn't even crack a smile. It only makes things much more awkward. I shift on my feet. "What's your question, Warren?" I say with a sigh.

He folds his arms over his chest and walks toward me. I

swallow my nervousness as he leans forward to speak to me, barely a foot away. "Do you just need someone to fuck you?"

Breathe in, breathe out.

Expand, contract.

Beat beat, pause. Beat beat, pause.

"What?" I say, dumbfounded. I'm positive I didn't hear him right.

He lowers his head a few inches until he's at eye level with me. "Do you just need someone to *fuck* you?" he says, with more precise enunciation this time. "Because if that's all it is, I'll bend you over the couch right now and fuck you so hard you'll never think about Ridge again." He continues to stare at me, cold and heartless.

Think before you react, Sydney.

For several seconds, all I can do is shake my head in disbelief. Why would he say that? Why would he say something so disrespectful to me? This isn't Warren. I don't know who this asshole is standing in front of me, but it definitely isn't Warren.

Before I allow myself time to think, I react. I pull my arm back, then make four punches my lifetime average as my fist meets his cheek.

Shit.

That hurt.

I look up at him, and his hand is covering his cheek. His eyes are wide, and he's looking at me with more surprise than pain. He takes a step back, and I keep my eyes focused hard on his.

I grab my fist and pull it up to my chest, pissed that I'm going to have another hurt hand. I wait before going to the kitchen to get ice for it, though. I might need to hit him again.

I'm confused by his obvious anger toward me for the past twenty-four hours. My mind rushes through anything I could have said or done to him that would make him feel this much hatred toward me.

He sighs and tilts his head back, pulling his hands through his hair. He gives no explanation for his hateful words, and I try to understand them, but I can't. I've done nothing to him to warrant something that harsh.

Maybe that's his problem, though. Perhaps the fact that I've done nothing to him—or *with* him—is what's pissing him off like this.

"Is this jealousy?" I ask. "Is that what's making you this evil, wretched excuse for a human being? Because I never *slept* with you?"

He takes a step forward, and I immediately back up until I fall down onto the couch. He bends down, bringing himself to my eye level.

"I don't want to *screw* you, Sydney. And I am definitely not jealous." He pushes himself away from the couch. Away from me.

He's scaring the living shit out of me, and I want to pack my suitcases and leave tonight and never, ever see any of these people again.

I begin crying into my hands. I hear him sigh heavily, and he drops down onto the couch beside me. I pull my feet up and turn my knees away from him, curling into the far corner of the couch. We sit like this for several minutes, and I want to stand up and run to my room, but I don't. I feel as if I'd have to ask permission, because I don't even know if I have a room here anymore.

"I'm sorry," he finally says, breaking the silence with something other than my crying. "God, I'm sorry. I just . . . I'm trying to understand what the hell you're doing."

I wipe my face with my shirt and glance at him. His face is a jumbled mixture of sadness and sorrow, and I don't understand anything he's feeling.

"What is your problem with me, Warren? I've never been anything but nice to you. I've even been nice to your bitch of a girlfriend, and believe me, that takes effort."

He nods in agreement. "I know," he says, exasperated. "I know, I know, I know. You *are* a nice person." He laces his fingers together and stretches his arms out, then brings them back down with a heavy sigh. "And I know you have good intentions. You have a good heart. *And* a pretty good right swing," he says, grinning slyly. "I guess that's why I'm so mad, though. I know you have a good heart, so why in the hell haven't you moved out yet?" His words hurt me more now than the vulgar ones he spit at me five minutes ago.

"If you and Ridge wanted me gone this bad, why did you both wait until this weekend to tell me?"

My question seems to catch Warren off-guard, because his eyes cut to mine briefly before he looks away again. He doesn't answer that question, though. Instead, he begins to prepare one of his own. "Has Ridge ever told you the story of how he met Maggie?" he asks.

I shake my head, completely confused by the direction this conversation has taken.

"I was seventeen, and Ridge had just turned eighteen," he says. He leans back against the couch and stares down at his hands.

I recall Ridge saying he began dating Maggie when he was nineteen, but I keep silent and let him continue.

"We had been dating for about six weeks, and . . ."

Scratch that thought. Can no longer keep silent. "We?" I ask hesitantly. "As in you and *Ridge*?"

"No, dumbass. As in me and *Maggie*."

I try to hide my shock, but he doesn't look at me long enough to even see my reaction.

"Maggie was my girlfriend first. I met her at a fund-raising event for children who were deaf. I was there with my parents, who were both on the committee." He pulls his hands behind his head and leans against the couch.

"Ridge was with me the first time I saw her. We both

thought she was the most beautiful thing we had ever laid eyes on, but, fortunately for me, my eyes landed on her about five seconds before his did, so I called dibs. Of course, neither one of us expected to actually have a chance with her. I mean, you've seen her. She's incredible." He pauses for a moment, then props a leg on the table in front of us.

"Anyway, I spent the whole day flirting with her. Charming her with my good looks and my killer body."

I laugh, but only out of courtesy.

"She agreed to go on a date with me, so I told her I'd pick her up that Friday night. I took her out, made her laugh, took her back home, and kissed her. It was great, so I asked her out again, and she agreed. I took her out for a second date, then a third date. I liked her. We got along well; she laughed at my jokes. She also got along with Ridge, which scored major points in my book. The girl and the best friend have to get along, or one of the two will suffer. Luckily, we all got along great. On our fourth date, I asked her if she wanted to make it official, and she agreed. I was stoked, because I knew she was by far the hottest girl I'd ever dated or ever *would* date. I couldn't let her slip away, especially before I was able to go all the way with her."

He laughs. "I remember saying that to Ridge the same night. Told him if there was one girl on this earth I needed to devirginize, it was Maggie. Told him I'd go on a hundred dates with her if that's what it took. He turned his head to me and signed, 'What about a hundred and *one*?' I laughed, because I didn't understand what the hell Ridge meant. I didn't understand at the time that he liked her the way he did, and I never really understood all the little gems he would spout. Still don't. Looking back on the whole situation and the way he would sit there and have to listen to the punk-ass things I said about her, I'm surprised he didn't punch me sooner than he did."

"He punched you?" I ask. "Why? Because you talked about screwing her?"

He shakes his head, and a look of guilt washes over him. "No," he says quietly. "Because I *did* screw her."

He sighs but continues. "We were staying the night at Ridge and Brennan's. Maggie spent a lot of time over there with me, and we had been dating for about six weeks. I know that's not long in virgin weeks, but it's a damn eternity in guy weeks. We were lying in bed together, and she told me she was ready to go all the way, but before she would have sex with me, there was something she needed to tell me. She said I had a right to know, and she wouldn't feel right continuing a relationship until I was fully informed. I remember panicking, thinking she was about to tell me she was a dude or some shit like that."

He glances at me and raises an eyebrow. "Because let's be honest, Syd. There are some really hot transvestite-looking dudes out there."

He laughs and looks straight ahead again. "That's when she told me about her illness. Told me about the statistics . . . the fact that she didn't want children . . . the reality of how much time she had left. She said she wanted to lay the truth out for me because it wouldn't be fair to anyone who saw something long-term with her. She said the likelihood of her making it to the age of forty or even thirty-five was small. She said she needed to be with someone who understood that. Someone who accepted that."

"You didn't want that responsibility?" I ask him.

He shakes his head slowly. "Sydney, I didn't care about the responsibility. I was a seventeen-year-old guy, in bed with the most beautiful girl I had ever seen, and all she was asking me to do was agree to love her. When she mentioned the words 'future' and 'husband' and not wanting kids, it took all I had not to roll my eyes, because in my head, those were a lifetime away. I would be with a million girls before then. I didn't know how to think that far ahead, so I just did what I thought any guy would do in that situation. I reassured her and told her that her illness didn't matter to me and that I loved her. Then I kissed her, took off her clothes, and took her virginity."

He hangs his head in what looks like shame. "After she left the next morning, I was bragging to Ridge about finally getting to bang a virgin. Probably went into way too much detail. I also mentioned the conversation we had beforehand and told him all about her illness. I was brutally honest with him to a fault sometimes. I told him that her whole situation kind of freaked me out and that I was going to give it two weeks before I broke up with her so I wouldn't look like such a douche. That's when he beat the living shit out of me."

My eyes widen. "Good for Ridge," I say.

Warren nods. "Yeah. Apparently, he liked her a whole lot more than he let on, but he just kept his mouth shut and allowed me to make an ass of myself for the whole six weeks I dated her. I should have caught on about how he felt, but Ridge is a lot more selfless than I am. He would have never done anything to betray what we had, but after that night, he lost a whole lot of respect for me. And that hurt, Sydney. He's like my brother. I felt like I had disappointed the one person I looked up to the most."

"So you broke up with Maggie, and Ridge started dating her?"

"Yes and no. We had a long conversation about it that afternoon, because Ridge is big on sharing his thoughts and shit. We agreed we had to honor the bro code, and it wouldn't really be good for us if he picked up and started dating a girl I had just screwed. But he liked her. He liked her a lot, and even though I knew it was hard for him, he waited until the term ended before he asked her out."

"The term?"

Warren nods. "Yeah. Don't ask where we came up with it, but we agreed twelve months was a decent length of time before the bro code became null. We figured enough time would have passed, and if he wanted to ask her out after a year, it wouldn't be so weird. By that time, she might have dated other people and wouldn't be going straight from my bed into Ridge's. As much as I could have tried to be cool about it, it would have been too weird. Even for us."

"Did Maggie know how he felt about her? During the twelve months?"

Warren shakes his head. "No. Maggie never even knew he liked her like he did. He liked her so much he didn't go on a single date for the entire twelve months I made him wait. He had the date circled on a calendar. I saw it once in his room. He never mentioned her, never asked about her. But I'll be damned if the day that year was up, he wasn't knocking on her front door. And it took her a while to come around, especially knowing she would have to interact with me. But things eventually worked themselves out. She ended up with the right guy in the end, thanks to Ridge's persistence."

I exhale. "Wow," I say. "Talk about devotion."

He turns his head toward mine, and our eyes meet. "Exactly," he says firmly, as if I just summed up his whole point. "I have never in my life met another human being with more devotion than that man. He's the best damn thing that's ever happened to me. The best thing that's ever happened to Maggie."

He pulls his feet up onto the couch and faces me full-on. "He's gone through hell and back for that girl, Sydney. All the hospital stays, driving back and forth to take care of her, promising her the world, and giving up so much of himself in return. And she deserves it. She's one of the purest, most selfless people I've ever met, and if there are two people who deserve each other in this world, it's the two of them.

"So when I see how he looks at you, it pains me. I saw the way the two of you watched each other at the party the other night. I saw the jealousy in his eyes every time you spoke to Brennan. I've never seen him struggle with his choice or the sacrifices he's made for Maggie until you showed up. He's falling in love with you, Sydney, and I know you know that. However, I also know his heart, and he'll never leave Maggie. He loves her. He would never do that to her. So seeing him torn apart because of the way he feels about you and knowing his life is with Maggie, I just don't understand why you're still here. I don't understand why you're putting him through that much pain. Each day you're still here and I see him looking at you the same way he used to look at Maggie, it makes me want to shove you out the damn door and tell you to never come back. And I know that's not your fault. I *know* that. Hell, you didn't even know the half of what he's going through until tonight. But now you do. And as much as I love you and think you're one of the coolest damn chicks I've ever met, I also never want to see your face again. Especially now that you know the truth about Maggie. And forgive me if this is harsh, but I don't want you getting it into your head that the love you have for Ridge will be enough to hold you over until the day Maggie dies. Because Maggie isn't dying, Sydney. Maggie's *living.* She'll be around a lot longer than Ridge's heart could ever survive you."

My head rolls forward into my hands as the sobs erupt from my chest. Warren's arm folds over my back, and he pulls me against him. I don't know who I'm crying for right now, but my heart hurts so much I just want to rip it from my fucking chest and throw it over Ridge's balcony, because that's where this whole mess began.

Ridge

Maggie has been asleep for a couple of hours now, but I've yet to sleep. That's usually how it is when I'm with her in the hospital. After five years of sporadic stays, I've learned it's much easier not to sleep at all than it is to get a half-ass couple of hours.

I open my laptop and pull up my messages to Sydney, then send her a quick hello to see if she's online. We haven't had a chance to discuss the fact that I asked her to move out, and I hate not knowing if she's okay. I know it's wrong to be messaging her at this point, but it seems even more wrong to leave things unsaid.

She returns my message almost immediately, and the tone of it already relieves some of my worry. I don't know why I always expect she'll respond unreasonably, because she's never once shown a lack of maturity or regard for my situation.

Sydney: Yeah, I'm here. How's Maggie?

Me: She's good. She'll be discharged this afternoon.

Sydney: That's good. I've been worried.

Me: Thank you, by the way. For your help last night.

Sydney: I wasn't much help. I felt like I was in the way more than anything.

Me: You weren't. There's no telling what could have happened if you hadn't found her.

I wait a moment for her to respond, but she doesn't. I guess we've reached the point in this conversation where one of us needs to bring up what we both know must be discussed. I feel responsible for this entire situation with her, so I bite the bullet and lay it out there.

Me: Do you have a minute? I really have some things I'd like to say to you.

Sydney: Yes, and likewise.

I glance up at Maggie again, and she's still asleep in the same position. Having this conversation with Sydney in her presence, as innocent as it is, makes me uneasy. I take my laptop and walk out of the hospital room and into the empty hallway. I sit on the floor beside the door to Maggie's room and reopen my laptop.

Me: The main thing I've appreciated about our time together over the last couple of months is the fact that we've been upfront and consistent with each other. With that being said, I don't want you to leave with the wrong idea about why I need you to move out. I don't want you to think you did anything wrong.

Sydney: I don't need an explanation. I've more than worn out my welcome, and you have enough to stress about without adding me into the mix. Warren found an apartment for me this morning, but it isn't available for a few days. Is it okay if I stay here until then?

Me: Of course. When I said I needed you to move, I didn't literally mean today. I just meant soon. Before things become too hard for me to continue to walk away.

Sydney: I'm sorry, Ridge. I didn't mean for any of this to happen.

I know she's referring to the way we feel about each other. I know exactly what she means, because I didn't mean for it to happen, either. In fact, I've done everything I could to stop it from happening, but somehow my heart never got the message. If I know it wasn't intentional on my part, I know it wasn't intentional on her part, so she has nothing to apologize for.

Me: Why are you apologizing? Don't apologize. It's not your fault, Sydney. Hell, I'm not even sure it's MY fault.

Sydney: Well, usually when something goes wrong, someone is at fault.

Me: Things didn't go wrong with us. That's our problem. Things are way too right between us. We make sense. Everything about you feels so right, but—

I pause for a few moments to gather my thoughts, because I don't want to say anything I'll regret. I inhale, then type out the best way to describe how I feel about our entire situation.

Me: There isn't a doubt in my mind that we could be perfect for each other's life, Sydney. It's our lives that aren't perfect for us.

Several minutes pass without a response. I don't know if I crossed the line with my comments, but however she's reacting to them, I needed to say what I had to say before I could let her go. I'm beginning to close my laptop when another message pops up from her.

Sydney: If there's one thing I've learned from this whole experience, it's that my ability to trust wasn't completely broken by Hunter and Tori like I initially thought. You've always been upfront with me about how you feel. We've never skirted around the truth. If anything, we've worked together to find a way to change our course. I want to thank you for that. Thank you so much for showing me that guys like you actually exist, and not everyone is a Hunter.

She somehow has a way of making me sound so much more innocent than I actually am. I'm not nearly as strong as she thinks I am.

Me: Don't thank me, Sydney. You shouldn't thank me, because I failed miserably at trying not to fall in love with you.

I swallow the lump forming in my throat and hit send. Saying what I've just said to her fills me with more guilt than the night I kissed her. Words can sometimes have a far greater effect on a heart than a kiss.

Sydney: I failed first.

I read her last message, and the finality of our imminent good-bye hits me full-force. I feel it in every single part of me, and I'm shocked at the reaction I'm having to it. I lean my head against the wall behind me and try to imagine my world before Sydney entered it. It was a good world. A consistent world. But then she came along and shook my world upside down as if it were a fragile, breakable snow globe. Now that she's leaving, it feels as if the snow is about to settle, and my whole world will be upright and still and consistent again. As much as that should make me feel at ease, it actually terrifies me. I'm scared to death that I'll never again feel any of the things I felt during the little time she's been in my world.

Anyone who has made this much of an impact deserves a proper good-bye.

I stand and walk back into Maggie's hospital room. She's still asleep, so I walk over to her bed, give her a light kiss on the forehead, and leave her a note explaining that I'm heading to the apartment to pack a few things before she's released.

Then I leave to go and give the other half of my heart a proper good-bye.

•   •   •

I'm outside Sydney's bedroom door, preparing to knock. We've said everything that needs to be said and even a lot that probably shouldn't have been said, but I can't not see her one last time before I go. She'll be gone by the time I get back from San Antonio. I have no plans to contact her after today, so the fact that I know this is definitely good-bye is pressing on the walls of my chest, and it fucking hurts like hell.

If I were to look at my situation from an outsider's point of view, I would be telling myself to forget about Sydney's feelings, that my loyalty should lie solely with Maggie. I would be telling myself to leave and that Sydney doesn't deserve a good-bye, even after all we've been through.

Is life really that black-and-white, though? Can a simple right or wrong define my situation? Do Sydney's feelings not count in this mix somewhere despite my loyalty to Maggie? It doesn't seem right just to let her go. But it's unfair to Maggie *not* to just let her go.

I don't know how I ever got myself into this mess to begin with, but I know the only way to end it is to break off all contact with Sydney. I knew the moment I held her hand last night that there wasn't a flaw in the world that could have stopped my heart from feeling what it was feeling.

I'm not proud of the fact that Maggie doesn't make up all of my heart anymore. I fought it. I fought it hard, because I didn't want it to happen. Now that the fight is finally coming to an end, I'm not even sure if I'm winning or losing. I'm not even sure which side I'm rooting for, much less which side I was on.

I knock lightly on Sydney's door, then place my palms flat against the doorframe and look down, half of me hoping she refuses to open it and half of me restraining myself from breaking down the damn door to get to her.

Within seconds, we're face-to-face for what I know is the last time. Her blue eyes are wide with fear and surprise and maybe even a small amount of relief when she sees me standing in front of her. She doesn't know how to feel about seeing me here, but her confusion is comforting. It's good to know I'm not alone in this, that we're both sharing the same mixture of emotions. We're in this together.

Sydney and me.

We're just two completely confused souls, scared of a much unwanted yet crucial good-bye.

19.

Sydney

Be still, heart. Please, be still.

I don't want him to be standing here in front of me. I don't want him to be looking at me, wearing the expression that mirrors my own feelings. I don't want him to hurt like I'm hurting. I don't want him to miss me like I'll miss him. I don't want him to be falling for me like I've been falling for him.

I want him to be with Maggie right now. I want him to *want* to be with Maggie right now, because it would make this so much easier knowing our feelings were less a reflection of each other's and more like a one-way mirror. If this weren't so hard for him, it would make it easier for me to forget him, easier to accept his choice. Instead, it makes my heart hurt twice as much knowing that our good-bye is hurting him just as much as it's hurting me.

It's *killing* me, because nothing and no one could ever fit my life the way I know he could. I feel as though I'm willingly forking over my one chance for an exceptional life, and in return, I'm accepting a mediocre version without Ridge in it. My father's words ring in my head, and I'm beginning to wonder if he had a point after all. *A life of mediocrity is a waste of a life.*

Our eyes remain in their silent embrace for several moments, until we both break our gaze, allowing ourselves to take in every last thing about each other.

His eyes scroll carefully over my face as if he's committing me to memory. His memory is the last place I want to be.

I would give anything to always be in his present.

I lean my head against my open bedroom door and stare at his hands still gripping the doorframe. The same hands I'll never see play a guitar again. The same hands that will never hold mine again. The same hands that will never again touch me and hold me in order to listen to me sing.

The same hands that are suddenly reaching for me, wrapping themselves around me, gripping my back in an embrace so tight I don't know if I could break away even if I tried. But I'm not trying to break away. I'm reciprocating. I'm hugging him with just as much desperation. I find solace against his chest while his cheek presses against the top of my head. With each heavy, uncontrolled breath that passes through his lungs, my own breaths try to keep pace. However, mine are coming in much shorter gasps, thanks to the tears that are working their way out of me.

My sadness is consuming me, and I don't even try to hold it in as I cry huge tears of grief. I'm crying tears over the death of something that never even had the chance to live.

The death of *us*.

Ridge and I remain clasped together for several minutes. So many minutes that I'm trying not to count, for fear that we've been standing here way too long for it to be an appropriate embrace. Apparently, he notices this, too, because he slides his hands up my back and to my shoulders, then pulls away from me. I lift my face from his shirt and wipe at my eyes before looking back up at him.

Once we make eye contact again, he removes his hands from my shoulders and tentatively places them on either side of my face. His eyes study mine for several moments, and the way he's looking at me makes me hate myself, because I love it so much.

I love the way he's looking at me as if I'm the only thing that matters right now. I'm the only one he sees. He's the only one *I* see. My thoughts once again lead back to some of the lyrics he wrote.

It's making me feel like I want to be the only man that you ever see.

His gaze flickers between my mouth and my eyes, almost as if he can't decide if he wants to kiss me, stare at me, or talk to me.

"Sydney," he whispers.

I gasp and clutch a hand to my chest. My heart just disintegrated at the sound of his voice.

"I don't . . . speak . . . well," he says with a quiet and unsure voice.

Oh, my heart. Hearing him speak is almost too much to take in. Each word that meets my ears is enough to bring me to my knees, and it's not even the sound of his voice or the quality of his speech. It's the fact that he's choosing this moment to speak for the first time in fifteen years.

He pauses before finishing what he needs to say and it gives my heart and my lungs a moment to catch up with the rest of me. He sounds exactly as I imagined he would sound after hearing his laughter so many times. His voice is slightly deeper than his laughter, but somewhat out of focus. His voice reminds me of a photograph in a way. I can understand his words, but they're out of focus. It's as if I'm looking at a picture and the subject is recognizable, but not in focus . . . similar to his words.

I just fell in love with his voice. With the out-of-focus picture he's painting with his words.

With . . . *him.*

He inhales softly, then nervously exhales before continuing. "I need you . . . to hear this," he says, cradling my head in his hands. "I . . . will *never* . . . regret you."

Beat, beat, pause.

Contract, expand.

Inhale, exhale.

I just officially lost the war on my heart. I don't even bother verbalizing a response to him. My reaction can be seen in my tears. He leans forward and presses his lips to my forehead; then he drops his hands and slowly backs away from me. With each move he makes to pull apart from me, I feel my heart crumbling. I can almost hear us being ripped apart. I can almost hear his heart tearing in two, crashing to the floor right next to mine.

As much as I know he should leave, I'm a breath away from begging him to stay. I want to fall to my knees, right next to our shattered hearts, and beg him to choose me. The pathetic part of me wants to beg him just to kiss me, even if he doesn't choose me.

But the part of me that ultimately wins is the part that keeps her mouth shut, because I know Maggie deserves him more than I do.

I keep my hands to my sides as he backs away another step, preparing to turn through my bedroom door. Our eyes are still locked, but when my phone sounds off in my pocket, I jump, quickly tearing my gaze from his. I hear his phone vibrate in his pocket. The sudden interruption of both of our phones is only obvious to me until he sees me opening my cell phone at the same time as he pulls his out of his pocket. Our eyes meet briefly, but the interruption of the outside world seems to have brought us both back to the reality of our situation. Back to the fact that his heart belongs with someone else, and this is still good-bye.

I watch as he reads his text first. I'm unable to take my eyes off of him in order to read mine. His expression quickly becomes tortured by whatever words he's reading, and he slowly shakes his head.

He winces.

Until this very moment, I'd never seen a heart break right before my eyes. Whatever he just read has completely shattered him.

He doesn't look at me again. In one swift movement, he grips his phone tightly in his hand as if it's become an extension of him, and he heads straight for the front door and swings it open. I step out into the living room, watching him in fear as I walk toward the front door. He doesn't even shut the door behind him as he takes the stairs two at a time, jumping over the edge of the railing to shave off another half a second in his frantic race to get to wherever it is he desperately needs to be.

I look down at my phone and unlock the screen. Maggie's number shows as the last incoming text message. I open it and see that Ridge and I were the only recipients. I read it carefully, immediately recognizing the familiar string of words she's typed out to both of us.

> Maggie: "Maggie showed up last night an hour after I got back to my room. I was convinced you were going to barge in and tell her what a jerk I am for kissing you."

I immediately walk to the couch and sit, no longer able to support my body weight. Her words knocked the breath out of me, sucked the strength from my limbs, and robbed me of any sense of dignity I thought I had left.

I try to recall the medium through which Ridge's words were initially typed.

His laptop.

Oh, no. Our messages.

Maggie is reading our messages. No, no, no.

She won't understand. She'll only see the words that'll hurt. She won't be able to see how much Ridge has been fighting this for her.

Another text shows up from Maggie, and I don't want to read it. I don't want to see our conversation through Maggie's eyes.

Maggie: "I never thought it was possible to have honest feelings for more than one person, but you've convinced me of how incredibly wrong I was."

I turn my phone on silent and toss it onto the couch beside me, then start crying into my hands.

How could I do this to her?

How could I do to her what was done to me, knowing it's the worst feeling in the world?

I've never in my life known this kind of shame.

Several minutes pass, full of regrets, before I realize the front door is still wide open. I leave my phone on the couch and walk to the door to shut it, but my eyes are drawn to the cab pulled up directly in front of our complex. Maggie is stepping out, looking up at me as she closes the door. I'm not at all prepared to see her, so I quickly step back out of her sight to regain my bearings. I don't know if I should go hide in my room or stay out here and try to explain Ridge's innocence in all of this.

But how would I do that? She obviously read the conversations herself. She knows we kissed. She knows he admitted having feelings for me. As much as I can try to convince her that he did everything he could not to feel that way, it doesn't excuse the fact that the guy she's in love with has openly admitted his feelings for someone else. Nothing can excuse that, and I feel like complete shit for being a part of it.

I'm still standing with the door open when she makes it to the top of the stairs. She's looking at me with a stern expression. I know she's more than likely here for anything other than me, so I take a step back and open the door wider. She looks down at her feet when she passes me, unable to continue the eye contact.

I don't blame her. I wouldn't be able to look at me, either. In fact, if I were her, I'd be punching me right now.

She heads to the kitchen counter, and she drops Ridge's laptop onto it without delicacy. Then she heads straight to Ridge's room. I hear her rummaging through stuff, and she eventually comes out with a bag in one hand and her car keys in the other. I'm still standing motionless with my hands on the door. She continues to keep her eyes focused on the floor as she passes me again, but this time, she makes a quick movement with her hand and wipes away a tear.

She walks out the door, down the stairs, and straight to her car, never speaking a word.

I wanted her to tell me she hated me. I wanted her to punch me and scream at me and call me a bitch. I wanted her to give me a reason to be angry, because right now, my heart is breaking for her, and I know there isn't a damn thing I could say to make her better. I know this for a fact, because I've recently been in the same situation that Ridge and I have just put her in.

We just made her a Sydney.

Ridge

The third and final text comes through when I pull up to the hospital. I know it's the final text, because it's pulled from the conversation I had with Sydney less than two hours ago. It's the very last thing I messaged her.

> Maggie: "Don't thank me, Sydney. You shouldn't thank me, because I failed miserably at trying not to fall in love with you."

I can't take any more. I throw the phone into the passenger seat and exit the vehicle, then sprint into the hospital and straight up to her room. I push open the door and rush inside, preparing to do whatever I can to persuade her to hear me out.

When I'm inside her room, I'm instantly gutted.

She's gone.

I press my palms against my forehead and pace the empty room, trying to figure out how I can take it all back. She read *everything*. Every single conversation I've ever had with Sydney on my laptop. Every single honest feeling I've shared, every joke we've made, every flaw we've listed.

Why was I so damn *careless*?

Twenty-four years I've lived without ever experiencing this type of hatred. It's the type of hatred that completely overwhelms the conscience. It's the type of hatred that excuses otherwise inexcusable actions. It's the type of hatred that can be felt in every facet of the body and in every inch of the soul. I've never known it until this moment. I've never hated anything or anyone with as much intensity as I hate myself right now.

20.

Sydney

"Are you crying?" Bridgette asks without compassion as she comes through the front door. Warren follows closely behind her, but he pauses the second his eyes meet mine.

I don't know how long I've been sitting motionless on the couch, but it still isn't long enough for reality to have been absorbed just yet. I'm still hoping this is a dream. Or a nightmare. This isn't how things were supposed to turn out.

"Sydney?" Warren says hesitantly. He knows something is wrong, because I'm sure my swollen, bloodshot eyes clearly give me away.

I attempt to form an answer, but I fail to come up with one. As much a part of this as I am, I still feel that Ridge and Maggie's situation isn't mine to be sharing.

Luckily, Warren doesn't have to ask me what's wrong, because I'm spared by Ridge's presence. He's barging through the front door, taking both Bridgette's and Warren's attention off of me.

He pushes between the two of them and heads straight for his room. He swings open the door, then comes out through the bathroom seconds later. He looks at Warren and signs something. Warren shrugs and signs back, but I can't follow their conversation at all.

When Ridge responds again, Warren looks directly at me. "What does he mean?" Warren asks me.

I shrug. "I failed to learn sign language between now and the last time we spoke, Warren. How the hell should I know?"

I don't know where my unwarranted sarcasm is coming from, but I feel Warren should have anticipated that one.

He shakes his head. "Where's Maggie, Sydney?" Warren points at the counter toward Ridge's computer. "He says she had his computer, so she had to come by here after she left the hospital."

I look at Ridge to answer but can't deny the fact that jealousy is coursing through me at watching his reaction when it comes to Maggie. "I don't know where she went. All she did was walk in, set your computer down, and grab her things. She's been gone for half an hour."

Warren is signing everything I'm saying to Ridge. When he finishes, Ridge runs a frustrated hand through his hair, then takes a step toward me. His eyes are angry and hurt, and he begins signing with forceful movements of his hands. His obvious anger makes me wince, but his disappointment in me fills me with my own share of anger.

"He wants to know how you could just let her leave," Warren says.

I immediately stand up and look Ridge directly in the eye. "What did you expect me to do, Ridge? Lock her in the damn closet? You can't be mad at me for this! I'm not the one who failed to delete messages I wouldn't want someone else to read!"

I don't wait for Warren to finish signing for Ridge. I walk to my bedroom and slam the door behind me, then drop down onto my bed. Moments later, I hear the door to Ridge's bedroom slam shut, too. The sounds don't stop there, though. I hear things crashing against his bedroom walls, one by one, as he takes his frustration out on any inanimate object in his path.

I don't hear the knock through the sounds coming from Ridge's bedroom. My door opens, and Warren slips inside. He shuts my bedroom door, then leans his back against it. "What happened?" he asks.

I turn my head to face the other direction. I don't want to answer him, and I don't want to look at him, because I know anything I say to him will only cause him to be disappointed in Ridge and me. I don't want him to be disappointed in Ridge.

"Are you okay?" His voice is closer now. He sits down on the bed beside me and places a comforting hand on my back. The reassuring contact from him causes me to break down again as I bury my face in my arms. I feel as though I'm drowning, but I have no fight left to even bother coming up for air.

"You said something about messages to Ridge. Did Maggie read something that upset her?"

I turn my head back over and look up at him. "Go ask Ridge, Warren. It's not my place to tell you Maggie's business."

Warren purses his lips in a tight line, nodding slowly while he thinks. "I kind of think it is your place, though. Isn't it? Does it not have everything to do with you? And I can't ask Ridge. I've never seen him like this before, and frankly, I'm a little terrified of him right now. But I'm worried about Maggie, and I need you to tell me what happened so I can figure out if there's anything I can do to help."

I close my eyes, wondering how I can answer Warren's question with a simplified response. I open my eyes and look at him again. "Don't be angry with him, Warren. The only thing Ridge has done wrong is fail to delete a few messages."

Warren tilts his head and narrows his doubtful eyes. "If that's the only thing Ridge did wrong, then why is Maggie avoiding him? Are you saying that the messages she read weren't wrong? Whatever has been going on between the two of you isn't wrong?"

I don't like the condescending undertone in his voice. I sit up on the bed and scoot back, putting space between the two of us as I respond. "The fact that Ridge has been honest in his conversations with me is not something he did wrong. The fact that he has feelings for me also isn't wrong, when you know exactly how much he's fought those feelings. People can't control matters of the heart, Warren. They can only control their actions, which is exactly what Ridge did. He lost control once for ten seconds, but after that, every single time temptation reared its ugly head, he walked in the other direction. The only thing Ridge has done wrong is fail to delete his messages, because by doing so, he failed to protect Maggie. He failed to protect her from the harsh truth that people don't get to choose who they fall in love with. They only get to choose who they *stay* in love with." I look up at the ceiling and blink back tears. "He was choosing to stay in love with *her*, Warren. Why can't she see that? This will kill him so much more than it's killing her."

I fall back onto the bed, and Warren remains beside me, quiet and still. Several long moments pass, and then he stands and slowly makes his way to my bedroom door. "I owe you an apology," he says.

"An apology for what?"

He drops his eyes to the floor and shifts his feet. "I didn't think you were good enough for him, Sydney." He slowly brings his gaze back to mine. "You are. You and Maggie both are. This is the first moment since meeting Ridge that I don't envy him."

He leaves the room, somehow having made me feel the tiniest bit better and a whole hell of a lot worse.

I continue to lie still on my bed, listening for the sound of Ridge's anger to return, but it doesn't. It's completely quiet throughout the apartment. The only thing any of us can hear is the lingering shattering of Maggie's heart.

I pick up my phone for the first time since I put it on silent and see that I have a missed text from Ridge, sent just a few minutes ago.

Ridge: I changed my mind. I need you to leave today.

Ridge

I pile a few things into a bag, hoping I'll actually need it once I get to her house. I have no idea if Maggie will even allow me to step through her front door, but the only thing I can do right now is be optimistic, because the alternative is unacceptable. It just is. I refuse to accept that this is it.

I know she's hurt, and I know she hates me right now, but she has to understand how much she means to me and how my feelings for Sydney were never intentional.

I clench my fists again, wondering why in the hell I ever had those conversations with Sydney in the first place. Or why I failed to delete them. I never thought Maggie would be in a position to read them. I guess in a way, I just didn't feel guilty. The way I've felt toward Sydney wasn't something I wanted to happen, but the feelings are there, and refusing to act on them since our initial kiss has taken a hell of a lot of effort. In an oddly sadistic way, I've actually been proud of myself for being able to fight it the way I have.

But Maggie won't see that side of it, and I completely understand. I know Maggie, and if she read all the messages, she's more upset about the connection I've made with Sydney than she is over the fact that I kissed her. The feelings I have for Sydney aren't something I'm sure I can talk my way out of.

I grab my bag and my phone and head into the kitchen to pack the laptop. When I reach the counter, I notice a piece of paper peeking out from the computer. I find a sticky note stuck to the screen.

Ridge,

It was never my intention to read your personal stuff, but when I opened your laptop, it was all right there in front of me. I read all of it, and I wish I never saw it. Please give me time to process everything before you show up. I'll contact you when I'm ready to talk in a few days.

Maggie

A few days?

God, please don't let her be serious. There's no way my heart will survive this for a few days. I'll be lucky if I make it through the end of today knowing how I've made her feel.

I toss my bag back toward my bedroom door since I won't need it for a while. I lean forward in defeat and rest my elbows on the bar, crumpling the note up in my fist. I stare down at the laptop before me.

Piece of shit computer.

Why the hell didn't I have a password on it? Why the hell didn't I take it with me when I left the hospital? Why the hell didn't I delete everything? Why the hell did I even write anything to Sydney in the first place?

I've never hated an inanimate object as much as I hate this computer. I slam the screen shut and bring my fist down on top of it with all my strength. I wish I could hear it crack. I wish I could hear the sound my fist makes each time I bring it down forcefully. I want to hear it crushed beneath my fist the same way my heart feels crushed inside my chest.

I stand up straight and pick the laptop up, then slam it down on the bar. I see Warren exit his bedroom out of the corner of my eye, but I'm too pissed to care if I'm making too much noise. I continue to pick the laptop up and slam it against the bar over and over, but it doesn't diminish the hatred I feel for it in the least, and it also doesn't do enough damage to the casing. Warren walks toward the kitchen and heads to a cabinet. He reaches inside and grabs something, then walks over to me. I pause my attack on the computer and look up to see him holding out a hammer. I gladly take it, then step back and bring the hammer down against the laptop with all my might. This time, I can actually see the cracks appear with each hit.

Much better.

I hit it over and over and watch as pieces fly in all directions. I'm also leaving a hefty amount of damage on the bar beneath my mangled computer, but I don't give a shit. Countertops are replaceable. What this computer destroyed of Maggie isn't.

When there isn't much left of the computer to destroy, I finally drop the hammer on the bar. I'm out of breath. I turn and slide down to the floor with my back against the cabinets.

Warren walks around me and sits on the floor in front of me, resting his back against the wall behind him. "Feel better?" he signs.

I shake my head. I don't feel better, I just feel worse. Now I know for a fact that it's not the laptop I'm mad at. It's me. I'm mad at myself.

"Anything I can do to help?"

I ponder his question. The only thing that could help me get Maggie back is to prove to her that there's nothing going on between me and Sydney. In order to prove that to her, I need to not have any interaction with Sydney whatsoever. That's kind of hard with her in the very next room.

"Can you help Sydney move?" I sign. "Today?"

Warren lowers his chin at my request, eyeing me with disappointment. "Today? Her apartment won't be ready for three more days. Besides, she needs furniture, and what we ordered this morning isn't even being delivered until the day she moves in."

I pull my wallet out of my pocket and remove my credit card. "Take her to a hotel, then. I'll pay for her room until her apartment is ready. I need her out in case Maggie comes back. She can't be here."

Warren takes my card and stares at it for several seconds before bringing his eyes back to mine. "This is kind of a shitty move considering this is your fault. Don't expect me to be the one to ask her to leave today. You owe her that much."

I have to admit, Warren's reaction surprises me. Yesterday he seemed to hate Sydney. Today he's acting as if he's protecting her. "I already told her I need her to leave today. Do me a favor, and make sure she gets moved in okay this week. Get her anything she needs. Groceries, extra furniture, whatever."

I'm beginning to stand up when the door to Sydney's room opens. She's walking out backward, pulling both of her suitcases. Warren scrambles to his feet next to me, and as soon as she turns around and her eyes lock with mine, she freezes.

The guilt over what I'm having her do hits me when I see the tears in her eyes. She doesn't deserve this. She hasn't done anything to deserve all that I've put her through. The way it makes me feel to know I've hurt her is exactly why I need her to leave, because I shouldn't care this much.

But I do. God, I care about her so much.

I break eye contact with her and look back to Warren. "Thank you for helping her," I sign. I head back to my room, not wanting to watch Sydney walk out the front door. I can't imagine losing both her and Maggie in the course of a few hours, but it's actually happening.

Warren grabs my arm as I pass him, forcing me to turn and look at him. "You aren't even going to tell her good-bye?" he signs.

"I can't tell her good-bye when I don't really want her to leave." I continue toward my room, thankful that I can't hear the sound of the front door closing behind her when she leaves. I don't know if I could take it.

I pick up my phone and lie down on my bed. I pull up Maggie's number and send her a text.

> Me: I'll give you however much time you need. I love you more than you even realize. I'm not going to deny anything I said to Sydney, because it was all true, especially the parts about you and how much I love you. I know you're hurt, and I know I betrayed you, but please. You have to know how much I've fought for you. Please don't end us like this.

I hit the send button and pull the phone to my chest. Then I fucking cry.

21.

Sydney

"Let me get those," Warren says as he bends to pick up my suitcases. He carries them down the steps, and I follow him. Once we make it to his car, I realize I don't even know where I'm going. I haven't thought this far ahead. As soon as Ridge told me he needed me to leave today, I just packed my things and walked out without even a plan for what I'm going to do for the next three days. My new apartment isn't ready, but I'm wishing I could be in it. I want to be as far away as I can get right now from Ridge and Maggie and Warren and Bridgette and Hunter and Tori and everything and everyone.

"Ridge wants me to take you to a hotel until your apartment is ready, but is there anywhere else you'd rather go?"

Warren is now sitting in the driver's seat, and I'm in the front passenger's seat. I don't even remember our getting into his car. I turn and look at him, and he's just staring at me. The car hasn't even been cranked yet.

God, I feel so pathetic. I feel like a burden.

"It's laughable, isn't it?" I say.

"What?"

I gesture to myself. "This." I lean my head against the headrest and close my eyes. "I should just go back home to my parents. I'm obviously not cut out for this."

Warren sighs. "Not cut out for what? College? Real life?"

I shake my head. "Independence in general, really. Hunter

was right when he told me I'd be better off living with him than on my own. He was right about that, at least. I've been in Ridge's life less than three months, and I've successfully ruined his entire relationship with Maggie." I look out the window, up to his empty balcony. "I've also ruined his entire friendship with me."

Warren cranks the car, then reaches over and squeezes my hand. "Today is a really bad day, Syd. A really, really bad day. Sometimes in life, we need a few bad days in order to keep the good ones in perspective." He lets go of my hand and backs out of the parking spot. "And you've made it this long without having to go back to your parents. You can make it three more days."

"I can't afford a hotel, Warren. I spent my savings on furniture and the deposit for the new apartment. Just take me to the bus station. I'll go stay with my parents for a few days." I pick up my phone in order to bite the bullet and call them, but Warren pulls it out of my hands.

"First of all, you need to stop blaming yourself for what's happening with Ridge and Maggie. Ridge is his own person, and he knows right from wrong. He was the one in the relationship, not you. Second, you need to allow Ridge to pay for this hotel, because he's the one making you leave without a notice. As much as I love the guy, he sort of owes you big-time."

I watch the empty balcony as we drive away. "Why do I feel like I've been taking Ridge's handouts since the day I met him?" I look away from the balcony, feeling the anger building in my chest, but I don't even know who I'm mad at. Love, maybe? I think I'm mad at love.

"I don't know why you feel the way you do," Warren says, "but you need to stop. You've never asked any of us for a single thing."

I nod, trying to agree with him.

Maybe Warren is right. Ridge is just as guilty in this as I

am. He's the one in the relationship. He should have asked me to leave as soon as he knew he was developing feelings for me. He also should have given me more than five minutes to move out. He made me feel like more of a liability than someone he's supposed to care about.

"You're right, Warren. And you know what? If Ridge is paying, I want you to take me to a really nice hotel. One with room service and a minibar full of tiny bottles of Pine-Sol."

Warren laughs. "That's my girl."

Ridge

It's been seventy-two hours.

Three days.

Enough time for me to come up with even more things I need to say to Maggie. Enough time for Warren to let me know that Sydney is finally in her own apartment. He wouldn't tell me which one, but that's probably for the best.

Seventy-two hours has also been enough time for me to realize that I miss having Sydney in my life almost as much as I miss Maggie. And it's enough time to know that I'm not going another day without talking to Maggie. I need to know that she's okay. I've done nothing but pace this apartment since the moment I lost her.

Since the moment I lost both of them.

I pick up my phone and palm it for several minutes, too scared to text her. I'm afraid of what her response will be. When I finally do type out a text, I close my eyes and hit send.

Me: Are you ready to talk about it?

I stare at my phone, waiting for her to respond. I want to know if she's okay. I want to be able to tell her my side. The fact that she's more than likely thinking the worst is killing me, and it feels as if I haven't been able to breathe since she found out about Sydney and me.

Maggie: I'll never be ready, but it needs to be done. I'm home all night.

As ready as I am to see her, I'm also scared to death. I don't want to see her heartbroken.

Me: I'll be there in an hour.

I grab my things and head straight out the door—straight back to the half of my heart that needs the most mending.

•   •   •

I have a key to her place. I've had a key to her place for three years, but I haven't had to ring her doorbell in all that time.

I'm ringing her doorbell right now, and it doesn't feel right. It feels as though I'm asking permission to break through an invisible barrier that shouldn't even be here in the first place. I take a step away from the door and wait.

After several painfully long seconds, she opens the door and makes brief eye contact with me as she steps aside to let me in. I pictured her on the drive over with her hair a mess, makeup smudged underneath her eyes from all the crying, and sporting three-day-old pajamas. The typical heartbroken attire for a girl who just lost all trust in the man she loves.

I think I would rather she looked the way I pictured her than how she actually looks. She's dressed in her typical jeans, and her hair is neatly pulled back. There isn't a smudge of makeup on her face or a tear in her eyes. She gives me a faint smile as she closes the front door.

I watch her closely, because I'm not sure what to do. Of course, my first instinct is to pull her to me and kiss her, but my first instinct probably isn't the best. Instead, I wait until she goes into her living room. I follow her, wishing more than anything that she would turn toward me and throw her arms around me.

She does turn to face me before she takes a seat, but she doesn't throw her arms around me.

"Well?" she signs. "How do we do this?" Her expression is hesitant and pained, but at least she's confronting it. I know this is hard for her.

"How about we quit acting like we're not allowed to be ourselves?" I sign. "This has been the hardest three days of my life, and I can't go another second without touching you."

I don't give her a chance to respond before my arms are wrapped around her and I'm pulling her against me. She doesn't resist. Her arms wrap tightly around me, and as soon as my cheek is pressed against the top of her head, I feel her begin to cry.

This is the Maggie I need. The vulnerable Maggie. The Maggie who still loves me, despite what I've put her through.

I hug her and pull her to the couch, keeping her secured against me as I sit with her now on my lap. We continue to hold each other, neither of us knowing how to begin the conversation. I press a long kiss into her hair.

What I wouldn't give to just be able to whisper all my apologies into her ear. I want her as close to me as possible while I tell her how sorry I am, but I can't do that and sign everything I need to say at the same time. I hate these moments in life where I'd give anything to be able to communicate the same way so many others take for granted.

She slowly lifts her face, and I reluctantly let her pull back. She keeps her palms pressed against my chest and looks me directly in the eyes.

"Are you in love with her?" she asks.

She doesn't sign her question; she only speaks it. The fact that she doesn't sign it makes me think it was too hard for her even to ask. So hard that maybe she doesn't really want to know the answer, so she didn't really want me to understand her question.

I did understand it.

I grab both of her hands pressed against my chest, and I lift them, kissing each of her palms before releasing her hands to answer her.

"I'm in love with *you*, Maggie."

Her expression is tight and controlled. "That's not what I asked."

I look away from her, not wanting her to see the struggle in my eyes. I close them and remind myself that lying won't get us back to where we need to be. Maggie's smart. She also deserves honesty, which isn't at all what I've been giving her. I open my eyes and look at her. I don't answer her with a yes or a no. I shrug, because I honestly don't know if I'm in love with Sydney. How could I be when I'm in love with Maggie? It shouldn't be possible for the heart to love more than one person at once.

She diverts her eyes away and scoots off my lap. She stands and slowly walks the length of the living room and back. She's thinking, so I give her a moment. I know my answer has hurt her, but I know a lie would have hurt her even more. She finally turns to me.

"I can spend all night asking you really brutal questions, Ridge. I don't want to do that. I've had a lot of time to think this through, and I have a lot I need to say to you."

"If brutal questions will help you, then ask me brutal questions. Please. We've been together five years, and I can't let this tear us apart."

She shakes her head, then takes a seat on the couch opposite me. "I don't need to ask the questions, because I already know all the answers. I just need to talk to you now about where we go from here."

I lean forward, not liking where this is going. I don't like it at all. "At least, allow me to explain myself. You can't come to a decision about what happens to us without hearing me out first."

She shakes her head again, and my heart clenches. "I already know, Ridge. I know you. I know your heart. I've read your conversations with Sydney. I already know what you're going to tell me. You're going to tell me how much you love me. How you would do anything for me. You're going to apologize for developing feelings for another girl, despite how hard you tried to prevent that from happening. You're going to tell me you love me so much more than I know and how your relationship with me is so much more important to you than your feelings for Sydney. You're going to tell me you'll do anything to make it up to me and that I just need to give you a chance. You're probably going to be brutally honest with me, also, and tell me that you do have feelings for Sydney but they don't compare to how you feel about me."

She stands and moves to sit next to me on the couch. There are traces of tears in her eyes, but she isn't crying anymore. She faces me and begins signing again.

"And you know what, Ridge? I believe you. And I understand all of it. I do. I've read your conversations. It's as if I was right there, sifting through it all while the two of you were attempting to fight whatever was developing between you. I keep telling myself to quit logging back into your account, but I can't stop. I've read those conversations a million times. I deciphered every word, every sentence, every punctuation mark. I wanted to find the spot in your conversations that proved your disloyalty to me. I wanted to find the moment in your conversations where you became this despicable excuse for a man by admitting that what you felt for her was purely sexual. God, Ridge. I wanted to find that moment so bad, but I couldn't. I know you kissed her, but even the kiss seemed excusable after the two of you had that open discussion about it. I'm your girlfriend, and even *I* began to excuse it.

"I'm not saying what you did is readily forgivable, by any means. You should have asked her to move out the second you felt compelled to kiss her. Hell, you shouldn't have ever asked her to move in if there was even the slightest possibility that you were attracted to her. What you did was wrong in every sense of the word, but what's so messed up is that I feel like I understand it. Maybe it's because I know you too well, but the fact that you're falling in love with Sydney is obvious, and I can't just sit back and share your heart with her, Ridge. I can't do it."

No, no, no, no, no. I quickly pull her to me, wanting the comfort of her to subdue the panic building within me.

She can be heartbroken. She can even be pissed or terrified, but the one thing I won't let her be is okay. She can't just be okay with this.

Tears begin to sting my eyes as I hold her as if my embrace is somehow supposed to convince her of how I feel. I'm shaking my head no, trying to get her not to take this conversation where I'm afraid it's headed.

I press my lips against hers in an attempt to make it all go away. I hold her face in the palms of my hands and try desperately to show her how I feel without having to pull apart from her again.

Her lips part, and I kiss her, something I've done on a regular basis for more than five years but never with so much conviction or fear.

Her mouth tastes of tears, and I'm not sure whose they are, because we're both crying now. She pushes against my chest, wanting to speak to me, but I don't want her to. I don't want to watch her tell me how okay my feelings for Sydney are.

They're not okay. They shouldn't be okay at *all*.

She sits up and pushes me away from her, then wipes her tears. I lean my elbow into the couch and cover my mouth with my trembling hand.

"There's more. There's so much more I need to tell you, and I need you to give me the opportunity to get it out, okay?"

I simply nod, when all I want to do is tell her how hearing her out is the last thing my heart can take right now. She adjusts herself and pulls her legs onto the couch. She wraps her arms around them and rests her cheek on her knee, looking away from me. She's still and quiet and contemplating.

I'm a complete wreck as I sit here and wait.

She unwraps her hands from around her legs and slowly lifts her head to look me in the eyes. "Remember the day we met?" she asks.

There's a faint smile in her eyes, and my panic eases slightly at the pleasantness in her memory. I nod.

"I noticed you first, before I noticed Warren. When Warren approached me, I was hoping he was approaching me for you. I remember making eye contact with you over his shoulder, because I wanted to smile at you so you would know that you caught my eye the same way I caught yours. But when I realized Warren wasn't approaching me for you, I was disappointed. There was something about you that tugged at me in a way that Warren didn't, but you didn't seem to have that same reaction to me. Warren was cute, so I agreed to go out with him, especially since I thought you weren't into me that day."

I close my eyes and soak in her words for a moment. I never knew this. I'm not sure at this point that I *want* to know this. After several quiet moments, I reluctantly open my eyes again and let her finish.

"For the short time I dated Warren, you and I would have these brief conversations and moments of eye contact that always seemed to make you uncomfortable, and I knew it made you uncomfortable because you were developing feelings for me. But your loyalty to Warren was so strong that you wouldn't allow yourself to go there. I always admired that about you, because I knew the two of us would have worked so well. To be honest, I was secretly hoping you would betray his friendship and just kiss me or something, because you were all I thought about. I'm not even sure I was with Warren for Warren. I think I was with him for you all along.

"Then, a few weeks after Warren and I broke up, I began to think I'd never see you again, because you never came for me like I hoped you would. The thought of that terrified me, so I showed up at your apartment one day. You weren't there, but Brennan was. I think he knew why I was there, so he told me not to worry, that I just needed to give you time. He told me about the deal you and Warren made and that you really did have feelings for me but didn't feel right pursuing them yet. He even showed me the date you had circled on the calendar. I'll never forget how that made me feel, and from that point on, I counted down the days until you showed up at my front door."

She wipes away a tear. I briefly close my eyes and try to show her respect by not allowing myself to pull her to me again, but it's so hard. I never knew she came for me. Brennan never told me, and right now, I'm struggling with wanting to let him know how pissed I am that he kept quiet and how much I love him for informing Maggie of how I felt.

"I fell in love with you during that year of waiting for you. I fell in love with your loyalty to Warren. I fell in love with your loyalty to me. I fell in love with your patience and your will-power. I fell in love with the fact that you didn't want to start things out wrong with us. You wanted everything to be as right as it could be, so you waited an entire year. Believe me, Ridge. I know how hard it was, because I was waiting right along with you."

I lift my hand and wipe a tear from her cheek, then let her finish.

"I swore I wouldn't allow my illness to interfere with us. I wouldn't let it prevent me from completely falling in love with you. I wouldn't let it be my crutch to push you away. You were so adamant that it didn't matter to you, and I was so desperate to believe you. We were both lying to ourselves. I think my ill-ness is the thing you love the most about me."

My breath catches in my throat. Those words hurt me more

than any words ever have. "Why would you say something like that, Maggie?"

"I know it sounds absurd to you because you don't see it that way. It's who you are. You're loyal. You love people to a fault. You want to take care of everyone around you, including me, Brennan, Warren . . . Sydney. It's just who you are, and seeing how Warren treated me back then made you want to jump in and become my hero. I'm not saying you don't love me for me, because I know you do. I just think you love me the wrong way."

I run my palm over my forehead and try to squeeze the pain away. My head can't take another second of listening to how incredibly wrong she is. "Maggie, stop. If you're about to use your illness as an excuse to leave me, I won't listen to it. I can't. You're talking like you're about to just give up on us, and it's scaring the living hell out of me. I didn't come here for you to give up. I need you to fight with me. I need you to fight for *us*."

She tilts her head to the side, slowly shaking it in disagreement. "I shouldn't have to fight for us, Ridge. I fight every goddamned day of my life just to survive. I should be able to *revel* in us, but I can't. I'm constantly living in fear that I'm going to upset you or make you angry because you want so badly to form a protective bubble around me. You don't want me taking risks or doing anything that causes me one iota of stress. You don't see the point in my going to college, since we both know my fate. You don't see the point in me having a career, because you think it's better if I just let you take care of me while I take it easy. You don't understand my yearning to experience the things that give people that rush of adrenaline. You get mad when I bring up the idea of traveling, because you don't think it's safe for my health. You refuse to go on tour with your brother, because you want to be the one to take care of me when I get sick. You give up so much of your life to make sure

I'm not having to give up any of mine, and sometimes it's so suffocating."

Suffocating?

I'm *suffocating*?

I stand up and pace the room for several moments, attempting to breathe the air back into my lungs that she's repeatedly knocking out. After I'm calm enough to respond, I return to the couch and face her again.

"I'm not trying to suffocate you, Maggie. I just want to protect you. We don't have the luxury of time like every other couple. Is it wrong that I want to prolong what we have for as long as we possibly can?"

"No, Ridge. It's not wrong. I love that about you so much, but I don't love it for *me*. It always feels as though you're trying to be my lifeguard. I don't need a lifeguard, Ridge. I need someone who is willing to watch me brave the ocean and then dare me not to drown. But you wouldn't be able to let me *near* the ocean. It's not your fault that you can't give me that."

I know it's just an analogy, but she's only using it to make excuses.

"You think that's what you want," I sign. "It's not. You can't tell me you'd rather be with someone who would allow you to risk the time you have left than have someone who would do whatever he could to prolong his life with you."

She exhales. I can't tell if she's admitting I'm right or if she's frustrated because I'm wrong. She looks me square in the eyes and leans forward, then briefly presses her lips to mine. As soon as I lift my hands to her face, she pulls back again.

"I've known all my life that I could die at any moment. You don't know what that's like, Ridge, but I want you to try to put yourself in my shoes. If you knew all your life that you were going to die at any moment, would you be okay with just barely living? Or would you live as hard as you could? Because you're needing me to barely live, Ridge. I can't do that. When I die, I need to know that I did everything I've ever wanted to do, and I've seen everything I've ever wanted to see, and I've loved everyone I've ever wanted to love. I can't just barely live anymore, and it's not in your nature to stick by my side and watch me do all the things I still have left to do in my life.

"You've spent five years of your life loving me like no one's ever loved me. My love has matched yours minute for minute. I don't want you to ever doubt that. People take so much for granted, and I never want you to feel that I took you for granted. Everything you do for me is so much more than I deserve, and you need to know how much that means to me. But there are times when I feel like our devotion to each other is tying us down. Keeping us both from really living. The past few days have helped me realize that I'm still with you because I'm scared to break your heart. But if I don't find the courage to do it, I'm scared I'll just keep holding you back. Holding *myself* back. I feel like I can't live the life I want to live for fear of hurting you, and you can't live the life you want to live because your heart is too loyal for your own good. As much as it hurts me to admit this, I think I might be better off without you. I also think that maybe someday you'll realize you're better off without *me*."

My elbows meet my knees as I lean forward and turn away from her. I can't watch her say another word to me. Every single thing she's saying is not only breaking my heart, but it feels as if it's also breaking the heart *within* my heart.

It hurts so much, and I'm so damn scared, because for a moment, I begin to think there's a possibility that she's right.

Maybe she *doesn't* need me.

Maybe I *do* hold her back.

Maybe I'm *not* the hero to her I've always tried so hard to be, because right now, I feel as if she doesn't even need a hero. Why would she? She has someone so much stronger than I'll ever be for her. She has herself.

The realization that I may not be what she needs in her life consumes me, and my regret and guilt and shame fold in on themselves, completely devouring the strength I have left.

I feel her arms wrap around me, and I pull her to me, needing to feel her against me. I love her so damn much, and all I want right now is for her to know that, even if it doesn't change anything. I pull her to me and press my forehead to hers as we both cry, holding on to each other with all we have left. Tears are streaming down her cheeks as she slides onto my lap.

She mouths, "I love you," then presses her lips to mine. I pull her against my chest as close as I possibly can without crawling inside of her, which is exactly what my heart is trying to do. It wants to embed itself within the walls of her chest, and it never wants to let go.

22.

Sydney

My cable won't be connected until next week. My eyes hurt from reading too much, and maybe also from crying. I finally put a down payment on a car with my leftover student loans, but until I get a job, I can't really afford the gas. I'd better find a job soon, because I'm pretty sure I've fictionalized how great living alone is. I'm tempted to try to get my job back at the library, even if I have to beg. I just need something to keep me busy.

I'm. Freaking. Bored.

So bored that I'm looking at my hands, counting random things that make absolutely no sense to even be counting.

One: the number of people constantly on my mind. (Ridge.)

Two: the number of people I wish would contract a sexually transmitted disease. (Hunter and Tori.)

Three: the number of months since I broke up with my lying, cheating bastard of a boyfriend.

Four: the number of times Warren has checked up on me since I moved out of the apartment.

Five: the number of times Warren has knocked on my door in the last thirty seconds.

Six: the number of days since I last saw Ridge.

Seven: the number of feet from my couch to the front door.

I open the door, and Warren doesn't even wait for me to invite him in. He smiles and slips past me, holding two white bags in his hands.

"I brought tacos," he says. "I was driving by on my way home from work and thought you might want some." He sets the bags on my kitchen counter, then walks to the sofa and plops down.

I close the door and face him. "Thanks for the tacos, but how do I know you aren't pranking me? What'd you do, switch the beef out with tobacco?"

Warren looks up at me and grins, impressed. "Now, that's a genius prank idea, Sydney. I think you might finally be getting the hang of it."

I laugh and take a seat next to him. "Figures, now that I have no roommates to prank."

He laughs and pats my knee. "Bridgette doesn't get off work until midnight. Want to go catch a movie?"

My head sinks into the back of the couch almost as quickly as my heart sinks into my stomach. I hate feeling as if he's only here because he feels sorry for me. The last thing I want to be is someone's worry.

"Warren, you don't have to keep coming by here to check on me every day. I know you're trying to be nice, but I'm fine."

He shifts his weight on the couch so that he's facing me. "I'm not coming by here because I feel sorry for you, Sydney. You're my friend. I miss having you around the apartment. *And* I might be coming by here because I feel a tad bit remorseful for treating you like complete shit the night Maggie was admitted to the hospital."

I nod. "Yeah. You were quite the asshole that night."

"I know." He laughs. "Don't worry, Ridge hasn't let me forget it."

Ridge.

God, even hearing his name hurts.

Warren realizes his slip-up when he sees the change in my expression. "Shit. Sorry."

I press my palms into the couch and stand up, wanting to

escape the awkwardness of our conversation. It's really not a subject I need to be talking about, anyway.

"Well, are you hungry?" I ask as I head to the kitchen. "I just spent hours slaving over the stove to make these tacos, so you'd better eat one."

Warren laughs, walks into the kitchen with me, and takes one of the tacos. I unwrap one and lean against the bar, but before I even bring it to my mouth, I become too nauseated to eat. In all honesty, I haven't slept or eaten very much in the six days since I moved out. I hate knowing that I had a part in causing so much hurt in another person. Maggie didn't do anything to deserve how we made her feel. It's also hard as hell not knowing how things have turned out between the two of them. I haven't asked Warren about it for obvious reasons, because whatever the outcome, it wouldn't change things. But now it feels as if I have this huge, gaping hole in my chest from the constant curiosity. As much as I've wished for the last three months that Ridge didn't have a girlfriend, it's nothing compared to how much I've hoped she could forgive him.

"Penny for your thoughts?"

I glance up at Warren, who's leaning against the counter, watching me think. I shrug my shoulders and set my uneaten food aside, then hug myself and stare down at my feet, afraid that if I look directly at him, he'll know what I'm thinking.

"Look," he says, dipping his head to try to get me to look him in the eye. "I know you haven't asked about him because you know as well as I do how much you need to move on. But if you have questions, I'll answer them, Sydney. I'll answer them because you're my friend, and that's what friends do."

My chest rises with my deep intake of breath, and before I can fully release it, the question spills from my mouth. "How is he?"

Warren clenches his jaw, which makes me think he wishes

he hadn't given me the opening to ask about Ridge. "He's okay. He'll *be* okay."

I nod but instantly have a million follow-up questions to ask.

Did she take him back?

Has he asked about me?

Does he seem happy?

Do you think he regrets me now?

I decide to take it one question at a time, because I'm not even sure his answers will be good for me at this point. I swallow nervously, then look up at him. "Did she forgive him?"

Warren is the one who can't hold the eye contact now. He straightens up, turns around with his back to me, and places his palms flat on the counter. His head hangs between his shoulders as he sighs uncomfortably.

"I'm not sure if I should be telling you this." He pauses for a moment, then turns back around to face me. "She did forgive him. From what he told me, she understood the situation between you and Ridge. I'm not saying she wasn't upset about it at all, but she did forgive him."

His answer completely slays me. I slap my hand over my mouth to muffle my cry, and then I turn away from Warren. I'm confused by my reaction and confused by my heart. I'm immediately consumed with relief to know that she forgave him, but the relief washes away with grief at the realization that she forgave him. I don't even know how to feel. I'm relieved for Ridge and grieving for myself.

Warren sighs heavily, and I feel awful for allowing him to see me react this way. I shouldn't have asked. Dammit, why did I ask?

"I wasn't finished, Sydney," he says quietly.

I shake my head and keep facing the opposite direction while he gets out the rest of what he wants to say.

"She forgave him for what happened with you, but what happened with you was also an eye opener about why they were even together in the first place. It turns out she couldn't find a good enough reason to take him back. Ridge said she's got a lot of life left to live, but she can't live it to the fullest when he's constantly trying to hold her back."

I bring both hands to my face, completely perplexed by my heart now. Just seconds ago, I was grieving because she forgave him, and now I'm grieving because she didn't.

Just three months ago, I was sitting outside on my suitcases in the rain, believing I was experiencing what it felt like to be heartbroken.

God, I was wrong. So damn wrong.

This is heartbroken.

This.

Right now.

Warren's arms wrap around me, and he pulls me to him. I know he doesn't want to see me upset, and I'm really trying my best not to appear that way. Crying about it won't help, anyway. It hasn't helped for the past six days I've been doing it.

I pull away from Warren and walk to the counter, where I tear off a paper towel. I wad it up and wipe my eyes with it. "I hate feelings," I say as I sniffle back more tears.

Warren laughs and nods in agreement. "Why do you think I chose to be with a girl who has none?"

The Bridgette diss makes me laugh. I do my best to suck it up and wipe away the rest of my tears, because, as I told myself before, the outcome of Ridge and Maggie doesn't matter to my situation. No matter how things turn out between them, it still doesn't mean anything for Ridge and me. Things are entirely too complicated between us, and nothing but space and time can change that.

"I'll go watch a movie with you," I say to Warren. "But it better not be a porn."

Ridge

"Give me my damn keys, Ridge," Warren signs.

I calmly shake my head for the third time in five minutes. "I'll give you the keys when you tell me where she lives."

He glares at me hard, still refusing to budge. I've had his keys for most of the day now, and I'll be damned if I'll give them back before he gives me the information I need. I know it's only been three weeks since Maggie broke up with me, but I haven't been able to stop thinking about how everything I've done to Sydney has affected her. I need to know if she's okay. I've gone this long without contacting her simply because I'm not sure what I'll say when I eventually do see her. All I know is that I need to see her, or I'll more than likely never sleep again. It's been more than three weeks since the last time I had a full night's sleep, and my mind just needs reassurance.

Warren sits across from me at the table, and I return my attention to the computer in front of me. Despite the fact that I want to blame my entire past few weeks on computers, I know it was all my fault, so I sucked it up and bought a new one. I still have to rely on a computer for income, unfortunately.

Warren reaches across the table and slams my laptop shut, forcing me to look up at him.

"Nothing good will come of it," he signs. "It's only been three weeks since you and Maggie ended things. I'm not giving you Sydney's address, because you don't need to see her. Now, give me my keys, or I'm taking your car."

I grin smugly. "Good luck finding my keys. They're in the same spot I hid yours."

He shakes his head in frustration. "Why are you being

such a dick, Ridge? She's finally on her own and making a life for herself and doing well, and you want to barge in and confuse her all over again?"

"How do you know she's doing well? Do you talk to her?" The desperation in my question surprises me, because I didn't know until this second just how much I need her to be okay.

"Yeah, I've seen her a few times. Bridgette and I had lunch with her yesterday."

I fall back against my chair, slightly annoyed that he didn't tell me this but relieved to know she's not holed up in her apartment, devastated.

"Has she asked about me? Does she know about Maggie and me?"

He nods. "She knows. She asked how things went with the two of you, so I told her the truth. She hasn't brought it up since then."

Jesus Christ. Knowing that she knows the truth should relieve my worry, but it only intensifies it. I can't imagine what she must think about my lack of communication with her now that she knows about Maggie. The fact that I haven't contacted her at all probably has her believing I blame her. I lean forward and look pleadingly to Warren.

"Please, Warren. Tell me where she lives."

He shakes his head. "Give me my keys."

I shake my head.

He rolls his eyes at our matched stubbornness and pushes himself away from the table, then storms off to his room.

I open my texts to Sydney, and begin scrolling through them as I do every single day, wishing I had the courage to text her. I'm afraid it will be easier for her to shut me out through a text than it would be if I were to show up at her front door, which is why I haven't texted her. Despite the fact that I don't want to agree with Warren, I know that nothing good will come from my contacting her. I know we're not in a place to start a relationship, and seeing her in person would only exacerbate how much I miss her. However, knowing what I should do and abiding by what I should do are two completely different things.

•   •   •

My light flicks on. Seconds later, my shoulders are being violently shaken. I smile through the grogginess, knowing by Warren's presence alone that I've got him right where I want him. I turn over and look up at him.

"Something wrong?" I sign.

"Where are they?"

"Where are what?"

"My condoms, Ridge. Where the hell did you hide my condoms?"

I knew that if stealing his keys didn't work, then stealing his condoms would. I'm just glad he thought to put on shorts before leaving Bridgette in his bed and storming into my room.

"You want your condoms?" I sign. "Tell me where she lives."

Warren runs his palms over his face, and from the looks of it, I think he's groaning. "Forget it. I'll go to the store and buy new ones."

Before he turns to walk out of my room, I sit up on the bed. "How do you plan on driving to the store? I have your keys, remember?"

He pauses for a second, and then his face relaxes when he's hit with a new epiphany. "I'll take Bridgette's car."

"Good luck finding *her* keys."

Warren stares at me hard for several seconds, then finally slumps his shoulders and turns toward my dresser. He grabs a pen and paper and writes something down, wads it up, and throws it at me. "Here's her address, asshole. Now, give me my keys."

I unfold the paper and double-check to make sure he actually wrote an address down. I reach behind my nightstand, and grab his box of condoms, and toss it to him.

"That should do you for now. I'll tell you where your keys are after I confirm that this is really her address."

Warren pulls one of the condoms out of the box and tosses it at me.

"Take this with you when you go, because that's definitely her address." He turns and leaves the room, and no sooner is he gone than I'm up and dressed and heading out the front door.

I don't even know what time it is.

I don't even care.

23.

Sydney

Sound triggers.

They happen a lot, but mostly when I hear certain songs. Especially songs Hunter and I both loved. If I listen to a song during a particularly depressing period, then hear it later on down the road, it brings back all the old feelings associated with that song. There are songs I used to love that now I absolutely refuse to listen to. They trigger memories and feelings I don't want to experience again.

My text tone has become one of those sound triggers.

Namely, Ridge's text tone. It's very distinct, a snippet from the demo of our song "Maybe Someday." I assigned it to him after I heard the song for the first time. I'd like to say that sound trigger is a negative one, but I'm not so sure it is. The kiss I experienced with him during the song certainly led to negative feelings of guilt, but the kiss itself still turns my heart into a hot mess just thinking about it. And I think about it a lot. Way more than I should.

In fact, I'm thinking about it right now as the snippet of our song pours from the speakers of my cell phone, indicating that I'm receiving a text.

From Ridge.

I honestly never expected to hear this sound again.

I roll over on my bed and stretch my arm to the nightstand, my now-trembling fingers grasping at my phone. Knowing that I've received a text from him has once again wreaked havoc with my organs, and they've forgotten how to function properly. I pull the phone to my chest and close my eyes, too nervous to read his words.

Beat, beat, pause.
Contract, expand.
Inhale, exhale.

I slowly open my eyes and hold up the phone, then unlock the screen.

Ridge: Are you home?

Am I home?

Why would he care if I were home? He doesn't even know where I live. Besides, he made it pretty clear where his heart's loyalty resided when he told me to move out three weeks ago.

But I *am* home, and despite my better judgment, I want him to know I'm home. I'm tempted to respond with my address and tell him to come find out for himself whether or not I'm home.

Instead, I go with something safer. Something less telling.

Me: Yes.

I pull the covers off and sit up on the edge of the bed, watching my phone, too afraid even to blink.

Ridge: You're not answering the door. Am I at the wrong apartment?

Oh, God.

I *hope* he's at the wrong apartment. Or maybe I hope he's at the *right* apartment. I can't really tell, because I'm happy he's here, but I'm pissed off that he's here.

These conflicting feelings are exhausting.

I stand and run out of my bedroom, straight to my front door. I peer through the peephole, and sure enough, he's at my front door.

Me: You're outside my door, so yeah. Right apartment.

I look out the peephole again after hitting send, and he's standing with his palm flat against the door, staring at his phone. Seeing the pained expression on his face and knowing it derives from the battle his heart is going through makes me want to swing open the door and throw my arms around him. I close my eyes and press my forehead to the door in order to give myself time to think before making any rash decisions. My heart is being pulled toward him, and I can't think of anything I want more right now than to open this door.

However, I also know that opening the door won't do either of us any good. He just broke up with Maggie a matter of weeks ago, so if he's here for me, he can turn right around and leave. There's no way anything could work between us when I know he's still heartbroken over someone else. I deserve more than what he can give me right now. I've been through too much this year to let someone screw with my heart like this.

He shouldn't be here.

Ridge: Can I come in?

I turn until my back is pressed against the door. I clutch the phone to my chest and squeeze my eyes shut. I don't want to read his words. I don't want to see his face. Everything about him makes me lose sight of what's important, what's best for me. He isn't what's best for my life right now, especially considering what he's gone through in his own life, and I should walk away from this door and not let him in.

But everything in me wants to let him in.

"Please, Sydney."

The words are almost an inaudible whisper through the other side of the door, but I definitely heard them. Every single part of me heard them. The desperation in his voice, combined with the simple fact that he spoke, completely slays me. I allow my heart to make my decision for me this time as I slowly face the door. I turn the lock and slide the latch loose, then open the door.

I can't describe what it feels like to see him standing in front of me again without using the term *terrifying*.

Everything about the way he makes me feel is absolutely terrifying. The way my heart wants to be held by him is terrifying. The way my knees seem to forget how to hold me up is terrifying. The way my mouth wants to be claimed by his is terrifying.

I do my best to hide what his presence does to me by turning away from him and walking toward the living room.

I don't know why I'm trying to hide my reaction from him, but isn't that what people do? We try so hard to hide everything we're really feeling from those who probably need to know our true feelings the most. People try to bottle up their emotions, as if it's somehow wrong to have natural reactions to life.

My natural reaction in this moment is to turn and hug him, regardless of the reason he's here. My arms want to be around him, my face wants to be pressed against his chest, my back wants to be cradled by him—yet I'm standing here trying to pretend that's the last thing I need from him.

Why?

I inhale a calming breath, then turn around when I hear him close the front door behind him. I lift my eyes to meet his, and he's standing several feet in front of me, watching me. I can tell by the tightness in his expression that he's doing exactly what I'm doing. He's holding back everything he's feeling for the sake of . . . what?

Pride?

Fear?

The one thing I've always admired about my relationship with Ridge is that we're so honest and real with each other. I've always been able to say exactly what I was thinking, and so has he. I don't like this shift we've made.

I try to smile at him, but I'm not sure if my smile is working right now. I speak to him and enunciate clearly so he can read my lips. "Are you here because you need a flaw?"

He laughs and exhales at the same time, relieved that I'm not angry.

I'm *not* angry. I've never been mad at him. The decisions he's made during the time he's known me aren't decisions I can hold against him. The only thing I hold against him is the night he kissed me and ruined me for every other kiss I'll ever experience.

I take a seat on the couch and look up at him. "Are you okay?" I ask.

He sighs, and I quickly look away. It's hard enough being in the same room as him right now, but even harder to make eye contact with him. He completes the walk into the living room and sits on the couch next to me.

I debated buying more furniture, but one couch was all I could afford. A love seat at that. I'm not so sure I'm sad about my lack of furniture, though, because his leg is touching my thigh, and the simple contact causes heat to roll through me like a riptide. I look down at our knees when they brush together and realize I'm still wearing the T-shirt I threw on right before I went to bed. I guess I was so shocked by the fact that he said he was at my apartment door that I didn't concern myself with how I looked. I'm in nothing but an oversized cotton T-shirt that falls to my knees, and my hair is more than likely a wreck.

He's in jeans and a gray Sounds of Cedar T-shirt. I would say I feel underdressed, but I'm actually dressed appropriately for what I was doing before he showed up, which was going to bed.

Ridge: I don't know if I'm okay. Are you okay?

I forgot I even asked him a question for a second.

I shrug. I'm sure I will be fine, but I'm not going to lie and tell him I am. I think it's obvious that neither one of us can really be okay with how everything has turned out. I'm not okay with losing Ridge, and Ridge isn't okay with losing Maggie.

Me: I'm sorry about Maggie. I feel awful. She'll come around, though. Five years is a lot to give up for a misunderstanding.

I hit send and finally look up at him. He reads the text, then eyes me. The concentration in his expression makes the breath catch in my lungs.

Ridge: It wasn't a misunderstanding, Sydney. She understood a little too well.

I read his text several times, wishing he would expand on it. *What* wasn't a misunderstanding? The reason they broke up? His feelings for me? Rather than ask him what he means, I cut to the question I want the answer to the most.

Me: Why are you here?

He works his jaw back and forth before responding.

Ridge: Do you want me to leave?

I look at him and slowly shake my head no. Then I pause and shake my head yes. Then I pause again and just shrug. He smiles endearingly, completely understanding my confusion.

Me: I guess whether or not I want you here depends on why you're here. Are you here because you need me to try to help you win back Maggie? Are you here because you miss me? Are you here because you want to try to work out some sort of friendship?

Ridge: Would I be wrong if I answered none of the above? I don't know why I'm here. Part of me misses you so much it hurts, while part of me wishes I never even met you to begin with. I guess today is one of the days I was hurting, so I stole Warren's keys and forced him to give me your address. I didn't think this through or come up with any kind of speech. I just did what my heart needed me to do, which was to see you.

His brutally honest reply melts my heart and pisses me off all at the same time.

Me: What about tomorrow? What if tomorrow is one of the days you wished you never met me? What am I supposed to do then?

The intensity in his stare is unnerving. Maybe he's trying to gauge if that was an angry response. I'm not sure if it was or not. I'm not sure how I feel about the fact that he doesn't even know why he's here.

He doesn't respond to my text, and it proves one thing: he's having the same internal conflict with himself that I've been having.

He wants to be with me, but he doesn't.

He wants to love me, but he doesn't know if he should.

He wants to see me, but he knows he shouldn't.

He wants to kiss me, but it would hurt just as much as it did the first time he kissed me and had to walk away. I suddenly feel uncomfortable staring at him. We're way too close together on this couch, yet my body is making it very clear to me that it doesn't think we're close enough at all. What it's wishing would happen right now are all the things that aren't.

Ridge looks away and slowly scans my apartment for a few moments, then returns his attention to his phone.

Ridge: I like your place. Good neighborhood. Seems safe.

I almost laugh at his text and the casual conversation he's trying to make, because I know we're no longer in a place for casual conversation. We can't be friends at this point. We also can't be together with so much against us. Casual conversation has no place between us right now, yet I can't bring myself to reply any differently.

Me: I like it here. Thank you for helping me out with the hotel until I could move in.

Ridge: It was the least I could do. Absolutely the least I could do.

Me: I'll pay you back as soon as I get my first paycheck. I got my job back at the campus library, so it should only be another week.

Ridge: Sydney, stop. I don't even want you to offer.

I have no idea what to say in response. This whole situation is awkward and uncomfortable, because we're both dancing around all the things we wish we had the courage to do and say.

I set my phone facedown on the couch. I want him to know that I need a break. I don't like that we aren't being us.

He takes the hint and lays his phone down on the armrest

beside him, then sighs heavily as he drops his head against the back of the couch. The silence makes me wish I could experience the world from his perspective for once. I find it almost impossible to put myself in his shoes, though. People with the advantage of hearing take so much for granted, and I've never understood that to the extent that I understand it now. There's nothing being spoken between us, yet I understand by his heavy sigh that he's frustrated with himself. I understand how much he's holding back by the way his breaths are being sharply pulled in.

I suppose his expertise in a silent world gives him an ability to read people, just in different ways. Instead of focusing on the sounds of my breaths, he focuses on the rise and fall of my chest. Rather than listening to quiet sighs, he more than likely watches my eyes, my hands, my posture. Maybe that's why his face is tilted toward mine now, because he wants to see me and get a feel for what's going through my head.

I feel as if he reads me too well. The way he's watching me forces me to try to control every facial expression and every breath. I close my eyes and lean my head back, knowing he's staring, trying to get a sense of where I am.

I also wish I could just turn to him and tell him. I want to tell him how much I've missed him. I want to tell him how much he means to me. I want to tell him how horrible I feel, because before I showed up in his life, everything seemed perfect for him. I want to tell him that even though we both regretted it, that minute we spent kissing was the one minute out of my entire life that I wouldn't trade for the world.

At moments like these, I'm thankful he *can't* hear me, or there would have been so many things spoken that I would regret.

Instead, there are so many things left unsaid that I wish I had the courage to say.

Ridge's weight shifts on the couch, and my eyes naturally

open out of curiosity. He's leaning across the arm of the couch, reaching for something. When he turns back around, he's holding a pen in his hand. He smiles softly, then picks up my arm. He turns his body toward mine and presses the pen to my open palm.

I swallow hard and slowly look up at his face, but he's looking down at my hand as he writes. I could swear I almost see a faint smile flash across his lips. When he's finished, he brings my palm to his mouth and blows softly to dry the ink. His lips are moist and puckered into a pout, and holy hell, it just got really warm in this apartment. He lowers my hand, and I look down at it.

Just wanted to touch your hand.

I laugh softly. Mostly because his words are so innocent and sweet compared to the things he's written on me in the past. I've been sitting here on this couch with him for ten minutes, wishing he would touch me, and then he goes and admits he was thinking the exact same thing. It's so juvenile, as if we're teenagers. I'm almost embarrassed that it pleases me this much that he's touching me, but I can't recall a time I've ever wanted anything more.

He hasn't released my hand yet, and I'm still looking down at his writing, smiling. I brush my thumb across the back of his hand, and he gasps quietly. The permission I just gave him with that tiny movement seems to have broken some invisible barrier, because he immediately slides his hand over mine and presses our palms together, then intertwines our fingers. The warmth of his hand doesn't come close to the warmth that just shot through my entire body.

God, if just holding hands with him feels this intense, I can't imagine what everything else with him would feel like.

We're both watching our hands now, feeling every bit of the connection pulsating through our palms. He brushes over my thumb and flips our hands over, then takes the pen and presses it to my wrist. He moves the pen slowly up my wrist, drawing in a straight line all the way up my forearm. I don't stop him. I simply watch him. When he reaches the crease in my elbow, he begins to write again. I read each word as he writes it.

Just an excuse to touch you here, too.

Without releasing my hand, he lifts my arm and keeps his eyes focused on mine as he bends forward and blows softly up and down my arm. He presses his lips lightly against his words and kisses them without once breaking eye contact. When his lips meet my arm, I feel a soft flick of his tongue tease my arm for a split second before his mouth closes over my skin.

That might have just made me whimper.

Yep. Pretty sure I just whimpered.

God, I'm so glad he couldn't hear that.

He pulls his lips away from my arm and continues to watch me, gauging my reaction. His eyes are dark and piercing, and they're focused all over me. On my lips, on my eyes, on my neck, on my hair, on my chest. He can't seem to take me in fast enough.

He presses the pen against my skin again, starting where he left off. He rolls the pen slowly up my arm, watching it intently the whole time. When he reaches the sleeve of my T-shirt, he pushes it up carefully until my shoulder is exposed. He makes a small mark with the pen, then slowly leans over me. My head falls back against the couch when I feel his lips meet my skin. His breath is close and warm against my shoulder. I'm not even thinking about the fact that he's drawing all over me. That can be washed off later. Right now, I just want his pen to keep going and going until it's completely out of ink.

He pulls away and releases my hand, switching the pen to his other hand. He pulls my sleeve back down over my shoulder, then slips his fingers inside the collar of my T-shirt, tugging it to expose more of my collarbone. He puts the tip of the pen on my shoulder and glances up at me while he proceeds with caution, making his way to my neck. His expression is heated, and I can tell he's proceeding with caution despite the fact that I know exactly what he wishes were happening right now and where he plans to go with this pen. He doesn't have to verbalize it when his eyes clearly state it for him.

He moves the pen slowly up my neck. I naturally tilt my head to the side, and as soon as I do, I hear a rush of air hiss quietly through his teeth. He comes to a stop just below my ear. I squeeze my eyes shut and hope my heart doesn't explode when he leans in, because it definitely feels as if it could. His lips press gently against my skin, and I swear the room flips upside down.

Or maybe that was just my heart.

One of my hands slides up his arm and grasps the back of his head, not wanting him to pull away from this spot. His tongue makes another quick appearance against my neck, but he doesn't let my desperation stall him. He lifts away and looks back down at me. His eyes are smiling, knowing how crazy he's driving me.

He rolls the pen from the spot below my ear, back down my neck, and around to the dip in the base of my throat. Before kissing the spot he just marked, he grabs me by the waist and lifts me up, sliding me onto his lap.

I grasp his arms and suck in a rush of air the second he pulls me against him. My T-shirt slides up my thighs, and the fact that I'm not wearing anything under it except underwear pretty much guarantees that I've gotten myself into something that's going to be damn hard to pull away from.

His eyes drop to the base of my throat as he slides a hand up my thigh, over my hip, and all the way up and into my hair. He grasps the back of my head, then pulls my neck against his mouth. This kiss is harder and not at all cautious like the rest of them. I slide my hands into his hair and keep his mouth pressed against my neck.

He works his kisses all the way up my neck until his mouth meets my chin. Our bodies are meshed firmly together, and one of his hands has found my lower back and is keeping me flush against him.

I can't move. I'm literally panting for breath, wondering where in the hell the strong Sydney went. Where's the Sydney who knows this shouldn't be happening?

I'll look for her later. After he finishes with his pen.

He pulls away when his lips come close to my mouth. Our bodies are as close as they can get without his mouth being on mine. He removes his hand from my lower back and brings the pen back around to my throat. When he touches the tip of it to my skin, I gulp, anticipating which direction he's about to go with it.

North or south, north or south. I don't really care.

He begins to scroll upward, but then he stops. He pulls the pen away from my neck and shakes it, then touches it to my neck again. He makes another movement upward with the pen but stops again. He pulls back slightly and frowns at the pen, which I'm assuming has just run out of ink. He looks back at me and tosses the pen over my shoulder. I hear it land on the floor behind me.

His eyes drop to my lips, which I'm assuming would have been the pen's final destination. We're both breathing heavily, knowing exactly what's about to come next. What we're about to experience again for the second time, knowing how much our first kiss affected us.

I think he's as terrified as I am right now.

I'm leaning all my weight into him, because I've never been this weak. I can't think, I can't move, I can't breathe. I just . . . *need*.

He brings both hands to my cheeks and looks directly into my eyes.

"Your call," he whispers.

Jesus Christ, that voice.

I stare at him, not sure if I like that he just put the control in my hands. He wants this to be my decision.

It's so much easier having someone else to blame when things go where they shouldn't. I know we shouldn't be putting ourselves into a situation we're only going to regret once it's over. I could put a stop to it right here. I could make it easier by asking him to leave now, rather than when things get even more complicated between us. I could slide off his lap and tell him he shouldn't be here because he hasn't even had time to forgive himself for what happened with Maggie. I could tell him to go away and not come back until his heart isn't confused anymore about who it wants.

If that day ever comes.

There are so many things I could and should and need to do, but none of them is what I *want* to do.

The pressure picks the worst possible time to break me. The *worst* possible time.

I squeeze my eyes shut when I feel a tear begin to work its way out. It trickles down my cheek, falling slowly toward my jaw. It's the absolutely slowest descent a tear has ever made. I open my eyes, and Ridge is watching it. He's following the wet trail with his eyes, and I can see his jaw growing more tense with every second that passes. I want to reach up and wipe it away, but the last thing I want to do is hide it from him. My tears say a whole lot more about how I'm feeling right now than I'm willing to say in a text.

Maybe I need him to know that this is hurting me.

Maybe I want it to hurt him, too.

When the tear finally curves and disappears under my jaw, he brings his eyes back to mine. I'm surprised by what I see in them.

His own tears.

Knowing that he's hurting because I'm hurting shouldn't make me want to kiss him, but it absolutely does. He's here because he cares about me. He's here because he misses me. He's here because he needs to feel what we felt in our first kiss again, just as I do. I've wanted that feeling back since the second his mouth left mine and he walked away.

I remove my hands from his shoulders and grab the back of his head, then lean into him, bringing my mouth so close to his that our lips brush.

He grins. "Good call," he whispers.

He closes the space between our mouths, and everything else falls away. The guilt, the worries, the concern over what happens after this kiss ends. It all melts away the second his mouth claims mine. He gently coaxes my lips apart with his tongue, and all the chaos running through my heart and head is eliminated when I feel his warmth inside my mouth.

Kisses like his should come with a warning label. They can't be good for the heart. He runs a hand around to my upper thigh, then slips it beneath the hem of my T-shirt. His hand glides across my back, and he grips me tightly, then lifts his hips at the same time as he pulls me harder against him.

Oh.

My.

Goodness.

I become weaker and weaker with every rhythmic movement he creates with our bodies. I find whatever parts of him I can hold on to, because I feel as if I'm falling. I grab his shirt and his hair while I moan softly into his mouth. When he feels the sound escape my throat, he quickly pulls away from my mouth and squeezes his eyes shut, breathing heavily. When he opens his eyes again, he's staring at my throat.

He pulls his hand from beneath my shirt, then slowly brings it up to my neck.

Oh, my dear, sweet God.

He wraps his fingers around my neck, gently pressing his palm into the base of my throat while he stares at my mouth.

The thought of him wanting to feel what he's doing to me makes my head swarm and the entire room spin. I'm somehow able to glance into his eyes long enough to see them transform from a calm desire to an almost carnal need.

With his other hand still curved around the back of my head, he pulls me to him with more urgency, covering my mouth with his. The second his tongue finds mine again, I give him more moans than he can possibly keep up with.

This is exactly what I've wanted from him. I've wanted him to show up and tell me how much he's missed me. I've needed to know that he cares about me, that he wants me. I've needed to feel his mouth on mine again so I could know that the way his first kiss made me feel wasn't just in my head this whole time.

Now that I have it, I'm not sure I'm strong enough for it. I know that the second this ends and he walks out the front door, my heart will die all over again. The more I open up to him, the more I need him. The more I admit to myself that I need him, the more it hurts to know that I still don't exactly have him.

I'm still not convinced that he's here for the right reasons. Even if he *is* here for the right reasons, it's still wrong timing. Not to mention all the questions still running through my head. I try to push them away, and for brief moments, it works. When his hands graze my cheek or his lips close over mine, I forget all about those questions that I can't seem to run away from. But then he'll pause to catch his breath, and he'll look me in the eye, and all those questions just cram right back into the front of my head, until they're so heavy that they're forcing more tears to want to escape.

I clench his arms when the uncertainty begins to take over. I shake my head and try to push against him. He pulls away from my mouth and sees my doubt building, and he shakes his head to get me to stop analyzing this moment between us. His eyes are pleading as he strokes my cheek, pulls me flush against him, and tries to kiss me again, but I struggle out of his arms.

"Ridge, no," I say. "I can't."

I'm still shaking my head when his hand grips my wrist. I slide off his lap and keep walking until his fingers fall away from me.

I walk straight to the kitchen sink and dispense soap into my hands, then begin scrubbing the ink off my arm. I reach into a drawer and pull out a rag, then wet it and press it to my neck. Tears are streaming down my cheeks as I try to wash away the reminders of what just happened between us. The reminders are going to make him that much harder to overcome.

Ridge comes up behind me and places his hands on my shoulders. He turns me around to face him. When he sees that I'm crying, his eyes fill with apology, and he pulls the rag from my hand. He brushes the hair off my shoulder and gently rubs my skin, washing away the ink. He looks incredibly guilty for making me cry, but it's not his fault. It's never his fault. It's no one's fault. It's both our faults.

When he's finished rubbing away the ink, he tosses the rag behind me onto the counter, then pulls me against his chest. The comfort that surrounds me makes this even harder. I want this all the time. I want *him* all the time. I want these tiny snippets of perfection between us to be our constant reality, but that can't happen right now. I completely understand his earlier comment, when he said that there are times he misses me and times he wishes he never met me, because right now, I'm wishing I never set foot out onto my balcony the first time I heard his guitar.

If I never experienced how he could make me feel, then I wouldn't miss it after he's gone.

I wipe my eyes and pull away from him. There's so much we need to discuss, so I walk to the couch, retrieve our phones, and bring his to him. I move away from him to lean against the other counter while I type, but he grabs my arm and pulls me back. He leans against the bar and pulls my back against his chest, then wraps his arms around me from behind. He kisses the side of my head, then moves his lips to my ear.

"Stay here," he says, wanting me to remain pressed against him.

It's crazy how being held by someone for just a few minutes can forever change how it feels *not* to be held by him. The second he releases his hold on you, it suddenly feels as if a part of you is missing. I guess he feels it, too, which is why he wants me near him.

Does he feel this way about Maggie, too?

Questions like this refuse to leave my mind. Questions like this keep me from believing he could ever be happy with the outcome of his situation, because he lost her in the end. I don't want to be someone's second choice.

I lean my head against his shoulder and squeeze my eyes shut, trying my best not to let my mind go there again. However, I know I have to go there if I ever want to find a sense of closure.

Ridge: I wish I could read your mind.

Me: Believe me, I wish you could, too.

He laughs quietly and squeezes me tightly in his arms. He keeps his cheek pressed against my head as he types out another text.

Ridge: We've always been able to say whatever is on our minds. You still have that with me, you know. You can say whatever you need to say, Sydney. That's what I've always loved about us the most.

Why do all the words he says and writes and texts have to pierce my heart?

I inhale a deep breath, then exhale carefully. I open my eyes and look down at my phone, terrified to ask the one question I don't really want the answer to. I ask it anyway, because as much as I don't *want* to know the answer, I *need* to know the answer.

Me: If she texted you right now and said she made the wrong choice, would you go? Would you walk out my front door without thinking twice?

My head stills when the rapid rise and fall of his chest comes to a sudden halt.

I can no longer hear his breaths.

His grip around me loosens slightly.

My heart crumbles.

I don't need to read an answer from him. I don't even need to *hear* it. I can feel it in every part of him.

It's not as if I were expecting his answer to be any different. He spent five years with her. It's obvious that he loves her. He's never said otherwise.

I was just hoping he was wrong.

I immediately break away from him and walk swiftly toward my bedroom. I want to lock myself inside until he leaves. I don't want him to see what this does to me. I don't want him to see that I love him the same way he loves Maggie.

I reach my bedroom and swing open the door. I rush inside and begin to shut the door behind me, but he pushes the door open. He steps into my bedroom and turns me around to face him.

His eyes are searching mine, desperately trying to get across whatever it is he wishes he could say. He opens his mouth as if he's going to speak, but then he closes it again. He releases my arms, then turns around and runs his hands through his hair. He grips the back of his neck, then kicks my bedroom door shut with a frustrated groan. He leans his forearm into the door and presses his forehead against it. I do nothing but stand still and watch him try to fight the war within himself. The same war I've been fighting.

He remains in the same position while he lifts his phone and responds to my text.

Ridge: That's not a fair question.

Me: Yeah, well, you didn't really put me in a fair situation by showing up here tonight.

He turns until his back is flat against my bedroom door. He brings two frustrated hands to his forehead, then lifts his leg at the knee and kicks the door behind him. Seeing him struggle with who he really wants is more pain than I'm willing to endure. I deserve more than he can give me right now, and his conflict is screwing with my heart. Screwing with my head. Everything with him is just too much.

Me: I want you to leave. I can't be around you anymore. It terrifies me that you're wishing I were her.

He hangs his head and stares at the floor for several moments while I continue to stare at him. He isn't denying that he'd rather be with Maggie right now. He isn't making excuses or telling me he could love me more than he loves her.

He's completely quiet . . . because he knows I'm right.

Me: I need you to leave. Please. And if you really care about me, you won't come back.

He slowly turns and faces me. His eyes lock with mine, and I've never seen more emotions flash through them than in this moment.

"No," he says firmly.

He begins walking toward me, and I begin backing away from him. He's shaking his head pleadingly. He reaches me just as my legs meet my bed, and then he grabs my face between his hands and presses his lips to mine.

I shake my head and push against his chest. He steps away from me and winces, looking even more frustrated with his inability to communicate with me. His eyes search the room for whatever will help him convince me I'm wrong, but I know nothing can help our situation. He just needs to realize this, too.

He looks down at my bed, then back at me. He grabs my hand and pulls me around to the side of the bed. He places his hands on my shoulders and pushes me down until I'm seated. I have no idea what he's doing, so I don't resist.

Yet.

He continues to lower me until I'm lying with my back flat on the bed. He stands straight up and removes his T-shirt. Before he even has it completely over his head, I'm already attempting to roll off the bed. If he thinks sex will fix our situation, he's not as smart as I thought he was.

"No," he says again when he sees me trying to escape.

The sheer conviction in his voice causes me to freeze, and I fall back against my mattress again. He kneels down on the bed, grabs a pillow, and lays it beside my head. He lies down next to me, and my whole body tenses from his close proximity. He picks up his phone.

Ridge: Listen to me, Sydney.

I stare at the text in anticipation of what he'll type next. When I notice that he's not even texting me a follow-up, I look at him. He shakes his head and pulls my phone from my hands, then tosses it beside him. He takes my hand and places it over his heart.

"Here," he says, patting my hand. "Listen to me here."

My chest tightens when I realize what he wants me to do. He pulls me to him, and I willingly allow it. He gently lowers my head to his heart as he adjusts himself beneath me and helps me get comfortable.

I relax against his chest, finding the rhythm of his heartbeat.

Beat, beat, pause.

Beat, beat, pause.

Beat, beat, pause.

It's absolutely beautiful.

The way it sounds is beautiful.

The way it cares is beautiful.

The way it loves is beautiful.

He presses his lips to the top of my head.

I close my eyes . . . and I cry.

Ridge

I hold her against me for so long I'm not even sure if she's awake. I still have so much I want to say to her, but I don't want to move. I love the way she feels when we're wrapped together like this. I'm afraid if I move, she'll come to her senses again and ask me to leave.

It's barely been three weeks since Maggie and I broke up. When Sydney asked if I'd take Maggie back, I didn't answer, but only because I know she wouldn't believe my answer.

I love Maggie, but I honestly don't think Maggie and I are best for each other anymore. I know exactly where we went wrong. The beginning of our relationship was romantic to the point where it was almost fictionalized. We were nineteen years old. We barely knew each other. The way we waited for an entire year only built up feelings that weren't based on anything except false hopes and idealized love.

By the time Maggie and I were finally able to be together, I think we were more in love with the idea of us, rather than with the actual us. Of course, I loved her. I still love her. But until I met Sydney, I had no idea how much my love for Maggie was built up from my desire to swoop in and save her.

Maggie was right. I've done nothing for the past five years but try to be the hero who protects her. The problem? Heroines don't need protecting.

When Sydney put me on the spot earlier, I wanted to tell her no, that I wouldn't take Maggie back. When she said she was terrified that I was wishing she were Maggie, I wanted to grab hold of her and prove to her how I've never, not once, wished I were anywhere else when I'm with her. I wanted to tell her the only regret I have is not realizing sooner which one of them I was better for. Which girl I made more sense with. Which girl I grew to love in a realistic, natural way, not in an idealized sense.

I didn't say anything because I'm terrified she won't understand. I've chosen Maggie over her time and time again, and it's my own fault that I've put doubt into Sydney's head. And even though I know that the scenario she's painting could never happen because Maggie and I both accept that it's over, I'm not so sure I *wouldn't* take Maggie back. However, my decision wouldn't be because I want to be with Maggie more. It wouldn't even be because I love Maggie more. But how do I possibly convince Sydney of that when it's hard for *me* to comprehend?

I don't want Sydney ever to feel like my second choice, when I know in my heart that she's the *right* choice. The *only* choice.

I keep my arm around her, and I pick up my phone. She lifts her head and rests her chin on my chest, looking up at me. I hand her back her phone, and she takes it, then turns away from me and presses her ear against my heart again.

Me: Do you want to know why I needed you to listen to me?

She doesn't respond with a text. She just nods her head yes, remaining pressed against my chest. One of her hands is slowly tracing up and down from my waist to my arm. The feel of her hands against my skin is something I never want to become a memory. I lower my left hand to the back of her head and stroke her hair.

Me: It's kind of a long explanation. Do you have a notebook I can write in?

She nods and slides off me. She reaches into her nightstand and takes out a notebook and a pen. I readjust myself against her headboard. She hands me the notebook but doesn't move closer to me. I grab her wrist and part my legs, then motion for her to lie against me while I write. She crawls toward me and wraps her arms around my waist, pressing her ear to my heart again. I put my arms around her and prop the notebook on my knee, resting my cheek on top of her head.

I wish there was an easier way for us to communicate so all the things I have to say to her could be instant. I wish I could look into her eyes and tell her exactly how I feel and what's on my mind, but I can't, and I hate that for us. Instead, I lay my heart out on paper. She remains still against my chest while I take almost fifteen minutes to gather my thoughts and get them all down for her. When I'm finished, I hand her the notebook. She readjusts herself until her back is pressed against my chest. I keep my arms around her and hold her while she reads the letter.

Sydney

I have no idea what to expect from the words he's just written, but as soon as he hands me the paper I begin to soak every sentence up as quickly as my eyes can scan them. The fact that a barrier exists in the way we communicate makes every word I receive from him, in whatever form, something I feel the need to consume as quickly as possible.

I don't know if I'm actually more aware of my own heartbeat than other people are of theirs, but I tend to believe I am. The fact that I can't hear the world around me leaves me to focus more on the world inside me. Brennan told me the only time he's aware of his own heartbeat is when it's quiet and he's being still. That's not the case for me, because it's always quiet in my world. I'm always aware of my heartbeat. Always. I know its pattern. I know its rhythm. I know what makes it speed up and slow down, and I even know when to expect that. Sometimes I feel my heart react before my brain has the chance to. The reactions of my heart have always been something I was able to predict . . . until a few months ago.

The first night you walked out onto your balcony was the first night I noticed the change. It was subtle, but it was there. Just an extra little skip. I brushed it off because I didn't want to think it had anything to do with you. I liked how loyal my heart was to Maggie, and I didn't want my loyalty to her to change.

But then, the first time I saw you singing along to one of my songs, it happened again. Only that time, it was more obvious. It would speed up a little faster every time I saw your lips moving. It would start beating in places I never felt my heart beat before. That first night I saw you singing, I had to get up and go inside to finish playing, because I didn't like how you made my heart feel. For the first time, I felt as though I had absolutely no control over it, and that made me feel horrible.

The first time I walked out of my bedroom to find you standing in my apartment, soaking wet from the rain—my God, I didn't know hearts could beat like that. I knew my heart like the back of my hand, and nothing had ever made it react like you did. I put the blankets on the couch for you as quickly as I could, pointed you in the direction of the bathroom, and immediately went back to my bedroom. I'll spare you the details of what I had to do while you were in my shower in order to calm myself down after seeing you up close for the first time.

My physical reaction to you didn't worry me. Physical reactions are normal, and at that point, my heart still belonged to Maggie. My heartbeats were all for Maggie. They always had been, but the more time I spent with you, the more you started to unintentionally infiltrate and steal some of those heartbeats. I did everything I could to prevent it from happening. For a while, I convinced myself that I was stronger than my heart, which is why I allowed you to stay. I thought what I felt for you was nothing but attraction and that if I let myself have you in my fantasies enough, that would suffice in reality. However, I soon realized that the way I fantasized about you wasn't at all how guys normally fantasize about girls they're attracted to. I didn't imagine myself stealing kisses from you when no one was around. I didn't imagine myself sliding into your bed in the middle of the night and doing to you all the things we both wished I would do. Instead, I was imagining what it would feel like if you fell asleep in my arms. I was imagining what it would feel like to wake up next to you in the morning. I was imagining your smiles and your laughter and even how good it would feel to be able to comfort you when you cried.

The trouble I had gotten myself into became obvious the night I put those headphones in your ears and watched you sing the song we created together. Watching those words pass your lips and knowing I couldn't hear them and feeling how much my heart ached for us in that moment, I knew what was happening was so much more than I could control. My strength was overpowered by my weakness for you. The second my lips touched yours, my heart split completely in two. Half of it belonged to you from that point on. Every other beat of my heart was for you.

I knew I should have asked you to leave that night, but I couldn't bring myself to do it. The thought of saying good-bye to you hurt way too much. I had planned on asking you to move out the next day, but once we talked through everything, the ease with which we dealt with our situation gave me more excuses to ignore it. Knowing we were both fighting it gave me hope that I could give back to Maggie the part of my heart I had lost to you.

The weekend of Warren's party was when I realized it was too late. I spent the entire night of the party trying not to watch you. Trying not to be obvious. Trying to keep my attention focused on Maggie, where it should have been. However, all the effort and denial in the world couldn't have saved me from what happened the next day. When I walked into your room and sat down beside you on the bed, I felt it.

I felt you give me a piece of your heart.

And Sydney, I wanted it. I wanted your heart more than I've ever wanted anything. The second I reached down and held your hand in mine, it happened. My heart made its choice, and it chose you.

My relationship with Maggie was a great one, and I never want to disrespect what I had with her. When I told you I've loved her since the moment I met her and that I'd love her until the moment I die, I was being honest. I have always loved her, I do love her, and I always will love her. She's an incredible person who deserves so much more than what life has handed her, and it pisses me off to this day when I think about it. I would switch my fate with hers in a second if I had that option. Unfortunately, life doesn't work that way. Fate doesn't work that way. So even after I knew I had found in you what I would never find in my relationship with Maggie, it still wasn't enough. No matter how much I cared for you or how deep my feelings for you ran, it would have never been enough to get me to leave Maggie. If I couldn't change her fate, I was at least going to give her the best damn life I could give her. Even if it meant sacrificing aspects of my own, I *would have done it without pause, and I never would have regretted it. Not even for a second.*

However, until three weeks ago, I didn't realize that the best life I could give her was a life without me in it. She needed the opposite of what I could offer her, and I know that now. She knows that now. And we accept it.

So when you ask if I would choose her over you, you're presenting a situation that I can't give you a straight answer to. Because yes, at this point, I probably would walk away from you if she asked me to. The majority of my loyalty still lies with her. But if you're asking who I need more? Who I want to be with more? Who my heart craves more? My heart decided that for me a long time ago, Sydney.

When I've read the last word, I pull the notebook against my chest and cry. He slides me off of him until I'm on my back, and he hovers over me, guiding my eyes up to meet his.

"It's you," he says aloud. "My heart . . . wants you."

A sob breaks free from my chest when I hear his words. I immediately grab his shoulders and lift myself up, pressing my lips to the area directly over his heart. I kiss him over and over, silently thanking him for giving me reassurance that I haven't been in this alone.

When I lower my head back to the pillow, he lies beside me, then pulls me against him. He touches my cheek with his hand and slowly leans in to kiss me. His mouth caresses mine so carefully it feels as if he's holding my heart in his hand and is afraid he might drop it.

As much as I'm convinced he would do everything he could to protect my heart, I'm still too scared to hand it over. I don't want to give it to him until I know it's the only heart he's holding.

•   •   •

I don't open my eyes, because I don't want him to know I hear him leaving. I felt him kiss me. I felt him slide his arm out from beneath me. I heard him pull his shirt over his head. I heard him search for a pen. I heard him write me a letter, and I heard him place it on the pillow beside me.

I feel his hand as it presses into the mattress beside my head. His lips meet my forehead before he pulls away and walks out my bedroom door. When I hear the front door shut, I roll onto my side and pull the covers over my head to block out the sunlight. If I didn't have to work today, I'd stay right here in this position and cry myself dry.

I brush my hand across the mattress in search of his letter. When I find it, I pull it under the covers with me and read it.

Sydney,

A few months ago, we thought we had it all figured out. I was with the one girl I thought I would be with forever, and you were with a guy you thought deserved you way more than he did.

Look at us now.

Wanting more than anything to be free to love each other but cursed by bad timing and loyal hearts. We both know where we want to be; we just don't know how to get there. Or when we should get there. I wish things were as easy as they seemed when I was nineteen. We'd grab a calendar and pick a date, and we'd start a countdown until I could show up at your front door and start loving you.

However, I've learned that the heart can't be told when and who and how it should love. The heart does whatever the hell it wants to do. The only thing we can control is whether we give our lives and our minds the chance to catch up to our hearts.

I know that's what you want more than anything. Time to catch up.

As much as I want to stay here and allow this to begin between us, there's something I want from you even more than that. I want you to be with me in the end, and I know that can't happen if I keep trying to rush our beginning. I know exactly why you were hesitant to let me in last night: you aren't ready yet. Maybe I'm not, either. You've always said you wanted time to yourself, and the last thing I want is to start a relationship with you when I've barely given enough respect to the one that just ended with Maggie.

I don't know when you'll be ready for me. It might be next month or next year. Whenever it is, just know that I have absolutely no doubt that we can make this work. I know we can. If there are two people in this world capable of finding a way to love each other, it's us.

Ridge

P.S. I spent most of the night watching you sleep, so that's one fantasy I got to check off the list. I also wrote lyrics to an entire song, which was unfortunate for Brennan. I didn't have my guitar, so I forced him to make a rough cut of it at five o'clock this morning so I could leave it with you.

One of these days, I'll play it for you, along with all the other songs I plan to write for you while we're apart. Until then, I'll be waiting patiently.

Just say when.

I fold the letter and pull it against my chest. As much as it hurts to know he's walking away, I also know that I need to let him. I asked for this. We need this. *I* need this. I need to get myself to a point where I know that we can finally be together without all the doubt running through my head. He's right. My mind needs to catch up to my heart.

I run the back of my hand across my eyes, then open my texts.

Me: Can you come over? I need your help.

Warren: If this has to do with the fact that I gave Ridge your address last night, I'm sorry. He forced it out of me.

Me: This has nothing to do with that. I need to ask you for a huge favor.

Warren: Be there when I get off work tonight. Should I bring condoms?

Me: Funny guy.

I close out the text to Warren and open up the song Ridge just sent me. I reach into my drawer for my headphones, then fall back against my pillow and hit play.

IT'S YOU
Baby, everything you've ever done
Underneath this here sun
It doesn't even matter anymore
Oh, of this I'm sure

'Cause you've taken me
Places I want to be
And you show me
Everything that I could ever
Want to see
You, you know it's
You know it's you

I think about you every single day
Trying to think of something better to say
Maybe hi, how are you
Not just anything will do

'Cause you've taken me
Places I want to be
And you show me
Everything that I could ever
Want to see
You, you know it's
You know it's you

24.

Ridge

Me: I'm looking at your schedule for March. You're free on the 18th.

Brennan: Why do I feel like I'm about to be busy on the 18th?

Me: I'm planning a show, and I need your help. We'll do it locally.

Brennan: What kind of show? Full band?

Me: No, just you and me. Maybe Warren if he'll sign for us.

Brennan: Why do I feel like this has to do with Sydney?

Me: Why do I feel like I don't care what you feel like?

Brennan: The ball is in her court, Ridge. You really should just leave things alone until she's ready. I know how you feel about her, and I don't want you to screw it up.

Me: March 18 is still three months away. If she hasn't made up her mind by that date, then all I'm doing is giving her a little shove. And when did you start giving relationship advice? How long has it been since you were in one? Oh, wait. That would be never.

Brennan: If I agree to help you, will you STFU? What do you need me to do?

Me: Just carve out some time for me between now and then to run through some new songs.

Brennan: Is someone over his writer's block?

Me: Yeah, well, someone once told me heartache is good for lyrical inspiration. Unfortunately, he was right.

Brennan: Sounds like a smart guy.

I close out my texts to Brennan and open one up to Warren.

Me: March 18. I need a local venue. A small one. Then I need you to get Sydney to go there with you that night.

Warren: Is she supposed to know you orchestrated this?

Me: No. Lie to her.

Warren: Not a problem. I'm good at lying.

I set my phone down, pick up my guitar, and walk out onto my balcony. It's been almost a month since I last saw her. Neither of us has texted the other. I know Warren still keeps in contact with her, but he refuses to tell me anything, so I just stopped asking. As much as I miss her and as much as I want to beg her to just let this begin with us, I know time is better for both of us right now. There was still too much guilt rolled up in the thought of starting something too soon, despite how much we wanted to be together. Waiting until we're both in a good place is definitely what needs to happen.

However, I feel as if I'm already there. Maybe it's easier for me because I know where Maggie and I stand, and I know where my heart stands, but Sydney doesn't have that reassurance. If time will give her that reassurance, then I'll give her time. Just not too much. March 18 is only three months away. I hope to hell she's ready by then, because I'm not sure I can keep myself away from her for longer than that.

I scoot my chair to the edge of the balcony and fold my arms over the railing, then look over at her old balcony. Every time I come out here and see her empty chair, it makes all of this so much harder. But I can't seem to find anything inside my apartment that reminds me of her anymore. She left nothing when she moved, and she really never had anything while she was here. Being outside on this balcony is the closest I can come to feeling her since it seems we're so far apart.

I lean back in my chair, pick up a pen, and begin writing the lyrics to another song, with nothing but her on my mind.

> *The cool air running through my hair*
> *Nights like these, doesn't seem fair*
> *For you and I to be so far away*
> *The stars all shimmer like a melody*
> *Like they're playing for you and me*
> *But only I can hear their sounds.*

I pick up my guitar and work through the first few chords. I want these songs to be enough to convince her that we're ready, so every single thing has to be perfect. I'm just nervous that I'm relying too much on Warren to help make it happen. I hope he's more reliable in this situation with Sydney than he is with his rent checks.

25.

Sydney

"I'm not going."

"Yes, you are," Warren says, kicking my legs off the coffee table. "I'm bored out of my mind. Bridgette works all weekend, and Ridge is off doing God knows what with God knows who."

I immediately look up at him with my heart caught in my throat.

He laughs. "That got your attention." He reaches forward, grabs my hands, and pulls me off the couch. "I'm kidding. Ridge is at home working, being a mopey little shit, just like you're trying to be. Now, go get pretty and come out with me tonight, or I'll sit on the couch with you and force you to watch porn."

I pull my hands from his and walk to the kitchen. I open a cabinet, then grab a cup. "I don't want to go out tonight, Warren. I had class all day, and it's my only night off from the library. I'm sure you can find someone else to go with you." I grab a container of juice from the refrigerator and fill my glass. Leaning against the counter, I take a sip as I watch Warren pout in my living room. He's kind of adorable when he pouts, which is why I always give him such a hard time.

"Listen up, Syd," he says, walking toward the kitchen. He grabs a bar stool and pulls it out, then takes a seat. "I'm about to lay things out for you, okay?"

I roll my eyes. "I doubt I can stop you, so go ahead."

He lays his palms flat on the counter in front of him and leans forward. "You suck."

I laugh. "That's it? That's what you needed to lay out for me?"

He nods. "You suck. So does Ridge. Since the night I gave him your address, you've both sucked. All he does is work or write music. He doesn't even play pranks on me anymore. Every time I'm over here, you're just focused on studying. You never want to go out. You never want to hear my sex stories anymore."

"Correction," I say, interrupting him. "I've never wanted to hear your sex stories. That's nothing new."

"Whatever," he says, shaking his head. "My point is that the two of you are miserable. I know you need time and blah, blah, blah, but that doesn't mean you have to give up fun while you're figuring your life out. I want to go have fun. No one wants to have fun with me anymore, and that's all your fault, because you're the only one who can put a stop to the misery you and Ridge are going through. So, yes. You suck. You suck, you suck, you suck. And if you want to stop sucking so much, then go get dressed so we can go out and not suck together for just a few hours."

I don't know how to argue with that. I do suck. I suck, I suck, I suck. Only Warren could put it in such a simple, straightforward way that would actually make sense. I know I've been miserable the past few months, and it doesn't help to know that Ridge has been miserable, too. He's miserable because he's sitting around waiting for me to get over whatever it is that's keeping me from contacting him.

The last thing he said in his letter to me was *Just say when*.

I've been trying to say when since the moment I read that letter, but I'm just too scared. I've never felt about anyone or anything the way I feel about him, and the thought of our not working out is enough to keep me from saying that one little word. I feel as if the longer we wait and the more time we have to heal, the better chance we'll have at our *maybe someday*.

I keep waiting for the moment when I know for sure that he's moved on from Maggie. I keep waiting for the moment when I know for sure that he's ready to commit fully to me. I keep waiting for the moment when I know for sure that I'm not going to be consumed with guilt for allowing myself to trust someone with my heart again.

I don't know when I'll get to that point, and it hurts to know that my inability to move forward is holding Ridge back.

"Now," Warren says, shoving me out of the kitchen. "Get dressed."

•   •   •

I can't believe I've let him talk me into this. I check my makeup one last time and grab my purse. As soon as he sees me, he shakes his head. I huff and throw my hands in the air.

"What now?" I sigh. "I'm not dressed appropriately?"

"You look great, but I want you to wear the blue dress."

"I burned that dress, remember?" I say.

"The hell you did," he says, pushing me back toward my bedroom. "You were wearing it last week when I stopped by. Go put it on so we can leave."

I spin around to face him. "I know how much you like that dress, and wearing it tonight while I'm out with you is a little too creepy, Warren."

He narrows his eyes. "Listen, Syd. I don't mean to be rude, but all this moping around for the past few months has caused you to put on a little weight. Your ass looks huge in those jeans. The blue dress may be able to hide a little of that, so go put it on, or I might be too embarrassed to go out with you."

I suddenly feel like slapping him again, but I know he's just got a peculiar sense of humor. I also know he might have a completely different reason for why he wants me to wear this dress and I'm trying not to let myself think it has anything to do with Ridge, but pretty much every situation I'm in somehow makes me think about Ridge. It's nothing new. But Warren is a guy who seems to put his foot in his mouth a lot, and I'm a girl, so I still wonder if his sarcastic remark has any truth to it. I *have* been replacing the void Ridge left in my life with food. I look down at my stomach and pat it, then look back up at Warren. "You're an asshole."

He nods. "I know."

The innocent smile on his face makes me instantly forgive any crudeness behind his joke. I change into the blue dress, but I am *so* cock-blocking him tonight. Jerk.

· · ·

"Wow. This is . . . different," I say, taking in my surroundings. It's nothing like the clubs Warren usually likes to go to. This one is a lot smaller, without even much of a dance floor. There's an empty stage along one wall, but there's no one performing tonight. The jukebox is playing, and several people are scattered around at tables, talking quietly among themselves. Warren chooses a table toward the middle of the room.

"You're a cheap date," I say. "You didn't even feed me."

He laughs. "I'll buy you a burger on the way home."

Warren pulls out his phone and begins texting someone, so I look around for a while. It's kind of cozy. It's also kind of weird that Warren brought me here. But I'm thinking he doesn't have any evil intentions, because he's not even paying attention to me.

His attention is on his phone, and he keeps glancing at the door. I don't understand why he wanted to come out tonight, and I especially don't understand why he chose this place.

"You're actually the one who sucks," I say. "Stop ignoring me."

He responds without even looking up at me. "You aren't talking, so technically, I'm not ignoring you."

I'm curious now. He's not being himself, the way he's so distracted. "What's up with you, Warren?"

As soon as I ask the question, he looks up from his phone and smiles over my shoulder, then stands. "You're late," he says to someone behind me. I look to see Bridgette walking toward us.

"Screw you, Warren," she says to him with a small smile. He wraps his arms around her, and they kiss for several uncomfortable seconds. I reach up and tap him on the arm when I'm convinced that neither of them can breathe. He pulls away from Bridgette, winks at her, and slides out his chair for her.

"I have to go to the bathroom," he says to Bridgette. He points at me. "Don't go anywhere."

He says it as if it's a command, and it irritates me even more because he's being really rude tonight. I turn and face Bridgette once he's left the table. "Warren said you were working all weekend," I say.

She shrugs. "Yeah, well, he probably told you that because of the elaborate scheme he has planned for tonight. He made me come so you wouldn't leave when you found out about it. Oh, and I'm not supposed to tell you any of that, so if he comes back, play dumb."

My heart rate escalates. "Please tell me you're kidding."

She shakes her head and raises her arm in the air, calling over a waiter. "I wish I was kidding. I had to switch shifts to be here, and now I have to work a double tomorrow."

I drop my head into my hands, regretting the fact that I let Warren talk me into anything. Just when I'm reaching for my purse to leave, he walks out onto the empty stage.

"Oh, God," I groan. "What the hell is he doing?" My stomach is in knots. I have no idea what he has planned, but whatever it is, it can't be good.

He taps on the microphone, then adjusts the height of it. "I'd like to thank everyone for coming tonight. Not that any of you are here for this particular event, since it's a surprise, but I feel the need to thank you anyway."

He adjusts the microphone once more, then finds our table in the crowd and waves. "I want to apologize to you, Syd, because I feel really bad for lying to you. You haven't gained weight, and your ass looked great in those jeans, but you really needed to wear that dress tonight. Also, you don't suck. I lied about that, too."

Several people in the crowd laugh, but I just groan and bury my face in my hands, peeking through my fingers at him up on the stage.

"All right, let's get on with it, shall we? We have a few new songs for you tonight. Unfortunately, the whole band couldn't be here, because"—he looks to his left at the small width of the stage, then to his right—"well, I don't think they all could have fit. So I'd like to present to you a small portion of the band Sounds of Cedar."

My heart falls to the floor. I close my eyes when the crowd begins to clap.

Please, let it be Ridge.

Please, don't let it be Ridge.

Jesus, when will this confusion go away?

I can hear commotion up on the stage, and I'm too scared to open my eyes. I want to see him sitting up there so much it hurts.

"Hey, Syd," Warren says into the microphone. I inhale a slow, calming breath, then open my eyes and hesitantly look up at him. "Remember a few months ago when I told you some-times we have to have really bad days in order to keep the good ones in perspective?"

I think I nod. I can't really feel my body anymore.

"Well, this is one of the good days. This is one of the really good days." He raises his hand in the air and motions to my table. "Somebody get that girl a shot of whatever will help loosen her up."

He moves the microphone to the stool next to him, and my eyes are glued to the empty chairs. Someone lays a shot on the table in front of me, and I instantly grab it and down it. I drop the shot glass back onto the table and look up just in time to see them walk onto the stage. Brennan is first, and Ridge is right behind him, carrying a guitar.

Oh, my God. He looks incredible. It's the first time I've ever seen him on a stage. I've been wanting to watch him perform since the first moment I heard his guitar on my balcony and here I am, about to watch my fantasy become reality.

He looks the same as he did the last time I saw him, just . . . incredible. I guess he looked incredible back then, too. I just didn't feel right allowing myself to admit it when I knew he wasn't mine. I must feel okay about it now, because holy crap. He's beautiful. He carries himself with such confidence and I can definitely see why. His arms look as if they were built for the sole purpose of carrying a guitar. It molds to him so naturally, it's as if it's an extension of him. There isn't a shadow of guilt clouding his eyes like there always was in the past. He's smiling, like he's excited for what's about to happen. His enigmatic smile lights up his face and his face lights up the entire room. At least it seems that way to me. He glances over the audience several times as he makes his way toward his seat, but he doesn't immediately spot me.

He takes a seat on the center stool, and Brennan sits to the left of him, Warren to his right. He signs to Warren, and Warren points at me. Ridge looks out into the audience and finds me. My hands are clamped over my mouth, and my elbows are propped up on the table. He smiles and gives me a nod and my heart crashes to the floor. I can't smile or wave or nod back at him. I'm too nervous to move.

Brennan leans forward and speaks into the microphone. "We've got a few new songs—"

His voice is cut off when Ridge pulls the microphone away from him and leans in toward it. "Sydney," Ridge says into the microphone, "some of these songs I wrote with you. Some of these songs I wrote *for* you."

I can hear a small difference in the way he speaks now. I've never heard him say so much at once out loud. He also seems to enunciate a little more clearly than the few times he's spoken to me in the past, like the subject in the photograph is slightly more in focus. It's obvious he's been working on it, and knowing he's continued to talk out loud makes my eyes tear up without even having heard a song yet.

"If you aren't ready to say the word, that's fine," he says. "I'll wait as long as you need me to. I just hope you don't mind this interruption tonight." He pushes the microphone away, then looks down to his guitar. Brennan leans into the microphone and looks at me.

"He can't hear what I'm saying right now, so I'll take this opportunity to tell you Ridge is full of shit. He doesn't want to wait anymore. He wants you to say the word more than he wants air. So please, for the sake of all that is holy, say the word tonight."

I laugh as I wipe a tear from my eye.

Ridge plays the opening chords to "Trouble," and I finally realize why Warren made me wear this dress. Brennan leans forward and begins to sing, and I remain completely immobile as Warren signs every word to the song while Ridge keeps his focus on the fingers strumming his guitar. Watching the three of them together, seeing the beauty they can create from a few words and guitars, is mesmerizing.

Ridge

When the song ends, I look up at her.

She's crying, but those tears are accompanied by a smile, and that's exactly what I was hoping I would see when I looked up from my guitar. Seeing her for the first time since I kissed her good-bye has a far greater effect on me than I thought it would. I'm trying my damndest to remember what it is I'm here to do, but all I want to do is toss my guitar aside, rush to her, and kiss her crazy.

Instead, I keep my eyes trained on hers while I play another song she helped me write. I begin the opening chords to "Maybe Someday." She smiles and clutches a hand to her chest while she watches me play.

It's times like these I'm actually thankful I can't hear. Not being distracted by anything at all allows me to focus on nothing but her. I can feel the music vibrating in my chest as I watch her lips singing along to the lyrics until the very last line.

I planned on playing a few more songs we wrote together, but seeing her has changed my mind. I want to get to the new songs I wrote for her, because I absolutely need to see her reaction to them. I start one of them, knowing Warren and Brennan will have no problem falling into step with the change-up. Her eyes glisten when she realizes that this is a song she's never heard before, and she leans forward in her chair, focusing intently on the three of us.

Sydney

There are only twenty-six letters in the English alphabet. You would think there would only be so much you could do with twenty-six letters. You would think there were only so many ways those letters could make you feel when mixed up and shoved together to make words.

However, there are infinite ways those twenty-six letters can make a person feel, and this song is living proof. I'll never understand how a few simple words strung together can change a person, but this song, these words, are completely changing me. I feel like my *maybe someday* just became my *right now*.

HOLD ON TO YOU
The cool air running through my hair
Nights like these, doesn't seem fair
For you and I to be so far away

The stars all shimmer like a melody
Like they're playing for you and me
But only I can hear their sound

Maybe if I ask them they will play for you
I try wishing on one, maybe I'll try two
It doesn't look like there's much for me to do

I want to hold on to you
Just like these memories I can't undo
I want to hold on to you
Without you here that's kind of hard to do

I want to hold
I want to hold on to you

The front seat's empty, and I know
When it's just me I seem to go
To places I never wanted to

I need you here to be a light
Star in the sky brighten up my night
Sometimes I need the dark to see

So come on, come on, turn it on for me
Just a little light, and I'll be able to see
Promise like a comet you won't fly by me

I want to hold on to you
Just like these memories I can't undo
I want to hold on to you

Without you here that's kind of hard to do
I want to hold
I want to hold on to you

Ridge

I finish the song and don't give myself time to look up at her before I begin playing another one. I'm afraid if I look at her, I'll lose every bit of willpower still keeping me up on this stage. I want to go to her so bad, but I know how important it is for her to hear this next song. I also don't want to be the one to make the final choice. If she's ready to be with me, she knows what I need from her. If she's not ready, I'll respect her decision.

However, if she's not ready to begin the life I know we could have together by the end of this song, I don't know if she'll ever be ready.

I keep my eyes trained on my fingers as they work the strings of the guitar. I glance at Brennan, and he leans forward into the microphone, his voice starting on cue. I glance to Warren, and he begins signing the words.

I slowly scan the crowd and find her again.

Our eyes lock.

I don't look away.

Sydney

"Wow," Bridgette whispers. Her eyes are glued to the stage just like mine. Just like every other pair of eyes in the room. The three of them make one hell of a team, but knowing that these words are Ridge's words and he wrote them specifically for me leaves me feeling more than overwhelmed. I can't look away from him. For the entire length of the song, I barely move. I barely breathe.

LET IT BEGIN

Time went fast
Time went fast till it was gone
You think it's right
You think it's right until it's wrong

Even after all this time
I still want you
Even after all my mind
Put me through

So won't you
Won't you let it begin
So won't you
Won't you let it begin

You hold it out
You hold your heart out in your hand
I snatch it up
I snatch it up fast as I can

Even after all this time
I still want you
Even after all my mind
Put me through

I stand here at your door
Until you come and let me in
I want to be your end
But you gotta let it begin

So won't you
Won't you let it begin
So won't you
Won't you just say when

Ridge

Our gazes never deviate from each other. Throughout the song, her focus remains solely on mine and mine on hers. When the song ends, I don't move. I wait for her mind and her life to catch up to her heart, and I hope it happens soon. Tonight. Right now.

She wipes tears from her eyes, then lifts her hands. She holds up her left index finger, brings her right index finger close to the left and circles it around, and then the tips of her fingers touch.

I can't move.

She just signed for me.

She just said "when."

Seeing her sign is something I never expected. It's something I never would have even asked her to do. Learning how to communicate with me the whole time we've been apart is the most amazing thing anyone has ever done for me.

I'm shaking my head, unable to get it through my mind that this girl is willingly mine and she's perfect and beautiful and good and, holy shit, I love her so much.

She's smiling, but I'm still frozen in shock.

She laughs at my response and signs the word again, several times. "When, when, when."

Brennan shoves my shoulder, and I look over at him. He laughs. "Go," he signs, nodding his head in Sydney's direction. "Go get your girl."

I immediately drop my guitar to the floor and rush off the stage. She pushes away from her table as soon as she sees me making my way toward her. She's only a few feet away, but I can't get to her fast enough. I take in the dress she has on and make a mental note to thank Warren later. I have a feeling he had something to do with that.

I look into her tear-filled eyes when I finally reach her. She's smiling up at me, and for the first time since the moment I met her, we're looking at each other without a trace of guilt or worry or regret or shame.

She throws her arms around my neck, and I pull her to me and bury my face in her hair. I hold her head firmly against me and close my eyes. We hold on to each other as if we're afraid to let go.

I can feel her crying, so I put enough space between us so I can look into her eyes. She lifts her head, and I've never seen tears look more beautiful.

"You signed," I say out loud.

She smiles. "You spoke. A lot."

"I'm not very good at it," I admit. I know my words are hard to understand, and I still feel uncomfortable when I speak, but I love seeing her eyes when she hears my voice. It makes me want to speak every single word I possibly can right here and now.

"I'm not good, either," she says. She pulls away from me and lifts her hands to sign. "Warren has been helping me. I only know about two hundred words, but I'm learning."

It's been several months since I last saw her, and while I've been trying to believe she still wanted to be with me, I did have my doubts. I was starting to question our decision to wait before starting our relationship. What I never expected was for her to spend those months learning how to communicate with me in a way my own parents didn't even care enough to learn.

"I just fell completely in love with you," I say to her. I glance at Bridgette, who is still seated at the table. "Did you see it, Bridgette? Did you see me just fall in love with her?"

Bridgette rolls her eyes, and I feel Sydney laugh. I look back down at her. "I did. Like twenty seconds ago. I fell completely in love with you."

She smiles and mouths her next words slowly so I can understand her. "I fell first."

When the last word passes her lips, I catch it with my mouth. Since the second I walked away from these lips, I've done nothing but think about the moment I would get to taste them again. She pulls me tightly against her, and I kiss her hard, then delicately, then fast and slow and every way in between. I kiss her every way I can possibly kiss her, because I plan on loving her every way I can possibly love her. Every single time we refused to cave in to our feelings in the past makes this kiss completely worth the sacrifices. This kiss is worth all the tears, all the heartache, all the pain, all the struggles, all the waiting.

She's worth it all.

She's worth more.

Sydney

We make it to my apartment somehow between all the kissing. He releases me long enough to let me unlock the door, but he loses his patience as soon as it's unlocked. I laugh when he shoves the door open and pushes me inside. He closes the door, locks it, and turns around to face me again. We look at each other for several seconds.

"Hi," he says simply.

I laugh. "Hi."

He looks around the room nervously before his eyes fall back to mine. "Is that good enough?" he asks.

I cock my head, because I don't really understand his question. "Is what good enough?"

He grins. "I was hoping that was enough talk for tonight."

Oh.

I get his question now.

I nod slowly, and he smiles, then steps forward and kisses me. He bends slightly and lifts me by the waist, wrapping my legs around him. He secures his arms around my back and begins walking me toward my bedroom.

As many times as I've seen this happen in movies and read about it in books, I've never actually been picked up and carried by a man before. I think I'm in love with it. Being carried into a bedroom by Ridge is quite possibly my new favorite thing out of any and all things.

That is, until he kicks my bedroom door shut behind him. Maybe Ridge kicking doors shut is my new favorite thing.

He gently lowers me to the bed, and even though I'm sad that he's not carrying me anymore, I'm a little bit happier to find myself beneath him. Every single move he makes is better and sexier than the last one. He pauses for a moment as he hovers over me, and his eyes roam sensually over my entire body, until they come to a pause on the hem of my dress. He reaches down and pushes it up, and I lift myself up off the bed just enough for him to pull it over my head.

He sucks in a breath when he looks down at me and sees that the only thing coming between him and a completely naked me is a very thin layer of panty. He begins to lower himself on top of me, but I push on his chest and shake my head, tugging on his shirt to let him know it's his turn. He grins and quickly pulls his shirt over his head, then leans in toward me again. I push against him once more, and he reluctantly lifts himself up, shooting me a look of amused annoyance. I point to his jeans, and he backs away from the bed, and in two swift movements, the rest of his clothes are somewhere on my bedroom floor. I don't quite catch where he tossed them, because my eyes are sort of preoccupied.

He makes his way on top of me again, and I don't stop him this time. I welcome him by wrapping my legs around his waist and my arms around his back and guiding his mouth back to mine.

We mold and fit together so perfectly it's as if we were made for this sole purpose. His left hand fits perfectly into mine as he brings my arm above my head and presses it into the mattress. His tongue melds perfectly with mine as he continues to tease my entire mouth as if it were made for this very purpose. His right hand seamlessly conforms to my outer thigh as he digs his fingers into my skin and shifts his weight perfectly against me.

His mouth leaves mine long enough to taste my jaw . . . my neck . . . my shoulder.

I don't know how being consumed by him could lend clarity to my purpose in life, but it absolutely feels that way. Everything about me and him and life makes so much more sense when we're together like this. He makes me feel more beautiful. More important. More loved. More needed. I feel more *everything*, and with every second that passes, I become more and more greedy, wanting all of every single part of him.

I push against his chest, needing space between us so I can sign to him. He looks down at my hands when he realizes what I'm doing. I hope I get it right, because I've practiced signing this sentence no fewer than a thousand times since I last saw him.

"I have something I need to say before we do this."

He pulls back a few inches, watching my hands, waiting.

I sign the words "I love you."

His eyebrows draw apart, and relief floods his eyes. He lowers his mouth to my hands and kisses them, over and over, then quickly pulls farther away, unwrapping my legs from around his waist. Just when I begin to fear he's come to some absurd notion that we need to stop, he lowers himself to my side but leans over me and presses his ear against my chest.

"I want to feel you say it."

I press my lips into his hair, then lightly secure him against me. "I love you, Ridge," I whisper.

His grip tightens around my waist, so I continue repeating it several times.

I keep his head pressed against my chest with both hands. He releases his grip on my waist and trails his hand over my stomach, causing my muscles to clench beneath his touch. He continues stroking his hand in sensuous circles over my stomach. I stop repeating the words and focus on where his hand is traveling, but he stops abruptly.

"I don't feel you saying it," he says.

"I love you," I quickly repeat. When the words leave my lips, his fingers begin moving again. As soon as I'm quiet, his fingers stop.

It doesn't take me long to figure out what game he's playing. I grin and say it again.

"I love you."

His fingers slip inside the top edge of my panties, and my voice grows quiet again. It's really hard for me to speak when his hand is that close. It's really hard to do anything. His fingers come to a pause just inside my panties when he doesn't feel me talking. I want his hand to keep moving, so I somehow breathe the words.

"I love you."

His hand slides further inside and stops. I close my eyes and say it again. Slowly.

"I . . . love . . . you."

What he does next with his hand causes me to repeat the words again instantly.

And again.

And again.

And again.

And again and again and again, until my panties are somewhere on the floor, and I've said the words so many times and so fast that I'm almost screaming them now. He continues to prove with the expertise of his hand that he's quite possibly the absolute best listener I've ever encountered.

"I love you," I whisper one last time between faltered and shallow breaths. I'm too weak to utter the words again, and my hands fall away from his head and land against the mattress with a thud.

He lifts his head away from my chest and scoots upward until his face is so close to mine our noses brush. "I love you, too," he says with a smug grin.

I smile, but my smile fades when he rolls away from me, leaving me alone on the bed. I'm too exhausted and spent to reach out for him. However, he returns to the bed as quickly as he left it. He tears open a condom wrapper and keeps his eyes focused on mine, never once looking away.

The way he's looking at me, as if I'm the only thing that

matters in his world, makes the moment take on a whole new feel. I'm completely consumed, not by waves of pleasure but by waves of raw emotion. I didn't know I could *feel* someone this much. I didn't know I could *need* someone this much. I had no idea I was capable of sharing this kind of connection with someone.

Ridge lifts a hand and wipes away a tear from my temple, then dips his head and kisses me, gentle and soft, coaxing even more tears out of me. It's the perfect kiss for the perfect moment. I know he feels what I'm feeling, because my tears don't alarm him at all. He knows they're not tears of regret or sadness. They're simply tears. Emotional tears stemming from an emotional moment that I never imagined could be this incredible.

He's waiting patiently for my permission, so I nod softly, and it's all the confirmation he needs. He lowers his cheek to mine and slowly begins to ease himself against me. I squeeze my eyes shut and focus on trying to relax, but my entire body is way too tense.

I've only ever had sex with one guy, and he didn't mean half as much to me as Ridge does. The thought of sharing this experience with Ridge, as much as I want to, makes me so nervous I'm physically unable to hide my discomfort.

He can sense my apprehension, so he pauses and stills himself above me. I love how in tune he is with me already. He looks down at me, his dark brown eyes searching mine. He takes both of my hands and pulls them over my head, then laces our fingers together and presses them into the mattress. He leans into my ear. "Want me to stop?"

I quickly shake my head no.

He laughs softly. "Then you have to relax, Syd."

I bite my bottom lip and nod, completely loving the fact that he just said "Syd" out loud. He runs his nose down my jawline, then brings his lips close to mine. Every touch sends waves of heat coursing through me, but it doesn't ease my apprehension. Everything about this moment is so perfect I'm afraid I might do something to mess it up. It can't get any better, so that only leaves things with one direction to go.

"Are you nervous?" he asks. His voice brushes across my mouth, and I slide my tongue over my bottom lip, convinced that I could taste his words if I tried.

I nod, and his eyes soften with his smile.

"Me, too," he whispers. He squeezes my hands tighter and then lays his head across my bare chest. I can feel the rhythm of his body rise and fall against mine with every tense breath. His entire body sighs, and one by one, each muscle begins to relax. His hands are still, and he's not exploring my body or listening to me sing or having me tell him I love him.

He's still, because he's listening to *me*.

He's listening to the beat of my heart.

His head lifts off my chest in one swift motion as he locks eyes with mine. Whatever realization he's just had causes his gaze to pierce mine with excitement.

"Do you have earplugs?" he says.

Earplugs?

I know the confusion can be seen in my expression. I nod anyway and point to the nightstand. He leans over me, opens the drawer, and feels around inside. When he finds them, he lowers himself beside me again, then places them in the palm of my hand. He motions for me to put them in my ears.

"Why?"

He smiles and kisses me, then trails his lips to my ear. "I want you to hear me love you."

I look down at the earplugs, then back up at him question-ingly. "How can I hear you if I'm wearing these?"

He shakes his head, then places his hands over my ears. "Not here," he says. He moves a hand to my chest. "I want you to hear me from right here."

That's all the explanation I need. I quickly put the earplugs in, then adjust my head on my pillow. All the noise around me slowly fades away. I wasn't aware of all the sounds I was taking in until they no longer run through my head. I don't hear the clock ticking anymore. I no longer hear the usual activity outside my window. I can't hear the sheets moving beneath us or the pillow under my head or the bed when he shifts his weight.

I hear nothing.

He grabs my hand and opens up my palm, then turns my hand around and places it over my heart. Once my palm is flush against my heart, he reaches to my face and brushes his hand over my eyes, closing them. He scoots himself away from me until he's no longer touching any part of me.

He becomes still, and I no longer feel him moving next to me.

It's quiet.

It's dark.

I hear absolutely nothing. I'm not sure this is working out the way he imagined.

I hear nothing but complete silence. I hear what Ridge hears every moment of his life. The only thing I'm aware of is my own heartbeat and nothing else. Nothing at all.

Wait.

My heartbeat.

I open my eyes and look at him. He's several inches away from me on the bed, smiling. He knows I hear it. He smiles softly, then pulls my hand away from my heart and places it against his chest. Tears begin to well in my eyes. I have no idea how or if I even deserve him, but there's one thing I know for sure. As long as he's a part of it, I'll never live a life of mediocrity. My life with Ridge will be nothing short of remarkable.

He rolls on top of me and lowers his cheek to mine, holding completely still for several long seconds.

I can't hear his breaths, but I feel them as they fall against my neck.

I can't hear his movements, but I feel him when he begins making the softest, most subtle shifts against me.

Our hands are still locked between us, so I focus on the beat of his heart, drumming against my palm.

Beat, beat, pause.

Beat, beat, pause.

Beat, beat, pause.

I can feel my entire body relaxing beneath him while he continues to make the subtlest of movements against me. He presses his hips into mine for two seconds, then relaxes and pulls back for a brief second before repeating the motion. He repeats this movement several times, and I can feel my need for him growing with each rhythmic movement against me.

The more my desire builds, the more impatient I become. I want to feel his mouth on mine. I want to feel his hands all over me. I want to feel him push inside me and make me his completely.

The more I think about what I want from him, the more responsive I become to the subtle shifts of his weight against me. The more responsive I become, the faster our hearts race against the palms of our hands.

Beat, beat, pause.

Beatbeat, pause.

Beatbeatpause.

Beatbeatpause.

The faster our hearts race, the quicker his rhythm becomes, matching each beat of my heart movement for movement.

I gasp.

He's moving to the sound of my heart.

I wrap my free arm around his neck and focus on his heartbeat, instantly aware that our hearts are perfectly in sync. I tighten my legs around his waist and lift myself against him, wanting him to make my heart beat even faster. He skims his lips across my cheek until they're flush against my mouth, but he doesn't kiss me. The silence around me makes me even more aware of the pattern of his breath falling against my skin. I focus on my palm against his chest and feel his quick intake of air, seconds before I taste the sweetness of his breath as he exhales, teasing my mouth.

Inhale, exhale.

Inhale, exhale.

Inhale, exhale.

His rhythmic breathing becomes quicker when his tongue slips inside my mouth, gently caressing the tip of mine.

If I could hear, I'm positive I would have just heard myself whimper. It's becoming a habit whenever he's around.

I move my hand to the back of his head, needing to taste more of him. I pull him to me with such sudden urgency he moans into my mouth. Feeling his moan without hearing it is probably the most sensual thing I've ever experienced. His voice as it passes through me does more than hearing it ever could.

Ridge slides his hand away from my heart and presses his forearms into the mattress on both sides of my head. He boxes me in with his arms, and I slide my hand away from his chest, needing to grab hold of him with all my strength. What little I have left, anyway.

I feel him pull farther back, and then, without hesitation, he pushes inside me, claiming me, filling me.

I . . .

Can't . . .

My heart.

Christ. He just silenced my heart, because I can no longer feel it at all. The only thing I feel is him moving against me . . . away from me . . . inside of me . . . into me. I'm completely consumed by him.

I keep my eyes closed and listen to him without hearing a thing, experiencing him silently, the same way he's experiencing me. I soak in every single beautiful thing about the smoothness of his skin and the feel of his breath and the taste of our moans, until it's impossible to tell us apart.

We continue to explore each other quietly, finding all the parts of ourselves we've only been able to imagine up to this point.

When my body begins to tense again, it's not at all because I'm nervous this time. I can sense his muscles clenching beneath my hands, and I grip his shoulders, ready to fall with him. He presses his cheek firmly to mine, and I feel him groan against my neck, making two final, long thrusts at the same second as I feel the moans escaping my throat.

He begins to tremble with his release but somehow pulls his hand between us again and presses it against my heart. He's shaking against me, and I'm doing my best to regain control of my own shudders while he begins to slow himself down, once again to the rhythm of my heart.

His movements grow so soft and subtle I can barely feel them through all the tears I'm crying. I don't even know why I'm crying, because this is by far the most indescribable feeling that has ever come over me.

Maybe that's why I'm crying.

Ridge relaxes on top of me and brings his mouth back to mine. He kisses me so softly and for so long my tears eventually subside and are replaced with complete silence, accompanied only by the rhythm of our hearts.

Ridge

I close the bathroom door and return to her on the bed. Her face is illuminated by the moonlight pouring through the windows. Her mouth is curled up into a soft smile as I lower myself down beside her. I slide my arm beneath her shoulders, then lay my head on her chest and close my eyes.

I love the sound of her.

I love *her*. Everything about her. I love that she's never judged me. I love that she understands me. I love that despite everything I've put her heart through, she's done nothing but support my decisions, no matter how much they destroyed her at the time. I love her honesty. I love her selflessness. Most of all, I love that I'm the one who gets to love all these things about her.

"I love you," I feel her say.

I close my eyes and listen as she continues to repeat the phrase again and again. I adjust my ear until it's directly over her heart, savoring every single thing about her. Her smell, her touch, her voice, her love.

I've never felt so much at once.

I've never needed to feel *more*.

I lift my head and look back down into her eyes.

She's a part of me now.

I'm a part of her.

I kiss her softly on the nose and mouth and chin, then press my ear against her heart again. For the first time in my life, I hear absolutely everything.

Acknowledgments

So many people to thank and so few words to do it in. First, not a single book I've started writing would ever reach the end if it weren't for those who encourage me and give me feedback along the way. In no particular order, these people deserve a huge thanks for always tagging along during the writing process.

Christina Collie, Gloria Green, Autumn Hull, Tammara Webber, Tracey-Garvis Graves, Karen Lawson, Jamie McGuire, Abbi Glines, Marion Archer, Mollie Harper, Vannoy Fite, Lin Reynolds, Kaci Blue-Buckley, Pamela Carrion, Jenny Aspinall, Sarah Hansen, Madison Seidler, Aestas, Natasha Tomic, Kay Miles, Sali-Benbow Powers, Vilma Gonzalez, Crystal Cobb, Dana Ferrell, the ever-supportive Kathryn Perez, and everyone else I've bugged along the way.

Thank you to my girls of FP. There are no words. Except these seventeen words, I guess.

Thank you, Joel and Julie Williams, for being amazingly supportive.

Tarryn Fisher, for being my confidence and also my reality check.

My husband and boys, for being the best four men on the planet.

Elizabeth Gunderson and Carol Keith McWilliams for your feedback, knowledge, and support. You are simply beautiful, and I couldn't have done it without either of you.

Jane Dystel and the entire Dystel & Goderich team for their continued support.

Judith Curr, publisher of Atria Books, and her team for going above and beyond their duties. Your support is unmatched.

To my editor, Johanna Castillo. To say I was nervous about delivering my first stand-alone to you is an understatement. I should have known better than to be nervous, because the two of us make a great team. I am so lucky to have you.

A HUGE thank-you to the *Maybe Someday* team: Chris Peterson, Murphy Fennell, and Stephanie Cohen. You guys rocked it.

And last, but definitely not least, Griffin Peterson. Thank you. A million times thank you. Your talent and work ethic can't go unmentioned, but your support and enthusiasm go above and beyond. There isn't even an emoji worthy enough.

Oh, and to Dave and Pooh Bear, just for the heck of it.

About the Author

COLLEEN HOOVER is the #1 *New York Times* bestselling author of the Slammed series, the Hopeless series, the Maybe Someday series, *Ugly Love*, *Confess*, *November 9*, *It Ends with Us*, *Without Merit*, and *All Your Perfects*. She is also the founder of The Bookworm Box, a bookstore and monthly subscription service offering signed novels donated by authors that supports various charities each month. She lives in Texas with her husband and their three boys. Visit ColleenHoover.com.

Dear Reader,

I had the pleasure of collaborating with musician Griffin Peterson in order to provide an original soundtrack to accompany this novel. Griffin and I worked closely together to bring these characters and their lyrics to life so that you will be provided with the ultimate reading experience.

It is recommended these songs be heard in the order they appear throughout the novel. To listen, please visit: https://www.colleenhoover.com/portfolio/maybe-someday/.

Thank you for being a part of our project. It has been so much fun for us to create, and we hope it will be equally as enjoyable as you read and listen.

Thank you,
Colleen Hoover and Griffin Peterson